John Harris

Wayside Pictures

Hymns, and Poems

John Harris

Wayside Pictures
Hymns, and Poems

ISBN/EAN: 9783744777278

Printed in Europe, USA, Canada, Australia, Japan

Cover: Foto ©Andreas Hilbeck / pixelio.de

More available books at **www.hansebooks.com**

WAYSIDE PICTURES,

HYMNS, AND POEMS.

BY

JOHN HARRIS.

WITH A PORTRAIT OF THE AUTHOR.

LONDON:

HAMILTON, ADAMS, AND CO.

1874.

LONDON:
PRINTED BY WILLIAM NICHOLS,
44, HOXTON SQUARE.

Dedication.

TO HIS LONG-TRIED FRIEND AND REVERED COUNTRYMAN,

ROBERT ALEXANDER GRAY, ESQ., OF LONDON,

THIS

COLLECTION OF POEMS,

THE LIFE-WORK OF THE AUTHOR, IS, BY PERMISSION,

Respectfully and gratefully inscribed.

Dedicatory Stanzas.

I.

Where slender harebells graced the garden hedge,
And granite pillars rose beside the door,
Split by the workman from the wondrous ledge
With lichen covered on the mystic moor;
And torrents tumbled on, with foam and roar,
By giant boulders sleeping in the moss;
And songful genii brushed the braken o'er;
A mountain minstrel, by the uplifted cross,
Sang when the heights were grand in evening's golden
    gloss.

II.

His father was with honest hinds enrolled,
Unskilled in letters, save the Book Divine.
Some mountain sheep he kept without a fold,
A steady horse, and still some steadier kine.
His mother's heart all gentle things enshrine,
Which filled his opening hours with rosy light,
As fancy-fraught he roved mid peak and pine,
And read the lore of Nature's loneliest height,
And ever taught himself by all things pure and bright.

III.

Then came the darkness of the dangerous mine,
His daily, nightly tasks of tedious toil,
Where never star, or moon, or sunbeams shine,
But sulphur-wreaths around the caverns coil;
Which health, and strength, and mental might might
    despoil,

Giving the feet of Time a tardy pace,
Through heated hollows, and rude rifts to moil,
When boyhood blossoms opened on his face,
And greenness clothed the tree which gave his being
    grace.

IV.

His study was the shadow of a rock,
O'erhanging the meek moss and lowly thyme,
Or flowery hawthorn, where the fleecy flock
Cropped the green herbage in the day's full prime.
And here he drank from rippling rills of rhyme,
Which lulled his spirit into blissful rest,
Till o'er the tree-tops rose the curfew's chime,
And the last wood-dove sought her sheltered nest,
And twilight lingered long in dalliance with the West.

V.

And as he sang beside the lonely tree,
In blissful brightness, by the glowworm's bower,
Where stone-crops nestled in the hedgerows free,
And fays stole forth from many a closing flower,
Enraptured with the mystery of the hour
That o'er his senses like a vision crept,
Filling his soul with the enchanter's power,
From the cloud-isles of eve a being swept,
With wondrous whisperings, as he watched and wept.

A 2

VI.

" The harp thou touchest with a trembling hand
Shall give thee comfort when the dells are dim,
And down the dingles of life's trodden land
Floats sad and slow the pensive evening hymn.
The cup of kindness, sparkling to the rim,
Shall cheer thee onward through thy after-days,
Proffered in gentleness and truth by him
Who Christian love and tenderness displays:
To whom I bid thee, then, inscribe thy simple lays."

VII.

The echo followed him when heaven was clear,
And when the clouds met in the angry sky.
It filled the breeze of every new-born year,
As one by one they swept before his eye.
In spells of song he oft would lyre-bound lie,
Until *he* came the cheerful meed to assign,
Bidding the care-shades to their coverts fly;
Whilst many stood aloof, with chilling whine,
He aided his song-skiff with gales of love benign.

VIII.

Now when his sun of life is in the west,
And length'ning shadows lie upon the land,
He yields the secret nurtured in his breast,
And thus fulfils the cloud-sylph's clear command,
Announced when roses were by faint winds fanned,
And gleams of song on hill and hollow lay,
Uniting kindreds in a golden band,
Till love shall reign, and war-feuds pass away,
And consecrates his psalms to ALEXANDER GRAY.

IX.

The friend of those whose earthly friends are few,
He fills the widow's heart with richest joy ;
To the Divine injunction ever true,
The weak to shield, to feed the orphan boy ;
The thorns along life's pathway to destroy,
And smooth the steep by drooping genius trod,
Who warmly thanks him in his loved employ,
Mid craggy cliff and cascade, music-shod,
And asks for ROBERT GRAY the guidance of his God.

X.

In fields, and lanes, and the o'erhanging wood,
These songs were written to the sound of streams,
Where the lark carols o'er the crystal flood,
And the dear daisy mid the grasses gleams,
And truly pure and righteous it beseems
To dedicate the nurslings of his lyre,
From bursting boyhood down to eve's dim dreams,
And Charity directs, clad in her meek attire.

XI.

Without his friendship these uncultured vines
In such a pleasant plot would not appear,
But, like the dodder neath the lonely pines,
Supported, cling amid the thickets drear.
May HE preserve his heavenly vision clear,
Till up the seraph slopes he takes his way,
Where spreads the tree of life in heaven's own
     sphere,
Amid the glories of unfading day :
REDEEMER, SAVIOUR, LORD, GUIDE THITHER ROBERT
     GRAY.

Contents.

SONNETS.

HYMNS.

PEACE POEMS.

THE LOVE OF HOME.

BOOK FIRST.

THE earth is fair with fields of
    happiness,
    With bowers that blossom ever-
      lastingly,
    With gems that sparkle on and
      never fade,
With streams that murmur sweeter and more sweet,
With flowers that wither not from moon to moon,
With gardens where the roses fill the year.
Affections cling around them ivy-like,
Entwining them for ever, till the hills
And silent valleys dimly fade in death.
Such is our birth-place, garlanded with green,
Fragrant with love-shoots of our early time,
Gemmed with pure thoughts that glow through after life,
Songful amid the sunshine of the Past,
And clinging to the memory evermore.

See yonder pilgrim with his hoary locks,
Sitting beside the streamlet in the vale
Which glides from rock to rock exultingly.
Before him, in that altered arbour's shade,
Lie the rough ruins of his father's cot,
Prostrate among the climbing ivy leaves,
And the rank grass which withers where it grows.
O how those granite blocks, untouched by Art,
Are murmuring to him on this April morn!
There's not a scattered fragment in that pile
But has a tongue, a most enchanting tongue,
Which captivates him with its eloquence,
And binds him to the mossy primrose bank.
They tell him of his mother and his sire,
His sunny sisters, lovely as the light,
The dear companions of his childhood hours,
And all the painted landscapes of his life.

Why does the tear-drop, gushing from his eye,
Steal over his sad face so silently,
Until it drops into the silver brook,
Startling the timid trout that watches there?
Why does he ever and anon start up,
Snatching his staff, then sits him down again,
And gazing still is still unsatisfied?
Why does he come among the early flowers,

As now he comes and lingers here alone
Among the ruins of that rended nest,
As if he saw a white-robed angel there?
This was that old man's birth-place. Four-score years
Have swiftly hurried o'er the pilgrim's head,
Leaving sad traces of decay behind.
But that pure principle which Nature gives,
And fosters in the breast of every one,
Burns on and on from youth to manhood's prime,
And smoulders not amid the snows of age.

"I'm travelling homeward," the old soldier said,
And aid his wallet down upon the stile.
Man, maid, and matron thronged to hear his tale.
"You see that village yonder mid the hills,
And that white house beside the aged thorn:
This was the soldier's birth-place. Yes, indeed,
The same old man that's talking to you now,
War-scarred and weary as he may appear,
With hoary locks crisp with the frosts of age;
The same old man that's talking to you now
Was once a little boy in that green vale,
Singing life's morning carols joyously."
And as he spoke he brushed away the tear
That slowly trickled down his furrowed face.

"One summer day—I well remember it:
Perhaps 'tis three-score years ago or more—
I had done something which displeased my sire,
And he reproved me, which displeased myself;
And I, to be revenged in my young way,
Caught up my clothes and left my father's roof,
And I ave not seen it since, till now it gleams
Upon my vision with a joy untold.

"I've been in battles both on sea and land;
I've heard the braying of the brazen trump,
And seen the flames of war, and heard its wail;
I've cut my way through walls of human flesh,
And flung my shriek upon the fearful flash,
And rolled myself in garments red with gore.
'Hair-breadth escapes' with me were multiplied:
I from the deck was toppled in the sea,
Down, down head-foremost on the coral reef;
And up I came again alive and well:
I met a lion once upon my track,
Which oped his horrid jaws to take me in;
I sent a bullet through the monarch's brain.
I've often drunk out of the stagnant pool,
And breakfasted upon the forest leaves,
And slept at night upon the naked rock.
Death met me once, swift-coming from his cave,
And aimed a dart at me: 'twas turned aside
By the unerring hand of Providence,

And lo! I see once more my native place.

"Home of my fathers, hail, all hail to thee!
When I have trembled in the Frigid Zone,
And languished in the land where Winter dwelt,
Making snow feathers in his crystal cell
To whirl around the world in hurricanes;
When I have shivered in this icy place,
My busy thoughts were revelling with home,
And leading me across those emerald meads.
Home of my fathers, hail, all hail to thee!
When faint and weary in the Torrid Clime,
Traversing day by day the arid waste,
Smarting with thirst, that keenest, bitterest pain,
How have I longed to be at home once more
Beside the bubbling fountain in the dell,
To quaff the waters of old England's springs!
When Battle raved, and shook his bloody blade,
And I was left on the red field as dead
Amidst the war-hacked mutilated heap,
Thoughts of my home, when wakening Reason dawned,
Came like a burst of music on my soul;
And up I rose, in spite of wounds and woes,
And rushed to conquer with my shattered sword.

"When storms were monstrous on the mighty deep,
And tempest-spirits rode upon the waves,
Blue lightning-wings were flapping through the sky,
And Thunder bellowed in his fiery caves.
When unseen monsters piped upon the winds,
And roared within the cordage of our bark.
Which soon went down where storms are never felt,
And I was cast upon the yielding sand,
Life came, and reason dawned,—my home was there;
I thought upon my mother and my sire,
My white-washed cottage here among the trees,
And up I got again and struggled on.
'Twas with me as I climbed the hill of life:
I reached the summit, and my home was there.
Then slowly I went down into the vale,
In foreign lands:—my home was still with me still.
Time drew his pencil from his rusty sheath,
And silvered o'er those scattered locks of mine;
Old age began to shake this house of clay;
And, fearing I should die on foreign fields,
I hastened here, to lay my bones with you,
And sleep securely in my native place."

He limped along, leaning upon his staff;
Inquired for those he loved,—but they were dead.
The stranger's icy eyes his native home
Froze the old man to sadness, and he wept.
He fell at last beneath the scythe of Death,
Among the summer flowers of fatherland,
And, where he wished, has found a resting-place.

The love of country is predominant
In every zone that belts the universe.
It lures the Indian to his loved wigwam,
Where sire and son, age after age, reposed
Beneath the peace-tree planted by their sires.
It binds the Afric to his sun-burnt soil;
I lies with the Arab through the wilderness,
So that he leaps not o'er his boundary-line;
Walks with the Swiss in his secluded vales,
Like an attendant spirit; flings its spell
Over the Islands of the laughing South,

And gilds the crests of Greenland's splintered crags,
Making home joyful bound with bands of ice!
The Scotsman sees no mountains like his own,
No glens so beauteous, and no fields so green;
And he whom fate consigns to sunny France,
And he the native of the Emerald Isle,
And he who claims his birth in Albion's vales.
Old music-murmuring England, thinks his home
The sweetest sublunary spot of all.
Born in the valley, nursed among the streams,
He loves the valley better than the hill:
Bred on the mountain, reared among the storms,
He clasps the crags that answer to the blast.
The love of home links man to fellow-man,
Binding earth's children to their native sod.

Upon the crest of yonder heathy hill,
Where the storm-spirits wrestle with the stars,
Flinging their flashing brands at the Great Bear,
And mutter in the hollows of the rocks,
Turning the timid man another way;
Upon the crest of this old granite mount,
I first beheld the breaking of the dawn,
And drank the morning zephyrs of young life.

Hail to thee, mountain birth-place! Not a rock,
O'er-written with the stanzas of the storm,—
And many rocks are shooting from thy crown,
And hanging from thy girdle,—not a rock
On which my sire and grandsire oft have stood.
And where I've climbed in childhood's cheerful spring,
Gazing into the deep blue summer sky,
And smiled to see the earth so beautiful,—
No, not a rock around my native place
But what I love, as if akin to me!
There's not a hedge-row, gemmed with ivy-leaves,
There's not a floweret in my father's lea,
There's not a sofa, with its seat of sod,
Where the tired pilgrim sits in Nature's hall,
And gazes on the portraits of the past;
There's not a moss-bower in the dear old croft,
Where the young Muses wooed the singing boy,
To list at evening to the harping breeze;
There's not a wild cave where the tempests roar,
Rolling their bass-blasts round the fire-scathed rocks;
There's not a flaw upon its furrowed front.
But seems even now a portion of my life!

Hail to thee, mountain birth-place! Other scenes,
In other lands, may press upon my ken,
And glow before my vision; other hills,
Lofty, majestic, mightier than thou,
Forcing their snow-clad crests above the clouds,
Where Winter sits and howls eternally,—
Ay, other hills may fill my mind with awe,
And startle me with wonder; but I'll turn,
Even in the midst of this excitement turn,
And fondly kneel among thy knolls again.
Sickness may blast this feeble frame of mine,
The tree of friendship may be rooted up,
The last bright star of earthly hope may fade,
Old age may twine its fetters round my clay,
A thousand happy memories may depart,
But I shall ne'er forget thee, mountain home!
The sweetest spot of earth! my native place!

It seems even now, in spite of hope deferred,

In spite of lassitude and all its ills,
In spite of cold neglect, which freezes more,
In spite of care, sleepless and wakeful still,
In spite of all the sorrows I endure,—
It seems even now, when wandering here alone,
Gazing upon the bowers where I have been
Tuning my lyre in Evening's dewy halls
Under the hawthorn in the daisy mead,—
It seems even now I feel inspired again,
And snatch my harp, forgetting all my woe.
O! when at last I'm sleeping in the grave,
Where the meek wildings whisper o'er my head,
And the soft breezes wail my mournful dirge
At vesper-time,—O! if an angel's wing
May stoop to brush the dew-drops from the down,
And visit scenes it loved,—then I'll descend,
Swiftly descend, beneath the purple eve,
Fanning the flowerets with my pinions bright,
And hover o'er this loveliest spot of all!

Cross this green meadow where the cowslips dance,
And gaze into that cot among the trees.
A father and his family are there:
How peacefully they dwell! Like sheltered birds,
They live together in their happy nest,
Beneath His wings o'ershadowing earth and sky.
The good man's home! Earth has no sweeter cup
Of sparkling happiness, surpassing thine!
Calm Evening comes, and o'er the quiet creeks
Spreads out her twilight mantle gracefully.
The flowers are sleeping in the dewy dells,
And, on the budding boughs, the singing birds
Have rocked themselves to slumber. All is rest,
And Silence muses where the Zephyrs sleep.
The sire returns from labour, and the boys,
The bigger boys, from work are thronging in,
And ruddy younglings rushing home from school.
The kettle sings upon the blazing hearth
A song of melting music to their ears;
Before the fire-place Puss enjoys her dreams,
Lark shakes his feathers in the general glee,
While Ponto whines to see their safe return!
And now they sit around the supper-board,
And make a hearty meal on homely fare.
The sire takes down the Bible, and aloud
He reads a portion of the holy Book;
And having round the altar knelt, they all
Retire to rest, and gentle sleep comes down,
And they are wafted to the isle of dreams:
Attendant angels hymn around their beds,
And shake rich music from their golden wings.

We visit them again in summer time.
Green grief is sitting on their hearts to-day,
And sobs come forth to load the mourning breeze,
And little sparrow on the chimney-top
Puts forth his ears to listen. Mother weeps,
And sister hides her face within her hands,
And brother gazes on his brother there,
And watch-dog shrinks into his nest and whines,
While little baby strikes his shrillest note,
And father silently is watching all!

Wherefore has sorrow seized them? On this morn
The circle of that happy family
For the first time is broken. A fair youth
Sheds on his sister's neck a flood of tears,

And takes his own loved mother by the hand,
Then rushes on, and on,—away, away!
The father followed to the moaning sea,
Saw his last foot-print left upon the land,
Beheld him standing on the vessel's deck,
Looking with wistful eyes towards the shore;
And then the old man knelt among the rocks,
Decked in their cloaks of slippery, salt sea-weed,
And wept and prayed,—and prayed and wept again,—
That God would guard him safely o'er the deep,
And save his son in dark temptation's hour.—
That old man never saw his child again!

On went the youth, lured by the god of gain,
Treading the hills and vales of a strange land,
Roaming the forest where the red man roved,
And climbing mountains in the far, far West.
He heard the solemn crash of waterfalls,
And gazed on dells immortalized in song.
He passed the spot where War's red blade had flashed,
And carnage howled upon the battle-field,
Drinking her wine-cups brimmed with clotted gore.
He heard the Siren's song in other lands;
He drank from rivers where the white man's lip
Had never pressed the sparkling wave before;
He gathered up rich shining gems in heaps,
And gained unnumbered friends where'er he went.
The rich came forth and shook him by the hand,
And little children blessed him as he passed,
And fair-haired maidens sang to him at eve.
He wished this moment, and the next enjoyed.

Deem not that he, in these exciting hours,
Forgot his home,—his home among the meads,—
His father's home,—that early home of homes!
It rose before him in his darkest hours,
And in his brightest moments. Not a day
But there it lay beside him, beautiful,
Sweeter and lovelier than it e'er had been!
And when the moon came forth at even-tide,
Silvering the summits of the ancient hills,
Weaving white robes of fleeting loveliness,
And flinging them o'er valley, lake, and stream;
When singing birds were sleeping in the brakes,
And the tired hedger laid aside his spade,
Well pleased to hear the evening story told;
When Silence slumbered in the vesper breeze;
At such an hour he oft would steal away,
To muse upon the home of early days,
And think the same wan moon was looking down
Upon the cottage roof he left behind,
And kindred eyes were then upturned to her,—
A weeping mother, and, perchance, a sire,
Brother and sister, and, yet dearer still,
The maid he left behind him fatherless!
Then, hastening back, he crept into his couch,
And saw it pass before him in his dreams!

Years fleet away: his face is homeward turned;
He can't forget his own beloved land;
He sees the white cliffs of his native shore;
And now is in the harbour, and is safe.
He hastens on, and on, from stage to stage,
And longs to see once more those sacred scenes
Where he in childhood with his brothers played.
He climbs a hill-top, where they oft have been,
In days of yore, watching his father's sheep.

He's on the highest crag ! He looks around,
And weeps for very gladness.—" Here's my home !
The smoke is curling upward through the trees,
Looking so beauteous in my misty eyes ;
And here my mother comes, my brothers too,
My little sister, like a flower in May.
One dear embrace, and then we'll weep our fill.
Home, home, sweet home ! we'll never part again !"

See'st thou that dwelling by the murmuring stream,
And those green fields where cows and horses feed,
And, coming with a pitcher in her hand,
That pleasant-looking woman ? 'Tis his wife,
The orphan girl he loved when far away !
This is his cottage, and that fertile farm
Is owned by him : he's now a happy man ;
He loves his home, he loves his family,
And, what is more than all, he loves his God.

The psalm of morning shakes among the hills ;
The lark is singing to the rising sun ;
Troops of grey sparrows gossip on the thatch ;
Reynard is slowly creeping to his lair ;
And far-off murmurs float upon the ear.
The satchelled poet is abroad betimes:
His path to school is through the quiet moor ;
And he delighteth to be lingering there,
Communing with the song-queen in her bower.
He bends him o'er the streamlet, as it plays
Its holy anthems in the ear of Dawn.
He listens to the lyrics of the trees,
Whose voices fill the galleries of morn.
On banks of dew-kissed flowers he sits thought-crowned,
Watching the swallows, as they dive and wheel
O'er brook and rock, glancing like spirit-wings ;
And as the vapours from Morn's brightening brow
Melt slow away, and glory-lines are cast
On her fair features, gazing, they appear
To the young school-bard rays of holy song.
And now he standeth by the woodland lake,
Peering far down into its silvery depths.
Shoals of strange Genii revel on the sands,
And ride upon the billows of the flood,
And climb the rushes to their pointed peaks.
Nature allured him from his mother's lap,
Enamoured of her woods and waterfalls.
No wonder that the boy grew up to fame.

Manhood has stamped its impress on his brow,
And the meek poet breasts the cares of life.
Just turn aside and look upon his home.
We find it in the valley, strange indeed,
And picturesque, and wild. Upon a rock
Is its foundation, and before it foams
The rushing torrent : rills, like silver threads,
Are trickling down the mount from slope to slope,
Gushing sweet music : o'er its reedy roof
The hollow crags ring to the eagle's scream,
And ancient oak-trees o'er the runnels rise.
Far down the vale amid the mounds of green
The shepherd's dog watches the fleecy flock,
And happy shepherd carols on his crook.
Woods in the distance on the mountains wave,
Upon whose summits towers and castles stand.
Flowers of all hues around his casement climb,
And look in at his door, whose hazel latch

Is almost hidden in a grove of leaves.

Among the ferns and furzes oft he walks,
By ruins grey, old wells, and haunted springs,
Or mid the wonders of the wilderness,
With book and pencil dangling in his hand,
Holding strange converse with ideal shapes
In dwellings trim, astride the gossamer
Which wraps him round as in Elysium.
Nature inspired him with her lays of love,
Carved on the mountains, ringing in the vales,
And pencilled on the flowerets of the field, —
Her book of wonders, strangely written o'er
By babbling breezes with their dewy pens,
Or angry hurricane with brand of flame,
Or silent zephyr with its quill of flowers,
Or Spring with roses, Summer with perfumes,
Autumn with golden grain, cold Winter's self
With icicles suspended from his locks,
Day with its rays of light that gem the page,
And midnight with the moonbeams :—Nature's book
Was read by him like some old ringing lay.

Hast ever climbed some old eternal hill,
Seared with the thunder-rod, whose awful crags
Confound thy senses with their stony glare ?
Hast ever scaled it in the black storm-cloud,
When the winds rattled 'gainst the thick rain-streams,
And the blue lightnings, with long forked tongues,
Chiselled their records on its jutting blocks ?
When Thunder flung his hissing bolts abroad,
Full of red vengeance, and the earth and sky
Roared to each other in the dreadful din ?
Hast ever, muffled in the cloudy night,
Bent thy stray steps up the untrodden wild,
With not a single walker at thy side,
Save those good angels, guiders of thy feet ?
And have thy thoughts leaped from their secret cell,
And mingled strangely with the shadowy slabs
That stooped to meet thee on thy rushing march ?
Here the true poet converse held alone
With shapes invisible and things unseen,
Clouds, lightnings, winds, rocks, meteors, misty rains,
Wild torrents, gentle streams, darkness and light,
Earth, sea, and sky, filled with the voice of God.
The mountains were his teachers: crags and storms,
Wild tumbling waterfalls, low-fluting rills,
And flowery valleys, fragrant with perfumes,
Woods, trees, birds, stones, the cattle of the field,
Stars, constellations, the chaste holy moon,
The filmy insect with its flashing wings,
And the dull reptile hiding in the fen,
Old Ocean, lifting up his awful voice,
And thundering in the ear of drowsy Night,—
Each atom of God's glorious universe
Was the fond teacher of the poet-born.
He loved the morning breezes, as they came
Laden with heavy dews : the breath of eve,
Tuning the tree-tops, stealing down the vale,
And murmuring up the shaggy mountain's side,
Was sweet to the poor bard : the lark's shrill song,
The woodland echo, and the tinkling stream,
Were things which seemed to mingle with his life.
His solitary rambles here and there,
By mead and moorland and the mountain mill,
And over giant rocks and echoing down,
Filled the rude cottagers with wondering awe,

Who looked upon him as a vacant man.
He loved the hill-tops of his fatherland,
And sang of home and its felicities,
Though wandering daily with the noisy herd,
Tortured and sad of heart,—longing for rest,
And pining for the paths of solitude,
Denied him in his battlings sore for bread.

Then came a day of darkness, dense and drear ;
Old friends forsook him. His beloved harp,
Which Nature gave him at life's early dawn,
Lay rusting mid the cobwebs of his cot.
A meagre host of skeletons arose,
And followed at his heels by night, by day,—
Want, Hunger, Famine, Pestilence, and Care,
And pale Exhaustion with his frame of bone.
His little children looked up in his face,
And cried for lack of food ; his wife grew sad,
And tears were streaming down the poet's cheek.
Thus crushed and broken, soon he bade adieu
To home and country, and, 'neath other skies,
In foreign vales his happy children played.

The rolling billows of the sea of time
For forty years had washed the cliffs of life,
When in his native valley once again
Alone he walked, the Pilgrim of the past.
His hair was hoary, time had marked his face ;
His step was slow, supported with a staff ;
And now and then a tear dropt from his eye,
As o'er the flowers the peasant minstrel hung.
He walked into the bower by Nature made,
The dear old arbour where he sang in youth,
And wooed the Muses from their breezy heights.
The ivy clung adhesive to the rock,
And the wild roses clustered over head ;
The swallows sported up and down the vale,
And merry birds were singing by the stream,
As musical as when he heard them last.
These seemed the same ; but, coming to his cot,
The narrow paths along the garden-ground
Were overgrown with grass ; they looked unpressed,
Untrodden for a series of long years ;
The shattered casements and the door unhinged
Told him of desolation and decay.
On a low rock the white-haired poet sat
In agony of soul, weeping aloud,
And calling on the names of those he loved.

His kindred had departed,—all were flown :
A hamlet showed its roof-tops in the vale ;
Tall handsome hinds were ploughing in the meads,
And stranger-faces peered among the trees.
None did he know, and he was known of none,
Forgotten in the valley of his birth,
Whose woods and streams inspired him with sweet song,
Calling forth music from his simple soul.
The image of his home, when far away,
Appeared before him as he saw it last :
But Time had changed it in his rapid flight.
He wiped his eyes, and turned him from the dell,
Slowly and sadly creeping up the hill,
And on its summit paused to look again
Back on his home.—He never saw it more.

BOOK SECOND.

Delicious Home ! within thy sacred shade
The weary man forgets the face of Care,
And the sharp thorns in Labour's hardened
    hands,
Smiling triumphantly at want and woe.
The mother, bending o'er her beauty-buds,
Sings in the breeze, and carols in the blast ;
The father sits within thy spring-green bowers,
And knows no melody so sweet as thine !
The ruddy youth pulls down thy clustering grapes,
And gives them to his sisters lovingly.
The mourner, poring o'er the blessed Book,
Flies to thy closet, ever-welcome Home !
And realizes there the joy of grief.
The weary wanderer gains thy fragrant seats,
All sprinkled o'er with sweets of other days,
And fondly woos thee to his wounded heart.
The wasted captive leaves his narrow cell,
And rushes homeward with electric speed.
The wrinkled warrior sheaths his shining blade,
Which now hangs resting on the pictured wall,
And in thine arbours twines the locks of Peace.
Thou treasurest up the tales of olden times,
And, when the gathering of dear friends is come,
Thou dost recite them in thy holy halls,
Uniting soul to soul with cords of love.

Oft when the chain of labour chills my heart,
Deep in the earth's great darkness, thoughts of home,
My children's voices, and my wife's glad smile,
Come, like the breathings of a seraph's lute,
Making the sad one joyous ! Free again,
With a glad heart I hasten to thy hearth,
And find no happier spot beneath the sun !

Among the rushes in a lonely fen
The miller lived ; a few small fields were his,
Which long were handed down from kin to kin.
His sire and grandsire, and his grandsire's sire,
Were born where now the busy miller dwelt,
And saw his ruddy children round him rise.
Delightful 'twas at summer eve to sit
Among the trees far up the mountain side,
To list the murmur of the gentle stream,
And hear the sheep-bells tinkling in the vale,
And far away the merry milk-maid's song.
His days were those of rural happiness,
Divided with his meadows and his mill,
Flowing along as smoothly as the brook,
That turned, and turned again, his wooden wheel.

But in the midst of his retirement sweet,
Strange rumours reached him of the land of gold
Across the mighty main. He rubbed his eyes,
And dropped his scoop to hear the tale again,
Which so o'ercame him that he closed his mill,
And left his little meadows half-untilled,
His fences half-repaired, his lambs unmarked,
The wide field-gaps, where wood-gates should have
    been,
Half-built with blocks of granite ; sheds half-thatched,
O'er which a meagre family of ropes
In his gold dreams were thrown, whose dangling ends

Unravelled in the rain. On the smooth lea,
Half-ploughed, half-planted with nutritious roots,
He left his spade still sticking in the earth;
And on the surges of the lucre-storm
He rolled into the field of blazing gems.

Armies were there before him; troops on troops
Came rushing on behind,—famed England's sons,
And Ireland's hardy swains, the Frenchman gay,
Old Scotia's mountaineers, and those afar
In isolated isles,—black men and red,
From Cornwall's miners, heroes of the rock,
To the smooth-featured children of the sun.
None seemed to heed his fellow: bent and bowed
With faces to the earth, they dug for gold
From morn till eve, nor did they dig in vain.
At night-fall in the camp's drear solitude,
After the gainful labours of the day,
His thatched home came before him,—wife and friends;
His prattling children clambered up his knees,
And told him stories of the wondrous bean,
With strings of other tales, and in his dreams
He heard the waters rushing o'er his mill.

That wheel is silent now,—he died abroad;
But his last thoughts were with his native vale,
And his last blessing was a prayer for it.

" I cull these flowers to deck my brother's grave.
He sleepeth in the village-churchyard now,
Surrounded with old elms and weeping pines,
Spreading their branches o'er his quiet tomb.
My mother rests beside him; and my sire
Has wandered from us, and returned no more.
She sweetly told us on her dying day,
That God would be our Father and our Friend;
And then she left us: so we lingered on
In love together for a little while,
Until my brother sickened, and then die,
And yesterday they laid him in the grave,
And I was left alone in this wide world.
I bring these flowers to place above his head,
That when the spring comes, they may blossom here,
The sweet memorials of a sister's love,
When I am far away, from whence we came.

" There is a country in the genial east,
Of which my mother oft has told us much,
And, as she spoke, the gushing tears would fall.
I think she called it England,—land of streams,
The isle of roses and the clime of song.
This is the country where we both were born,
And twined life's morning flowers in fresh festoons,
To hang around the beauteous neck of Love.
I scarce remember now the primrose-bower,
In ivy-mantled, happy fatherland,
Where we have played when life was fresh and green.
But more than this I know not. In the night
We left our home upon the mountain's side;
And the next day I heard the ocean roar,
And felt the billows toss our bounding bark.

" On went the vessel o'er the trackless blue,
The white-winged eagle of the stormy deep,
Careering, like a wind-god, westward still,
Until the cry of ' land ' bade all rejoice.
We stepped ashore, and found the settler's home;

O how unlike the dwelling left behind!
Soon father fled, and mother pined away,
Still wasting, till she dropped into the tomb :
My little brother quickly followed her;
So swift does sorrow sorrow overtake!
To-morrow I depart, and haste away,
To seek once more my earliest playing-place.
May gentle dews descend on these pale flowers
I plant upon the grave of him I love ;
And may the sunbeams kiss them into life,
And mantle them in rainbow-coloured robes,
That they may weep, at holy evening-time,
For those who sleep so quietly below.
When I am far away, I know not where !"

The morrow dawned : the flapping sails were spread ;
The ocean-eagle floats along her way ;
The maiden looked behind her on the land,
And it had dwindled to an atom-speck.
One tear of sadness, and she smiles again :
" My face is turned towards my earliest home :
Almighty Father! guide me safely there."

Her prayer was answered. Soon her native land
Rose fair and beauteous, clad in Spring's green robes :
And she through England's vales inquiringly
Pursued the way to her ancestral mount.
Behold her at the foot of the old hill,
Gathering king-cups and nodding hyacinths,
And kissing them in rapturous ecstasy !
O how she listens while the robin sings,
On the old hawthorn, snowy with May-flowers,
And lifts her hands, and wipes her streaming eyes!
Then hastens on across the moorland meads,
Where the young lambkins sport among the grass ;
And stops and listens to the cuckoo's voice.

But who is he, with sandals sadly worn,
With dusty garments, and a knotty staff,
Sitting among the lichen-covered rocks,
Wrapped in a fit of musing ? 'T is her sire,
Thus strangely piloted to meet her here !
He had been wandering over foreign fields,
In quest of gold, that glittering deity ;
And, travelling back to live and die at home,
He came this way, to see the cherished spot,
More dear to him than hills with cedars crowned.
She soon was standing near him : questions rose,
And rapid answers followed, till the whole
Came gathering round him, like a murky cloak,
'Gainst which the keen blast chattered. Pale he stood,
And pressed his daughter to his beating heart,
And cried in all the ecstasy of grief,
" I am thy long-lost father, dearest one,
Come back to cheer thee in thy solitude.
O, be mine angel through this wilderness,
And lead me gently downward to the tomb !
We'll make this vernal spot our dwelling-place,
And live together here till life be past,
In the old cot where both of us were born."

'T was one of England's ancient cottage homes,
Straw-roofed, and clasped with ivy. Sweet woodbine
Around the Gothic casements strangely crept,
And o'er the porch the clustering roses hung ;
Beneath the eaves the sparrows built their nests,
Upon the tree-top little robin sang,

And sky-larks carolled o'er it merrily.
Behind it, rose the mountain's ragged crest;
Beside it, paced the shepherd with his crook;
Below it, walked the murmuring rivulet.
A bard might linger there, and hear old rhymes
In every breezy murmur,—winds and waves,
And silent-speaking flowers, and singing-birds,
And tuneful zephyrs harping on his ear!

Delicious Home! beside thy blazing hearth
What griefs are softened, and what bruises healed!
What loves, what friendships, cherished and matured!
What cares beguiled to silence! Little words,
Conceived within thee, travel on and on,
Increasing on their earthly pilgrimage,
Till they become the watchword of their day,
The flashing oracles of mighty states,
The awe of kingdoms, and great Europe's dread.
They live and move for ever, till the last
Dire, awful death-groan of the universe;
And then these little words appear again,
In the bright daylight of eternity,
Radiant with life and immortality!

See'st thou that mother, at the evening hour,
Gathering her children round the cheerful hearth,
And telling them of God? Plain her address,
So that the smallest in that happy band
May comprehend it, and the elder ones
Weep, when they hear that tale she tells so oft,—
The Saviour's love to save us from the fall!
Angels are bending o'er their shining seats,
To listen to the teacher; and their hands
Rest, for an instant, on their living lyres.
The storm that rocks the mountains, tearing off
Huge, splintered fragments of the rifted oak,
Twisting the branches of the giant palm,
And battling with the spirits of the dark,—
The storm that roars so furiously without,
Is scarce regarded by this band within.
They listen to the voice of her they love,
Breathing in their rapt ears plain Scripture lore;
They drink the gushing music from her lips,
And feel the first fresh buddings of delight,
The early promptings of the better part.
The seed is sown that will spring up again.

We pass along the rush of numerous years,
And look into that happy home once more,
Strange faces seem to greet us from the hearth,
Whose beaming eyes reveal the mind within.
They are the same we saw in days gone by,
In the fresh pastures of Life's April fields,
Now standing on the crest of Manhood's mount,
Stretching their eagle gaze at Fame's green crown.
But where is she who sat among her flowers,
Her little children in their early time,
And taught them how to shun the paths of Vice,
And walk in Wisdom's flower-enamelled track?
Stand on her silent grave,—the dust is there,
But her freed spirit has gone up on high,
To sing the song of Moses and the Lamb!
But that same voice is heard at evening-time,
Along the garden walks, beside the stream,
In the green fields, and by the hallowed hearth,
And coming from the churchyard's sacred sod,
In sweetest accents still, for evermore!

On comes the rushing separation blast,
Scattering the olive branches of this house
In different sections of the busy world!
One makes his home where the green Islands smile,
In the Pacific Ocean. Sitting there,
Beneath the branches of the bread-fruit tree,
What time his life lay in the snows of age,
These little words, the voices of the past,
Come thronging round him, with their tones of love,
Bringing fresh tear-drops with them: down he kneels,
And blesses God for such a parent gone!
Another carols on the desert sands
Lays which he heard his sainted mother sing.
Another plants his dwelling far away,
Beside the silver lake, in a strange land;
And little ones come clustering round his board,
The joyful issue of the marriage-bed.
He now has reached the autumn of his years;
But, coming o'er the summits of the past,
Along the hills of life, her living words
Are ringing round him wheresoe'er he goes,
To her he owes the comforts God has given:
"It was my mother made me such a man!"
Another climbs the towering mount of Fame,
From crag to slippery crag, until at last
He feels the laurel pressing on his brow,
And drinks the voice of praise with ravished ears.
Men bow before him, wondering at his might,
The awful mystery that wraps him round,
The unseen halo moving where he moves!.
He writes his name in living characters,
To glow for ever in the hearts of men.
He freely sows the seeds of life and light,
Which are to vegetate eternally:
And, drawing near the banks of Death's dark stream,
He breathes to those who watch Life's dropping sands,
"I owe my mother everything I am!"
Another, with the Bible in his hands,
Girding the Christian's glittering armour on,
Goes forth to meet the erring sons of men,
To tell the simple story of the Cross.
Methinks I see him in his pilgrim weeds,
Way-worn and weary, by the fountain's side,
Sitting upon the earth. Beside him stands
The fierce barbarian, stained with stormy strife,
To whom he tells the tale he loves so well,
Heard in the halls of home in early time,
When sitting on his sainted mother's knee.
The savage hears, and trembles, and believes;
Old things are past with him,—all things are new,
And floods of glory fill the moral world!
How honoured are the ministers of Christ,
The trumpeters of Zion, thus to be
The messengers of hope to those that mourn!

How gloomy are those frowning prison walls,
O'er which Despair flaps his dark raven-wings!
Gaze through that grating; look upon the floor:
What's that we see there, sitting on the straw,
Looking like Misery's self? 'Tis an old man,
Wasted away to shadow, wasting still,
Though twenty years have found him wasting here.
How sad is his lament! and yet a hope
Is tingling in his melancholy dirge,
Sobbed forth to-day upon the rotten reeds:
"Another year of slow revolving Time,—
For, O how slow he travels in my cell,

Trailing his leaden limbs along my track!
Another year, and yon dark iron door
Will ope, to let the prisoner out again
Into the world, unchained, at liberty!
Where are the friends and kindred of my youth,
I left behind me in my early home,
In the green wood o'ershadowed by the elm?—
And twenty years have since crept o'er my head!
Perhaps they all are gone!" And the old man
Roared in the corner of his prison-house,
So that the echo came, and came again,
And went and came: and still among the straw
He moaned in very bitterness of soul!

Days, months lag on; and as the period wanes
Which brings him nearer to the happy hour,
Hope kindles in his bosom, kindling still,
As, day by day, the added notches rise.
At last the old man, through the grating, saw
The wished-for morning ope its dewy eye;
For he all night had rolled upon his reeds,
Weeping for very joy. It broke at last,—
The blushing dawn of liberty to him:
The severed links fell from his wasted arm;
The manacles were lifted from his flesh;
The grating door upon its hinges turned;
And forth he went into the dazzling light,
'Neath the blue arch of heaven, free as the birds
That sang on high their songs of liberty;
His song as happy and as free as theirs!
Standing upon a rising hillock, he
Surveyed the lofty prison walls behind,
And, resting on his staff, wept a farewell.
And now he bounds along with jocund tread,
Not on the highway, but across the meads;
Now sits him down, recounts his sorrows o'er;
Now runs again, now whirls his staff in air,
Now halts and dances with excess of joy.

Where are his eager footsteps bending? Where?
List, and you'll hear him as he rushes on:
"A few miles more, and I shall reach the wood,
The birth-place of my honoured sire and me,
Where, years ago, amid the vines I left
A weeping mother and her little ones.
I saw them often in my prison-cell,
In the dim land of dreams, when I lay down
And groaned myself to slumber on the straw.
Home came before me, like sweet fairy-land,
Even in my darkest moments, gilding oft
The blackening pall that o'er my dungeon hung!
And shall I see my birth-place once again?
Quaff the pure breezes murmuring through the wood?
Drink the clear water from the welcome well,
And hear the song I heard in days gone by?
Shall I, in the old chamber of my youth,
Where I was born amid September fruits,
Meet the stern slayer, and lie down and die?
O, grant me this, kind Heaven! I ask no more."
Wiping the perspiration from his brow,
And brushing his hoar locks, away, away,
With quickened pace, the weary wanderer went.

He had his wish,—had all he wished to have,—
And in the chamber where his grandsire died,
He closed his eyes on all material things.

" Blaze bright, ye lightnings! send your steeds of flame
On messages of death around the world!
On your fierce fiery travel hiss and burn,
That cruel man may shudder with affright!
Roar loud, ye thunders! echo in your ire,
And crack your sulphurous tongues, that scathe the vales.
And twitch the stone-caps from the mountains' heads,
Hurling them to destruction! Rend the skies
With your dread echoes, that the heart of man
May melt within him at God's awful voice!
Wail loud, ye winds, till the shook welkin splits,
And the storm-spirits on their rattling cars
Drag up the forest-trees like shrivelled reeds,
Turn o'er the villages like tufts of down,
And stir the ocean deeper than 'tis wont,
That its proud billows may usurp the land,
And pull back to its depths the pride of man!
Ye waters, streaming from the muffled cloud!
Pour down your ruin floods on this grave-dark night,
Wherein my master turns his slave abroad,
Whipped, branded, fasting, fettered to the bone,
To make my bed 'neath this o'erhanging rock,
Up which the blue flames clamber, leaping high
From crag to crag, loud crackling o'er my head!
Stream from your secret reservoirs, ye rains,
And wash the mountains from the woodless wild!

" Surrounded with the war of wrestling winds,
Deserted by the friends of human-kind,
Forced from my master's dwelling, at this hour
A vision comes before me:—'tis my home,
Far from the slave-man's country, far away
In the sweet vale of reeds. In early youth
We dwelt together, brothers, sisters, friends,
Mother and father, in one pleasant home,
Loving and loved, a joyous family.
Brief were our days of happiness, too brief:
Down from the mountains came the fierce white man
Like an unchained tornado, scattering friends,
And wringing blood-drops from the patriot's heart.

" 'T was a bright summer morning; the past night
I lay down in the corner of my shed,
And slept so sweetly! Dreams of fatherland,
Its streams, its rivers, hills, and aged woods,
Where the huge, shaggy forest-king resides,
And birds of silvery plumage gem the trees,
And carol wildly,—dreams of fatherland
Were floating through the chambers of my brain.
For, O, methought my own dear mother came
And kissed me as I slept, and bade me rise,
Calling upon her boy. I started up,
And felt a cold hand clasping both mine own,
Dragging me swift away. My arms were chained,
My feet were fastened, and on board a ship
They brought me to this country, wet with tears.

" Youth has been broken here on slavery's wheel,
Manhood has writhed upon the withering rack,
Age has been chilled beneath the tyrant's chain,
Whose gore-dyed rivets fastened on my soul.
My life has been an age of servitude,
Black, sunless, woful, winter-like, and drear:
No spring, no summer has adorned the scene:
Before, behind, on this side and on that,
And over head, oppression's thunder-clouds:
The frightful whip has dug into my back,

Until the blushing gore crept through the holes;
The hissing brand has burnt into my bone,
Until I shrieked the name of that dread God
Who of one blood has made the sons of men.
But in the midst of those conflicting pangs
And jerks of nature, Afric's sunny home,
My forest birth-place, swam before my sight.

" My wife long since was hurried from my side,
Ere Time's rude razor had slipped o'er my head,
Or his rough ploughshare furrowed up my brow.
My children have been sold before mine eyes,
And torn from my embrace, and whipped away
Where fields are moistened with the mourner's tears,
And blood is rusting on the planter's spade,
And human bones are bleaching in the sun,
O'er which the death-bird flaps his heavy wings,
And wails in concert with the rocking trees.
Filling the night with dirges,—where is heard
The crack of the slave-whip, and the shrill cry

Of the poor sufferer smitten to the earth :
Ay, there my children were compelled to pine.
I've drunk the bitter waters of despair,
Shrunk from the frosty fingers of Neglect,
Eaten the crust of bitterness, and bowed
Me like a beast of burden to the yoke :
But, in the midst of sorrow's briny sea,
That fair home-spirit rode upon the waves.

" Flash, flash, ye elements, and lay me low !
I'm a forsaken, desolate, poor slave,
Cast out from home, and its society,
Whom now ye toy with :—whirl me to the grave,
That I may hide me there in endless night !
For I shall never see my boyhood's bowers,
Or drink out of my native wells again.
I'm weary of existence, and would sleep."
And from the cleft sky an electric blaze
Freed the cold clay from his enfranchised soul.

WAYSIDE PICTURES.

BOOK FIRST.

THE

HONEST WORKMAN.

HE fairest flowers, the fullest
sea of sight,
The costliest pearls, the most
inviting gems.
The grandest, greatest, meekest,
noblest minds,
Are often shining in this dark-
some world
Where least expected, and their glory's beams
Remain unnoticed in the general glare.
How many an honest man in homely weeds,
Whose name is odour in his little sphere,
Dwelling in vale obscure by sea or stream,
Or where the city darkens, many-tongued,
Or in the hamlet's hollow, as the rill
Trickles soft-singing over slippery stones,—
How many are there living thus obscure.
Scarce known on earth, but much esteemed in heaven,
The gems of Adam's race, whose royal names
Are deep engraven in the Book of Life !

So have I heard from some low cottage porch,
Reed-wrapped and woodbined over like a bower,
With lattice low, and rude walls, boulder-built,
Sweet-scented mid the mineral of the mine,
What time the milk-maid brushed the early dews,
A gentle carol warbled from the lips
Of moorland maiden, rarely caught by kings.

Some court " great gluts of people," houses, towns,
And cities drunk with riot ; but, for me,
I woo the reedy meadow and the fen,
Where rushes rustle, or the rock where climbs
The shining ivy, and the wild bird sings.
Quaint do ye call me, that I love such scenes,
For evermore with Nature ? Be it so;
I am her child, and she my mother is ;
And so you must not blame me. Up the hill,
And down the vale, and through the breezy bourn,
By the sea-shore, and on the ragged ridge,
I read her legends, living lays of love.
My own old county is my copy-book.
From which I cull my pictures ; and its leaves
Are like her mines, exhaustless in their worth.
My hero-miner is no gilt ideal.
Pulled in to make a poem, but a man
Who really lived, and acted, and expired ;
A noble man, a man to imitate.
But, see, two riders and their foaming steeds
Burst from the coppice like a thought of flame.

c

Still onward dashed the horsemen. Through the mist
Loomed the grey granite crags and castle-top
Of mineral-marked Carn Brea, whose awful head
Was drenched with rain, and smitten with the storm.
The rabbit cowered within its mossy cell,
The wild bird sat in silence 'neath the ledge,
With half-shut eye, and beak beneath his wing.
As marched the winds across the weltering wild,
Hurling the rain-drops on the groaning world.
Still onward dashed the horsemen. Bank and brier,
And deep morass, and ditch with water drowned,
And rivers wildly tumbling o'er their rims,
Rough ruins green with age, or grey with years,
And bogs with torture boiling,—all were passed,
And in a cottage clinging to a rock,
Where sat a lonely dame in linen garb,
They turned at last for shelter, while their steeds
Stood in an outhouse 'neath a roof of straw.

A Christian had been buried, one whose gifts
Were great in secret, whose heart-prayers were made
More in the closet than the crowded church ;
Who spoke with pity to the lowest hind,
And wiped the tear from Sorrow's softened face ;
Who called the children round him when the day
Expired in purple o'er the forest falls,
And told them tales, and fed upon their smiles,
Laughed with their laugh, and shouted with their
    shout,
Mingling the lays of age with early life;
Then led them far beyond the roofs of time.
He stood between the oppressor and oppressed,
Healing the wounds which cruelty had made.
He sought the bed of sickness, and, when found,
Refreshed the sufferer with his purse and prayer.
With liberal hands he wrought most liberal things.
The widow found in him a constant friend.
The wandering orphan, shivering through the world,
Ne'er stopped in vain before the good man's gate.
His bounty, like the sky-lark's joyous song,
Gladdened the hearts of all within its range.
He stooped to wretchedness, and, with kind words
And kinder deeds, lightened the grey-haired man.
Familiar was he with Dame Nature's laws,
Nor sealed her book of wonders ; but his soul
Held endless converse with the Eternal Word.
Messiah was his pattern. Morn and eve,
And busy noontide, found him toiling on
In the Redeemer's footprints. By his life
He preached the Saviour to the multitude,
And cried to all, " Walk in the narrow way."
He stood among his fellows like a tree,
Of foliage rare and verdure beautiful,
Whose summer greenness never knew decay.

The Sabbath bells are ringing, vale and wood,
And rock, and ridge, and slope with mosses dressed,
Are hung with echoes ; wandering voices flow
Upon the spirit, lulling it to peace,
And gentle visions fill the mind with heaven.
Beneath this honeysuckle let me sit
In quiet meditation. As for man,
His days are swifter than the eagle's wing,
Or river rushing down the wildest steep ;
To-day he rises in his summer prime,
To-morrow bends along the vale of age.
How near the days of happy childhood seem,

Though forty winters block them up with clouds !
I stretch my arms forth with a gush of joy,
And seem to touch my daisy-gathering hours.
Alas ! alas ! old Time hath hurried on,
And left them far behind the farthest hills,
With king-cups sparkling over all the land :
And now I battle with the storms of life.
But there is peace at last for all our woe,
And comfort for the weary, if we trust
The kind and loving Saviour, in the home
Of Eden-music higher than the stars.

Peal on, ye gentle preachers. Day is done,
And Eve steals down the vale in garments grey :
I ponder in her shadows. One sweet spot
Is ever with me, as your echoes float
Above the tree-tops, like the sweep of wings.
A little grave it is among the hills,
Beside a Gothic chapel, and I seem
To hear the tread of those who haste to prayer,
Through primrose lanes, although I'm far away.
Here have I long desired to sleep at last,
When life, with all its cares, is at an end,
Among the honest, pious villagers,
Just at the foot of my old granite mount ;
That when the cottager, his day's work done,
Sits in the dusk with baby on his knee,
What time the first few tapers gild the pane,
He, listening to the river at his gate,
May think of him who carolled through his moors.

Sweet honeysuckle ! let me linger here,
Among thy fragrance issued in a shower.
How blissful thus to muse where Nature pours
Her incense forth in hollows watched with hills,
And roofed with stars, and floored with living flowers !
O what a temple is the leafy wood,
The rude old rock, the ocean's solemn shore,
The valley's bosom, and the meadow's lap !
I love thee, Nature, with a fire unfeigned,
And ever at thy feet thy child would sit
In pleasant meditation, where the eye
Of selfish man beholds not my retreat,
In storm or calm, when heaven is blue or black,
Learning thy lore, and treasuring up thy truth.
Could I have had my choice, my home would be
Among the reefs and rivers, fens and ferns,
From human hives as lonely as a loch.
Here, hermit-like, I'd pass away my hours,
Drinking at Nature's fountain, undisturbed
By trump or tumult, writing simple song,
With wife and bonny bairns, until life's last
Long evening shadow fell upon the plain.
But Providence has given me other work,
And other wonders, and I bless His name.
Now to our story mid the spreading thyme.

The dame heaped up the fuel on the hearth,
Which cracked a joyous carol, while the blast
Drove the rude rain-drops rushing on the thatch,
And hissing on the casement. Then she spoke,
With much of love and Cornish courtesy.
" I give you greeting to my lowly home,
Ye storm-caught strangers. Nearer draw you now
My turf-baked cake upon the shelf,
I have a turf-baked cake upon the shelf,
And milk and cream upon the pantry board :

Pray let me fetch them for you." So she placed
Before her guests these simple elements.
They ate, and drank, and chatted each with each,
Giving their hostess space to speak between.

She told of trials past, and tempests near ;
Of storms blown over, and of gales to come ;
Of blank bereavement, like the rush of war;
Of kindred lost, and relatives betrayed ;
Of beauty blighted in her summer morn ;
Of tear-drops shed upon the infant's grave ;
Of Hunger sitting with the household flowers,
As still as Death, amid the charnel dews ;
Of sickness entering with its fever-face,
And laying low a loving family ;
Of harvest-time, when earth was wet with rain ;
Of noise and show acquiring shouts of praise,
And meekness pining in its empty shed ;
Of Horror, stalking through the heavy night ;
Of Desolation, coming like the sea,
With blackened breakers, bearing with a roar
The hopes of man upon the rocks of doom.
But more than all were they intent to hear
How first she walked the way of widowhood.

Her husband was a miner, toiling where
The light of morning never found its way,
Or star-beam gilt the gloom ; where night remained,
Blacker than Boreas when he hides the hills,
And shrouds the valleys with his dismal wings.
His eldest boy strove with him, twelve springs old ;
A bud in shade, a blossom in the dark.
And they were wont the ladders to descend,
Tied in a rope. At one end was his sire
Going down before, and after him the lad
Came clinging to the staves. Around their waists
The cord was fastened ; so that, if the child
Fell, he might save him as he downward dropped,
And bring him to his mother and his home.
He was a tributer ; a man who worked
On speculation, digging through the ground
In search of ore, the sweetener of his toil.
If found, he flourished ; if not found, he fell ;
Nor fell alone, fell wife and family.
But much of misery was he doomed to feel.
Long months of disappointment, nights of woe,
And days of strife, and mental agony :
He dug, and found not ; dug and dug again,
Again to be the loser—all was dead.
He ventured till his clothes were heavy rags,
And the last shilling glided from his purse.
Yet hope sang with him in the sulphur-rifts,
And pictured bright to-morrows. And when green
Tinctured the rock, or copper stained the stone,
In fancy he beheld his stores increase,
His pile of mineral levelled on the floors,
His debts discharged, his wife in new attire,
His household songsters warmly clothed and fed,
His new home rising by the running brook,
His farm enclosed, his pretty meadows tilled,
Poultry and pigs rejoicing in the stye,
And Molly 'neath the hawthorn by the gate
Chewing her cud in quiet. So he dug,
With eyes the home of tears, and heart in heaven :
But when men elbowed him along the street,
And frowned upon him in his patched-up vest,
And cries of hunger echoed in his home,

His heart sank in him, and the angel Hope
For a short season travelled from his side.

One weary day he laboured in the smoke,
Pale with prostration, while vexed Fortune's wheel
Turned round and round in utter emptiness.
He left his working-place a clouded man,
And in his white-washed home among the stacks
A wail o'ercame him such as Misery mourns
Among the famished in her shattered shed.
His darling children, cold and hunger-pale,
Cowered in his hovel, crying much for food.
On a small stool, scoured white with straw and sand,
His eldest boy bent, broken in the bud,
Weeping aloud with redness in his eyes.
A little girl sat sobbing on her chair,
With hunger-marks upon her lovely cheek.
In the wood-cradle baby found a voice,
Thrusting his faded hands in empty air.
The mother's face, beneath her apron hid,
Appeared a sky of drops ; while through the gloom
Words wandered woful, " Father, give us bread."

Meanwhile the moon's face blushed behind a cloud ;
Strange footfalls echoed on the threshold stone ;
The door was rudely opened ; when at once
Two men rushed in, with wildness in their looks,—
The landlord and a towering officer,
Who, spite of tears, and sighs, and hunger-moans,
Took an inventory of their furniture,—
Clock, dresser, table, settle, stools, and chairs,
Bed, bedding, clothes-press, pewter pans and plates,
Old faded pictures, jostled much by time,
The hour-glass, and the cage without the lark,
And other items, such as knives and spoons,
With numerous tin cans shining on the shelf,—
And, scowling on the good man, left his home.
O God of Jacob, succour the distressed !

Sleep came at last, and bound them in their tears,
When he, with many arrows in his soul,
Knelt in his chamber, with uplifted voice,
Praying and sobbing, " Father, hear Thy child,
O hear Thy child ! Have mercy on a worm !
Yes, I have sinned against Thee ; with high hands
And outstretched arms defied Thy just commands.
Yet, O, have mercy on me, for the sake
Of Thy dear Son, who tasted death for me.
Give me Thy Holy Spirit, gracious Lord,
To lead me in the path of rectitude,
And fill my erring soul with light Divine.
Thou seest my wasting household : all day long
Have they been pining in my breadless home ;
The stamp of famine is upon their face ;
Weakness in every limb, mist o'er their eyes,
And untold gnawings shake through all their frame.
Have mercy on us, Father ; let our cry
Bring down Thy bounty on our shrouded hearth,
All-gracious Benefactor. Thou art He
Who ever feed'st the raven of the rock,
The wild bird of the wood, and all the forms
Of unseen life that throng this wondrous world ;
And Thou hast promised, those that trust in Thee
Shall feel no lack of anything that's good.
O, Father, Father, shield us from the woe
Of wasting hunger ; let my little ones,
And her that bare them, speedily be saved

From creeping down to death with feet of bone.
Be merciful, O God, to sinners vile ;
Open a door of hope, a path of life,
That we may bless and praise Thy mighty name.
But if, by Thy inscrutable decree,
My poor petition may not move Thine heart,
And we all die, Thy righteous will be done."
He wiped the hot drops from his eyes, and heard
A voice of sweetness, " Go to Widow Worth."

The shipwrecked sailor, rescued from the deep
Moaning in mountains round its struggling prey,
And tossed half-naked on a stranger shore,
Clothed, warmed, and fed, and guided to his home ;
The limb-lopped soldier, hunted by the foe,
And bidden with the mercy of the good,
Whose sons and daughters he had sworn to kill,
Until the howl of murder drooped and fell,
And he in safety reached his friends and fire ;
The friendless orphan on a winter's night,
Blue with the blast, and crying with the cold,
Snatched from his doom, and sheltered from his fate,
By those who never knew his father's name ;
The hungry man, in valleys not his own,
Fed from the table he had never seen ;
The thirsty pilgrim, o'er life's burning sands,
Refreshed with waters from the limpid brook,
A little girl the cheering minister ;
A starving labourer, borrowing precious loans
From one whose dwelling towered above his own,
Which saved his feeble wife, and feebler ones,
From rushing o'er the rapids of despair ;—
These know the worth of true benevolence.

Within a quiet, pious fishing-town,
Snug in the west, resided Prudence Worth ;
A lady famous for her charity,
Both in her native place, and far beyond.
The unsuccessful, striving fisherman,
Who in his little boat went paddling forth,
Singing his hymns, and looking up to heaven,
With net, and hook, and bait, to lure his prey,
On the blue fields of ocean wonder-filled,
Where the great gull rode kingly, and the winds
Spoke in a language heard not on the shore ;
Returning when the moon twined her chaste rays
O'er the white billows breaking on the sand,
With not a single fish for all his pains,
To creep into his shed, distressed, and sad ;
Emptied his sorrows in the widow's ear,
And felt his wants abundantly supplied.
The failing farmer in the western vales,
Craving her bounty, drank it like a stream
Of living waters, healing greedy woe ;
The toiling artisan who sighed for help,
Found help in her, when other helpers failed ;
The pale mechanic and the delving hind,
The heart-crushed struggler sighing on through clouds,
The weeping widow and the orphan slim,
All found in her an angel of relief.
In the sick chamber, and the home of pain,
She sat, like Love, with honey on her lips,
Dispensing bounty with a smile of joy.
Like Him, who left the glory of the heavens
And stooped to suffering manhood, walking o'er
This woful world with healing in His heart,
Both for the bodies and the souls of men;

So Widow Prudence passed her pilgrimage :
Her goodness, like an odour wafted far,
Had reached the honest miner ; and he took
His staff in hand to travel to her bower.

The morning light was wooing the green earth
To wake from slumber, when he kissed his babes,
And westward turned his face toward the hills,
Whose blue peaks caught the sunshine, while they
　　　　seemed
To roll him welcomes from their rocky tongues.
He walked along, conversing with his thoughts,
Which rose in mystic phases, many-hued ;
Now winged with hope, now blank with rayless doubt.
Through long, rude lanes he travelled, charmed with
　　　　birds,
That trilled sweet measures on the fresh free air ;
Or awed with Nature's wonders, mount and main,
And forest full, and river rushing clear,
And height, where quiet slumbered, hid in moss ;
Or farm, or cottage, peering through the trees,
With apple-blossom laden ; and his soul
Discoursed, meanwhile, in silent speech with God.

He reached the lady's residence, and told
His simple story,—how in a dark mine
" Bad speed " pursued him ; though he laboured long,
And toiled with zest unchanging, nothing came ;
And now his goods were all distrained for rent,
Which would be sold at once, unless a friend
Would lend him money to escape the blight.
'T was a great trouble which had touched his soul,
And so he prayed she'd help him. " Where's your
　　　　home ? "
Asked Mrs. Worth ; "pray tell me,—and your friends ?
For aught I know, you are a wicked man,
A drunkard or impostor ; tell me all."

" O, Madam, I am neither," he replied ;
" But what I say is honest, simple truth.
No bread is in my cupboard, and the cry
Of fainting hunger pierces through my frame.
My neighbours know, but will not heed, my woe.
If you will kindly lend me this small sum,
I promise that, when four short months are flown,
I'll come and pay you, as I hope for heaven."
" How much do you require ? " asked Widow Worth.
" Three guineas," said the miner ; " this would make
The world a glory and my life a joy."
Her heart, unused to anything but love,
Yielded to his entreaty : so she placed
The money in his hand, saying, meanwhile,
" Here, take it, though I never see it more."
And he, o'ercome with gratitude, retired,
Sobbing between his thanks, " I'll come again
In four short moons, and each bright guinea pay."

BOOK SECOND.

CARN BREA.

How often hast thou fed my early Muse,
Crag-heaped Carn Brea, when from my father's
　　　meads
I scanned thy front, mist-clad or clear, and deemed

My mount and thee twin-sisters beautiful !
One bright May morn, when violets were rare,
I tricked old Labour, and equipped myself
With poets' baggage, pencil, sheet, and lyre,
And, walking o'er the moors, I turn'd my face
Towards its summit shining in the dawn,
As 'twere an old bard welcoming the young.
I crossed the meadows, followed by our dog,
Who snuffed the air and barked among the flowers,
Itight happy to be free ! The larks were up,
Singing among the cloudlets, and sweet song
Gushed from a hundred hollows. In the fields
The cottagers were busy with their spades,
And ploughs, and harrows; and perhaps they thought
I was a crazy fellow wandering weird.
I reached the mountain's base, where an old man
And a young lad were cutting granite blocks,
Perchance to build a cottage of their own ;
And hard enough they worked. So on I went
To gain the summit of this famous carn,
Which looked so distant from my father's door,
That oft in childhood I have thought the sun
Stopped on the rocks and started forth again,
Renowed by resting on its ridgy brow ;
And in my dreams within my own dear bower
I oft believed, if I could wander there,
I should be sure to see great Phœbus' bed,
And mark the door from whence the moon came out,
And view the' uncovered stars. O, childhood, fair
Art thou, and innocent as fair, and sweet
As breeze-blown odours from the banks of broom,
And fleet as sweet,—gone like an uncaged bird.
I gain'd the hill-top, saw its boulders bare,
Some worn by time, some carved by Druid art,
Where oft perhaps the painted Briton prayed
To Thor and Woden, offering human blood,
When moral darkness filled our blessed isle.
Thank God, the light has come. the living light,
Chasing the shadows, gilding house and hall,
And guiding Albion in the way of truth.
Even then, boy as I was, I learned to list,
Beside the banks and rocks and hedges low,
For any tones of Nature's poetry
Straying upon the zephyr ; and methought
I heard the tramp of feet along the down,
And saw, as in a mirror, bearded chiefs,
With battle-bows, and skins about their loins,
And paint upon their cheeks, calling aloud
On gods which having eyes could never see,
And ears could never hear; and such a sound
Rushed from the rocks, that, snatching up my lyre,
I hastened from the hill, and at its foot
Stopped for a moment, gazing up its side,
To pluck some flowers with white-and-yellow leaves,
Which I bore home, calling my brothers round,
And little sister, giving them the whole.
They seemed to wonder where such flowers could grow,
And begged me I would tell them. Sitting down
On a green hillock 'neath our hawthorn tree,
I pointed to the mountain far away,
And told them that its rifts were covered o'er
With those dear beings pale with gentleness.
They shouted in their mirth, "Brother has been
Up in the sky, and plucked those pretty flowers,
And brought them to us." So they tripped about,
Well-pleased to have my nosegay for a toy.

I had been on the mount, and breathed its air,
Bathed in its glory, worshipped in its glow,
Clambered its stairs, beheld its chambers huge,
Paused by the quoit, and listened by the cave,
Harped on its wild gorseddau,* light-enthroned,
And the rock-basins, stained with mysteries;
Read cantos on the castle, where each ledge
Is a rude poem from the pen of Time ;
And felt repaid, and then paid o'er again,
For my rough climbing; wishing, too, that May
Would reign without a rival. Walking-back,
I travelled on, through song from bird and stream,
The lark in air, the cuckoo on the bough,
And, meeting with a cottager, I caught
The following echoes struggling through the broom.

The speaker was a pilgrim, and he wore
A cloak of beaver, streaming to the grass.
His eyes were black and bright, and on his brow
There was a dignity by thought impressed ;
And this the import of his story strange :—

" The moon was resting on a broken cloud,
Bright as an angel, when, beside that rock
Deep-channelled yonder, two fond lovers sat
Reading each other's faces. As they gazed,
Tears fell, and sighs were uttered, which the dark
Revealed not, as their sweet lips met again,
And kissed like streamlets. Each far star appeared
A burning seraph with a harp of joy,
And the old world was Eden. O'er the reeds
Glanced white-robed visions, and the swelling wind
Wafted their names upon it. From her bower,
O'erarched with ivy, Happiness looked forth,
And sang her tenderest vesper, while the heath,
Brown in its beauty, wooed bright angel-feet,
And shook with solemn breathings. Thus they sat,
Embowered with blossoms from the tree of bliss.
How beautiful the dawning of young love,
Gilt with the glory of the sun of hope,
Fresh, Eden-odoured ! On the mountain sides,
In the still vales and hamlets, rustic-robed,
And clover farms, she lingers, clad in white,
Amid the ruins of this blighted ball.

" Like a fair flower had their affection grown
In the dear dingles of their fatherland,
Sweet-scenting every action ; first the bud,
And then the bloom, and then the perfect rose,
Ripe for the white-robed angel. When she walked
In gentle girlhood through the peat-hedged meads,
To milk the cows beneath the flowery thorn,
He whistled at the gate, and saw her home.
And if at eve she took her waterpots,
To fill them at the fountain, there was he,
Conversing by her side, and aiding her
To cross the narrow stiles with granite steps,
Bearing her pitchers even to the door.
And when she rode from market, holding fast
The basket on her lap, he strove to steal
Across the lane, with business on his brow,
Or true or false, he cared not, so he caught
A smile from her to gladden all his care,
And one May eve he washed and combed his curls,
And brushed his best coat lustily. and took
Some wild flowers in his hand, which he had plucked,

---

* Judgment-seat of the Druids.

Searching the moorland for them when the sun
Showered his warm kisses on the sheltered banks,
Or hedges tipped with green, and bent his steps
Towards her dwelling, lighted up with love.
For she was ill, and those sweet offerings pale
Were for his Laura, beautiful in gloom,—
Daisies and blue-bells, buttercups and moss,
And primroses, with sonnets on their leaves.
The wakening world looked like a petted bard
Shining in fresh-won laurel, and the sky,
Blue in its brightness, seemed the gate of heaven.
He touched the latch, it rose, and soon the door
Turned on its hinges, and he found himself,
For the first time, sitting beside his love
In her own home. They blushed and blushed again;
And then the father spoke, the mother too ;
And the youth felt his tremor wane away,
Even as the wind falls on a summer eve,
And leave him chainless. In the porch she came
At parting, sweetly bidding him good night.
Thus step by step the Graces led them on.

" Summer was past, and in the leafless wood
Autumn lay down to die. Deep mourning tones
Arose from Nature, and the sky wept tears
Upon the sounding earth, as, one gray eve,
They climbed the old hill with elastic tread,
And, sitting on a moss-bank, hand in hand,
Conversed in whispers. On her path the moon
Walked robed in silver, and the white rocks looked
Like saints assembled on the hills of heaven.
He spoke delighted ; as he spoke, love words
Came thronging on him, till his speech surprised
The speaker, and the gentle listener smiled ;
Then bent her head, even as the lily bows
When the sun blushed too deeply on its face.
' How happy must we be when you small home
Among the rushes shall be wholly ours ;
And we dwell there like honeysuckles dwell
In the green covert, shedding sweet for sweet !
How will we tend the crocus, how the rose,
And how the woodbine climbing to the thatch !
How beautiful shall be our walks at eve,
Twilight descending, and the day's toil done !
And when the Sabbath, like a traveller, comes
From the peace-shore, with hymns upon its harp,
And prayers and praises flowing from its tongue,
How will our hearts rejoice beneath the vine
Of holy Israel, rich with clustering love !
And should the crow of baby-ones be heard,
And baby-feet patter along the floor,
And baby-music shiver by the hearth,
How will we love them for the Giver's sake,
And dedicate our rose-buds to the Lord !
Speak, speak, my angel, shall it not be so ? '

" He listened, and the silence deeper grew ;
The wild bird screamed among the naked blocks,
The wind came rustling, and deep shadows stalked
Along the hill-side, whispers filled the air
Mysterious, weird-like. ' Answer me, my love,
My light, my life, my summer in the cold,
My fountain in the desert, answer me.
Shall not our love grow stronger year by year ?'
Still no reply, but silence deep as death.
Gently he touched her hand,—it fell like stone.
Then, stooping down, he looked into her face.

Her eyes were fireless, and the roses fled.
He kissed her lips ; but they were cold as rock.
A shudder shook him, all his pulses beat,
And coals seemed heaped upon his burning brain ;
Life's courses almost stopped, as with a shriek
Her name rushed from him, echoing o'er the wild.
He knelt and wailed, then rose, and cried again,
Gazed on her face, and wondered in her eyes,
Entreated her to whisper but a word,
Or smile upon him ; but she stiller lay,
And colder grew, and waxed more pale, until
The truth hissed through him, that the foe had
        quenched
An arrow in her heart, and she was dead.
Yes, she was dead ! In Love's enchanted bower
Blissful she lay, when death came, like a breeze
Laden with wings, and lulled her into rest.
Her pillow was the moss, her couch the fern,
Her canopy the star-bespangled blue,
Her curtains Cynthia's tissues, and the rays
Which play about the blessed in their dreams
Her free attendants. So she gently died,
As dies the moonlight on a harvest morn ;
And angels came and carried her to heaven.

" Darkness o'ercame him, harp and tabor ceased ;
The glory of the old mount waned away ;
The face of man grew strange. He sought the fields,
And sounding wilds, and caverns cloaked with shade,
And moors with marshes mournful, till his hair
Grew as the shaggy common, and his form
Spare as the lonely alder. Boy, and girl,
And timid matron, shunned him in their walk,
And village gossip gave him twilight fame ;
And one clear evening, when the moon was full,
Two harvesters returning from the meads,
Beheld him sitting on his favourite bank
Where Laura's spirit left her. He appeared
Like one conversing with some mystic shape,
Or far-off brightness. On his head he wore
A hat of oaten straw, and in his hand
He held an oaken staff, rough-knotted round,
And he was gazing eastward. Days, and months,
And heavy years lagged by, with sorrow fraught ;
Yet he was seen not, and returned no more."

The peasant wiped his brow, and, sobbing, said,

"An aged man was sitting by his door
One quiet evening, listening to the sounds
That rose from Nature, and a tale he told
Of war and want, that smote the listener's ear.
Two sons had he, his comfort and his stay,
His all in life ; he had no kin besides ;
For they had ripened quickly, and lay lopped
Beneath the reaper's sickle. Years passed by,
And Peace slept in their dwelling, till, one morn,
The brazen trumpet brayed among the hills,
And forth they rushed to battle. What they saw,
And what they heard, and what they suffered there,
Can hardly be imagined :—sounds that made
The hill-sides tremble, and the stately pines
To wag their weeping tops ; hoarse howls that drove
The timid beast beyond its trodden lines,
The wild bird from its covert ; dying groans
Upon the pulses of the laden breeze,
As if had dawned the dreaded day of doom ;

The crash of arms, the roar of musketry,
The thunder of the cannon, at whose sound
The great rocks seemed to bellow, and the heights,
Studded with tongues, appeared one awful clang ;
The rush of armies, as their spear-points met,
Hustled and wavered like the black north wind
Among the forest branches ; towns on fire
And cities roaring in one horrid blaze ;
The widow murdered, and the fatherless
Stabbed, shrieking for their parents : greybeards felled
At their own table, the sharp-pointed steel
Pinning their stained locks to the social board ;
Men dying in the darkness, wailing loud
For distant friends, some with torn scalps, and some
With limbs hewn like a tree ; some hot for thirst,
With tongues cracked and glazed eyes, and some
Bleeding away in quiet, gleams of home
And face familiar passing through the mind ;
Some uttering prayers a mother's love had taught,
And some with curses on their closing lips ;
Some starving in the bushes, peeled with shells
That blazed and crashed, and left them there to die,
Forgotten by their fellows, who had wheeled
As the foe drifted, maddened with the charge,
Lorn now of reason, staring at the stars.

"A young man by a river stained with blood,
His school-gift Bible lying at his side,
With clotted hair, and jaw-bone rooted off,
Lay gazing at a locket.   'Twas the shade
Of one who loved him, where the roses twine
About her father's cottage.   Death had set
His impress on his features, and full soon
He crossed the river, and his name was lost.
A father and his four sons in a trench
Lay heaped together, marked with many a scar.
Down-toppled from a rampart.   They had fought
In noise and blood, till, overcome at last
By pressing thousands, they were speared, and shot,
And hacked, and sabred, and then wildly tossed
Upon each other, spear-points broken off,
Out-gushing from their bodies, and their limbs
Shattered or lopped ;—in a green vale beyond
Leaving a mother childless and a wife
In lonely widowhood and endless tears.
The old man's boys beheld them lying there,
The warm blood mingling as it faintly flowed,
And penned a letter to him.   Hunger sharp
Was then their portion, watching and fatigue.
They begged his prayers, and hoped that heaven at last
Would be their meeting-place.   They wrote no more.
In a few days a fearful fever came
And hurried them away, and in one grave
They both were tumbled, without board or shroud,
On a lone prairie where the wild beast roars.

"The tiding reached him, and his hair turned grey,
Turned in a single night, and the blow bent
His body, even as the slim reed bends
When the cold tempest mutters.   Then, like Job,
He stooped submissive, asking for His love
Who doeth all things well, who gives all good,
And for our profit taketh it away.
And oft at eve, when murmurs fill the vale,
And loiter up the mountain, when the air
Is faint with softness, and the purple hills
Seem thronged with angels, many a villager

Is startled in his cabin as he sings
His war-dirge to the moaning of the main.
The traveller, passing by his rushy home,
Beholds him at his door, oft scattering crumbs
To feed the sparrows, or conversing low
With little redbreast on the hawthorn tree,
Straining his eyes beyond the distant hills
As if he saw the gateway into rest."

More more of Thee, my Saviour : though the winds
Wail, and the waves rise higher than the land ;
Though poverty come rushing like a blast,
Or persecution meet me on my way,
Or pain or weakness ; Saviour, more of Thee !
Even like the mariner upon the plank,
Whose bark has foundered and whose mates are
        drowned,
Not heeding the bright stars above his head,
Or the full moon of silver, but whose eyes
Are rivetted on the approaching ship,
Steering to save him, so would I behold
The Man of Sorrows crucified for me.
More, more of Thee, my Saviour, when the morn
Breaks o'er the mountains, or hot noontide pants
Along the dingles, or pale Evening sits
Singing her vespers by her glow-worm lamp,—
More, more of Thee, my Saviour !   Though I learn
But little of the world and the world's ways,
And men pass by me in their rush for fame,
And friends forsake, leaving me lone to pine
Where leafless branches rustle, and the ice
Of cold neglect hangs on the withered spray,—
More, more of Thee, my Saviour !   Though the bars
Of some dark dwelling shut me from the light,
And pains press on my limbs, and I sit there,
An utter outcast, gnawing a dry crust,
And sipping stagnant waters, while the hands
Of Want and Woe pluck off the wasted hair,—
More, more of Thee, my Saviour !   Seas are crossed,
Rude lands are traversed, for the dust of wealth.
Bright blades are bared, red armies meet in strife,
Dark plots are laid, and, O, what blood is shed !
Men ponder night and day, and day and night,
How they may fill their coffers.   "Give me gold,
O give me gold," cry out the multitude,
Pursuing gain in paths all dark with gloom.
I sigh not for earth's treasures.   As Thou wilt,
Thou great Disposer, give or take away.
More, more of Thee, my Saviour !   If I walk
Through thorns and briers, or o'er beds of moss
Where Plenty spreads her table ; if my path
Is rough with trial, or all smooth with joy ;
If Favour sing my praises in her poems,
Or Calumny deface the precious page ;
Whatever be my lot, where'er my place,
If high or low, or be it rich or poor,
In cloud or light, in sunshine or in shade,—
More, more of Thee, my Saviour, till I gaze
Upon Thy glory in the land of love !

How many mercies meet me on my way,
Making my life delightful !   Loving friends,
Like sunlight in the darkness, wife and home,
And little children running at my call,
Climbing my knees, and mingling in my joys,
And sometimes sharing in my draught of woe.
O blessed Saviour, thank Thee for the buds

Around my table, lovelier than the green
Which robes the valleys redolent with rills.
And when I see the pining little one,
In other households, or the empty chair
And playthings left in quiet; when I mark
The scalding tear upon the mother's face,
From mention of her darling whom the grave
Holds in the darkness; when I sometimes hear
The church-bells toll among the solemn trees
For childhood in its greenness; words of praise
Press to my lips, and gush up from my soul,
For those Thy love preserveth, blooming fair
In my home-garden by the blue sea-shore,
The breeze of health flowing among the leaves
Pencilled with lines of beauty, yielding me
An everlasting summer. O what joy
To meet them at the hearth when evening comes,
Each like a ringing poem, and their eyes
Gleaming with glances of a brighter day!
And when they sit around the frugal board,
Enjoying what our Father has bestowed,
My cup of bliss uprises to the brim,
Bubbles and overflows, inspiring strains,
That echo only in the home of love.

Once more I shake me from dull worldly thoughts
That twine into my being, and look up
Where dwells the' Incarnate pleading for a world,
Praising Thy name, O Jesus. If I not
Unnumbered blessings ever at my side,
Both when I wake and when I rest in sleep,
Which others know not, and do not enjoy?
Troubles I have, in common with my kin,
And sorrow upon sorrow, which all feel
Whilst journeying homeward through a land of foes.
But he who saw the humble fishermen,
On the wild billows near Bethsaida,
Toiling in rowing, and who walked the waste
Of surging water with majestic step,
Proving His Godhead, quelling their hot fears,
And speaking down the tumult of the storm,
So that the winds fell powerless, and the blast
Shattered its trumpet, hurrying through the void,
Sees me a toiling rower on the sea
Of dark distress, tossed with the fretful waves;
And in His own good time will surely come
And whisper, " It is I ; be not afraid ;"
Guiding my vessel to the port of peace.

Our horsemen linger by the widow's fire,
Where we may meet at the next chapter's close,
In fields of story, fresh from fatherland.
We left our miner by the lady's lodge,
Blessing and blest, within his heart a joy
That gladdened every object, driving far
The clouds of gloom which hung above his head,
Filling with light the glowing firmament,
The trees and dancing flowers, as forth he walked
Into the glory of the outer world.

BOOK THIRD.

FIRESIDE STORIES.

MUFFLE thy chords, my harp,—England's dear
          Queen
Is now a widow, clad in widow's weeds.
Her heart is bleeding, and a nation mourns.
Commerce was rife, the hum of merchandise
Rose from the earth, old ocean's argosies
Swept shoreward, and the noisy tongue of Time
Told of a world in action, when disease
Rushed like a sable warrior in the dark,
And forced his spirit from him. The brave Prince
Lay in the Royal castle, like a tree
Torn up in summer by the fierce monsoon,
In all its leaves apparelled, and a cry
Of mortal anguish shuddered o'er the globe.
Music sat wounded at her instrument,
With hot drops running o'er the silent wires.
Painting let fall her pencil with dim eyes,
And one sad vision on the canvass lowered.
Poetry, with frozen thought, struggling for birth,
Ran o'er wild walks in blank bewilderment.
Amazement seized the senator, and wrapped
His utterances in mourning; and a wail
Rose from unnumbered hearts, heavy with grief.
O wondrous Prince! drinking the wine of Peace,
And dying in her arms, with vest unsoiled,
And name untarnished, leaving love behind.
O, pray we for our country and our Queen,
That red-robed War may never stain our shores,
That strength be given her in this hour of need,
And all the scions round the Royal board,
To bear this dispensation which rolled by,
Leaving thick blackness on its midnight trail.
The cup is drunk, our widowed Sovereign walks
Without her partner. We will hope her heart,
Soft as the sunshine on the morning flower,
Will feel yet more for poverty and woe,
The widow and the orphan. Thus we pray,
" O Prince of princes, save our dearest Queen."

Leave the light boat upon the pebbly strand.
The shore is green with verdure, and the leaves
Dip down into the waters: murmuring streams,
And singing birds, and echoes from the dells,
And cottages like fabrics of the fays,
And flowers as numerous as the lights of heaven,
And many-coloured as the bow of truth,
Make it a royal haunt where princely feet
Brush the bright mosses of a favoured isle.
Turn down you lane, loved for its crookedness,
Where bats wheel in the twilight, and the vow
Of early lovers trembles on the air;
And on the green hill's side behold a cot,
Guarded by angels. Softly walk ye now,
Nor let your garments rustle as ye pass
The woodbined window. In that cottage home
An old man lies afflicted on his bed,
And by his side a lady in dark weeds
Sits reading from the Bible. Gentle words
Float on the peasant's ear, and visions bright
Pass and repass before him,—battlements
Gilt with the sheen of harpers glory-clad,

And valleys trod by seraphs, whose white wings
Murmur delicious music; streets of gold,
And cities turreted with fadeless light;
Flowers smiling sweetly in the upper sphere,
Where friends departed mingle; and he longs
To shake life's burden off and be at rest.
And then a silent prayer ascends on high,
That God would bless the lady, whose dark weeds
Hang mournfully about her. Blush, O man
Denying truth, for this is England's Queen.
O happy nation, blest with such a head!
Ten thousand voices, like the rush of waves,
Rise from the hills, and echo from the vales,
And thunder from the waters, " Saviour God,
O save our Queen, save, save our dearest Queen!"

How are we tossed and drifted ! Each high tide
Drags back our hopes into the black abyss.
And leaves us floundering on the shore of change.
Three pleasant homes, since busy life began,
Have closed their doors upon me, and I've gone,
Leaving their feathers dewy with my tears.
My first was reed-surrounded and reed-roofed,
A cottage on the crag where free fern-fays
And moorland fairies danced among the broom,
And music trilled o'er Druid-trodden thyme,
From bank and boulder, bush and bending brake,
Or spanned the welkin like a choir of chords.
Silence and Peace walked round it arm in arm,
And Poesy sang beneath its shaven eaves,
Or warbled by the hearth-stone, and the lore
Of lofty legends lingered in its light.
O blessed home, next to my home in heaven !
With sunlight covered, when all else is gloom ;
I loved thee as a bridegroom his young bride,
And twined thy buds around my youthful harp.
I roamed among thy fissures, like a thought
From the hot brain of some fame-foolish bard.
I heard within thy echoes trumpet-tongues,
Blown by the blast, and read upon thy rocks
Immortal cantos, chronicled by Time,
And in the twilight of the summer eve
Visions descried,—great hosts of bearded seers,
Or towers far distant on which harpers stood,
Or mountains crested with the sheen of heaven ;
And travelling through thy thickets, verse-imbued,
Whispers have floated round me, heard by those
Whose lives have lengthened in the love of song.
Sweet home, all-precious, through revolving years!
I turn my thought toward thy rude-built walls,
Now prostrate on the common, like the tar
Rowing to land, not seen for many moons.
Love drew me from thee with a thread of gold ;
But evermore along life's bustling track
My spirit meets thee like a saint from bliss.

Among the mine-pits was my second home.
Here grew our earliest flower, still opening fair,
In childhood's garden, like a plant from heaven,
Until the first dear word tripped from her tongue,
Filling our hearts with rapture, and we gazed
Into the future, beautiful with hope.
Here, too, my harp gave pleasure deep and still,
Although the hand of hard, incessant Toil
Pressed on my limbs like metal, and my nerves
Tingled with weakness like a crazy chord.
My third was 'mid the rushes by the rill,

Babbling its beauty to the tall blue-bells,
Which kissed its waters as they sparkled by.
'Twas a small house, with pleasant garden-ground,
Built for myself. My own hands raised the stone
From an adjoining quarry, and our croft
Yielded me granite, which I split and brought.
And I had thought to pass my life away
In its seclusion, till the call arrived
To leave the shadow for the shadeless shore.
But no; it must not be. One autumn morn,
We started up, and left it in the mist
Which gathered thick between our eyes and it,
And by the sea-shore with our babes we came.
Not all. There is a grave beneath the trees,
Small, daisy-covered, where the glow-worms shine,
And green grass grows, and freedom's favourites sing;
And here one slumbers like a rose entombed.
But fifty moons have scarcely come and gone,
Ere we must leave again, and sorrowing go
To seek elsewhere a humble dwelling-place.
But God will surely guide us on our way.
With my dear wife and loving little ones,
And harp, and book, and friendly brother-bards,
A hovel were a home, with hollow walls
And rended roof wind-swept upon a rock.
On Cornwall's moors, or 'mid the Alpine snows,
Sun-streaked with beauty from the isle of love.
These changes, treading on each other's heels,
Will surely wean us from this world of woe,
And bind our spirits to the home of heaven.

One miner left the town, as if a weight
Was severed from his person. All things changed,
A grandeur filled the universe, and glowed
Above the highest hill-tops, streaming round
The gladdened welkin like a zone of gold.
Sometimes he cried, sometimes he laughed, for joy.
He travelled on his way, as through a grove
Of beauteous blossoms painted by the bard.
The flowers, and trees, and sparkling waters smiled,
With other faces fairer and more dear ;
And every man and country bairn he met
Seemed far more friendly than they were before.
His wife and dear ones rose before his view,
Wooing his feet like angels, and his eyes
Beheld them imaged wheresoe'er he turned.
Elastic was his step, his song all flame,
And warm thanksgivings rushed up from his soul.
The sounds of Nature altered ; voice of bird,
And running brook, and wonder-working wind,
And humming insect steering o'er the down,
And ploughboy whistling on the sloping lea,
Were far more musical than heretofore.
As suddenly as thoughts troop through the brain
The old dark World had put his wrinkles off,
Enamelled with the rosy streaks of youth.
So have I often felt when pay-days came,
With little hope for that which I required
To purchase blessings for my family,
Denied me, though I laboured hard and long :
If but an unexpected trifle dropped
Into my pocket, earth was dark no more,
And, hastening home to kiss my little ones,
I felt as happy as a nation's king.

Return we to the cottage, where the wife
And loving mother waited wearily.

The children oft had started in their sleep,
And uttered sobs of anguish ; now awake,
They cried for food ;—nor did they cry in vain.
A neighbour poor, whose husband was a hind,
Broke her brown loaf in two, and brought them half,
Which, with a jug of milk, refreshed them all,
And seemed like manna to their hungry lips.
But as the day declined, and on the hills
Huge shadows rested, they with tears inquired,
" Is father coming? Why is he so long ?
Wherefore is evening here, and he away ?
We have been looking through our window-square
For long, long hours, and yet he does not come.
Why does he tarry when we feel such pains
Shooting through every artery like a fire?
You told us that a lady of the west,
Whose soul was softer than the multitude,
Would surely send your hungry ones relief.
Haste, mother, to the corner of the road,
And see if father's coming," Then she took
Her faded cloak and bonnet, and crept up
The narrow path, with thistles overgrown,
Where stood the waymark with its stony hands,
Pointing along the common ; but she saw
No husband through the halo of her tears.

The moon was rising, and the wild bird slept
In the still thicket, when he reached his home,
And dandled baby once more on his knee.
His children gathered round him, glad to hear
Of that day's travel, glad to grasp and eat
The sweetest bread that ever strengthened life.
He watched them with a heart from whence a stream
Of waters issued, bursting from his eyes.
" Could you have seen us," the pale widow said,
" Kneeling together in our little room,
And heard my husband's earnest prayer of praise
For mercies countless as the grains of sand,
Or drops of dew upon the locks of Morn,
You surely would have cause to weep anew.
But darker visions crowd upon my sense,
Beings of blackness, whose mysterious shapes
Hid for awhile the sunlight from my soul."

She paused amid her sobbings, which burst forth,
Stronger and stronger, as her tale unrolled,
With sorrow-streaks along each wetted page,
Like winds that whistle ere they wound the world.
Then spoke the horsemen, wondering by the fire.
The first, with forehead bold and quiet eye,
Peered through the Gothic casement, uttering loud,
" How the great mountain like a rocky king
Stands silent in the tempest ! Not a gust
With water laden, rushing with fierce front
Against his temples, but he shakes it off,
Like filmy atoms from an insect's wing.
The thunder roars upon his rocky head,
Echoing from cave to cave, and every crag,
Carved by the Druid in the olden time,
Seems like a fiery pillar, as the flames
Leap from the clouds, and lash their knotty sides.
He, awful in his calmness, shakes his locks,
And gazes up into the solemn sky,
As if a strain of music shook the air.
O wondrous mountain, 'neath thy ribs of rock
Lie beds of precious mineral, which, when Time
With tardy feet hath crept through other years,

Shall cheer the seeker with their shining store.
Rude ridge of boulders, carn of polished crag !
Eternal utterer of the Deity,
I muse within thy shadow, and look up,
As on the face of the Invisible.
I need no other monitor to show
The impress of Jehovah. Thou art full
Of the Eternal, and His voice is heard
Among the Druid relics of Carn Brea."

Then spoke the second rider, with a face
All summered over like a July lake :
" There's not a sound vibrating from the chords
Of the hill's harp but thunders of the Lord,
The mighty Maker of this beetling dome.
Beside yon lodge, with lichen covered o'er,
Once stood a cottage, where an old man dwelt,
Grey as the granite round the castle's base.
He wore an ancient hat, and shaggy coat,
With buttons white as silver ; on his shoes
Were shining buckles, and where'er he went,
His curly dog would bear him company.
But on his face there was a settled gloom.
He was a mighty reader, and devoured
Books by the parcel, books of baser sort,
Shadowed with doubt, and doleful with despair.
The Bible he believed not, never read
Except to cavil ; and the sun, and moon,
And silver stars, green earth and sounding sea,
Were on his calendar as imps of chance.
He turned his forehead to the blushing sky,
And with his lips he uttered blasphemies,
And madly shouted, ' There's no God, no God!'
He vowed that heaven and hell were fables both,
And man would perish like the roving kine ;
That all went down and rotted in the earth,
And there it ended. At the judgment day
He laughed, and wildly laughed at death, and said,
That when it came, he'd meet it without fear,
And go to sleep in quiet. Thus he grew
Yet hard and harder every passing hour,
Until his soul was crusted o'er with wrong,
And childhood fair and staff-supported age
Passed by him, whispering, 'That's the infidel.'
Poor hopeless outcast, blinded in a blaze
Of heaven's own glory gilding the great world !
Open thine eyes, blank idiot, and behold
God in the meanest newt or noblest form.

" The morning sun illumed the castle's crest,
And shot his rays athwart the solemn steep,
As forth he wandered, listening to the lark,
Trilling his sonnets on the spires of light ;
When, mingling with his anthem, he o'erheard
A gentle carol trembling through the dews ;
And, looking, he beheld a little girl,
Now half way up the mountain, climbing still
A narrow sheep-path, singing as she rose,
' I thank Thee, Father, that mine eyes behold
Another morning. All night long hast Thou
Been my protector, so that no rude thing
Came near my dwelling, sickness or alarm ;
And now Thy little lamb would come again,
O gentle Shepherd, asking Thee to guide
My youthful feet into the way of life.
And when I die, O take me home to heaven.'
And every rock and toppling stony heap,

And flower, and fern, and furze-bush beautiful,
And matin breeze, sweet murmuring o'er the down,
Seemed strangely echoing, 'Take me home to heaven.'
Through the fresh air, from myriad tongues unseen,
Floating on cloudlets or the zephyr's wing,
Or borne by birds across the mossy turf,
These words came ringing, 'Take me home to heaven.'
In his dark soul it sounded like a bell
With muffled cadence, 'Take me home to heaven.'
The old hill seemed to shout it, and on high
A shining seraph, sweeping through the dawn,
Chimed it upon his harp with golden strings.
He stood, as if with sudden sickness seized ;
His limbs were paralysed, a heavy weight
Was resting on his person, all his sins
Stood naked round him, while dread Tophet's flames
Seemed redly rising even at his feet.
He roared like one touched with the tongue of Fire.
' There is a God. O yes, there is a God.
I feel it now, it burns through every vein.
That little angel, climbing, with her prayer
Of simple sweetness, up those quiet heights,
Seems more than mortal. God has used this child
To lead an aged sinner to Himself ;
So that the weak has overcome the strong.
Be merciful, O Lord, be merciful.
I here renounce my wickedness and crime,
And fall upon Thy goodness : save, O save,
The vilest wretch that ever trod the ground.'

" Weeks crept away, with blackness on their wings,
And still he groaned, in agony untold ;
Till, one soft evening, as the sun went down,
A voice came murmuring through the bending broom,
' I blot thy sins out, for the Saviour's sake ;'
And he was happy. So his latter life
Was full of faith and deeds of charity.
He bore the fruits of love to God and man.
His curse was turned to prayer, his sneer to praise,
And joy was beaming from his aged eyes ;
The winter of despair had left his soul,
And summer glory overflowed the void ;
He drank from clearest rills, and walked with God.
Dying at last, he entered into rest,
Leaving no scion to prolong his name ;
And soon his rude-built cottage walls decayed,
The roof fell in, and on a night of storm
It lay upon the highland in a heap,
And now the site is a smooth bed of moss.
'Tis thus we fall, and perish from life's page."

Then spoke the rider of poetic eye :
" To-day a tale came tear-hung to our home,
Filling our souls with sadness. Woe of woes,
Death on a door-step 'neath the frosty stars.
Not age down-drooping, but a green young girl,
Blackened and broken in the porch of June.
She turned aside from virtue, and went down
The way of wrong, with poison-fruit o'erhung,
Slipping at every step, until she fell
Where tears are shed not, and the heart is rock.
Behold her in a den of infamy,
Quaffing the cup of crime with front of fire,
Singing lewd songs, and uttering woful words,
In fluttering feathers, faded like herself,
The very queen of Satan's high-fumed court.
Too soon a change passed o'er her : she grew old

Before her summer, and the rose of youth
Died like a blasted primrose on the moor.
Her lovers all departed, hope fell dead,
And tongues of torture shot through every vein.
She dared not look above : the frowning heavens
Poured withering curses on her sinking soul.
She gazed around, and all her May-day friends
Had vanished, leaving her to writhe alone,
With fall-eyed Hunger staring from his stand.
No ray of light gleamed in the cave of gloom.
The snow fell fast, the wintry winds were loose,
Rolling their white ears o'er the frozen hills.
Muffled in rags, she stole into the street,
And laid her down beside the rich man's gate.
Within were happy faces, pleasant cheer,
Great blazing fires, a sounding sea of song,
Beauty on cushions, mirth and sparkling wines.
Outside the door, in withering loneliness,
A dying wreck, with snow, and wailing wind,
And biting frost, her cruel ministers.
Thus beaten by the tempest's wing she lay,
Till from a chasm of the fearful gale
Death dropped and slew her. Still within went on
The feast and song, the wine and revelry ;
And Morning, struggling through her icy doors,
Revealed a vision sad as sin can stain."

BOOK FOURTH.

FIRESIDE STORIES.

I HAD been busy with a little poem,
  Making and mending, when I took my book,
  And started up to walk into the fields,
To gather inspiration from the flowers,
And happy birds, and lyric-laden breeze ;
And, turning round a corner by a stile,
I saw a blind man with his violin,
Singing and playing to some villagers,
Led by a little girl of six years old,
Ruddy and beautiful, and thinly clad,
Who caroled cadence to her father's chime.
He wore a coat of bargain, and a hat
Long mocked by tempests and the pelting rain ;
A green eye-shade concealed his sightless orbs,
And on his face the powder-grains had left
The impress of their riot, pits and ruts
And fearful scars, with bottoms black and sides.
One hand was splintered, half the fingers gone,
And the dried wrist, all blackened with the blast,
Seemed like a moving cinder of charred wood,
Guiding the bow across the warbling strings.
O what a wreck he looked, a human wreck !
And yet he sang and played so pleasantly,

As if he were the happiest man alive,
I stood to listen, and the pity-drops
Came to my lids to hear those ringing strains,
Rising and swelling on the evening air.
If he were happy, blind and blackened so,
Half fed and weary, on whom wind and rain
And bitter cold poured all their violence,
How should my song of gratitude arise
For mercies, numerous as the countless sands,
Strewn on my path, and clustering round my board!
His little girl sang with him, and her eyes
Oft looked imploringly on those around.
'Twas a sad sight. Within a reedy shed,
On a wild height, six little ones were left,
Wrapped up in woe, and wrung by wasting want,
Watched by a loving mother, woe-begone,
With scarce enough to keep them from the worms.
And day by day this pensive couple passed
From town to town, to sing for daily bread,
Not only for themselves, but those at home.
I gave the child a trifle, and passed on:
But through the rushes and among the ferns,
Beside the hedgerow and along the lane,
Over the pools and quivering through the trees,
Their touching ditty sounded, and I heard
The sharp shrill shiver of the violin.
O ye enjoying eyesight, when you gaze
Upon the beauties of this under-world,
On moon and stars, comets and wandering clouds,
That glow serenely in the upper sphere,
Think of the poor blind player, and relieve
The wandering minstrel singing through the gloom.

His history is soon told. One Autumn morn,
He left his cot, and travelled to the mine;
But not before he bent above the beds
Where slept his treasures, kissing every one.
He hastened down the ladders, and full soon
Was at his labour, boring the hard rock.
He placed a charge of powder in the hole,
Filling it half-way up, and the top part
With a soft stone he had designed to fill,
Tamping it to the top. Alas, alas!
When beating down the second floor, a spark
Ignited the closed charge, and off it crashed,
Like a great peal of thunder, dashing him
Back several fathoms; and when consciousness
Came, like a stranger, wondering at the change,
His eyesight had departed, and his limbs
Hung like the blasted branches of the beech,
Lashed with the livid lightning. If you ask
His first fresh thoughts as he lay groaning there,
He'll tell you that his soul was uppermost,
And then his wife and children. Poor, poor man!
'Twas sad to see him, after weeks of pain,
And long, long months of anguish, borne in trust
And Christian meekness, sitting by his fire,
Feeling the faces of his little ones,
And playing with their ringlets, telling them
That he should ne'er behold their eyes again,
Or gaze upon their beauty, but their hope
Must now be in the God who made the heavens,
And whom they should behold each other there.
Then, as his limbs grew strong enough to bear
His wasted body, and his children's cries
Rose loud for help, he took his cottage-harp,
Which he had practised when he was a boy,

And with his little maiden wandered forth
Among the hamlets, singing for their bread;
And day by day is heard the violin
Amid the mountains and upon the moors.

Then spoke the rider, twisting round his chair:
"'Tis sad the havoc the great foe hath made,
Since first let loose to blight the wicked world.
Fire, sword, diseases, haggard pestilence,
Storm, earthquake, famine, with ten thousand ills,
Like whetted scythes, mow down the field of man.
I knew a farmer, who went step by step
O'er misery's steep, until his end came on,
As sudden as the warrior blade to blade.
Wine was his mocker, till it madly hurled
Him, blinded, from the earth before his Judge.
One market-day he left his injured wife
And gentle babes, and promised to return
When evening shadows fell upon the flower.
But eve approached, a summer eve and still,
And night with all its stars and blessed dreams,
And yet he came not. At the farm-yard gate
She crept to listen, then went back again
To weep and wonder. Shadows flitted round,
Or scowled among the pictures on the wall,
Perched on the chairs, or sat upon the stools.
She hid her face, and silent was her prayer.
The clock struck two; she sought the gate again,
Again to feel no comfort; not a sound
Passed through the stillness, save the river's moan.
The clock struck three: she heard the horse's hoofs,
And, rushing through the door, beheld, sad sight!
The steed without its rider. Months lagged on,
And years of sorrow trailed into the dark.
The widow's hair turned grey upon her brow;
Her eyes had ceased to weep, her heart to bleed.
Her children gone, she lived in loneliness,
With heaven before her shining like a sun,
And yet no tidings of the lost one came.
Conjecture's page was rife;—the assassin's blade,
The river's bed, the mine-pit's awful gloom,
The sea's dark grotto, or the hungry bog,
Perhaps engulphed him. This is all that's known.
He left the highway inn at one o'clock,
Weltering in wine, and dizzy with the dose.
The cunning landlord helped him on his horse,
Received his money with a gracious smile,
Bade him good night, and turned the pony's head
Into the lone lane leading to the moor.
He swaggered in his saddle, and rode on.
The widow died, and gone is all her kin.
Long hath the landlord slunk into the grave.
Mysteries have risen, shook their dark drapery off,
And stalked about the world in weeds of light;
But till this hour a haze has overcast
The fate of this poor drunkard, which, perhaps,
Will lie beneath the cloudy hill of doubt
Until the judgment of the last great day."

"How differently our friend we left behind,
In the green graveyard, 'neath the castle walls,
Lived!" said the other, resting on his hand.
"And living well, he died in perfect peace.
The stranger lingering 'mid our lodes, who saw
His face among his fellows, and o'erheard
The gentle words that murmured from his tongue,
Felt in his heart he was a man of God.

The April of his life, his May-day hours,
His summer season and rich autumn brown,
Were all devoted to the cause of truth.
Sobriety sat down in plain attire
Beside his table, and, where'er he walked,
It bore the pilgrim pleasant company.
His conversation, like a purling brook,
Even for ever, though the rude storm strove,
Flowed freely, never rushing o'er its bounds.
The neighbours prized him, and believed his word,
And sought his counsel when discomfort came,
Or trouble rolled upon them, which he gave
Free, without grudging, tilling life with love.
The Bible was his compass, chart, and guide.
He took the lowest place, and deemed himself
Unworthy as an officer of Heaven.
He feasted with Humility, and sat
Among the rich grapes in her porch of rest.
Religion with him was an awful thing,
Too dread to handle lightly : hence he fell
In awe before her, all unworthiness.
He wrestled in his closet, all alone,
On hill and valley, with the Lord of life.
'Twas there he won his greatest victories,
And drank more largely of the wine of heaven.
At times he lifted up his voice in prayer
In public places, feeling it a cross.
At times he uttered words which served to cheer
The faint disciple of the blessed Christ.
At times he warned the sinner to repent.
But all was managed meekly, and much good
Was oft accomplished in his Master's name.
The great God blessed the labour of his hands,
So that he prospered daily, and his alms
Oft dropped into the shrivelled palm of Want.
He went about the country like a balm
For hearts care-broken, by his look, and word,
And cheerful deed, performed with earnest prayer.
His life was one convincing homily,
To win the wicked and to serve the saint.
Death came, and in his little upper room,
With glory filled, fronting the morning star,
Bright angels gathered, and he fell asleep
With Canaan's odours passing o'er his soul.

" Now take another scene from memory's page :
Amid the rocks he dwelt, and waterfalls,
And Druid hills with strange-carved crags a-top :
An easy man, with brain enough to think
How cattle sold, and corn, and farming crops,
And just no more : this was enough for him.
A small horizon bounded by the heights
And drowsy downs, distinguished from his door,
In which his mind revolved for sixty years.
The seasons came, with wisdom on their wings,
And teachings for the thoughtful, morn and eve,
And day and night, the sun, and moon, and stars,
Telling of God, and whispering of His love.
And yet he heard not, saw not, and his soul
Grew dark and darker every passing hour.
The flowers arose and cast their fragrance forth,
Breathing of Him who made them ; and the birds
Sang in the valleys their Creator's name :
And every stone, and steep, and rushy rill,
And roaring torrent, rolling down the rocks,
And cowslip clinging to the shelly ledge,
And shining insect humming o'er the heath,

Had each a tongue which trilled the name of God.
And yet he heard it not, but closed his ears,
And shut his eyes, and groped about in gloom,
Quenching the light within him, till he seemed
Almost as callous as his native crags ;
And many shook their heads in sage debate,
Saying, ' Alas ! there's little hope for him.'
But good art Thou, O Father, and Thy love
Extends to every atom Thou hast made ;
Chiefly to man, the noblest of Thy works,
Drawing the farthest wanderer to Thyself,
Refusing none, receiving all mankind,
Not willing that the vilest should be lost,
But giving Jesus that the world might live.

" Strange that within the landscape of his thoughts
There should be found a phantom men call fame,
Glistering in raiment brighter than the morn,
And that, amid the stillness of his home,
Where rushes waved and hawthorns marked the
              meads,
This easy man should sigh to be renowned,
And hunger after immortality.
Yet so it was. On every New Year's Day
He dropped a trifle in a small tin box,
Which, he had said, when lying with the worms,
Would buy his tombstone, and his name would live
Within the village when the tower turned grey.
And so the box remained, a sacred thing
Not to be opened till was oped his grave.
One April morn, when buds were on the brea,
And primrose clusters from the coppice peered,
Like angel-eyes, inspiring thoughts of song,
And waking melodies that slumbered deep
Within the soul, a Bible-reader came,
And eyed the treasures of the holy book
Before his eyes, and bade him gaze and live ;
And, passing on, he left him to his thoughts.
All this was new to him, a region fair.
And bright, and wonderful, and rich with hope.
Man lost and ruined, but redeemed and saved,
Justice appeased, the Father reconciled,
And the great Conqueror spoiling Death and Hell,
Opening the gates of glory to a world,—
All this was new to him. The Spirit shone
Into his heart, and one by one the scales
Fell from his eyeballs, till he clearly saw
The path of life, and walked the way to heaven.

" Daylight was done, and night came stealing on,
A night of cloud and tempest. How they rush
Above the hills, and hurry through the air,
Like muffled monarchs marching on to doom !
The angry Wind lifts up his dreadful front,
And shouts in fury on the trembling heights,
Shaking the earth and stirring up the sea,
Roaring around the reedy hamlet-home,
And knocking like a robber at the door.
Such was the world without, as he sat down
Beside his fire of peat, with new-born thoughts
Thronging the galleries of his wondering soul.
His wife, in linen weeds, and spectacles,
Was mending an old garment ; on the shelf
The hour-glass stood, with brown sands trickling down,
Where pewter plates and pewter teapots shone ;
In the wood-corner's entrance slept the cat,
And o'er the flower-pots by the lattice hung

A cage, and bird with beak beneath its wing.
Gone were their children, married all, and gone;
And so life's autumn closed them in its calm.
At last he spoke, and said, 'Yes, I'm resolved
That when to-morrow's sun looks o'er the hill,
I'll ope my box, and, be it rain or shine,
I'll take the money to the minister
To help the cause of Christ. This is my all,
And long have I been thinking it would buy
My tombstone, and our famous village bard
Might write my epitaph, and I should live
For generations 'mid our moors and meads.
All this I now abandon for His sake
Who scattered my thick darkness with His light,
That others may believe and feel like me.'
And year by year he walked with humble feet
The road to Zion, and his influence,
Silent as dew, was felt where'er he moved,
And many feared, and sought and found the Lord.
His last hour came. With shining armour on,
He stepped into the boat, and reached the shore,
And landed where a dart is never hurled.

" How does it thrill through every chord of life
To hear of princes clad in peasant weeds,
Monarchs in frieze, and kings in coarsest vests,
Or queens apparelled like the cottage dame,
Wielding the Spirit's sword with mighty power,
Moving Jehovah on His throne of stars.
And bringing down upon the sons of men
A flood of blessing from the sky of Love!
I knew a mother, living on a moss,
Who quietly pursued her humble way
Along life's road, communing with her Lord.
She had a froward son, who took his seat
Among the scorners, greedy after wrong.
He laughed at goodness, in whatever form,
And ridiculed religion, saying they
Were easy souls who sought her sacred shade.
He walked unblushing to the drunkard's den,
And roared his ragged carol, stealing home,
With reason reeling round an airy ring,
When Midnight sat upon the darkened hills,
Or Morn came blushing through her golden porch;
And as he lay, all feverish, on his bed,
She softly stole into his room to pray.

" Time rolled along upon his cloudy car
By wild-winged coursers drawn, till one spring morn,
When buds were bursting to the gush of song,
And rills stole softly round the primrose banks,
He left his native land, and o'er the seas
A vessel bore him to another clime.
Here he remained for years, as rock, unchanged,
Turning his back upon the cause of Christ,
And seeking rest to find increasing woe;
Till one rude night, when Horror was abroad,
And thunder rushed from groaning hill to hill,
As reeling through the forest to his shed,
A change passed o'er him swifter than the light.
Nought was or is, above, around, below,
Without, within, but with an angry tongue
It raised reproof. In the red thunder's roar
Deep condemnation rattled: every sheet
Of lurid flame that dashed across the dark
Glared like a dreadful monster, uttering doom.
The black pine forest shook its mighty arms,

And seemed to menace wildly, while his guilt
Rose like a great hill, covered o'er with clouds.
He fell upon the ground, and cried to God,
Rose and pursued his way; then fell again,
And cried, yet louder. Feeling no relief,
He reached his injured home, and wailed till morn;
And after many bitter days and nights
Rose up renewed. He turned away from sin,
And lived another life, of faith and love,
Preaching the Cross he had despised before.
That praying mother, in her little room,
By angels guarded, still exists in peace.
But day is dying, and we fain would hear
Our widow's story. Will you end it, dame ? "

The matron wiped her eyes, and thus began:
" My path through life has been marked out by Him
Who cannot err, and so I know 't is right.
Sometimes in cloud, sometimes in brightest sun,
Sometimes in mist, sometimes in clearest blue,
Sometimes o'er flowers, and oft where thorns abound,
Such has my journey proved towards my rest.
But life all summer would have chained my heart
To lower objects than the bliss of heaven;
Prosperity unbroken would have bound
My spirit to the creature; and a walk
All smoothness would have led me to the pit.
Sweet was my childhood, sweet my hymnful youth,
And sweet my womanhood and married life,
Though cares came creeping as my steps advanced.
And now, when lone and wintry, I look up,
With much of thankfulness, and trust, and hope
For help below and happiness above,
And like a lonely plover on the moor,
With night approaching, I awake my cry,
If haply I may soon regain my mate."

And then she told them how, when ripe fruit hung
Within the orchard, and the harvest-wain
Rolled laden from the corn-field, when among
The changing leaves the swallows held their court,
Ere they departed to a warmer clime,
And robin sang in silence, drawing near
The open casement with his whistling note,
Her husband donned his Sunday dress, unlocked
A little chest, and gladly took therefrom
Three guineas for the lady. Then he kissed
His olive-branches, bade his wife good bye,
And said, "Expect me when the moon's locks rest
Upon the mountain: Heaven preserve you all!"
And, resting on his staff, he crossed the brook,
And hasted up the footpath o'er the stile,
And soon was lost among the rising hills.
She scanned him from the casement, till her eyes
Grew dim with gazing, and a sudden rush
Of pale presentment bowed her to her chair.
Never had warrior to the fearful field,
Or mariner on long discovering voyage,
Or traveller to pile of ancient fame,
Intenser watching than she gave her lord.

BOOK FIFTH.

STERLING HONESTY.

He walked along, delighted with the world,
Delighted with himself, and all he met ;
His eyes beheld, in everything around,
The grandeur of the Highest. In the hills,
Golden with autumn, he discovered God ;
In the rude rocks that raised them, and the clouds
That gathered on their summits, and the light
Which oped their revelations, clearly he
Saw God ; and in the valleys shining, God ;
In the dear wayside flowers, and narrow rills,
The trees, and shrubs, mosses, and blades of grass,
And humming bees, and sporting butterflies,
And white sand-grains along the sea-shore, God ;
Above, below, and all around him, God.
His mind was full of light, his soul of prayer,
As, climbing hills and threading quiet dales,
He thus soliloquized 'mid ferns and fens :
" What joy to taste the stillness of the moors !
I feel afraid to shake their holiness
By breathing freely. Silence, beating heart,
And let me listen to the feet of God.
He walks among the mosses, where the flow
Of Nature's anthem murmurs on the ear.
I rush away from man, to pour my thanks
Forth in my temple filled up with the Lord.
The rivers are my trumpets, and the trill
Of tongues unnumbered my sweet choristers.
What bliss to worship here beneath the blue
Of heaven's broad ceiling, without fear of man !
Sweet breeze, O bear upon thy odorous wings
The praises of my Saviour ! Hear it, heaven,
And echo it, O earth, and roll it far,
Thou everlasting ocean. If I die
On some sharp crag, alone and hunger-pierced,
I'll breathe the name of Jesus. If the sea
Engulph me in its grottoes, struggling hard
To foil the monster, that all-precious Name
Shall bubble from the breakers. If far off,
In some thick forest, where the wild beast roars
And serpents lick the dust, the hovering bird
Behold me pining, watching for my fall,
The name of Jesus from my closing lips
Shall but half-scare him from his quivering prey.
If, in the quiet of our moorland cot,
My spirit breaks its fetters, or within
The workhouse walls life's burden I lay down ;
Or fall on Time's highway o'errun with care ;
My latest utterance shall be His great name.

" I turn my face towards those rock-crowned reefs,
Silently solemn, feeling that the law
Of God condemns me, and my trembling soul,
Beclouded, cries, ' Where shall I look for hope ? '
And the deep desert rolls the query back,
' Where shall I look for hope ? ' The towering trees,
Nature's true prophets, ranged along the vale,
Look kindly on me in their green-leaf robes,
Fresh, beautiful, lyre-hung, and wonder-fraught ;
And so I ask them, weeping at their roots,
' Where shall I look for hope ? ' and their firm trunks

Echo aloud, ' Where shall I look for hope ? '
Over the brook I bend, the wayside brook,
And kiss its murmuring waters clear as truth,
And as dear songs float to me, borne along
By gentle wavelets to its grassy shore,
I ask the purling poet, loitering through
The dingle, with its idyls on its lips,
' Where shall I look for hope ? ' and the clear stream
Sobs in the shade, ' Where shall I look for hope ? '
I gaze above, below, on either hand,
On steep and stone, on river, reef, and rill,
Asking them all, ' Where shall I look for hope ? '
And back returns, ' Where shall I look for hope ? '
The great rocks frown upon me, and the flowers
Hang down their heads in silence ; bird and beast,
And grass, and grove, the earth, and sea, and sky,
Are silent, and my words wander through space
Like orphan forms, ' Where shall I look for hope ? '
O blessed Bible ! let me turn to thee,
Full of my Saviour, shining with His love !
Here is the door of mercy, shut to none
Who rest on Jesus, the chief Corner-stone.
Here, here is hope, built on the oath of God.
Shout it, my soul, and let the happy winds
Waft it upon their wings to farthest shores,
Till all mankind rejoice in its embrace.
Shout, God is love ; He gave His only Son
To die for sinners, to atone for guilt,
Vast without compass, piled upon a world."

And thus he journeyed on, with pilgrim pace,
As through Elysium, gathering purest joys
From meditation, where the robin sang,
Or through the hawthorn soared the shepherd's lay,
Or from the thickets rose the mighty rush
Of the rejoicing rivers. On he stole,
Companioned with the comforts of the skies,
So soon to be where sin has left no stain.
Joyous was he ; his soul was like a well
Of living waters, bubbling o'er its brim,
As thus he poured his fervid feeling forth :
" Forbid it, that I e'er should seek for rest
But in my loving Saviour. Do I not
Desire Him more than gold, or precious stones,
Or friends, or fame, or house, or fruitful farm ?
Thou knowest, Father, that I dare not build
My hopes on earth's foundations. None but Thee
Do I desire, O precious Prince of Peace ;
No, none but Thee, nor less than Thee be given.
But, ah ! how slowly do I learn Thy love !
Like infant faltering o'er its mother's name,
Or staggering from the cradle to her arms.
Forgive me, Saviour, and inspire my heart
With grace and strength to serve Thee more and more.
O come, Great Spirit, scatter all the mist
Which hangs about the summit of my hopes,
And fill the' horizon of my faith with light.
Jesus is all, my Comforter, my Friend,
Refuge and Rock, my Fortress and my Tower,
My First and Last. I drop into His arms."

Ah, world, how changeful art thou ! Morning dawns
On hopes in embryo, withering ere the Eve
Draws her grey cloak around her. All things here
Have marks of change upon them, and a sigh
Is ever creeping at the heels of Joy.
He passed an old man, sitting by a tree,

Whose hair was white as winter. He had left,
Within the churchyard, by the belfry porch,
Each vestige of his kindred ; so that now
He had no child but Nature, whom he loved
With all a poet's fondness. They exchanged
Few words of kindness, greetings of the heart,
And then, as quickly parting, went their way.
He reached Hayle River at the rising tide,
And, glad to save three miles of weary road,
Resolved to ford the channel. Be it known,
That in those days no Causeway spanned the void ;
But Art has now another daughter here.
His feet are in the water, which becomes
Deeper at every step, yet deeper still :
Now at his loins, and now above his breast,
And now it reaches even to his chin.
Hope leaves him blinded. A black-chambered wave
Rolls with a roar upon him, the loose sand
Yields underneath, when, thrusting up his arms,
A prayer to Jesus rushes from his lips,
And down the good man sinks to rise no more.

"Come, little ones, and lay your toys aside,"
Said the fond mother ; " kiss me once again,
Kneel at your prayers, and creep into your beds.
The moon is come before your loving sire.
I'll sit and read my Bible." Then they clasped
Their little hands, and prayed that God would bless
Their father and their mother, make all good,
And take them up at last to heaven's bright home,
And, lying on their couches, fell asleep,
With summer landscapes sweeping through their dreams.
How sweet is home when day's hard task is done,
And Labour's forge is silent ; when the song
Of village milkmaid warbles from the mead,
And twilight idyls tremble through the trees !
I oft have felt, when sitting in my cot,
After a day of trial, such as those
Who dig in darkness only can conceive.—
I oft have felt, as round me shook the buds
With household music which my Father gave,
To deck my dwelling on the pensive moor,—
I oft have felt, when loving eyes have turned
Upon my face, and loving words have dropped
Upon my ears, that I would not exchange
My Cornish cabin, fragrant with the breath
Of richest roses, for a gilded court,
Where little children fill not life with love ;
And when those gentle song-strains have been hushed
By sleep's enchantments, and a solemn spell
Has dropped upon me, I have snatched my harp,
And its wild music, rushing round my hearth,
Has quite o'erturned the wasting wail of care,
And lulled me in a land of pleasant dreams.

She read, re-read, and then read o'er again,
The precious page of promise : " Let your heart
Be free from sorrow ; rest upon My word.
Beyond the stars are mansions, where the sun
Scorches no more, nor pang is felt of pain ;
And those who love Me shall be where I am,
And see My face for ever ; " and the tears
Fell on the page that cheered the worshipper.
" O, there are times," she said, and raised her eyes
From the worn Bible, " when my spirit longs
To leave this prison, and go home to rest,
Like a lorn bird confined in cruel cage,

Fluttering its wings, and picking at the bars,
Longing to break the wires, and mount away ;
So does my spirit pant for its release.
But soon the silver cord shall be unloosed,
The bird shall leave its cage of closing clay,
And like the lark among the morning clouds,
Whose song is sweeter as he higher soars,
So shall I feel upon my angel-ear."

And then a rustle, like a hundred wings,
Seemed to sweep by her. Starting quickly up,
She hastened to the door to look for him,
Her light in darkness, wondering why the stars
Shone clear, and solemn midnight long had past.
And he not come to brighten all below.
She kissed her babes again, and knelt in prayer.
The night was spent in watching, and when morn
Called up the ploughboy from his bed of sedge,
And robin shook his wings among the leaves,
And sparrow on the housetop, down the lane
Came a pale man, with sorrow in his face,
And words of sadness stealing from his tongue.
Their import, like a dreadful monster, rushed,
And felled her to the floor, and when this flash
Of faintness left her, she was shattered so,
They scarcely knew her ; yet with feeble voice
She gently murmured, " God hath given me all.
And He hath taken, blessed be His name !
My dear-loved treasure to the land of flowers.
O be my Husband, great eternal King,
And shield my blossoms from the ice of want.
And as I travel through this lonely world,
O let Thy face illuminate my path,
And cheer me with Thy presence, till beyond
The blue of ether I regain my mate,
Where Paradise reveals her living streams."

And then the messenger, with faltering voice,
Told where her husband in a fisher's shed
Lay shrouded in a sail-cloth, dead, and drowned ;
And she informed him, trembling, how he took
Three guineas, purposing with it to pay
Their debt of kindness to good Mrs. Worth.
He hastened back and published what he heard.
They searched his pockets, but no gold was there.
They looked along the beach, among the shells,
And in the sand ; but it could not be found.
Some one observed his right hand firmly clenched.
'Twas opened, and Surprise brushed back her hair,
And Wonder stared with silence on his lips,
To see it shining in the dead man's palm.
His promise seemed to occupy his mind,
When the last life-string cracked beneath the wave.
The funeral day came, laden with the mist
Of lazy clouds that covered all the heavens.
The mourning train moves down the mossy moor,
Singing a solemn dirge, through hamlets lone,
And meads all mournful, to the churchyard stile.
The coffin was lowered down, the good man read
The sweetly-solemn service, as great sobs
With heavy utterance labour from her soul.
Strangers were there, and loving relatives,
And neighbours wiped their eyes. His children, too,
Were there, in weeds of mourning, and their feet
Sank in the slimy mould which soon will hide
Their loving parent underneath the ground.
A little robin on a cypress limb

Poured forth a dirge for the departed one,
As pensive as the trickle of a stream.

Hail, honest miner! such true worth as thine
Has more of glory than the din of blades.
Thou wert among the dwellers of the earth
Like moonlight on the mountains, guiding feet,
All prone to stumble in the gloom of sin,
To haloed bowers of rectitude and right.
Life's closing drama, like the blaze of heaven,
Flashed out in darkness ; the black curtain fell,
With thy free thoughts, like sea-boat, missing barks,
Steering towards the harbour they had left,
Where friend was longing to embrace his friend,
And love to weep upon the neck of love,
Fatally foundering even at its mouth.
Hail, honest miner ! to thy ashes peace !
Entombed in quiet 'neath the blessed flowers,
Where country winds are sighing, and the stars
Look down on tower, and tree, and village spire.
The great Recorder, in the land of leaves
That never wither, shall reveal thy name
Among the noble on Life's mighty page.

And now the rain had ceased, the wind was gone,
The clouds had fled behind the farthest hills ;
The thrush came forth, and on the dripping thorn
Sang his last vesper to the peering star ;
The swollen rivers through the valleys rushed
With lofty voices, each a solemn song ;
The rustling sea-gull wheeled along the void ;
The old mount with its altar of grey rock,
And a few tears upon its shining face,
Rose in the blue of heaven with quiet crowned.
Beneath the eaves of a thatched cottage near,
A miner's child was singing to the moon,
Whose crescent gleamed above the castle's roof.
Strains softly sweet gushed from a thousand lyres,
And down the lane beside the lover's well
The thatcher whistled walking to his home.
Up rose the riders, musing to depart,
But not before she told them how her sons
And grown-up daughters left her one by one ;
Some for the seas, some for the vale of gold,
Some to seek lands, and some slept in their graves.
But God upheld her alway. His kind care
Was like a cloak around her ; food, and rest,
And peace, and hope, were with her evermore ;
And still she trusted that the Lord would bring
Her safely through the wilderness, and guide
The weary pilgrim to the home of heaven.

Buttoning their coats, one to the other said :
" You know the poor corn-gleaner, with a hood
Over her bonnet, whom we saw to-day
Crossing a stile, leading her little girl
With paleness on her forehead ? Her sad tale
Would move a heart of diamond. O'er yon hill
That sends a gale of odour through the moors
From furze, and fern, and broom with golden bells,
So that the dweller in the city-street,
Treading our turf and breathing the pure air,
Exclaims renewed, ' What floating fragrance here !'
Over you hill trod by the feet of bards,
Who love to walk within its hoary caves,
And trill their sonnets, smiles a cottage-home,
With reedy roof, and honeysuckle porch,

And pretty garden, like an isle of bloom :
And here, a blithe corn-nymph, she sweetly passed
Her girlhood, and ten years of marriage life,
As happy as a princess, love-o'erflowed,
Until the winds of wild adversity
Came howling in their chariots, bearing off
Her summer glory to the land of cloud.
Then earth appeared a gloomy sepulchre,
And for a season heaven was hung in black.

" 'T was summer time, the sun was on his march,
The white clouds drifted to their western homes ;
Beauty lay down, and dreamt upon the thyme,
Or carolled through the thicket ; swallows skimmed
O'er glassy pools, or dashed athwart the dells ;
Breeze followed breeze, in amorous pursuit,
Kissing among the rushes, or on high
Murmuring their loves in the fresh fields of air,
And now descending to the limpid rill,
Brushing its wavelets with their welcome wings,
Stealing into the little lattice low,
Where sickness bound the sufferer, cheering him
With freshness gathered from the fields and flowers ;
Now shaking through the hoary locks of Age,
Resting upon his thorn-staff, thought-o'ercome ;
Now kissing the fair child, whose hands were full
Of gathered flowers, not fairer than herself ;
Now murmuring o'er the hamlets, now away
Among the lichen by the great sea shore ;
Now in the meadow, now along the mine,
And now beyond the farthest flight of thought,
Song filled the welkin, song o'erflowed the dell,
And gushed from every crevice of the cliff.
The bright sea-waves stole singing to the shore,
With music in their chambers ; and the world
Above, below, was one rejoicing note
Of love and thankfulness to the Supreme.

" Her husband was a fisher, and that day,
On a large rock beneath the Lizard Lights,
He sat and chimed his psalm, as heretofore,
With hook and bait, in patient watchfulness
To capture that which brought his household all.
Nature was grand with wildness ; crag, and creek,
And curious cliff, and sea-birds perched around,
Or ricing on the waters like a plume,
All undisturbed within their tuneful doors,
And scarcely stirring at the approach of man.
The bright blue sky, the ever-moving main,
And fanes of serpentine o'erflowed with praise,
While voices rolled from billow, bank, and brake,
Or crashed from organs hidden in the heights.
His cottage, up the valley by a brook,
Was plainly seen, and at its rustic door
His wife and children watched him on the moss :
She knitting, and they playing, bright with bliss,
Wher suddenly a great wave, growing still,
And rising higher as it onward rolled,
Rushed o'er the rock, and fell in sparkling foam,
Tumbling him in the water quick as thought ;
And as they gazed, he struggled with the waves,
Which bore him seaward, onward, outward still,
Until he sank exhausted, and gave up
His ghost beneath the billows. Still they gazed
And wrung their hands, and wailing tore their hair :
They saw his body rise bereft of life.
It drifted from them still away, away ;

E

Then from the highest, farthest, fullest crag,
A huge sea-bird dropped on the floating corse.
They gazed, and wiped their eyes, and wailed again,
Until the body and the great sea-bird
Shrunk into haze, and dwindled out of sight.
Nothing on earth but merges into change.
That morning shone on their unsevered band ;
The evening saw them lone and desolate.
The green reed bruised, the blossoms crushed and torn ;
They fatherless and friendless in the strife,
She entering on her night of widowhood."

Full hastily they sang their parting lay,
Then from their purses cheered their hostess' heart,
Mounted their steeds, and turned a parting look
On the calm monarch in the evening's gloom,
Marking distinctly just above its base
A little glow-worm shining in a rift,
Channelled long since by the wild water sprite,
And garnished over with the god of flowers.
They gazed, yet spoke not, pleased with quiet thought;
When all at once a meteor, like a stream
Of purest silver, shot athwart the heavens,
And on its march it almost seemed to sweep
The summit of the mountain. This aroused
Them both to action : they exclaimed, " How grand ! "
And onward dashed the horsemen.

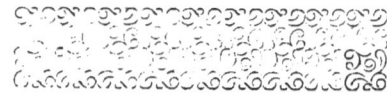

BOOK SIXTH.

THE TRUE HERO.

WHO comes along Cornwallia's hills and dales,
   In ministerial garb, with Book and staff,
   Scattering the doctrines of the Holy One,
Like flaming lights, around on either hand ?
And, lo ! they drop upon the barren wilds,
Giving the rocks a tongue ; in the green vales,
And the delicious flowerets smile for joy ;
Stream sings to stream, and, in the shady wood,
Trees clap their hands, and murmur their delight !
There's not a village on the low hill's side,
There's not a hamlet here with trees embowered,
There's not a town in all our western land,
A singing bird, a wood, a mound, a stream,
A silent flower, a shining blade of grass,
Or granite cross amid the boulders here,
But ever whispers Wesley's wondrous name.

The stars are glittering in their crystal homes,
The moon looks o'er the summit of the hill,
Peace walks with Twilight through her dusky bowers:
The harper is abroad in the lone vale ;
You hear the dying music of his lyre
Float through Eve's curtained halls, now high, now
                                                low,
As if an angel sang his holiest song !
A mother bends beside her lowly couch,

Placing her hands upon her baby-boy,—
Who kneels beside her like a cherub fair,—
And prays aloud that God would bless the lad !
His rest is sweet : he rises with the morn,
And hastens forth to greet the early lark,
Soaring and singing high above the mist.
The sportive lambkin in the emerald mead
Was not more joyous than that little one :
He plucked the flowers, whose eyes wept tears of dew,
Pressing them to his bosom ; and a voice
Came in the music of the little birds,
And in the treble of the piping winds,
And in the hum of wakening life around,
" O give thy heart to Me, My little one ! "
And the young prattler listened, till his lips
Instinctively replied, " I will, I will."
'Twas the Good Spirit striving with him there.

On ran the boy along his flowery track,
Till summer sunshine lighted up his face,
And painted his fair tresses beautiful ;
And on his blossomed way the Spirit's voice
Rang in his ears, still ringing, ringing still,
" O give thy heart to Me, My little one ! "
And the boy wiped his eyes, and said, " I will."

Decided now to be a Red-Cross Knight,
And fight the battles of Immanuel,
He girds the Spirit's sword upon his thigh,
To war with enemies without, within,
And hastens forth upon the battle-field.
He joins without delay the Church of Christ ;
Becomes in youth a follower of the Lamb,
And feels the freedom of his new-born soul.
While many in the Valley of Desire
Lingered and lingered on, until grey hairs
Hung on their temples, and old Time had ploughed
Deep furrows on their faces ; till their limbs
Were palsy-shaken, and they fell at last,—
Fell in the middle of this murmuring vale,
And sank into the bottomless abyss ;—
He stepped beyond its winter-smitten line,
Into the country where the upright walk,
And gathered grapes which clustered round his path,
And drank the waters flowing from Life's stream,
And plucked the leaves that prophets feed upon,
And heard the crystal hymnings of the blest ;
And, through the living telescope of faith,
The soul-eye of the Christian, he would oft
Gaze on the Golden City far away.
With sheeny battlements, and silver towers,
And glittering turrets, blazing in the Sun
Which never sets in all that wide domain !

Linger not in the Valley of Desire :
Dry reeds are here, and ferns, and dwarfish things,
And vegetation seems but half awake ;
It is the abode of sullen Discontent,
Unthankfulness, and withered Unbelief.
Despair's own cave, hung round with rusty swords,
Cracked scimitars and muskets tanned by time,
Old haggard ropes, and nails congealed with blood,—
Despair's own cave, under a beetling crag,
Is in the centre of this horrid dell.
Owls hoot within its shadows, and the ghosts
Of murdered thousands nightly visit here.
Don't linger in this melancholy vale ;

Step o'er the ridge of those dark frowning rocks,
Which lie between thee and the better path.
Don't starve thy soul, and lose thyself at last.
Haste from this dreary valley ; haste ! O haste !
The dread avenger is pursuing thee ;
His flaming sword is lifted o'er thy head :
Another step, and it may be too late !
He did not linger here,—with instant speed
He quickly crossed its withered boundaries,
Left its dark deserts and its windy wilds,
Soared high above its blasted scenery
Into the region of perpetual spring,
Drank the balm-laden breeze of Paradise,
And on the hills of hope conversed with God.

There are within this teeming universe,
This land of deserts, thorns, and prickly briers,
This vale of tears, this wilderness of grief,
This mire of heartfelt sorrows infinite,
This dungeon-home of Care, this rocky bourn,
This tangled labyrinth of false complaint,— ,
There are along its valleys, on its hills,
Beside its streams, in wood and flowery lea,
Among the ragged rocks, the wiry heath,
The sandy deserts, and the hungry crags,—
There are green spots,—green in the midst of death;
Green in the storm-time, when the sere leaves fall;
Green in the track of War, when his hot rain
Is shaking old Time's furrowed battlements ;
Green when gaunt Famine stalks along the streets,
With haggard Pestilence upon his heels ;
Green when the blade is blighted, and the ox
Is withering in the stall ; green when Decay
Fastens his putrid fingers on the flower;
Green when the heavens are angry, and the great
Dark cloud of judgment shrouds the weeping sky ;
Green, always green! e'en in the winter-time,
When Nature wears her covering of snow!

One of those green spots in the waste of life
Is where the children of Messiah meet,
To worship at the footstool of the Lord ;
To climb the golden ladder Jacob saw,
Dropped from the presence of the Deity ;
To sweep their hands across the holy lyre
Tuned by the cherubim in Paradise ;
To sit beneath the vine-leaves of delight,
And eat the food that angels live upon.
How many spots like these around us lie,
Kissed by angelic breezes ; bowers of bliss ;
Gems in the rubbish ; sparks amidst the gloom ;
Streams in the desert ; flowers in solitude ;
Suns in the chaos ; fire amidst the frost ;
Life in the house of bones and rottenness,
Watered by living dews from Eden's isle,
And warmed with hallowed flames from Love's great
    Sun !

How often, with the Bible in his hand,
Would he walk up yon narrow shadowy lane,
O'erhung with hawthorn and sweet-scented brier,
Till Evening put her starry mantle on,
And the bat floated by the shadowy grange !
How often would he read his Bible here,
Away from noise and strife, and feel the while
As happy as a ransomed man can be !
'T was here he treasured up those burning words

Which tinged the colour of his future years,
And made him such a Christian conqueror !

Hast ever seen a mine ? Hast ever been
Down in its fabled grottoes, walled with gems,
And canopied with torrid mineral-belts,
That blaze within the fiery orifice ?
Hast ever, by the glimmer of the lamp,
Or the fast-waning taper, gone down, down,
Towards the earth's dread centre, where wise men
Have told us that the earthquake is conceived,
And great Vesuvius hath his lava-house,
Which burns and burns for ever, shooting forth
As from a fountain of eternal fire ?
Hast ever heard, within this prison-house,
The startling hoof of Fear ? the eternal flow
Of some dread meaning whispering to thy soul ?
Hast ever seen the miner at his toil,
Following his obscure work below, below,
Where not a single sun-ray visits him,
But all is darkness and perpetual night?
Here the dull god of gloom unrivalled reigns,
And wraps himself in palls of pitchy dark !
Hast ever breathed its sickening atmosphere ?
Heard its dread throbbings, when the rock has burst?
Leaped at its heavings in the powder-blast ?
And trembled when the groaning, splitting earth,
Mass after mass, fell down with deadliest crash ?
What sayest thou?—thou hast not ?—Come with me ;
Or if thou hast, no matter, come again.
Don't fear to trust me ; for I have been there
From morn till night, from night till dewy morn,
Gasping within its burning sulphur-cloud,
Straining mine eyes along its ragged walls,
And wondering at the uncouth passages
Dashed in the sparry cells by Fancy's wand ;
And oft have paused, and paused again, to hear
The eternal echo of its emptiness.

Come, let us leave the fields and flowers behind,
The murmuring brooklet where the poet walks,
Weaving life's cobwebs into silken flowers
To beautify the homes of fatherland.
Come, let us leave the lovely light of day,
The bower of roses, and the Muses' haunt,
Where the green ivy roofs us over head ;
And go down, down into the earth's black breast,
Where, in the bottom of a shaft, two men
Prepare e'en now to blast the solid rock.
The hole is bored ; the powder is confined ;
The fuse is fixed,—it cannot be drawn forth.
They negligently cut it with a stone
Against a rod of iron. Fire is struck !
The fuse is hissing : and they fly, both fly,
Towards the bucket, taking hold thereon,
Shrieking the well-known signal. He above
Strove, but in vain, to put the windlass round.
One could escape,—delay was death to both !
One of them was our hero. Stepping back,
He looked a moment in his comrade's face,—
O what a look was that !—and cried, "Escape !
A minute more, and I shall be in heaven."
On sped the bucket up the sounding shaft:
The man was safe ! Eager to watch the fate
Of his sublime deliverer, down he stooped,
And bent him o'er the shaft, just when the roar
Of the explosion rumbled from below.

Up came a fragment of the rifted rock,
And struck him on the brow, leaving a mark
Which changing time will never more efface
Till Death shall wrap him in his murky pall!

They soon began, among the fallen rock,
To burrow for the corpse. At last they heard
A cheering voice among the shining flints,
Ring in the rattling fragments! Here he was,
Roofed over with the rock,—alive and well!
Forth from his fearful grave the hero came,
And smiled on all around him. Daniel's God
Had saved His servant in this dangerous hour.
All he could tell was, that, when left alone,
He sat down in a corner of the shaft,
And held a slab of stone before his eyes,
To wait the issue. And when asked why he
Gave up his life to save his friend, he said,
" His little children would be wet with grief,
While I had none my sudden death to mourn."

I look abroad on earth's great battle-field,
And from the hall of heroes, wrongly named,
I drag some laurelled wight, whose crimson robes
Are dripping in the blood his hands have shed ;—
I take the northern Czar.—him who, to build
A city, and to call it by his name,
Once sacrificed a hundred thousand men !
I take him with his soul besmeared in gore,
And place him, crowned, and worshipped, and adored,
Beside this Christian miner, who to save
His comrade's life, sublimely gave his own !
I take them, and I place them, side by side,
Upon the world's great platform, and I ask,
" Which of them is the hero ? "

                                        Line on line
Day dawned along the dingle ; from his hut
Among the mosses, where he lived alone,—
Except his dog and goat and favourite bird,—
With flowing beard and forehead high and broad,
And eyes that flashed with an unearthly fire,
Clad in a garment streaming to his feet,
The Mountain Prophet came : while the sweet flowers
Drank on the down their cups of morning dew,
Waiting among the willows wet with tears,
He raised his eyes and sang his matin hymn.

" Good, gracious Being, throned in endless space,
And stooping down to such a mite as man !
Accept the morning psalm I offer Thee.
I hear Thy voice flow through the gates of morn ;
I see Thy hand in every folded bud ;
I trace Thy wonders in the meanest worm ;
I feel Thy goodness in the fanning air ;
I read Thy bounty in the drops of dew.
Great is Thy name, and marvellous Thy power :
Thou art the same to-day and evermore.
Men change, and creeds evanish ; but Thy love
Unfailing stretches through eternity ;
And though sometimes to ever-erring man,
Stumbling along the stony path of life,
Thou wrapp'st Thyself in awful mystery,
The grand design is his eternal peace.

" How beautiful the summer of my life,
And the young bride Thou gavest me! Then there came

The image of her mother, and my harp
Was ever strung to notes of thankfulness ;
The earth was Eden, Eden were the skies.
Thou saw'st these were my idols ; so in love
The fever came and bore them both away.
How bowed my soul beneath this winter-cloud !
No light broke in from the eternal Sun.
I shivered like a lost man mid the ice,
And groped about, not knowing where I went.
Then rose my soul in prayer, O God, to Thee,
And poured out all its sorrows ; balm came down,
And gleams of glory glowed through all my frame ;
And closer walked I with the Blessed One,—
Lived less on earth, and mingled more with heaven.

" Years passed ; rich mercies thronged my temporal
                        path ;
I walked the earth in sunshine : lands increased,
And gold and silver, houses, friends, and fame.
The love of lucre chilled my love for Christ :
My heart had grown too worldly : then a scythe
Was sent by Thee to cut those brittle cords.
A storm arose and rent the watery waste,
And down went ships and costly merchandise ;
My cattle perished in the blighted fields ;
And sickness, like a strong arm from Thyself,
Pulled me upon the borders of the pit ;
And when I woke, like dreamer in strange land,
I found myself a poor man in my hut,
Alone within this shaggy wilderness.
O blessed God, I thank Thee for it all !
This way alone would lead me to Thyself :
My own marked path would issue in despair.
Here in these moorlands much I learn of Thee,
And riper grow for the white fields above.
All praise, all glory to Thy mighty name !
Among the dews of morn I shout Thy love,
And with the birds now trembling into song
My hallelujahs float into Thine ear."

And then he changed his theme and changed the key,
As starting to his feet he seemed to hear
A marvellous echo from the land of lays.

" The cruel war had ended ; from the field
The shooters had retreated, and the sword
Of the fierce soldier rested in its sheath.
The dead in heaps were rolled into a pit,
And buried in their armour. Far away
The wounded had been carried ; some in sheds,
And some in barns, and some in hospitals,
Were panting for dear life. Legless were some,
And some were eyeless, moaning in the dark ;
Some were bereft of hands, and some of feet ;
And some had splinters driven into the brain ;
And some with more than half their faces gone,
And some whose ribs were shattered, groaning loud,
And some with bullets pressing near the heart,
And some with scalps half-blown into the air,
And some with broken arms and rooted joints :
And others rolled in fearful agonies,
With teeth hacked out and shoulders hewn away,
Gashed in the battle with a hundred blades.

" Lift up thine eyes, and look upon yon hill ;
Blood stains the blushing verdure. Here, last night,
Huge armies met in combat, and a name

Was won, and writ in characters of gore.
Here lies a headless hero, there the head
Split like a shell in halves: yonder a steed,
And under it its rider black in death.
Pinned to a battery with quick-broken blades,
A hapless gunner dangles stiff as steel.
Here a grey veteran, grasping hard his spear,
Lies dead beside a youth cropped in his teens.
A father and his son, tossed side by side,
With stony eyeballs stare into the skies.
Here shreds of armour, there a heap of heads ;
And here a hand, beside a crimson rill,
That strangely grasps a shattered bayonet.
And here are legs in wild confusion hurled
Of crushed war-steeds and men ; while far away,
Beside a rock, a wounded youth has crawled,
To read his Bible and lie down to die.
A dismal dolour presses on the ear,
And over all dark pitchy wings are spread,
And Glory, shrieking, flies the bloody spot.

" In a farm-cottage on the craggy cliff,
Half-hid with oak and leafy sycamore,
Dwelt Pitt the ploughman, singing merrily
Among the sky-larks and his leaping lambs.
His wife and children loved him tenderly,
For whom he laboured with a happy heart ;
Till one dark day, when loitering through the town,
An officer o'erwrought him with his speech,
And he became a soldier, laying down
The spade of peace to grasp the warrior's knife,
And wreak it with a vengeance. Then a cloud
Fell on his dwelling darkening evermore.
He had been told of glory, and he thought
To win her trappings 'neath the wing of War,
To have his name enrolled among the great,
Green in his country's story. Ah poor man !
To seek for honour cutting human throats !
His conscience should have whispered better things,
And warned him of his error ; and no doubt
It gently chid him mid his golden sheaves.
But he was deaf to all but fame's red song,
Which only lured him from the crimson marsh.
Poor erring wanderer, dazzled by a spark !
The truly generous are the truly great.

" The night is chill and rainy : through the vales,
And up the hills, and o'er the boggy plains,
The weltering winds are writhing. Sad and slow,
The lone hours, one by one, are stealing out,
As by the fire a weary watcher sits
In sorrow for the absent, who has been
Through months of conflict on the hills of strife.
Sometimes her moist eyes gaze into the fire ;
Sometimes she listens at the creaking door ;
Sometimes she lifts her hands with freezing moan,
And a chill shiver shatters all her frame.
Sometimes she kneels upon the stony floor,
And sobs her sorrows in the ear of Heaven :
And then an angel with white wings of hope
Calms into peace the conflict of her soul.

" This stricken creature is the soldier's wife,
Once Pitt the village ploughman. Dark the day
On which he left his home for tented plain,
The flail-staff for the cannon, spades for spears,
The reap-hook for the rifle, and the song

Of the sweet sky-lark for the wail of war.
Since his departure to the field of fate,
Sickness blew on the flowerets of his home,
And with a fell swoop Death destroyed them all ;
And so the mother, desolate and lone,
With bleeding heart and eyes that cannot weep,
Waits for her husband, who, the letter says,
Has left the battle covered o'er with fame.

" A few days since, when passing by his door,
I saw the broken hero : he had crept,
Upborne by crutches, to his garden-gate,
And looked a corse for paleness. Sad it was
To see a leg was missing, and his face
Was scarred in furrows fearful to behold.
'Twas plain he had but little time to live.
His wife was standing by him, and her cheeks
Were almost fleshless, though her eyes were flame.
Has Glory nothing more than this to give,—
Limbs shattered, health destroyed, and life lopped
        short ?
Last evening, as the leaves dropped quietly,
And robin whistled on the ivy wall,
The funeral-bell was echoing up the moor,
And in the vale was filled the soldier's grave."

He paused upon his harp, while o'er him wheeled
A flock of sea-birds, and the mower's scythe
Was rustling sweetly in the dewy grass,
And, coming down a little pensive lane,
A village girl was singing an old psalm.
The smoke curled from a cottage chimney near,
The ploughman to the furrow led his team,
As thus he sang among the opening flowers :—

" 'Twas at the time when early lambs appeared
In meads half flowerless, that a labouring man,
A man of books and study, as he walked
Across the moorlands, thus apostrophized :
' O gentle Spring, sweet maid of tears and sighs,
And shining shoots and blossoms numberless !
Hail, hail to thee, thou damsel of the dews !
I feel thy breath upon my pallid cheek ;
It floats across the valleys like a balm,
And all the air seems full of imagery
The poets picture, and my soul of song.
I know thou comest ; for I feel thy fire ;
And from the weeping South I welcome thee,
With primrose clusters for the lap of earth,
And blue-bell cushions for the pastoral Muse,
And rills of sonnets for the rural bard.
Winter away ! we've had enough of thee ;
Thy storms have almost rocked the ragged hills,
And tossed the ocean up to meet the clouds,
Or torn it into rents like gulfs of doom,
Quick closing o'er the drowning mariner.
Thy chilly fingers, cold and shining ice,
Have almost petrified us into stone ;
So that, when stealing out beside the wood
In overcoat, and muffled like a bell,
Our teeth have chattered at thy frigid roar.
Good bye, good bye ! we've had enough of thee :
And hail, meek Spring, thou damsel of the dews ! '

" And then his thoughts assumed another form,
And childhood rose before him, soft with sweets,
And milk-white blossoms from the tree of May ;

His play-hours bright, beside the cot of thatch ;
His mother's story, in the faggot's flash ;
The prayers of one he never could forget ;
The songs he sang behind the hazel plough,
Or when he watched the sheep, or threshed the sheaf;
His father's counsel at the household board ;
His slides in winter, on the moorland pool ;
His bird-nest rambles in the ferny creeks ;
His first departure, his long stormy sail
O'er seas all billows, and his safe return ;
His walks with Mary in the clime of love ;
His marriage-day, when earth appeared a heaven ;
His firstborn son, his home among the hills
Shining with treasures from the mint above ;
And standing by the lattice of his cot,
What time the taper on the table burned,
He saw bright eyes glance on him through the panes.

" There is a joyous utterance by the hearth
Unknown to other bowers, and gentle thoughts
Flow in the fire-light winged with words of balm.
Sweet was the converse of that cottage choir
Which classic chiefs might envy, and Delight
Sat on the cushion with a smile for all ;
When at the door was heard the postman's knock,
And soon a letter with a foreign seal
Was lying on the table. Much amazed,
The children whispered and the parents smiled,
Conjecturing whom it came from. ' Break it, sire,
And let us see what's in it,' said they all.
And soon they saw the writer's autograph.
It was a letter from a daughter's hand,
Penned many miles away, bearing within
A precious portrait of their absent one,
A money-order, and a line to say,
' Expect me, mother, with the cuckoo-bird.'
How much they joyed 't is not for bard to sing :
Sad that such joy should be so near to pain.

" That night a fire devoured them. From the heavens
A mass of flame dropped like the arm of Fate,
And whelmed them in destruction ; dwelling-house,
Barn, corn-rick, store-shop, cattle with their sheds,
All scorched to ashes, save one little boy
Tossed by his mother, in a blanket wrapped,
Through the hot casement on the garden shrubs,
As the red chamber sank beneath her scream,
And all went down to ruin : he was saved ;
And when his sister reached her native land,
She found him like a lone bird on the wild,
And took him to her nest, and lived with him,
And brought him up to manhood, when his name
Rolled like an echo through the realm of mind.

" How sweet the music of the mellow morn !
Each bush that trembles in the dewy dawn
Seems a cloaked minstrel bursting into praise.
The shining flowers, wet with the tears of night,
With silent voices sing upon their stems :
Each zephyr has a lyre upon its wings,
Each fern a harper, each white crag a harp.
Up from the rushes flocks of swallows float,
Wheel o'er the rocks, and dash into the dell,
And glimmer round like brilliant shreds of song.
The bard-thrush carols from the golden brake ;
The rill sends up an anthem, and the wood
A shout of praises to the Great Supreme.

How beautiful to catch the first fresh burst
Of harmony from Nature's morning choir !
That little cow-herd, whistling o'er the field
To lure the sky-lark in his upward flight,
And brushing back his hair to see the sun
March from his mansion o'er the tissued mount,
Is happier here than Sleep upon his silk.
He mine the joy to watch the breezy Morn
With tears upon her face, to breathe her sweets,
And worship God on Nature's dewy throne."

Then kneeling down among the fragrant thyme,
Alone with silence in her mossy home,
He bowed before his Maker. On the clouds
Bright beings floated from the meads of Morn,
Drifting away in space, and smiled to see
A pilgrim praying with his face in tears.
A stream of joy fell from the Fount of Life,
Gladdening his happy soul, so that the gorse,
And ragged rocks, and hoary heights around,
Seemed gilded with the glow of Paradise ;
And when he left his closet on the crag,
A holy light was resting on his brow,
And peace was flowing through his bounding heart,
The rich reward of intercourse with Heaven.

I know a man who dwelt among the meads,
A labouring man, a man without a pound,
Who wrestled with the Lord in mighty prayer,
Until he moved the heart of the Most High,
Who sent bread to him by the birds of heaven.
One morn in Spring, when I was yet a child,
And had a childish passion for field-flowers,—
As I have now, though stumbling down the hill,—
I strolled into the leas in search of buds ;
And, feeling thirsty, sought this good man's door,
To ask a cup of water. All alone
I found him, praying in his only room,
With hands and eyes raised upward : though I spoke
Three times in earnest, me he heeded not,
Entranced in his devotion. God was there,
And beings brighter than in palaces.
Such tracks of earth, thus trod by holy feet,
Are hallowed ground for ever. He who walks
Amid those grottoes treads the skirts of heaven.
Again I spoke, but spoke once more in vain ;
And so I left him talking with the Lord.
One eve in April, as the primrose flowers
Closed in the coppice 'neath the twilight star,
His soul went forth to rest for evermore.
O, many years have passed away since then,
And many images of by-gone days
Lie in the chambers of forgetfulness
Mid skeletons dust-covered ; but this saint
Alone with Jesus in his humble home,
Grows brighter still as old Time steals away,
Bringing me nearer to the door of death.

BOOK SEVENTH.

THE MOUNTAIN PROPHET.

Noox filled the world with strivers. In his
    bower
The Prophet mused enraptured: swallows strove
To peer upon him in his quietude,
And moorland breezes fanned his flowing hair.
Oft in the fever of the fulsome town
Such dear haunts rise before me, full of God,
And running over with the breath of praise;
And tears flow down for what I can't enjoy.
The genii of the Muses hover here,
And sweep the mosses with their starry wings;
And oft at evening in the primrose time,
When my dear home was on the golden height,
And Silence drew me from my ready cot
Into her moss-house hung with leaves and flowers,—
When wandering softly in the falling dews,
I seemed to hear the footsteps of the Lord,
The very stones are precious in my sight,
And the peat hedges thrill like chords of song.
My spirit, panting through the universe,
Floats back to it, and settles down in peace.
Though clouds are heaped upon the world like hills
From zone to zone, sunshine is always here.
My thoughts turn to it in my sea-wash'd home,
And the pale flowers and springs among the ferns,
And crags that cry to the wild tempest's shout,
Rise on my view like ministers of hope.

Mid such a scene, in such a golden grot,
The white-haired Prophet mused at burning noon:
" Methinks, as listening on this bed of thyme,
I hear a voice across the distant waves:
' Come to me, darlings, cluster round the log,
Get near the fire, and warm you in the blaze.
Snow hangs upon the mountains, and the pines
Look white as angels in their feathery robes:
The rills are silent, and the shaggy bear
Prowls in the darkness near the homes of men.
I've brought a treasure from the British shore,—
That blessed book, the Bible; and I fain
Would read a portion to you ere we rest.
The Minister who freely gave it me
Said how it told of God who made the world,
And Jesus Christ, His well-beloved Son,
Who suffered for our sakes, and went to heaven.
And I desire to know those things myself:
So I have called you round our happy hearth,
And ask you now to listen.' Then he read
And wondered much, and read and wondered more;
And every night and every day he read,
Till light streamed in to cheer them, and they walked
In golden sunshine through a clime of clouds.

" Yonder, beside the orchard, sad and slow,
A funeral train moves on; the dead a man
Who dearly loved his Bible, and who lived
In close communion with the Lord of life.
He leant upon the precious promises,
Like trembling traveller on his long-used staff.
Disease o'ertook him on his mid-way course,

And laid his hot hand on him. On his couch,
Beside his pillow, lay the Book of God.
I saw him when the green corn clothed the meads,
Clasping the Bible to his throbbing breast;
His eyes were full of waters, while his lips
Showered forth the everlasting promises.
A few days since, upon a car of light
His spirit passed the boundaries of the world,
And rested on the overlasting hills.
O Love eternal! thank Thee for the Book
Above all books, that shows the way to heaven!
No charter like the Charter of the skies.
Its gold gems glitter mid the dust of time
To woo the weary to eternal rest.
A full free river, clear and beautiful,
Its healing waters gladden every land.
It cheers the peasant, and exalts the poor;
It sheds a halo o'er the hedger's hut,
And adds a glory to the noble's hall.
In every clime, in every age the same;
Black men and white men, freemen and the slave,
All learn salvation from the written Word.

"How beautiful the measures of the day,—
Morn, noon, and eve, and legend-loving night,
When stars and comets and the floating moon
Teach their Creator in the blue-built heavens,
And musing Silence, by the ruined tower,
On the dark steep, and in the village lane,
Or stealing like a presence through the streets,
Is softly whispering, Holy One, of Thee!
Then when the week is ended, and its sighs
And crushing sorrows, prayers and burning tears,
Are all recorded by a seraph's pen,
How like an angel in its snowy robes
The Sabbath comes, with blessings on its brow!
And in its stillness men think of their sins,
And lift their hearts in prayer, O God, to Thee.
A holy anthem fills the universe,
And heaven and earth are mingling into one.

"Jesus, I thank Thee for the Sabbath-day,
When grapes are given me from the tree of life,
And angels, climbing hill-sides purple-hued,
Gleam on my vision, lifting me with song!
What myriads throng Thy courts at Sabbath-time,
To bow before the Root of Jesse's stem,
And climb communion's halo-covered head!
Ye brooks and breezes, summer's gentle lyres;
Ye ferns and furzes, birds and bleating kine;
Rock, tree, and flower, and grasses numberless;
Ye shining rushes, drinking at the rills;
Ye rills, that murmur music as ye flow;
Ye mosses, blinking at the waterfalls;
Ye waterfalls, that crash with endless praise;
Ye thunderbolts, that cleave the flinty hills;
Ye lofty hills, that lift your fronts to heaven;
Earth, sky, and ocean, every living thing,
Man, beast and reptile, fish and floating fly,
Join with a worm to laud your Maker's name,
And praise Him for the healing Sabbath-day.
Shout Hallelujah! shout it high, ye winds,
And let the rain-drops pour it from their urns,
And zephyr bear it on its tuneful wings;
Glory to Him who made the Sabbath-day!

" How calm the spirit brooding over all!

Beside yon rock, white in its lichen robes,
A being sits with beauty on her brow.
Sweet notes gush from her, like to those we hear
A pensive poet playing on his harp,
When he forgets the world and the world's cares.
She wears a vest of blossoms ; in her hand
She holds a corn-sheaf, on her head a crown
Of burning berries beautifully bright,
And words of love and plaintive tenderness
And free goodwill are flowing from her lips.
Men drive her from the city ; so she hides
In lonely places, praying evermore
That war and discord may die.
Her name is Peace, her home is with the good.
Though born in heaven, she glides the warring globe,
And woos the nations 'neath her leafy wings.
She woos them, but they will not come to her ;
Rave, rush, and stab, and stumble in their graves.
Yet Peace will soon appear : she comes, she comes,
To link the world in loving brotherhood.

" Night waned away in silence ; then the morn
Broke like a mystery o'er the ancient hills,
Filling the vales with music. By a stream
A humble cottage, perched upon a mound,
O'erlooked with sycamore and English oak,
Where rooks were cawing and gray sparrows chirped,
Glowed in the glory of the rising sun.
Nature awoke all dewy from her rest,
And donned her cloak of sunbeams, while her heart
Poured forth a flood of God-accepted praise.
Each bird and bee, and sweetly-flowing stream,
And crag and creek, and sun-illumined height,
And moor and mead and marsh, and stirring wood,
And common brown, and cliff and murmuring sea,
Sent up its anthem in the ear of Heaven.

" Pause we a moment by this rustic porch,
And gaze upon the cottage. Sweet indeed
Are tree and trellise, walk and hanging flower,
And reedy roof, and chimneys ivy-wreathed ;
But yet a sombre sadness hangs o'er all,
Pressing into the spirit, and a voice
Seems sadly sobbing of decay and death.
No eyes peer through the lattice ; by the door
No merry voices mingle ; on the seat
Beneath the woodbine, in the grotto still,
No father sits to breathe the morning balm ;
Blinds hang o'er all the windows ; not a sound
Is echoing here, but all is still as death.
A few days since, within that upper room,—
You scarcely see the casement for a fir,
Whose graceful branches fall like folds of air,—
A mother lay a-dying, and her face
Was pale as marble, yet more beautiful.
At the bed's foot two little sisters sat,
The only children of the sinking one,
Conversing in a tone subdued and low,
With tears upon the roses of their face.

" ' Don't weep, Racele : o'er yon frowning steep,
And higher up, beyond those gathering clouds,
And higher still, behind the solemn sky,
Amid the stars, upon His throne of light
Our heavenly Father sits, and He looks down
To bless the weeper trusting in His care.
Have we not often heard our mother say

That not a sparrow drops upon the ground
Without His notice, and the very hairs
Upon our heads are numbered by His love ?
And when dear father perished in the wood,
That night of snow and roaring hurricane.
She sweetly told us of the God of heaven,
And bade us cower beneath His spreading wing.
Have not our wants been hitherto supplied ?
And if our mother fade away from earth,
And walk an angel mid the sweets of bliss,
And we are left alone upon the world,
Our father's God will feed and clothe His own.'

" But dear Racele's eyes still rained hot tears,
And throbbed her little heart as if 'twould break,
As, looking in her sister's face, she sighed :
' But 'tis so very, very hard to part ;
To have no mother when my tears run down,
And my sad heart is wounded ; all alone
To feel the stinging hand of poverty,
And plod my hungry way across the world ;
To lose her look, her smile, her healing kiss,
And never more to hear her speak to me ;
To leave our home, and go I know not where.
O, this is hard indeed ! But I submit ;
And as you say our Father up in heaven
Will feed us then, so I believe it all.
Indeed the prayer she taught us says so much.
So I commit my future ways to Him.'
The mother's face grew paler, paler still ;
And as these two, alone and comfortless,
Gazed hard upon her, suddenly her lips
Moved slow in prayer, while from the streets of gold
A glory beamed upon her countenance,
And, like the moon behind a summer hill,
Her spirit passed into the land of stars.

" The day is strangely quiet ; far away
Is heard the mill-wheel in the rushy vale,
And robin sings among the shining sloes.
The flowers seem praying on their mouldering stems,
Before they drop into their autumn graves.
The hedger whistles on the spacious moor ;
And down the river by the changing wood
The boatman carols to the falling leaves.
Within a churchyard sloping to the sea,
Where mounds rise thick on the uneven sward,
And the thatched belfry in its ivy-robes
Stands like a Druid o'er the epitaphs,
And yew-trees shadow many a silent urn,
Two orphan girls are kneeling on a grave,
O'er which a rose-tree dangles its last flower.
They both are sad, and both are shedding tears ;
Below them sleep their mother and their sire,
And overhead an unseen presence floats
With fragrance in its pinions, gazing down
Upon her orphans in this world of woe.

" Behind yon hedge with hawthorns covered o'er,
Behold a weary toiler : drops of sweat
Are falling from his forehead, and his face
Is seamed and saddened with the plough of care.
Old Time has led him till his hair is hoar,
And now he totters down the steep of Age
Into the vale of skeletons below,
Where Death sits monarch on his throne of skulls.
The sun shines hotly on him ; his dry lips

And burning tongue are almost cracked for thirst.
From morn till noon has he been hard at work,
Trimming the sod to make his winter fire,
His body bent to earth, his thoughts in heaven;
He looketh upward through the mists of time
For the grand coming of the Blessed One,
With flaming seraph and the trump of God.
Poor happy toiler, rich in royal hopes!
Time passed and left the weak one weaker still.
One day, when snow was falling, he lay down
And fell asleep. High o'er the highest hill
His spirit mounted on ethereal wing.
They dug his grave among the falling snow;
And when the earth was white, they buried him,
And mid the snow his funeral rite was read.
He left no wife or child or living thing,
And, like a bird whose mates were gone before,
He passed away into the twilight sphere."

Now gazing on the West, before him passed
A sunset vision, beautified by prayer,
As thus his song unrolled upon the breeze:—

"Eve changed to purple, purple were the skies,
The clouds were purple, and the distant hills,
And whispering trees, and lone heights summer-still,
The far-off lake, the flags upon its brink,
Sweet little flowers that gemmed the banks of moss,
Rills dropping music down the mountain sides,
Sea, rock, and castle, and the soft sweet air
That filled the heavens, were purple, purple all.
And 'neath the purple canopy a saint
Walked with his Bible; as he walked, he prayed;
And up to heaven was borne his earnest cry,
And rich the blessing falling on the good.

"Again he prayed; again the high heavens oped,
And filled his soul with visions. He beheld
The war-god's funeral in the land of peace:
He wasted till the fiend could waste no more,
And then he died in horrors: so he lies
On smashed artillery, shells, and broken blades,
Cracked dagger-edges, knives and shattered spears,
Gore-rusted shields, and prongs with poisoned points,
Bullets, gunpowder, rifles, tomahawks;
Down deep in earth, with hills heaped o'er his head,
And seas of blood upon him, while the heavens
Resound in thunders, 'War shall rise no more!'
And earth re-echoes, 'War shall rise no more!'
He saw the Jews all gathered to their home,
Jerusalem re-built, and Christ their Lord.
He saw Idolatry dashed from his throne,
Sad Antichrist and Error; and he heard
Messiah's songs thrill through the universe.
The lion fondled with the snowy lamb,
And kids and tigers played among the flowers,
And little children joined them in their sports.
From hill and valley, stream and rocking sea,
Hamlet and city, the wide wilderness,
Island and rock and broadest continent,
Mine, moor, and mead, and solitary hut,
One universal song swept up to heaven:
'Jesus, Immanuel, Saviour of the world!'

"Yes, Jesus, Thou art all, and over all;
Thy love is stamped on all created things;
Thy glory blazes through these lower worlds;

And Thou art heaven itself, where heaven is found.
Thy power is potent o'er the rich round globe,
And where the moon and stars and sun converse.
Thou shinest like a jasper in Thy Word,
And more than Adam lost we gain in Thee.
Have we a hope-prop, plodding down life's steep?
That prop is Jesus, and that hope Thyself.
Have we a solace in the shadow-land
Over whose hills the wings of Death are spread?
That joy is Jesus, and that comfort Thou.
Have we a heaven when dust returns to dust,
A land of fadeless beauty far away,
Where waters murmur by the tree of life,
And seraphs dip their wings in lakes of love?
'Tis all through Jesus: He the First and Last,
The great Beginning and the mighty End.
I strip myself of every selfish thread,
And fall a beggar at Thy blessed feet.
Hail, Jesus, Saviour, hail for evermore!"

Night stole forth pale with moonbeams: o'er the farms
And wayside hovels, woods and hamlets lone.
Wide whispering wastes, bright rills and bended flowers.
And ivy-pulpit grey with Druid lore,
Old hazel-hedge, still bluff, and daisy-mead,
The silver network hung, tissuing the locks
Of Silence musing in her rushy robes,
High on the white crags of his own dear hill
The Mountain Prophet stood, with hands upraised,
While flaming meteors flashed along the sky.
Beneath the burning stars he moralized:—

"How dark yon dwelling by the solemn grove!
The woodbine is neglected, and the grass
Grows rank around the doorstep; wildest birds
Perch on the roof and hover o'er the place;
The very air that staggers through the trees
Is sick with moaning, and the moon looks down
Upon a picture stained with loneliness.
A story meets you with a tear upon 't.
Here dwelt a pair beloved by earth and Heaven;
Child after child was added to their home,
Until four sons stood at their father's side,
And helped him in his labours. Tidings came
That o'er the seas the river-banks were gold,
And gold was shining in the river-sands,
And glancing brightly in the torrent rifts,
And lying heavy in the great bear's den,
Or heaped upon the summit of the hills;
That folk went there, and very soon returned
As rich as Crœsus in his gilded court.
And so the father and his four brave boys
Sailed for the gold-land, leaving Ruth behind.

"Years passed; a letter came with lines of cheer,
And words of sweetest comfort. When the Spring
Brought golden sunshine, flower and meadow-song,
She might expect them in their English home,
With gold enough to drive lean Want away.
But how unsearchable to human ken
Are Thy dread ways, O God! My soul adores
And breathes enchained among Thy lesser works,
Nor scarcely dares attend Thy loftier march.
The stately ship rode safely o'er the waves,
Till from the deck the sire and son beheld
The castle-cliffs of England. Fancy drew
Their joyous meeting on a sheet of light.

Where tears and kisses blended, till they sat
Within their dear home, telling travellers' tales.

"Then rose the winds and sighed among the cords,
Still rose and sighed again, and heavy clouds
Assembled seaward, mounting to the stars;
The lightnings strode the welkin with blue swords,
Followed by moaning thunder rattling loud;
The sails cried in the rushing river-rains.
The vessel groaned for torture, as the storm
Waxed loud and louder, tossing the torn bark
Upon the breakers, where it rolled in two,
And down went every soul into the deep.
A few were saved on spars and floating casks;
And some were killed, whose life-blood stained the
      waves;
And some did pray, and some did wildly scream;
Some clasped their hands, and sank without a word;
Until the seething waters foamed o'er all,
And morning saw the beach with treasure strewn,
Large heaps of wreck, and corpses stiff and pale.
The father and his sons were seen no more.

"Ruth fainted at the tidings; a dark cloud
Passed o'er her being; reason reeled and swam,
And left her a sad maniac, till she died
In the asylum on yon lonely heath.

"In a clay cottage, on the common's edge,
Dwelt a pale widow with her little one,
Unknown to almost all the warring world,
Kings, nobles, heroes, wielders of the pen;
Or even those a few short miles away:
Unknown to them, but not unknown to God.
He watched her in her weeds of widowhood,
And cheered her with His presence. On a day
When rains had fallen on the weltering world,
And earth and heaven were once more free from mist,
And they three days had fasted in their hut
Without complaining, save a mouldy crust
Broken between the two, in water soaked
And eaten with their tears; the widow drew
An old chair near the fireplace, when she kissed
A wasted tear-drop from her daughter's cheek,
And in a low voice whispered, 'Kneel, my love,
And let us ask our Father up in heaven
To send us bread, so that we perish not.'

"One eve that summer, as the sinking sun
Tinged the white faces of the hilly steeps,
And spread his gold-clouds o'er the distant heights,
Her husband sat within their cottage porch.
Reading his Bible in the holy hush,
When suddenly, without one warning step,
Death came and took him. Ere a week had passed,
With stealthy stride he stole away two girls,
Her brightest and her best; and she was left
With one lone floweret on life's wilderness.
And now those two are kneeling side by side,
Pleading the faithful promises of Heaven;
And up the hills, and o'er the mountain pines,
And far above the vapours of the marsh,
Beyond the clouds and blue bright firmament,
And higher than the highest crystal orb,
Up through the vales of Eden rose their prayer,
And moved Jehovah on His lofty throne.
Seraphs were bending o'er their shining seats,

And looking down upon them, while their harps
Hung for some moments on the Tree of Life.

"Who stands without that dwelling on the down,
Wrapped in sweet thought, with basket on his arm,
And hand upon the latch, listening with awe,
And ever and anon wiping a tear.
And lifting up his eyes towards the sky,
As if he saw an angel with his lyre?
It is a farmer from a distant field,
Who in the furrow left his ancient plough
And oxen standing still; for, as he toiled,
A voice came to him from the depths of heaven:
'Relieve the widow on the common's side.'
And so he filled his basket to the brim
With bread and meat and eggs and wholesome cheese,
And came and heard them praying. Joy was there
And holy harpings in that humble home
Which emperors might envy. Thus saith God:
'Before thou callest, I will answer thee.'

"I knew a rustic poet by a brook; .
He woke one morn in boyhood's golden dream,
And, while the lark was singing o'er the mist,
God placed the lyre within his trembling hands.
It was a priceless treasure: day and night,
In cloud and sunshine, here was joy for him.
When sorrow smote, or cruel Death bereaved,
The Muse brought comfort to his stricken heart.
But though his soul was as some precious thing,
Dwelling apart among the works of God,
And shining like a diamond in its cell,
So very humble were his ways and words
That men passed by him as a common thing,
Nor heeded they his mission. Like a well
That bubbles up among the village homes,
And glides into the meadows unperceived,
Refreshing fern and floweret on its way,
And adding greenness to the thing that's green,
And beauty to the already beautiful;
So passed the poet through this weary world.
I met him yester-eve among the rocks:
I knew him by his striking breadth of brow;
And, pausing where the banks were gay with flowers,
He looked towards the setting sun, and said,
'I have two visions with me evermore:
One is an aged matron, kind and good;
The Bible her chief comfort, heaven her home.
She dwells upon the borders of a croft,
In a low dwelling fronting the grey morn.
This is my loving mother. Hid with firs,
Within a valley watered by a rill,
A lonely chapel stands in Gothic garb
And dim seclusion, holy as a saint:
Before it a small grave-yard always green,
Save when a new tomb opens; and a mound
Beneath a young elm, where the daisies grow,
Is ever with me—'tis my daughter's grave.
She faded quickly, home's all-cheering flower,
Even while I gazed upon her loveliness,
Then heaven's bright portals let her in to God.'
And down the ravine stole the pensive bard.

"In moonlight mantles these hoar rocks stand up,
And woo me to their cloisters. I have learnt
In whatsoever state to be content.
This Thou hast taught me, Father. I feel not

The least desire to leave my native heights.
This mountain is my world, these crags my throne,
And glancing fairies are my retinue ;
The night-bird is my poet, and the rill
My sweet musician trickling down the rocks ;
Winged spirits, bearing harps, my ministers ;
And God my audience, looking down from heaven.
O hear me while I lift my heart to Thee !
I thank Thee for Thy guidance : Thou art Love ;
Thy name is sweeter than the breath of flowers ;
Thy heart is full of holy tenderness.
Hast Thou not promised to uphold the weak,
To be the prop of age, and in the stream
Of death itself to cheer the trusting saint ?
O what a strong tower has Thy presence been
In days of darkness and in nights of woe !
When the fierce tempter, as a lion roused,
Rampant and huge, alarms the quaking wood,
The rushes raving through the tangled brake,
With red fire flaming from his rolling eyes,
Lashing his great sides with his shaggy tail,
And shaking dew-drops from his monster mane ;
So rushed the devil down upon a worm.
But Thou didst save me in that perilous hour,
And drive the monster back into his smoke.
And Thou wilt save me to Thyself at last,
And clothe me with a fair immortal vest,
Safe in the jasper home of the redeemed.

" Enter yon room, and mark that praying one :
No voice to hers responded. Through the heavens
The black clouds wandered weeping evermore,
With thunder on their fronts and wings of flame.
Dark were the moon and stars, and frantic winds
Rushed down the mountains like a sea of waves,
So that the grateful cottar in his home
Thought of the sailor through a shining tear,
Half-oped his door, and murmured, ' What a storm ! '
High in her chamber, all alone with Heaven,
As she was wont, a pious mother prays
That God would bless her and her household train
With grace to bear the chastenings of His hand,
And lead them all to Christ the loving One :
And peace hung brooding o'er her brightened soul.
That day Disaster like a sheeted ghost
Stole through her dwelling, scaring each in turn.
The boys shrank from the spectre, some to play,
And some to riot with companions rude,
And some to revel in the glow of wine,
Which only makes the sad one sadder still ;
The maids to dress and parties, she to God :
They to return with anguish more intense ;
She, bright with radiance from the' eternal throne.

" Hers was an influence quiet as the dews
That drop at nightfall on the golden flower,
To cheer it opening in the light of morn ;
And day by day thus secretly she shed
A holy halo over all her house,
Till by the Spirit love filled up the place.
For one cold winter's eve, beside the fire,
Her six brave sons, to ruddy manhood grown,
Were sitting musing on the chequered past,
When down upon them fell the breath of heaven,
And one by one prayed silently and still ;
And one by one determined for the Lord ;
And one by one confessed the second birth,

And passed from darkness into Zion's light ;
Till all embraced the promised Comforter,
Rejoiced in hope, and praised the Trinity.
How grand the gracious scheme to save mankind,
Wrought in the halls of old eternity,
And perfected on Calvary's rocky crest !
The living doctrines of the Saviour hang
Like golden sunbeams round the icy north,
And span the summits of the spicy south ;
And soon their light shall fill the gladdened globe.

" Time travelled on with much of care and change ;
Her children had departed ; some at sea,
And some on land, and some were in their graves ;
All, save a darling daughter, like a bud
Left by the March blast on a stricken spray.
And so she loved her with life's latest love,
That lingered in her bosom like a brand.
Go to the church beside the ancient bridge,
When Sabbath songs are caroled by the choir :
They both sit down together side by side,
That widowed mother, and her darling dove,
With tearful eyes fixed on the Minister.

" No day without its mercies : how they throng
The gates of morning and the doors of eve,
Blessing each hour and moment of our lives,
And teeming round our path, a loving host !
I knew five men who laboured in a mine,
Five in one party in a cave of tin,
And o'er them hung huge rocks as if by hairs,
Nodding to fall ; and yet they knew it not.
These five were teachers in a Sabbath school :
And one bright summer noon they were regaled,
With tea and cake, in a wide field of flowers.
These five were present ; their dark cell below
Was empty then : and at that time there fell
Some tons of flint upon the very spot
Where they were standing just twelve hours before,
And where no doubt they had been standing then,
To be all marred and mangled, crushed to death,
Had not the Lord in His compassion drawn
Their hearts to serve Him in His blessed work."

Just then the post came rushing up the hill ;
And as the horn rang through the village trees,
A pensive picture passed upon the page :—

" Soft eve was still with worship ; flowers slept sweet
On beds of down ; and birds that loved the brake
Sang not, save here and there a pensive note
Passed with the dying daylight. On his bed
Within a cottage, by the elfin elm,
The postman lay a dying : wiping off
The perspiration from his burning brow,
He gazed upon his little girl, and said,
' Run, Anna, to the fountain in the dell,
That bubbles up among the shining moss,
And bring some water to your sinking sire,
Clear, bright, and beautiful, that I may drink
And be refreshed once more before I die.'
So, taking a clean cup, the little girl
Ran to the well, and soon was back again
In that lone chamber, when the dying man
Kissed her pale face, drank heartily, and said,—

" ' May Heaven reward thee, child, when I am gone,

F 2

And be thy friend and father. This cool draught
Is sweet indeed : but sweeter far within
I feel the waters of the Well of Life
Flowing through all my frame. When I was young,
I sought this Fount, and it was sweet indeed.
Ten thousand times since then I've come to drink,
And it has always cheered me ; but its streams
Have ne'er refreshed me as they do to-day.
'Tis Christ, my darling, in the trusting soul.
Farewell. my love : the white-robed choir is come,
And hymnings not of earth float on my ear.
I soon shall be where thirst is never known.'
Then at the bed-side knelt she in the hush
Of that dim chamber, praying to her God,
While Death with soft feet stole in to her sire.
Again she wiped her eyes, and prayed again :
And as the postman's horn rang o'er the reeds,
Her father's spirit floated up to heaven.

"Two youths I well remember : gentle, one,
And kind and loving, striving to obey
The laws of God and man : the other, fierce
And cruel as a serpent, swearing loud
And plotting mischief on his midnight bed.
And once they met together in a town
Where the meek youth had business, and he strove
To turn him to the harlot's guilty shed,
And stain his soul with sulphur : but he flew
Far from its shadow, and knelt down to pray.
God heard his prayer, and filled his mind with peace ;

And he went on his way with praise and song.
The other staid behind him till dark night
Looked down upon him sinning, and the stars
Blushed as they sank behind the hills of morn.
A few short years of infamy and crime
Passed o'er him, and upon a foreign land
He died alone within the wilderness,
Without a friend to lift his sinking head,
Or breathe the name of Jesus to his ear :
And now the wild beasts howl upon his grave.
The other lives, a loved and honoured man,
Striving to labour for his Lord and Christ,
His back upon the world, his face to heaven.

" How the bright stars, conversing as they shine,
Invite my gaze among them ! Eyes of love,
They smile upon me in my hill of rock,
And bid me think of summer homes on high,
Where wife and husband, child and parent meet,
To part no more for ever. Bless the Lord !
While I have breath, I'll bless and praise the Lord.
The song dies on my lips, but when at last
This clog of clay is shook off in the grave,
And my freed spirit walks with the redeemed,
How will I sing and bless and praise the Lord !
Praise, praise the Lord ! O bless and praise the Lord !"

So, taking up his staff, he passed away
Among the moonlight shadows, with his face
Bright as an angel's.

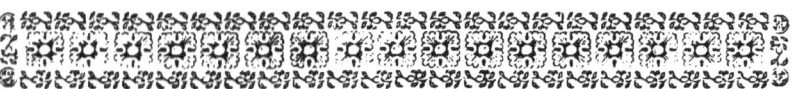

AN INDIAN STORY.

CANTO FIRST.

...usic among the mountains ! How
it streams
Along the hollows where the fern-
queen trills
Melodious matins by her door of
moss,
Shakes the bright ivy shimmering
on the rock,

Thrills through the thicket like a throbbing trump,
And overflows the happy voiceful vale !
It is a queenly morning : the great globe
Is rife with whispers from a world of wings,
Each bush and tree a temple. How the psalm
Of the green wood soars in a sound of praise,
And every quiver from the brambled brake,
Dew-pearled and gleaming in the rising sun,
Is like a priest conversing with the Lord !
I'll bow me down and worship :—
　　　　　　　　　　　　Lord of life !
Great Spirit in the centre of all worlds !
Thou King eternal, lone, invisible,
Monarch of all things, mighty Potentate !
Giving, upholding, guiding, Thee I praise,
And dare approach, through Jesus Christ, Thy Son.
I thank Thee for the morning, when the earth
Is adoration, and the heavens are praise.

I bless Thee for the noontide full and free,
When every wilding by the leaping brook,
Or grass-blade shining where the soaring lark
Sings up his glory-path, repeats Thy name.
I laud Thee for the evening's holy hush,
When over all things fall the wings of rest;
For night, and stars, and sleep; for all fair forms,
And beautiful and bright; for wind and rain;
For gentle airs and dews on summer flowers;
For teaching seasons changing evermore;
For Sabbath days; for food and reason rich,
Eyesight and hearing, and the springs of hope
Which bubble up among the mounds of care;
For childhood blossoms and the fruits of age;
For promises which fill the Holy Book;
For manna in the desert; for soft slopes
Along life's pathway, thickly gemmed with green;
For hill and vale, and sunsets flocked with clouds—
Like one I saw a few fair eves ago,
As if the gate of glory met my gaze;
For songs that fill this lovely universe;
For thunder rumbling through the startled void;
For shepherd's pipe, and ocean's solemn roar;
For solitude, and books, and fireside friends;
For light and darkness, and ten thousand joys,
Which die unuttered on my stammering tongue;
But, more than all, for intercourse with Thee
Through Him, my ever blessed Substitute,
'Neath temple-roof, or where the crags are still,
Adored for ever be Thy holy name!

The velvet moss is voiceful. I have heard—
In bygone summers streaked with ruddy youth,
Stealing among it with my shouldered harp—
Words never uttered by the tongue of man;
And when I've stretched me in my father's croft,
In boyhood's brightness, with the sky above
And the great world around me, each small cup
By fairies handled, shaken with the breeze,
Seemed a rich goblet with rare nectar full.
O, how I loved it and the rocks around!
And when the quarry-man, with drill and wedge,
Split an old crag on which I've often stood
To watch the storm twist up the angry heavens,
And battle through the welkin, when the sky
Was one vast echo of the grandest song,
I seemed to lose a portion of myself.
And in the thoughtful, sober autumn-time,
When leaves were falling on the quiet earth,
And robin whistled on the meadow-gate,
How have I joyed, perched on some granite block,
When echo almost mocked the linnet's chirp,
To clap my hands and hear it in the vale!
Where mosses climb, there Nature teacheth much,
And poets learn what schools cannot instil.

Hark! what is that? What music do I hear?
'Tis not the lark, though he is up betimes
To cheer the morning with his passion-lay;
I marked him long ago rise from the corn,
And shake his wings, and soaring sunward sing.
'Tis not the lark, or the tree-loving thrush,
Piping his pleasure on the dewy thorn,
Though every crevice in the old hill's side
Seems studded thick with harpers. List again!
A breeze comes full and breaks among the ferns.
O, what a shower of notes! See! there she steals

Along the pathway leading to the gate,
Straw hat in hand, Lila, the Mountain Maid!
Her hair falls loosely on her shoulders white,
Her arms are bare, her eyes are large and black,
Her brow like chiselled marble, her fair cheeks
Outvie the lily by the moorland brook,
Herself a lily shedding odour round.
And then her mind, O, it is like a well
Of clearest water, cheering where it flows.
She is her aged mother's only child;
A gentle widow wandering down to death;
They live together in a reedy home
By the wood's entrance, near the old highway;
And the sole light the stricken mother has
Is this lone planet and her God in heaven.
So very humble is the mountain maid,
She scarcely knows that she is beautiful,
Or deems that she is good.—On in the dews,
And this her carol:—

"Father, hear Thy child.
My mother taught me to obey Thy voice,
And praise Thee for Thy goodness. Flowers are
Thine,
And forest, fen and fountain, hill and vale,
Ocean and sky, and everything I see,—
The little birds that twitter on the boughs,
The cattle grazing on a thousand hills,
Thou feedest all, and givest them their meat:
And yet Thou mindest not! I'll praise Thy name
While I have being. Let me trustful lay
My hand in Thine, and Thou shalt guide Thy child."
And sweeter than the music of the morn,
Down the hill-side, and up the sun-full vale,
And over the thick forest, music-stirred,
These words swelled sweetly, "Thou shalt guide Thy
child."

Under a hawthorn, lonely as a cross
Upon the common, William Collingrew,
A youth half through his teens, a peasant's son,
Who guides the plough along his father's fields,
Sits watching Lila with a lover's gaze:
His right hand shades his eyes, on which the curls
Of brown hair fall bright with the kiss of dawn.
The hymn she sings with morning at her feet,
Floats through his soul like some angelic lay;
He heedeth not the skylark o'er his head,
The river at his side, leaf-hidden thrush,
Or song-burst from the thicket, but, enwrapt,
Bathes in the music of the maiden's psalm.
He watches her till down behind the hill
She sinks in beauty like the moon at morn.

Young Collingrew was nurtured on the heights
Where echo answered echo 'mid the rocks,
And waterfalls went tumbling down the steeps.
His mother taught him early to obey
The laws of God and man, to shun all vice,
Which stains too oft the morals of mankind,
And heed the Spirit's monitory voice:
And much she laboured to instruct her boy
To practise evermore the Golden Rule,
Which the despised Redeemer gave the world,—
To love his neighbour as he loved himself,
And give to others as he would receive.
Pleasant it was, on evenings passed away,
To hear that mother's counsel to the lad,

Who by her side sat gazing in her face.
She told him of the new unpeopled earth;
Of Adam in the land of Paradise;
Of Eve, the mother of the human race;
Of our first parents' sin, whereby all fell;
Of Jesus Christ, the Saviour of the lost,
Promised to Adam and his sinning seed;
Of Cain, who killed his brother; of the flood
Of whelming waters, with the ark and dove,
And the first rainbow spanning the great sky;
Of Hagar wandering in the wilderness;
Of Isaac and the altar on the hill;
Of Joseph sold and prisoned, courted, throned,
And saving those who would have spilt his blood;
Of Israel's bondage in the land of crime;
The plagues, the flight from Egypt, when the king,
Cruel and cold, and harder than a rock,
In the red waters perished with his host;
Of Samson and Delilah; of fair Ruth,
The maid of Moab, gleaning in the field:
And oft she told him of the shepherd-boy
Who slew the great Goliath with a sling
And a smooth pebble from the silver brook;
And how he afterwards became a king,
And sang the glory of Messiah's reign;
Of the three Hebrew children and the fire;
Of Daniel in the darkness of the den,
Where lions roared and glared into his eyes;
Of Jonah, swallowed by the mighty whale,
And mourning underneath the smitten gourd;
With other stories from the pen of Truth,
Which shed a sweetness o'er his opening mind.

But, more than all, that mother taught her boy
Of One who, stable-born, grew up to man,
And lived a life of holiness and love:
He healed the sick, and raised the buried dead;
Opened the blind man's eyes, so that he saw
The teeming wonders of the universe;
Hushed the wild tumult of the raging sea
By the sweet breath of peace. The ear, sealed up
With stony deafness, opened was by Him,
So that sweet sound filled the awakened soul.
He walked the waters of the troubled deep,
And reached the ship where His disciples mourned,
Cheering them with His presence. The great storm,
With broken wings, fell powerless at His word,
Murmuring for lack of might. Forgave He, too,
The sinner's sins, bidding him err no more.
The dumb one spake, and praised the Healer's name;
The leper felt His touch, and rose renewed;
Back from the land of death the damsel came,
When He exclaimed, "Arise!" and at the gate
Of the full city, standing by the bier,
He speaks the dead to life, and the fair youth
Leaps from the coffin to his mother's arms.

Listened the pupil, while his earnest orbs
Were full of wonder-gleams and passions strange;
And gentle were the teacher's simple tones,
As she described the suffering Son of Man,
Maker and Monarch of the universe,
Not having any place to lay His head;
Seeking His lodge upon the mountain-top,
And praying in the valley. Birds had nests,
But He no home or shelter from the storm.
Wild creatures of the forest, the wise fox

In the great thicket had a safe retreat;
But He no cover save the roof of heaven.
His life was nought but love and charity,
Yet sin and hate pursued Him, till at last
The hour of darkness rolled upon His soul
In agony unuttered. Drops of blood
Pressed through His skin, and spread the blushing
    ground.
Crushed in the Garden of Gethsemane
With the world's wrongs, the sins of all mankind,
His prayer arose, and smote the ear of Night:
"My Father God, if it be possible,
Remove this cup, which is so hard to drink;
However, not My will, but Thine be done!"
And down from Eden shining angels dropped,
And ministered unto Him. Through the gloom,
With torch and staff, the wretched Judas came,
And with a kiss betrayed Him. Then they dragged
The lowly One to Pilate's dreaded bar,
And scoffed and mocked Him, hooting in His ear,
Crowned Him with thorns, and spat upon His face;
They beat Him with their palms, and plucked His hair;
Then stretched Him on the wood, and hammered nails
Into His flesh, and crucified the Lord;
And as He hung upon the lifted cross
Between two thieves, they gave Him gall to drink,
And pierced His side, and howled in anger round.
"Father, forgive them," said the dying Lamb,
"They know not what they do." And then His last
Atoning utterance through creation rolled:
"'Tis finished!" and He bowed His head and died.
All Nature shuddered, the great sun grew dark,
Light left the universe, day reeled and fell;
Clouds rushed against each other; sheeted dead
Rose from the tomb, and glided through the streets;
Rocks, bulging from the hill-side, crashed and rent,
And one great groan filled up the astonished void:
The unbeliever, startled at the scene,
Cried out, convinced, "This was the Son of God!"

And the boy listened as she told him how
They laid Him in a new tomb in the rock;
And when three days had passed, the Saviour rose,
And soared to heaven, a conqueror over death,
Where He now lives to intercede for man:
That He requires us to obey His voice,
And yield our hearts to Him, by which we gain,
In life and death, the promise of both worlds:
That all mankind are only travellers here,
Swift-journeying to the shores of the unseen;
To-day the tree is clothed with foliage fair,—
To-morrow stripped, and whistling in the wind.
The only stay for erring man is Christ—
All other props rest on the unsettled sands,
Which in the eddy of the last great whirl
Shall be dashed down to darkness. By and bye
The dread archangel shall descend from heaven,
And blow his trumpet on the drifting cloud,
At whose huge echo the high firmament
Shall be burnt up like to a shrivelled scroll,
The sun shall blaze no longer, and the moon
Shall glare like blood upon the plain of night;
The stars shall fall, and heaven be desolate;
The crashing earth be one great globe of flame;
Thunder shall leap to thunder, horrid, high;
And lightnings follow lightnings, till the wreck
Sweep utterly across the empty air;

And Time shall tumble from his azure throne.
But those who love the Saviour will not fear
This host of horrors, but shall safely sail
Into the city on a sea of fire.

Listened the boy, with aspirations high
Sunned with this solemn teaching. He grew up
Familiar with the verities of God,
E'en from his very cradle. In the wind
He heard His voice, and in the linnet's lay;
And when his mother joined his hands in prayer,
As Eve came pensive musing in the dews,
Sometimes a tear would glisten in his eye.
Thus he grew on, a sapling pruned by truth;
He dared not lie, he dared not swear nor steal;
Vile words he never uttered, but obeyed
The voice of conscience, by the Spirit led.
When old enough, that mother taught her son
To read the Bible, which he valued much.
Good books were his companions, which he searched
Under the trees, or by the river sides,
Or on the rocks at sunset purple-hued,
Or by the log-fire in his mother's home,
Soul-full of pleasure exquisite as light;
And many friends had William Collingrew.

How like his home to mine, where childhood dwelt
Among the low peat barriers! Here I caught
The spell of song high-lifted on the hill,
Midway between two worlds. The strife of tongues,
The blast of bickering, and the howl of hate
Roars not among its caverns. Nature here
Trills her own carols with the pipe of peace.
She woo'd me from my marbles; her sweet voice
Made me her lover ere I was aware;
And so I trod the rhyme-fields, quill in hand,
Diverted with my whistle. Fleeting years
Have only bound me to my teacher more,
With bands that death can only rend away.
How long I now to hide me in the heath,
Where man cannot behold me, rapt with strains
That murmur from the higher firmament!

He wandered where the hilly heather hung
O'er brake, and bank, and burrow. Here he dwelt
In his own temple, placid as a priest,
Harped to by winds and waters; not a thought
Ruffled his spirit; tranquil as a lake
Among the hills, till underneath the thorn
Love wounded him, and left him in amaze.
Then walked he wilds, paced the great rugged tarns
And sounding fens, with Silence at his side.
Or meadows green, with footpaths like a cord,
If haply he might meet the mountain maid,
And whisper how he loved her. One still eve,
Just when the full moon rose upon the moor,
He met her by a stile, and spoke to her,
With trembling in his speech : and she was free,
And kind, and gentle ; so he turned aside
From his own track, scarce knowing what he did,
Chatting and smiling till they reached the door,
Where stood her waiting mother ; then she breathed
The sweet good night, and left him blind with bliss.

Soon intercourse grew thicker than the weeks
That pressed on one another. In the woods
They walked at sunset,—she his sun and light;

Wandered by streams which murmured Lila's name ;
Travelled through lanes where love tuned every tree ;
Discoursed on flower banks,—she his fairest flower.
Where the low thyme was sweetly eloquent,
He told her of the deep well in his soul,
Which with love-waters freely bubbled o'er.
Oft when the eve came like a gentle dove
In twilight valleys, arm in arm they walked
Where hawthorns flung their fragrance, hearing sweet
Celestial music in the earth and heaven.

Day wanes among the willows ; the great sun
Has disappeared behind the western hills,
Leaving his purple track upon the sea,
Headland, and hoary height. Along the lane
The thatcher whistles, followed by the bat ;
And gentle murmurs fill both hemispheres.
Lila has cleaned her cottage, swept the floor,
And laid the hearth in order. On a chair
Her mother sits, with needle in her hand,
In linen cap, and " spectacles on nose,"
Clean as a pebble on the sandy shore.
The cat purrs on the cricket ; the pet bird
In the small cage is musing like a bard,
While the clock ticks upon the oaken stand.
She drops her book, and, by the hazel door,
Peers down the narrow lane, and soon descries
Young Collingrew come pacing up the hill,
Twirling his stick for gladness : on the air
Is borne his whistle, floating 'neath the eaves.
What holy transport rushes through her soul !
Soon the door opens, and he enters in,
Cheered with a smile from Lila, and a glad
" How do you do ? " from the cap-crested dame.
At first he's slow and bashful ; by and bye
Speech trickles freer—then it flows—and then
They are all chatting, mother, maid, and youth.
How swift the moments fly ! The wicked clock
Seems bent to gallop with an untold pace.
And then he slowly rises, takes his hat,
Still lingering in the doorway, lingering still,
Till forced to part within the ivy porch.

Next evening spoke the widow, as they sat
Drinking their tea, what time the twilight fell,
And listened Lila, purple with the speech :
" I have respect for William Collingrew,
He is an honest lad, and humble, too,
Taught at the feet of sterling piety.
Like thee, he looks a cowslip by the well,
Hanging its head in native loveliness,
No treachery lurks beneath his trustful glance,
Nor in his smile deception. I have seen
Much of mankind, and read it in his face.
The looks of some men tell us what they are.
That thou art thus esteemed by Collingrew
Much pleaseth me, my daughter. May he be
A husband like thy father, kind and good,
And gentle as the fanning wind to-night !
Well I remember now our wooing days,
And what dear bliss it brought us : not a breeze
Or woody warbler sweeter than his speech,
Or limpid runnel clearer than his eye ;
No gloom was in his soul for aught but love.
And then we married. Our small home was bright,
As if an angel dwelt beneath the roof ;
And surely angels harboured with us then,

And harbour with us still; for they abide
Unseen within the dwellings of the good.
When thou wert born, how swelled my prayer of praise!
We walked to church together, read at home,
And served the Lord in spirit. Years passed on,
And not a hand-cloud rose upon our sky,
Or drop was dashed out of our cup of joy.
On market days we rode into the town,
Returning when the wood-bird sought its nest.
Old Time for us had sunshine on his face.
Then darkness filled the horizon : sickness came.
And Death put out the light of our abode,
And snatched your father from us. In the dark
How bowed I low, dripping with sorrow's rain !
But there was light above this fearful gloom :
I looked, and saw my Saviour. ' Unto Me
Commit thy way, and I'll direct thy path.'
This promise stayed me as it were an arm.
And, in a dream which came to me one night,
I saw your father standing by a lake
As clear as crystal, in the land above,
Clad in white robes, and white wings graced his sides ;
A crown of glory glittered on his head,
And in his hand he held a golden harp ;
And, sweetly smiling on me, I awoke.
He is in heaven, my Lila. When he died,
His last words were, ' I'm safe through Jesus Christ.'
And then he slumbered like a weary child.
But soon I go to meet him, where the trace
Of parting tears shall never more be seen."

Soon into autumn slid the shortening days ;
The fruits were gathered in ; the leaves fell fast ;
The ploughman and his team were on the mead ;
The sportsman was abroad,—echo was rife
With shout and halloo swelling on the air ;
The plovers whistle o'er the ancient tarn,
And whirl and whistle, whistling round and round,
Until they drop to be the fowler's prey.
'Tis pleasant now to leave the city's smoke,
And be alone with Nature. Rusty fern,
Cloud-catching peak, stern ruin, grasses grey,
And tree-bough season-streaked, have each a psalm
Of holy cadence for the listening ear.
Lila is watching by her mother's bed
With all a daughter's fondness ; she had been
For long, long days afflicted. On a thorn
Beside the casement little robin sings ;
And through the open window floats his song.
Cheering the weary sufferer. Then she speaks :
" Come, read to me, my daughter,—read once more
Of the bright streets of gold in Eden-land,
Where rest the good for ever,—where the King
In beauty dwells, and I shall soon appear.
I feel my days are numbered ; every hour
Adds to my weakness : ere another sun
Is lost behind the waters, heaven is mine.
Nay, do not weep, my daughter ; think of Him
Whose word is firmer than the firmament ;
Trust, and He'll be thy helper. Lift me up,
That I may once more see the autumn hills
Kissed with the lingering sunset. Now good bye ;
I see a chariot coming on the cloud,—
Fine are the horses, fire the charioteer,
And fire the car which takes me through the air !
Hark ! don't you hear the rumbling of its wheels ?
Nearer it comes, and nearer ! O what light !

The room is full,—'tis glory everywhere !
Dear Jesus, I am coming." Then she fell
As falls a meteor when the skies are clear.

Now, with an aunt lived Lila by a brook,
Beneath a bending mountain. Here were fields,
And there a green wood, courted by the thrush ;
And on the right a dingle full of notes.
Here Lila wandered often, like a bird
Whose nest was beaten by the howling blast
And blown to ruin ; here she wandered oft
In pious meditation, filled with thoughts
Which only cluster round the mind of peace ;
But much she felt the woe of orphanage
In such a world of evil, where the good
Are oft pursued by hunger and distress,
Or left to perish in the biting air ;
Then like a friend, beside her ever walked
This precious promise, cheering her with light,
" When all forsake thee, I will take thee up."
And where was Collingrew ? In vales remote
Across the seas he worked, from dawn to dusk,
With Lila's presence ever by his side.

One summer eve—the twilight had begun,
And murmurs filled the forest, when she walked
Down her accustomed pathway. Over head
The grand old hill seemed clad in priestly robes,
Sounding his solemn vespers. On the winds
A voice came murmuring, " We must work and wait."
And every echo in the far-off fen
Took up the utterance, " We must work and wait."
Her spirit felt it, " We must work and wait."
For Collingrew had promised to return
And take her o'er the waters, where a home
Awaited her beneath the beechen bough.
But days, and weeks, and months had slowly passed,
And yet he came not, lingering, lingering still ;
And still she felt that she must work and wait.

With staff and bundle, pleasant to behold,
Comes o'er the bridge, across the village stream,
A tall young man, with candour in his face,
And sunshine in his features. By the door
Of a lone cottage, where the ivies climb,
He asked a mother, kissing her sweet babe,
If Lila, whom they called the Mountain Maid,
Still dwelt beside the forest ? Then she paused,
And raised her head, and softly answered, " No ;
Her mother died when leaves began to fall ;
She's buried in the churchyard on the hill,
And Lila's home is with an aged aunt.
Among our damsels she the fairest is,
The kindest, best, the gentlest of them all,
And happy he who wins her." So he turned
Out of the road, taking the narrow path
With rushes skirted, singing like a bird :
"Twas William Collingrew come home again.

They met among the bushes. Yes ; they met,
Lila and William, sudden as the moon,
Which then came up behind the eastern hill,
Round, full, and fair, paler than she was wont.
They met, and kissed each other. O, what joy
Held that dear moment, bursting with delight !
Earth cannot give a holier cup than this,
Nor can it offer one similitude
So rich in precious treasure. A new thought

Which fires a poet's fancy, shooting life
Throughout his being, is a symbol tame.
They met, and kissed each other. Her fair face,
Silvered with moonlight, and suffused with grief,
Had never looked so beautiful before.
They drank from cisterns purified by tears,
And fed upon the fragrant fruits of love.
Then, as he led her down the village lane,
He told her of his labours in the west,
Where the Red Indian hunted ; how a home
Awaited her beneath the forest boughs,
Built by his own hands, near the river side,
Where Plenty sat, and pressed the juicy grapes ;
Though, till she came, no light illumined it,
But it was dark and cheerless. Would she go ?
And Lila bowed her head, and answered, " Yes,
I'll go and share it with you." Throbbed his heart,
And beat his pulses quicker than before ;
And earth and heaven seemed blended into one.

Soon after this, the village bells rang out
Their merry chimes upon their wedding day,
And they were one for ever. Blessings pure
As crystal rain-drops fell upon their souls
From man and matron, as they walked from church,
Clad in their bridal garments. Flowers were strewn,
Hymns gaily sung, quaint psalm-lines chanted o'er,
And joy o'erflowed the hamlet. Then they sighed
A gentle farewell to their native land,
And sailed upon the waters.

CANTO SECOND.

Sways the primeval forest like a sea
Stirred with sweet summer breezes ; the great
trees
Sigh in the silence of the summer air,
Rife with poetic fancies ; their strong arms
Are lifted as in prayer, and every leaf
Trills tuneful tribute to its Maker's name.
In venerable ripeness stands the wood,
A miracle of grandeur, flinging back
Reproof in showers upon the scoffer's head.
Here silently, for centuries unperceived,
Nature has used her only husbandry
To cultivate the soil of solitude,
And rear her trophies nurtured with the dews,
And rain, and air, and sunshine beautiful ;
No planter's spade has ever delved the ground,
Or settler's hatchet trimmed the sturdy boughs ;
She is her only pruner, lopping off
And rooting up by hurricane and time.
Her book is full of wisdom : read it well,
And thou shalt feel there is a great First Cause.
The swaying forest sighs, " There is a God ; "
And every leaflet on the lifted bough,
Tuned with the zephyr, murmurs, " There's a God ; "
And the mysterious thicket, " There's a God."
The beasts that shelter in the underwood ;

The birds that gleam and sing till set of sun ;
The thunder crashing through its arches grand ;
The lightnings flaming up its avenues ;
The tempest striving with the creaking trunks ;
And every whisper slowly walking where
The tendrils cluster, echo, " There's a God."

Within a clearing by a rushing stream
Is a log hut, and a low barn of logs,
And several log sheds, by a farmer used,
For cattle, pigs, and poultry. The few fields
Have each log fences, saving here and there
A tree is left to grow, half lopped perhaps,
Half green, half dry, and there a heap of stumps
Piled up to form a barrier. The rich mould
Requires but little culture, bringing forth
Abundant crops to cheer the settler's soul ;
Fruits in their season, corn, and milk, and wine,
And game in handfuls, captured without toil.
Children are playing underneath the porch,
And by the river is a gentle boy
Sailing his boat : his mother calls him now
To meet his father at the supper-board,
And sisters sweeter than the lotus-flowers.
This is the home of William Collingrew.
Long has he laboured, toiling many a year,
And this his increase blessed by Providence.

Sometimes they sailed upon the wooded lake
With fishing-tackle 'neath the maple boughs,
Where perched the mocking-bird and robin red,
Catching the bright fish, William and his boy.
Sometimes they wandered in the forest dim
To watch the squirrel on the hickory tree,
And pull the berries from the bounteous brake :
And when the winter came in garments white.
Sometimes they tracked the rabbit in the snow,
Or swiftly sleighed across the open ground,
Hooded and fur-clad, wondering at the speed.
Then sweet it was to cluster round the log
In the wide chimney, happy boy and girl,
To list to Lila's lays of early life
In blissful England, where throughout the year
Dear daisies grow, and lawns are always green.
She told of tracks her youthful feet had trod,
Of banks where violets grow mid moss-cups rare,
Of rivers warbling music ; of the cot
Among the rushes where her mother dwelt.
And where she grew beside her, sunned by love :
Of evenings spent with story, nights with dreams,
And days with visions burning far beyond ;
Of her dear parent, and her teachings pure.
But when she whispered of the little church
Among the pine trees, where she worshipped oft,
And found the Lord, and bade them seek Him too,
Tears trickled slowly over every face.

Some cannot bear prolonged prosperity :
When all is pleasant, they forget themselves,
And Him who gives the blessing ; sitting down
And rising up without a thought of thanks ;
Going out and in unmindful of the Lord.
And such was William. First, he ceased to pray
Within his closet : then the sacred Book
Remained unopened on the dusty shelf
Month after month, with no desire to search
The oracles which testify of Christ ;

And then his lips unwatched would utter wrong,
Slowly at first, then like a rushing stream.
His heart grew cold, and selfish was his soul.
Forgotten were the teachings of his youth,
His years of love forgotten. Like a skiff
Borne by the current in an adverse course,
In spite of brawny arm and well-set sail,
So drifted he upon the tide of wrong.
This fell like hail upon the settler's home.

It is a soft and lovely eve in June :
The sun is set, though over all the sky
Glow radiant tints, which fill the gazer's soul
With visions of the future land of rest,
Where Eden's waters murmur, and the gleam
Of seraph wings falls on the holy lakes ;
The full moon mounts above the solemn pines,
And cherry trees, now rich with crimson fruit,
And Indian corn just bursting into ear,
Revealing every feature of the scene.
Tall, muscular, and strong, preparing scythes
For the approaching hay-time, Collingrew
Is sitting on the door-step of his home,
Busy at work, so that he does not see
An Indian hunter drawing near his door,
Until he speaks in supplicating tone :
" Will you not give a poor unfortunate
Some supper and a lodging for the night,
Whose way has been mistaken in the wood ? "

The farmer eyed him with a look of scorn.
Anger was in his eyes as he replied,
Uncourteous and cruel : " Heathen dog !
Begone, begone, you shall have nothing here ! "
The Indian turned, then, facing Collingrew,
In accents low and musical he said :
" But I am very hungry ; it is long
Since I have eaten. Only give a crust,
A bone to cheer me on my weary way."
Then answered he with fury and a frown,
" Go, get you gone, you red-skin heathen hound !
I've nothing for you ; get you gone, I say."
A struggle seemed to rend the hunter's breast,
As if two beings were contending there
To gain the mastery,—fainting want, and pride.
The former conquered. With weak voice he said :
" Give me a cup of water, cool and pure ;
For I am very faint, and ready to fall."
E'en this appeal moved not his heart of rock.
He bade him seek the river. Turned he then ;
His weak steps showed that he was much in need :
Haughty and high, necessity was sharp
To urge him thus, the warrior of the wood.
And so he turned from one of Christian name
With proud yet mournful air, as turns a king,
When all his hopes are in the battle lost.
But woman's heart is tender : to the cry
Of suffering sorrow she will lend an ear,
Whether in deserts, or in cities fair.
Hushing her infant, Lila heard this speech,
And through an open casement watched the steps
Of the weak dusky native, till he sank
Exhausted near her dwelling. Then she took
Some bread and milk, parched corn, and roasted kid ;
And soon was at his side, when, bending down,
She whispered with a voice of tenderest love :
" Will my red brother rise, and eat and drink ? "

He rose and fed ; then, kneeling at her feet,
He pressed her hand so gently to his lips,
And thus spoke he in soft melodious tone :

" The eagle shall not pounce on the white dove,
For Carcoochee will save it. For her sake,
The unfledged young shall shelter in their nest,
And her red brother seek not for revenge."
Then drawing from his bosom a gay branch
Of heron's plumes, he took the longest out,
And, giving it to Lila, spoke once more :
" When o'er the hunting-grounds the white dove's mate
Flies in the chase a-near our dear wigwams,
Bid him to wear this feather on his head."
Then with a graceful nod the warrior turned,
And, gliding through the woods, was lost to view.

The summer passed, the harvest came and went,
The wheat and maize had all been gathered in,
The garden pumpkins graced their winter-homes,
And tints adorned the forest, which the hand
Of Autumn paints upon the changing leaves.
It was the time of hunting. A small band
Asked Collingrew to join them in the chase,
Beyond the river and the vale of pines.
Active and bold, he used the hatchet well ;
Expert, too, with the rifle, and his joy
Had heretofore been much to scour the wood ;
But now his heart misgave him. The dark form
Of the poor Indian he had so abused
Struck terror through his spirit. Night and day
It haunted him with horror unsurpassed.
At length he called his gentle wife, and said :

" My conscience lashes me like thongs of fire,
I have a wounded spirit hard to bear.
You know the native who last summer came,
And begged some bread, and begged of me in vain ;
It haunts me, O it haunts me. Ever since
All that my mother taught me has been here,
My duty to my neighbour and my God :
Both have been much neglected. I repent,
And live a different future. No, dear wife,
I cannot join to-morrow in the chase.
For I have strange misgivings in my mind.
Say, would you go, my Lila ? "

            Then she smiled,
Gazed in his face, and told him how she fed
The exhausted red man, keeping to herself
This flower of kindness fragrant in her heart,
For fear she might offend him. From the press
She fetched the heron's feather, telling him
The Indian's words, that he had nought to fear,
If this bright plume was seen upon his head.
Then Collingrew :

           " These Indians ne'er forget,
Nor evermore forgive an injury."

" Nor let a kindness unrewarded pass,"
Said gentle Lila, with her hand in his.
" I'll sew this feather in your hunting-cap ;
Then trust you to God's keeping, though I know
He could take care of you as well without ;
Yet we must use the means. My father said,
'Trust like a child, and labour like a man.'

Would we have help, then we must help ourselves.
No miracles are wrought on our behalf,
While we do nought but idly fold our arms.
O we are wrong; dear William, we are wrong.
Let's humbly bow before the Lord our God,
And ask His mercy." And that night they knelt,
For the first time, in earnest social prayer.

The morn was clear, the forest beautiful;
Hush, rush the trees, shook with the western wind;
No cloud was on the brow of Collingrew,
His fears had vanished with the rising sun.
The hunters had assembled, dogs and guns
Showed underneath the maples, and his heart
Was beating high with a prospective joy.
So buoyant were his spirits, that he seemed
Inclined to take the feather from his cap,
When Lila held his hand, and whispered, "No."
And he obeyed her, saying, "If you think
The plume will save me from the redskin's knife,
I'll wear it for your sake." Then on he put
His hunting cap, shouldered his gun, and soon
In the wild woodland gladly sought for game.

Then day grew dim, and night came calmly on;
The hunters sheltered in a mossy cave,
Which was a bear's they killed at red sunset,
As he came out upon the river's bank.
His flesh made steaks for supper; his soft skin,
Spread on a bed of leaves, pillowed their heads
Throughout the night; and, when the dawn began,
They left their rude room, and resumed the chase.
With ardent footsteps, following a fawn,
William became bewildered in the wild,
Apart from his companions. Not a mark
Could he discover which would tell him where
To bend his footsteps, so that he might leave
The great thick forest shutting out the sun.
He could not read the lichen on the trees,
Which served as waymarks to the Indian tribes;
And thus for hours he wandered on in vain.
Ofttimes he started, fancying he beheld
The bright gaze of a red man in the bush;
And, hasting on, was more bewildered still.

The trees grew thinner as the sunset came;
And then he reached a prairie stretching far,
Covered with long grass, and with brushwood low.
Through this extensive tract a river ran,
Bursting in freshness down the solitude:
On its low banks were bushes. Collingrew
Approached with caution, being weak and faint
From fasting since the morning; and his gun
He held half-cocked, for fear of beasts of prey.
When on its brink, he paused, for he could hear
A sudden rustling in the underwood;
And the next moment a huge buffalo
Rushed out like wind unloosened. His great head
He bent full low, and on the intruder dashed,
Who raised his gun, and fired: the beast, though hit,
Drove on with fiercer fury. His strong arm
Was weakened in the march, but danger nerved
His soul for battle: and he seized the brute
By the long hair which on his forehead hung,
Drawing his knife, if haply he might strike,
With his left hand, his adversary's throat.
Unequal was the combat. On the ground

The buffalo had hurled him, ere he trod
The prostrate man to death; when, in his woe,
The sharp click of a rifle smote his ear;
And, in an instant, the fierce animal
Sprang roaring in the air, and then fell dead,
Partly upon the wounded Collingrew.
Then, in a moment after, a dark form,
In Indian garb, came gliding through the grass,
And in the neck of the dead buffalo
He plunged his hunting-knife, then stood erect,
While Collingrew was struggling to his feet,
Who thus addressed the red man at his side:

"From dawn till dusk have I been wandering here,
Apart from my companions in the chase;
Cut with the hanging trees and tangled brake,
And mocked by vistas opening to deceive;
Now this, now that way hurrying; shouting now,
And now as silent as the falling leaf.
With bleeding feet I reached the prairie's edge,
And sought the river, when this startled brute
Came roaring down upon me. All the rest
Is known to thee to whom I owe my life.
I have a wife and pleasant little ones
Waiting to greet me to my forest home,
Sheltered by oaks and melancholy pines.
Canst thou direct me to the nearest town
Where my white brethren cluster?"

                          "If, till morn,
The weary hunter will consent to rest,
The eagle will direct him where to find
The nest of his white dove."

                          And then he took
Him by the hand, and led him through the dusk
To an encampment by the river side,
Under the trees that grew upon its banks.
Here the kind-hearted Indian bade him sup
On hominy and venison; spreading out
Some bison skins, the trophies of the chase,
He signed that he should take them for his bed,
And then he left him to his lone repose.

The east had scarce a shimmer of the dawn,
When Collingrew was wakened by his host:
And, after sitting to a slight repast,
They started on their journey. In advance
The Indian kept, through the still darkened wood,
Precise and rapid, showing that he knew
The secrets of the forest, led by signs
Which never failed him in the hour of need;
And, ere the sun had once more clothed with gold
The far-off Rocky Mountains, Collingrew
Stood gladly gazing on his precious home.
Yes, there it lay, in gentle, calm repose;
And, at the sight so dear, a cry of joy
Burst from the hunter's soul.

                          "I thank thee much
For thy great kindness. Yonder is my home,
Which, but for thee, I should have seen no more.
Lo, there my children come, and there my wife,
Straining their eyes along the forest paths,
And wondering much that I so slow return,
Hark, dost thou hear the crow of baby boy?
Accept my thanks, who cannot thank enough."

G 2

The warrior turned, and fronted Collingrew:
His face had not been seen by him before,
Save in the glimmer of his rude wigwam:
The sun's rays fell upon him, and revealed
To the astonished settler, smitten dumb,
The features of the red man, who had been
Five months before repulsed so cruelly.
Yes, this was he whom he called "Indian dog,"
When driven from his dwelling. In his face
A dignified, yet mild, rebuke was seen,
As he addressed him:

　　　　　　　　"Five short moons ago,
When I was faint and hungry at your door,
You called me 'heathen hound,' and drove me forth
Into the woods, a weak and famished man.
I might, last night, have sated my revenge,
And felled you in the forest. The white dove
Fed me, and called me 'brother.' For her sake
I spared her mate, and led him through the wild!
Now Carcoochee would bid you hasten home:
And if hereafter you should ever see
A red man need your kindness, do by him
As Carcoochee has treated you this day!"

He waved his hand, in turning to depart;
But the abashed and humbled Collingrew
Now sprang before him, with entreaty free:
"As one dear proof of your forgiving love,
Come with me to my dwelling; there my wife,
My gentle Lila, shall prepare you food
Fit for a prince's table. The best chair
Our room contains shall be your welcome seat;
And little loves shall blossom on your knees,
And shed sweet fragrance round you. By the well
We have a field; and in the field a lamb,
As white as snow, and nurtured tenderly;
The choicest of the flock: this shall be yours.
O, come and sup with us, and I shall know
That we are friends for ever." And, at last,
He gave consent, and to his cottage came.
Lila beheld them walking down the wood,
As in the door she held her baby up,
Who crowed to see his father. O, what joy
There was in meeting; and what gratitude
The wife expressed to noble Carcoochee,
Who thus repaid her for her deed of love!

The red man here was now an honoured guest,
A brother, and a blessing. Oft he came
To visit them, with joy from friendship's store;
And once he told them how he had escaped
Upon the burning prairie. He had rode,
With his companions, far into the noon,
When, lo, behind them, the great fiery flood
Rushed like a seething monster. On they dashed,
Spurring their coursers, racing for dear life;
While fiercer, faster, flashed the flaming sea!
The horses glared for terror: trees stood charred
To solid blackness: the high heavens were red,
And flared like crimson: roared the beasts of prey

Before the rocking, rolling element:
Birds whirled and fell, and turned to cinders dark:
And all was whelming horror. Stopped they then,
And, leaping to the ground, tore the long grass
Up with their hands, till a clear space was made;
And with a flint and steel they struck a light,
Burning the grass around them. The black spot
Grew larger still, on which they led their steeds:
And when the great fire reached the place, it fell
For lack of fuel; and they all were saved!

And Collingrew the grandest lesson learnt
From the untutored savage: how to love
His fellow-men, as sons of one great Sire;
To give to others, as he would receive:
And, step by step, he climbed a holier height,
Led by the Spirit where the Saviour hung,
Upon the cross; and heard His pardoning voice,
And felt the sweetness of the second birth.
And Lila, too, was changed; she gave her heart
To Jesus Christ, and fed upon His love:
Together walked they to the land of rest,
'Mid luscious fruits they never plucked before.

And, by and bye, light came to Carcoochee,
And liberty, and life, the light of truth,
From love's pure firmament; in which he read
His sins forgiven, and saw his Eden home.
The teaching of his white friends had been blessed
To his conversion; and the prayer of faith
Had oped for him the treasury of the skies.
And, when the white-haired Missionary came,
Some two years after, in the river-waves,
Baptized was Carcoochee: the first to join
The infant church among the forest-rills.
Now, the red warrior, who had wielded long
The tomahawk in slaughter, went forth, armed
With weapons from the armoury of Heaven,
To battle for the mighty Prince of Peace!
And thus he laboured for his living Lord,
Till age crept slowly on him: then he sought
His white friends' home, where he might die in peace.
His last hours passed in simple praise and prayer:
And, like a sailor coming into port
From voyage of hazard, brightened with his home,
So lay he gazing on the great unseen.
One cloudless summer morning, when the winds
Were vocal with a thousand instruments,
And the soft airs were laden with perfumes,
He closed his eyes, and slept the sleep of death.

Years, long and many, through the silence swept;
The Collingrews are sleeping in their graves
Within the churchyard, on the forest edge,
Where lie the bones of noble Carcoochee.
But their descendants in the township dwell;
And oft the grey-haired grandsire, seated low
Beneath the great magnolia, tells this tale
To his grandchildren, gathered on the grass.
And what he teaches them, was taught by Christ:
"Give unto others, as ye would receive!"

REUBEN ROSS.

DRAMATIS PERSONÆ.

REUBEN ROSS . . . . . . *A returned Emigrant.*
A WOODCUTTER.
A COUNTRY WOMAN.
MATA . . . . . . *A Village Maiden.*
A COTTAGER.
A WELL DRESSED MATRON.
AN AGED WIDOW.
    THE STORM KING, &c.

PART FIRST.

SCENE—*Hill-Top.* TIME—*Noon.*
REUBEN ROSS *alone on the heath.*

Reuben Ross. On this hill-top whose
    face looks up to heaven
Again I'm breathing freely. Years
    have passed
Since last I left it with a great
    resolve,
Which filled my soul like water fills the sea,
Or air the welkin to the distant poles,
Leaving no vacuum for a lesser good;
And I have won it, which the years shall tell
And marriage bells shall jingle. This fresh air
Lifting my locks is like the kiss of love,
When the moon gilds the ash leaves. Thus it is
In life's encounter: from the conquered heights,
The thorny plain, and moor with boulders strewn,
And rough ascent, seem nothing. Conflicts past,
Fierce storms outrode, and dangers overcome,
Give zest to our existence. True, the scars
Of wasting warfare are upon my flesh,
And my arm fails in fighting; the reward
Of honest labour recompenses all;
So that the earth rejoices in the wealth
Of summer suns, blue seas, and lovely flowers,
Whence incense rises ever. Birds have wings
To sweep the air above the loftiest pines,
Where blast to loud blast rattles: fishes sport
In ocean's chambers which the heart of man
Has never sounded: beasts are fleet of foot
To scour the earth with hoofs that aid their flight,
With instinct strong and mighty as their speed:
But man is king of all: he holds the rein,
And beast and bird obey him. [*He still soliloquizes.*
                 Let me turn,
And view the scene all other scenes beyond—
My own dear birthplace. There the old house stands,
With woodbine wall and windows near the eaves,
With roof of thatch, and hawthorn by the gate,
And white lambs feeding in the quiet fields,
As when I was a boy. Long years have run
Since last I saw it, when a mother's lips
Were pressed to mine, with the sad slow farewell;
And I passed forth beyond its sacred porch,
With the great world before me, a lone man,
To tread the way of life, to face its frowns
And guard against its smiles. I crossed the yard,
Passed o'er the stile, and entered on the leas;
Then turned and saw her standing by the door,
Holding her apron to her weeping eyes,
Watching her child depart. This was enough:
I could hold out no longer, and a sigh
Which seemed to rend my bosom scared the birds
Among the withs, and tears ran down my face;
My heart beat loud and knocked against my side,
And my knees trembled like the branches shake
When Thunder leaves his closet, and pours out
His smoking censer on the quaking hills.
I thought I should have fallen to the ground,
But her prayer smote my ear and smote my heart,
And I passed onward. O how oft since then
Have I in fancy seen her by the door,
Watching my slow departure! and her prayer
Like some sweet spell has lingered round my steps,
And o'er the roar and tumult of the world
My mother's voice has sounded. Is it well?
Does she still live, and is my father here?
And by the shoulder of that sloping moss,
With one tree near it like a watching saint,
Does Mata dwell,—the fair, the beautiful?
The Maiden of the Mountain, whose love-gleams
Lit up my path and sunned my soul with hope

When youth was in its morning ? Sporting round
The gentle birds hop on from twig to twig
With bright eyes turned upon me ; but their notes
Have no revealings which I fain would grasp
Like miser hugs his hoard.   I soon shall know.
But, hark, a footstep !   [*Enter a* Village Woman.
Village Woman.   It is pleasant here.
Art thou a stranger 'mid our silent moors.
Where wild birds breed, and airy echoes hide,
And Cupid shoots his arrows ?   Hast thou heard
The news that our small valley gives the world ?
The parson's maid is married, and the hind
Of Farmer Ford is much in love with Meg,
The thatcher's younger daughter.   Felix Fir
Has oft been seen near Widow Watson's cot,
What time his horses have left off the yoke,
Returning home by moonlight : gossips say
There must be something brewing in the wind.
Last night the seines were shut by Raddo's Rock,
Enclosing fish in hundreds.   Miner Joe
Has cut a lode of copper in his croft.
Ben White has signed the pledge ; 'twas time he
       should,
For drink had stripped him to the very skin.
Old miser Riff has starved himself at last,
And his poor bones are buried.   I have seen
Him hobbling forth with holes along his hose,
And in his shoes tied up with draggling yarn,
Through which his blue skin gazed like hungry eyes
Upon the frowning Winter.   Bless you, Sir,
His clothes were rags, his bed a heap of filth,
His food dry crusts and water.   When he died
They found a brown bag underneath his head
Stuffed full of gold he had no heart to spend.
They say the old fool's ghost is in the lane
When midnight stars are shining ; but I think
He's far too lean to walk this world again.
Reuben Ross. Thy words bring pleasure to my listen-
      ing ers ;
Like one long pent in darksome prison house,
Longing to flee, but cannot break his bars,
Who, when his cup of sorrow is o'errun,
Hears the sweet voice of Mercy.   Dost thou know
Aught of a damsel living by the brook
With a fair face and air of gentleness,
Modest, retiring, bashful in her speech,
As full of goodness as a bubbling well,
Whose name is Mata ?
Village Woman.   Bless you, know her ! yes !
A gentler soul ne'er walked the whispering world.
She would not bruise a spider, and they say
She has a love for every living thing.
I saw her once beside a widow's bed,
In a small cottage underneath the oaks,
Reading the blessed Bible.   On her brow
A light was resting which was not of earth,
And her words floated through the sufferer's room
Like whispers at the sunset.   Gifts were there,
And little services her hands had wrought,
Which drew the tears upon the sick one's face.
I sat in silence overcome with awe,
And felt the place was holy.   If this world
Has one fair angel, Mata must be she.
Reuben Ross. That there are angels we cannot deny,
Whose wings sweep by us at the hour of prayer
And in the time of danger.   Let me hear
A little more of Mata : speak, I pray :

Thou canst not talk too much of such an one.
My ears would not be weary, though thy speech
Ran on into the thickest of the night,
Or till the day broke smiling.
Village Woman.   It is well
To feel we have a watcher at our side,
Upholding us in conflict.   By the brook
Grew up a stripling straight as river reed,
In all his actions just.   He scorned to walk
In the dissembler's path, made God his Guide,
And studied Nature with an artist's eye.
No wonder Mata loved him.   Like the leaves
Expanding in the perfect light of heaven,
Or the corn-stalk to ripeness, so their love
Grew into fulness in the fields of hope.
But duty called him unto other climes,
From whence his letters cheered her, till the sound
Of wailing rose that he was fading fast
Under the hand of sickness.   Then the maid
Sighed in her chamber, calling on his name ;
Her joyfulness departed ; sorrow's shade
Blent with the lines of beauty on her face.
The weight became too heavy : she arose
And packed her trunk and paid her passage fare,
And now awaits the stately steamer's sail.
A love like this makes our poor world a heaven.
Reuben Ross (*aside*).   How oft the heart is gladdened
      in its grief
By lips unconscious !   Gold could not procure
What this good dame has brought me.   Mata lives,
And loves her Reuben.   This is everything.
I walk through roses and by lily lakes.   [*Exeunt.*

Scene—*Wild moor.* Time—*Midnight.*   *Enter the*
Storm King.

Storm King. Amid these boulders let me raise my throne,
And cease awhile to ravage.   Thus I fold
My ebon wings, and on these huge blocks sit,
Resting my chin upon my cloudy hands,
Swift-staring through the blackness.   Strange exploits
Have been performed by me and my compeers,
Since Night sat in his chamber.   O'er the hills
I've turned my steeds, where they have raced unreined,
Pawing the clouds beneath them, champing loud,
With manes of flame, and hoofs of thunder-stone.
Beside a well, where ferns and ivy grew,
And rushes raised their plumes, two lovers sat,
When Eve came forth to sing her twilight song ;
No fairer she than this delightful maid.
Her eyes were like the beams of Jupiter,
When no cloud walks the farthest firmament :
Her hair was bright as gold ; her cheeks were pale,
Her fair hands small and snowy, and her waist
No bigger than a brook-nymph's.   Down we came,
And smote her lover with the roar of fate,
Dashing him headlong in the treacherous spring ;
And while her cry went up in agony
For him who struggled there and grasped at leaves,
Her foot slipped, and they perished.   In the vale
She had an aged mother, he a sire ;
And when the tidings reached them, overpowered
With a great sorrow, they fell suddenly
As the fruit falls when blasted.
          [*He still soliloquizes.*
          On the cliff
A young wife watched a ship upon the sea,
And raised her handkerchief with words of cheer

When she beheld her husband on the deck,
And felt how soon he'd press her in his arms,
And give the kiss of welcome. In her home,
Among the woodbines near the narrow creek,
The cottage fire was burning, the cloth laid,
The supper cooked, the favourite book prepared,
His chair wheeled in the corner, and the lamp
Ready to be rekindled. Fierce I spoke,
And at my roar the angry waters rose,
And swallowed the proud bark and all the crew,
As if it were a nutshell; down it went,
With a great shriek that shook the shattered trees.
She stood upon the bench and saw it all.
Her hair blew wildly round her. Once she spoke,
In piercing tones which rose above my rage,
" O God, I am a widow ! " Days and nights
Beheld her watching on the lonely cliff,
And then she wandered far from sight and sound.
　　　　　　　　　　　　　[He still soliloquizes.
A straw-thatched dwelling rose beside a wood
Where an old dame was knitting. Years had passed
Since first she owned it, led there a young bride
By him whom storms can never more affright.
Beside it towered an elm which was a tree
At her own mother's wedding. Far it spread
Its knotty arms, and swung them in the air,
And its huge trunk noteworthy was for girth ;
Fair childhood loved it, and old age admired ;
It was the praise and glory of the glade.
This tree was in our passage. With one shout
We rent it like a giant rends a reed,
And hurled it on the cottage. Morn arose
With tears upon her eyelids, but the dame
Lay 'mid the ruin, raised beyond alarm.
A ferryman came rowing in his boat
A pleasant damsel ; half the passage crost,
She sat admiring Nature. Up we came
And rolled our fury on them, driving back
The rended craft against the broken quay,
Shivering it into fragments. The old man
Clung to the railing with a desperate grasp,
While the white waves beat o'er him. Tiles were
　　　　tossed
From warehouse-roofs, tall chimneys quick destroyed,
And slates went hissing by the traveller's ears.
The maiden had sunk once, and when she rose
The boatman caught her by her spreading dress,
And soon the two were safe upon the land.
I drove my coursers onward at swift pace,
And the proud bent to hear me ; the young child
Clung to its mother, the dumb mother moaned,
Woods rocked, and were uprooted ; but I know
There is a Power that holds my might in thrall,
And chains my rage within a given sphere.
　　　　　　　　　　　　　　　　[Exit.

SCENE—*The Hill-Top again. Enter* REUBEN Ross
and a WOODCUTTER.

Woodcutter. Good day, young master ! May I
　　make so bold,
Is not this prospect charming to the eye,
Where wood and waters mingle, and blue hills
Rise in the distance with a crown of clouds ?
O what a place to breathe in ! It was hard
And much exhausting, toiling up the turf,
And twenty times I wiped the sweat away

Amid the pauses of my upward march ;
But here I am, with heaven above my head,
O'errun with beauty, and great thoughts like ships
Gliding across the waters of my soul ;
The earth below me like a teeming mart.
So renovated, so refreshed am I,
If I had wings I'd flash into the air,
And strive with all the marvel of a sage
To grasp this growing grandeur. In the woods
At summer twilight, I have heard strange songs
Travelling among the shadows, and my strength
Grew as the notes waxed louder, till I felt
The sinews of a giant, and strode on
With supple limbs through seas of solemn sound,
Feeling no weariness, forgetting pain,
And followed by an angel. But this height,
So near the chamber of the Mighty One,
Brings organ swells, and crash of lifted trumps,
And sounding odes from choirs whose wings are flame,
Whose harps are moulded in the fires of love,
That I grow big with blessing.
Reuben Ross. 　　　　This bright world
Has much good gifts to comfort cheerfulness,
Which grumblers never win. If I have light,
And bread and water, and a soul to feel,
This is full theme for praising, and I hear
A thousand harps among the ripening corn.
That cottage yonder by the forest side
Is my own birthplace. It has power to draw
The hot tears from their fountains, though I've been
'Mid other scenes for long eventful years,
Struggling with hardships which I overcame,
And left behind in ruins. O how sweet
To view the porch, the walls, the roof of home,
After long travel ! Trees have disappeared,
Boulders have vanished, lakes have left the land,
And barren wastes grown fruitful ; but below
Is the dear sanctum of my early life,
Wooing me like a vision, and I weep,
And clasp my hands in prayer.
Woodcutter. 　　　　　Coming here
I passed a poet where the moss was close,
And rushes waved, and willows. By his side
A grey rock rose with lichen on its front,
And overhead from out the great hill steep,
With roots half bare for lack of helpful mould,
A tree gave grateful shadow. He was pale,
Much worn with musing, and his pensive eyes
Were wells of thought where hallowed figures hid,
Ready to flash forth at the sound of song.
I saw he had been weeping. By him lay
A written fragment, moistened with his tears ;
And when I spoke of homes and warm firesides,
With books and loved companions, I could see
Him freely use his kerchief, and I knew
The mountains were his closet. Oft I hear
Sublime intonings when my sharp axe strikes
The monarch of the forest : then the woods
Are full of murmurs solemn as the sea,
Nor need I other harpings.
Reuben Ross. 　　　　　　　Ever flows
From Nature's lyre the voice of harmony.
Has this provincial bard the holy fire
Which the Divine One to His true-born gives ?
And has he written words which stir the soul ?
Woodcutter. The world should thank him for his
　　wondrous book,

Which lives when tombs are ashes: but he's poor,
And hence neglected. Money rules the world
And bridles genius. By him dwells a man
Whom Fortune has much favoured : gold and land
Have come almost unsought for, and he's rich.
He gives of his abundance to the poor ;
He builds a home to shelter widowhood ;
And praises crowd upon him. Slaves bow down
And worship at his footstool, and his deeds
Shine in the columns of the journalist.
Men meet in conclave, and their voices shout,
" His charity shall be his monument :
A noble man, the noblest of his kind."
And they are satisfied, and so is he.
Amid this swell of praise the bard is lost,
Although his lofty thoughts shall burn and blaze
When monuments are powder. Comes the moth,
The rust, the ravage, water-fiend, and fire ;
And riches vanish: but the poet's lay
Shall gild the globe with glory evermore.
               [*Exit Woodcutter.*
Reuben Ross (aside). How like the full moon o'er
     the castled hill,
With scarce a sign to herald her approach,
Wooing the earth to watch her loveliness,
Steals the true poet on the wakeful world !
No flash of arms, no boom of brazen guns,
No sound of trump, no clang of ringing bells,
Announce him to his fellows ; but he spreads
His thoughts before them like the silent heavens.
Hark ! hark ! what music ! these dear vales are full,
And every moss bank has a harper on't ;
The doors of song seem open, and out pours
More melody than this small sphere can hold.
Is it some angel wandering near the world ?
Again the music ripples on mine ears,
Again it swells and rises, and the flowers
Shake with the sweetness. On my fancy steals
A lovely vision, which was wont to cheer
Me in the bliss of morning when my life
Was heavy with the honey of delight.
My precious Mata ! it is surely she.
Thus I repose and listen.

Mata sings in the distance.

     There grew a flower on Albion's strand,
     The fairest flower in all the land :
     But came the winds one cloudy day,
     And swept my gentle rose away.

     There sang a bird by English lakes,
     No sweeter caroled from the brakes :
     But sighed the seas, my thrush was flown,
     And now I'm in the world alone.

     In British woods a sapling throve,
     A greener never graced a grove :
     But burst the lightning's livid glare,
     And passed my plant I know not where.

     O Reuben, Reuben, where art thou !
     My rose, my thrush, my greenwood bough !
     The hills may melt, the valleys flee,
     My love shall not depart from thee.
                 [*Exeunt.*

PART SECOND.

Scene—*Cave on the cliff with* Reuben Ross *before it.*
Time—*Morning.*

Reuben Ross. No Providence ! The thought itself is
     sin,
And burns like lava. Hence, ye cloudy doubts,
And hide with Error in his vault of gloom,
Where never daylight pierces ! In the heavens
I see His hand, and trace it on the earth.
The hurricane that travels in the dark
With ruin on his wings ; the northern winds
That twist the oaks like straws ; the thunder roar
That awes the rocking mountains ; the great sea,
The forest-trumpets, the swift river's voice,
The changing seasons, sun and moon and stars,
Comets and clouds, the hues of morn and eve ;
Birds on the boughs, the flowerets of the fields,
The rain among the roses, sounds and sights
At every angle, fill their cups of praise,
And gladly hymn the God of Providence.
He feeds the widow and her weeping babes,
Though to the cold world strangers. The poor man
With sackcloth on his loins, begging his bread
From door to door, the road his only home,
Has his wants met by Him who succours all.
Once in a cottage by a shelly creek
I saw an aged matron at her meal,
A crust of bread and water. I had found
Her door half open : so I entered in
Somewhat abruptly. At her table's end
By a small window, sheltering a few flowers,
Sat this contented pilgrim. Need I say,
Her linen weeds and linen cap were clean
As when they left the mangle ? Her two hands
Were clasped together and her eyes upraised.
I watched her face, and saw two tears upon't
Shining like crystal, slowly gliding down
Where wrinkles long had wasted. 'Twas a sight
To fix the gaze of angels, a fit theme
To engage the artist's pencil, this grey saint
Left lonely in the desert, praising God
For a dry crust and water. May not kings
And thankless princes learn a lesson here ?
              [*He still soliloquizes.*
" There is a Providence," the hills reply,
When shouting to each other : valleys urge
The echo onwards to remotest dells,
And wood and waste proclaim it. Cities vast,
And hamlets brown, and cottages of reed
Tell the same holy story. Cornfields wave
The truth in living billows, and the vine
For ever whispers its Creator's name.
I see Him in the firmament of stars,
And in the blue of ether ; in the clouds
Marshalled at sunset round the crimson west,
With banners stained with glory ; in the flowers

That fringe the skirts of Nature; in the leaves
That rustle music to the milkmaid's song;
In the proud eagle's wing-flash, as he leaves
The highest peaks behind him; in the wren
That chirps among the brambles; in the rain,
The ice, the snow, the sunshine, and the gloom:
The merest atom, the sublimest height,
The heavens, the earth, are full of Providence.
Nor do I fail in meaner things to trace
The hand of the Upholder. The poor swain
Whom ills detained to reach the bark in time
Which foundered in its passage; the young girl,
Met in her sorrow by the hand of love
Which led her to the altar; the old pair
Drifted with adverse winds o'er angry seas,
Swift-sailing till the currents drew the hulk
Safe into harbour where the woods were green;
The book left open where the scoffer read
Words sharp as arrows, leading him to light
And bliss which never endeth: these attest
The grace and guidance of the Power Divine.
Nor do I fear to trust Him, though the way
Is blocked with marble higher than the hills,
And no path lies before me. He is God,
And will not leave His people.

[He still soliloquizes.

Hear, ye hills,
And list, ye solemn valleys! Did I not
Do all for Mata? labour, live for her,
Keep her before me like a rose-leaf shrine,
All purity and odour? Did she not
In fancy follow me from place to place
With silent footstep, raining on my soul
An influence steeped in Eden? Did I stand
Among my fellows trafficking for gold?
Her bright eyes seemed to scan me. Did my gains
Swell more and more, as the slow years crept by,
Until the wine of riches warmed my brain,
And the great earth put out her garden flowers
To summer's fullest music? on me beamed
A smile like Mercy's from my Mata's face.
Did I encounter winds, and dismal rains,
And thunder shocks, and rushing lightning fires,
'Mid barrenness and blackness? Mata's mien
Shone in the conflict, till the mighty storm
Staggered amid its triumph, and fell back
Tamed with its own great passion. She was all,
My light, my life, my sum of happiness,
The spring of every action; and the sky
Which canopied my future, seemed to be
All blue with beauty. Home I came at last
To claim her as my own for evermore
Without a jot of hinderance, when a spell
Mysterious as the darkness covered all:
I heard her voice, a living voice it seemed,
Where harebells bent their faces. Thrilled I was,
And ran to meet her at the cottage porch,
Where we had whispered love in other days:
But Mata was not there. I shrieked her name
Till echo mocked me and the rocks replied,
And yet she came not; no, she never came.
The earth grew dark; its glory disappeared:
I sought this cavern. Oft the little birds
Come twittering round me; but they cannot tell
Where I may find my Mata. Silence, speak:
Is she on earth, or dwells my love in heaven?
Does she wear weeds that fairy fingers weave,

Or is she clad in robes which angels own?
How lag are my surmisings! but no sound
Reveals the secret; and I harbour here
Amid the trumpets of the mighty crags,
Till death shall solve the riddle.

[Exit.

Scene—*Mountain Top.* Time—*Twilight.* Enter
the Storm King.

Storm King.   What of tears?
Think you my heart will soften for a sigh
From weaker woman? that a few poor moans
From stricken starvelings will affect my soul?
Think you a prayer from Agony's lean lips
Would thwart my purpose, or my plans subvert,
Stay my ripe fierceness, or impede my march?
Shall I for shrieks from a few timid swains
Fold my black wings, and cower behind the poles?
Shall babes affright me on their mothers' knees?
No truly! Though old age twitch his white hair,
And beat his hard palms gory; though the rose
Fade out of Beauty's visage, and her eye
Lack all its living lustre; though the voice
Of wailing rise like ocean in his wrath,
And hot tears roll in rivers; though Distress
Lift up his wrongs in thunder, I'll go forth
With savage tread, and on the humbled earth
Pour out the vengeance of my fury-cup.
How will I shake the mountains by their hair,
Until the valleys tremble! how arouse
The spirit of the ocean, till the waves
Boil in their anger, surging ship and crew!
The pines shall ring for fear; the awful rocks
Grind in their chambers; the grand cedars mourn;
Man in the uproar of the earth and heaven
Shall lowly bend and worship. Love shall sigh,
Mirth drop his mask, and Pleasure hide her head.
Fair habitations built upon the rock
Shall reel and waver, wailing to their fall;
The strong trees raise their arms, to be dashed down
And rise no more for ever. A great swell
Shall surge across the land and smite the sea.
Hiding the heavens from vision. Babes shall cling
Close to their mothers, wondering at the woe,
And lift their eyes to scan the saddened face.
Cloud shall meet cloud, and wreck ride over wreck,
As 'twere the end of all things; but I'll sit
Upon my throne, and lift my hands, and roar
At the tremendous frolic. Thus I blow
My azure trump, and call my servants round.
Go ye and do my bidding!

[Exit.

Scene—*High Cliff.* Time—*Morning.* Enter a
Cottager.

Cottager.   All night long
I've heard oppressive moaning, and dull sounds
Have walked the moors with Midnight. I came out
And paced my little garden, musing much;
Then leant upon the wicket. O how black
Was everything around! I strained mine eyes
In vain to pierce its thickness, raised my hand,
But could not see it, thrust it in the gloom,
And drew it back with a mysterious chill.
The mighty heavens and the big earth seemed one.
And still those sighs! I sought my door again;

Crept to my chamber; pressed my pleasant bed;
But sleep forsook me. So when Morn arose
With dew upon her hair, before her veil
Was laid aside, I sought this lofty cliff
To look and listen. Yonder comes a boat
Without a rower, drifting here and there,
At mercy of the billows. Strange indeed!
Let me descend this pathway to the sea,
And labour to secure it. [*He secures the boat.*
                         What is this?
No oar, no oarsman, but a maiden fair
Lies in the small boat's bottom. On her face
The curls are clustered. O how white that face,
How beautiful those hands! That snowy neck
Is full perfection; and that lovely brow!—
Can so much beauty be in league with death?
I almost fear to test it. Heavens! she breathes.
Still lives the gentle maiden. From what isle
Has such a blossom drifted? and where dwells
The idol of her being? Is her home
Where palms are graceful, and the honey-bee
Lays up her stores, where the gay red-bird breeds?
Or is her garden by this beetling cliff,
Where sea flowers woo the waters? See, she moves,
And opes her eyes like Summer to the dawn.
But comes a stranger singularly clad,
Prying about him with an earnest look,
As if he sought adventure. [*Enter* REUBEN ROSS.
Reuben Ross.   Truly this
Has been a night of roaring. Down and dell,
And fen and forest, earth, and sea, and sky
Appeared one awful trumpet, uttering woe.
My cave became too small to hold my thoughts,
And so I left it for the great sea-shore,
To watch the waves and wonder. In the rage
Of loosened elements methought I heard
A voice like Mata's, calling on my name:
A hundred times I heard it, as I paused
A hundred times to listen to the gale.
What mean these symbols in the arc of strife?
The sweetest word that ever charmed mine ear
Is hurled along the air in shocks of doom
With horror and the thunder. It foretells
Intelligence as rapid as the roar
Of whirlwinds on the desert. What is this?
A peasant with a boat upon the sand,—
Perhaps a smuggler. Ho! what have you here?
Cottager. As I stole out to watch the angry deep,
This boat came tossing, which with my two hands
I pulled where now thou see'st it. Start not back:
It holds a damsel fairer than a queen,
The diamond of the waters. Speak to her,
If thou hast aught that presses to thy lips.
Reuben Ross. A precious freight! Why is it thou art
      here,
Voyaging across the salt sea all alone,
Like daughter of the ocean? Is the ship
That bore thee wrecked, and thy companions gone?
Or didst thou lose thy way, and lose thy oars,
And toss thou knew'st not whither? Let me know:
Tell me thy name, and wherefore art thou thus.
Maiden. Give me a little water, and I'll speak.
I had a lover once, a kindly youth;
And if he lives, I'm sure he loves me still.
He left me for the seas, and came no more:
But night and day I seemed to see his face
And hear his voice, so like an April bird;

And then a rumour reached me he was ill
And fading among strangers. This was sad;
And every hour it sadder, heavier, grew,
Till I no more could bear it. Tears I shed
And burning sighs, until the listening Night
Grew paler as it watched me, and a voice
Was strangely sounding, sounding evermore,
"Go seek him where he suffers." So I turned
From home and its endearments, sire and friends,
With a great love like fire within my soul,
Burning more fiercely as the dangers swelled;
And in a ship careering o'er the sea
I met the raging tempest. Days and nights
Our bark was tossed and battered, driven back,
And then advancing, then again repelled
With sevenfold fury, till the timbers groaned
And the seams sucked the water. Back we came,
And neared the shores of England, when a rock
Drew her upon its flint, and all was lost.
I sprang into a boat, and drifted here.
The rest I need not tell you. God is good:
He willeth not the sinner's overthrow,
But rather all should turn to Him and live.
Now guide me to my mother: by the wood
Is her abode, with ivy overgrown,
Where, when the swallows wheel along the moors,
I'll kneel and pray for Reuben.
Reuben Ross.   Maid, thy name:
Thou hast not told me this. What is thy name?
Speak quickly, firmly: gaze into my face.
Thou canst not tell the weight that hangs on it:
No alchemist had ever such a power:
It has a spell to change these rocks to gold,
To turn December into pleasant May,
My painful night to morning. Speak, O speak;
A world of sweetness hangs upon thy name.
Maiden. If my poor name is such a weight with thee,
I blush not to reveal it. Ever since
I've known the sweetness of a mother's love,
And at her feet put up my evening prayer,
When all the earth was holy; ever since
I've worn a necklace of dear daisy-flowers,
When hand-in-hand with Innocence I walked,
And shouted to the cuckoo; ever since
I've been a child, and now when older grown,
They simply call me MATA.
Reuben Ross.   Blessed girl!
Come to my arms, thy Reuben meets thee here:
Misfortune's winds which strangely stranded us
Have brought us thus together. Night is gone,
And sudden morn has dazzled me with joy.
Let's kiss thy face, more lovely in distress.
                              [*He kisses her.*
Another, and another. Precious maid!
This is no dream: no, no: I am awake,
A spirit cannot charm as Mata does.
I seem to tread a sphere where goodness dwells,
And sin approaches never. This great bliss
Walks with me like a moon, so that my path
Is on through glades of silver. Kiss me, love:
I have a history long and intricate,
Which if unravelled now would tire thine ears;
Suffice it that this hour all pleasure-fraught
Atones for years of anguish. Let it go.
I grasp the future, 'mid the rush of song
From copse and corn-field; and sweet marriage-bells
Seem floating o'er the waters. Mata, come. [*Exeunt.*

SCENE—*Country lane.* TIME—*Evening.* *Enter*
REUBEN ROSS *and* MATA.

Reuben Ross. How sweet these woodbines arching
 overhead !
But sweeter is thy breath than honey-flowers ;
Thy speech than lark's spring warble. Look on me,
And let me read the mystery in thine eyes :
Within their depths are images of light
With snowy wings, reclining in their dreams
On emerald banks, where droop the buds of peace.
How lovely does my Mata make the world !
Her presence fills the desert with perfume,
And clothes the waste an Eden ; the dry ground
Is barrenness no longer ; verdure smiles,
And lilies grow amid the water-springs.
The coming years, with plenty in their arms,
Rise on my vision like a pleasant poem,
Which it is rapture to bend o'er and read.
We'll walk the world together ; let it frown,
And both our hearts are wounded ; let it smile,
And summer suns shall kindle up our souls :
Thus will we share the bitter and the sweet.
Lean on my arm, dear Mata. Did I hear
A murmur in the thicket ? It was Love
Wooing us to her arbour. Here we'll sit,
And lose ourselves in kisses.   [*Exeunt.*

SCENE—*A small Village.* TIME—*Noon.* *Enter a*
well-dressed MATRON.

Matron.   O how true !
Whate'er we sow, that shall we also reap ;
The thistle-seed will never bring forth figs ;
Nor yields the hawthorn grapes. A life of wrong
Will cause remorse and sorrow, and the stings
Of deep contrition, wretchedness, and woe.
Sobriety shall win its own reward,
And gain a solid footing. Give me this,
Although the struggle ends where heaven begins.
Let Reuben Ross this truthful lesson teach :
He gave his hand, his heart, to honesty,
And in a land where strong temptations lure,
He struggled with his fate. Slowly he rose,
Step after step, gaining the world's esteem,
And adding gold to gold, till he was rich,
And now he comes to pass his latter days
Beside his native fountain. Hark, the bells
Among the oaks are ringing merry peals,
And maids in white come tripping o'er the stiles ;
It is a wedding : Reuben takes to wife
My only daughter Mata. Thus 'twill be
When the young world grows older, bells will ring,
And bridal feet go brushing through the flowers,
While mourners pass them with the silent bier.
    [*Enter an aged* WIDOW.
Widow. My prayers for Reuben. Those are truly
 good
Who live for others, overcoming self.
How many hearts have Reuben's gifts made glad !
How many widows thanked him ! Wreaths of praise
Have circled up to heaven, and reached the throne,
Which shall descend in blessings on his path,
Like rain upon the verdure of the fields.
O how much better would the wide world be
If there were other Reubens, men who feel

The fatherless and widow, and where'er
The toiling pilgrim trod with weary feet
Would hail him as a brother ! It will come,
Although the clouds are congregated now
Upon the distant mountains, and the roar
Of rude artillery rattles : it will come,
The golden age of plenitude and peace,
When Friendship's arms shall circle all the globe.
Bless you, these bells are ringing showers of joy,
And wafting gladness to a hundred hearths ;
'Twould do you good to see the gladdened dames
In straw-roofed sheds, with clean washed garments on,
Talking of Mata, Reuben's happy bride,
And calling her an angel. Earth has frowns,
Which often chill the tender leaves of Hope,
And on the face of Meekness force the tear ;
But days like this bring balm for other hours.
    [*Exit* WIDOW.
Matron. 'Tis always best to take the pleasant path,
And leave sharp thorns behind us ; always best
To hand the cup of kindness, and to greet
Mankind as brethren on the march of life.
How many are there using rough command,
And treading on their fellows, causing pain,
Where kindness would bring pleasure ! Not a blow
Should fall on human form to cause a tear,
Or harsh word wound the spirit, could my prayer
But win an echo in the soul Divine.
A traveller climbing up a rugged hill
Beheld before him in the hanging mist
An object which he thought was some wild beast
Slow-prowling through the stubble. On he passed,
The huge thing getting nearer, and it seemed
More hideous than before. He wiped his brow
And struggled onward ; but when face to face,
He found 'twas his own brother. Thus it is
Upon the highway to the upper hills.
But here is Reuben's home. I'll enter in
Amid the bridal music.
    [*Singing in the distance.*

The world may seem an endless round,
Through briers and thorns and stony ground,
Still up the steep with strife and strain ;
But virtue its reward shall gain.

The winds may frown, the earth be bare,
And we like those who beat the air ;
But courage ! courage ! danger's past,
And virtue wins the prize at last.

Why should we hang our heads and moan ?
The shepherd sometimes gains a throne ;
And perseverance shall succeed,
For virtue wins its honest meed.

Gay vests of silk and broadcloth rare
Oft hide a bosom genius-bare ;
And though from these we be debarred,
Yet virtue wins its own reward.

Then let us chant our songs to-day
In praise and hope, as well we may,
And pour our psalms forth full and fast ;
For virtue shall succeed at last. [*Exeunt.*

THE MINE.

PART I.

OME from his pit among the reeds
    and flags,
Where he had dug for months, and
    dug in vain,
The pale man came to dinner.
    Lost in thought,
Upon a bench, and the low table's
    end,
      He ate the remnant of their only loaf.
His lean dog scanned him by the three-legged stool,
And in a cage beside his lattice small
An old thrush chattered with a marvellous glee.
His wife, her face upon her wasted hands,
Sat in the chimney by the red peat fire,
Watching the smoke ascend the smutty stack,
And lost meanwhile in wondrous reverie.
Laying his knife upon the wooden plate,
He broke the silence with a heavy sigh :—

"'Tis no use, Maggie, digging any more.
I've ventured till we've only one goat left,
The weakest of the flock : the kids are gone,
And all the sheep and lambs have long been sold :
The cows have vanished from the untilled fields,
And all the horses have been driven away,
Save that poor pony, lean, you see, and long :
The pigs and poultry feed in other yards,
And every sack of corn has left the barn.
I sold the straw last night to farmer Jones,
And our next neighbour bought the rick of hay.
Not a potato in the outhouse lies :
The furze is taken from the under croft,
And all the turf is carried from the carne.
My bran-best hat and breeches waterproof,
My buckled boots, my best, my yellow-topped,
Bridle and saddle, and my darling cane,
With silver head and silver studded o'er,
I bought when we were married,—all are gone,
And I am left alone, a ruined man.
Dame, look around you : where the chest of drawers ?
Where all the pewter ? where the copper pans ?
Where the old china, rich indeed for age,
The bright tin teapots, and the oaken chairs ?
Gone ! and the cracked panes echo, ' Gone !'
I've worked until my bones are almost bare,
And Hope has weeping left me ; and, to fill
This dark-lined cup to overflowing quite,
Our only boy could bear distress no more,
And so last night he left us for the seas.
O God, have mercy on us and the lad !"

The poor man groaned and shook his streaming locks,
Resting his back against the cupboard door,
He fixed his eyes upon an empty shelf.
Then Maggie's full heart poured its treasures forth.
She told of many men of humble birth
Who persevered in duty's upward path,
And won estates, rich fortunes, and a name.
"Last night," she said, "I dreamt 'twas summer-time,
And we were walking by a limpid lake,
Whose face was crystal as the mirrored heavens,
And overhead the tall trees shadowed us,
And shook their leaves with gladness. We sat down,
And listened to the birds, and marked the kine
Feeding upon the lawn, while round us lay
Orchards of fruit and fields of waving corn ;
And all was ours, and all the gift of Heaven.
But I awoke, and, lo, it was a dream."
And then she bade him not to be dismayed,
But trust in God, who made the mighty hills,
And placed the minerals in their hidden cells ;
That nothing came of him who ceased to act,
And wept at every steep he had to climb.
The navigator, hoping against hope,
Still steered his vessel over darksome seas,
Until new lands were added to his chart.
So he should never give despair a place,
But go and try again another week.—
That week brought fortune in a mine of wealth.

It happened thus. Down from a distant moor
An old man came, with wisdom in his face ;
Mean his attire, and homely was his speech,
But warm his heart that beat beneath a frieze ;
And calling at the tinner's rustic door
The following morn, he gently knocked, and said,
"Cheer up, faint heart : I'm come to give thee aid."
And forth upon the plain of pits they went,
Conversing by the way of lodes and veins.
Meanwhile a cloud went marching up the sky,

And blacker grew and blacker, mounting higher,
Until it reeled and staggered o'er their heads,
And sent forth streams of fire that rolled along
The rocky valley like a flaming beast.
The two men gazed, and cloud and fire were gone.
Then much they chatted in the light of morn.
Spoke the old man with warm heart wrapped in frieze,
"'This is the dragon of the mineral vault:
He's out but rarely, and his presence shows
A mine of riches wheresoe'er he rolls.
His track was down the sheep-path by the oak,
Close to the pit where you were digging last,
Sad and discouraged. But this augurs well
For you, my neighbour: and we'll try once more
What virtue's in the famous dowzing-rod."

So from a white thorn, with his large clasp-knife,
The old man cut a twig formed like a V,
And, holding it in both his steady hands
Point uppermost, he paced along the vale
From north to south, till, near the ancient oak,
The point turned downwards with a sudden twitch,
And rays of joy shot from the old man's eyes.
Then back he went, and forth he came again,
Holding the rod point upwards as before,
And down it went over the same marked spot.
So he was satisfied, and said, " Sink here:
There is a mineral-chamber underneath
Will well repay you for your little loss.
Behind yon mount o'er which the sun has soared
They saw a fire like this : I used the rod,
And where it turned, two labourers sank a pit,
Who now have coaches, titles, and estates.
I'll wager, sinking here, you'll have a mine."
And o'er the hills the dowzer passed away.

The vale is silent, silent are the trees,
And still the waters of the sleeping lake :
The lark's last note has floated up to heaven,
And down the stream the merry boatman glides,
And louder sings as drawing nearer home.
The smoke is curling upwards o'er the pines,
And merry voices ring among the flowers,
As Eve reposes in a glade of green.
Amid the reeds a gentle damsel sighs
Like harper in the thicket, and the wren
Puts out his ear among the springing ferns,
To listen to the sorrows of the maid.

" He's gone, he's gone, my loving Henry's gone :
To-day we parted by the village gate,
What time the sun had reached his highest noon.
He shook my hand, and tears came in his eyes ;
And seeing his, mine own were dim with rain ;
And when he told me he should sail away
Across the ocean to a land of heat,
And seek his fortune in a grot of gold,
Because his father with a hero's heart
Lost all his little digging for a mine,
My heart seemed bursting in me, and I thought
I should have sunk upon the flinty ground.

"'Dont weep,' he murmured ; 'when a few short years
Have passed like visions, Henry will return,
And the church bells shall ring our wedding chime,
And we be one and happy. Far away,
Alone with strangers and a selfish world,

Thine image shall be with me, going out
And coming in, and sitting by my chair,
And mirrored on the universe of light.
I'll wear thee visioned on my heart of hearts ;
And when the daylight dies among the hills,
And Eve steals onward with her urn of dews,
I'll think I see thee by thy cottage door,
And hear thy song float o'er the listening trees,
And feel thou prayest for thy Henry gone.'
He kissed my hand, and soon was out of sight."

In a rude land he laboured with success,
Till one bright morn beneath an ancient tree
A group of men are standing. Some have rings,
And some have purses, little boxes some ;
And some have letters crammed with lines of love ;
And some have bits of gold, and some have coin ;
And some have strings of pearl, and some have shells ;
And some have portraits of their household flowers,
Loved, happy faces, grouped in miniature ;
And some have books, and some have curls of hair,
And ribbons some, and some have metal pens,
And some have landscapes lengthened on a leaf,
And some have little poems wet with tears.
All eyes are bent upon a fair young man,
With staff in hand and bundle on his back,
And face towards his home in fatherland ;
And these are trifles for their distant friends,
Child, mother, wife, and lover : so he placed
Each tiny treasure in his travelling-bag,
Shook hands with all, and hastened on his way.

Return we to the tinner of the moor.
Soon as the dowzer left him, he went home,
And took his pickaxe, pipe, and well-worn spade,
And ancient canteen swinging in his hand,
And down the sheep-path once more travelled he
Into the place of pits, a hopeful man.
Laying aside his outer vest, his eyes
Instinctively turned upwards, and he sighed,
"O Father, if it be Thy holy will,
Prosper the labour of Thy servant's hands.
The gold is Thine, the tin and copper Thine :
Direct me where to labour with success.
However, not my will, but Thine be done."
And down into the earth the pickaxe went,
As if a giant dashed it in the ground.

Down went his shaft through various strata-crusts,
Thick layer after layer, till he came
Upon a hope-reviving bed of blue.
He brought up samples with a gladdened heart,
And washed them in the rill among the reeds,
And they produced some grains of precious tin.
Next day a boy came with him, and they placed
A windlass on the shaft, and wound the ore
Up in a goatskin fashioned like a bag.
Each day the lode grew richer, and more tin
Was lying on the surface. Then he made
A wooden wheel, and placed it in the vale,
And on some stakes of oak put iron heads,
To stamp the rough stones into powder fine.
Then o'er the wheel he turned the limpid stream,
And round it went ; up rose the heavy heads,
And falling bruised the stones to mineral sand.
So cleaning it, the old man's pony bore
The treasure to the far-off smelting-house ;

And he returned with twenty pounds or more.
And as it chimed within his mole-skin purse,
How Maggie's bright eyes twinkled with delight!
That eve a grateful prayer rose up to heaven.

Then weeks and months and seasons passed away,
And tin was wound up in the goatskin bag,
And cleaned, and carried to the smelting-house ;
And he returned with guineas in his purse ;
Till one still eve he sat upon his bench
Much pondering. Leaping quickly up, he said,
" I have a whim now whirling in my brain :
I'll work it out to-morrow. " When day dawned,
And to the covert slunk the full-fed fox,
He cut down wood and nailed it like a cage
With horizontal slabs and slabs oblique,
And through the centre a rough forest tree
Placed for an axle, and from out its side
Ran two arms like a giant's. Near the shaft
He set it up, and round it twined a rope,
Brought o'er a pulley by the tin-pit's mouth ;
And to the rope a wooden barrel swung,
Made by a cooper in his village shop.
He harnessed pony to the great wood arm,
And round and round and round again it went,
Pulling the barrel up and down the shaft,
Till heaps of tin upon the surface lay,
And fortune filled his mole-skin purse with gold.
And seasons came and passed, and came again ;
Rains fell, and sunshine kissed the gladdened earth ;
The crops grew up and fell before the scythe ;
Men wooed and married, feasted, failed, and died.
Levels were driven, and other shafts were sunk ;
An adit from a valley drained the mine ;
Great heaps of tin upon the surface lay,
And still went round the whim and waterwheel.

There dwelt among the hills a thoughtful boy,
Whose mother was the model of her sex ;
And he was very forward for his years,
Fond of good books and study. Other lads
Were only happy when engaged in play ;
He when with God and nature. On a time,
As he sat musing by his cottage-grate,
The boiling kettle hissed upon the hearth,
And so he stopped the steam and stirred the fire,
His mother looking on with chiding eyes,—
Until the power confined thrust out itself,
And burst the kettle in his rage for fame.
This led the student on to higher things,
From steep to dizzy steep, until at last
He made the great steam-engine, when the world
Received a boon to bless it evermore.
And so Watt's name is carved among the great,
And chimed in song, and decked with summer flowers.

Meanwhile the mine extended and grew rich,
And every month the workmen multiplied ;
The water gushed from countless cracks unseen,
Ran down the levels' sides, and bubbled up
Within the adit, keeping the bold men
From sinking far beneath it, till the wheel
Was laid aside, and in its place arose
A small steam-engine newly wonderful ;
And wonderful the ease with which it wrought,
Draining the mine as strangely as a spell.

After the shaft was sixty feet in depth,
Ends were extended eastward, westward far ;
Then winzes sunk for air from level to level ;
And so it ever was and ever is.
And as they sunk from rugged stair to stair,
The troubled entrails of the rifled world
Changed hard as marble. Drills were introduced,
And mallets rang where picks had clinked before.
Then holes were blasted in a dangerous way,
By rushes thrust into the powder-charge
Through a small hole made by a copper wire,
Igniting it as sudden as a thought ;
Ere the poor wretch could say one word of prayer,
Destroying limbs and often life itself.
Then quills were used. Still very dangerous they
And more expensive. Lastly came the fuse,
Unparalleled for safety. Turn we from the fields,
And ladder after ladder quick descend,
Until we reach a labourer's working-place.
It is the hour of morning : on a plank
A father and his elder son sit down,
A boy with fourteen Aprils on his face,
With thought of home and brothers in his mind,
And sunny slopes and lawns of laughing flowers,
Denied him here, denied the lad so soon.
A flask of water dangles to a nail,
And here a can of powder; candles there,
A pair of scissors, and a bunch of quills.
Their dinners lie beside them, and beyond
Are drills and hammers and long iron bars.
Ere they begin to labour, child and sire
Kneel down among the rocks, and that dark cave
Is visited by angels, whose bright wings
Float through the darkness to the voice of prayer.
Aloud the father intercedes with Heaven
For blessings on the labour of their hands,
And blessings on his darling ones at home,
That He would spare them, if it were His will,
To meet at eve around the supper board.
But if they fell and died among the rocks,
He prayed that they might dwell in heaven, and sit
Down at the marriage-supper of the Lamb.
And then he wrestled for his comrade-boy ;
And in his earnestness he seemed to grasp
The arm of the Most High, and so prevailed
That human kissed earth and dropped into the mine.
Could you have peered into that youngling's face,
Hidden in both his hands, you would have seen
Great shining tear-drops roll down on the stones.
That boy grew up to bear the cross of Christ.

PART II.

YEARS stole away; the rich mine richer grew;
Another lode was added richer still:
It strangely shot out in the engine-shaft,
And so he hailed it as a friend with gems,
Who came to pour the treasures in his lap.
It was a vein of copper bright as brass,
Which soon became the theme at every hearth.
Copper has colours different in the ores,
As various as the rainbow,—black and blue
And green and red and yellow as a flower;
Gold-coloured here, there dimly visible,
Though rich the same in measure and in meed.
'Tis found alike where glittering granite gleams,
Where killas darkens, and where gossans shroud,
And oft where wise ones write it cannot be,—
Thus wisely scattered by the Hand Divine.
Tin is more secret far, with duller eye
Oft hiding in the river's shingly bed,
Or the flint's bosom, near the central fires,
In chambers wide, or veins like silken lace;
So that the labourer, stumbling on a start,
Wipes his hot brow, and cries, "Lo, here is tin."

The slime of earth is only on the skin;
That of the serpent stains into the soul.
The honest miner, pale and sulphur-streaked,
Basks in the brightness of the eternal Sun,
And muses through the halls of intellect
As largely as the man of wealth and power,
And walks as blest with calm-eyed Piety,
Behold him in his honeysuckled home,
Kissing his children in the day's young prime,
Even while they lie sweet-smiling in their dreams;
Then hasting forth with prayer upon his lips
To tug with Danger in his darksome den
Beneath the hills' foundations. Noon arrives,
And in a level far below the light,
With flint on either hand, a band of men,
From different chambers of the mighty cave,
Frieze on their loins and slime upon their limbs,
Sing, pray, and praise the Lord, and fruit Divine
Is gathered by them from the banks of bliss.

Old Timmy was the driver of the mules,
And he kept sixty shaggy skinny things,
Fed upon grass and very little grain;
And with his mules he visited the mine,
A tramping troop, to carry off the ores
In little bags upon their bony backs,
Two upon each, up hill and down deep dale,
To the sea-port where it was shipped away
Across the waves, and fused to metal slabs,
And years passed by, and still he drove his mules
Through cloud and sunshine, storm and pleasing calm,
Summer and winter, smoking as he went,
Or whistling tunes and cracking his short whip,
Telling strange tales to singing birds and flowers,
Familiar with each hedge, and crooked turn,
And ragged rut from long lane's end to end,
Till he grew grey as the grey herd he drove:
Then, as the ores increased, the farmers came,

With waggons wide and woeful, and lean steeds,
Which panted o'er the highways rough and rude,
With perspiration dropping off like rain,—
A sight to sadden every sorrowing heart.
But one spring morn, awaking from his dreams,
He heard the steam-horse rushing o'er the rails,
Bearing more ores behind it than his troop
Could carry in a fortnight. So he turned
His old friends on the common, where they failed,
And failing failed, till they could fail no more,
And Winter slew them with his sword of frost.
He could not weep, for all his tears were gone;
And in his reedy lodge a heavy sigh
Let out his ghost into the land unseen.
His grave is by the chancel of the church;
And on it many years a grave-board stood;
But time has blotted out the epitaph,
And left him sleeping in a nameless shroud.

A travelling youth hastes down the village lane
All fevered with excitement. By the well
He meets a matron who her pitcher bears;
And as she dips it in the crystal fount,
He asks her, pointing with his hazel staff,
" Who lives across the coppice in yon house
They say was haunted many years ago?
Though for my part I can't believe a ghost
Would quit the bowers of angels for this place,
To dwell with rats and cobwebs. Fie on it!
I've heard my father say how oft strange lights
Would flare along the damp rooms windowless,
And solemn dirges at still midnight rose,
And songs were heard when nought but winds were
    there:
And so the people said the manor-house
Was haunted with the strangest, wildest things.
Old women's fancies! why, I've walked o'er graves,
And fields of dead, and mounds of rotting bones,
When stars were blinking in the deeps of heaven;
And I have often prayed to see a ghost,
If ghosts are palpable to mortal ken;
But not a phantom raised his shadowy arm.
When last I saw this dwelling, years ago,
'Twas weeping in its ruins: now it looks
The abode of plenty, where red faces meet.
Pray, can you tell me who the owner is?"
And when she told him that its present lord
Was once the tinner living on the moor,
Who ventured till the mice forsook his shelf
And lornness seized upon him, he exclaimed,
" O change of changes! 'tis my father's home."

Full soon he crossed the greenwood, praising much
The grand old trees that seemed to welcome him
To linger in their cloisters. Then he stood
Within the ivy archway, lost in thought,
And now his hands are playing with the vine
About the porch; and now he knocks the door,
And soon is weeping in his mother's arms,
Then father comes, but how unlike the man
He left half-starved within his frigid hut,
Still struggling, striving, hoping against hope!
A portly person now with manly air,
And much that's pleasant peering from his eye.
Then tales were told and loving questions asked,
And lengthy queries answered, till the moon
Slid into midnight with her suite of stars,

And prayer uprose among the listening trees.
Then he lay down to dream of other days,
And one bright vision flitted though his brain.

Next morn his father took him on a hill
Within his own estate, where cattle grazed
And finest sheep were feeding. Far below,
Upon the very spot the dragon rolled,
Where the bold honest tinner lost and won,
A mine spread out its vast machinery.
Here engines, with their huts and smoky stacks,
Cranks, wheels, and rods, boilers and hissing steam,
Pressed up the water from the depths below.
Here fire-whims ran till almost out of breath,
And chains cried sharply, strained with fiery force.
Here blacksmiths hammered by the sooty forge,
And there a crusher crashed the copper ore.
Here girls were cobbing under roofs of straw,
And there were giggers at the oaken hutch.
Here a man-engine glided up and down,
A blessing and a boon to mining men :
And near the spot where, many years before,
Turned round and round the rude old water-wheel,
A huge fire-stamps was working evermore,
And slimy boys were swarming at the trunks.
The noisy lander by the trap-door bawled
With pincers in his hand ; and troops of maids
With heavy hammers brake the mineral stones.
The cart-man cried, and shook his broken whip ;
And on the steps of the account-house stood
The active agent, with his eye on all.

Below were caverns grim with greedy gloom,
And levels drunk with darkness ; chambers huge
Where Fear sat silent, and the mineral-sprite
For ever chanted his bewitching song ;
Shafts deep and dreadful, looking darkest things
And seeming almost running down to doom ;
Rock under foot, rock standing on each side ;
Rock cold and gloomy, frowning overhead ;
Before, behind, at every angle, rock.
Here blazed a vein of precious copper ore,
Where lean men laboured with a zeal for fame,
With face and hands and vesture black as night,
And down their sides the perspiration ran
In steaming eddies, sickening to behold.
But they complained not, digging day and night,
And morn and eve, with lays upon their lips.
Here yawned a tin-cell like a cliff of crags,
And Danger lurked among the groaning rocks,
And ofttimes moaned in darkness. All the air
Was black with sulphur burning up the blood.
A nameless mystery seemed to fill the void,
And wings all pitchy flapped among the flints,
And eyes that saw not sparkled mid the spars.
Yet here men worked, on stages hung in ropes,
With drills and hammers blasting the rude earth,
Which fell with such a crash that he who heard
Cried, " Jesu, save the miner !" Here were ends
Cut through hard marble by the miners' skill,
And winzes, stopes, and rizes : pitches here,
Where worked the heroic, princely tributer,
This month for nothing, next for fifty pounds.
Here lodes ran wide, and there so very small
That scarce a pick-point could be pressed between ;
Here making walls as smooth as polished steel,
And there as craggy as a rended hill :

And out of sparry vagnes the water oozed,
Staining the rock with mineral, so that oft
It led the labourer to a house of gems.
Across the mine a hollow cross-course ran
From north to south, an omen of much good;
And tin lay heaped on stulls and lovel-plots ;
And in each nook a tallow taper flared,
Where pale men wasted with exhaustion huge.
Here holes exploded, and there mallets rang,
And rocks fell crashing, lifting the stiff hair
From time-worn brows, and noisy buckets roared
In echoing shafts ; and through this gulf of gloom
A hollow murmur rushed for evermore.

And then the father and his wondering boy
Crossed the rude moors, conversing as they went,
When the youth learnt his sire had sold the mine
For thousands upon thousands, keeping still
Large shares of profit for himself and son.
And as they lingered by a broken stile,
Watching a flock of rooks wheel o'er the wood,
And breathing odours from the banks of flowers,
A group of mining men came down the lane,
With footsteps fleet, and very sad of face,
Bearing a burden on some unplaned boards
Nailed carelessly together. 'Twas a youth
Who left his mother on the lonely wild
At dead of night, to dig within the mine.
He was her only son ; the rest were drowned,
And so this boy became her sole support.
And rumour ran he courted a fair maid,
Whose fame was like a rose-bud, and next moon
They would be married in the village church.
But Providence had ordered otherwise ;
For while he laboured, tamping up a hole
In a hard cross-cut, ninety fathoms down,
It crashed around him, killing him outright ;
And so his mangled form, lashed to a spar,
Was drawn up through the shaft, and borne along
By his sad comrades to his mother's hut ;
And fleetly passed they over hill and dale,
Till lost among the rising mists of morn.

There was a miner living by a rock
They called " The Giant's Marble :" with him dwelt
His wife and six young children, and he strove
By dint of labour with his head and hands,
Early and late, above ground and below,
Both in his little farm and in his pitch,
With manly courage wondrous and sublime.—
More of the hero than the man of spears,—
To feed the flock the Shepherd of the world
Placed in his fold upon the brambled plain.
But months passed by, and he no mineral found
Within the rock he blasted : pay-days came,
But not for him ; and on his famished cheek
Despair had almost stamped his frightful name.
Late one long eve the weary tributer
Was digging in the darkness, when he found
A prill of copper larger than his fist,
Which led the labourer to a course of ore ;
And ere three weeks had passed, the worthy man
Had gained enough to cheer his drooping wife,
To pay his debts, and buy his fruitful farm.

A cottage girl is wandering by a brook,
Gathering wild flowers, and singing, " From the isles

My love is coming with his heart for me.
His letters have been sweet with tenderest lore,
And musical with gladness. Since he left,
His sire one morn awoke in rifled rags;
And ere the sun went down behind the waves,
He was a rich man, courted and caressed.
And will success estrange my only love,
And lure him to some less devoted maid ?
Away with such a thought! it cannot be;
And so I pluck these flowers to bind his brow,
And kiss them as they smile baptized with dews.
He loves the primrose: thus, ye cherubs, come,
And let me pull you for an offering sweet."
And as she drew them from their homes of moss,
Pressing them gently in her little hand,
A fair young man came tripping down the banks,
With summer sunshine glowing in his face.
It was her Henry, and full soon their tears
And sighs and kisses mingle as they flow.

"Why do the bells ring out such merry chimes?"
An aged dame asked, pausing on the road
To meet her daughter from the market town
With basket huge and heavy. "All this morn
A sea of echoes has been rolling round,
So that the rooks have scarcely had a note
To offer to the sunshine; peal on peal
Has travelled through the valleys, and the hills
Have almost thrust their ragged caps aside.
I've seen the horses prick their pointed ears,
And pause amid the clover; and the dogs
Have barked and danced, not knowing what they did.
Boys clap their hands, and maidens sing for glee,
And matrons, arms a-kimbo o'er the fence,
Converse and smile, and kiss their wondering bairns.
Why, every tree now shining in the sun
Seems wagging with a bell upon each branch.
I never heard such stunning peals before;
No, not when our good squire and lady fair
In bridal robes walked to the dear old church.
Do tell me, daughter, why the bells ring so."

"It is a marriage, mother. The rich man
Who lives in yon high house across the gorge,
Environed with a wood of English oak,
Who drew his riches from a mining pit
When almost dead with fasting, this still morn
Has seen his son united to a girl
As beautiful as summer, whom he loved
When Want stood shivering in his father's home
With Famine on the doorstep. Far away
The young man laboured, prospered, and returned
To find his father rich in friends and fame,
Himself a partner in his hard-earned gains.
But richer to his eye the cottage girl,
Who sang among the green fields like a bird,
Than heaps of diamonds piled up to the moon,
Or farms, or friends, or any other thing;
For he was true, and love to him was heaven.
So they are married, mother, and the bells
Ring that the grand old steeple seems to nod."

See'st thou that mansion on the woody slope,
Where trees stoop down and kiss the river-waves,
Or whisper on its marge; and graceful sails
Glide up and down, and sea-birds float and dive?
Along the shrubbery walk a lady comes

Leading her children by the evergreens,—
Two boys, with brows like bards and eyes like space;
And one bright girl, with April on her checks.
Grey deer are leaping round them, snowy swans
Steer over silent lakes, and cooing doves
Drop from tall trees to drink at glassy falls,
Whilst in the noble dwelling Wealth sits down
Dangling his shining keys with wagging sides.
This hall is Henry's, his that lady fair,
And his those children beautiful as morn,
Now placed among the worshipped of the world.

GLOSSARY.

Adit—An opening beneath the surface of the earth, to carry off the water from the mine.
Cobbing—Breaking the stones with an iron hammer, to separate the mineral from the refuse.
Course of ore—A wide vein or lode.
Cross-course—A hollow vein intersecting the lodes.
Cross-cut—A level driven to intersect the lode.
Crusher—A sort of iron mill used to crush the ore.
Dowsing-rod—A white thorn used by the ancient miners to ascertain the position of uncut lodes.
Dragon—A fiery meteor, said to be indicative of the earth's riches.
Drill—A bar of steel used for boring the rock.
End—A local name for level, the extremity of the subterranean passage.
Fire-stamps—A steam-engine used to stamp the rough ores.
Fire-whim—A small steam-engine used to draw up the broken earth.
Fuse—A flexible material, similar to common yarn, bound with twine, and filled with gunpowder; used in blasting.
Gigger—One who sifts the ores through a small sieve into a hutch or large box of water.
Gossan—Consists principally of per-oxide of iron, mixed with earthy matters, quartz, &c.
Killas—A dark-coloured stratum of rock, composed of clay, slate, &c.
Lander—The man who empties the bucket when it reaches the mouth of the pit.
Level—An excavation along the mine.
Level plot—A floor of wood where the miner fills the bucket.
Lode—A mineral deposit, generally running from east to west.
Man-engine—A machine to let the miners up and down the shaft.
Mine—An excavation of the earth.
Pitches—Cells of copper or any other mineral, where the labourer has a certain tribute.
Prill—A lump of solid mineral or metal.
Rises—Chambers raised from beneath.
Smelting-house—A place where raw ores are converted by fire into metal.
Start or *sturt*—Among miners an extra month's wages; chiefly, the good fortune of tributers.

Stopes—The upper and lower parts of levels broken up by miners.
Stulls—Large beams of wood across the lode, on which rough boards are nailed.
Tinner—One who works on tin.
Tributer—One who works for a certain part of the profits of the ores he may raise.

Trunks—Hutches let into the ground.
Windlass—A simple roller of wood with an iron handle, around which is wound a rope or chain, which is let up and down the pit.
Winze—A sink from one level to another.

CALEB CLIFF:

A DRAMATIC FRAGMENT.

PART FIRST.

Scene—*Wild Moor.* Time—*Spring Morning.* *Traveller alone on the heath.*

Traveller. The larks sing April welcomes. Here they soar
And carol in their gladness; there they float
In streams of song along the firmament;
Now bubbling like a fountain, tender now,
In quivering drops out-gushing from the clouds,
Filling the muser's listening ear with love.
The moors are full of music: everywhere
These blessed warblers kindle up delight,
Suddenly dropping with their viols full
Of holy sound o'erflowing all the air,
As if heaven's gate half-opened, and let forth
Bright jets of fervour. Here on banks they stand
Warbling and whistling, till mine eyes are full,
And praises leave my lips. All thanks to Thee!
The earth has still some lays of Paradise.
But what poor wretch is this?—a female form
Half-clad in weeds, and by the hand she holds

Her white-faced boy. I'll cross the heath and see.
How pale she is! how pale!

Scene—*Beer-shop on the common, with the traveller and the poor woman before it.*

Poor Woman.   Alack, alack!
O Sir, my heart is breaking. See my boy,
The first dear flower that graced our marriage home.
Came other flowers, and flowers they passed away:
I'm thankful to my God that it is so,
Or my dark sea of woe would wider be,
And the waves thicker, blacker, and the storm
Beat with a fiercer fury on my head.
Why, dost thou ask? Because this slender thing,
My Hubert here, pines now for lack of bread;
And if they faded not upon their stems,
I should even now have other mouths to fill.
But they are with the worms, thank God for that,
Where I too wish to be.
Traveller.   I grieve to mark
A form like thine so sadly sorrow-stripped,
Though life is in its summer. Shipwrecked bark,
Fierce-flashed with storms and on the breakers bulged,
With shrivelled shroud and mast rent like a reed,
Looks not more desolate. What is thy wrong,
And what its source?
Poor Woman.   My wrong were great to tell,
High as a hill, and wider than the waste,
And bigger than a mountain. How it swells
Even as I turn to face it! Shade thine eyes,
And look across the dingle. Thou canst see

That little dwelling standing by the stream,
With a few trees beside it, and behind
The great blue ocean surging on the shore.
Here was I born, and there my mother taught
Her child to pray to the great God of heaven;
Yes, yes, to *pray :* why don't I do so now?
　　　　　　　　　　　　　　　[*She weeps.*
Traveller. Go on until thy tale wears to a close:
'Tis good to pour out sorrow to a friend :
Thus the heart drops its burden. Pray go on.
Poor Woman. I grew up with the flowers, like one
　　　　of them,
With summer all around me: hill and vale
Were clothed in sunshine, and my heart was glad.
The future looked a garden full of sweets
Zoned round with beauty; and I dared not dream
Of coming winter settling on the soul.
How could I, when my leaves were free from stain
As are the lily's ? By and bye the years
Led me to womanhood, when from the hills
Down came a youth with honest open face,
And saw me in my freshness. I was fair,
I know I was; and he was handsome too.
I thought him then like David with his sheep.
How my heart fluttered when he spoke to me !
And I blushed so and turned away my face.
Yes, he was handsome then, and so was I.
But now—I really shudder to go on.
　　　[*Here she trembles, and wipes her eyes.*
Traveller. Proceed, I pray thee. My attention grows
And interest deepens as thou lead'st the way,
Like pilgrim drawing near some fabled shrine.
Poor Woman. The months brought frequent visits
　　　　from the youth,
With joys love-winged, full fraught with holiest bliss.
My parents knew him well, and praised him much.
Oft by the sea we wandered, and the waves—
So thought I then—would murmur Caleb's name :
The sighing streams sang sweeter; rill and rock
And dale and down were love-clad. How we joyed
To hear the larks sing o'er the mossy moor,
And watch the clouds at sunset ! Still their strains
Fill up the welkin, but I heed them not.
The evening clouds drift seaward purple-hued,
And hang around the doorway of the dark,
As if to light the dim day to repose;
But grief has such a dwelling in mine eyes
That all is bitter blank. Alas! alas!
That sin's dark wings should sully so much sweet !
Traveller. Sit on this bench, and let me hear thee out :
Thy legs shake with much standing. Give the child
This bread and cheese : he looks half-dead with want.
No wounded hart wrecked by the hunter's gun,
And hid among the bushes, seemed more bare.
How eagerly he eats it !
　　　　　　　　　　　[*The child eats.*
Poor Woman. Yes, poor wretch !
He's fasted all the morning, and two crusts,
Broken and hard, were all the day before,
With one small cup of milk. But to my tale,
Which bears me on to blackness which thou seest
Thick-gathered round me and my hungry child.
Suffice it that we married. No two doves
So happy dwelt as we within our nest;
For Caleb loved me and his pleasant home.
We read our Bible ; to the church we went,
And worshipped God together; and I've thought,

Ay, often thought, no household was so blessed.
And then our boy was born ; he looked a rose
Dropped down from Eden. Other children came,
And, as I told thee, died as soon as born.
Thus time passed by until seven years were gone,
And then a cloud came gathering o'er our path.
At first 'twas small and scarcely visible,
And then it grew as large as human hand,
And then it spread and widened, spreading still
And blackening as it rose, until the heavens
Were sackcloth, and the great round sunless earth
Reeled on in blindness. Groped I in the shade,
And shrieked in anguish, shrieking still in vain,
Even as thou seest me.
Traveller.　　　　　　Sad it is to hear
From sorrow's lips the sigh of misery,
But sadder still to feel its fellest fang.
Now to thy story, for I wait thy will.
Poor Woman. Yes, thou shalt hear it. Caleb took
　　　　to drink ;
Yes, took to drink, which brought with wind and hail
A sea of ruin on us. First he walked
With heedful step along the slippery brink,
And said, "I'll go no further." Then he strode
A little nearer, nearer, nearer still,
When one thick morn, entirely off his guard,
And charmed with poppies growing near the brink,
He slipped and fell, and dragged us all below.
I groaned, and cried, and wrung my hands, and prayed,
But is was all in vain, yes, all in vain;
For still he flounders in the black abyss.
Traveller. Wilt thou be somewhat more minute and
　　　　clear
In thy description of his downward course ?
Poor Woman. One eve returning from a sharp day's
　　　　work
In the pine forest, loading some large trees,
He met with Edmund Connor on the moor,
Which thou didst cross when coming o'er to me ;
And Edmund asked him to go in and take
A glass of ale in the Spread Eagle here,
Only a glass, and then they'd leave full soon.
So Caleb went and drank ; and the next eve
Was there again, and drank a little more,
And praised the ale, and said 'twas really prime ;
Then sang a song, and left at ten o'clock.
So it went on, my Caleb drinking still,
And wildly wasting what should bring us bread.
I watched for him at night, at first with sighs ;
And then with tears that fell upon the floor,
And prayed upon my knees, and prayed again :
But the high heavens were brass. How changed he
　　　　grew !
His love all left him—Caleb cast me off,
And this was like a dagger in my soul.
He learnt to swear. Still I was kind to him,
And hoped for better things. We could not starve,
I and my boy; for wages there was none ;
And so I parted with my wedding-ring,
And then the presents which my mother gave,
And then the trinkets treasured from a child,
And then my Sunday dresses one by one,
And then the plates and dishes, chairs and stools,
And other items, till the walls were bare.
But why should I go on ? An attic now
Is our abode within a filthy court,
Where ragged urchins in the puddles scream.

Traveller. 'Tis a sad tale, and saddens me to hear.
But where is Caleb now ? From what thou sayest,
I cannot doubt he is a drunkard still.
Poor Woman. No change for good. His heart is
     harder grown,
His soul more sottish, and his ruin sealed.
My home—'tis scarcely worthy of that word—
Is like a desert trodden with simoon.
The only thing for which I care to live
Is this poor babe, now worse than fatherless.
Often at night I lay him on the straw
Covered with rags, and then beside the grate,
Fireless and frigid, watch I for his sire.
Sometimes I moan, and wring my withered hands,
And wail to Heaven. Sometimes I pace my room
Hungry and sad, and stare upon the walls.
Sometimes I strive to weep, but the tears freeze
In their worn channels. Oft I leave my shed,
When the grey tower-clock treads the hour of twelve,
To list his footfall sounding down the yard.
O heavens! the stars look angry, and the moon
In mockery smiles upon me : shadows strange
Frown from the doorways, and my tattered shawl
I tighter draw, and hasten back again
Where Misery meets me with a startling howl.
Then by and bye he comes, mouthing the night,
Reeling and banging, roaring like a storm :
He swears for supper,—what have I to give?—
And then he swaggers forward to the child,
Who screams affrighted at the drunken man.
I bow my head upon my wasted hands,
And blows come down upon me, blows from him
Who swore to shield me from the cruel world :
Then dizziness and darkness, and a prayer
For peace where worms run riot.
Traveller.   'Tis indeed
A history woful which thy lips declare :
And well may all who love the voice of truth
And peace and joy unite in earnest toil
To roll the the headless monster in his grave.
Is thy tale finished ?
Poor Woman.   Earth has no such woe
As weighs upon the wife of him who walks
The broad highway trod by the drunkard's feet.
Oft when the snow has fallen I've gone forth
With shivering limbs, desirous of a meal;
Smote with the joy of firesides comfort-crowned,
Snug blazing hearths, the smell of viands rich,
Where songs of childhood trickled, winning love
And sweetest kisses from a father's lips :
Here Happiness amid the circle sat,
With eyes upturned to heaven. Alas for me,
Companioned with the storm ! The fierce winds struck
With swords of ice into my very bone,
So that life halted with excess of strife,
And the soul knocked against its prison walls
To be let forth for ever. Back I crept,
The monster Hunger following to my shed,
Where he lay down and gnashed his horrid jaws
With glare unearthly. Groaned my boy and I,
And the blast mocked our sorrow.
Traveller.   The land mourns
With the red vintage, adding woe to woe,
And cramming gaols and churchyards. Hast thou done?
Poor Woman.   A few more drops from the full cup
     of grief
Will end my canto. Yesterday at four

He left our attic, staggering then with drink.
See'st thou this mark upon my beaten brow,
Where his hand smote me ? Yes, my husband's hand !
All night I watched, but Caleb never came ;
The cock crew and the owl hooted no more,
While from his grassy nest springing the lark
Sang up his morning path ; a sparrow chirped
And knocked our lattice, when I dressed my boy
In the few rags thou see'st upon him now,
And brought him fasting forth. Cupboard and shelf
Were bare as the black beach ; the very mice
Have ceased long since to come there ; and the cat
Sleeps on another floor, starved out of place,—
Starved out of place, I say. A wicked thought
Frowned, smiled upon me : *poison*—that was it.
I staggered, reeled, half yielded, then I rushed
Into the alley followed by my brat
Who screamed to see my terror. Here we came,
And found his father in this wretched den,
Drunk, by the dirty table. Though I've asked,
Yet he won't leave this dark ill-fated place.
Beseech him for me : he may heed thy voice :
'Tis not so low but I may grasp at hope.
          [*The traveller enters the beer-house, when
               the drunken man sings :*

          Here I'll sit, and here I'll sing,
          Till the ancient rafters ring ;
          Here I'll sit, and here I'll drink,
          Till the tallow candles wink.

          What care I what parsons say ?
          I will drink till break of day.
          What care I for child or wife ?
          Halloo, landlord, this is life.
                              Hurrah ! hurrah !

Traveller (aside).   Poor drunken idiot ! his tossed
          brain is hot
And melting in the fire. 'Tis ever so
With him who tramples on sobriety,
Breaks o'er the fence, and roves the wilds of wrong.
          [*The drunken man sings :*

          Fill the tankard to the top ;
          I will drain it every drop.
          This is life indeed for me,
          This is rarest jollity.

          What care I though moon may wink ?
          What care I though stars may blink ?
          What care I for child or wife ?
          Halloo, landlord, this is life.
                              Hurrah ! hurrah !

Traveller (advancing towards him).   Outside the
          porch, standing beside the gate,
One waits to see thee with a message strange ;
And I'm desired to ask thee to go forth
And take it with good will.
Drunken Man.   Ha ! ha ! good Sir,
I'm not the chap to launch your squibs upon.
Try some one else. My tankard holds some drink,
And drink holds me ! so I won't move an inch,
Though a prince beckons with a royal nod.
Traveller.   I'm grieved to hear this answer. 'Tis a
     friend

Who craves thy audience, and no smooth-faced foe
With dagger 'neath his mantle : 'tis the weak
Whom we are called to succour, and lift o'er
The thorns and thickets of this selfish world.
I would not care to bear him company,
Or call him man, who thought but of himself,
And shut his ears to every cry of pain.
Away with such a fellow from the world,
And let him herd with tigers, bears, and brutes !
Mankind can do without him. Come, good man,
And meet the weak one at the gate of grief.

Drunken Man. A sermon truly ! I'm too deep in
  drink
To be drawn out by any crotchy text
Or verse of Scripture. You talk well, you do,
And my old granny taught me several things,
Long words of meaning winged with points of law,
Which once I thought were very wonderful,
But now have quite forgotten.

  [Here he strikes the table and sings :

  Drink, more drink !
  Why should I care if others swim or sink ?

Traveller.   Listen, man :
We have no warrant for our length of life,
Or health or strength, which we receive from Heaven.
He gives, He takes, and none can stay His hand.
What if the lightnings from the gates of fire
Should lash thy limbs, and singe away thy sight,
And lay thee riddled on the hungry earth !
What if disease dry up the fevered blood,
And leave the body prostrate ! Would'st thou not
Thank some kind hand to wipe away thy tears,
And feed thee with the bread that perisheth,
And smooth thy passage to the land of worms ?
Think well and answer truly.

Drunken Man. Yes, indeed ;
I feel as if a cord were drawing me
Towards the doorway whither you would guide ;
But see, I stagger, take me by the hand.

  *[They leave the beer-house, and join the poor
  woman, when the drunken man proceeds :*

Ha, ha ! my wife and little dirty brat !
What brought you here ? You've seen me drunk before,
I guess you have, and reeling like a bark
Smote by the moaning billows. Have you brought
My breakfast from the cupboard ? O, I feel
As hungry as a serpent. Ha ! ha ! ha !
I'm glorious this grand morning. Go away,
If you have nothing for me : go away,
And let me drain the tankard. Ha ! ha ! ha !

  [Drunken man sings :

  Fill the tankard foaming o'er ;
  For I love it more and more.
  I will drink till blinks the day ;
  I will drink while parsons pray.

  Fill the foaming tankard, fill ;
  For I'm thirsty, thirsty still.
  I will drink while misers snore ;
  Then I'll tumble on the floor.
    Hurrah ! hurrah !

Traveller. Behold thy wife whom thou hast sworn
  to love

And shelter from the tempest, and the child
Whom God has given thee, beaten with the blast
Raised by thy furious folly. See them stand
Like reeds upon the mountain stripped and bare
And peeled by thine own fingers. On their cheeks
The tomb-flower glitters, graven by thy hand.
O mark them pelted with the ire of hate
And woe and want, which by thyself is hurled.
Does it not grieve thee that they shivering stand,
Starved in the porch of shelter ? Shame on thee !
Dost think thou wilt escape the thunderbolts
Of angry Heaven ? I tell thee, sinner, nay.
Repent, and do thy duty : love thy wife,
And take her to thy bosom : let thy child
Feel that he has a father. Snatch the cup,
The inebriate cup, and dash it from thy lips,
And ask thy God to help thee. Turn, O turn,
Or on thy head fierce judgment will be poured
In hissing streams from the unfathomed gloom.
Already art thou branded " infidel,"
And curst by Him who made thee. Fly, O fly,
Or ere the ground shall ope to take thee in,
Or unseen monsters drag thee to thy doom.

Drunken Man. O Lord, have mercy on me ! Round
  my head

  *[Here the drunken man labours under delirium
  tremens.*

Whirl fiery circles, and the moor is full !
Imps with long tongues are licking at my brow,
And snakes with wings of flame crawl up my breast ;
Huge monsters glare upon me, some with horns,
And some with hoofs that blaze like pitchy brands ;
Great trunks are some, and some are hung with heads.
Here serpents dash their stings into my face
All tipped with fire ; and there a wild bird drives
His red-hot talons in my burning scalp.
Here bees and beetles buzz about my ears
Like crackling coals, and frogs strut up and down
Like hissing cinders : wasps and water-flies
Scorch deep like melting mineral. Murther ! save !
What shall a sinner do ?

Traveller.   Pray to thy God,
And ask Him for forgiveness. On thy knees,
And supplicate His favour and His arm
To help thee in thy trouble.

    [He falls on his knees.

Drunken Man. Pity me,
Great Lord : I'm drunken Caleb Cliff.
Thou knowest me, the wicked Caleb Cliff.
O pity me : I'm drunken Caleb Cliff.
Without Thy help I'm weakness.

Traveller.   Come along,
And let us seek thy dwelling with thy wife,
And fading scion, whom thy love must prune.
For there is love yet in thy hardened soul
Which will thaw out and flow in tenderness
Under the streaming sunlight. Take my arm :
Come home and read thy Bible.

      [Exeunt.

PART SECOND.

Scene—*Lecture Hall*—Caleb Cliff *on the Platform.*

Caleb Cliff. Five years, dear friends, have run
    their cycles out
Since I came here, a melancholy man,
With grief enough upon my wretched self
To hide the highest mountain. Know you not
That men looked at me as a blazing ship,
Rushing to ruin, hurried by the storm?
The great Disposer saved me. Though the masts
And sails and spars flamed to the water's edge,
Thank God, by one great effort I escaped,
And leaped upon the rock of temperance,
And so was saved,—I who before was steeped
So deep in sin that I sank down below
The strong-horned brute. And ask ye why, my friends?
No, no: you know how Caleb Cliff has left
His wife who loved him when he cursed her name,
And smote her with these hands, to starve in rags,
And that dear boy whose cries went up for bread
At morn and eve, went up for bread in vain:
He pined like roe amid the forest firs
Left by his mates in fear. I heeded not,
But sucked the cup of fire, and kissed the rim,
While my child starved and staggered, and his eyes
Gleamed in the midst of famine. Fool I was,
And raving maniac, hurried strangely on
By appetite more foul than gorging wolf:
But came a hand, and stopped me, bless the Lord!
A mighty arm which dragged me from the mire,
And placed me where I stand.
                    [He still goes on:
    Five years ago
I entered this same hall more desolate
Than watch-tower in the waters. On my back
Were hanging rags that hissed in every wind:
I wore no shirt, nor had I for a year:
My hat was bulged and battered like a drum
Left with the slain upon the battle-day;
My uncombed hair in knots hanged round my brow:
My beard was like a forest; and my hose
Cracked, gashed, and gaping. On my feet were shreds
Of hardest leather which had once been shoes,
Tied up with dastard strings, and worn awry,
Through which my toes peered as I passed the street:
And these were all I had, yes, all I had.
The drink had drowned my best coat long ago,
And left it steeping in the butt of sin.
I blushed to show my face or lift my head;
And my limbs shook like rushes when the moor
Is walked by Winter, and the savage winds
Lift up their fists like robbers. On my heart
A rocky burden rested, and my eyes
Were like a blind man's. Thrice I tried to speak,
And thrice the words died in me, till at last
With one tremendous effort up I sprang,
The great sweat-drops down-hanging from my hair,
And dropping from my chin and finger-tops,
And splashing thickly on the floor like rain.
This was a moral combat, and I fought
With foes dart-armed and fiercer than the fire,

And threw them all at last, and victory gained.
With one tremendous effort up I sprang,
While my voice shivered through the edifice,
And angels bore the news to Paradise:
" I'll turn my feet, yes, Caleb Cliff will turn."
A weight that moment tumbled from my heart,
A burden from my back, and the thick film
Left the eye-sockets, while the name of brute
Slipped from me, and I shouted like a boy,
" By God's good help, the cup of scorching drink
Shall never pass these lips of mine again!"
Then the bad angel left me: in his place
A seraph stood, and he is with me still.
Yes, he is with me still in robes of white,
To lead me by the hand when paths are dark,
And keep my feet from dashing on the stones.
                [He still goes on:
Good news this for my wife. I hastened home,
And told her all: but she, poor thing, looked strange,
And deemed me crazed. But when I washed my face
And combed my hair, and left her for my work,
I thought I saw a brightness in her eye
Which had been hidden in the dark for years.
I worked on through the week, though oft a crust
Was all I got for dinner: yet I smiled,
Nor ever uttered murmur, and it seemed
As sweet as honey. Drank I of the streams
That murmured from the hills and murmur still.
Yet oft Temptation like a warrior came
With buckled armour on, and hurled his darts
So thickly that I should have surely fallen
But for the right arm of Omnipotence
Which held me up amid the horrid whirl.
I looked to Him, and He was nigh to save.
The sixth day ended, and I hastened home,
And threw the whole week's earnings in her lap;
Then sidled round to watch her. First she smiled,
The only one that I had seen for years;
Then a few tears came out upon her face;
And then a ring of joy rang through the room;
And then she clasped her hands in words of prayer,
And lifted up her eyes towards the heights
Where dwells the King of Glory. I was dumb,
I could not bear it, and I gently came
And fell upon her neck, and kissed and wept
And prayed to be forgiven. Forgiveness came,
And with it an embrace which angels give,
And kisses such as angels can bestow.
" Yes, Caleb dear, we may be happy yet."
                [He still goes on:
I left the room and rushed into the light:
The future lay before me :—fields of grain
Ripe for the harvest, orchards wide fruit-hung,
And vines with clusters juicy, which I felt
Determined to do battle for and win.
I stood upon the earth a different man;
The sun of heaven was shining on my brow,
And Hope was at my side with hand outstretched
To lead me on to summits yet beyond.
I went into the world with giant power
To wrestle with its hatred, woe, and wrong,
And do the right, that I the right might gain.
And if at times the warfare grew too fierce,
And the blows bulged my shield, her words came back
Like balm to bless me on my battle march.
I have an angel watching in my home,
And all good wives are angels breathing airs

That taste of Eden and its holiness.
The way were long to lead you how we throve:
Suffice it that we struggled, strove, and prayed,
And worked together, and success was sure.
First from the pledge-shop came the furniture,
And then the other items. Soon we dressed
In Sunday suits, and sought a place of prayer,
And bowed in humbleness before the Lord,
And found His mercy. By and bye we changed
Our place of residence, and bought a shop
In the front street, which proved a great success.
We added house to house and field to field,
Until they call us rich. A ship of mine
Now sails upon the ocean, which I trust
Will anchor here to-morrow. Am I not
A wonder unto many, saved from woe
Both in this world and that which is to come?
None could sink lower down than Caleb Cliff
Who stands before you by the grace of God:
So there is hope for all. Come let us sing.

[*They sing:*

There is no drink like water clear
That gushes through the silent mere,
Or bubbles from the mossy well,
And murmurs down the rushy dell.
So give me water, water clear,
That gushes through the silent mere.

The traveller 'neath Arabia's sky,
Whose water-skins have long been dry;
The miner in the mineral cave;
The sailor wrecked upon the wave;
Feel there is nought on earth so dear
As sparkling water fresh and clear.

There was a time, alas! alas!
I loved to drain the drunkard's glass:
But this to mine brought deepest woe,
And darkened everything below.
So now I'll drink from year to year
Nought save the sparkling water clear.

A little well among the trees,
Where sports in love the passing breeze,
And birds are hopping on the brink,
And pretty children come to drink,—
This is a sight I love full dear:
So give me water, water clear.

How pure it is in cup or glass,
Or sparkling onward through the grass,
Where little lambs delight to play,
And maidens meet at close of day!
I'll not forget, while wandering here,
To thank the Lord for water clear.

[*Exeunt.*

SCENE.—*A Hill—Poet musing on a Bank.*

Poet. O what a storm we've had! the wild sea rocked
And roared in all his caverns, and the waves
Rolled headlong over hoary crag and cliff
Into the very cornfields. I stood here
And listened to his great grand awful voice,
Until the ground shook which I trod upon,
And the broad ash-trees trembled. The huge winds

Twisted and wrangled like a host spear-armed,
And coast and cliff were white with sparkling foam.
I never heard such thundering, though mine ears
Wait, watch, and wonder at the gates of sound.
But who comes here?
[*He is joined by a Coast Guard.*
Coast Guard. Hast heard the mournful news?
Last night the "Lila" on the gull-rock struck,
And foundered like a bullet. All were lost,
Except a damsel fair and beautiful,
Washed on a rude plank to the rocky shore.
Thou shouldst have seen her rescued from the deep,
Her black hair dripping with the salt sea-wave,
Falling upon her shoulders, and her face
White as a seraph's 'mid the trees of heaven:
Thou shouldst have seen her; it were subject good
For poet or for painter. I'm right glad
The sea has lost the maiden; for I hear
She'll soon be wedded to our countryman,
Young Hubert Cliff the merchant.
Poet. I came out
Last eve to watch the sunset. By and bye
A little cloud rose from the ocean's rim,
No bigger than my lady's photograph,
And scudded up the heavens with wondrous speed;
And then I lost it. Soon a larger one
With edges ragged started on the chase
With blacker crest and bolder: then a mass
Sprang from the water, circling half the heaven;
And then a never-ending multitude
Without a chink of daylight, covering all.
The reeds sighed heavily, the forest-tops
Moaned to the rising tempest, ocean boiled
And fretted, tossed, and floundered, sea-birds screamed
And lashed along the breakers. Then came night,
And then—
Coast Guard. I am right glad the "Eagle" rode
In safety through the tempest, and now lies
Moored and secure behind the castle's head.
She is a queenly vessel, strong, well-built,
And manned with British heroes: for I deem
The mariner who battles through the blast
In the pitch night, while Wealth snores on his down,
To swell his country's comforts, rightly wins
The name of hero. Glad am I, I say,
That Caleb's ship rode safely through the dark,
Whose sails now whiten in the gentle air.
There's no lack, sure, of subject for your muse.
[*Exeunt.*

SCENE.—*A Country Village—Traveller advancing.*

Traveller. I've been delighted with the pealing bells,
As I came o'er the meadows. How I love
To list and linger to these holy sounds.
Rising and swelling over the great earth!
It seems as if an angel raised his voice
And uttered words of sweetness. List, my soul,
And fall before thy Maker. But to-day
They ring a merry peal, as if they said,
"Rejoice, rejoice; the earth is beautiful,
And there is more of heaven than woe and sin:"
And I believe it. But I'll ask this dame
Dancing her baby in the morning sun,
Why all this jingle?
Country Woman. There's a marriage. Sir:
Young Hubert Cliff has won his Honnymead,

And brought her from her birth-land. She is good,
They say, and rich, and very beautiful ;
And well does he deserve her. He's a youth
As noble as the noblest ; and his sire,
Though once a poor man, lives in that high house
With trees around it on the shaven lawn,
Where dines the wedding party. He has lands
I cannot tell how much, and sheep and kine,
And ships, and gold, and servants plentiful :
And poor men's prayers go up to heaven for him,
To whom his hand is liberal. For my part,
I say it frankly, I am always glad
When the good prosper.
Traveller (pursuing his way). Yes, the very same
Whom I found wrecked upon life's broad highway,
An abject slave of vice in iron chains ;
Reformed and lifted in the moral scale !
But nothing is too wonderful for Him
Who guards and guides the rolling universe.
That he is rich astounds me. But it comes
From walking in the land of soberness,
And listening to the counsel of his God :
His blessing only can true riches bring.
But here is Caleb's dwelling. Song and mirth
Are sisters in it. What if I go in

And see my daughter's husband, Hubert Cliff ?
So be it. Now I'll knock.
[*Door opens, and he enters. Villagers surround
    the house, and sing :*

Sing we low, and sing we high ;
Let our strain soar up the sky,
And bring blessings white as May
Down on Hubert's marriage-day.

Every boy and maiden meet,
Beating cadence with their feet,
Join to chant a cheerful lay
Now on Hubert's marriage-day.

Little birds on twig and tree,
Sing your carols lustily ;
While the dancing brooklets play
Hymns on Hubert's marriage-day.

Hubert's bride is rich and fair ;
Hubert is his father's heir :
Strew the leaves and roses gay
Now on Hubert's marriage-day.

[*Exeunt.*

BULO.

DRAMATIS PERSONÆ.

SELANDO	*A City Merchant.*
ANLEAF	*His Wife.*
BULO	*Their Daughter.*
RUPEDO	*The Serving Man.*
WALLA	*A Shipwrecked Mariner.*
FARDO	*A Shrimp Catcher.*
TAMSON	*His Wife.*
ITARA	*A Street Organist.*
COUNTRYWOMAN.	
TEEMU	*A Lost Child.*
AN AUSTRALIAN STOCKMAN.	
DITTO SHEPHERD.	
THE LOST CHILD'S MOTHER.	
FIRST REAPER.	
SECOND DITTO.	

PART FIRST.

SCENE—*A country residence near
the sea.* TIME — *Midnight.*
ANLEAF *and her daughter* BULO
in their sleeping apartment.

Anleaf. And still this knocking !
What intruder scares

The dark-winged Night, and hurries sleep away
Where torrents lift their voices, and the bat
Sports with the moonbeams in the old church lane
Beside the woodman's cottage ? Bulo, up,
And call the serving-man. The racket roars
As if a cliff had tumbled headlong on the beach
And dammed the roaring ocean. Ring, I say,
And let the bell cry something terrible.—
That Jeopardy stands frowning. Strange the dark
Should harbour deeds that injure honest worth
Which lives as innocently as the flowers,
And would not harm a beetle : strange, I say,
That brazen Wickedness should swagger forth
In garb unseemly, lifting his harsh voice,
And trampling virtue, honour, so that thorns
Are often scattered on the good man's path,
And prickles in his pillow. So it is,

Whilst we as pilgrims travel o'er the earth,
Which in itself is lapped in loveliness:
The sober suffer for the woes of wrong.
But hark, the door is opened, and methinks
I hear the sound of footsteps. What is it?
Rupedo calls my name.

[*A room below. Enter* Rupedo, *the serving-man,
leading* Walla, *a shipwrecked sailor.*

Rupedo. I found this poor man, Madam, at the door.
He says he's shipwrecked. See, his hands are cut
With climbing up the cliff, and the salt sea
Is dripping from his garments. Does he not
Demand great succour in this hour of need?

[*Exit* Rupedo.

Walla. Necessity needs small apology:
A starving man will eat a mouldy crust,
Nor think to growl for butter. If my house
Were burning round me, and the sound of " fire "
Smote on my ears and flamed before mine eyes,
Think you I'd scorn the only gate of hope,
To leap half-naked in the crowded street?
What if the ice should break beneath my tread,
Bearing me outward, onward? think you I
Should be ashamed to shout and shriek for help,
So that the echoes wondered in their caves?
No, Madam, life is precious. Gold and gems
Are sordid dust compared with such a boon
Alike to prince and peasant: all we have
We give for it, and deem the bargain cheap.
Last night the hurricane o'ertook our bark,
And dragged it on the breakers. I alone
Escaped with life, flung high upon the land,
And, feeling through the darkness, crossed the downs,
And found your door.

Anleaf. Right welcome art thou here.
May life surcease when Charity expires!
She is the queen of virtues, suffering long
And ever hopeful; blessing those that curse,
And showering smiles where harrowing frowns are
hurled.
I saw her once in weeds of modesty,
With long hair streaming, leading by the hand
Towards her door her bitter enemy,
To feed him at her table. Ever since
She's been my guest and guardian in my home,
Where now her bright face cheers us.

Walla. Not alone
With one small nation does this angel dwell,
Or race or people, howsoe'er refined.
Once, marching through the forest, I was lost,
And left by my companions. Eve passed by,
The night closed round me, and another day
Broke burning through the heavens. Hunger and
thirst,
Faintness and fever, had their work fulfilled
And dashed me earthward. Prostrate there I lay,
Gasping away my being. The great winds
Went thundering through the prairies, and wild
beasts
Howled in close coverts, till their voices fell,
Seeming none other than a small bird's chirp.
A few more tugs and life would be o'erpowered
And lose the solemn conflict. O'er me crept
The haziness of watching, and I longed
To mingle with the sleepers in the past;
When from his war-path burst an Indian chief
As swiftly as a fire-tongue. Armed he was

With bow and arrow, spear and scalping-knife,
And on his forehead waved the heron's plume.
He wore a belt of wampum, a skin cloak
Hung from his shoulders, and his eagle eye
Flashed as he scanned the arches of the wood.
And mark you, Madam, this same warrior chief,
This red marauder, by his wrongs had sworn
To be the white man's endless enemy;
For they had slain his children, burnt his home,
Destroyed his all, and sent him naked forth
Amid the wild and woful wilderness,
A houseless wretch, the last of all his race.

Bulo (aside). I never heard a voice like his before,
Or saw a face so charming. Nature keeps
Her treasures in the shadow, hid sometimes
By leaf and rock and water. Speak again:
If all who go in ships are like this man,
Then I would wed a sailor.

Walla. Seeing me
All pale and gasping underneath the leaves,
With Famine watching on a horrid rock,
And in the tree-top a big bird of prey
Whetting his beak against the broken boughs,
And eyeing me with ardour, he drew near,
And in his language spoke most soothing words,
Which fell upon my ear like summer rain;
And then he brought me water from the stream,
And ripe fruit from the thicket; took my hand,
And bade me rise, and led me to his tent,
And fed me from his table. Night came on,
When I lay down upon the red man's mat,
And slept till morning. Three whole days I stayed
Within his wigwam: then he gave me bread
And steaks of venison, bade me seek my band,
And took me o'er the deer-tracks, till I saw
Our fort beside the river. O, his words
Were like a harper's echo. " Go," said he,
" And mingle with thy people; trim their fires
And gladden them with laughter: let fair maids
Rejoice to hear thy music, and young men
Thy pleasant story. Cheer thy mother's heart,
And guide thy father's footsteps to the grave;
Water the tree of peace, and may its leaves
Hide thee for ever from the flame of war:
Be thou thy nation's blessing. But, amid
The summer of thy comfort, cherish still
The forest warrior whom the white man's hand
Stripped in the blood-feud, cutting off his sons
And loving daughters like hoar frost the flowers,
Leaving his home all winter: think of him
Feeding his enemy with his own bread
And rendering good for evil: think of him,
When sitting calmly with thy pale-face friends,
And go and do thou likewise.'

Anleaf. Deeds like these
Are watched by angels, and by angels loved;
So God-like is their nature. Does He not
Lift up the weak to overthrow the strong,
And silence wisdom with simplicity?
I've seen a beggar tottering on his staff,
Whose answers were sublime philosophy:
And much I've wondered. I remember well
A palsied man slow hobbling through a lane,
Of whom a child said, " Mother, can you see?"
This s mote his ear, and smote the old man's heart.
He pa ised upon his staff, and sharply cried,
" Ay, little maid, and what is it you see?"

K

A poor old wanderer in a suit of rags.
I've been in places where I've seen the king,
Who ne'er said, ' Can you see ?' " The moral here
Is worth preserving. But strip off thy weeds,
And put on dry apparel: take some food,
And rest a little ; then we'll gladly hear
The *finis* of the matter.
                                    [*Exit* WALLA.
Bulo (aside).   Yes, he is
A very prince in action. Sweetly shines
A moral dignity upon his brow
Which dwells not with the wasteful. His high mien
Becomes a monarch. And this kingly man
Has been abroad upon the dreadful deep,
Smote with the hurricane, and tossed ashore
Amid the drift-wood like a useless cork.
Some wondrous genii must have led him here
To fill my soul with longing. My poor life
Was like a flower for ever in the shade,
But he has brought it sunshine. Shine, O sun,
And let no cloud force its black breast between
Until my plant is perfect. Hark, he comes.
I'll watch him like a fowler, and may be
An arrow from my lids, a shaft of light,
May wound him in at a venture. [*Re-enter* WALLA.
Anleaf.   Once I stood
Beside a roaring torrent. Down it dashed
With foam and shiver, shaking the great ground ;
And wondering there my foot slipped, and I fell :
A peasant's arm sustained me. Seeing how
The grass-tufts left my hands, and I slid on
Towards the thunder, he sprang down a rope
And caught me falling. This was Providence ;
For chance and luck are liars. Ope thine eyes,
And thou shalt see HE fills the universe.
Now let us hear the story of thy woes.
Walla. It was a night of watching : from the
        heavens
Strange voices broke, and muttered in the clouds ;
Blue rills of fire flamed through the hemisphere,
Succeeded by the thunder ; and the sea
Boiled in the strife, and struggled, surged, and
        swelled.
Our bark rose like a feather on the foam,
And then sank down into the horrid depths ;
And thus we drifted, losing all command,
The mighty winds being master. Soon the helm
Broke, and the creaking masts crashed overboard.
" Lost," cried the captain, and the face of Death
Frowned in the flashing foam. We had with us
A lovely maiden from another isle,
Whose tale of love was passing pitiful.
Her look was not unlike your daughter's here.
A chieftain wooed her, of a noble race,
And came the eve of marriage. Hark ! the storm
Is rolling in his chariot ! rains descend,
The rivers rise, and valleys overflow ;
A hapless wretch is struggling in the flood ;
The chieftain strives to save him ; both drift down
Towards the ocean, and return no more.
She saw him from the window, shrieked, and fell ;
And when she rose another day had dawned,—
The earth had lost its glory. She was rich ;
And, gathering up her gold and precious stones,
She bade farewell, and left her home behind,
To seek the sons and daughters of distress,
And cheer them in their sorrow. Gentle maid !

A wave came thundering, and I saw her borne
Into the arms of ocean : her black hair
Streamed on the water, and her white hands rose,
Then sank for ever on a bed of shells.
Bulo (aside). How much I love the dear old country
    lanes,—
The songs they bring, the pleasures they impart !
The flowers have gentle teachings, and the leaves
Are all o'erwritten with the psalms of truth.
And if the bells among the churchyard trees
Peal out in sweet devotion, and I see
A grey tower in the twilight, earth appears
Imbued with much that Eden must bestow ;
The soul is healthier here, breathes more of bliss,
And walks with One who loved to be alone.
But all sweet sounds that changing Nature yields
To his dear words are harshness. I have heard
Woman commended for her soft sweet tone,
Which is a virtue much to be desired,
And one which scatters discord ; but this man
To my poor ears outdoes my gentler sex,
And overpowers me with sweet harmony.
What if the Fates have ordered that I should
Be wedded to a sailor ? Let it be. [*Exeunt.*

SCENE—*A village on the sea-coast.* TIME—*Early
    morning. Enter* FARDO, *the shrimp catcher.*

Fardo. Hang it ! Ill luck attends me. The east
        wind
Came blow, blow, blow, banging my net about ;
And, ere I was aware, up came a tide
And hemmed me in a gully. There was I,
With rocks around me, all the blessed night ;
And the cold crags had faces, and great eyes
As big as a chair-bottom. I heard sounds
Unlike to human,—barkings, such as dogs
Make when they dream of robbers,—piercing screams,
More shrill than wretches drowning, and my hair
Turned white upon my forehead. I'll go round
And speak to my old woman. Bless her heart !
Tamson (at the window). Who's there ? I have been
hot with fear and ghostly surmisings all night, so that
excitement has bathed me in perspiration. I believe
my head is much swollen, for the beating was intoler-
able. I heard such sounds in the chimney and on the
roof ! and every gust of wind seemed the footfall of
my dear old man. To make the matter worse, the
magpie upset my snuff-box, and the cat threw down a
flower-pot, and broke a pane of glass. I never passed
such a night in my born days. And I all alone here,
with no old man to comfort me ! But who are you ?
Fardo. I'm Fardo the shrimp catcher, your old man,
Who led you to the altar. Ope the door,
And let me kiss you.
Tamson. Go along with you ! You have white hair,
but Fardo's hair is as black as the feathers of the raven.
Fardo's face is red with the sun and sea, but yours
is sallow and sunken. Go along with you ! I know
that wonderful things happen now-a-days : fire horses
run upon wheels, men go up in the air in bladders,
and love-letters are sent along on the bottom of the
sea : but if your white head belongs to Fardo, why,
this is the strangest thing of all. And now I recollect,
Fardo was once injured so that his left hand is like a
rake ; hold it up and I shall know. [FARDO *holds up
his hand.*] Well, it must be Fardo or his spirit. I

am in one solid tremble, and was never so nervous
since the blind fiddler knocked at my lattice. I'll let
this apparition in; and may all good angels help me!
But it is the strangest thing that has happened since
Shakespeare wrote his Hamlet. [*Exeunt.*
[*Re-enter* ANLEAF, BULO, *and* WALLA.

Walla. O how strange
The last few days with their events appear!
A dream had never such significance.
Allow me, Madam, now my heart is full,
To make another mention. In our crew
There was a man it is a grief to see,—
A desperate drunkard. He had spent his lands
And drunk away his houses; with them went
His reputation, and he lost his all.
His children suffered; his heart-broken wife
Sighed in the sorrow of her home's eclipse.
The light of love flashed out, and by the hearth
Sat desolation with black wings outspread.
Friends stared, and left her weeping in her woe.
He fell as low as erring man may fall.
We took the wretch on board; and when our ship
Sailed from the harbour, on a neighbouring hill
She watched us from the rocks, and we could see
Her rags wave in the distance, and her hand
Pointing to heaven. Just then the half-moon dipped
Behind a bank of cloud, and she was gone,
And our bark met the tempest. Still he drank,
Though the wild winds marched in dread fury forth,
Grasped the great waves and dashed them in his
face,
And spoke of death and darkness: still he drank,
Although the thunder in the opening heavens
Echoed rebuke, and the red streams of fire
Lit up his horrid visage: still he drank,
Till madness seized him, when, with yells insane,
As a fierce thunder-bolt tore up the deck,
He sprang into the blackness of the night,
And perished shrieking. Madam, this is sad;
But bad ways have bad ends.

Anleaf. Yes, it is true,
The way of wrong is oft a smooth incline
Which tempts the careless footstep. On and on
The unwary go, till, passed the porch of crime,
They rush to deeds that shame the face of day.
Of the first step beware.

Walla. I love to hear
Your words of wisdom: for they take me back
To trustful childhood, when my mother's hand
Passed through my curls, and pointed me to heaven.
We had a poet with us, one who read
The secret signs of Nature. Born he was
Of lowly parentage, and learnt to sing
Among the breezy moorlands. Streams and flowers,
Birds, buds, and mosses, taught the truthful bard.
This was his one great object which he sought
In joy and sorrow, jingling evermore.
His brother-toilers up the hill of life
Cared not to pause and listen, and he lay
Neglected 'mid his music: so he left
His native moors and wandered o'er the world,
Taking his song-love with him. I have seen
Him, when the brilliant meteors were abroad,
And the big stars were brightest, feed his thought
With earnest glances up the deep profound
Until his eyes brimmed full of lofty lays.
Some say a nymph was ever at his side,

To us invisible, still breathing airs
As sweet as rose-scents to his listening soul.
He stood amid the storm like one entranced,
And shouted to the thunder. With one hand
He grasped the stern, and gazed into the sea,
So bending forward that the curling waves
Lapped him in foam, at which he strangely laughed.
The hurricane grew stronger; the crushed ship
Lurched to its fate; and he went singing down
To meet the mermaids where the sea-weeds shine.

Anleaf No race is more erratic than the bards;
This moment low, then towering o'er the hills,
Sighing in shadow, smiling in the sun,
And visited with visions pearl-beset.
Theirs is a wondrous mission, and the world
Grows brighter for their beauty, deserts bloom,
And crime is chased where wildernesses moan.
That he should perish thus is the world's loss.

Walla. I fain would close with one whom love did
blight,
A native of the forest. He grew up
Amid the pine trees, softened with their sound.
Once, near a brook which shimmered 'neath the
leaves,
He met a maiden. They had met before
Beneath the leafy ceiling of the grove
With interchange of words; but now they stood
Long lingering in the twilight, till the youth
Felt he was passion-wounded. Days passed by,
And months sped onward with an even course,
Opening his love-bloom, when a cloud arose
Which covered him in sackcloth. She was cold,
And shunned his presence, would not heed his words,
And frowned when he addressed her: it was plain
Her spirit was another's. This great blow
Smote like a hammer, and he reeled and fell.
His native woods grew painful. Battle rose:
He rushed into the thickest of the fight,
And longed to die, but left the field unscathed.
Where'er Danger forced his fiery front
Amid the blazing ruin, there was he.
He sought the seas and sailed to many lands,
Aimless and hopeless, like a wildered bird.
We took him in our bark, that pale, sad man,
With mystery in his eyes; and when the storm
Rolled o'er our heads, he sat quite motionless,
With his hands clasped, gazing into the gloom,
And sank without a sigh.

Anleaf Our mortal life
Is rife with wonderful vicissitude,—
Sighs, sorrows, smiles,—to-day a quiet sky,
To-morrow rent and darkened. This should tend
To lift us higher than the hills of earth,
Where truest rest remaineth.

Walla. Madam, good-bye.
I thank you much for what you've said to me,
And much for what you've done. When death comes
quick,
And snatches all your mates and leaves you lone,
Bruised and bewildered in the sudden strife,
To babble forth the story, much that earth
Calls sterling gold takes wings and disappears.
The honours of the world are but a dream,
And fame a leaf the wild winds howl away.
There is a greater, more enduring good
Which beacons my pursuit. I'll search it out,
And wear the jewel nearest my poor heart;

My good resolve is strengthened by your speech.
'Tis kind of you and your fair daughter here,
This patient audience. When I'm far away,
Amid my native valleys, you shall be
A portion of my study. There in hope
Waits an expectant mother, who is now
This moment praying for me. Ah! her prayers
Have saved her boy and snatched him back from
    death.
If you could see her, Madam, love would be
Let loose to bind her captive. Dear old saint!
Her face is shining with the light of heaven.
And there my father dwells; his silver hair
White as the moonlight falling on the hills:
And there my little sister, like a fawn,
Will climb to kiss me on my glad return.
Forgive me, Madam, if I say her eyes
Are love-full like your Bulo's. Thrice a day
She climbs the green to watch the passing ships,
O'er anxious for her brother. Tears are come:
The fount of feeling is fresh broken up,
And down my face it courses. Thus I'll sing:
                    [WALLA *sings.*

   The fierce, foul winds the ocean tossed,
   When ship and comrades all were lost,
   And I was cast ashore to find
   The fairest form of womankind.

   I've seen bright beings o'er the sea,
   Where wealth and song for ever be,
   But Bulo's beauty makes me blind,—
   The fairest form of womankind.

   Now, like a star behind a cloud,
   Or flower with sudden sunshine bowed,
   I bear away within my mind
   The fairest form of womankind.

                    [*Exit* WALLA.

Bulo (aside). He's gone, and my heart with him.
O, I feel
I've passed from sunlight into sudden gloom,
Blinded with darkness. Hush, ye rising sighs!
'Tis only woman's weakness. Let it be.
No king were half so dignified as he!
                    [*Exeunt.*

PART SECOND.

SCENE—*An office in the city.* TIME—*Morning.*
SELANDO, *the merchant, alone at his books.*

Selando. Round goes the world, and round I
    go with it
In one wild whirl of business! Day by day

My face is earthward, stained with sweat and dust.
And yet what profit do I win withal,
But raking straws together which ere long
The fretful fire may suddenly consume?
Within my ears are heard for evermore
The wheels and cranks of Commerce. On I go,
Beating the air and grasping at a shade,
My thought pelf-bound within this narrow are.
Joy sometimes meets me with a few poor smiles,
And then the blast of sorrow wounds mine eyes.
Accounts to-day, accounts again to-morrow,
And thus my years are made up with accounts.
So hot has been the battle, so severe
The earnest struggle, that this world was all,
Though nought is certain here but grief and pain,
Twin-sisters in the combat. Houses, lands,
Fame, fortune, friends, pass from us like a dream;
And I've been plodding on step after step,
Forgetting that I have a child in heaven,
A seraph in the city, clad in white,
For ever watching her poor father's feet.
O God, forgive me! quicken my poor life,
And lift me from the closing webs of care!
Her angel presence visits me again;
I yield to tears and watching.   [*He weeps.*
          [*Enter* ITARA, *a street organist.*
Itara.   Rest I here.
'Tis no use playing in the street to-day;
The town is all excitement: children run;
Old age is in the doorway, mute with doubt;
And matrons mount to windows opened wide;
Youths on the roof-tops huddle,—some climb trees,
And some high garden walls; whilst two o'er-bold
Tall workmen scale the lofty monument,
With eyes towards the north, and all cry, "Fire!"
My organ-pipes are silenced in the din,
With not an ear to heed me. All this morn
I've turned my music-barrel round and round,
Glanced high and low, with face this way and that,
Nodded and winked, and looked what I would say,
Nor won a single farthing, though I know
Not where to get my dinner. Birds have nests,
The fox a shelter, and the mole a bed;
But I am friendless, houseless. In the heavens
There is a God who fills the world with good,
Who sends the wren his satisfying meal,
And rears the cony by the naked rock,
And He will be my helper.
Selando.   Answer me,
In what direction is this fearful fire,
Which so alarms the people?
Itara.   Hearing much,
I climbed a hill and looked towards the sea,
And saw the fire-fiend fling his arms about.
The very waves that broke upon the beach
Were ruddy with his anger, and the sky
Appeared enkindled. Never saw I sight
That flashed me with such wonder. I have been
Amid the ranks upon the battle plain,
Stood face to face with War, and saw him drink
The gore of captains, raze the city walls,
And in his winepress tread the pride of kings.
His fiery breath has scorched the fighting ships,
As if they were a shaving, and whole fleets
Have vanished at his thunder: but this fire
Propels alarm like to a comet's birth.
I'm frightened at the uproar. Let me say,

All wars are wicked, all attacks of arms
The grossest insult to the King of love.
The time is speeding when the reign of swords
And battle-spears shall be for aye o'erthrown,
And peace shall fill the world with holy song.
Selando. Is there a wood beside this monster fire,
The trees in rows and sloping to the creek,
And to the right a castle and a moat,
Where slowly walks the warden on the wall?
Tell me, for I am anxious.
Itara.   Even so;
And to the left a river winds along,
With boats upon its bosom. Furthermore,
There are fair farms around it; in the fields
The teams stand idle; for the workmen go
Where the high flames shoot forth and lap the air,
And rooks scream in the tree-tops. Rumour says
There is a damsel 'mid this wasting wreck
More fair than ever decked an Eastern hall
In danger of destruction, and the bells
Throughout the district ring the rage of fire.
How fearful to awake and feel the flame
Upon our foreheads, knowing that our all
Which life has given us smoulders into smoke,
To be regathered never! 'Tis a thought
All winter woe and utter wretchedness.
But you are trembling, Master; on your brow
The perspiration stands. Thanks for your coin:
I pray no human life may suffer wrong
In this great conflagration. Thus I go,
And trust for bread and water.   [*Exeunt.*

Scene—*Farmyard.*   Time—*Moonlight.*   *Enter*
Fardo *on horseback.*

Fardo.   Gee up, gee,
Gee, gee, my Hannibal! Thus I alight,
And the horse goes to stable. I have had
A gleesome time, such riding with the fays!
These little velvet-coated gentlemen
Would perch themselves upon the horse's ears,
And clap their hands, and shake their silver swords,
While their gay helmets, like a bead of dew,
Gleamed in the moon's white fulness. Such a host
Swung on the leaf-tips over Mary's grave
Who died for love, that I could scarcely pass,
And Hannibal grew restive. Then the king
Of all the fays came riding on a moth,
His rein a cobweb crossed upon his neck,
And pressed a shining goblet to my lips,
Which filled me with excitement. I rode on
Through long dark arches lit by glowworm lamps,
While from the distant ruin the dull owl
Shook out his sobs of dolour: so I took
A little drop of whisky from my flask,
Shouted, and sang, and reached this pleasant bed,
And press at once its whiteness.
          [*He goes in the horsepool and lies down.*
                              Where am I?
Where, where am I? O murther, where am I?
The waters rise around me. What looked sheets
So smooth and thin upon a pleasant bed,
Was only treacherous moonlight, and I'm lost!
O yes, I'm lost! my Tamson, I am lost!
Do you not hear me drowning? I am lost,
And I shall never, never see you more.

O treacherous! treacherous! your own Fardo's lost!
          [Tamson *rushes from the house to his rescue.*
Tamson. What is here? Fardo in the horsepool!
This is more than I can stand. I shall give way under
this, like the side-wall of Jeremiah's house, and fall
flat upon the ground. Some people are always ancle-
deep in mud, and the reason is, they take the wrong
way in the beginning. The wrong way! I wonder who
isn't going in the wrong way. As if my poor old
shrimp catcher couldn't jog quietly home and come in
to me without taking a bath in this green gutter! But
it all comes from the flask of whisky. I should be so
glad if all the whisky in the world was in the bottom
of the sea. A pretty piece of business, isn't it, to be
watching and waiting for him whom I have loved and
cherished for more than forty years, and to hasten
forth and find him disgraced like this? O there is a
curse in the whisky, a curse in the whisky! But I
suppose it is best to pull him out!
          [*She pulls* Fardo *out of the horsepool.* *Exeunt.*

Scene—*A wide common.* Selando *amid the rocks.*

Selando. And is it come to this? In one short hour
Disaster puts his fiery fingers forth;
And what I owned is shrivelled into nought,
And mounts the clouds in smoke. But yesterday
Men called me squire, and doffed their hats and
                              smiled;
To-day I'm hurled upon the stony ground
With but a beggar's portion. What is life
But the bright gauze upon the insect's wing,
Bruised by the blast, up-broken, and is gone?
The fire which comforts oft o'erleaps its right,
And like an angry giant strips me bare,
And thrusts me naked on a selfish world.
O what a blow is this! my very bones
Seem broken in the struggle, and my flesh
Smarts 'neath the cruel, keen, dissecting blade,
And on the earth has dropped a huge black shroud,
Behind which frown the Furies. Prince Divine,
Have mercy on a sinner!
          [*Enter* Anleaf *and* Bulo.
Anleaf.   Here we are
Amid the roots and berries. Nature's hand
Spreads a moss carpet for us, soft as down;
The clear lakes are our mirrors, and the clouds
And graceful moonbeams curtain us to rest;
Bright birds our glad domestics, and the sun
In the great heavens our grand chronometer;
The twilight is our poet, when the dells
Are full of harpers and the heights of praise;
Our books are leaves and the pure eyes of flowers;
Our music, murmuring waters, brooks, and streams;
Our furniture, the drapery of the hills;
Our friends, the bees and pleasant grasshoppers;
And more to be desired are they than man,
Whose heart is like a cage of unclean birds,
A desert of deceit, where poison flowers
Flaunt in the woful herbage. God hath given,
And He hath taken what was never ours;
For all is His, and we too are the Lord's.
Dear husband, do not murmur. From the dust
Jehovah raiseth princes, and the seed
Of the low labourer fills the seat of kings.
In having you I feel I am not poor,
And Bulo, too, is left. Let the winds rise

And rage upon their coursers, let the snow
Come in a whirlwind, burying half the globe,
Let the hot thunder dash his brands about,
Let rivers rise and ocean overflow,
Till the deep din affright the humbled world,—
In having you I'll face it. Hunger, thirst,
Fatigue, and pain are feathers in the scale.
Content can lead me with you over seas
Where icebergs hold their revels, or by tracks
Where lions roar and serpents lick the sand,
Where wild men wander and where mountains burn.
Think you I'll wound your ears with foul complaint?
No, never, never, though these bristling rocks
Be all the home the wicked world affords.
I'll sing you songs as when our youth was green,
Lull you to rest with tales of other years,
Soothe you in sickness, humour you in joy,
Weep when you weep, kneel by you when you pray,
And travel star-ward with no thought of loss.
Selando. O queen of women, best of mothers, wives!
Thy words revive me like the richest wine.
Earth had no spring if woman ceased to be,
But darkness would possess it, such as ne'er
Assailed a globe so rich in light as ours.
I sigh no more. The pangs at our great loss
Were much for you and Bulo. Let all go :
I still am rich in the most costly gifts,
Whilst I have you to light me on my way.
What if our table be the solid slab
With lichen fretted, and our seats the sod?
What if our dinner be a mess of herbs,
In wooden bowls, with water from a shell?
What if our bed be rushes, and the heath
A pillow for us in the rudest hut?
What if a fir-cone serve to give us light,
As round the hearth we gather, where the thorns
Crack, flash, and blaze, and suddenly expire?
What if our clothing be the humblest weeds
A century from fashion?—I would bear
The whole of this, ay, doubled o'er and o'er,
So you complained not, looking up to Him
In simple confidence for better things.
How beautiful upon the mountain tops
Where Morning walks, and in the silent vales
Where Twilight muses, on the mighty sea,
In the dim wood and echoing wilderness,
Is the dear goddess Nature! Fair is she
In all her changes, gemmed with sun or star.
Man stains whate'er he touches : his rude hands
Despoil the landscape and corrupt the scene.
Here we shall be her children, loving much,
In her great temple swept with airs Divine.
Anleaf. Still weeping, Bulo? Dry your maiden's
tears,
And leave with Heaven the future. How He leads
His trusting children o'er the safest path!
Bethink you how the fire enwrapped our house,
Leaping from beam to beam, while you stood pale
And shrieking at the window? Know you not
Who scaled the wall, and saved you in his arms?
The sailor whom we succoured. He, it seems,
When passing by on business near at hand,
Perceived the fire, and rushed to rescue life.
Thus kindness lives insuring its reward.
Bulo. This sudden change has left me quite o'er-
powered,
Like one swift-passed from sunlight into gloom.

I seem not to be Bulo ; yet these hands
Belong to me, and those two feet are mine.
Let me rejoice that I possess so much ;
And since I have my parents, all is well.
I cheerfully bow down to humble things,
Content with you, whatever may betide.
Like a white vision in the vale of night
Comes the young sailor, and my sweetest dreams
Are tell-tales of his presence. Never more
Can I forget a sympathy so strong,
And yearn I to repay it.
Anleaf. Glad am I
That we so oft the pilgrim's heart have cheered
With the full cup of kindness. Not a child
Or hoary sufferer asked us alms in vain.
And as we sow, so may we hope to reap.
I trust as truly the Eternal Word
As a meek child its mother. Corn and oil
Are for His people as Jehovah wills.
A cup of water given in His name
Shall win rewards which swords cannot attain.
The earth shall be destroyed, the heavens shall burn,
The stars shall rush to ruin, the fair moon
Blush into blood, thick darkness seize the sun,
And Nature fall an overwhelming wreck,
But His sure word shall never pass away.
       [Enter a COUNTRY WOMAN *bearing a basket.*
Country Woman. Weeding the corn, I heard of
your distress,
And came with those few trifles. Once you saved
My little maid from starving, when we lay
Beneath the fever's fury, and my prayer
Has been for you o'er since that trying hour.
May His bright sunshine soon dispel the clouds
And fill your sky with glory! Pray accept
What love returns for benefits received.
How oft the good are smitten with distress,
And earthward bowed by sorrow! tears are shed
In homes whose aspects are extreme delight.
How sad that these should suffer! Once I lay
In the cold clime of hunger: work was none,
And sickness smote my husband. He was good,
Gave alms and read his Bible ; thrice a day
He prayed within his closet. Round me flocked
My four small children, sobbing sharp for bread,
With features pinched and looks of utter woe ;
And I had none to give them. Ah! that cry
Grew sharper, shriller, wounding my poor heart ;
And then I prayed that He who fed the flocks
Upon a thousand hills would help afford.
O how I prayed! and succour soon arrived.
Yes ; Anleaf came herself on a wild night
With Bulo, smiling, and our wants were met.
My children ate their food and crowed for joy,
Whilst I stood gazing through my mother's tears,
And lifting up my thanks. A love like this
Meets from the Master its supreme reward.
The time may seem to linger, but at last
It comes like spring with cheering song and flower.
       [Exit COUNTRY WOMAN.
Anleaf. Eggs, bread, and fish, a knife, a fork, and
spoons,
Cheese, bacon, milk! How kind of the dear dame!
Come, husband, take your dinner. Bulo, round.
This moss well serves us for a table cloth ;
And whilst we eat, our thankful thought shall claim
Elijah and the ravens. See, the thrush

Is watching us on the green holly bough,
And flies buzz o'er the fern-brakes; flowers stand
　　round
With urns of perfume filling the fresh air,
Whilst over all a watchful presence broods,
A cheerful grace, my Bulo.
　　　　　[BULO *repeats grace, when they all eat.*
Selando. 　　　　　　　O how sweet
These viands to my taste! the honeycomb
Was never more delicious. Circumstance
Oft smoothes its own ascent, and on the wild
Creates an arbour where the bramble blooms.
Wealth has no wings when sickness bows it down.
I'd rather be a herdsman on the height,
Whistling my dog, and watching my few kine,
Surrounded with the mysteries of the moors,
Sustained by humble fare in humblest shed,
Contentment for my guest, than I would reign
A thankless monarch on an irksome throne.
Of all the graces in the golden train
Contentment stands the fairest. Her sweet face
Has never frown nor wrinkle, and she smiles
Alike when barns are full and harvests fail.
Then let us court her presence. She is here
At our moss board, encircling us with love.
Though pain assail us wandering on our way,
Hunger and thirst, and hurricane, and fire;
Though we plod through bereavement, where the vale
Is full of bitter waters, and the winds
Wail through the weeping willows; though no friend
Stand by us in our trial, she shall be
Our smiling guest for ever. 　　　[*They sing.*

　　Who hastes to heap up gold shall find
　　A heavier burden on his mind;
　　But happy he who is content
　　With what the hand of Heaven has sent.

　　Contentment is the loveliest lot:
　　She dwelleth oft in lowly cot
　　With him who is of humble mind,
　　And leaves the palace far behind.

　　Of all the nymphs in Virtue's train
　　That haunt the wood, or hill, or plain,
　　However low my lot may be,
　　O may Contentment dwell with me!
　　　　　　　　　　　　　　[*Exeunt.*

PART THIRD.

SCENE—*Section of the Victoria gold fields.* TIME
　—*Summer evening.* SELANDO, ANLEAF, *and* BULO
　in a shepherd's hut.

Anleaf. 　How the sun glows behind the western
　　　　　creeks!
　　And round about him the soft gorgeous clouds
　　Are marshalled in much splendour,—purple isles,
With crimson turrets on their floating crests,
Fantastic in their changes. O, I love
To think these cloudlets are the golden gate
Which lets the spirit home to perfect rest,
Behind which shines the city. Do they not
Remind us of a country far away,
Where tower and church would woo the feet to prayer
When solemn bells are pealing? We have sat
Within the doorway of our dearest home
When Evening walked the meadows, blest with sounds
From English hill and valley. O what love
O'erflows my heart for precious fatherland!
This well of waters never will dry up
Till the last tear is bottled and I dwell
Amid the upper palms.
Selando. 　　　　　These purple strips
That strangely stream along the firmament
And stain the tree tops, speak to me of home.
I used to watch them from my native hill,
With all a poet's wonder, till they seemed
The paths of angels through the silent heavens.
Our God is with us here: His Spirit fills
This boundless wilderness, and gives us joy.
My wearied thought will oft fly back with yours
To Albion's pleasant valleys, where the springs
Bubble among the mosses, and the lark
Soars singing up the ether; then the drops
Fall from my eyes unbidden. Oft the smell
Of fragrant hayfields seems to greet my sense,
When rocks are swinging to their evening home,
Which fills me with such longing. Happy years
Were ours in native England, till the fire
Came in swift fury, scorching up our joy:
Deeds, notes, checks, parchments, fed the furious flame.
Alas! our earthly all, the fruits of life,
Lay at our feet a cinder. This was best,—
A chastisement of mercy.
　　　　　[*Enter a* STOCKMAN, *leading a little boy.*
Stockman. 　　　　　Audience, all!
My herd was out upon the wilderness,
Where human life puts forth no other sign
Than the dark wild man's trail in the long grass,
Towards the river's angle. Here free winds
Sweep the low myal which the cattle love,
And eagle-hawks and flocks of curious quail
Flash o'er the clear lagoon. The kangaroo
Revels unscared along the river banks,
Where the great emu sometimes comes to drink;
Far off the gum trees nodded, their white trunks
Gleamed in the sunset like the robes of saints;
And crimson parrots, green, and snowy white,
Whistled and shrieked among the winking leaves.

The Day was driving down his twilight path,
Drawn in his crimson car by crimson steeds,
And round about him his attendants hung
Like servants at his bidding, when I turned
My drove towards the sundown.
Anleaf.   Take a chair;
Much standing makes us weary, and the tongue
Runs all the freer when the limbs have rest.
Give the poor child this morsel; he looks thin,
As if a woe had passed him.   [*The* CHILD *eats.*
Stockman.   Three full days
Had we been journeying when we reached the sand,
A wailing desert sick with poison-air,
And travelling o'er it felt the pangs of thirst.
Then came a lane of blackness, silent, lone;
The earth was cracked, the heavens appeared on fire;
I gnawed a leaden bullet, which allayed
The fierceness of the fever; and the herd
With lolling tongues lifted their heads and moaned.
And then came water, verdure, and a prayer
Rose from my heart to Heaven.
Anleaf.   How beautiful
Bubbles a well of water! No rude sounds
Foretell its issue as it gurgles forth
Amid the moss in limpid loveliness,
Refreshing all around it, murmuring on
In streams of blessing till it reach the sea.
So would I choose to pilgrimage through life.
Stockman. As I sat listening a gay cockatoo
Which kept the marsh in motion, a faint cry
Rose from the brushwood; hearing which, my dog
Did prick his ears and raise a feeble whine,
Then dashed into the dingle. He came back,
And licked my hand, and looked into my face,
Barked, scampered round my feet, then closed his teeth
Upon my garment, and I followed him
Into the bush a winding round and round,
The little cry that scarcely stirred the air
Still waxing louder, when he dropped his grip,
And barked and bounded from me. By a tree,
With white hands clasped and "mother" on his lips,
I found this little stranger. He came out
To gather berries, when he lost his way,
And could not find his parents. He had called
And called again, and wandered farther on
Until his clothes were torn, his small feet bled,
And his eyes burned with weeping. The full moon
Rose o'er the wilderness, and he sat down
Calling upon his kindred in great sobs,
Even where I found him.
Selando.   Is there then no clue
To find his parents? What a vacant place
He makes in one sad household!
Stockman.   I have urged
This rumour onward with the speed of tongues;
The pen has babbled it, the printed sheet
Borne it far north and south; but it remains
A mystery of the future, which the scroll
Of other years may open to the light.
To me he looks a wanderer from the stars,
Where he was owned of angels. What bright hair
And loving eyes and pretty mouth are his!
He is too tender for a stockman's tent,
So often pitched, so often struck again;
And yet 'twere pain to lose him.
Anleaf.   Leave him here:
We'll feed him at our table, nurture him,

Teach him to read, and fold his hands and pray,
As if he were our offspring. Seek thy herd,
And follow thy employment; and when time
Permits thy absence, visit us again,
And we will cover nothing.
Stockman.   So be it.
And may Jehovah bless the boy and you!
                    [*Exit* STOCKMAN.
I could not deem it was so hard to part.
This pretty wanderer rescued in the wood
Has stolen o'er me like the breath of prayer,
Making my life more holy. Seeds of truth
Sometimes spring up thus quickly, growing on
Until the flower is perfect.
Bulo.   Pretty child!
He says his name is Teemu, and his home
Is where the parrots flutter. There he left
His wooden horse, his whip, his battledore,
Mother and brother, and his box of toys;
And now he's pouting for them. Come to me,
And let me be thy sister. Teemu, come!
                       [*Exeunt.*

SCENE—*A surgery in Victoria.* *Enter* TAMSON.

Tamson (addressing the doctor). O sir, my husband's
     ill, my husband's ill!
One eve, when shrimping by the Lady's Rock,
A tall mermaid, with bright shells in her hair
And pearls about her neck, rose suddenly
What time the moon came out above the trees,
And fixed her eyes upon him. They were large
And shining like a furze-brand, and her feet
Were covered o'er with seaweed. Thrice she waved
A wand of coral, and then disappeared,
Leaving a light upon the yielding wave.
This was a sign, he said, of something wrong;
And five nights after, when the sky was clear,
By some mischance he got into a pool,
From which I dragged him not a tick too soon.
And Fardo has been ailing ever since.
O, he grew worse on shipboard, ay, much worse,
And saw a sad thing standing on the deck,
A week's fair sail from England. Woe is me!
And now he's ill, he's ill, my Fardo's ill!
O come and save him, ply him with your pills.
Hasten, dear doctor, do not risk delay.
He's precious to me, precious! and the means
Are ours to practise: Heaven will do the rest.
Quickly, good doctor, mount your handsome horse,
Ride to our dwelling; I'll come on behind.
Carry your phials with you, drench him well.
O save my Fardo, save the old shrimp-man
Who saw the mermaid, and my silver box,
My marriage portion, ring, and all, is yours!
Would I could shout still louder. Save my man,
Good doctor, mighty doctor, save my man!
The tenderest, kindest, very best old man!
Mount, gallop, spur your horse, O save my man!
       [*On her return* TAMSON *meets* FARDO.
Fardo. I'm better, Tamson, better. All my fears
Have taken wings and flown I know not where.
The powerful medicine set me on my legs;
No second dose was needed, and I ate
A roasted chicken and came off to you.
I hope to-morrow, if the day be fine,
To yoke my oxen to the new swing-plough,

And labour in the paddock. Don't look scared:
Dangers when boldly fronted shrink away.
Tamson. Well, this beats everything. This beats
all.—Napoleon, Shakespeare, and everybody. To think
I should leave my old man dying, hasten for the doctor,
and then meet him walking without a stick on my
return home! I wonder what the world is coming to!
Perhaps we may soon have flying ships and railways
in the air. Well, I never! I am perfectly smashed
with amazement. O dear! O dear! O dear!
[*Exeunt.*

SCENE—*Settler's home.* TIME—*Morning.* The
MOTHER *in much sorrow.*

The Mother. Heavy blow! O heavy, heavy blow!
The days
Drag on in twilight with the rain of tears,
And bring no comfort, for they bring not back
The gentle Teemu to his mother's arms.
Perchance the wild beasts have him, or he's drowned
Within the dull lagoon; perchance he sits
Starving amid the thicket, and his cry,
Feebler than when a baby on my breast,
Lags with the name of mother. If I knew
That he had crossed life's threshold, and gone o'er
Into the awful future, it would be,
Methinks, a glad relief: but this suspense,
This dread uncertainty, is like a fire
That scorches up my marrow. Such a woe
Is surely greatest in the list of ills:
To lose a child whose tender, pleading face
Meets you at every turn from Memory's shore,—
To lose a boy so beautiful as mine,
With such a brow and such a depth of gaze,
And know not where he lies,—this is a blow
That cannot be repeated. But I bend
Beneath the stroke, and sigh, "Thy will be done!"
[*Enter a* SHEPHERD *with a lamb in his arms.*
Shepherd. As this white lamb went straying from
the fold,
Torn by the hanging branches, I pursued,
And overtook it by a shallow pit
Where coiled the reptiles. The bewildered brute
Knew my familiar voice, and when I spoke
Came bounding at my call, licking my hand
And baaing with delight, as if it said,
"Dear master, pity me!" I took it up,
And bore it in my arms across the bush;
And by a gully where a path was made
I found this chip of paper, which I've brought
For your especial reading. May it be
A messenger of comfort! [*Exit* SHEPHERD.
The Mother. What is this?
A child found by a stockman in the bush,
With curly hair, black eyes, and handsome face,
Whose age is near four summers, and his name
Is only Teemu. This must be my boy;
The angels have been with him, and he's spared;
And I shall surely see his face again,
Look in his eyes, and read his loving thoughts,
And feel his kiss, and wonder at my joy.
Already the horizon of my hopes
Glows like the kindling morning. I stand here
And look into the future, and his arm
Supports my feebleness, and leads me down
Into the vale of dimness, where the winds

Leave the same point for ever, and the house
Shakes with its keepers while the grinders cease.
But let me run with this news uppermost
To give my neighbour word. [*Exeunt.*

SCENE—*Selando's hut.* SELANDO, ANLEAF, BULO, *and*
TEEMU *within.*

Selando. There is a stranger coming o'er the flat,
And he seems much in haste. Lifting his cap,
He wipes the perspiration from his brow,
Swinging his arm, and taking rapid strides,
As does full oft a courtly messenger.
'Tis evident he makes our house his aim;
He's o'er the fence, and nearing the fruit trees.
I'll ask him in. Thus hospitality
Has sometimes sheltered angels.
[*Enter* STRANGER.
Stranger (embracing TEEMU). Yes, 'tis he!
Thou art my darling brother. Why is it
Thy little feet have borne thee thus away?
Dost know thy mother has refused her food?
That smiles have left her face, and light her home?
That tears have been her portion, and Distress
Sat by the hearth in sackcloth? Her dear boy,
Her younger-born, had left a vacant seat,
Nor could she catch a whisper of report
Whither her love had drifted. How she'll clasp
Her treasure to her bosom, sing for joy,
And cover thee with kisses! Thanks to those
Who rescued thee from ruin, and who gave
Thy hapless head a shelter.
Bulo (aside). 'Tis no dream
That thus o'erpowers me with deliciousness:
I am awake and conscious, and I hear
A voice like falling waters. What is this
That o'ertakes me as the news of home?
I wander in a garden, and appear
Like one swift passed from utter barrenness
Into a land of blossoms, where the birds
Warble among the roses, and the air
That fans the lake is thick with harmony.
I'll screen me in this pleasant summer bower,
Peer through the leaves and listen.
Anleaf. Take a seat.
This child was brought to us by one who found
Him starving in the swamp. An unseen chain
Of many links full oft unites events,
And draws the whole together. Didst thou not
In thy loved England rescue from the fire
A timid maiden, as the beams gave way,
And roof and rafters flashed into the hall?
Behold her in this dwelling!
Bulo (aside). Yes, 'tis he!
The mystery of my being, the one star
For ever twinkling in the sky of of love:
A star no longer, but a blazing sun.
I would I were the little earth it warmed
And kissed into perfection.
Walla. This great joy
Flows o'er me like a tide, and leaves me stunned
Amid the waters. I have this to crave,
Which if denied me fills the world with shade,—
Your daughter's hand in marriage. I have gold
And flocks of kine enough for us and you.
Come, let us live together. Three months since,
When with a comrade digging by a tree,

We found a nugget in the native soil,
Which I struck with my pick, and when unearthed
We sold the monster for nine thousand pounds.
It was God's hand that led me, whom I serve.
Selando. We place no barrier in our daughter's way,
But leave her free to take or to refuse.
This, not because thou art increased in goods,
And that much gold is added. What is gold?
A glittering ruler seizing on the heart,
A shining burden crushing comfort out!
How hardly shall a rich man enter heaven!
No, not because of this, but for His grace
Who calls thee to repentance. Hear me out.
I would not have my Bulo wed a man
For money only, whose all-grasping hands
Are stained with avarice, whose eyes are dull
To beauty's vision and affection's power,
Who views the world through the false glass of pelf
And barters truth for gain, who ever weighs
Life's dearest interests in the scale of wealth,
And stoops to coin more than to sterling worth.
I would not have my Bulo wed this man
If he had half Golconda. Verily
I'd rather pick a carrier from the yard,
Whose soul was glowing with the beautiful,
Who felt the force of Heaven-born charity,
Than she should marry such a gilded clod.
How many limbs are torn on Mammon's wheel!
How many homes are darkened by his wings!
How many lives are yearly sacrificed—
Daughters and sons—upon his altar fire!
Unions for gold are marriages for strife.
One drop of love is worth a titled name;
One spark of pure affection is more dear
Than the most noble dowry. Give me love,
And then let Fortune treat me as she will.
Love makes an Eden of the wilderness,
A palace of the cottage, and green fields
Where only dry reeds rustle. Would my voice
Could girdle the great globe, I'd raise it high
Until it marched like thunder through the land,
Till hill and valley caught it, and 'twas rolled
From clime to clime upon the hurrying winds,
Arresting human ears like shrill cloud-trumps:
" Don't wed for gold! let marriage be for love.
Beware ye be not yoked unequally;
This brings a blight upon the lovely world.
Follow affection, prize it more than pelf.
Begin with Heaven; and let Heaven's finger guide,
And earth shall yield the fruits of Paradise."

SCENE—*A moonlit arbour.* *Enter* BULO *and* WALLA.

Walla. On this old tree trunk by the river side
We'll bathe ourselves in moonlight. See what spires
Of shining silver gem the forest boughs,
And shoot along the hill sides in a shower.
What purity of sweetness! far more pure
Because thy lips are here to welcome mine.
The little fays are fairer in thy smile,
And loveliness more lovely. Ne'er a king
With dainty helpmeet was so blessed as I:
So perfect is my measure of delight
Another drop would mar it. Bend thy face,
And kiss me once again. On those white clouds
Slow sailing through the ether, it is said,
The angels glide at evening, looking down

Upon this little planet. Can their bliss
In saintly vesture far exceed mine own?
Methought sweet sounds rose from the distant bank:
'Twas the dear music of thy beating heart.
Still rest it on my bosom, it is thine,
While stars shine down approval. When the sun
Creates another day, we two are one,
Blent like the light and rose-leaves. Blessed hour!
I seem to bathe in nectar, and the waves
Come murmuring round me more delicious still,
A preface to my volume of delight.
Now let me lead thee homeward at slow pace,
Loitering at every turn, as lovers will,
Creating seraphs out of every leaf,
And theme for dalliance from the softest sound.
Thus we depart with kisses.   [*Exeunt.*

SCENE—*Harvest field.*   TIME—*Noon.*   *Enter* Two
REAPERS.

First Reaper.   O how cool
The shade of this old tree! Let's rest awhile,
And listen to the music of the bells
Across the woody dingle. It is sweet
To pause sometimes amidst our earnest toil,
And think how we are steering o'er the tide
Of solemn waters all so fleetly cross.
The bells teach much if we would understand.
Second Reaper. Oft when my sickle cuts the precious
stalk,
And it lies flat upon the stubble ground,
I think of human life and human ends,
And pray that when the silent mower comes
I may be ripe and ready. But to-day
It seems ill-timed to hurry sadness on,
To cloak the brow, and play the hypocrite,
When Joy has wings and Mirth is drunk with bliss.
The miner leaves his gold, the smith his fire,
The shepherd boy his flock upon the plain,
The stockman's axe is silent; in the shade
The driver's team is resting, and the boys
Throw up their caps and wildly dance and shout.
Ring out, sweet bells, over the vales away;
Let the world know 'tis Bulo's marriage day!
                                    [*Exeunt.*

SCENE — *Stockman's   dwelling.*   TIME — *Sunset.*
WALLA *and* BULO *standing before the hut.*

Walla. Dost like this lodge, my Bulo? To mine eyes,
A cottage home among the watching hills,
Where the brook babbles, and the roses cling,
And hawthorns guard the gateway, is more fair
Than towering palace in the city's roar.
And when I die, methinks if I could choose
The place of my departure, it would be
A lonely dwelling by the waterfall,
Encircled with the mountains, from whose tops
My ransomed spirit should escape to heaven.
See how the roses o'er the doorways hang
Along the fair verandah! The high posts
Look fragrant pillars sweetly budded o'er,
Festooned with creepers and bright passion-flowers;
Grapes hang about the lattice; on the roof
Of strong tree bark the water-melons grow,
And bees hum here when morn is in the vales;
Behind it rise the fruit trees. Here the beans

And blossomed peas stand up in even ranks,
While fowls are roosting on the spreading boughs.
Dost like this lodge, my Bulo ?
Bulo.   Beautiful !
No fairy ever had a home more sweet.
Mine eyes drop tears to see it. Blessed spot !
Which cherubs visit when the night is young.
Its influence moves me like a sacred psalm
From lips prophetic. O if it were mine !
Walla. And it *is* thine, my Bulo ! all is thine ;
These hands have reared it for thee. Day by day
I've toiled and tugged with sunshine in my heart ;
And when I fixed a stake, or raised a beam,
Planted a rose bush or an apple tree,
Fashioned a lattice, or planned out a door,
Modelled a path, or raised a rural fence,
Delved the rich soil, or pruned the pleasant vine,
I felt 'twas all for Bulo. This great joy
Of yielding it to my dear lady love
Knocks at my soul for language, but it fails ;
The bliss is far too exquisite for words.
See how the sunset lingers 'mid the leaves,
Kissing the rose-buds in their bowers of green,
As if to sanctify our future home.
Here we will dwell in Love's own tenement,
Watched by the smiling Graces. Future years
Shall aye mellow what has been begun,
Which ripens in the fields without a cloud,
Beyond the swelling Jordan. I have been
Year after year like poor neglected bard,
Longing for quiet, chased from room to room
And door to door, nursing his new-born thought,
Till driven forth beneath the pitying sky
To woo his Muse : so have I longed for rest,
To find it here with Bulo. Come, my love,
Let's ope the gate and enter.   [*Exeunt.*

SCENE—*Room in Walla's dwelling. A table spread
   with provisions. Enter* SELANDO *and* ANLEAF.

Anleaf (embracing Bulo).   Darling child !
This is a home befitting thy true love,
And thou art worthy of it. May no wind
With foulness laden over blight its walls,
And its green roof-tree have perpetual spring,
Fed with the dews of goodness ! Well thou know'st
The Gospel precepts lodged within thine heart :
Now let them sway thy future. Without this,
The fairest bower becomes a brambled brake.
Where wild beasts tread the thicket. Live for love,
And rather bleed thyself than wound thy friend.
Serve only for thy husband. Be his sun
When clouds assemble, his adviser sweet
When foes assail or dreadful crosses burn,
His harp in storms, his lute in piercing winds,
His star in sorrow ; and when sunshine bathes
Your groves in beauty, his expanding flower !
Then in your lives shall earth and Eden meet.
Selando. I'm pleased with all I see, with all I feel,
With all my ears are greeted. It is good
To stand upon life's hill-side, and look o'er
The history of our journey. One great Hand

Upholds and governs all things : let this be
The comfort of my daughter.
            [*Enter* WALLA'S MOTHER, *leading* TEEMU.
The Mother.   Sit, my boy,
And wait till all is ready. Bulo comes
To kiss thy face and stroke thy shining curls :
She now is Teemu's sister. Pretty place,
Where all is ordered in simplicity !
How bright and shiny are the knives and forks
Laid on the strong deal table ! Of blue delf
Are all the plates and dishes. On the hob
Potatoes steam, and simmer peास and greens ;
The smell of pork, peach pie, and orange tart
Mingle with beef and mutton, and a smile
Is on the faces of our honest friends.
            [*Enter* ITARA *the organist.*
Itara. You meet with grumblers, walk which way
            you will.
The world, say they, is drifting on through space
In a false orbit, soon to be a wreck.
There is no order : everything is launched
Upon a sea where false winds roar and rage
And roll from every quarter. Government
Is on the shoulders of poor sightless Chance,
To toss and writhe for ever. Out on ye !
I dare not hug such jargon. Earth has love,
And love makes heaven : the strongest power is love.
And earth has smiles and sunshine, light and flowers,
Music and friendship, and fair childhood's wiles,
And hopes in rainbow clothing. For my part,
I seem o'erwhelmed with blessing ; and my woes
Are as a feather weighed against my gifts.
I thaw to see you, friends, to feel your joy,
And quaff your cup of welcome. We will keep
Our glad hearts warm with praises, then the clouds
Dare only show their frontlets in the sky,
And hurry off like shadows. Let us leave
Rank weeds and thorns, and pluck the fragrant flowers
That cluster ever round our daily track,
As free to reach as thistles. By your leave
We'll sit and dine, and then in simple tones
My organ-pipes shall greet you.
[*They surround the table, after which* ITARA *sings.*

Along the streets and through the lanes
    I long have woke my simple strains,
And love has been from year to year
    The theme which I have sung so dear.

The shepherd-boy upon the moor,
    The maiden by her mother's door,
Have paused amid their sighs to hear
    The theme which I have sung so dear.

In every clime it telleth true ;
    'Tis over old and over new ;
It bringeth on the cheek the tear,
    The theme which I have sung so dear.

And thus its power will ever be
    Acknowledged wide from sea to sea,
The sweetest strain from year to year,—
    The theme which I have sung so dear.
                              [*Exeunt.*

L. 2

A TALE OF THE MANACLES.

DRAMATIS PERSONÆ.

MEENA . . . . . *The Drunkard's Wife.*
ERNO . . . . . *A country Maiden.*
FIRST BOATMAN.
SECOND DITTO.
MEENA'S DAUGHTER.
COTTAGE WOMAN.
RIDO. . . . . . *Meena's Son.*
MEENA'S HUSBAND.

STORM SPIRITS, &c.

SCENE—*A Common in Cornwall.* TIME—*Evening.* MEENA *walking up the hill.*

Meena. The sky is red and glowing;
  all below
Is streaked with beauty, whether
  cloud or crag,
Wind-waving fern or wondrous
  firmament,
Pine-clump and peak and river
  fringed with reeds;
And there are echoes from the hollow hills
And mystic marshes, which the busy noon
In the full swing of labour heedeth not.
My mother oft, when Eve lay down to dream,
Watched by the gathering twilight, called me near,
And bade me listen while the moon arose
Above the crags that watched us, turning tears
To beads of silver on her thoughtful face;
And then she pointed westward, where the light
Was like a crimson curtain, whispering low,
As if her words were harsh 'mid such a psalm
From lutes unstrained by action : " List, my child,
These murmuring voices are the sounds of prayer
From thickets thronged with trumpets, each a tongue
Which utters praises in the ear of God !"
Then came a blast with poison on its wings,
Smiting her in its march, and she dropped down
Where bitter dews were falling, and the sigh
Of sickness swelled upon the leaden air.
A second blast, and when a third arose,

Rushing with rolling force, she smiled no more,
But lay upon her bed in love with death,
Pale as a lily when the storm descends;
And through the portals of the purple sky
Her spirit passed into the field of flowers.
From the high hills of heaven she watches me,
And knows my path of sorrow. [*She weeps.*
            Let me weep !
These thoughts bring tears, and tears will ease my load.
They have not flowed like this for many a day ;
For the cold hand of Care has dammed them up
With walls of tribulation. Blessed tears !
I'll thank the Giver for these rills of truth,
In which I see the hopes of other days,
Fair plans and prospects, figured and achieved.
Then from the poison-marshes rolled a stream,
Thick, black, and burning, bearing life away,
Leaving behind it brokenness and death.
What am I now but a storm-wrangled wall
Which the great sea of grief has undermined,
And still the waves come dashing to its doom ?
My home is a wild wreck upon the deep,
Swept with big billows, where sea-monsters herd
And shapes unnamed by mortal : on it drives
By shores of thunder with the lightnings torn.
No food is in my dwelling ; on the straw
A dying daughter with no fire to warm
Or cordial to refresh her. By the hearth
With brand unkindled, Famine sits and scowls,
And sparrows pick the casement paper-blotched,
Alarmed to hear her wailings, fluttering off
To other doorsteps joyous for a meal.
Methinks her sorrow, like a phantom slim,
Follows for ever, treading in my steps,
And sighing in mine ears, and meeting me
With ashy features wheresoe'er I turn.
Her father is a drunkard. Once his light
Illumed our dwelling, chasing gloom away ;
She ran to meet him when his work was done,
And in his arms he held her high in air,
At which she crowed and clapped her pretty palms.
She told him stories sitting on his knee,
Shared in his meals and laughter, nor withheld
Her earnest kisses, sweet as gales of May.
O, home was holy then ! beneath our vine
An angel sat with benedictions bright,
And the soft music awed us into prayer.
Too soon was it supplanted : in its place
A thing of gloom lay cowering all day long.

And moaning until morning : light was gone,
And darkness crammed it to the very roof.
The voice of prayer died out, and fiercely wild
Rose words of clamour. Drink has done it all ;—
Affection, friends, health, happiness, and home,
Reason and right, wisdom and heaven for drink!
In these poor rags I've wandered through the lanes,
If haply I might meet the wretched man,
And lure him to his dying daughter's side,
Whose wasting cry is lifted up for help,
So soon to be a seraph. Let me go
Where all the miseries meet !
          [*Enter* Erno, *a country maiden.*
Erno.   Is sorrow thine
Beyond a pilgrim's portion, that thy face
Is channeled like a hill-side by the sea,
Where meet the four winds, followed with the rain
And sounding thunder ? Sighs thy bosom heave
Like her deserted when the rose of love
Seems bending to her fingers, and thine eyes
Deep-set and shining flash forth more than words.
Would talking ease thee ?
Meena.   '   I have much to bear.
Mine is a great woe wresting life away,
Filling the land with hailstones. Summer fruits
Are changed to rottenness, and the green grass,
By the huge grief-cloud drifting up my path,
To prickly stubble where strong reptiles brood.
Thou mayest draw near and look with pitying eyes,
But canst not reach such agony as mine.
Erno. All have their suffering: some a greater share,
And some a lesser : some have grievous ills
Out-jutting on their journey, sharp as swords;
And some have angry seas where waves run high,
And whirlpools roar, and winds come tumbling down;
And some have valley, meadow-path, and stream:
Sunshine have some, clear sky and level plain ;
And some more days of darkness than of dawn :
Thrice happy he who takes what Heaven assigns
With grateful heart, and rests upon His rod !
Meena. What is there in the feverish swamp of ills
With mien more mournful than the drunkard's wife,
Crushed out of comfort by a weight of wrong,
Heaped on by him whose hands should hold her up ?
And such am I, with all my garments stained.
Far better be a watcher in the fields
Till the moon rises, lonely as the lark
Whose mate fell when the winter winds were wild.
Pass by our garden : there the nettle stings,
And brier and bramble riot ; thistles wave,
And dock-weeds flaunt and frolic. The low fence
Is broken to the turf, and the lean hog
And hungry horse prowl o'er it at their will.
The hovel's roof is greatly reft of reed,
So that the wood lies bare. The monster blast,
One muttering night when darkness drowned the moon,
Thrust in his hands, close followed by the snow,
And opened cruel gaps which wider stared
As the north raised its trumpet. The porch rose
Is draggling in the earth, with no fond hand
To train it to the timber : once it won
The praise of all who saw it ; now, like me,
It is a target for the darts of scorn :
Yet still I trim the lingering lamp of love.
Erno. 'Twere ill to banish hope, and let the mind
Drift like a feather. I have had my share
Of what the world calls trial. Once a fire

Came in the darkness when the city lay
In a still sea of slumber, stretching out
Great lurid arms which stained the firmament ;
And when I woke the room was full of sparks,
And red tongues smote the lattice. Then a hand
Came through the sulphur, taking hold of mine,
And the next moment there were shouts of joy.
Ah ! I was but a child, and my first care
Was for my mother, whom I saw no more.
My father too fell ill from harms received
That fearful hour, and shortly after died,
Leaving an orphan in the workhouse walls.
Soon I was sent to service. Cruel hands
Inflicted bruises on my tender frame,
Which would command the tears from eyes like thine.
Long suffered I in silence with a prayer
To Him who soeth in the secret place ;
And when my grief increased with stripes of pain,
I ran away and begged from door to door.
Sometimes I hungered much, and lay in barns,
Or by the rich man's pillar ; oft a crust,
Soaked in the stream on whose green banks I sighed,
Sustained me from the morn till morn again.
My feet were shoeless, my thin garments torn,
My tangled hair uncovered. Once a voice
Rang in me when the hunger pang was high :
" Steal !" and I trembled as my wasted hand
Was stretched to take what never had been mine :
I drew it back, and cried, and cried again ;
Then prayed for help, and soon the Helper came.
A lady found me on the rift's rough edge,
And led me thence, and placed my willing feet
In other paths, where flowers of knowledge grew ;
But trouble followed still. Beyond the woods
Young Rido dwelt, of aspect delicate
And loveful as a river. We met oft
Where branching elms gave shadow, and one theme
Entranced us ever, murmuring in the brook
And ringing in the echoes of the trees.
He sought for me when eve came down the west,
And led me to the door, and talked of love ;
And oft some little present would he bring :
But stern his father. When the truth came out,
How his son wooed an orphan, he was wroth ;
And in the night, when rain-floods roused the hills,
And torrents rumbled through the rocky gorge,
He drove him forth with many a bitter word
And stamp of foot, forbidding his return
Till the pure love-plant perished in his soul.
I cried until my tears appeared like fire
Burning upon my lids, and my limbs shook
With daily fasting ; yet he never came :
And still I listen when the eve is calm,
And the mill-brook is gurgling round its banks,
To hear his whistle ; but no whistle rings.
'Tis dark without him : when will it be light ?
Meena. 'Tis even so : the earth has woes for all.
But mine are blacker, bolder, more intense,
More fraught with horrors, saddening human ears,
Than those that throng the pathways of the world.
What blighted being is so sad as she
Who shivers in the ruin of her home,
Made blank by drink which scorches like a fire ?
I stand like one for whom the ocean roars,
Cast lorn and naked on the hungry strand,
Whose earthly all is in the waves entombed.
         [*Exit* Erno. Meena *soliloquizes.*

Meena. How strange the leaflets of our human life !
Some are replete with conflict, some as smooth
As lakes in summer ; some have jets of song,
And some adventure cramming half the page.
Why has this maiden crossed my weary path,
Murmuring for love ? and Rido is my son.
Yes, Rido is my son. His angry sire,
When full of drink and swaggering in his words,
Bade him be gone and seek his home no more,—
Bade him be gone because an orphan girl
Had won his heart's affection. O how sad !
He did not know her beauty or her worth ;
Powerless and friendless was enough for him ;
There was no gold, and so the balance turned,
And merit was rejected. This is life,
Or be he bard or barber. Show your purse,
And cunning tongues will praise your cleverness.
If you have none, why, you have friends to seek.
No strains of music can atone for this ;
No lofty talent, no invention huge ;
The gilded idol wins the bended knee.
And yet she loves our Rido, weeps for him,
And watches all the passes of the hills
With eyes that weary not and heart that yearns.
And what is gold to this ? a water-drop
To seas of milk and honey ! Shame, O shame !
This maiden is a treasure unsurpassed ;
A garden of sweet spices. Who wins her
Will have a fortune in her. Once our boy
Has written, and the letter reached our shed.
Rough seas were crossed, and plains and rivers wide ;
And in a country thick with tangled wood
He trod the lion's track, and heard the wolf
Howl in the coming darkness : the wild man
Peered from the bushes, and the condor screamed.
He may be on the sea or on the land,
Or in his grave : God knoweth, and not I.
But for this damsel's sake I'll pray once more
That Heaven may shield him. Now I sadly go
Where ills are gathered, shutting out the day,
Worse than Egyptian darkness. *[Exeunt.*

SCENE—*A cottage on the Cornish cliff.* TIME—*Midnight. A storm.* *Enter* TWO BOATMEN.

First Boatman. Perils huge !
I've been abroad in gloom and savage strife,
When heaven and earth were roaring, and the sound
Was like a falling mountain ; but to-night
The waves rise high until they burst themselves
In frantic fury, weltering o'er their bounds,
And flash and foam into the very streets.
No craft can stand such anger. Crags are torn
From their primeval footing, and great trees,
That watched the centuries, cry as if in pain,
Uprooted like a bulrush. Hark ! a gun
Speaks in the tumult. Let us to the door,
And watch the flash upon the heaving sea.
Second Boatman. A flash again ! If my discernment serves,
It must be near the jutting Manacles,
Which all night long are watching for their prey.
Methinks I hear the shouting mariner,
Or was it the wild echoes of the more ?
Another gun, and there the signal lights !
Let's to the rescue : duty needs no guide.

[Exeunt BOATMAN. *Enter* MEENA, *leading her daughter.*

Meena. We have no home, my daughter, but the heath
Where vapours haunt the marshes ; rain and storm
Vent their ill humour on us, and the cold
With wakeful harshness make th life severe.
O, we had friends when sunshine was our lot,
And mirth and music, conversation bright,
Nod and hand-shaking ; but when trouble came,
Stark want and ruin, by the demon drink,
Then friendship's face was hidden, and cold eyes
Froze sheer into the spirit. I stood lone
Among my sex with a great gulf between,
Which widen yawns with desperate doors of doom,
As my thin rags grow thinner where they hang.
It grieves me, child, to mark thy pallid face.
Severely hast thou fasted, till thy life
Seemed swinging by a hair ; then the sun shone,
And the crushed lily rallied. Mine own woes
Are limping dwarfs, nor worthy to be named,
And dwindle into straws, whilst thine are trunks
Whose girth might shield a lion. Watched I long
And saw thee sinking with a dearth of bread,
And heard thy sorrow while relief's high gates
Were barred up by thy father, and dark waves
From whose cold chambers issued wailing words
Went washing through my dwelling. How I sighed
None but Jehovah and the angels know.
And then came food from whence I cannot tell,
But it was Heaven who sent it. Yet he drank,
And reeled from slope to slope still lower down,
Whirling with greater force, till the last plunge
Was most terrific, levelling every hope
And dashing it in anger to the ground.
Then my brain reeled, thick darkness veiled mine eyes :
A shadow lay before me. When I woke,
My home was gone and its endearments changed,
A heap of wasting ashes. A great sigh
Swelled to the clouds, and underneath the stars
We wandering went, thou whispering in mine ear,
"I'll go where mother goes, and starve with her ;"
Till the wide south grew angry, and huge clouds
Rose from the roaring waters ; darkness dropped
Upon the mountains, and along the rifts
Walked the wild thunder,—we were in the storm.
Thanks for the safety of this reedy shed
And a kind-hearted hostess !
Cottage Woman. Let my hands
Be free to help a sister in distress,
And shield the daughter of calamity.
We all are drifting on a sea of change,
And know not where the tide may carry us.
Monarchs to-day in regal vestments clad
Are mendicants to-morrow, and the hall
Where music sits enamoured of itself,
And painting spreads the canvas, yields to cells
Where stone and plaster are the ornament.
Right welcome are you to abide the gale,
Which its own rage must shatter in the clouds.
As now I help, let timely aid return.
Meena. I have two storms which roar upon me now
Like fields of icebergs,—one a ruined home,
And one the horror of this hurricane
Marching the earth in fury. On the sea
My boy may now be drifting, thrust with winds
And thunder-heavings. If I look above,

There is a black arch which I cannot pierce,
And on each side a fearful wall of black,
And black beneath me. Once the sky was fair,
And bright stars journeyed with the watery moon,
And gay flowers decked the landscape : now I stand,
Like some fond lover of the beautiful,
With lakes beneath, beyond the waving pines,
Behind bluff tarns and peaks with sunset stained,
And in the distance barks and the blue sea,
And a high hymn of praise to gladden all.
I stand like one thus blest with loveliness ;
And as I gaze the glory disappears,
And a waste wilderness, where monsters breed
And reptiles batten, quickly hems me in.
The children know me, strangers read my curse,
Neighbours forsake, the wealthy wag their heads,
And gather in their garments as they pass
For fear of great pollution ; and the brutes
Which stand on their own level seem to feel
By wondrous instinct I'm the drunkard's wife.
Like one who toils through trial, treading on
And struggling eve and morn until he roars
A dwelling by his birthplace, saying oft,
"Now I shall rest securely," but whose door
Is much besieged by callers whose free talk
So interrupts his quiet ; or like him
Whose hand did aid his fellows, struck with age
And withering sickness, pushed aside and scorned
As if unworthy of the ground he trod ;
Or the poor wretch who labours for a fire,
And when it is enkindled, is thrust out,
And others feel the comfort of the flame :
Too faint these emblems are of woes like mine.
O, why do not the elements unite
In rage unwonted, and with one vast turn
Of the strong key which looses the dread bolt,
Unravel the great future ? Better lie
In the still grave, watched by the loving moon !
Cottage Woman. O what fierce arrows of blue scorch-
  ing fire
Shoot through the heavens ! The wild, crag-shaking war
Of thunder rises, roaring as it rolls
More stunning still the last ear-piercing peal.
Disaster's catalogue will swell to-night,
New widows mourn and orphans, and the sea
Entomb its sleepers without board or shroud.
Hear'st thou the minute gun ? Trim the night lamp
Which blazes in the window : it may be
A guide to some poor sailor. Now sit down
And take this cup of tea and slice of bread.
You both look famished. Never part with hope :
It is the spirit's anchor ; and a calm
Follows the storm and lulls the ruffled wave.
  [MEENA *and her daughter eat. Enter the* STORM
      SPIRITS, *singing in a circle.*

From cloudy chariots we unchain
The noisy winds that march the main.
Uncurbed, unchecked,—away, away,—
They sweep the earth, they lift the spray,
They hoist the sea with haughty swells
Around the mighty Manacles.

The stately vessel homeward bound,
Where wealth and absent friends are found,
Rich-freighted from yon spicy shore,
Shall plough the emerald waves no more.

Her keel shall bruise the hidden shells
That stud the mighty Manacles.

The maiden at their base shall sleep,
While mystic watch the mermaids keep ;
The ancient mariner shall rest
With ocean-pearls upon his breast,
Where everlasting silence dwells,
Down by the mighty Manacles.

Here dirges rise from deep sea-caves,
And foam is ever on the waves,
In storm and calm, by day and night,
When boards are cleared, when fires are bright,
And roar the waves the rock repels,
' Beware the mighty Manacles."   [*Exeunt.*

[*Re-enter the* TWO BOATMEN, *leading a youth.*
First Boatman. A splendid bark, with all her boards
      unbulged
And not a stain upon her ! yet she seemed
A very plaything on the angry deep,
Rocked like a fairy's cradle, till she fell
Right in the rage of the stern Manacles,
Which ground her to destruction. Sounds arose,
And muffled echoes which I dare not name,
And shrieks which rent the darkness ; then the roar
Of the great ocean overwhelmed the whole.
All hands were lost, except this ruddy youth,
Who bound himself to the disabled mast,
And, when the timbers parted, washed ashore.
We found him lying in the awful surge,
Cut the wet ropes, and set the prisoner free.
His eyes were closed, his locks were wet with brine,
Part of his clothing wrested from his limbs,
And a black bruise upon his shining brow.
With proper treatment he was soon restored,
And we have brought him hither.
Meena (*aside*).   Do I dream,
Or gaze I on a vision ? This fair youth,
Sea-washed, sea-smitten, surely is my son !
He has his eyes, his hair, his smiling mouth,
His graceful bearing, and his look of truth.
His speech will soon convince me. Passions strange
Light up their fires, and beat me at the blaze,
And such a shaking overtakes my limbs
As I have never witnessed. See, his lips
Tremble to speak ! I wait to catch the word.
Youth. I thank you, friends, for these your deeds of love.
I have a mother somewhere on this moor,
Bruised with an early sorrow, whose kind eyes
And gentle words have followed in my steps ;
And, looking homeward, I have seen her tears.
I left a sister, too : a staggering sire,
Draining the cup of wrong, whose liquid light
Dazzled the halo of our holy home,
And piled around it hills of horrid gloom.
His anger fell upon me like a rock,
Crushing and grinding ; and when I came forth
With hideous scars and bruises, I was forced
To leave the maiden whom my soul adored,
And face the cold world and its freezing frown,—
This at my father's bidding. I took ship,
And on the deck beheld the hills recede,
The play-paths of my childhood, and through tears
The cot where roses hung and Erno dwelt.
O how I mourned the maiden ! Day and night,

In sun and rain, my heart was sad for her;
And every wave which washed the vessel's side
Would murmur, "Erno!" I have suffered thirst,
Cold, nakedness, and hunger: savage men
Have been my rude companions, and my feet
Bled with excessive travel. Once a bear,
Warm from his bolster, rushed forth for a meal,
And I escaped aim favoured by a tree.
In this great storm our ship was overwhelmed ;
But more I need not mention. Know you now
If my dear mother lives, and Erno too,
My sister and my father?
Meena (rushing into his arms). Precious boy,
Behold thy loving mother! Let this kiss
                              [*She kisses him.*
Suffice for thee that tenderness like mine
Is not extinguished by the winter winds
Or frosts of dark December. Frowns may drop
Like two-edged swords upon a mother's soul,
Lean-featured Want confront her on the way,
The cry of hunger murmur through her house,
The night of separation fill the void,
And those she bore neglect her,—but her love
Outlives the fire, the flood, the fever's touch,
The flight of days. the changing hues of years,
The blast of desolation, and survives
The roughest rigour and the keenest care.

SCENE—*A narrow valley.* TIME—*Evening.* Enter
RIDO and ERNO.

Rido. Does not this mound of moss with ferns o'erhead,
And at our feet the river, seem a shrine
Where lovers worship when the moon is young?
List to the waters ! What a low sweet hymn
They murmur forth upon the ear of Eve !
I never heard the wavelets washing so.
Methinks the reeds are harpers, and the flowers
Upon its margin throng with tuneful elves.
It is thy presence, Erno ! all the earth
Is music where thou walkest. and thy steps
Are pretty poems musical as May.
The sorrows of my life, my wrong, my woe,
My parting struggle, my distress and fear,
Hardship and hunger, bonds, imprisonment,
Stripes, shipwreck, travel.—all appear as nought,
Light as the seed-down wafted by the wind,
Now thou art with me. O ! thy precious smile
Uplifts me like the morning, and the light
Of thy dear eyes imparteth second life.
Bend on me now another tender gaze,
Like those bestowed by angels. Seas of bliss
Smile in the distance, on whose silver tide
Sail ships of merchandise and vessels fair,
From climes where blaze the topaz ; on their shores
Are trees of orange, grape, and cinnamon,
Where birds of every colour flutter free,
And rich fruits ripen for us. In our bark
We'll float among the islets where the rose
Dips in the crystal water, and the world
With lovely Erno shall be Paradise !
Such tenderness doth now abide with me,
'Tis Paradise already, and the sky
And earth and ocean burn with hues Divine.
Come, love, a little nearer. One kiss more,
One goblet of pure nectar, and we leave
This holy place where cherubim abide,

And ere another moon shall gild with light
The ivy of the chapel, we shall be
One in our joys and sorrows.
Erno.   It is sweet
To hear the falling waters, and afar
The murmur of the forest, the rich song
From yonder cottage window, where a girl
Sings at her sewing ; but my Rido's voice
Is more delicious, far more exquisite :
Nor find I on the teeming earth around
The faintest shadow of similitude.
I revel in the future, which spreads out
In lawn and shining laurel. Let it be
As Rido willeth !   [*Singing in the distance.*

How many homes in every land
Made sacred by the household band,
Where prayer arose when night had fled
And friendship's smile was hourly shed,
Have had their altars overthrown
By darkly, deadly drink alone !

How many wives in England dear
For ever shed the bitter tear,
On whom the winds and rains have power
In scanty clothing hour by hour,
Whose hopes and hearths are overthrown
By darkly, deadly drink alone !

How many damsels bright and fair,
With flashing eyes and flowing hair,
A brother's pride, a mother's stay,
A father's prop when hairs are grey,
Now sleep beneath the churchyard stone
By darkly, deadly drink alone !

Then let us aid as best we may
To lift this cruel curse away,
The source of untold wrongs and cares,
The darkest blot which England bears,—
To such unkind proportions grown,—
The darkly, deadly drink alone !   [*Exeunt.*

SCENE—*Farmhouse in an orchard.* TIME—*Noon.*
Enter RIDO, ERNO, MEENA, her DAUGHTER and
HUSBAND.

Meena's Husband.   Bright and blessed time !
I need not tell you that my happiness
Is only now completed. I have been
Like some lone traveller floundering through a marsh,
And every plunge, drawn by the *will-o'-the-wisp,*
Increased my blindness. Dawn at last appeared,
And then day broke along the splendid skies ;
The green trees clapped their hands; and from the reeds
The rills sent up an anthem. I beheld
The glowing landscape, and rejoiced to feel
The healing breezes. O, what music rose
From valleys new-created, where the dews
Of morning glittered on a thousand flowers !
Bright birds of beauty flashed along the lakes,
And winged the woody mountains. The strong chain
I forged myself with liquid links of fire,
And wrapped so tightly round me, was rent off
And hurled into the darkness. I went forth
Without my shackles. The Almighty King
Has sent His angel, and the lion's mouth

Is closed on me for ever. My dear wife,
So crushed with care and watching, now revives
In social sunshine, kindled by our love.
Unnumbered blessings on her! When the waves
Of bitter waters rolled her hopes away,
And she sat cold and hungry, shedding tears
As salt as sin can mingle; when the heavens
Were brass above her, and the earth was ice,
And I drank on in spite of fearful dreams
And shrieks and visions; her affection burned
As steadily as starlight. Words of scorn
And bitter menace, rough as raging fire
And rude as thunder, could not quench the flame
Or thrust the idol from its saintly throne.
She watched for me when night-newts were abroad,
And phantoms throng the moorlands, when the bats
Float by old ruins, and the churchyard gates
Creak in the silence, and bold chanticleer
Proclaims the day-streak. Yes, she watched for me
With tears upon the furrows of her face,
And hunger in her bosom. Then her love
Won me to deep repentance. I stole forth,
And kissed her brow, and bade her hope and live.
She smiled as angels do, and I shed tears,
And lifted up a cry to the great God
For help in time of need; and succour came.
Thou knowest this, my Meena. Like a plant,
Long trodden in the mire, now lifted up
And cherished and restored, so dost thou raise
Thy gladdened eyelids to another morn.
Meena has saved me with the power of love.
How beautiful along this fallen world
Stands lovely woman, perfect in herself!
Her footsteps leave a sweetness where they pass,
And cheer the desert like the gentle rain,
Refreshing man with visions of the skies.
Without her earth would have small trace of heaven.
Rido. The trees which bend above us seem to bear
A record of our pleasure, and the birds
Are full of grateful welcomes. For my part,
I feel like one surprised with sudden calm
After a night of tempest most intense.

Erno makes May, and May is beautiful.
A thousand blessings on that holy man,
Who, in the chapel by the torrent's track,
Twined the white bonds about us, love-impelled,
To be unravelled with the hand of death.
Meena. My husband gives to you these fruitful lands,
Orchards, and tenements,—an uncle's gift.
Bequeathed by will: enjoy them and live long.
We have enough to last life's passage out,
And satisfy the sexton. Darkness reigns
Throughout the night, but at the morning's dawn
Joy lieateth on the sunbeams.

[*Singing in the distance.*

The wells are clear, the rivers free,
A glory hangs upon the sea;
A mystery fills the shady wood,
Expands the flower, unfolds the bud,
By lonely cave or fountain's brink:
But earth is darkened by the drink.

The heavens receive a solemn strain
From waste and water, mount and main;
And notes of sweetness float along
Where hamlets chant their vesper-song.
And sparrows 'neath the thatch-roof clink:
But earth is darkened by the drink.

The seasons speak by moor and mead,
That he who runs may ever read;
Their voices rise in holy lays,
However long or short the days,
When skies are black or moonbeams blink:
But earth is darkened by the drink.

Yet comes the time when love shall reign
From vale to vale, from plain to plain;
When strife and hate shall be o'erthrown,
And peace extend from zone to zone,
When truth shall conquer link by link,
Nor earth be darkened by the drink.

[*Exeunt.*

THE LAND'S END.

PART I.

.. es, there are voices, echoes of
the Past,
That rise from old Earth's silent
solitudes,
And sound along the crowded courts of
men.
They flow among the roses of the spring.

On the stream's wavelets, in the wooing winds,
And n id the fresh drops of the vernal shower.
They ride upon the coursers of the storm,
Wail round the ruins of the lonely shed,
And murmur by the cold forsaken hearth.
They float upon the billows of the deep,
Or howl among the breakers near to land:
They tremble in the flowing forest-odes,
And sing beneath the hamlet's spreading trees,
When morn is breaking, or the early Eve
Calls home the swallow 'neath her dusky robe:

M

Or when old Night is walking with the stars,
The earth is full of utterances sublime.

For me the rocks have language, and I've thought,
When gazing on those lichened chroniclers,
So stony-still, like giants clad in mail,
And slumbering on in awful dreaminess,
Of wondrous things that walk below the moon,
And feed on night-winds by the coppice-cave,
Or drink the dew from woven cups of moss,
Or dance upon the gilded lily leaves,
Or swing within the chalice of the flowers,
And glide around with golden imagery.
Nor gaze I on those hoary sentinels,—
By field or fell, by castle or by cliff,
Lone in the waste, or by the village stream,
Or piled in dreadful heaps, crag over crag,
Like those around the wondrous Loggan Rock,
Bare in the sunlight, dimly scanned at eve,
Tissued with moonbeams, garnished with the stars,
Or frowning 'neath the sable weeds of night,—
But tones of olden times come back again,
With dreams of song and visions of romance.

I walked the storm-swept, boulder-bound Land's End,
And mused within its sea-washed galleries,
Whose granite arches mock the rage of Time.
I revelled in the mystery of its shades,
And my soul soared up on the wings of song.
I treasured up the lore the sea-gulls taught,
Which in white clouds were cooing to the breeze.
I quaffed the music of this granite grove,
And read rude cantoes in the book of crags,
When morn was breaking, and the light-house seemed
An angel in the waters, and the rocks
Rang to the music of a thousand throats.
I looked upon it as an awful poem,
Writ with the fingers of the Deity,
Whilst the proud billows of the mighty deep
Rolled on their crests the awful name of God.

Who told thee that the scenes of other lands
Were far more beautiful than aught in mine?
Who told thee that the soothing sounds of song
Fell on the ear from classic fields afar
More musical than down our thymy braes?
Who told thee that the Alps and Apennines
Had more of wildness in their very names
Than all the wonders of our Cornish coast?
Ramble among our valleys, climb our hills,
Gaze on our bulwarks red at setting sun,
Mark well our bays strewn with the whitest sand,
Muse on our moors, and wonder in our mines;
Linger among our ivy-covered walls:
List the sweet breezes playing through the ferns,
Where sings the robin, and o'erhead the lark;
Stand by our castles and our monuments,
Our towns and hamlets and religious fanes;
And look upon the dark-green rocks that lie
Beneath the Atlantic surges, or on those
That tower on high in awful craggy peaks,
Rolling eternal diapasons wild
To the great billows' bass; and when within
The pillared grotto of the famed Land's End,
Bethink thee of the scenes of other shores,
And let thy heart be friendly to mine own.

Oft in my sleep I've trod the land of dreams,
And worshipped mid its still sublimity.
I've climbed the back of some dark jagged cloud,
Rolling through chaos; and methought I've heard
The breathing spirit of infinity.
I've wandered by clear streamlets far away,
Which seemed more musical than aught of earth;
I've travelled valleys starred with radiant flowers,
And wept upon my silent harp for joy;
I've scaled black mountains where the huge rocks rose
In grim array, a ghostly multitude,
Lifting their rough heads to the icy moon,
And shivering there in silent majesty;
And I have walked among them joyously,
Feasting my spirit on their visioned forms,
And then, awaking, wondered 'twas a dream.
But when I found me on the rough Land's End,
Conning the numbers which the winds and waves
Had channelled on its pillars, not a dream
But seemed outrivalled by this craggy host.

Time plucks the coronet from kingly brows,
And scathes the laurel in the wreath of fame;
The glory of man's greatest work departs,
And o'er it drops the drapery of decay.
The hero, and the hero's blazoned deeds,
Though carved in marble, drizzled o'er with blood,
From memory fade, and shrink into the dark.
The fancy-palace built up by the bard
With its own echoes breaks and disappears;
But those eternal everlasting rocks
Sing the same cadence to the solemn sea,
And stand up strangely in their bright shell-cloaks,
With their great Maker's name upon their tongues,
As when King Arthur to the midnight marsh
Resigned his diamond-girt Excalibar.

The morn is breaking, and the daylight flows
Among those bearded bards, and from the sea
A freshness and a melody uprise
Which seem to tremble from another sphere.
A pretty boy is playing by the peak,
A rosy little fellow, and the lark
Is wooing him to imitate his song.
He whistles wildly to the poet-bird
With eyes uplifted, while his flaxen locks,
Sparkling with dew-drops, stream upon the breeze.
He has no brother, and his sister fell,
When putting forth her earliest leaflets green,
Beneath the sickle of the world's great foe.
Thus sisterless and brotherless he plays
Upon the down, deeming the wondrous earth
A glowing garden of unplucked delight.

Sometimes he sits upon the mossy mounds
That fill our moors like hillocks o'er our chiefs,
Weaving the rushes into little boats,
In imitation of the fisher's craft,
Straining his eyeballs o'er the rolling sea,
And wondering where the bounding billows rise,
And why they lash the cliffs for evermore,
And why the ships come sailing every day,
And where they swim to on that great blue pool;
And if the moon's home is upon the waves,
Or if the red sun on his evening car
Goes down into the brine depths fathomless,
To rise again on t' other side the world;

And when the wild winds howl among the rocks,
And the sea-foam is hurried o'er his head,
And sounds of sorrow fill the furious air,
Sporting among the muttering elements,
He seems to dally with the angry storm.

Thus lived the boy, the scion of the hills,
A wanderer in this rocky wilderness;
And there were breathings which he sweetly heard
At morn, and noon, and softened evening-time;
Mysterious throbbings of the outer world
To the young heart within. From flowers they came
That tipped the hedge-rows round his reedy lodge,
From limpid runnels chiming down the cliffs,
From pebbles polished by the restless wave,
From birds and breezes mid the waving corn,
From rocks and rushes and the hollow reeds,
Or rising from the gorse-brakes wooingly:
And oft, when playing in the shell-paved rifts,
These mystic monitors addressed his soul.

In a low hut among luxuriant ferns,
Where heath is plentiful and rocks abound,
Near a deep bay not far from the Land's End,
Dwelt the fond parents of this lonely lad.
His father was a famous fisherman,
And knew the secrets of the finny tribe.
His mother carolled at her spinning-wheel,
Turning the hour-glass with its drifting sands.
She kissed the forehead of her little one,
And bade him cheerfully to go and play.
He rode their pony o'er the prickly down,
And gathered grasses for him by the spring;
And father praised the boldness of his boy.
But words of admonition or reproof
Were never uttered in that youngling's ear,
And soon he wandered from his native hearth.
And as we journeyed from the Loggan Rock
Away, away towards the famed Land's End,
Up hill and down hill, through the muddy moors,
And over heath-crofts, 'gainst a driving mist
Which wrapped the mountains in a dropping shroud,
Stopping the harvester amid his sheaves,
And hiding Nature's wonders from our ken;
Two weary worn pedestrians, pilgrim-aimed;
We glanced among the noisy peasant-lads,
Thinking he once had played in these old lanes,
And rode his pony o'er those misty mounds.
The crooked hedges, as we passed along,
Seemed full of tongues as well as searching eyes;
And murmurs straggled from the ferny brakes,
From brambled dykes and rippling rushy pools,
And clambered over ruins ivy-clad,
And rose from plants upon the ancient stones,
And rolled along the highway of the waves,
And walked the chambers of the summer air.

In a lone vale, a few miles to the south,
An old tin-streamer dwelt, who long had been
The hoary oracle of all the hinds.
The dells he ransacked for the precious ore,
Delving and digging with huge might and main.
Large boots he wore when standing in the stream,
Washing the dirt, to find the polished grain;
Boots reaching to his knee, with wooden taps,
And upper leather almost bullet-proof:
And when the clouds were heavy, and thick showers

Pattered upon the pools, he shelter found
Within his peat-shed by the reedy dyke,
Covered with rushes chopped up by his spade.
A little girl lived with him, like a flower
Among the rough rocks of this western wild.
Tradition says, he found her by the sea,
And reared her up to cheer his lonely life:
For he no mother had, or wife, or babe;
And so she called him father, which he loved.
She brought his dinner to him at the stream,
And sat down with him in his rushy hut,
While he devoured it with an eager zest,
Giving a portion to the little one.
She climbed upon his knees, smoothed his thin locks,
And kissed him as she left him at his work;
And when the shades of evening gathered round,
And the red sun seemed sinking in the sea,
Before the redbreast crept into the bush,
She ran to meet and lead him to his home.

The boy, all brightness, playing on the down,
When life was budding, left his father's roof,
And found a home within the streamer's shed.
He ate his brown loaf off the old man's board,
And drank the milk his speckled goats supplied.
He slept upon the ground-floor of his cot,—
The only floor that hollow dwelling had,—
And dreamt till morning brought him to his meal.
He laboured with the old man at the stream,
And chatted to him at his honest work:
He jogged home with him at the close of day,
And seemed to love him much more than his sire:
And when at evening in the chimney-nook,
The huge old chimney full of smouldering peat,
Whilst the old man was smoking dreamily,
He glanced into the pretty maiden's eyes,
As if he saw a thousand wonders there.

Sometimes they stole into the silent carn,
Mid mossy hedges and low banks of thyme,
To gather whortle-berries from the brake:—
Not altogether for the fruitage sweet.
Sometimes they wandered by the limpid stream,
While she in beautiful simplicity
Sang to the waters that went singing by:—
Not altogether that the waves might bear.
Sometimes they chatted in the lowly dell,
What time the cuckoo sang his wandering song,
Pulling the blue-bells wet with evening dew:—
Not altogether for their love of flowers.
Sometimes they sat upon a rising knoll,
Where the wood-sorrel blinks among the ferns,
Watching the sunbeams stream upon the earth,
Themselves as beautiful as rays at dawn.
Thus they grew up together year by year,
As much in love as blossoms and the light.

It cheers the soul, when angry storms are gone,
To breathe the quiet of the soothing calm:
It fills the mind with high poetic glow
To press the foot-marks of earth's gifted ones:
It gives the flow of thought a keener zest
To hear the trickling waters after rain:
It adds a beauty to the beautiful,
When eyes of love are mingling with our own:
It warms the spirit's innermost recess
To view the picture-halls of snowy eld:

M 2

It stirs the deepest fountains of the soul
To list the rolling echoes of the past.
So thought I in this rocky citadel,
Stretched on the moss in morning's early light,
While round me th ronged a thousand mysteries.

I musing lay amid the marvellous,
While the blue breakers bounded at my feet,
And the wild sea-birds screamed to me of wreck
And sad disaster by the Lady's Rock,
And fearful drownings in those ghostly rents.
O, if old Johnson's Head had but a tongue,
What chapters would it chatter, till the flowers
Wept at December's dismal tragedies!
I lay among the golden buds and bells
And meads of camomile and fragrant song,
When morning breezes chimed their instruments,
And larks were singing at the gates of dawn ;
And down upon this host of stony bards
A gentle breathing fell, a soothing calm,
Which seemed to flow into my inner soul.
Then Fancy led me past those hoary kings
To my low cottage by the streamlet's rim,
Where oft the Muses deign to visit me,
And oft the song of thankfulness is heard ;
And other rocks and other rills uprose,
And other scenes came crowding on my brain.
The bower I love, the paths across the peak,
The streams all fringed with boyhood's fairest gems,
The meads that slope adown my mountain's side,
The rugged ruins on its furrowy crest,
The friends that winter with me on the moor,
The few choice books that stand upon my shelves,
The mine whose caverns mock my smothered groans,
And, in the churchyard by the ivied wall,
The small green grave of my beloved one.—
All marshalled round me musing on the moss ;
And as my tears fell on those craggy leaves,
I started up to travel on my way.

My heart is wounded, and it will not heal :
I pray not that it should ; no, let it bleed.
The world is cruel ; there's relief in tears ;
I pour them out upon the far Land's End.
Methought a spirit winged and glistering
In Eden vesture sat upon the rocks,
And cried, " All flesh is grass, and like the flower
So fade away the beautiful of earth.
All flesh is grass.   The prophets, where are they ?
And where the fathers of an ancient age ?
Ay, where the travellers of the mighty past,
Who roamed among those fearful trumpeters,
And drank the echoes of this mammoth choir ?
Gone like the exhalations from the fen !
The truly wise obey their Maker's voice,
And love the Being that created them,
They arm themselves to meet the fleshless foe,
Ere he overtake them mid the damps of time.
All flesh is grass."   And the Atlantic waves
Thundered the spirit's dirge, " All flesh is grass."

PART II.

Haunt of the sea-bird, city of the crag,
Kingdom of granite, gallery of the Muse,
Poem of wonders, page for poet's eye,—
Storm-brewing chamber, whence the winds are loosed
That crack and tumble through the universe.—
Nature's great organ-hall, where blasts of song
Shiver among her mossy-mantled priests,
And swell across the mountains and the vales,
Thundering at storm-time, murmuring in the calm,
Flowing at day-dawn, rumbling through the dark,
And crashing mid the music of the main,
Stirring the soul's depths like a lofty psalm.
When standing here with Nature and with God !
How thy full chorus lifts the wanderer !

The Cornish streamer was a rare old man :
Strange stories by the firelight he would tell,
When angry winds went roaring round the rocks,
And not a star looked down upon the snow.
His audience were the petted girl and boy,
And on the oak-stock's end the favourite cat.
Strange stories bordering on the marvellous :—
How once these valleys were brim-full of tin,
Before King Solomon's great fane was built,
When Jews did smelt within those curious coves ;
And oft a streamer's fortune had been made
By stumbling on a Jews'-house wonderful ;
Of giants living in those mighty rocks,
With heaps of pearl and waggon-loads of gold ;
Of shining creatures coming from the sea,
And making poor men richer far than kings ;
Of horses running swifter than the winds,
And bearing fiery comets on their backs ;
Of little pixies, wearing small red cloaks,
And mightily riding timid wights to death ;
Of wizards changing brands to silver bars ;
Of fiery dragons rolling through the air,
Uprising from old Cornwall's copper-caves :
And one dark evening, when the winds were high,
And the fierce lightnings hissed across his shed,
And thunder rumbled up the steep Land's End,
He filled his pipe and told these cheerful tales :—

" I knew an old man living in a cave :
White locks had he, white as the winter snow ;
And he was washed here on a vessel's wreck ;
He told of countries where gold nuggets lay
As thick as pebbles roll upon our beach ;
Of towering trees, whence honey sweetly gushed ;
Of forests with the fragrant cedar filled,
Where birds of every colour sat and sang ;
Of boats, whose rowers handled golden oars,
And played on instruments of orient dye ;
Of strange men strutting round in silver boots,
And wearing silver caps upon their heads ;
Of little ponies drawing silver ploughs,
And lazy labourers plying silver spades ;
Of ladies clad in robes of glittering gold,
And bearing vessels studded o'er with gems.
And once I saw him with a golden wedge
A dark chief gave him in this fabled isle.
And as he came, so passed this hoary man :
One wild November night he sailed away

Upon a portion of a stranded ship.
I've heard my granny, older than the pines,
In linen cap, and hooded cloak of red,
When cowering o'er the smouldering brands of wrecks,
Say, how into the west a wizard came,
And told the miller's man a silver tongue
Was hidden by a hawthorn in the vale;
And if he travelled there at dead of night,
Nor spake one word to any whom he met,
And dug the earth up with his fingers' ends,
He'd find this strange thing 'neath the prickly tree.
He went and dug, and found no silver tongue,
But heaps of gold, and chests of glittering coin."

That night the bright boy slept not; through his brain
A thousand thoughts were wandering, and his soul
Drank from the founts which stole o'er golden sands.
So when the light of morning clothed the hills,
And thatcher whistled on the reedy eaves,
And Colin carolled in the clover meads,
What time the sparrow shook him from his rest,
Awakened by the mower's rustling scythe,
He started up, and bade adieu to all.
But as he hasted down the rocky road
Which slid into the valley awkwardly,
He looked behind him, and the maiden ran
To pour the streamer's blessing on his head,
And shake hands with him by the violet-bank.
She said, "When absent, shall I be forgot?" "No."
And Edwin wiped his eyes, and murmured, "No."

Within the gold dells of a fabled clime
The young man wrought and prospered. Year by year,
He added something to his little store,
With which he hoped to cheer the loving maid.
He heard her voice among the giant trees,
And saw her image in the crystal lakes.
The unknown flowers, with dew upon their lids,
All spake of her, and told him of her love:
The gorgeous birds that sang upon the boughs
Made the hills ring with her beloved name:
The rivers rolled it to the wandering winds,
Which trilled it back upon his eager ear:
It sighed among the thickets, and it sobbed
In the sweet murmurs of the summer eve.
So, after years of absence which had made
His love the stronger, gathering up his all,
He stepped into a vessel far away,
And turned his face towards his dear Land's End.

The sky is blue, the earth is beautiful,
A gentle gale flows sweetly from the shore,
And, though November, 'tis a quiet time.
A ship comes up the Channel; all her sails
Are filled with wind and spread before the breeze;
The sailors idly lounge upon the deck,
And carol songs of rising fatherland.
But in the black rifts of that wandering cloud
The spirits of the angry elements
Are brewing mischief in their airy caves.
Another hour, and all things wear a change.
The gulls are flying shorewards, and the leaves
Are flapping on the branches. The wild winds
Now wrestled fiercely with a strife insane.
The huge black billows bounded o'er the rocks,
Until the Light-House seemed a hill of foam.
The sea-birds screamed; the pitchy night came on;

The ship heaved in the waters awfully;
A sea stove in her starboard, and away
Went binnacle and compass in the deep.
The captain shrieked in agony of soul.
"Lost, lost!" and the wild storm howled, "Lost!"
Great consternation fell on all the crew;
And when consulting whither they should steer,
The life-blood curdled in their freezing veins
To hear those awful words, "Breakers a-head!"
And the next moment she was on a rock.
The sea beat over her with furious howl;
Her masts went one by one, her bowsprit split,
Her rudder was rent off, and the wild waves
Rushed through her bottom with terrific roar;
Despair seized all; the sailors were confused,
And to the rigging clung the passengers.
A wild shriek rose,—the vessel split in two,
And hills of foam rolled o'er the Indiaman.

How rapid are the changes of the earth!
How fall the mighty, and how sink the brave!
Death still devours his millions at a meal,
On sea and land, above ground and below.
With stealthy step he strides along even here,
And reaps his harvests mid those granite hills.
The flight of years, the withering blasts of time,
Have acted on the dwellers of those cliffs,
And left them mouldering on their hurried march,
Or charged from boyhood into manhood's form,
While those huge heaps still wear the vest of youth.
The story-telling streamer is no more:
The little girl he picked up on the sands
Is grown to womanhood, and lives among
The healthy farmers of those western wilds;
And on the evening of that stormy night
Which made the sea so fretful, she had climbed
A heathy hillock, gazing on the ship,
And wondering if the boy of other days,
Whose image she has worn within her heart,
Was coming back to bless her with his love.

"Why art thou lingering thus, my loving one?
How long I've waited for thee! Spring has passed.
And other springs have put forth other leaves,
And summer after summer taken flight;
But still thou comest not. I had plucked for thee
A bunch of violets from our parting-bank;
But they have long since withered. Come away!
My eyes are dim with watching for my love.
And day and night I feed upon his name.
My couch is wet with weeping, and the earth
Is cloaked with shadows, dying in his light.
O, is he in that ship? If it were so,
How quickly would my feet be on the foam!

"Last night I dreamt we wandered on a hill,
To take our farewell of the setting sun,
Which sank before us like a golden globe.
A lone thrush whistled on an aged thorn,
And by the fountain sang the village maids.
A pilgrim, leaning on his knotty staff,
Whose white locks floated in the evening breeze,
Carolled his vespers, moving o'er the marsh.
Methought my Edwin pressed my hand in his,
And kissed my cheek,—the dew is on it still,—
And gazed into the galleries of mine eyes
So tenderly, so kind and lovingly,

That very quickly they were blind with tears.
And then he talked to me of foreign fields,
Of countries strange, of perils on the deep,
Of home, sweet home, among those mineral hills,
And future happiness when we were one.
Methought his voice was like an angel's lyre.
But when the moon came sudden on my sight,
Like a chaste vestal wandering on her way,
My loving Edwin vanished from my side,
And I awoke, loud calling on his name.

"How oft at sunset have my weary feet
Climbed up this rugged path! How oft I've strained
My aching eyeballs o'er the glassy sea,
Watching the ships that near my native strand.
Another comes, with white sails fully spread;
And is my Edwin gazing from the deck
Upon the rude hills of his rough birth-land?
O Thou great Builder of the universe,
The God, the Guide of all created things,
Who studded heaven with stars, the earth with flowers,
The sea with isles, its hidden caves with gems,
And filled the air with music exquisite!
I worship on my knees among the dews;
I lift my hands, my heart, my soul to Thee!
O spare the mariner, my Edwin spare,
And lead him home to fatherland and me!"

Yes, he was in that bark; his eyes e'en then
Beheld the white cliffs of his own dear land,
Whilst tears of thankfulness ran down his cheek.
Kind Providence had blessed him far away
With gold and silver and the choicest gems,
And home he came to share it with his love.
Then Memory stood beside him on the deck,
And bade him look upon her gilded scroll,
The panorama of his early life,—
His first old home, the fisher's home of thatch,
His play-morn on the common near the sea,
The tunes he whistled labouring at the stream,
Old stories heard here many years ago,
And, rising like an angel on his gaze,
The girl he loved in darkness and in light.
'Twas on the eve of merry Hallowe'en,
When after long, long years the hills of home
Rose on the vision of the voyager.
Then Hope stood by him like a damsel fair,
And drew the curtain of the future back,
When dazzling images burst on his sight:
Where he had played upon the echoing down,
A polished villa rose, with flowers and shrubs,
And laurel walks, and sweet laburnum bowers.
Within a parlour, reading the good Book,
The western floweret sat, his life's bright star,
With matron meekness shining in her face;
While round him danced his laughing little ones.
But he was startled from his sunny trance
By howling billows struggling with the storm,
The crash of shipwreck, and the shriek of dread.

The stout bark in the anger of the gale
Writhed like a living thing, and then the winds
Twitched her in pieces with tremendous rage,
And hurled the fragments howling on the rocks,
Or drove them shivering high upon the heath.
Edwin is riding mid the seething waves,

Which ope their foamy mouths and moan for prey,
And snap the ringing crags: lo! Edwin rides
Upon a portion of the wrenched mainmast,
Which dashed him fainting 'neath the cliff's high brow.
With mighty effort he climbed up the crags,
And sat above the beating of the sea
By the same hillock where at set of sun
The faithful maiden knelt and prayed for him
Who now, half-dead, lay bruised upon the turf,
Lone in the darkness, till the light of morn
Fell like enchantment on this rocky world,
And the first thing the shipwrecked youth beheld
Was the fair Eda, his soul's dearest life.

Imagine what he felt. A sudden light
Seemed shed upon him from the hills of heaven.
He gazed like one awoke from some sweet dream;
And, gazing long, he knew her. They embraced
And parted, and full soon embraced again,
And kissed each other in the rosy light,
And wept and smiled, gazed long, embraced again,
O'ercome with sweetest transport. Then he told
The sad slow story of his own distress,—
How the great sea had glutted all his store,
And tossed him naked on his native strand,
With nothing left her but his heart's true love.

"Lament not that thy treasure is concealed
In solemn ocean's silent house of shells.
Adversity may strip thee of thy all,
And poverty may freeze thee with its frost.
Thy love is what my hungry soul requires.
Ay, should we travel o'er this barren world
In beggar's weeds, 'twere Eden with thy love.
O, let me kiss the tear-drops from thy face,
And smooth thy ringlets wet with ocean's brine,
And bless thee with the yearnings of my heart.
I have the streamer's savings in my trunk:
'Twill throw a sunshine o'er our future path.
How pale thou lookest, love! Come, come away."

And now, Land's End, the pilgrims would return;
The voice of duty summons from the shore.
Yet let me linger 'neath thy rugged robes,
And kiss thy forehead golden with the dawn.
I thank thee for the breeze thou givest me,
Fresh, full, and flowing with eternal song.
I thank thee for the visions which the Muse
Has seen among thy channelled monuments.
I thank thee that I ever turned aside
From life's rough track and plunged into thy calm,
Awed by the lore of ocean's lofty voice.
The Almighty's name is pencilled on thy flowers,
And deeply graven on thy granite leaves,
Glittering within the mosses of thy vest,
And rolling through the thunders of thy harp.
I leave thee with a bright thought in the bud,
And on my eyelash a fresh falling tear.
There's much that thrilled me in thy eloquence,
And drew the waters from my flowing soul.
Thy aspect, like the face of faithful friend,
Will often cheer me mid life's weariness;
And when I'm gasping in the smoky mine,
And pining for the fresh breeze of the hills,
Thy wind-awakened melodies shall soothe
My panting spirit like the song of hope.

RADO REEF.

DRAMATIS PERSONÆ.

RADO REEF . . . . *The reformed Inebriate.*
POLLY PEER . . . . *The Story-teller.*
PHILIP REEF . . . . *Son of Rado Reef.*
MYLA . . . . . . *An Orphan Maiden.*
FLOWER GIRL . . . *Daughter of Rado Reef.*
POOR WOMAN . . . *Wife of Ditto.*
CHILDREN OF RADO REEF, SINGERS, ETC.

SCENE — *A sea-port.*
TIME — *Noontide.* RADO
REEF *walking from the
quay.*

Rado Reef. How longs my soul for
quiet! Like a spar
On the wild waters where the rocks
are rude,
Now wafted landward, now drawn
back again,
Bleached, blackened, bended, scarred
with jostlings huge
Into the boiling billows,—so am I
Upon the sea of trouble. Mates, farewell
For a long season! and our own good ship,
Which bore me safely, unimpaired by leagues
And change of seasons, heat and piercing cold,
Hailstone and thunder, o'er the endless deeps,
From clime to clime and distant isle to isle,
Until the years wore on, like silken threads
Unravelled by Time's fingers, fare thee well!
We part like brothers when the harvest fails
And provender is little. In my heart
I'll wear thee like a jewel, though the surge
Of the world's warfare welter to my feet.
But who is this in cloak of crimson drest,
And curious long-shaped bonnet, creeping down
The narrow lane that leads into the wood?
'Tis Polly Peer, or I am not alive;
Old Polly Peer, the story-telling dame,
Who lived in a reed cottage on the earn,
Built with rude boulders, with one boulder stack

And two quaint-casements. How we loved to sit
The twilight out beneath her cottage-eaves,
Whilst she her knitting handled, listening much
To histories tinged with fiction, though we deemed
In boyish rapture they were sterling truth!
I'll much my footsteps quicken, and perchance
Shall soon o'ertake her. Thus I walk the world.
[*He overtakes her.*
Good day to Polly! Let me have your hand,
The same that stroked my curls by boyhood worn
When other summers filled the earth with joy.
Well met where roses cluster! I have been
A wanderer from my kindred, with no rest,
No solid footing; now upon the sea,
Driver like a vapour; now upon the land,
Toiling and wasting. Yes, your eyes are dim.
Wipe from your spectacles those grains of dust,
And then survey me. Ah! I know I am changed
As much as man can be; this bushy beard,
These cheeks of bronze, and brow where furrows hide,
Are not like Rado Reef's. But I am he,
Come back to home once more.
Polly Peer. A welcome then
With all the warmth of age! My strength is changed
Since thou hast left us, and is changing still;
My knees are weaker, weaker are my hands,
And my feet fail me, while my feeble gaze
Deals oft in fiction, and the trees go round
The fields and hedges ; but my heart's the same.
I welcome Rado back to home and rest.
Rado Reef. To rest thou sayest? let me find it so,
And ease my wanderings, though it may not come,
Shut out of Saturn. How the love of home
Burns in my bosom standing by this stile,
And overpowers me like the rush of song
From master spirits! See, the road-side trees
Reach out their arms of greeting, and the leaves,
Shook with the murmur of the gentle air,
Are like melodious voices heard at eve
When the dew droppeth, each a welcome home.
The faces of the hills assume no change ;
Their sun-crowned heads are lovely, and the vales
And shadowy hollows wear their ancient hues,
And great tarn-temples, while the little brook
Glides through the grass as ever. Where, O where,
Are those that loved me, father, mother, wife,
My sons and daughters? to the grave gone down
Where all is dust and darkness? Or alive

Breathe they upon these moorlands with sad thought
For him who grieved them, wandering from their fire?
He cometh! yes, he cometh with the tear
Of penitence unbottled. Knowest thou,
Good Polly Peer, aught of the suffering Reefs,
And where located?

Polly Peer.   Small my scrap of news,
And scarcely readable. Bethink I now
These voices by the fire one winter's eve,
When the great comet awed us, and the heavens
Seemed full of thrusting swords and horsemen huge
That pawed the staggering moon,—bethink I now
How through the darkness came a struggling voice,
" The Reefs are scattered!" Then my fire died out;
The flaming comet through the door of stars
Passed on its orbit, the white moon went down
Behind a sea of silence, and the morn,
Like a green hunter, travelled through the woods.
I listened near the lattice, and a rush
Passed by my grating, sharp as eagle's wing,
And in the rush the same mysterious words,
" The Reefs are scattered!" and I heard no more,
Save overhead the wailing of the wind
Which smote the thatch and left the rafters bare.
They travelled none knew whither. May'st thou have
Much joy in meeting!   [*Exit* POLLY PEER.

Rado Reef (soliloquizing). Let me say Amen,
Though with a faintness lagging from my lips!
But He who giveth darkness, bringeth light.
The Reefs are scattered! Yes, like lowering sparks
When Boreas blows the embers. Have I not
Passed through more anguish than my fellows share,
Riddled with doubt, and stunned with monster thrusts
From enemies in armour who came down
In sheets of mist and left me with the slain?
Have not the clouds of famine lowered their wings
And hemmed me in with barrenness and death?
Have I not stood among the naked peaks,
With arm uplifted, calling on the winds,
Whose war-trumps rattled through the rended skies,
To whirl their chariots, by the Furies drawn,
And I would ride with them through watery ways
Over the edge of the tremendous globe?
Have I not sat on ledges with my heels
Dangling o'er gulfs a hundred feet below,
Till the great burden of my loneliness
Drank the clear rill of reason, and I raved
Like one whose finger-tops were burnt with fire?
Have I not drifted on a doleful log,
Washed with the moaning waters, till my limbs
With the salt sea were hardened like a rock,
And my orbs gave no vision save quick gleams
Like wild-wood flashes? Have I not stood lone
And shivering in the tempest, craving help,
And earning thongs of hate and cords of jeer,
Till my knees smote together and my tongue
Declined its office, dry as withered leaf?
Have I not wept till tears would come no more,
And my hot temples burned with fever-pain,
And great sighs mocked each other as they rose?
And why all this? Ah! I have played the fool,
And the game overmatched me; down I fell,
To rise with ashes in my twisted hair.
I pressed the fire-cup to my heated lips,
And drank my senses wild. Oft was I warned
And oft entreated with the voice of love;
And yet I kept within this dangerous clime,

Where maniacs rove, and lords in foul attire,
And women dry and shrivelled, wrapped in weeds,
With fierce eyes flashing; merchants clad in rags,
With ruin on their foreheads, and good men,
Brought down to dust, raved by the boiling springs
Where herbage withered and the hollow earth
Was hot and smoking as a burning hill!
                     [*He still proceeds.*
No tears could move me, no appeals avail;
The voice of childhood charmed not: hunger-cries
And Famine's awful groan smote my deaf ear.
Winter and cold and nakedness and want
Lifted their hands in anguish, but no sound
Touched my seared spirit. Mid the ranks I reeled,
Where foaming tankards in foul fulness winked,
Till all my honour vanished, and my name
Was like a rag thrown to the muddy street.
My children starved, or begged, or died for me,
And curses pierced my wife like points of steel.
High Heaven was challenged: I could sink no more;
Then justice seized me. To avert its arm
I fled my native place, and far away
Sorrowed and sighed and sought the Lord in prayer,
Dashing the dregs of misery to the ground,
Trailing my chain of suffering, till the links
Left fearful channels which will never fill.
And now I come to seek those precious ones
Whom my shame bruised and bended, and a voice
Sobs from the moorland and the wide morass,
" The Reefs are scattered!" This the fruit of sin;
And I must reap what I have swiftly sown.
                            [*Exit.*

SCENE—*Path on the cliff.*—TIME—*Evening.* *Enter*
     PHILIP REEF *and* MYLA.

Philip Reef. Art thou an orphan in this world of wrong,
Drooping unpropped, like a luxurious rose
O'erfed with richness? Lean upon my arm:
I'll be thy glad supporter. Nevermore
Shall bramble wound thee when my hand is near,
Stone strike thy foot, or prickle pierce thy frame.
Dost thou remember our first meeting-place?
The moon was full just as she is to-night,
And in the woods the murmur had begun
Which comes at twilight, when from distant stars
Good spirits visit us with hymns of heaven;
Beside the lake, pulling white tufts of down
From bending rushes, thou alone didst stand.
My sheep were penned, and I was loitering home,
Humming an ancient ditty which describes
The blessedness of loving, when my feet
Bore me towards the mere. Beside a bank
With one hand on my crook lake-ward I looked,
And on the further side beheld thy face
Reflected in the water. Pardon me,
But I stood speechless, pulseless, feeling sure
It was an angel; nor was I deceived.
Thou art an angel, Myla, pure and good,
And wearing in thy soul the gem of truth.
I glided round and bade good eve to thee,
Met thy sweet gaze and wondered. Then I pulled
Some leathery rush-tufts, offering thee the whole,
Bringing the thanks upon thy pretty lips.
No farce was used, no artifice contrived;
But love grew up uncultured, growing on
Until the tree-boughs bend with ripened fruit.

The next eve found us there, and eve by eve.
The rest needs no narration. Here we are
In moonlight chambers where no sound is heard
But love's soft footfalls on the mossy floor,
Enriched with one another. Winds may howl,
Wild winters beat, huge thunders split the heavens,
But nought shall sever the eternal cord
That binds our souls together. Myla, speak !
Myla. Thou know'st my portion. Little birds have nests
And beasts their shelter : I have nothing here,—
No gold, no silver, no ancestral fame ;
Nought but a spirit overcharged with love
Which pours it out to bless thee. Seek'st thou more ?
Thou canst not have it, for I give thee all.
Philip Reef. I am contented, gladdened, overjoyed,
Delighted beyond language. My poor heart
Is like to burn with sunshine. In mine ears
Are shafts of music like the summer trees
Shake when the rose is brightest. This is love,
And gold to it is granite. These two hands,
If God gives health, shall bring whate'er we want ;
And kings can have no more. A shepherdess
Shall Myla be among the little hills,
And all the lambs shall love her. We will live
Where flowers are freshest by the waterfall,
And birds are building in the hollow glen
Where echo follows echo, dingle-born,
Attended by the seasons ; and our songs
Shall blend with morning matins and eve chimes.
The spreading globe in all its gear of green
Shall seem created for us : rivers, woods,
And rising mountains shall be ours alone.
On the weird heights we'll offer sacrifice
Of praise and prayer and loving gratitude,
Like priest and priestess. The great God above
Created us to cheer each other's hearts
Along the journey of our mortal life.
Thy mother sleeps where the lone belfry stands
With ivy arches, and the restless sea
Entombs thy father ; sister thou hast none,
Nor loving brother. I am these to thee ;
And more than brother, more than father, friend.
Rest thou on me, and I will bear thee up.
We met like two stray fawns where leaves were green,
Who sought companionship, and fondly found
A well to slake their thirst and food to cheer.
Our lives were lonely, till love's crown of flowers
Adorned thy temples ; then the weariness
Of winter vanished, and sweet spring returned,
And the glad turtle triumphed in the trees.
                                  [*He still proceeds.*
Thou know'st my father through the wine-cup fell,
And with him all our house. 'Twas a sad day
When mother wept, and little sisters sighed,
Because he went and never more returned.
We waited until midnight, and the moon
Bent down behind the castle ; then our tears
On the worn floor fell splashing, Food and fire
Were long extinguished, and no candle burned ;
And in the agony I plainly heard
Our hearts beat wildly. Morn awoke like fire
Where sand-plains widen, and my mother's voice
Rose in a shriek that scared the early bird,
" The deadly drink has triumphed !" She went wild,
And then they tore her from us. With my hands
On a lone hill held star-ward, I resolved
Never to taste the poison, that my drink

Should be the sparkling waters cool and pure
From Nature's fountains, which the midnight heard,
And the great darkness, spreading out its wings,
And over all the Presence of the heavens ;
And I have kept it, and I hope to keep
This earnest vow till silence sealeth all.
But, sea, a stranger ! On his face are lines
By travel written : he essays to speak.
Let's step behind these willows !
                        [RADO REEF *advancing.*
Rado Reef (aside).   It is sad
To lay our hopes in disappointment's tomb,
And bury up our prospects. It is sad
When early love is overborne by wrong,
Nipt with the hoar-frost of a sudden fall ;
And sad it is to tread our native land
After an absence of a few brief years,
And find no face to greet us. Such am I
Among my mountains, like some wandering bird
Which man can name not. Old familiar spots,
The spring, the lane, the seat beneath the vine,
The hamlet trees, the old barn near the stile,
The cottage where we dwelt when joy was ours
And bliss and blessing, seem to wear no smiles
Or looks of greeting. Why had I not died
Ere the great foe o'ercame me, and I fell
As falls a city when the earthquake roars ?
Beneath the ruins lay my little ones
And loving wife, with haughty heaps hemmed in ;
And when they crept into the searching light,
Their countenances altered, and they sat
Amid the wreck and moaned to the great moon,
Whose pale gleams showed their faces paler still.
Thick rains fell splashing down, the wild winds rent
Their hair in anger, thunder-echoes rolled,
Hunger and famine mocked them, their bare limbs
Stiffened with frost, and ice drank up their blood,
Whilst I stood swaggering by,—the cause of all,
Without one thought to help them. Wicked man !
The censer of His vengeance then o'erturned,
And my scorched spirit yielded. I went forth
To wet my bread with weeping, where the hills
Were smote with bitter blasts and cut with storms ;
And no man cared to take me by the hand,—
The weful wages the inebriate earns.
And now, unknown, where childhood lay in dreams,
And wove the web of fancy with bright threads,
Supremely golden, would I raise my voice
So that the farthest hill-tops catch the cry,
And the deep hollows all reverberate,
" Look not upon the wine when it is red ;
In it an adder coileth which will sting
Thy soul to sadness, shouldst thou not forbear!
Receive what nature giveth : fountains clear
And wells like crystal gushing at thy feet.
Receive it, and be grateful ; then thy life
Shall be as pure as the breeze-breathing roe
Or chamois of the fastness. Lofty thoughts
Shall visit thee at even, when the stars,
Those angel-ladders, throng the heights of space ;
And to the grave thou shalt at last go down,
Crowned with hoar hairs, the glory of thy lot."
                             [*Exit* RADO REEF.
Philip Reef. How like my father ! His warm words
                        were winged
With fire enough to shake me where I stood,
And bring the scalding tears upon my face.

N

I scarce refrained from rushing to his arms,
So strongly was I drawn, and a whole life
Seemed centred in a circle. This foretells
A future hung with fruitage, where bright streams
Glide over golden pebbles, and the lawns
With kine are studded for my love and me.
But, hark! a canzonet among the cliffs!
Lean on my arm and listen. [*Singing in the distance.*

 'Tis sad, 'tis sad, where all is gay,
 Where little children dance and play,
 Where old men talk and matrons sing,
 And maidens linger by the spring,
 Where tales of love and song have birth,
 To be a stranger at the hearth.

 The buds are bursting on the trees,
 The corn is springing in the leas,
 The swallow floateth o'er the plain,
 The wild rose bloometh in the lane,
 The valley-bowers are gay with mirth;
 But I'm a stranger at my hearth.

 The wren is twittering 'neath the leaves,
 The thatcher shaves the cottage-eaves,
 The lark is singing overhead,
 The flowers adorn the path I tread,
 The woodman trills of trodden worth;
 But I'm a stranger at my hearth.

 'Tis sad, 'tis sad, 'mid scenes so dear,
 Which witnessed many a pleasant year,
 And where I deemed my life would close
 In quietude and dear repose,
 To feel this sympathetic dearth,—
 A stranger at my native hearth. [*Exeunt.*

SCENE—*Ruin on the sea-shore.* TIME—*Noon.* RADO
REEF *amid the ivy.*

Rado Reef.   Much I love
To muse where ruin moulders, where the stones
And broken fragments lift their voice in sighs
For beauty bowed for ever. Every block
Where ivy fastens and smooth mosses blend
Is an historic chapter, graven o'er
With strange occurrence and unique event,
Which should command the study of the wise.
Our human hopes, our human plans and schemes,
And best contrivances, too often fail
Like these rent walls and loopholes. On the arch
Sits Desolation, with a mocking laugh
At his own mischief, huddled at his feet.
Is not this ruin emblematical
Of my poor state amid the ways of men?
I bring my sorrows to it. Full, my tears,
And wash the ivy from these prostrate stones!
'Twill ease a heart where Misery long has lodged,
And his dark-visaged partners. Here we feel
How little earth can offer from its store
To ease a wounded spirit. List! a voice:
Some wandering maiden selling summer sweets.
       [*Enter a Flower Girl.*
Flower Girl (*singing*). Primroses from the lanes!
  Who buys? who buys?
With fragrant lips and pretty yellow eyes!
Rado Reef. Come hither, little maid, and speak to me.

Thou lookest worn and hungry, and thy dress
Like one who sits where suffering beareth rule.
Hast thou no father to supply thy wants?
Where is thy mother? Where thy humble home?
Do let me hear: thy voice will comfort me.
Flower Girl. You judge me hungry, and you judge
  me right.
I have not tasted bread since yesterday,
And then I earned a crust by selling flowers,
And shared it with my brother; but to-day
I've travelled through the town from end to end
Without one ear to heed me: so I turned
With sad steps homeward. Is it very wrong
To ask you if you ever purchase flowers
For your dear children? Pray forgive me, Sir.
Rado Reef. Go on, go on! I wait to hear the end.
Here, take this money-piece; 'twill do thee good.
       [*He gives it to her.*
(*Aside.*) A wondrous mystery shineth in her eyes!
Flower Girl. My thanks are many more than I can
  speak.
How will it help my mother, pale and thin,
And overcome with watching! 'Tis the Lord:
He brought you here to cheer her broken heart.
When I knelt down this morn, and clasped my hands
To say my prayer, she sweetly told me this,
That all our blessing cometh from His love;
And prayed I in the street from door to door
As I walked onwards, knowing 'twould be so,
Though all hearts hardened: and relief has come.
I thank you, Sir, with gratitude unfeigned.
Rado Reef. My precious child, thou hast not told me all.
Where is thy father? where thy home? and where
Thy loving mother, teaching thee so much,
A knowledge above rubies?
    (*Aside.*) O what strength
Has simple innocence! Her words refresh
My sinking spirit as a water-spring
The traveller of the desert. On my ears
Old tones come back I had forgotten long,—
The music of my merry marriage bells,
And hymns which floated round the festal board.
Flower Girl. There is a cabin halfway down the cliff:
You see it from this arch-stone. There we live,
And there you'll find my mother. Poverty
Weeps on the woven rushes; and long grass,
Rent from the hollow, is our only bed.
I have no father here; he ran away;
Perhaps he's dead, perhaps he's living yet,
And may come back again and kiss his child;
For every day at morn and even-star
I pray for him, with face upturned to heaven,
"O blessed Saviour, send my father home!"
I know he'll come to make the promise sure.
Rado Reef. What was thy father's name, my pretty
  child?
Flower Girl. The people simply called him Rado Reef.
They say the drink destroyed him. But the low
Are not too prostrate never more to rise:
Our Father helpeth those who help themselves.
Would he were come! then I should have a sire,
Like other children, and be clothed and fed;
For every day I pray he may be good.
Now let me lead you where my mother mourns.
       [*They enter the hovel.*
Rado Reef (*addressing the Woman*). I met your
  child beside the abbey walls,

And she has brought me hither. You look pale,
Much scorched by sorrow, and your pensive eye
Tells of a pressure wearisome to bear.
You have a treasure in this pretty girl:
She told me how the dark cloud rose and fell
With heightened horror on the hills of hope,
Leaving no streak of glory on your path;
And yet she prays that father may come home.
Has he sent letters? know you if he lives?
And whether you may hope his safe return?
Poor Woman. The whole is so mysterious I am blind.
What I have suffered let no chronicler
Reveal to mortal. Shipwrecked mariner,
Bound to the mast, dashed onward through the dark,
Bruised, thunder-smitten, was not more forlorn,
Or miner in the cavern, with his lamp
Crushed out and blackened. Once the sun was high,
And beauty filled the landscape, birds sang sweet,
And flowers were filled with perfume. Love arose
And stocked the universe with hidden sweets,
Matured by seasons and the march of years.
I little thought the wind would come so soon
And overturn my hive, and fill with dust
My cells of honey, whirling all around.
Yet so it was. The husband of my youth,
The idol of my girlhood, tore away
The prop that stayed me, leaving me to fall,
Like a bruised tendril draggling on the stones.
Suffice it that the fire-wave scorched his soul,
And burnt affection out. And yet I loved,
Though bruised by hands I oft had kissed before,
And would kiss then, but that his rage was high.
And then he left me,—left me with my babe
And other children,—left me without food,
Or fire, or raiment, or a single friend,
Like a dismasted hulk amid the seas:
And yet I loved him, and I love him still,
Although he should despise me, and his words
Wound me like daggers,—though his hard hand falls
Upon my face, leaving its trail behind,—
Though he should spurn me from him with his foot,
And lift his threatenings higher than the hills:
I still will love him, faithful unto death!
Rado Reef. My dearest wife! come to my arms once
    more! [*Embracing her.*
I am thy Rado, softened and subdued,
Unworthy of a treasure like thyself:
But let the past be buried. Coming years
Shall prove my true repentance, and great griefs
Shall be outbalanced by thy greater joy:
Thy woes and wrongs are ended. Lift thine eyes,
And see a summer spreading o'er the earth;
The blackness has departed, and soft airs
Come stealing up the valleys. Let this kiss
    [*Kisses her.*
Atone for long desertion, crime, and care.
And come, my darling daughter, fling thine arms
About my neck, and kiss thy father's face.
    [*They embrace each other.*
Thy prayer is answered and thy heart made glad.
Thou wert my guide to lead me to your door.
Without thee I might long have stumbled on,
Not knowing where you sheltered. From henceforth
Your lot is altered. I have gold and lands,
Enough to fill the year with ripened fruits.
Come, leave this hovel! [*Exeunt.*

N 2

Scene—Village in the valley. Time—*Morning.*
    Enter Polly Peer.

Polly Peer. Ding! ding! dong!
Ding! dong! the bells are swinging! Philip Reef
Has married Myla, and the village rings.
His father now is rich, and Woodclose Farm
Is given to Philip as his marriage dower.
I'll linger here and mark the wedding train
Pass on among them. It is meet
To make a holiday and fling joy-shouts
Upon the air of summer. May their path
Be overshadowed by the wing of peace,
As free from envy as their hearts from guile,
Till in the western sky their red sun sinks.
The scattered Reefs are sweetly gathered home!
    [*Exit* Polly Peer. *Enter* Philip Reef, Myla,
        Rado Reef, *his* Wife *and* Children.
Philip Reef. Beyond those trees thou see'st that
    pretty home:
It is thine own, my Myla. There thy hands
Shall twine the rose and woodbine, and sweet birds
Shall sing thee to thy slumbers. In Love's bower
The months shall glide so smoothly that old Time
Shall be astounded at his rapid march,
And rub his brow and ponder. We will drink
Nought but dear Nature giveth pure from wells
And bubbling fountains and rush-hidden rills.
Our moderation shall be known to all.
Under the purple heavens we'll worship God,
And thank Him for our mercies. Swaying pines
Shall give us music, and clear waterfalls,
And far off rivers thundering down the steeps;
And the true seasons, as they travel round,
Shall teach us solemn lessons, till we fall,
And loving children sorrow o'er our tomb.
Myla. Joy fills my heart so that it overflows,
And my poor lips are silent. Let it be!
In weal or woe thy Myla clings to thee.
Rado Reef. One sweetness brings another. Not
    alone
Is he who tastes it: other hearts rejoice,
And so the circle widens, widening still,
So that a whole community is cheered.
This is our portion. These good people round
Catch the contagion, and shouts wound the clouds.
Of all my days wove in the loom of Time
This has the happiest visage, and I feel
Like one awakened from some dismal trance,
Walking where blossoms dip into the pools.
Your joy, my children, gives my joy new wings,
So that I soar where goodness sits enthroned,
And majesty and beauty, and the air
Is one vast concert of eternal praise.
The trial-land from which we have emerged,
Led by our guardian angel, leaves a voice
Of mercy in our souls, a lesson sage
Which we should hold with hands that slacken not,
And strength that never wanes,—to trust in God,
And never hang an issue on ourselves;
Forego the poison, use what Nature gives;
Love all as brethren; rather give than take;
Uphold the weak, encourage those who strive;
Thrust not a suppliant from the beaten path;
Labour to bring upon the sons of men
The reign of the millennium, when the earth
Shall bud and blossom with the trees of heaven.

[*Voices singing in the orchard.*]

The earth in spring and summer dress
Has much of Eden's loveliness ;
What purity appears below,
Even in its winter robe of snow !
Nor God nor Nature has decreed
That man the tempter's voice should heed.

Resist thy foes on every hand,
And He shall give thee power to stand ;

Pursue thy way with zeal unfeigned,
And love and fame and gold are gained !
Due strength be thine till day is done,
The conflict past, the victory won !

Along the heavens a voice is heard ;
The vales, the mountain-peaks are stirred :
On, on it speeds throughout all lands ;
The listening nations clap their hands:
That sword and strife and wrong shall cease,
And earth repose in perfect peace.   [*Exeunt.*

CHANONCHET AND WETAMOE.

ALM was the waning hour : the day
On the great hill-tops died away ;
The setting sun's last golden gleam
Had tinged the ripples of the stream ;
The fair young moon's chaste robe
was thrown
O'er tangled wilds and mountains lone ;
The fox was peeping from his lair,
The squirrel munched his evening fare ;
The wolf had planned his midnight prowl ;
Astir was seen the ghostly owl,
Staring from out his ivied den,
To hoot within the haunted glen.

A wigwam, by the blue lake's side,
Whose simple door was open wide,
In moonlight shadow might be seen ;
And, entering now, with placid mien,
An Indian youth, with locks of jet,
Smoking his peaceful calumet.
Beside the hearth-stone's flickering ray,
Sat a bright girl, as sweet as May,
Fair as the Morning's orient eye,
In the blue landscape of the sky.
To her he gave the pipe, and she
Quenched it in sweet simplicity.
He pointed to the lake's calm face,
Which winded round the mountain's base,
And forth she walked beside him there,
With dark blue eyes and flowing hair,
And wondrous music in her voice,
That bade the listening woods rejoice.

O rapturous hour ! He silence brake,
And thus it was Chanonchet spake :—

"Thou know'st my sire in battle died,
And with him fell our country's pride.
Curst be the white man's pale-faced host,
That prowl along our wooded coast !
And cursed be their savage hands,
That fired our towns with lightning-brands !
Like angry gods they strangely came,
And scorched us with their hissing flame,
Till all the hero died,
Covering the warrior's face with shame,
Scattering destruction wide !
My father in the centre stood,
Fierce, although wounded ; and the blood
Was rushing through his swelling veins,
Spurring his spirit's warrior-reins.
The pale-face chieftain by his blade
Was on the trampled wood-sward laid :
And ere his reeling followers came,
My father smote with deadly aim.
O'ercome with numbers,—sad to tell,—
At last my sire heroic fell,
Covered with wounds, with death-stripes crossed,
On half an army's sword-points tossed,
His manly features pale and gory,—
Ha, ha ! they falsely called it glory !
I saw him on the battle-plain ;
I strove to stanch the oozing vein.
The blood was clotted on his cheek,
And thrice I heard the red man speak :
' Come hither, son, and let me trace
My image in my darling's face.
Wet my dry lips ! O how they burn !
I go from whence there's no return ;
Thy father dies ! My only son,
Revenge my death when I am gone ;
Let the war-cry thy bosom swell,
And chase them with thy angry yell.

So shall my sated ghost be blest,
When hunting in the' unclouded West.'
He said, and sank upon his side,
Shivered his shattered lance, and died.

"Athwart yon dell our wigwam shines,
Sheltered by trees and clustering vines,
Where oft at eventide is heard
The carol of the forest-bird;
Where flower-buds, tinged with rainbow-hues,
Are drinking up the summer-dews.
Sweet flowers! Can I forget them? No,
For oft I twine them round my bow,
And cease to hunt the leaping roe.
Can I forget my fleet canoe,
That glides across these waters blue,
As swiftly as the eagle flies?
Dear are ye in Chanonchet's eyes.
And she who hugged me on her knee,
And sung her wild-strained lullaby;
Who often kissed my boyish face,
And nerved and clad me for the chase;
O how she praised my courage, when
I slew the panther in the glen,—
The first that 'neath my arrow bled,—
And dragged it to our wind-rocked shed!
She told me I should hunt the deer,
And cause the pale-face man to fear;
Should scare the lion from the wood,
And thrice revenge my father's blood!
Yet at thy name, a magic word,
What throbbings of my heart are stirred!
Strange tremors through my body run,
Falters the song ere well begun,
And I impatient watch the day
That lingers ere it haste away,
When night's first star, mid skies of blue,
Shall light me to my Wetamoe.
Then in the mild beam of thine eye
I thrill with holiest ecstasy.
Dost thou perceive what makes me tame,
And darts like lightning through my frame,
When whispering Wetamoe's sweet name?
Dost know?—'Tis love's celestial fire,
The gushing flood of pure desire:
Thy fond Chanonchet knows to feel
What time may soften, but not heal.
To-morrow both our lives shall run
Like two clear streamlets into one."

He spoke.—The young moon smiled on high,
A star or two looked through the sky,
The fishes sported in the lake,
The eve-bird warbled in the brake,
The dew-beads hung upon the trees,
And distant harp-notes filled the breeze.
'Twas solitude and silence here,—
An emblem of the' Elysian sphere.

He would not deem, beneath this sky,
That danger was so very nigh;
But, suddenly a host of thieves
Came leaping from among the leaves,—
White savages, men-stealers they!—
Who pounced upon their helpless prey,
Careless of colour and of clan:—
How true that "man's worst foe is man!"

Resistance would have been in vain;
It only would increase their pain;
And so they yielded to the chain.

How quickly are our prospects crossed,
And every ray of hope is lost!
The sun withdrawn, the sky o'ercast,
And young buds fall before the blast!
Chanonchet, and the cherished flower
He deemed would deck his forest bower,
Are severed by the Christian's hand,
And quail beneath black slavery's brand:
To different districts both are driven,
From love, and home, and kindred riven.

It was Chanonchet's fate to be
Surrounded with the sugar-tree,—
A slave, where all save man was free!
And he would sigh, with grief oppressed,
When labouring pains upheaved his breast;
And oft he sought the wild wood's shade;
And there, where many waters played,
He mused upon his banished maid.
His cruel master whipped him sore,
And blushed not when he saw the gore,
But cut and lashed him with a frown,
And beat him till the blood ran down,
And poor Chanonchet sank away
With faintness on the crimsoned clay.

Deem not, when tortured and oppressed,
Home-feelings died within his breast.
Deem not, at this afflictive hour
He had forgot his boyhood's bower;
Or that the proud oppressor's steel
Benumbed him, that he could not feel.
O no! his home was with him there;
And, floating on the balmy air,
He heard his own melodious birds,
And listened to his mother's words,
Drank Wetamoe's soul-stirring strain,
And lived his childhood o'er again.
And when the world was drowned in sleep,
It was Chanonchet's time to weep,
To pace his little garret-room,
And wring his hands, and wail his doom;
And, through his broken casement, he
Would oft peer forth upon the sea,—
What time the moon had decked the night,
Flooding the solitudes with light,—
Smarting beneath the tyrant's rod,
And muse upon his native sod.

One night,—thick darkness veiled the sky,
And not a star-beam shone on high:
The clouds, in wild commotion hurled,
Were striking terror through the world;
The angry tempest-spirit growled,
And every outward aspect scowled;
The household had retired to sleep,
The patient sufferer to weep;
For from Chanonchet's back, that day,
His master whipped the skin away.
He raised him from his straw-made bed,
And paced his murky prison-shed.
Poor fellow! O how sad was he,
Resolving in his mind to flee!—

"The angry winds I hear without,
Whirling the rifted pines about,
Riving the knotty oaks in twain,
And shaking Neptune's dread domain,
Are far more pitiful and kind
Than those wild bears I leave behind:
Therefore I'll nerve myself for flight,
And leave this cruel house to-night."

He said, and through the lattice flew:
The wild-bird shrieked as he withdrew;
And, creeping onward through the dark,
He thought he heard the bloodhound's bark!
He reached the gloomy wood, and there
In silence knelt him down to prayer,
That the Great Spirit's hand would guide
Him to his native valley's side.
Within a hollow tree he crept,
Lay down at night, and sweetly slept,
Forgetful of the furious boar,
And scared not with the tiger's roar;
And when the morning broke, he rose,
Cheerful and gay, and off he goes
He with his knife and hatchet here
Lived happily on forest cheer;
Vessels of earth he fitly framed,
Rubbed the dry wood until it flamed,
Made bows and arrows wondrous strong,
Killed wild game as he hied along,
Plucked clustering berries from the tree,
And drank from rivers pure and free;
The earth his bed, his roof the sky,
He fattened where a wolf would die.

At last he reached his native wild,
Where he in life's bright morning smiled,
And, from the hill's head, down he gazed
Where erst the festive faggot blazed.
What were his feelings when he found
His cabin prostrate on the ground,
The peace-tree scathed, his mother gone,
And not a kinsman left,—not one!
He asked,—he heard the sad, sad tale:—
The white men stalked into the vale,
Killing and burning as they came;—
His mother perished in the flame!
'Twas told him,—and he sought the wood,
To end his days in solitude.
A mossy cave became his den,
And here he lived apart from men,
On herbs and roots, with naked breast,
The Indian Hermit of the West.

The river's side, at close of day,
Where Wetamoe was stole away,
He oft would visit, and his mind
Would picture scenes of saddest kind.
He saw her tortured, whipped, oppressed,
With mighty woes and wrongs distressed,
Bruised, broken, scourged, made dumb with pain,
And bending earthward 'neath the chain,
And when this rose before his eyes,
The wild woods echoed with his cries.

One eve he left his mossy cave,
And sat beside the limpid wave,
And sang his melancholy song,
That floated sad the trees among:—

"The young cub seeks its mother's breast,
The eagle hastens to his nest,
The lion slumbers in his lair,
A shelter has the shaggy bear;
The wanderer to his mates will come;
But poor Chanonchet has no home!
My father, on the battle-field,
Fell conquered on his broken shield;
And, hark! along my native coast,
I hear my mother's wandering ghost,
Invoking me fierce war to wage,
And scathe the foeman in my rage,
Who thrust her to the smouldering fire,
And burnt our wigwam in his ire.
My mother and my sire are gone:
I've not a kinsman left,—not one.
And she, poor sad Chanonchet's sun,—
How quickly were we both undone!
She loved me;—this I felt, I know,
And for it loved my Wetamoe:
But they have dragged my flower away,
Turning to night my sunny day!
My sweet wigwam, alas! is missing;
The angry serpent there is hissing.
And where the son and mother slept,
The fierce envenomed snake hath crept:
And there the owl his haunt is making,
And the wild beast his fast is breaking.
No human voice is heard; 'tis dumb,
And poor Chanonchet has no home!
Where now shall the sad lone one flee?
The red wild warrior misses me;
The grey deer round my cave is leaping,
And there the soft young fawn is sleeping.
Yes, this is all that does me gladden;
For sights of other objects sadden:—
My wigwam burnt, my father slain;
My mother's ashes strew the plain;
My Wetamoe for ever banished,
And every ray of hope evanished!
No, not a star is in the sky;
There's nothing left now but to die!"

Backward he turned; his tears were streaming;
Blue lights were on the mountain gleaming,
Black clouds were gathering thick before him,
And the wild winds were wailing o'er him,
Clashing with fury on his ear:
He paused, the striving storm to hear.
When suddenly around him came
A flashing sheet of livid flame,
And awfully athwart the heaven
A blazing thunderbolt was driven!
It rived an aged tree in twain,
Which fell and shook Chanonchet's brain,
Shattered the skull, and cleft the head,
And in a moment left him dead,—
A piteous corse, with gore imbrued,
Hallowing the awful solitude!

But who across the green wood hies,
A bow upon her shoulder slung,
Sad sorrow streaming from her eyes?
She weeps, although so young.
'Tis Wetamoe.—The bitter cup
Of slavery hath the maid drunk up;
And now the wild wood does she rove
In search of him, her only love!

She dreamt—within their wonted bower
They sat, at summer's twilight hour,
Charmed with the note of many a bird,
That in these solitudes was heard,
Breathing forth vows of love and truth,
And smiling in the' embrace of youth!
Again she dreamt—at eventide,
When roving through the forest wide,
A bristled boar, with foaming bound,
Struck poor Chanonelet to the ground,
Was tearing the live flesh ;—and she,
Shrieking, awoke in agony ;
And, rushing from the tyrant's den,
Alone she sought her native glen.
In hunter's garb the maid doth go
With battle-axe, and spear, and bow,
Roaming the woods, devoid of fear,
In search of him, to her so dear.

Hast thou not seen the little flower,
The earliest spring-bud of the bower,
  Smote by the wintry blast ?
So the struck maiden bowed her head,
When first she saw her lover dead ;
  Her life had nearly passed ;
And, with a shriek that rent the sky,
As dark clouds dimmed her closing eye,
She fell beside his mangled clay,
And fluttering reason fled away !
At shut of eve, across the dale,
What time is heard the nightingale,
The Maniac Maid will quickly pass,
Brushing the dew-drops from the grass.
Her clustering ringlets, sunny-brown,
Dishevelled, fall her shoulders down ;
Unplumed, unbonnetted is she,
The vacant child of misery.

She pauses oft, and oft her song
Of melancholy floats along,
Which seems some wild, unearthly strain,
Flashing across her tortured brain :—

"Behold, on high the eve-star gleams,
Silvering our rippling, flower-fringed streams ;
But though so winning, mild, and clear,
'Tis not Chanonelet's fit compeer ;
For he, upon his lowly stem,
Would far outshine this sparkling gem.
I'l tell you where my love is laid :
O stranger, hear the Maniac Maid !
Beneath the tree he slumbers sweet ;
W'ld wood-leaves are his winding-sheet ;
And sapless boughs that o'er him wave,
The victory-scalps that deck his grave.
The forest-bird sobs for him ever,
Nor stops his plaintive murmur never!
His spirit through Elysium wings
Its rapid flight, and sweetly sings :
Or with his ponderous, twanging bow
Sweeping the forests he doth go,
Hurling his cedar-shafts with dread,
And stalking o'er the prostrate dead !
Of all our tribe he was the flower,
The best, the brightest in our bower !
His heart would bleed when sorrow came,
And danger roused his slumbering flame.
They stole him when our hope-tree budded,
And with green leaves the boughs were studded ;
And when again I sought and found him,
The hungry wolves were roaring round him.
The eagle o'er his head was screaming,
How shrill !—but, O ! my love was dreaming.
He sleeps beneath the tall tree's shade :—
O stranger, hear the Maniac Maid !"

KYNANCE COVE.

—

've been to fairy-land, and seen
    the fays
Unvested in their workshop.
    Scenes are here
That hold a poet captive with
    their charms,
And mock his fancy like a thing
    of gloom.
The wondrous cliffs are polished
    with the waves,

And flash and flicker like huge mineral walls.
Their scaly sides are clothed with leafy gold,
And burn with beauty in the light of day.
The sands that lie on this Elysian cove
Are all ring-straked with painted serpentine :
The hollow caves the waves have fretted out
Are dashed with images of flowery hues ;
And on the rocks, like beautiful psalm-leaves,
Are odes of music lovely as the light.
Trilled by the sea-nymphs in their watery robes.

I'm fond of travelling old deserted paths,
Searched by the winds and soft with solitude ;
Of matchless Nature in her robe of crags,
Or fringed with flowers, or edged with velvet moss ;
Of grand old forests, where the trees stand up

And shout together, " God hath made us all ! "—
Of odorous heaths, that oft inspire my Muse,
And lift me high on Inspiration's steep ;
Of musing lonely by old Ocean's shore,
And roaming widely through the fields of thought ;
While castles, towers, and palaces uprise,
Built with chaste light, and roofed with burning gems.
But, starting from my song-trance one bright morn,
And turning down you crooked curious lane,
These fancy-pictures floated in the dark,
As rock on rock uncurtained to my gaze,
And rolled upon my vision like a spell.

Hail, fairy-featured, beautiful Kynance !
A loving smile is ever on thy face,
And Beauty revels mid thy gold arcades.
Along thy glittering grottoes tones are heard
Like songs at evening by some distant lake.
Thy coloured crags, on which the sea-birds perch,
Are tuneful with the tread of tiny feet.
No harsh discordant sound is heard in thee ;
And he who journeys through these sculptured creeks,
And gazes on those hills of serpentine,
Where Nature sits upon her chiselled throne,
Smiling benignly in her samphire robes,
Wearing her best, her craggy crown of gems,
When clustered once more in his loving home,
Will feel a sweetness flowing through his heart,
And more exalted views of Nature's God.

Why seek for beauty in the stranger's clime,
When Beauty's state-room is the gay Kynance ?
Why seek for visions courted by the Muse ?
When Kynance opens like a mine of gems ?
Why seek for language from the waves' white lips,
When ocean's organ fills this pictured Cove ?
Why seek for caverns striped with natural lays,
When they are stained here by the surging sea?
Why seek for islands girdled with the main,
When Kynance holds them in her feathery folds ?
So mused I in the sea-damp Drawing-Room,
While through the Bellows rushed a flood of song.

Heath ! heath ! what forests fill those fragrant fields !
My lot has been to dally with these flowers,
And walk among them like my kind compeers.
I twined them with my boyhood's tissued wreath,
And manhood found me roving mid their sweets.
I bound them into brooms so beautiful
To decorate my rhyme-mill on the moor.
I wove them with my lyre-chords lovingly,
And ran to meet them with a smile of joy,
At dawn, at noon, and music-breathing eve ;
And from life's early morn these moorland fays
Have chimed around me with their bells of gold,
Till now they seem a portion of myself.
But O, those poets of the rocky range
Stand up in armies round the fair Kynance,
On hedge-side, moss-bank, field, and craggy cliff,
Streaking the valleys, carpeting the hills,
And wooing kisses from the amorous sea ;
So that, when wandering with those sweet-robed queens
That July morn, my cup of joy ran o'er.

Behold this little creek among the thyme,
Whose sloping sides abruptly tumble down
To meet the tide that stately rolls up

To kiss the shell-fish thickly clustered here.
The rocks are golden, like the flowers they screen,
And every cell is hung with ornaments,
That seems the palace of King Oberon.
Here graceful swallows glide, and singing birds
Mingle their music with the billows' lay.
It is in sooth the song-house of the Muse.
And as I lingered by a tiny stream
That trickled'neath some flat rocks fringed with flowers,
A comely Image issued from the ledge,
Like studious pilgrim clad in thymy robes,
With shoes of moss and hose of ivy-stems,
Inwoven with the grasses of the glen :
Upon his head, among the rushy hair,
Were gems of light that shed a halo round ;
And, leaning on his knotty holly-bough,
He oped a worn book strangely charactered,
And read, like some old bard, these mystic chimes:—

" There is a valley deep among the hills,
Split down by Nature in a passion-freak ;
And evermore it wears its wild rough weeds,
And lies a cold untrodden wilderness ;
And evermore a melancholy wail
Moans through its hollow caverns, and a sound
Like grief's dark dirge is labouring on the blast.
And in its centre, by a rapid stream,
That brawls among the shingles, lies a cot,
Torn into ruins, called ' The Haunted Home.'

" The sun was setting on a summer's eve,
And all the gentle brooks were full of song ;
The swallows glanced and wheeled along the wild ;
The white lighthouse seemed whiter in the dusk ;
The sea-birds gathered on the gilded cliffs ;
And soon a holy quietude came down,
That filled these moorlands with the breath of heaven.
A pious youth is kneeling here alone,
And praying to his Father. O'er his head
Angels are hovering with their wings of flame;
Smiles play about their lips, like rays of light
When morn is breaking o'er the woody hills,
To see a Christian wrestling with his God.
The young man prays, and as he prays, his face
Grows bright and glorious ; in his eye a ray
Of heaven's own light is kindled, and his soul
Is full of love and tenderness divine.
He rises from the earth celestialized ;
And when again he mingles with the world,
Men mark him for his kindness, and they smell
The sweets of heaven upon his earthy robes.

" For many happy days and months and years
The pious youth ran well : he watched, he prayed,
He read the Bible in his closet-home,
And worshipped God amid the groves and fields,
And bowed before Him in His holy fane.
He served his Maker with a perfect heart,
And did his duty with a willing mind.
Thus filled he foreshadowed bliss above.
But in an evil hour the tempter came
With soft seducing. See him listening now,
And now resisting, till the wily fiend
Entrapped him in his meshes, and he fell
Deep in the mire of sin, to rise no more.

" Within a lone cot by an aged mill,

O'er which a hollow alder spreads its arms,
Twisted and turned by many a winter storm,
A simple maiden dwelt, as innocent
As blooms the white rose by the waterfall.
Her song was sweeter than the throstle's lay,
And Eve unveiled her face among the dews,
And stood on tip-toe in the murky marsh,
To hear it rippling on the vesper breeze.
She loved the vales and mountains, woods and streams;
And Nature filled her heart with melodies,
And taught her wisdom with a silent tongue.
Nor was the God of Providence forgot,
To whom she prayed in young simplicity.
Thus lived she with a sire of hoary hairs,
And aged mother bending to decay.
Diffusing light and beauty everywhere;
Till the seducer with a flattering tongue
Ruined and left her a poor shattered wreck,
Over which angels mourned and cherubs grieved,
To pine and die in want and loneliness.

"A few years glided by like noiseless dreams,
Though oft he trembled when the unseen hand
Had written strange lines on his closet-wall,
And conscience smote him with a fiery sword.
The wild night-winds, unbridled from their steeds,
Crack through the welkin with an echo rude;
And in the inky blackness of the storm
He strangely perished on the hedgeless height."

The tall Corn Prophet turned the lengthy leaves,
And trilled distinctly : "Streams are beautiful
That run along among the rushy tufts
With silvery clearness; blossoms on the trees,
Or flowers among the grasses of the field,
Or rich with beauty in the garden-ground,
Are passing lovely ; but the poet's child
Was lovelier than the best ; she far outshone
The sweetest tints of Flora, growing up
As grew the lily by the running brook.
How much he loved her is a thing unknown ;
But sickness came, and weakness and decay;
And in the sweetness of the Sabbath morn,
When earth was worshipping in hallowed robes,
Her loving spirit passed to Paradise.

"Now sadly weeping in the hawthorn shade,
When summer dews are hanging on the flowers,
And evening shadows walk the dim hill-sides,
A gentle vision haunts him in his tears,
And gleams upon him from the heights of heaven.
Along the living slopes of Eden-land,
Where fadeless roses fringe the shining banks.
His angel-babe is gliding, and her robes
Are whiter than the snow-wreath. Wandering here
Amid the sun-bright scenery, her fair hands
Are filled with treasures from the tree of life,
And fragrant flowers that never know decay.

"If thou shouldst meet on this romantic cliff
A pensive man with tear-drops in his eye
And hand upon his breast, scanning the rocks,
Or looking mournfully upon the deep,
Or pausing when the distant church-bells sound,
As if he read a memoir in their toll,
Disturb him not ; this is the stricken bard.
His thoughts are climbing hill-tracks far away,
And glancing o'er the journey of his life.
His Sabbath hours, his children, wife, and home,
With all the sweet endearments of the past,
Throng tearful round him : so disturb him not."

The Vision paused a moment, turning o'er
The thick book-leaves that noisy rustling made ;
Then read again in sad funereal tone :
"There is a lone grave on this golden cliff,
Where long has slept a shipwrecked mariner.
A broken oar thrust in the mossy mound
Serves as his monument : long grass and heath
And prickly brambles mingle on his tomb.
Tradition says, one night a storm arose,
And a small craft was dashed upon the rocks,
And fell in fragments. When the Morning rose
With tears upon her lids, two fishermen
Secured a body rolled up by the surf,
And buried it a few yards from the sea :
And here it lies in silent loneliness.
A Bible with his name inscribed thereon
Was all they found on him, which one of them
Lodged on a shelf within his reedy home.

"Time passed, years fled, the fishermen were gone :
An only daughter occupied the shed,
Married and blossom-blessed, when one dark night
A wrinkled grandam stepped the threshold o'er.
Strange were her vestments, and her tale as strange :
Her only son had left his mother's home,
And smiled upon the seas ; and he had said
That after three long years he'd come again,
And give his mother much. Three years expired,
And three times three brought no relief to her.
The wanderer came not. Then Distress and Want
And Hunger chilled her with their grisly stare.
Her household trifles went : the bench and stools,
And pewter plates upon the dresser-shelves.
The clothes-press quaint, carved chest of ancient make,
Table and form, and old clock on the stairs,
The tin canteen and bottle with entwined,
Till, not a vestige left, she wandered forth
To beg the cold world's colder charity :
And lying one night by a moorland hedge.
She dreamt she found the Bible of her boy,
With his own name upon the known fly-leaf.

"If, when the trees are stript and fields are bare,
And rear the winds along the hungry coast.
You see an old crone on the moaning corn,
Sitting upon the sad grave with bare head,
Catching the big rain in her wasted palms,
And chattering strangely wild, O turn and weep !
This is the mother of the mariner."

A heavy groan rose upward from the rocks.
Rushed from the waves, out-rumbled from the cloud
And rolled across the moor in plumes of black ;
And as it died away, the Seer began :
"In a rude dwelling shivering on the cliff,
An old blind pilgrim dwelt, whose eyes were dimmed.
When Beauty wove a garland for his brow.
'Tis sad to think of this afflicted one.
Suffice it that he loved a gentle maid,
And she returned her own into his heart ;
And they had purposed on their marriage-day
To walk among those flower-robed choristers

That trill their silent hymns along the strand.
But down upon them came a fearful doom;
Pale sickness seized her like a hungry beast,
And dragged her to the dust, and, as he mourned,
Pierced to the soul with sorrow's briny sword,
Blackness crept o'er his vision, and dull night
Dammed up its natural doorways, till he groped
About in darkness like a frame of bone.
You might have seen him stumbling o'er the heath,
Creeping towards the churchyard in the dusk,
Where every new grave is a novelty,
Searching among the rank grass with his hands,
Until he felt the small board o'er her head;
Where he would sit and mourn most dolefully.

"Don't pass that thatched cot, whose low roof is crushed,
With one lone tree upon the garden-hedge;
Nor think of the old blind man. Here he lived
His life away in darkness, and was fed
Nobody could tell how. The neighbours say
That oft at evening gentle songs were heard
Around his lonely casement rose-entwined,
Like angels singing in the fields of air.
And when he died, he passed away to heaven."

The shining Phantom paused with heated brow:
Wiping his forehead with a tuft of ferns,
He gave the last page of that song unread:
" The birds are joyous on the garden-trees,
And noontide floods the welkin. In her home
A mother sings her pensive lullaby
To little baby in his cradle-couch,
Who thrusts his arms up in a fit of rage,
And sobs his dawning-odes. 'Hush, little one;
Thy father plougheth in the sloping field;
I see him where the limpid fountain springs,
And cheerfully he guides the labouring team.
Art weeping so to call thy father home?
'Tis thy fond mother rocks thee patiently.
O sleep, my pretty one, sleep, sleep, my love!'

" A few stray zephyrs meet upon the hills,
Kiss in the hollows, separate and run
Among the rocks in very wantonness.
Sunshine is streaming down upon the vales,
And decking Nature in her robes of gold.
Among the lambkins on the grassy lawn,
New kite in hand, behold a happy boy,
Anxious to see it fly. He tries and tries,
And, though he often fails, he tries again,
Till in the air it rises, rising still
And fluttering o'er him like a thing of life.
He shouts, he halloos, dances, shouts again;

So that the very flowerets of the field
Are gently shaken with his gust of joy;
And when at supper by his mother's side,
How does he talk of what he has achieved!

" A studious youth is wandering where the rocks
Are bright with sonnets woven with the waves.
There is a mystic brightness in his eyes,
And strange outbeamings from their inner depths.
He seeks not intercourse with selfish man,
But fellowship with mountains and the muse;
And in a hollow grot of serpentine,
Where dwell the genii of the snowy surf,
He reads aloud the song-lines on the walls,
Sweet mingling with the harmonies of eve:—

" 'The gentle Anna, sweeter than the rose,
And bright as waters sparkling through the grass,
Sat at cool twilight in her lover's bower;
And pleasant was their language learned by love.
They talked of streams that tinkle down the dells,
Of reed and ragwort wooing in the moss,
Of flowers and trees, blue hills and setting suns,
And golden summers many years away;
Whilst Providence was worshipped and adored;
And roaming mid the pictures of Kynance,
Leaning upon her Edward's arm, she cried,
"O Cove enchanting! much is said of thee;
But of thy beauty half has not been told." '
And as the young man opened from his dream
Amid those gems from Nature's lavish hand,
He shouted high in joyous ecstasy,
' O Cove enchanting! half has not been told.' "

He closed the volume with a magic clasp,
And hid it in his bosom. How I longed
To woo it from the stranger, that kind friends
Might joy to trace its wonders, and my soul
Be gladdened with the freshness of new thought!
But through the golden doorways of the rocks
He vanished while I gazed; and, looking round,
The twilight had descended; far away,
My lingering mates were calling; the great sea
Was sounding like an organ: so I turned,
And turning turned to look a long farewell.

One word at parting from thee, fair Kynance.
Although I travel to my inland bower,
And mingle in the war of busy life,
With many a mile between thee and my home,
There is a cell within my memory,
Where thou shalt nestle like a song enshrined,
And oft thy beauty, like a sky of gold,
Enclose me in a wilderness of gems.

LUDA:

A LAY OF THE DRUIDS.

BOOK FIRST.

THE ALARM.

s there not on the ground we tread,
In the rough rock-heaps round us
    spread,
In every hollow of the hill,
In flowing river, creek, and rill,
In silent dingle, down, and dell,
    And shady wood, and mossy cell,
On crag and cross, and castle lone,
On tor, and tarn, and Druid-stone,
Some olden tale the Muse to lead,
So that whoever runs may read?
Who has not heard at evening hour,
When seated in some lonely bower,—
What time the ploughman leaves the lea,
And dances baby on his knee,
And down the lane the milkmaid sings,
As she the full pail homeward brings,—
Who has not heard from fern and fen,
From whispering wood and grassy glen,
From mystic marsh, and ruin wild,
And altar-stone on stone up-piled,
Mysterious voices, song-o'ercast,
The genii of the mighty past?

'Tis eve, 'tis calm; the winds are still;
Not e'en a whisper walks the hill;
In silent groups the lilies lie,
Nor tremble as the stream steals by;
The closing flowers in garments fair
Beneath the twilight seem at prayer;
The rushes stir not by the lake,
The bramble bends not in the brake;
The oak is moveless on the moor;
The hawthorn near the herdsman's door,
The larch adown the lengthened lane,
The willow by the warrior's fane,
The ivy o'er the fortress gray,
No leaf is lifted on the spray,
And Peace in many a fair festoon
Is singing to the rising moon.

With cautious footsteps up *Carn Brea*[1]
A palmer climbs in vest of grey.
A staff he carries, and a Book,
In which he solemnly doth look;
And oft he lifts his pensive eye
In prayerful glance towards the sky,
As if for souls of guilty men
With Heaven he interceded then.
His face was brown, his hair was long,
His agile limbs were spare and strong;
A shaggy deer-skin cap he wore;
A horn within his belt he bore;
A wallet from his shoulder fell,
Which held his roots and drinking-shell;
His sandals were both soiled and worn.—
'Twas plain long travel they had borne;
And on his brow were lines of care,
As if distress had been his heir.

In sooth he was a thoughtful man,
And seemed to study Nature's plan.
He scanned the rocks as if he read
Strange records where the lichens spread.
He watched the flowers with rich delight,
And kissed the little mosses bright.
The birds that glanced from tree to tree,
Or 'mid the berries carolled free;
The limpid brooklet dancing down;
The curling smoke from cottage brown;
The drifting clouds that travelled by,
Like seraph-ships across the sky;
The evening airs that round him stole,
Brought echoes from the palmer's soul:
And when the wind with gentle swell
Passed slowly through the eastern dell,
Fanning the heath as it rose higher,
And murmuring like a lonely lyre,
Filling with melody the place,
The tears came out upon his face.

A moment pause, to mention here
A soothing scene he deemed most dear.
Beside a cromlech on the bluff,
Upheld by pillars rude and rough,
A youth with raven hair and eyes
Walked underneath the evening skies,
Driving his wandering, grazing herd,
While homeward flew the latest bird;
And thus in pensive strain sang he:

" Come. pretty maiden, live with me :
My home is where the ring-doves call
Beyond the foamy waterfall.
I have no silver vessels fair,
But love's rich roses blossom there.
A rushy mat is at my door,
A rushy mat is on the floor :
My couch of sedge is softly spread.
Where thou canst gently lay thy head.
A guileless heart I give to thee :
Then, maiden, come and live with me.

" And are there those who offer more,
And promise thee a greater store ?
Let not their flattery lure my dove ;
For riches cannot purchase love.
The little rill with noiseless flow,
That glides along so clear and slow,
Is more refreshing in its course
Than yon dark river swift and hoarse.
That little rill am I to thee :
Then, maiden, come and live with me.

" Thou canst not tell how much I prize
The holy light within thine eyes.
I ever feel, when thou art near,
'Tis summer-time and always clear.
It can't be darkness where thou art :
The clouds to see thee quickly part,
And sliding shadows fleetly fly,
While sunshine fills the earth and sky.
Thy face brings joy where'er I be :
Then, maiden, come and live with me."

Before the castle wall he stood,
Gazing around on rock and wood.
The scene was grand from sea to sea,
From east to west, from tarn to tree,
From brook to brook, and stream to stream,
Which through the withs and rushes gleam.
A few small huts in brakes apart,
Where dwelt the hunter of the hart.
Or rude marauder, shunned and feared,
Were nearly all that then appeared.
Some sod-fenced farms. refreshed by rills,
Like sentinels among the hills,
Where corn.fields waved and orchards smiled,
Were thinly scattered o'er the wild.
No mine-heaps on the surface lay,
No engine-stacks to dim the day ;
No hiss of steam, no hammer's bang,
Or anvil's ring. or bucket's clang,
Or iron horse through hill and dale
Swift hurrying on the wondrous rail ;
But Solitude and Silence lone
Sat musing on a seat of stone.

I said no mine-heaps filled with gloom
Those hills and vales of fragrant broom :
But here and there, where rushes grow,
And where the streams in clearness flow,
A solitary man was found,
Turning with eagerness the ground,
And washing it in search of tin.
Which lay concealed the sand within.
And Fortune on him oft bestowed
A prill of copper from a lode.

Which served in after years to show
The way to hidden heaps below.
Tall trees bend o'er the limpid lake ;
The wild birds whistle from the brake ;
The grey fawn in the dingle feeds ;
The ducks flash up from dells of reeds ;
The fish abound in crystal streams.
And Nature murmurs in her dreams.

The palmer saw it all, and smiled :
A voice seemed echoing from the wild,
Which floated over wold and wood :
" And He pronounced it very good."

" There are." said he. as on the dell
And distant scene his vision fell,
" Who walk the earth, and yet deny
The power of Him who made the sky.
I hear His voice in every breeze
That shakes the tresses of the trees.
I see the impress of His hand
On every flower that gems the land ;
And morn and eve, and day and night,
The changing seasons in their flight,
The harvest waving in the vale,
The shining grasses of the dale,
The moon and stars, the earth and sea,
Proclaim the power of Deity.
The wind at midnight moaning loud,
The lightning breaking from the cloud,
The welkin wide with thunder trod,
All tell me plainly there's a God.

" My native land, my native land,
With healing gales of fragrance fanned !
How sweet to climb thy hills once more,
Replete with legendary lore !
How like a dream thy glades appear,
Where streams are gliding fresh and clear !
Below me is the dell of thyme
Where I have passed my early prime,
And drunk of brooklets issuing lone
From fairy fountains hope-o'ergrown.
Then siren voices lured me on
To richer scenes when years were gone.
I cannot tell how much I prize
Thy greenwood glades and placid skies,
Thy rivers murmuring to the sea,
Each rock and rill, each tarn and tree.
When oft I've climbed some foreign mound,
And heard the sighing winds around,
No matter where I chanced to roam,
They seemed to murmur songs of home,
And gentle forms would round me rise,
Until the tears streamed from my eyes.
The dreams of youth may pass away,
And friendship's flowers droop and decay ;
Dark clouds of care hang o'er the land ;
Old age may lead us by the hand ;
Our shattered idols round us lie ;—
The love of home will never die."

He knocked the castle's heavy gate :
The warder asked him why so late,
And what his message was ; and he
Told him of journeyings by the sea,

Of wanderings over hill and dale,
Of prayers in lonely forests pale ;
Of frequent fastings far away,
Where the fierce robber prowls for prey ;
Of battle-fields where dying men
    Blessed him for words of love,
Before their lingering spirits took
    Their flight to joys above.
Oft had he stood, this prayerful man,
Beside the lonely caravan,
And marked the pang and heard the sigh
When the last bottle had been dry,
And on the sand sank son and sire,
As thirst drank up their blood like fire,
And hardly flapping over head
The great bird's heavy wings were spread ;
Encouraging with promise high
The fainting ones so near to die.

More had he seen. Suffice it now
That he had reached the mountain's brow
Through peril huge o'er waste and wold,
With message for Rouanes bold ; [*]
Escaping spear and arrow keen,
When winding through the forest green,
And fording rivers where the roe
Drank only underneath the sloe,
Pursuing tracks the beasts had made
Down mossy moor and dim arcade,
Sustained by truth and love to save :
And now quick audience would he crave.

The castle by the old green wood [3]
On a vast ledge of granite stood,
With hollow arches in the stone,
O'er which a bridge of rock was thrown.
The walls were thick with holes, to show
And shoot no doubt the approaching foe,
Through which the arrow whistled oft,
As the hot Dane came up the croft.
The owl along the turret flew ;
The oak among the boulders grew ;
A mystery hung upon the rocks,
And walked in whispers 'mid the blocks.

The warder drew the bolt aside,
And oped the castle portal wide,—
A hole it was the rocks among [4]
Beneath the rude foundation strong,—
And bade him enter with his prayer,
For holy men were welcome there.
An inner screen was open flung ;
Here shields and heavy crossbows hung,
With many a battle-axe and spear,
And antlers of the graceful deer
Arranged in order on the wall,
Within the chieftain's audience-hall.
A mastiff by the chimney lay,
Which was with age and service grey ;
And as the palmer passed the door,
And placed his foot upon the floor
So strangely paved with granite rock,
From end to end one solid block, [5]

* *Rouanes*—Among the Britons a name of dignity, signi-
fying "Royal."—BORLASE.

He raised his head and growled, and then
Lay down in loneliness agen.

Rouanes was advanced in years,
And taller far than his compeers,
Of aspect stern, and strong of limb ;
To dare and do was part of him.
His small grey eye had fire enow,
A few spare locks were on his brow ;
His nose was large, his eyelids grey,
His beard had all been trimmed away ;
A scar was frowning on his face,
A trophy of the war or chase ;
And his huge hands and arms of length
Showed that he was a man of strength.

The chieftain bowed with courtesy meet,
And bade the palmer take a seat ;
For he looked travel-stained and tired :
And then his message he desired.
The stranger rose, and thus replied :

" Returning home from travel wide,
Yes, *home* where first I saw the light,
And watched the moon steal o'er the height,
And felt devotion's holy flame,
And murmured mild a mother's name ;
And in the cot yon rill above
I sat beside the maid I love,
The gentle Luda, whose blue eye
Has followed me when none were nigh.
I ever hear her voice of song,
Whether the winds be still or strong,
Whether the moon be young or old,
Whether the year be hot or cold,
Whether the oak be green or bare;
Like note Elysian on the air,
A spell to cheer my footsteps on :
But, warrior, more of this anon ;
For thou hast weightier words to hear,
And draw thy hand towards thy spear.

" Yestreen beyond the Druid's ford
I passed a dell with lichen stored,
Whence issued by a fountain small
A band of Northmen fierce and tall.
Their ships were lying near the strand
A few yards from our western land.
A sword of brass their chieftain wore,
And heavy spears his followers bore ;
And wildly scanned these warrior men
Each hill and dale, each glade and glen.
Their armour rattled as they rose,
As if they were in view of foes.
I hid myself behind an oak ;
When thus the Danish leader spoke :

" ' To-morrow when the light is spent,
And stars adorn the firmament ;
When silence like a robe shall rest
Upon the forests of the west,
Your fearless captain leads the way
Towards the castle on yon brea.
Where you, my warriors wild, once more
Shall dye your blades in princes' gore,
Shall trample on the furious foe,
And lay the haughty archers low.'

" He said, and waved his sword on high ;
I saw it flash as they passed by.
And heard their tramp, and felt their ire
Burn through my being like a fire.
The raven wheeled and croaked o'erhead ;
The tall trees trembled at their tread ;
The fox slank off as if in fear,
And scampered by the timid deer ;
And birds that chirp and birds that sing
Were frightened all, and all a-wing.

" And here beneath the boughs I lay
Till eve and night had passed away,
And Morning, like a lovely bride,
Came stealing down the mountain side,
Brushing the dews with naked feet,
And walking vales with roses sweet.
Then I rose up, poured forth my prayer,
And read my Book with serious air :
Ate my dry roots, and drink did I
From the clear stream which babbled by,
Asking His guidance whom I see
In every flower and every tree ;
For in a land where strangers dwell,
Whose kindness caused my heart to swell,
I found a higher, greater good
Than Druid ever taught in wood,[6]
Or cave, or carn the crags among,
In pleasing fable or in song.
Nor ever felt I such desire,
When standing near our altar-fire.
What think you was the lesson high ?
That there's a God who made the sky,
The earth, the sea, each stream and stone ;
And we must worship Him alone.

" So when the shades of eve again
Fell like a covering o'er the plain,
And by the spring the glowworm's lamp
Was sparkling 'mid the mosses damp,
I left my covert on the moor,
And stood before thy castle-door.
The rest thou knowest. Bestir thee then,
Call up thy hardy battle-men.
Forbid it that their cruel hands
Should bind our sons in captive bands,
Despoil our wives and daughters bright,
And quench in blood our household light,
Or dash our darlings on the stones,
And fill the land with guilt and groans.
Another hour may be too late ;
The foe, the foe is at thy gate ! "

Rounnes strode across the hall,
And reached the warder on the wall,
And bade him blow his whistle shrill,
Which echoed sharp from hill to hill ;
When from each shed and oak-clump round
The war-men started at the sound.
Some rose from ferns which shield the fox,
And some from hollows in the rocks ;
Some up from thickets strangely dashed,
Their helmets in the moonlight flashed.
They hastened to the castle lone,
For well they knew their chieftain's tone ;
And thus he spake :

" There's danger near :
Amid my band I've nought to fear.
Our valour and our arms are tried ;
Full oft we've conquered side by side.
Let the foe near us if they dare
To beard the tiger in his lair :
Our homes are dear, our households bright ;
For them we yield not in the fight.
The Danes approach us. Watch, my men ;[7]
They'll find us lions in the den.
Our blades are sharp, our spirits high,
And fall we may, but will not fly.
Each to his post be firm again,
And we shall triumph o'er the Dane,
And save the dwellings of our birth :
Our battle cry, OUR HOME AND HEARTH ! "

Thus spake the spearman bold, and then
Arranged in order his brave men,
Some high, some low, some here, some there,
Behind the battlements with care ;
And through the loopholes they could see
The approach of friend or enemy.
By this the moon rose o'er the mere,
The stars did in the heavens appear ;
The thrush was silent by the lake,
When, hark ! a crackling in the brake,
The tread of feet upon the hill !
" The Dane, the Dane ! be still, be still."
The warriors watch the approaching foe,
Each with his hand upon his bow.

NOTES ON BOOK FIRST.

NOTE 1, PAGE 99.

With cautious footstep up *Carn Brea*
A palmer climbs in vest of grey, &c.

Carn Brea is an enormous tor in Illogan, Cornwall,
crowned with granite blocks and boulders, having an
ancient castle on its head.—See history of the palmer,
&c., in BORLASE's " Antiquities of Cornwall," p. 335.

NOTE 2, PAGE 100.

Where cornfields waved and orchards smiled.

" The island is well peopled, full of houses, built
after the manner of the Gauls, and abounds in cattle."
—CÆSAR. See DR. SMITH's " Religion of Ancient
Britain," p. 29.

NOTE 3, PAGE 101.

The castle by the old green wood.

" *Carn Brea* hill has all the evidences that can be
desired of having been appropriated to the use of the
British religion. The top of this hill is thick set with
karns, and the spaces between and below were in the
memory of the last generation filled with a grove of
oaks. The castle is footed on a very irregular ledge
of vast rocks, and the architect has contrived so many
arches from rock to rock as would convey the wall
above. The walls are pierced everywhere by small
holes, to descry the enemy, and discharge their
arrows. This is certainly a British building, and
erected in those uncultivated ages when such rocky
hideous situations were the choice of warlike, rough,
and stern minds." — BORLASE's " Antiquities of
Cornwall," pp. 113–319.

NOTE 4, PAGE 101.

A hole it was the rocks among, &c.

" It" (the castle) "hath but one way of access or entrance into it, through a hole artificially cut in the rock under the foundation of the wall."—GILBERT'S " Parochial History of Cornwall," p. 237.

NOTE 5, PAGE 101.

From end to end one solid block.

"What they call the parlour here, marked in the plan of the castle, is floored with one rock."—BORLASE'S " Antiquities of Cornwall," p. 115.

NOTE 6, PAGE 102.

Thou Druid ever taught in wood, &c.

" Parents and guardians thought they could not do better for children of the highest birth than send them to the Druids to be instructed. This instruction was instilled into youth in the most private manner; some cave, or retired and sacred wood, or some rocky karn, being the appointed place of tuition; their education not being completed in less than twenty years. Under the direction of the Druids, the most singular part of instruction was that of learning a great number of verses by heart. They used also allegory and fable."—BORLASE, pp. 81, 82.

NOTE 7, PAGE 102.

The Danes approach us. Watch, my men, &c.

" Plunder and power were the sole and darling objects of the Danes; and by degrees they came to use the Cornish as bad as the rest of the kingdom. They practised every kind of severity unprovoked; fire, sword, and desolation attending them wherever they marched; so that Cornwall is supposed to have been utterly ruined by them, and to have continued as a forest for several ages."—BORLASE, p. 49.

BOOK SECOND.

THE SUSPENSE.

THE furze and heather are in bloom,
The moors are fragrant with perfume;
Afar is heard the hum of bees,
Whose murmurs mingle with the trees.
The waters flow the fens among,
The skylark fills the glades with song,
And in the wood where Summer strays
The throstle like a poet plays.
O now to tread some hillock high,
To catch the breeze that murmurs by
From banks of thyme and beds of flowers,
Where Nature rears her own green bowers,

And tunes her harp, and sings for aye
Her soothing everlasting lay!
My Cornwall! what a land is thine
For crag and cross, for moor and mine!
Thy hills are zoned with copper ore;
Thy vales yield tin, a precious store;
The greenest grass thy glades afford;
Thy sheltered bays with fish are stored;
Thy granite carns are castle-crowned,
Where altar-heaps and forts are found.
No brooks are clearer than thine own,
Which steal by cave and cromlech-stone;
And every hill-top in the land
Is marked by rude tradition's hand.
Sweet wild-flowers hang their lamps of love
By path below and rift above.
Thy sons are brave, thy daughters fair,
And none can with thy wives compare.

The sun was shining on the lake,
When the good palmer sought the brake.
Leaving the castle on the right,
He walked along the ledgy height
Towards an opening in the wood,
Where a rough Druid temple stood.[4]
For well he knew by sight and sound,
From distant vale and rising ground,
And cottage nestled by the mere,
That a religious rite was near:
And hence he travelled on, and strove
Before mid-day to reach the grove[2]
Beyond the rude *gorseddau-seat*,[3]
Where the wild worshippers would meet.

Adown the glen on palfrey white[4]
An aged Druid comes in sight:
His long beard on his breast is spread,
And oaken leaves adorn his head;
A sash does round his body meet,
And shoes of wood are on his feet;
His snowy garments reach his heels,
Which the light prancing palfrey feels;
And figures on his vest appear,
A serpent's head and crescent clear.
Six different badges mark his store;
The King could only wear one more.
The horse-rein doth his right hand hold,
His left uplifts a hook of gold;[5]
And as he climbs the sacred mound,
His eyes are fixed upon the ground.
Behind him comes a motley throng,
Thus chanting as they walk along:

" The crescent moon, the crescent moon,[6]
Is six days old this pleasant noon:
Again the new year is at hand,
Green leaves and flowerets till the land.
So to the silent grove we go
To cut the golden mistletoe.[7]

" Tramp, tramp along, tramp, tramp along;
Teutates is our war-god strong.[8]
And he will save us from the host
Of wicked Danes that spoil our coast.
So to the silent grove we go
To cut the golden mistletoe.

" The shady trees, the shady trees.
How pleasant here to feel the breeze
We know our great Taranys' power
Will save us in the battle-hour.
So to the silent grove we go
To cut the golden mistletoe."

They reached the oak,—a sturdy tree,
And yet withal 'twas fair to see,
With green leaves fluttering in the light ;
And then the priest, in robe of white [9]
And golden hook, ascends the bough,
And cuts the shining mistletoe,
Which on a snowy cloth is laid,
Spread for that purpose in the shade.
Two white bulls, never yoked, are there :
And so they for their feast prepare,
With rising shouts that seem to shake
The very blocks among the brake.

Subsides at last that echoing cry;
Oak-leaves upon the altar lie,[10]
And sprinkled is the holy ground,
While the assembly wait around :
Some naked forms are standing there
With paint upon their bodies bare.
The Druid's prayer is now begun ;
Turning his body to the sun,[11]
He walks around the excited throng,
His thick beard streaming white and long.
The fated victim's hour is come ;[12]
The trumpet clangs, and sounds the drum ;
Shake the hour rocks, and bows the wood ;
Full fifty arrows drink his blood.
The altar-fire flames up the sky,
And the straw image blazes high :
Intemperance howls with hideous roar—
Thank Heaven, these rites will rage no more.

The palmer left this savage scene,
And walked along the brakes between,
Until he reached a fountain lone,
That bubbled from a granite stone
Far from the Druid's holy pile,
And musing sat him down awhile.
The fairest ferns were hanging there,
And little velvet moss-cups rare ;
Green rushes in the hollow grew.
And dainty flowerets white and blue ;
Delicious murmurs filled the vale,
And floated down the quiet dale,
And every zephyr seemed to say
That cruel man was far away ;
And, stretched the whispering reed among,
He sweetly sang this tender song :

" Whate'er I do, where'er I be,
I have a presence still with me,
A whispering angel by my side.
To cheer me o'er the desert wide.
She comes, she comes, by day or night ;
For Luda is the palmer's light.

" Sometimes, where clouds and darkness are,
She shines upon me like a star :
Or do I climb the cliff of care,
She is my moon to guide me there ;

And oft within the blooming bower
My Luda is the loveliest flower.

" O come, my Luda, come away :
Without thee it is never day.
Dost thou not hear thy palmer sing
His lay of love beside the spring ?
My light, my life for ever be ;
O lovely Luda, come to me ! "

The pensive palmer ceased his strain,
And wiped the falling tear again ;
Shouldered his wallet, and essayed
To leave the fountain in the glade ;
When suddenly a form he saw
Which filled his very soul with awe.
Was it some vision of the night,
That lovely lady clad in white,
Stealing along from mound to mound,
Whose feet seem scarcely on the ground ?
He gazed again.   Who can it be,
So bright and beautiful to see,
Fair spirit of the wilderness
In garb of youthful Druidess?
Her hair and outer robe were white ;
Her linen cloak with clasp made tight [13]
And snowy gown were without speck,
And plaited ringlets graced her neck ;
A brass-work girdle bright she wore,
And in her hand a rod she bore,
Which was in sooth a magic wand,
And oft she waved it o'er the land.

Yes, who was she, that vision bright,
So like an angel clad in white,
Stealing beside this little well
Of limpid water in the dell,
Whose naked feet scarce move the grass,
As they among the flowerets pass ?
She started like a timid hare
When she beheld the palmer there.
And turned to flee, still looking back,
As if love bound her to the track,
Until in holy hour their eyes
Met underneath the smiling skies.
The gentle lady's magic wand
Dropped useless from her trembling hand :
She had no will or power to flee,
But sweetly faltered, " Yes, 'tis he ! "
Then down the pretty maiden sank
In faintness on the flowery bank.

You should have seen the palmer then,
And heard him sighing in the glen,
As he supported Luda's head
Upon its soft and thymy bed.
For this was Luda : yes, 'twas she.
The cooing doves came forth to see ;
The robin sang his wonder-lay ;
The wren kept twittering on the spray ;
And fleet-winged swallows brushed the hair
Of breathing Beauty slumbering there.
Of broadest leaves he made a fan
To cool her cheek, this pious man.
He bathed her forehead from the well,
Bringing the water in his shell ;

And prayed he in this lonely place,
And kissed with tears that lovely face.

At length she smiled, and oped her eyes ;
More blue they were than summer skies ;
Then passed her hand across her brow,
And whispered,

      " Where is Luda now ?
Is this Elysium that I see,
And is my palmer here with me ?
I left my home when noon was high,
To travel to the grove to die :
For it was rumoured in mine ear
That he to me than life more dear
Had perished by the ruffian's hand,
And lay entombed on savage strand.
And so the Druid of my clan,
A learned, brave, and powerful man,
Who eats and drinks and takes his rest
In yon high palace of the west,[14]
And sways upon a golden throne
A powerful sceptre all his own,
Bade Luda give her life away[15]
Upon the funeral pile to-day,
And I my palmer's love should gain,
And meet him on the spirit-plain,
Where heaps of scattered riches lie.
But tell me, palmer, where am I ? "

" Rise, Luda, let me kiss thy face :
Surely thou know'st this pleasant place.
When we met here a while ago,
The moon was like thy father's bow.
Dost thou remember how she hung,
And radiance o'er the grove-tops flung ?
Rise, Luda, call me thine once more :
I'll guide thee to thy mother's door.
From travel wide did I return,
And sought thee mid thy native fern :
For thou art dearer to mine eyes
Than rocks and hills and summer skies,
Or war-steed strong, or armour bright,
Or tempting gold, or silver white :
And as I lay beside this well,
Thou camest : the rest I need not tell.
But, dearest, show thy palmer now
Why like a Druidess art thou ;
Why, Luda, dost thou talk of fire,
And burning on the unholy pyre ? "

" Yes, thou shalt hear. First fill thy shell
With water from my native well,
And let me drink, O palmer mine,
And then my secret shall be thine.
The mouths with heavy feet trod on
And came again since thou wert gone,
When one dark eve a horseman rode
In fury to our loved abode,
And told us that a savage throng
Waylaid my love the hills among,
And slew him ; and a cloud of black
Hung evermore upon my track.
'Twas when October's face was pale,[16]
And through the tree-tops rose the gale
To hear November's heavy tramp
Come sounding down the hollows damp.

Our holy fires were blazing bright
On stony cairn and sacred height,
When forth I went, procured a brand,
And bore it homeward in my hand
To light within our dwelling lone
The faggot on the chimney-stone :
And as the sepulchre I passed,
And reached the old hill's foot at last,
I met a Bard. Slow was his pace,
And much high thought was on his face ;
And as he walked, his mystic verse[17]
In solemn tone did he rehearse ;
His eyes were fixed upon the ground :
Methinks e'en now I hear the sound,
And see the Druid. Much said he
Which I've not time to tell to thee.

" Once when the dog-star broke the sky,
Nor sun nor moon appeared on high,
They stood within the silent glade
To dig the vervain in the shade,[18]
By which the future they foretell,
Distempers heal, and fevers quell.
An iron instrument they use,
And honey on the earth diffuse.
Around the plant with the left hand
They make a circle on the land ;
And then they lift it from its bed,
And wave it high above their head ;
Then dry it, and the same infuse
In water which they ever use,
When laughter lags, and feasts are slow,
That merry staves may merrier go.

" He said by this the Eubates knew,[19]
And by the selago that grew[20]
In quiet places fresh to see,
That thou wouldst ne'er return to me.
That morn, as neighed their horses white,[21]
The same dark image came in sight ;
So then the great Bard bade me pray
To Jupiter, and went his way ;
But not before he showed that I
Within the sacred fire should die,
Which was the only way to be
In immortality with thee.
This I believed ; and when the flame
Up from our stony altar came,
I sought the scene, and reached the fire,
The wild cries ever mounting higher,
And in the pile a letter hurled[22]
To cheer thee in the other world,
And bid thee watch the doors of day,
For Luda soon would come away.

" See'st thou that little cave of moss
Just a few steps the brook across,
Where stone-crops hang the entrance o'er,
And reeds and rushes make the floor ?
There oft methought I've heard thy name
In every gust of wind that came,
And felt thy voice, and seen thy face,
And wept I in this lonely place.
Behold this wreath : I wove it there ;
That shining knot is Luda's hair,
And these dear flowers did sweetly grow
A few yards from my lattice low :

And this was thine, with roses set,
When on the shores of joy we met.
No words are strong enough to name
The anguish which devoured my frame,
When thou didst roam mid stranger men :
My heart was like a ruin then.
To-day I donned this sacred dress
Worn by the British Druidess,
And left my mother moaning loud
To die amid the excited crowd,
And join my palmer in the isle
Where everlasting pleasures smile.
Hark ! sacred sounds o'ertop the height,
Scaring the wood-dove in his flight.
Thou know'st the sequel. Wipe the tear :
Minerva's blessing crowns us here."

The palmer gently raised her now ;
A light seemed beaming on his brow,
And shining genii thronged the glade,
As stooping down he kissed the maid ;
Then in a voice both sweet and clear
Those words fell softly on her ear :

" Dear Luda, one brief hour of bliss
So sweet, so exquisite as this,
Is worth long years of toil and care,
And much of penitence and prayer.
How have I waited, sweet, for thee !
And this is rich reward for me :
Another kiss, and yet one more,
And then an endless love in store.
But, Luda, list, our gods are wrong ;
Thy palmer now reveres the Strong.
To Him alone direct thy prayer,
The one great Ruler everywhere,
Whose presence speaks in every place,
The one Redeemer of our race.
I've seen your sacred rites to-day,
And sad and sighing turned away ;
And as I walked among the trees
So gently murmuring in the breeze,
A voice came floating from the cloud
Which down the western hill-peak bowed :
' Your heathen feasts and holy fires,
The dark religion of your sires,
Your Druid lore and temples lone,
Shall very soon be overthrown :
Your powerless gods shall faint and fall,
And He shall reign that ransomed all.' "

Could you have seen that maiden's face,
So lovely in this lonely place,
You'd surely deem some angel bright
Had wandered from the land of light,
The blissful clime of the forgiven,
To cheer the earth with gleams of heaven.
She spoke not, as along the glen
They walked in holy transport then ;
But thought was beaming in her eyes
Like fields of blue in rainbow skies.
Overhead a lark sang sweet and long,
Filling the moorlands with his song,
Whose gushes gladdened all the air,
As if a cherub's home were there.
Like raindrops when the sunshine fills
The April valleys and the hills,

Glittering from clouds through quiet skies ;
So fell the tears from Luda's eyes.

Along the dingle then they hied
In sweetest converse side by side,
Charmed with the ripple of the burn,
And swallows wheeling mid the fern.
The bramble-bud and woodbine there
Flung showers of fragrance on the air ;
And tangled tufts of heather smile
By pleasant banks of camomile.
Beneath a hawthorn on the moor,
The nearest to her mother's door,
Whose spreading top with flowers is white,
They stand at last, and view the sight :
When thus the palmer :
                          " All things here
Are changing with the changeful year.
Oft Gentleness is left to mourn,
While Pride has much to call his own ;
And Pomp with high caress appears,
While Merit walks in weeds and tears.
Love is beneath the spreading sky
The only thing that will not die :
And such is ours. Distress may come
And famine crouch within our home ;
The wolf of want may stand and stare
Upon our table blank and bare ;
Disease may smite us with his hand ;
As in the clime of cold we stand,
Our half-clad limbs benumbed and spare
May shiver in the icy air ;
Mid thunder-roar or lightning-flame
Our mutual love is still the same,
To die not till our spirits rise
To walk the groves of Paradise.

" But listen, Luda, bend thine ear :
Thy palmer knows there's danger near.
The foe, the foe,—the cruel Dane
Is stalking through the land again.
I've seen within yon shaggy glen
A portion of their armed men.
How flashed their blades so reckless thrown !
Their words were sharp as pointed bone.
Our homes and friends we hold so dear
Are all unsafe while they are near.
Itonanes' mandate is gone forth
From east to west, from south to north,
To summon all his warrior train
To shield their own firesides again,
And save their wives and blossoms bright
From cruel fate more dark than night.
My path is ta'en : I see my way :
I see it, love, and must obey.
This is no time for sighs and tears
And gentle lays to lady's ears :
My country calls me, and I go
To meet the bold invading foe ;
May be, some fainting chief to cheer,
When strife is high, and death is near.
Another kiss. Love, do not weep.
Hark, hark, the trumpet on the steep !
Corn Brea is rife with spear and bow :
We meet in heaven or meet below."

NOTES ON BOOK SECOND.

Note 1, Page 103.

Where a rough Druid temple stood.

" It is by no means to be questioned but that they" (the Druids) " retained and publicly exercised their other more innocent rites of worship,—and in private it is much to be suspected that they continued also their ancient bloody customs,—even till Christianity itself appeared. Indeed, after Christianity their fondness for human victims continued; and some of their rites seem also to have reached down far below the date of their conversion to Christianity."—BORLASE's " Antiquities of Cornwall," pp. 148, 149, 331.

Note 2, Page 103.

Before mid-day to reach the grove.

" The principal times for ordinary devotion were either at mid-day or midnight."—BORLASE, p. 119.

Note 3, Page 103.

Beyond the rude *gorseddau-seat.*

Gorseddau—" seat of judgment." See BORLASE, "Antiquities," p. 114.

Note 4, Page 103.

Adown the glen on palfrey white, &c.

The Druids were clothed in white. On their head they had a diadem or tiara. They wore a badge of honour on their garments next in dignity to that of sovereign princes. The Druids had the privilege of wearing six colours in their robes, the king and queen seven, the nobles five. Their shoes were of a singular shape, made of wood, of a pentagonal form. The general distinction of their order was the figure of a serpent's egg. They wore also on their garments a crescent. The Druids had white horses. The younger Druids were without beards, the old had very long ones, and sometimes a wreath of oaken leaves round their temples. Their garments reached down to their heels, and generally their eyes were fixed upon the ground.—BORLASE, pp. 120, 121, 134.

Note 5, Page 103.

His left uplifts a hook of gold, &c.

In gathering the mistletoe they used only the golden hook.—*Ibid.*, p. 92.

Note 6, Page 103.

The crescent moon, the crescent moon, &c.

The beginning of their year was July, the moon six days old ; and an age or generation was thirty years. When the end of the year approached, they marched with great solemnity to gather the mistletoe of the oak, inviting all the world to assist at this ceremony with the words, " The new year is at hand : gather the mistletoe." The Druids accounted nothing more sacred than the oak mistletoe, which was approached with great reverence, principally when the moon was six days old.—*Ibid.*, pp. 91, 92.

Note 7, Page 103.

To cut the golden mistletoe.

The mistletoe was of a golden colour, an adventitious plant of the climbing kind ; and therefore the golden bough is compared to it by Virgil.—*Ibid.*, p. 92.

Note 8, Page 103.

Teutates is our war-god strong, &c.

" Mercury was their chief deity. After Mercury they worshipped Apollo, whom they called Balenus, and sometimes Belis: by him they meant the sun. Then Mars, whom they called Hesus, and Teutates, and next Minerva. Apollo cured diseases ; Minerva taught all works of ingenuity and handicraft ; Jupiter reigned in heaven, and Mars presided in war."—*Ibid.*, p. 104.

Note 9, Page 104.

And then the priest, in robe of white, &c.

" They prepare the sacrifices and religious feasts under the tree, and lead forth two white bulls, never yoked, nor their horns till then bound with ropes : the priest, clothed in white, ascends the tree, and with a golden hook cuts off the mistletoe, which is received in a white garment spread for that purpose."—*Ibid.*, p. 92.

Note 10, Page 104.

Oak-leaves upon the altar lie.

Without the leaves of the oak were first strewed on the altar, no sacrifices could be regularly offered. The priest first prayed, then the victim was offered, wine and frankincense attending.—*Ibid.*, pp. 150, 120.

Note 11, Page 104.

Turning his body to the sun, &c.

The Druids turned their bodies sun-ways in their worship, and during the prayers walked round their assemblies, their holy cairns, and their religious fires. —*Ibid.*, pp. 124-127.

Note 12, Page 104.

The fated victim's hour is come, &c.

" Variety of deaths they had for those miserable victims. Some they shot to death with arrows ; others were crucified in their temples. One Druid sacrifice was still more monstrous. They sometimes made a huge image of straw, which they filled with human beings and wild beasts, burning the whole together in honour of their gods, the drums and trumpets drowning the cries of the miserable victims. Intemperance in drinking generally closed the sacrifice."—*Ibid.*, pp. 122, 123.

Note 13, Page 104.

Her linen cloak with clasp made tight, &c.

" The Druidesses are described by Strabo to have had white hair, white gowns, linen cloaks joined together by clasps, to have been girt with a girdle of brass work, and their feet naked. In their hand they carried a magic rod."—*Ibid.*, p. 121.

Note 14, Page 105.

In yon high palace of the west, &c.

The Druids sat on golden thrones, lived in large palaces, and fared sumptuously. They were the principal governors of the state.—*Ibid.*, p. 79.

Note 15, Page 105.

Bade Luda give her life away
Upon the funeral pile to-day, &c.

Some willingly threw themselves into the funeral pile of their friends, in order to live with them after death.—Borlase, p. 94.

Note 16, Page 105.

'Twas when October's face was pale, &c.

The Druids had their solemn fires on the eve of November, to which the people were obliged to resort, and re-kindle the private fires in their houses from these consecrated fires of the Druids, the domestic fires in every house having been for that purpose first carefully extinguished.—*Ibid.*, p. 130.

Note 17, Page 105.

And as he walked, his mystic verse
In solemn tone did he rehearse, &c.

The Druids comprised all the particulars of their religion and morality in hymns, the number of which was so great, that the verses which composed them amounted to twenty thousand. The bards were remarkable for an extraordinary talent of memory, and teaching by verse was very likely their office.—*Ibid.*, pp. 83, 84.

Note 18, Page 105.

To dig the vervain in the shade, &c.

"The Druids were excessively fond of the vervain. They used it in casting lots and foretelling events. Anointing with this they thought the readiest way to obtain all that the heart could desire, to keep off fevers, to procure friendships, to heal all distempers. It was to be gathered at the rise of the dogstar, without being looked upon either by sun or moon ; in order to which the earth was to be propitiated by a libation of honey. The iron instrument dedicated to the rite was to describe a circle round the plant, and then dig it up ; in doing which the left hand was to be used, and to wave it aloft after it was separated from the ground. The leaves, stalk, and roots were to be separately dried in the shade; and if their couches were sprinkled with an infusion of it in water, the feasts were thought in a fair way of being much the merrier for such a sprinkling."—*Ibid.*, p. 91.

Note 19, Page 105.

He said by this the Eubates knew.

There were three degrees of Druids. The superior class were called *the* Druids. They had under and next them the Bards, who, though inferior in rank, are said to be prior in antiquity. These were the poets of the Britons and Gauls. The Eubates, or *Vates*, were of the third and lowest class. Their business was to foretell future events.—*Ibid.*, p. 67.

Note 20, Page 105.

And by the selago that grew, &c.

"With great care and superstition did the Druids gather the selago. Nothing of iron was to touch or cut it, nor was the bare hand thought worthy of the honour ; but it was first covered with a sacred vesture taken privately from some holy person. The gatherer was clothed in white, his feet naked and washed in pure water. He was first to offer a sacrifice of bread and wine. The selago was then gathered, and carried from the place of its nativity in a clean new napkin."—*Ibid.*, p. 23.

Note 21, Page 105.

That morn, as neighed their horses white, &c.

The Druids had certain white horses, which were carefully fed in their sacred groves ; by observing the neighing of which future events were foretold. Not only the common people, but the nobles and priests, placed great dependence on this way of divining.—*Ibid.*, p. 134.

Note 22, Page 105.

And in the pile a letter hurled, &c.

"Others threw letters into the funeral pile, to be read by the deceased in the other world."—*Ibid.*, p. 94.

BOOK THIRD.
THE ATTACK.

There is a Book all books above ;
  Its every line is traced by love.
  Here gems and choicest pearls abound,
  And richest mines of wealth are found.
Here streams of living waters run,
To gladden all beneath the sun ;
Destined to cheer the seeking soul
From zone to zone, from pole to pole,
Through every age, on every shore,
Till changing time shall be no more.
The son of suffering here may find
A solace for his burdened mind ;
The child of want and woe and wrong,
The poorest pauper of the throng,
The beggar-man, the harlot ill,
The rich, and whosoever will,
May open it themselves, and read
Of such a Saviour as they need.

How brightly does this teaching shine
Amid the oracles Divine,
That war shall die the wide world o'er,
And man shall trample man no more !
From battle sword and spear shall cease,
And change within the land of peace
To implements of comfort rare,
The pruning-hook and shining share ;
And on each vale and mountain-head
The knowledge of the Lord will spread,
Until the earth o'erflowed shall be
As swelling waters fill the sea.
The wolf within the flowery mead
Shall with the sportive lambkin feed :
The leopard and the lion strong
The little child shall lead along ;

And o'er all lands in sweetest strains
Shall float, " IMMANUEL EVER REIGNS."
The time must come, it will not stay ;
His word shall never pass away.

I can't forget a lonely bower,
O'ergrown with moss and many a flower,
A gentle covert mid the hills,
Refreshed by reeds and mountain rills,
Where swallows wheel and robins sing,
And glowworms sparkle by the spring :
I love it much, because I found
My harp within its sacred bound ;
And thought revisits it full oft,
And finds a *sanctum* in the croft,
Though I am now so far away
Mid human suffering and decay.
Here childhood has its story told,
Some fairy tale or legend old,
Which charmed the listening Eve until
The harvest moon rose o'er the hill,
And Georgie with the empty wain
Came trotting down the Lovers' Lane.
Those days are gone like dreams which were,
But tale and legend linger there.

Tradition says on *Carn Brea* land,[1]
Near where the rough rock-basons stand,
A dreadful battle once was fought
'Twixt saints and Satan on this spot.
With fury fierce huge blows they wage,
Then hurl these boulders in their rage,
Shaking the old hill to its bed,
And echoing through the air o'erhead,
Till beaten Beelzebub gave way,
And groaning in the valley lay.
But other theme demands our verse,
Which now we hasten to rehearse.

The castle-ground is thronged with men,
And warriors hasten from the glen
On horse, a-foot, all armed and brave,
Resolved their own firesides to save,
To fall or conquer in the fray,
But ne'er to yield : true patriots they.
And soon the foemen are in view
Marching in fury near *Reddrew*. [2]
A savage band they are, and strong,
And haughtily they dash along,
Spoiling the land from stage to stage
In spite of innocence and age.

Rouanes saw them from the wall,
And bade his warriors heed his call,
And form themselves in phalanx good,
Then boldly sally from the wood.
And march to meet this robber-horde,
Nor suffer them to cross the ford.
He blew his trumpet loud and shrill :
Its echoes rolled from hill to hill,
From peak to peak, from plain to plain,
Over the woods, then back again.
The stag rose up and snuffed the breeze,
Then fleetly bounded through the trees :
The charger neighed to hear the sound,
And flocks of wild birds wheeled around.

The foe stood still that blast to hear,
And seemed at once o'erta'en with fear.
So sudden was it, they fell back,
Their spear-heads resting on their track.
Upon that issuing host of men
The Normans fixed their eager ken,
As down the mount with armour bright
The British bowmen came in sight.
From rank to rank the Druid flies,[3]
The wild fire flashing in his eyes,
With drawn sword and extended spear,
Bidding the soldiers banish fear.

" Behold," said he, " yon plundering band,
How ravage they our native land !
Our gods will surely shield the right,
And aid our warriors in the fight.
With lifted hands for you I pray,
Who to the rescue rush to-day.
Go forth and conquer. In the shock
Stand, spearmen, like your native rock.
By signs that sweep before my view
I know that victory waits on you.
Wade deep in slaughter. Let your bow
Twang to the downfall of the foe.
But should you on the field be laid,
And fall beneath the Northman's blade,
A pleasant passage you shall gain
Into the land where riches reign,
And fragrant gales from fadeless flowers
Float on you in Elysian bowers.
Then your accounts shall settled be [4]
When the fair groves of love you see,
And mid the stars ye speed along
In bodies beautiful and strong.
There you shall ride on horses fleet,[5]
In glittering armour most complete ;
And food and clothes and riches own
Which on the earth were never known.
So, warriors, onward ! Fight, or fall !
A rich reward awaits you all."

The Druid waved his sword on high,
Which cleft the air as he strode by.

Rouanes in his chariot rode ; [6]
The horses' full manes richly flowed :
Of polished yew the beam was made,
Its seat with smoothest bone inlaid ;
Sharp scythes and hooks, made thin and bright,
Were to the axis fastened tight.
High sat the kingly charioteer ;
In his left hand he held a spear ;
A quiver full of arrows keen
Behind his shoulders might be seen ;
And o'er the steeds he somewhat leant,
As if to aid them as they went.
Before him marched his spearmen strong,
Behind him came the archer throng,
With many a noble charioteer,
And troops of horsemen close the rear.
Swept down the hill this warrior train,
And drew up grandly on the plain.

No spear was thrust till eve appeared,
And then the war-steeds foamed and reared :

Plumes rose and fell, band fronted band,
Now foot to foot and hand to hand.
From lifted arms the broad swords flashed.
The trumpets brayed, and helmets crashed;
The arrow from the twanging bow
Let out the life-blood of the foe,
And shrieks of fury rent the air.
For Slaughter's gory arm was bare.
The sun went down in skies of red.
And scarlet were the clouds o'erhead;
And scarlet were the crags which lay
Like watchful warriors on *Carn Brea;*
And scarlet were the tree-tops then
On mountain peak, and echoing glen,
And castle-top, and narrow pass;
And crimson drops were on the grass.—
The blood of men with weapons gored,
Which stained the waters of the ford.

The warfare had not long begun
Ere many daring deeds were done.
I only mention Corma's might,
For ever foremost in the fight.
Born was he by a Cornish loch.
And reared amid the mountain block.
A Briton brave, a warrior bold,
Nor shrank he from the heat or cold.
His arm was like an arm of oak,
Which felled the foe at every stroke;
Nor thrust he o'er his lance in vain,
But left behind him hills of slain.
Once, near a rift where water flashed,
Three daring Northmen on him dashed
With brazen blades and darts of bone;
But mighty Corma stood like stone:
He stooped to avoid a well-aimed blow,
Then dead in dust he laid his foe.
Amazed the second Norman stands;
He lopped his limbs like willow-wands;
Then thrust him through; the strong blade bent
And snapped within the gory rent.
His third man dealt him thrusts of wrong
With sinewy limbs and muscles strong,
So quick and sure that one of these
Caused him to stagger to his knees:
Then to his feet great Corma sprang
Amid the battle's rising clang,
And caught the *Viking* * by the locks,
And flung him o'er the frowning rocks;
And ere he reached the chasm's floor,
An arrow drank his issuing gore.

Ronanes bade his men fall back
A few feet from the river's track,
Form in a mass, and then rush o'er
With flashing blade and thundering roar,
And deal a desperate final blow
Upon the already quailing foe,
Till every Northman left the land
Or fell before the British band.
Sudden as thought they wheel around,
Then clear the river at a bound,
Which through the invaders strikes dismay,
For like a wall of blades were they.

* Sea-King

The Normans paused, and shook, and fled,
Leaving the hill-side strewn with dead.
The chieftain mid his followers stood,
And left his chariot by the wood.
At once the swift pursuit began,
And rushed along each armed man:
Rose up to heaven an awful cry,
O'er hill and dale, and down they fly.
The arrow hisses through the air,
The sword and spear are flashing there;
Huge blows are dealt by heroes strong;
Victor and vanquished rush along,
Away, away, by dyke and dell:
At every thrust a Northman fell:
Away, away, o'er moss and mound,
Through wood and waste and rocky ground ;
Away, away, o'er hillocks high,
Away, away, beyond *Karn-kei;*
Away, away, through mineral lands,
Where now my native *Camborne* stands;
Away, away, pursued and pressed,
Towards the waters of the west ;
Away, away, by tor and tarn,
Till war-men rose on every carn.

Just then an arrow sped full fast
Which pierced Ronanes as it passed ;
And in a moment they fell back,
The gore-drops falling on their track.
They laid him on their weapons strong,
And bore the wounded chief along ;
His martial cloak they o'er him threw,
And crossed the ford beyond *Reddrew;*
Then up the hill-side wound their way,
And reached the castle on *Carn Brea.*
The ancient hall they quickly passed,
And placed him on his couch at last.
He drained the silver goblet dry,
And thus addressed his warriors nigh.

"My end is near, an end of bliss :
Ronanes always longed for this,—
To fall where Battle's banners wave,
And gain the booty of the brave ;
To give life's latest lingering sand
In striving for my own dear land.
Already in the clime of stars
I see the dwelling-place of Mars ;
He beckons me to come and share
The treasures which await me there.
The foe is routed, never more
To pillage on our sea-washed shore.
How did our swords like lightning fall,
And blanch and blight the Northmen all!
The field is ours. 'Tis glory now
To feel the death-dew on my brow.
Farewell, farewell ! So rest thee, blade !
Entomb me where our chiefs are laid.
But hark, methinks I hear the drum ;
I would that holy man were come."

The palmer up the mountain strode
Towards the chieftain's high abode ;
For as he o'er the wounded bent,
And by the dying warrior leant,
Whose latest words a blessing bore
For him whose love was known before,

But whose clear face serene and mild
Now seemed some genius of the wild,
Sent by the gods to calm their ills
With waters from Elysian rills,
And give their passing souls relief,—
He knew the danger of their chief.
So, with a priest of hoary hair,
Whose acts of love were sacred there,
He left his feeble charge, and went,
On mercy's holy mission sent,
Towards the castle on the brea,
Where in his wounds Rouanes lay.

And as he through the bracken pressed,
With serious thought within his breast,
A sharp shrill sound afflicts his ear,
Like one deep pierced with pain or fear.
It seemed some female voice, and he
Turned from the narrow path to see
From whence and whom this utterance came
Which sent a shudder through his frame:
When, lo, beside a narrow rill
Which trickled slowly down the hill,
Whose shallow edge with blood was dyed,
A maiden lay and faintly sighed.
An arrow from the flying foe
Had laid the gentle damsel low ;
And here upon the turf she lay,
As ebbed her lovely life away.

The palmer reached this fading flower,
Thus strangely bruised in Nature's bower;
And spoke some words of holy trust
From Him whose ways are true and just,
Whose path is on the earth and sea,
Whose grace for all is rich and free.
And as he laved her forehead white,
And laid aside her tresses bright ;
He gazed upon her features fair,
And knew 'twas Luda dying there,
His Luda : and the palmer sank
Beside her on the mossy bank ;
Then lifted up his hands and prayed,
As oped her eyes the sinking maid.
She knew him, and a loving smile
Passed o'er her beauteous face the while :
Her pale lips murmured faint and clear :

" My precious palmer, art thou here ?
I little deemed that this would come,
When last we parted near my home,
Stoop down and kiss my icy brow :
Our tree of hope is blighted now.
Death comes to smooth my latest bed :
Hark, hark, I hear his welcome tread.
With thee, my love, the flowers, and sky,
And twittering birds, 'tis bliss to die.
And now a faintness on me falls ;
Upon the cloud a spirit calls.
How sweet the music floats along !
The very heavens are filled with song.
Your words are lodged my heart within :
There is a God who pardons sin.
I trust in Him ; there's safety there,
And not in any Druid's prayer.
Another and another kiss,
And then for aye the heaven of bliss."

The breeze sighed slowly o'er the tarn,
Stirring the heather of the carn ;
Passed through the tree-tops bending nigh,
And shook the ferns as it stole by.
The lark soared up his path of air,
And sang as if no woe were there ;
The swallows sported o'er the heath,
Though sin and suffering lay beneath ;
And gales of fragrance filled the moor,
And spread the rocky mountain o'er.
Across the hill, the gorse among,
An aged woman walks along :
Her piercing scream is on the air,
Her head and streaming locks are bare :
And as she hastens through the wild,
She sadly sobs, " My child ! my child !"
She heedeth not the raven's wing,
She heedeth not the rabbit's spring,
She heedeth not the earth or sky,
Or shining flowers that blossom by,
Or singing bird, or mossy stone ;
But evermore she makes her moan,
Whose echoes reach the mountain's brow.

" My dying daughter, where art thou ?
Call on our gods, and they shall come,
And take thee to their glorious home.
Great genius of the rocks and glens,
Thou silent watcher of the fens,
Whose powerful voice I ever hear,
O lead me to my daughter dear,
That I may see my child once more,
Before she gains the richer shore."

She hastened on with earnest pace,
With grief's dark shadow on her face :
But ere she reached that brooklet's bed,
Her lovely Luda's life had fled.
The palmer kissed her marble brow ;
His burning tears fell freely now,
And uttered he such sighs of woe
As severed love alone can know.
But though a shadow veiled the sun,
His heart replied, " Thy will be done !"
Then in the stricken matron's care
He left that lifeless form so fair,
And climbed the carn with trembling feet
Towards the warrior's rough retreat ;
And as each footfall bore him higher,
These words rang from him like a lyre :

" How soon the earth is dark for me !
How soon the green has left the tree !
How soon life's choicest flower is flown,
And I am on my path alone,
With no star beaming over head
And hope's inviting landscape fled !
I've nothing now to lure my stay,
But Heaven's behests I must obey.
Henceforth my life shall only be
A willing sacrifice for Thee,
To spread the knowledge of His name
Who for the vilest rebel came.
I hear the holy tidings now
Roll grandly o'er the mountain's brow,
That war and wickedness shall die,
And perish underneath the sky ;

Nor round the world shall battle moan ;
  For Christ shall reign, and Christ alone."

He hastened on at duty's call,
Nor paused he till he reached the hall,
And saw the warrior lying low,
Whose great life ebbed at every throe.
O, he had only time to read
From his best Book that better creed,
And one short prayer of import high,
When thus Rouanes made reply :

"I thank thee for thy words of love :
Another light breaks from above,
Another glory meets my view.
My warriors all ! a last adieu :
The air is full of swords and spears,
And battle-trumpets shake mine ears.
My horsemen, on !"—

                    And down he lay,
With nothing left of him but clay.

And when the moon at twilight hour
Was rising over brake and bower,
Within the dim religious gloom
They laid the war-chief in his tomb,
Within a stone-chest by the flags,
Just underneath the old hill's crags.
In his *kist-vaen* they placed his spear,[7]
His battle-bow, and war-trump dear,
His helmet, hunting-cloak, and shield,
And brass sword which he oft would wield,
When War walked wildly on his way,
And victory led him in the fray ;
Then blew their trumpets loud and long,
And chanted thus his burial-song :

"Rest, chieftain, rest ! The rocks around
Shall watch for aye the hero's mound.
The plover oft shall wing the hill,
And drop for thee his whistle shrill,
And lichen-leaves and mosses spread
Above Rouanes' battle-bed.

"We leave thee now 'neath clouds and stars,
Thou favoured of the mighty Mars.
The crossing lightnings here shall flash,
And thunders o'er thy crag-house crash,
And wailing winds and tempests strong
For evermore thy fame prolong.

"Lie down, lie down. The seasons here
Shall watch our mighty leader's bier ;
And morn and eve and listening night
Repeat the mystery of thy might,
Until the earth grown old and grey
In flaming fire shall pass away."[8]

Then down the mount the warriors came,
And left the chieftain to his fame,
With nothing there to mark his bed,
Save the big boulders over head.

Beside a war-path on the brea
An urn with Luda's ashes lay,

And oft the palmer sought the hill
To visit it when winds were still ;
And here, when twilight filled the land,
His head oft resting on his hand,
He sat and listened, while his eyes
Were fixed upon the distant skies,
And drops fell down his thoughtful face,
And wet the mosses of the place.

One eve, what time the moon was new,
And all the sky was clear and blue,
He bade farewell to scenes so dear,
And parted from them with a tear,
To preach in homes the hills between
The doctrines of the Nazarene.
Nor paused he till our western land
Had heard the Saviour's just command,
And where the thorn choked up the wild
The Rose of Sharon sweetly smiled.
And when the Roman rose to reign,
Then fell the Druid and the Dane.

With Arthur's name we close our tale,
Who fought in *Vellan Druchar* vale,
When not a Sea King lived to tell
How swift their latest remnant fell.
In *Genvor Cove* the daring Dane
Had landed from his ships again ;
And here and there along the land
They pillage armed with spear and brand.
The beacon-fires threw out their ray
From rude *Trecrobben* to *Carn Brea :*
St. Agnes and *Cadbarrow* black
Soon fling an answering signal back,
And *Roughtor* and *Brownwilly* high
Sent up their war-sign to the sky,
Which roused King Arthur and his men,
Who at *Tintagel* feasted then ;
And buckling on their armour bright,
Forth sallied many a valiant knight.
Nine full-armed kings with Arthur go,
And in two days they reached the foe,
And fought with such a desperate will
That blood was shed which worked the mill.[9]
The wind arose with dirgeful roar,
And cast their ships upon the shore,
And blades were snapped and helmets cleft,
Till not a single Dane was left.

Like seers from the recording seat
The cycles of the ages meet.
No savage frowns their features mar,
No thirst for blood, no battle-scar :
The sword of strife is spent with rust,
The spear is splintered in the dust,
The bow lies broken on the plain,
And friendship's arms embrace the Dane.
She comes, she comes, the Princess fair,
From *Denmark's* dells to Albion's Heir ;
And welcome Alexandra brings
For *England's* isle a line of kings.

NOTES ON BOOK THIRD.

Note 1, Page 109.

Tradition says, on *Carn Brea* land, &c.

See Elihu Burritt's "Walk from London to the Land's End, and back," p. 329.

Note 2, Page 109.

Marching in fury near *Reddrew*.

"In this hill of *Karnbrea* we find rock basins, circles, stones erect, remains of cromlechs, karns, a grove of oaks, a cave, and an enclosure of a religious kind; and these are evidences sufficient of its having been a place of Druid worship. The town about half a mile across the brook which runs at the bottom of this hill was anciently called *Red-drew*, that is, the Druid's Ford, or Crossing of the Brook. *Red-drew--Redruth*."—Borlase's "Antiquities of Cornwall," p. 116.

Note 3, Page 109.

From rank to rank the Druid flies, &c.

The Druids frequently attended military expeditions, praying with great fervency to their gods with hands uplifted to heaven. Their presence was extremely useful in the field; for in the day of battle their office was to animate their troops by inculcating the immortality of the soul, and assuring them either of victory or a passage into a state of happiness.—*Ibid.*, p. 79.

Note 4, Page 109.

Then your accounts shall settled be, &c.

"So confident and assured of a future life were the Druids, that they very often put off settling their accounts till they met in the other world."—*Ibid.*, p. 94.

Note 5, Page 109.

There you shall ride on horses fleet, &c.

"They imagined that in the other life the man had all the same wants and the same passion for horses, armour, food, clothes, the same rights and claims to money, slaves, and every other property, which he had in the present life."—*Ibid.*, p. 96.

Note 6, Page 109.

Romance in his chariot rode, &c.

For description of British war-chariot see Du. Smith's "Religion of Ancient Britain," p. 29.

Note 7, Page 112.

In his *kist-vaen* they placed his spear, &c.

Kist-vaen—"stone chest." "They inserted such things in the grave, urn, or funeral pile, as the person deceased used or delighted in when alive."—Borlase's "Antiquities of Cornwall," p. 96.

Note 8, Page 112.

In flaming fire shall pass away.

"The Druids believed in a future state, the immortality of the soul, and that the world would be destroyed by fire."—*Ibid.*

Note 9, Page 112.

That blood was shed which worked the mill.

Arthur gave the Danes battle near *Vellan Druchar*. So terrible was the slaughter that the mill was worked with blood that day. Not a single Dane escaped. See Hunt's "Popular Romances of the West of England," Second Series, p. 62.

MINOR POEMS.

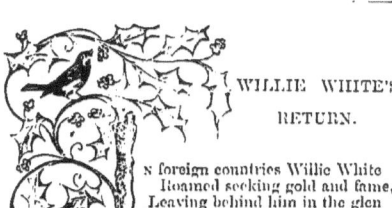

WILLIE WHITE'S RETURN.

In foreign countries Willie White
  Roamed seeking gold and fame,
Leaving behind him in the glen
  A poor but loving dame;
Leaving a sister and a sire,
  A brother by the streams,
And Mary, cherished more than all,
  The angel of his dreams.

The sun was shining on the lake,
  The lark was in the sky,
The milkmaid carolled by the bridge,
  As Willie White passed by.
He saw the mill-wheel in the vale,
  Which filled his heart with joy.
Where oft he whistled by the brook,
  A careless happy boy.

And then his cottage came in sight,
  He marked it through his tears;
O, he had not beheld its roof
  For many, many years.
Conflicting feelings filled his soul,
  As he stood listening there;
And from his lips warm praises rose,
  And from his heart a prayer.

His brother ploughed the hill-side farm
  Beside the orchard hedge,
Where little robin built its nest
  Among the moss and sedge ;
His sister to the great round pond
  Drove down the thriving kine ;
He waved his cap, and called their names,
  And they returned the sign.

His father shouted from the yard,
  Where he the reed did spin,
" Here's our own Willie home again :
  Come in, my boy, come in !"
His mother left the cake unturned
  Upon the great fireplace,
And rushed into his open arms,
  And wept upon his face.

The hours sped fast, as tales went round ;
  And when the day was flown,
Two blue eyes met him in the dusk :
  O, they were Mary's own !
He clasped the maiden to his breast,
  And all his secret told ;
And she that night had Willie's heart,
  And Willie's bags of gold.

THE FATHER'S GIFT.

" COME, John, we'll cease a-ploughing now :
    You turn the horse a-field,
    And bring the cows into the yard,
  Their luscious milk to yield.
Build up the old gap by the cairn,
  While it is evening light ;
Then hasten home ; for I have there
  A gift for you to-night."

John trotted down the narrow lane,
  To let the horses drink ;
And while they quaffed the cooling draught,
  The boy began to think :
" I wonder what my father has
  At home to give to me :
A little orphan lamb perhaps ;
  I know not what 'twill be."

A-feeding in the grassy mead
  He left the weary team ;
And, plodding on his homeward way,
  Indulged in many a dream.
And soon he passed the clinking mill,
  The stile, the barn of thatch,
And stood within his father's porch,
  With hand upon the latch.

The supper ended, grace was o'er,
  The playful girls and boys
Enjoyed themselves in leafy nooks
  With picture-books and toys;
When, sitting on a grassy seat
  Beside his rustic shed,
The old man called the boy to him,
  And thus he sweetly said :

" I offer thee no bags of gold,
  Or gems from fabled mine ;
No jewels bright, or costly robes,
  Or title-deeds are thine.
But thou, with health and honesty
  And industry and care,
Canst win those treasures for thyself,
  If thou wilt do and dare.

" But what I now present to thee
  Will prove of higher worth,
If rightly read and understood,
  Than all the gems of earth.
O, take this Bible from thy sire ;
  And may its light Divine
Illuminate thy path of life,
  As it has brightened mine ! "

Then kneeling down among the flowers
  In twilight's deepening shade,
Placing his hands upon his boy,
  The good old father prayed.
O, sweetest music filled the void,
  Low murmuring o'er the shed,
Floating upon the evening clouds
  From angels over head.

Time passed along with rapid flow,
  And upward grew the boy
To manhood's form : his father's gift
  Was evermore his joy.
He prized it more than glittering gold :
  And now he takes his stand
Among the gifted of the earth,
  The honoured of the land.

SAMSON SIDD.

AMONG the miners, Samson Sidd
    Was underground a digger ;
    He loved a damsel of the down,
  A graceful fairy figure.
They told him gold shone in the ground
  A month's fair sail from Dover,
And those who sought it always found :
  Said Samson, " I'll go over ! "

So he took ship, and sailed away,
  Leaving the maiden weeping ;
And through the years their first fresh love
  She in her soul was keeping.
The winds blew loud, the winds blew still,
  Through all the seasons swelling ;
But she was faithful to her vow
  Within her mother's dwelling.

One eve when bats flew by the church,
  Where yew-trees stood so stilly,
The tea was on the cottage-board,
  Where sat the gentle Milly ;
When on the porch a timid tap
  Came in the sparrows' chatter,
And up the mother gently rose
  To see what was the matter.

And when the door was opened wide,
  Among the wall-rose bushes,
A handsome man was standing there,
  And, O, how Milly blushes!
You'll guess, I know, 'twas Samson Sidd,
  With gold and jewels laden,
And a true heart within his breast,
  Come back to claim the maiden.

The old man rose to welcome him,
  And held his hand out lightly,
Stepping across the kitchen floor,
  And Samson grasped it tightly.
His wife smiled much to see him come,
  As she the biscuit buttered,
And brought the fresh cream in the cup,
  While Milly's bosom fluttered.

They placed the best chair on the mat,
  And kindly him they greeted:
Blush after blush warmed Milly's face,
  And Samson soon was seated.
And oft along the table-top
  With deep delight he glances;
As Milly meets his look of love,
  Her heart with pleasure dances.

And then he told them how his path
  Had been where gold was shining,
And that his fortune still held on
  Without the least declining.
And ere a month had passed away,
  Its blissful visions bringing,
For Samson Sidd and Milly May
  The marriage bells were ringing.

REVERIE.

Thought now is like a bark,
  Tossed where the waves are dark,
Drifting bewildered on some nameless clime:
  And so I turn my skiff,
  And clear this dangerous cliff,
And anchor in the peaceful port of rhyme.

Here soothing sounds delight,
  And on my gladdened sight
Stretch emerald landscapes, sweetly summered o'er:
  Castle, and old grey tower,
  Rude ivy-mantled bower,
And harpers, rush-screened, trilling on the moor.

No hours so sweet to me,
  With harp upon my knee,
On some smooth moss-bank, circled round with fays:
  Or be it wild with broom,
  Or still with solemn gloom,
'Tis ever sunshine, where I chant my lays.

If from my lattice low,
  As evenings come and go,
The mountain tops and purple clouds I see;
  Or hear the shepherd's strain,
  The wind, or gentle rain,
I'm not alone—this is enough for me!

Through the hot dust of strife,
  On the broad road of life,
The rhyme-paths of my youth my dim eyes fill:
  When morn, and noon, and night,
  Deep vale, and dizzy height,
Wore robes song-covered, as they ever will.

O, bliss! to turn my feet
  To some old cave's retreat,
Far from the tumult of the torturing crowd;
  Where nothing meets the eye,
  But sea, and earth, and sky,
And Cynthia riding o'er a snow-white cloud;

To hear the tinkling rills,
  To mark the fading hills,
To watch the light wane from the marshy moor;
  To catch the labourer's song,
  As home he hies along,
To kiss his children, watching by his door.

Perchance, some old weird mill,
  With buckets bulged and still,
May on the common, like a Druid, stand:
  Whose shadow in the lake
  Shall sweet psalm-dreams awake,
Leading the muser into fairy land.

O, may this joy be mine,
  Even till life's decline,
At dusk of day to watch the dwindling spire!
  So, take the crowd for me;
  I am content to be
Alone with Nature, and her mighty Sire!

MY MOTHER'S VOICE.

My mother's voice! it haunts me when
  I'm sitting in my cot,
  Surrounded with my little ones,
  The sharers of my lot!
Their voices chime, like music-chords,
  Within my humble bower:
But this is heard above them all,
  In sunshine and in shower.

I hear it when the midnight winds
  Are rushing o'er my head,
And busy thought drives sleep away
  From visiting my bed.
It comes on slumber's downy wings,
  'Tis blended with my dreams,
When wandering over unknown lands,
  Among the crystal streams.

I hear it when the storm is high,
  And when the winds are still;
I hear it in the sheltered vale,
  And on the storm-beat hill.
Yes! floating o'er its locks of heath,
  That silvery voice I hear,
Above the ruins of the past,
  In cadence sweet and clear.

I hear it in the busy throng ;
  I hear it when alone ;
I hear it in the darksome earth,
  The same melodious tone !
I hear it when my heart is sad,
  And when my lips rejoice ;
It floats around me everywhere,
  That same mysterious voice !

It leads me back when life was new ;
  Tells of those happy hours
I passed in childhood's sunny vale,
  Among the opening flowers :
Brings back again my early home,
  That home of homes to me,
Engraven on my heart of hearts,
  For ever there to be !

The music of this voice I hear,
  Above the world's rough roar,
Like whispers from another sphere,
  Some calm Elysian shore ;
Sweet harp-notes from the lyre of Time,
  Around me and within,
They gush with conquering ecstasy
  To lure my soul from sin.

I hear it in the moonlight bower,
  And by the murmuring stream ;
I hear it when spring's earliest flower
  Smiles in the sun's glad beam.
In weal, or woe, where'er I be
  On this revolving sphere,
Above the thunderings of the world
  My mother's voice I hear !

BESSY BRIGHTON.

"PUT on your hat, my darling :
    The summer sun is bright ;
    The greenwood leaves are beautiful,
  And winking in the light ;
The gossamer is floating
  Along its winding way :
So you may kiss your mother, dear,
  And go an hour to play."

Then little Bessy Brighton,
  Eight years of age or more,
With eyes as clear as dew-drops,
  Skipped from her cottage-door ;
And down a sandy channel
  Among the rocks ran she,
Where shells and shining shingles
  Were washed up by the sea.

Her mother plied her needle
  As fleet as rhymer's lay.
And scarcely thought of Bessy
  Who had gone out to play.
But when upon the table
  The tea-things all were spread,
She ran in haste to seek her
  With an uncovered head.

She called the name of Bessy
  Among the weeping flags ;
She shrieked the name of Bessy
  Among the ringing crags.
Nought but her own wild echo
  Came back upon her ear,
Or moaning of the ocean,
  Which filled her soul with fear.

A peasant lad, returning
  From labour on the lea,
Said, " Pretty Bessy Brighton
  Is floating on the sea.
I saw her as I travelled
  Around the fretted caves ;
I saw, but could not save her ;
  She's drowned among the waves."

She shrieked not at the tidings,
  But meekly bowed her head,
And quaked for inward anguish :
  " It is the Lord," she said.
Now in her cottage lonely
  Her daily task she plies,
With tears upon her pale face,
  And Eden in her eyes.

QUEEN VICTORIA AT THE ROYAL MARRIAGE.

IN Windsor's Royal Chapel,
    The nobles of the land,
    The flower of dear old England,
  Assemble heart and hand ;
And mitred Bishops cluster
  Around the Royal Pair,
Far Denmark's bud of beauty,
  And Albion's noble heir.

Within this holy structure,
  How many prayers ascend
For the good Prince and Princess,
  That Heaven would them befriend !
Standing before the altar,
  Their precious vows to plight ;
Whose future oped in glory,
  A hemisphere of light.

See, in the Royal Closet,
  The Queen in sad attire ;
Weeping, and wiping tear-drops,
  As crashes forth the choir !
Singing, in stately numbers,
  A chorale of the kind
"Albert the Good," who vanished,
  Leaving a light behind.

Intrude not on her sorrow,
  But bless those sacred tears,
Which flow from visions rising
  Out of departed years :
The dawn of love ; the bridal ;
  The first delicious flower ;
Bud after bud ; affliction ;
  And the sad parting hour.

Intrude not on her sorrow,
　O, let the fountain flow;
There's sweet relief in weeping,
　It blunts the edge of woe.
It softens much that's earthy,
　And sheds a power benign
Upon the chastened spirit,
　Which surely is Divine.

Did not our blessed Saviour,
　On hill and grassy glen
In hamlet-home, and city,
　Weep as He walked with men?
Then, break not on her sorrow,
　But let the drops run down
Upon her sable garments;
　"*She* wept to wear a crown!"

O, voices by the river,
　And voices on the sea,
In city, cot, and castle,
　On lawn and flowery lea,
Uprise from hearts unnumbered,
　While tears flow down the while,
"God bless our dearest Sovereign,
　The Queen of Britain's isle!"

TO MY BOWER.

DEAR natural bower! what a pleasure to greet
　Thy heath-hanging roof and thy moss-covered
　　　seat!
'Tis not very long I have fled from thy sight;
Yet since, in perspective, I've seen thee so bright,
So clothed with a mantle of sky-coloured light,
That I'd leave the great world at this tear-dropping
　　hour,
Could I muse once again in my heath-covered bower!

From the bustle of life how delicious to steal
To this grotto of quiet, my sadness to heal!
'Tis like balm to my spirit, like rest to my frame,
When I gaze on the height whence my forefathers came.
How familiar each rock in its ivy-clad throne!
How each hedge to my eye-ball distinctly is known!
How I love the fresh breeze! How I prize the young
　　flower
That smiles forth at spring in my heath-covered bower!

How sweet in this cave of retirement to kneel,
When the hallowing awe of devotion I feel!
And when to the God of my being I pray,
Who has guided me over life's thorn-piercing way,
How delicious the feast 'neath the mantle of even,
To drink of the streamlet meandering from heaven!
'Tis a sacred retreat where the song-spirits cower,
And sing their soft lays in my heath-covered bower!

We've been friends a long time in sorrow and glee;
Each day thou art dearer and dearer to me.
I love thee so well, I cannot but sigh
When I think,—O, how sad!—we must part by and bye.
The sigh of the rill in the distance is heard,
And mingled with this is the plaint of the bird;

A seraph's bright pinions are brooding above,
And around me is floating the music of love;
Angelical lays, on the drops of the shower,
Fall down from the sky in my heath-covered bower!

And when the wan moon, from her throne in the sky,
Gilds the mountain's crisp heath-locks that rustle
　　hard by;
When the sky-lark has hung his mute lyre on the
　　cloud,
And the light dews are dropping on twilight's dim
　．shroud;
When under the hawthorn my closet is made,
And I look to my Father, imploring His aid;
Methinks I then feel such a life-giving power,
As lifts me to heaven from my heath-covered bower!

What a peaceable spot! Not a motion of strife
Disturbs you, or ripples the current of life.
The din of the city affrights you no more:
At peace you may talk with the heroes of yore,
With spirits that long have departed on high,
To the home of the blest in the beautiful sky!
'Tis the fane of the Muse, where no sadness can lower:
The breezes have lyres in my heath-covered bower!

It is rough in its aspect, when seen from afar;
But to me it shines forth like a beautiful star.
'Tis more precious to me, the lone warbling one,
Than the wood-waving land where my kindred have
　　gone.
I would dwell in its quiet my life's little day;
And when the tired spirit shall flutter away,
O lay me to rest where will bloom the wild flower,
And the breezes sing sweet,—in my heath-covered
　　bower!

MY LITTLE WIFE AND I.

OLD Time has run with rapid race
　His journey to the tomb,
Since first I met my own dear Jane
　Where honeysuckles bloom.
I wonder, as I sit and muse,
　How swift the seasons fly;
For we've been married twenty years,
　My little wife and I.

Our path is sometimes overgrown
　With thorns and thistles drear;
But oftener it is smooth and sweet
　From changing year to year;
And if to-day the heavy clouds
　Should gather in the sky.
We have a moon of cloudless blue,
　My little wife and I.

When first I met her by the stile
　Within her native leas,
She was the fairest, daintiest flower
　E'er kissed by summer breeze.
Dame Nature kindly petted her;
　No gold her worth can buy,
As we go toiling on our way,
　My little wife and I.

Now children cluster round our board,
   Which oft is simply spread :
With thankful hearts and beaming eyes
   They eat their daily bread ;
And though my locks are thinning fast,
   As down the hill we hie,
We take the stony with the smooth,
   My little wife and I.

Oft when my rhyme-scrap is complete,
   Whate'er that scrap may be,
I read it to my gentle Jane ;
   A faithful critic she :
She stops her needle for a while,
   The thread hangs from the eye,
As we con o'er the written sheet,
   My little wife and I.

And how we chat above the brand
   That flickers in our home !
We make the best of what we have,
   And trust for days to come.
There is a loving Providence
   Who watches from on high,
And He will guide and He will guard
   My little wife and I.

What though we own no equipage
   Or servants in our train ?
Though lords and ladies know us not,
   My birdies or my Jane ?
We have our legs to carry us
   O'er mead or mountain dry,
Where Nature's beauties ever charm
   My little wife and I.

How leniently these forty years
   Have led her in their flight !
No place is like her own fireside,
   Her home is her delight.
We strive to live within our means,
   No useless things we buy,
Nor do we spend " 'tis buts " in drink,
   My little wife and I.

I reck not where our lot may be
   On this broad field of care ;
Give me my wife and children dear,
   I'm happy anywhere.
Thus hopeful, trustful, on we go ;
   And when at last we die,
O lay us where the daisies bloom,
   My little wife and I.

TO THE SWALLOW.

WELCOME, welcome, little swallow,
   Floating round my heathy hollow,
   Stooping down to kiss the flower
Bordering my balmy bower !
Many a by-gone tale thou bringest,
As away, away thou wingest,
Gliding o'er my native heath,
Sweeping down the vale beneath ;

Through the merry meads thou strayest,
With my mountain's locks thou playest ;
Now above my head thou wheelest,
Now through yonder dell thou stealest.
Welcome, welcome, little swallow,
Floating round my heathy hollow !

Bird of bright and glossy wing,
Coming to us in the spring !
Dost thou love these rocks so rude ?
'Tis the cave of solitude.
Here I've lingered many an hour ;
Bird, this is the poet's bower !
Float around me, little stranger ;
Float around me,—there's no danger.
Startling sounds won't here alarm thee :
Can a poet's musings harm thee ?
Other birds, the woods among,
Cheer us with their summer song ;
But thou'rt welcome, little swallow,
Floating round my heathy hollow !

DAVIE DRAKE.

A COTTAGE mid the moorland reed
   Smiled by the fabrics' turning ;
   And there it was that Davie Drake
First saw the light of morning.
He had a pleasant loving face ;
   His eyes with joy were beaming ;
And he among his native flowers
   Appeared like April dreaming.

The seasons ran their annual rounds,
   The sun and stars grew older ;
Ambition seized his thoughtful soul,
   And Davie Drake was bolder.
A voice seemed sounding on the hill,
   And whispering through the brier :
"Climb, Davie, climb ; the way is free
   To higher things and higher."

His friends were poor, his kindred few ;
   His father was a hedger ;
His only uncle on the cliff
   A weather-beaten dredger.
He had no one his mind to guide
   To teach him e'en the letters :
So Davie said, " I'll teach myself,
   And climb towards my betters."

The way was long, the hill was high,
   The rough ascent distressing ;
But Davie boldly persevered ;
   Still step by step progressing.
Hope walked beside him, chanting sweet,
   In rainbow-rich attire :
"Climb, Davie, climb ; the way is free
   To higher things and higher."

The people raised uncertain sounds,
   Which through the air were sighing,
As they looked on with folded arms,
   " 'Tis no use, Davie, trying."

He placed his fingers in his ears,
Impelled by warm desire,
And upwards through the mist arose
To higher things and higher.

At last he reached the golden height
With streaks of glory laden ;
He gained the Lily of the Loch,
The banker's matchless maiden.
He gained the honour of his race,
Who bowed before his lyre.
Still Davie Drake this motto bears :
" To higher things and higher."

GREEN FIELDS.

Home of the healthy breeze,
Ye song-inspiring leas !
I wake my reed upon your lap once more ;
And not a dear wild flower,
That woos the sun and shower,
But seems more lovely than in days of yore.

Here oft, beside this stile,—
The moon looked down the while,—
Have I sat gazing on the village spire ;
And as the solemn bell
Pealed through the hollow dell,
My buried thoughts rose high o'er mound and pyre.

Ah ! what is human life,
Its constant toil and strife ?
What, but a Spring bud beaten by the blast ?
Or cloud at dawning-time,
Or mist at morning's prime :
So soon they vanish, and so life is past.

Beside this hedge of thorn,
How sweet to muse at morn,
What time the skylark shakes him in the grass ;
Then spreads his dewy wings,
And soaring sunward sings,
Pouring his lyre-notes in a liquid mass !

Around me steals his song,
Soft, musical, and strong,
Trickling amid the mosses of the mead ;
Or where the daisies he
With dew-tears in their eye,
Or swelling sweetly through the oaten reed.

Dear rural sight and sound,
With pastoral graces crowned,
Throng round me musing by this meadow gate ;
And sheep-bells far away
Blend with the thatcher's lay,
While wren in earnest calls upon his mate.

O, sweet from man to fly,
And mid your flowers to lie,
Winding my simple fancies into rhyme !
And sweet your halcyon calm,
And sweet your breezy balm,
Like fragrance wafted from some holier clime.

I dare not love the town ;
Its full stream bears me down ;
But here my soul breathes fetterless and free ;
And round my vision throng
The genii of sweet song :
O, life is joyous passed upon the lea.

And when eve's purple vest
Hangs round the sleepy west,
And twilight's dusky gates wide open stand,
I ask no higher bliss,
No fuller cup that this,
To rove in rhyme-dreams o'er the meadow land.

And so, green fields, to you,
'Neath heaven's ethereal blue,
A pensive poet turns his weary feet :
For none will miss him here,
None mark the falling tear,
But the great Father on His shining seat.

THE CHILD'S FIRST PRAYER.

Weary with play, the little boy
To his fond mother ran,
Who kissed his pretty smiling face
As only mother can :
And bending o'er her little one,
She wept, although she smiled,
And taught him this, his first sweet prayer,—
" Our Father, bless Thy child ! "

Along the fragrant fields of May
He and his mother walked :
Summers and winters had passed by :—
How lovingly they talked !
Sweet was the music of their lips
That so the hour beguiled :
He knelt among the flowers, and said,
" Our Father, bless Thy child ! "

Behold him in the churchyard shed
Tears, bitter tears of woe :
His mother weeps beside him, too :—
His father is laid low !
But suddenly he stills the storm
Of bursting passion wild ;
And, bending o'er the grave, he says,
" Our Father, bless Thy child ! "

He stood upon a foreign shore,
To stately manhood grown ;
His mother to the better land
A long, long time had flown.
And here, where Nature's sentinels
In frowning ranks were filed,
He raised his eyes to heaven, and said,
" Our Father, bless Thy child ! "

This, through the changing scene of life,
Did not from memory part ;
His mother's voice was in his ear,
Her lesson in his heart.

And wheresoe'er his lot might be,
  In storms and tempests wild,
This was the pilgrim's sweetest prayer,—
  "Our Father, bless Thy child!"

His locks were silvered o'er with age,
  And dim his thoughtful eye,
When on a Christian Sabbath-eve
  He laid him down to die.
He fell asleep so peacefully,
  And, O! so sweetly smiled,
And whispered with his dying breath,
  "Our Father, bless Thy child!"

THE STORY OF ROBIN REDBREAST.

I'VE been down in the valley, and O, I have seen
Young Spring tripping on in her mantle of green:
A garland of buds on her forehead she wore:
I sang her a song, for I'd seen her before,
Flinging daisies and buttercups round the rough brae,
And studding the vales with the gems of young May.

By the brink of the rill, as it murmured along,
On a bud-bursting twig I awoke a new song,
And I saw where the waters delicious did lave
A cluster of primroses kissing the wave,
And a violet or two seemed to welcome my trill,
As I mingled my notes with the plaint of the rill.

Then I hopped on a bough of the green-budding thorn,
Where my mother has told me Cock Robin was born.
In an ivy-lined hole I directed my eye,
Where sightless and featherless once I did lie:
And when I beheld it, I warbled for glee,
That Robin was hatched in this bud-covered tree.

I flew o'er the valley, and rambled at will
To a straw-covered cot on the brow of a hill;
Where I crept from the tempest a short time ago,
When Winter was puffing around the white snow.
And I sang a whole day, but they gave me no meat,
And poor little Robin had nothing to eat.

So I fluttered away, faint, hungry, and weak,
The home of a good-natured poet to seek;
Crept forth to the door, hopped up on the sill,
Shook the snow-feathers off, and then knocked with
  my bill;
When out came the bard, and he gave me my fill.
So I sang him a song, with significant look;
He nodded, and wrote it all down in his book.

Night closed in around me, and fearful to say,
How affrighted I shrank from the storm-spirit's fray.
The frost-dews adhered to my ice-bitten toes,
And I thought my faint breathings were come to a
  close.
I saw a poor sparrow drop down from the thatch,
And flutter and die underneath the cold latch.

Then off to a snow-covered cow-house I crept,
Where in a cold cranny I shivered and wept;

And a pert little wren from the rafter did prate,
And no single whit seemed to pity my fate.
The storm howled tremendous, and groaned overhead,
And at midnight it tore off the roof of the shed.

I thought the fire-circle, amid all the crash,
Around little Robin incessant did flash;
And I deemed I was dead, but here I am still,
On the walls of the cow-house awaking my trill.
'Tis a trill of affection. But poor little wren
Has never been seen by Cock Robin since then.

How gloomy the fields were a short time ago!
But now they are covered with daisies,—not snow.
How fearful the wind was that wailed through the trees!
But now there is mirth in the voice of the breeze;
And poor little Robin exulting can sing,
"Hail, hail to thy coming, Spring, beautiful Spring!"

MANKIND ARE ALL REDEEMED.

THERE is a glorious sentiment
  Which earth and heaven rehearse;
  It flows from all material things,
  It fills the universe.
It rolls along life's rugged path,
  It on our fathers streamed:
'Twill echo down Time's latest march,
  "Mankind are all redeemed."

A thatcher at the early morn
  Sang on the roof-top clear,
And in the dew-damp sycamore
  The sparrows bent to hear.
The daylight, quivering through the brakes,
  O'er mine and mountain streamed,
As with a cheerful voice he sang,
  "Mankind are all redeemed."

A miner in his smoky cave,
  Amid his coarse employ,
In clouds of darkness visible,
  Thus sweetly sang for joy.
His toil-wet face and brow were pale,
  And very ill he seemed,
When carolling those thrilling words,
  "Mankind are all redeemed."

A sailor, sailing on the seas,
  A hundred leagues from land,
Amid the angry hurricane,
  Poured forth his carol bland:
And though the lightnings flashed around,
  And through the rigging gleamed,
His voice was heard above the storm,
  "Mankind are all redeemed."

A shepherd on the low hill's side
  Sat in the trees' cool shade,
While round him fed his fleecy flock
  Upon the tender blade.
Bright visions filled his thoughtful mind,
  As 'neath the oak he dreamed;
And lifting up his voice he sang,
  "Mankind are all redeemed."

A pilgrim by the waterfall
  Sang in the light of eve ;
A poet sauntering by the rill,
  A cheerful song to weave ;
A woodman in the breezy dells,
  Where fragrant flowerets teemed ;
A pale mechanic at his board,—
  " Mankind are all redeemed."

A little girl went singing where
  A streamlet slid along ;
And sweeter than the brooklet's flow
  Arose that maiden's song.
Methought the high hills rolled it back,
  That with eve's glory gleamed ;
And every valley echoed it,
  " Mankind are all redeemed."

STEER STRAIGHT FOR ME.

"THE fog is thickening, mother,
  And hanging o'er the bay ;
  I fear my dearest father
Will miss his homeward way.
He kissed me much this morning
  When stepping from our door ;
Then in his boat he left me,
  And pushed it from the shore.

" Look how it spreads and darkens
  On creek and cliff the same ;
I'll hasten o'er the shingles,
  And call my father's name.
Perchance his daughter's message
  At once he'll understand,
And my dear loving father
  Will safely steer to land."

And then the little maiden,
  With soft and silken hair,
And eyes brimful of beauty,
  And features round and fair,
Ran down the sandy hollow,
  And reached the sighing sea,
And, stooping to the billow,
  Cried, " Father, steer for me."

Bewildered in the darkness,
  He knew not where to glide ;
When her sweet words of welcome
  Came floating o'er the tide.
'Twas like an Eden whisper
  From shores where seraphs be,
That murmur on the waters,
  " Steer, father, straight for me."

He shouted in his gladness
  To hear his daughter's cry,
And soon upon the pebbles
  His boat was safe and dry ;
And he had clasped the maiden
  Within his fond embrace,
And lovingly imprinted
  Sweet kisses on her face.

O with what joy at evening
  They told the story o'er,
When safely by the ingle
  They sat in peace once more !
And how he loved his daughter,
  And felt his bosom swell
With gratitude unuttered,
  Is not for bard to tell.

Soon after this she sickened,
  And then she gently died,
Upon her lips " Our Father,"
  Like rose-bud in its pride ;
But from her grave it echoed
  Beneath the old yew tree,
" I'm up in heaven, dear father,
  And so steer straight for me !"

'Tis said that he was careless
  Of precious Gospel lore,
But his dear daughter's message
  Came from the higher shore,
Where angels walk in whiteness
  Beside the glassy sea :
" I'm up in heaven, dear father,
  And so steer straight for me !"

These words were with him ever,
  At morning, noon, and night :
" Steer straight for me, dear father,
  On Canaan's holy height ;"
Till, yielding to the Spirit,
  He prayed, and was forgiven :
And now he's with his daughter
  Upon the plains of heaven.

THE EMIGRANT'S DEPARTURE.

HE stood upon his native mount,
  And gazed along the sky :
  'Twas bluer than 'twas wont to be,
Or *looked* so to his eye.
And when the evening sun went down
  Behind the wavy west,
The tear-drop glistened in his eye,
  And heaved his labouring breast.

The music of the evening bells
  Came on the harping breeze ;
And O how sweet, how passing sweet,
  It floated through the trees !
Dame Nature tuned her sweetest lyre,
  Or *seemed* to tune it, then :
He never heard such melody,
  Nor hoped to hear again !

The peasants in the vale below
  Were at their evening meal ;
And when the merry village hum
  Did o'er his senses steal,
He turned away his saddened eye
  From scenes so dear beneath,
And dropped a tear in solitude
  Upon the rustling heath.

O! there were notes too sweet to last,
   That trembled o'er the plain ;
And there were shadows of the past,
   That swept across his brain :
And there were in his watery eye,
   Around him and above,
In every portion of the sky,
   Sweet images of love !

He thought the first bright flowers of May
   Had never looked so fair,
As when his last long lingering glance
   He bent upon them there.
He kissed the little murmuring stream
   Within his native dell,
And, as the evening star came forth,
   He sighed his last farewell !

The moon arose, and showered her beams
   Upon the ivied rocks,
And twined her silver tissues with
   The mountain's murmuring locks ;
When, with his hawthorn staff in hand,
   He left his cottage door,
And wandered to a foreign land,
   To see his home no more.

TO BE WHERE MAN IS NOT.

AMID the emerald meadows
   The lark unfolds his wings,
   And in the blue of ether
He high and higher sings :
The slender harebell bendeth
   Where mosses mark the spot :
How sweet in silent musing
   To be where man is not !

To walk by falling waters,
   And little lonely rills,
Which murmur 'mid the rushes
   Among the watching hills :
O, here the swallow glideth
   By many a fairy grot :
How sweet in solemn silence
   To be where man is not !

The murmur of the forest,
   The woodbine and the rose,
The thorn and tangled thicket,
   Along the dingle flows.
No music is like Nature's,
   By bird and breeze begot :
How much the soul may profit
   To be where man is not !

O, could my wish be granted,
   My dwelling-place should stand
Alone amid the mountains,
   With woods on either hand,
Where limpid runnels ripple,
   And thrush-notes link the thought ;
Contented thus for ever
   To be where man is not.

Full oft through sorrow's portals
   I sadly enter in
Where want and wrong are lying
   Upon the couch of sin ;
And pallid faces meet me   -
   In many a mouldy spot :
How yearn I in the clamour
   To be where man is not !

And oft where woe is wasting,
   Where noise and tumult reign,
Where pomp and pride are worshipped,
   And crowned with wondrous fame ;
Where merit lies in shadow
   To struggle with its lot ;
I long with tears for ever
   To be where man is not.

THE MOTHER'S TEACHING.

WITHOUT, the angry elements
   Were raging in their ire ;
   Within, the mother spoke of Christ
Beside the cheerful fire.
Her little ones were sitting round,
   To whom the world was new,
Drawing the honey from her lips,
   Like flowerets drinking dew.

She told how Christ a baby was
   In Bethlehem of old ;
He came from heaven in human form ;—
   So holy men have told.
He came from heaven in human form,
   His frame a human clod ;
He suffered, wept, and died below,
   And then went back a God.

The seed thus sown in early life
   Was like the precious grain,
When warmed by vernal suns, and cheered
   By spring's refreshing rain.
Dark days of weariness and cloud
   May often intervene ;
But then the little blade smiles forth,
   And then the ear is seen.

The parting blast of years hath blown
   Upon this little band,
And scattered them, like forest-leaves,
   Around their fatherland.
And that loved mother sleeps below,
   Beside the village fane ;
But, written on the earth and sky,
   Her living words remain.

Those lessons by the holy hearth
   Are travelling on and on,
Although the voice which uttered them—
   That mother's voice—is gone.
From age to age their course will be
   For evermore the same,
Till children's children joy to bless
   That mother's sainted name.

THE VILLAGE LANE.

O'ERSHADOWED, still retreat,
    Track trod by tuneful feet,
Haunt of the swallow, robin's rich domain,
    The freehold of the wren,
    The fairies' chamber when
.The moon is fullest! welcome, village lane.

    Beneath the spreading trees,
    Shook by the sighing breeze,
A few roods past the last house and the mill,
    Bubbles the village well,
    Where lads and lasses tell
The hamlet's wonders when the day is still.

    How sweet to wander here,
    When vespers murmur clear,
Tuning my harp betwixt the day and night!
    Then pictures, fairer far
    Than sky or peering star,
Throng on my vision o'er the dusky height.

    At such a quiet hour
    There comes a soothing power,
Found only in the path of solitude;
    And voices in the breeze,
    And voices in the trees,
Are richly laden with the spirit's food.

    Why crowd the sickly street,
    With noisy, feverish heat,
Where not a bud or living leaf is seen,
    But hills of brick and stone,
    Where weary wretches groan,
When you may wander where the walls are green?

    Come to the village lane,
    Enjoy its calm again,
As Eve steals forth to bend her favourite flower;
    Beneath the woodbine sit,
    Where bats in silence flit,
And muse on life beyond earth's little hour.

KATE.

SHE stood beside the old field-gate,
    Wiping her eyes, poor homeless Kate.
    Her lover played the traitor's part,
And left her with a bleeding heart:
To distant lands the sinner stole
With crime like fire within his soul.

Dark, blank, and wild the future lay
Before her without hope of day;
The hills were hung in clouds of gloom,
The valleys looked like dells of doom;
A frown was on the earth and sky,
And Kate, poor Katie, wished to die.

Where should she turn, where hide her head?
Her lover gone, her parents dead!
A stain was on her honest name,
Upon her cheek the blush of shame;
The tears kept gathering in her eye,
And Kate, poor Katie, wished to die.

The night came on; no home had Kate:
Still stood she by the old field-gate;
The rains came down, the winds did blow,
And smote her bosom white as snow:
She drew her torn cloak round her head,
And in the morning she was dead.

Rest, maiden, rest: there's peace for thee
Beneath the solemn cypress tree.
The voice of slander comes not near
To violate thy sleeping ear;
But little birds in twilight's gloom
Shall twitter ditties o'er thy tomb.

And shall the wretch who thus betrayed
The lovely, honest orphan maid,
And left her desolate to die,
Escape the judgments of the sky?
No, surely no. A poisonous dart
Shall ever rankle in his heart.

MY OWN BELOVED HILLS.

MY own beloved hills!
    How beautiful ye rise,
    In all your silent majesty,
    Ascending to the skies!
A cottage here and there
    Is glancing from your crest,
And many a little tender flower
    Is nursed upon your breast.

My own beloved hills!
    My thoughts will to you soar,
When deep in Plutus' copper-caves
    Hard-toiling for the ore.
My own beloved hills!
    The dwelling-place of Rest,
The summer-home of Solitude!
    Of silent heights the best!

And when I dream of peace,
    I always dream of you:—
Of sublunary happiness?
    Then ye are present too!—
Of spots of purest joy,
    Gladdened by sun and shower?
O, then my spirit quaffs the breeze
    Within my mountain bower!

And here I am again
    On Nature's rocky throne,
Weaving the locks of Solitude!
    Once more I am alone!
And as on each dear spot
    I rest my watery eye,
I'm thankful that I have again
    The happiness to sigh;—

The happiness to weep
    Apart from human eyes,
Watched only by the birds and flowers
    Of myriad hues and dyes!

Watched only by my Father God,
Who all creation fills,
Who made the flower-enamelled vales,
And my beloved hills!

CILDA AND THE SAILOR.

DAYLIGHT on the yellow moors
With the dusk was dying,
Cilda by the empty board
In their cot was sighing.
"We are hungry, mother dear,
Sadness is our measure ;
Can we have another meal ?"
"I have none, my treasure !

"And we owe a twelvemonth's rent,
Which augments our sorrow :
The hard landlord turns us out
In the lanes to-morrow.
Houseless, homeless, we must be,
Smote in form and feature ;
But there is a Providence
O'er the meanest creature.

"Sure I hear a manly step
Where the elms are rocking :
'Tis a sailor clad in blue :
Hark ! my love, he's knocking.
Ope the door and let him in,
Our sad secret keeping :
Do not show the mariner
That we have been weeping."

"Can you tell me, mistress, say,
Where lives Thomas Tilly ?
Is it somewhere hereabouts
Where the fields are hilly ?
Years have passed since last we met,
Ere I was a whaler,
Sailing over swelling seas :—
Hear an honest sailor."

"In the grave he lieth low ;
There the thrush is singing ;
Freshly too the churchyard grass
O'er his head is springing.
I'm his widow : Cilda here
Is his only daughter :
For the sake of Tilly gone,
Welcome o'er the water !"

"Thomas Tilly lent me gold
When I was in trouble :
Jack will nothing do by halves,—
Here it is, and double !"
Saying this, ten guineas shone
In her hand together :
"Honesty shall win at last,
Spite of wind and weather !"

O'er the threshold then he stepped
While their tears were flowing,
And along the river walked
With a bosom glowing.

"Bless the Lord !" the mother cried ;
"He hath seen our sorrow."
"Yes," said Cilda, "He will give
Strength for every morrow."

THE MOTHER'S CLOSET.

THERE is an elm-tree by the rock,
Within a hollow glen :
A branchless trunk it is, and far
From the abode of men.
It is indeed a lonely place,
Scooped out by Nature's hands ;
O, there is solitude enough,
Where the old elm-tree stands.

It must be many years ago
When it was in its prime,
Because they say it flourished there
Before my father's time.
But now the old trunk stands alone,
Clasped with the ivy green :
And not a bud o'er decks its crown,
The pilgrim of the scene.

Once on a time the woodman came,
With sharpened axe in hand,
To cut it down, and cast it forth,
Like refuse of the land.
But, thinking when he was a boy
'Twas beautiful to see,
He dropped his axe, and walked away,
And spared the old elm-tree.

O, blessings on his hoary hairs,
And blessings on his brow,
And blessings on his children dear,
For sparing it till now !
For where would pious Mary pray,
Where would her closet be,
If hands of other days had hewn
The trunk of this old tree ?

But now 'tis Mary's holy haunt ;
The twilight finds her here ;
She kneels and prays with weeping eyes
For those she holds so dear.
Bright angels watch her from the skies ;
For unto them 'tis given
To minister unto the wise :
Her prayers were heard in heaven.

MY LITTLE MAID AT SUPPER-TIME.

THE daylight on the hills
Was fading fast away ;
The labourer to his home returned,
And children tired of play ;
When, in my own dear home,
Beneath our Father's eye,
We sat down to our evening meal,
My little ones and I.

That day had been a day
    Of trial and of care;
And I was musing on the past,
    Not heeding who were there.
I fear I ate my meal
    Not thinking whence it came;
Not thanking God at supper-time,—
    I speak it to my shame!

But when my little maid
    Had laid aside her cup,
And kissed her mother many a time,
    And picked the fragments up,
She clasped her hands, and said,
    As sweetly as could be,
" I thank Thee, Father, for my food,
    For sister and for me."

My heart is not *all* stone;
    The adamant gave way;
My child had taught me in that hour
    Just what *I* ought to say.
The simplest note we hear,
    The humblest flower we see,
Oft teach us, Father, in dark days,
    Our gratitude to Thee!

I STEAL AWAY TO WEEP.

THE day is come I long have wooed:
    "Tis April's budding hour,
And I, with sister Solitude,
    Am seated in my bower.
Across the lawn the zephyr's chime
    Melodiously doth sweep;
But, though it is the budding-time,
    I steal away to weep!

The lark is singing in the sky,
    The redbreast on the wall,
And, in the rushy moor hard by,
    I hear the cuckoo's call:
The sparrows on our dear old cot
    Their merry-makings keep;
But, though they seem so musical,
    I steal away to weep!

The furze-bush waves its golden bells
    Where vernal breezes run,
And every little daisy tells
    A story to the sun;
Blue violets, 'neath the hawthorn tree,
    And nodding cowslips peep;
But, though a thousand flowers I see,
    I steal away to weep!

Around I hear the shout of joy,
    Yet shun the merry choir:
A mother loves her singing boy,
    A sister and a sire;
A loving wife, a daughter dear,
    Around my heart-strings creep:
But like a banished man I'm here,—
    I steal away to weep!

And when my comrades smile so gay,
    So jubilant and glad,
I wonder why I turn away,
    And seem so very sad.
I wonder why within my bower
    Alone I love to creep,
And, though it is the budding-hour,
    I steal away to weep.

KIND WORDS.

'TIS strange to feel, as on we plod
    O'er the rough path of life,
    What power is in a few kind words,
Breathed in the midst of strife,
Or murmured o'er the sick man's bed,
    Or in the orphan's ear,
Or by the hearth so desolate,
    The widow's heart to cheer.

Once, winding through the noisy streets,
    I met an aged hind;
His face was shaded o'er with grief,
    The reflex of his mind.
I took the stranger by the hand,
    And spoke with gentle air:
The clouds departed from his brow,
    And sunshine settled there.

By the road-side, beneath a tree
    A weary wight sat down,
With garments patched and dust-bedimmed;
    His face and hands were brown.
"Man, look to God," a soft voice said,
    "And cast on Him thy care:"
The beggar rose as if new life
    Were granted to him there.

The day was fading into eve,
    When by a lowly cot
A pretty maiden, weeping much,
    Bewailed her lonely lot.
A few kind words fell on her ear
    Like music from above,
And grief and sorrow, dread and fear,
    Were swallowed up in love.

A poet, sobbing o'er his lyre,
    Sat in the hawthorn shade;
Its silent strings were rusted o'er,
    And not a note they made.
A kind friend cheered him with his voice,
    Who through the vale did plod;
The poet sang as if his strain
    Dropped from the hills of God.

Within a dingy shop, smoke-black,
    A husband and a sire,
Whose hands were bronzed with iron toil,
    Stirred up a furnace-fire.
Why does he work so free to-day,
    The foremost of his clan?
A few kind words have made him feel
    And know himself a MAN.

Is gold a thing too great for thee ?
Are gems beyond thy reach,
To give to cheer thy fellow-man ?
Thou hast the gift of speech.
Speak kindly to the weary one,
The erring souls that stray:
So shall thy deeds like sunshine stream
Along life's rough highway.

THE MOTHER'S PRAYER.

" God bless thee," said the mother,
As her boy did by her stand,
With his bundle on his shoulder,
And his hawthorn in his hand.
" God bless thee on thy pilgrimage
Along life's rugged race !"
And o'er the threshold stepped the lad,
With tears upon his face.

He wandered down the rushy flat,
Oft pausing in his dream,
And gazing back to see once more
His old home by the stream :
And every bird and fly and bee
That gladsome hummed along
Seemed with the silver brook to sing,
" God bless thee," in their song.

A mill-wheel turning round and round
Beneath a willow bank,
Where swallows dipped their flashing wings
And merry robins drank,
Where he with his bright-eyed compeers
A-playing had been found,
Seemed echoing his mother's prayer,
When turning round and round.

On board a ship and o'er the seas
Now sailing on in haste,
The flapping sails, the piping cords,
The weary watery waste,
The mystic voices heard around
On ocean and in air,
Were all replete with words of life,—
His mother's holy prayer.

This nerved him as he toiled through lands
Unknown to poet's song,
When sorrow smote, or green-eyed grief,
And disappointment strong.
And in the silent hush of life,
Though crushed with cruel care,
His soul drank in this healing strain,
And felt his mother's prayer.

And when the God of Providence
So blessed him that his name
Was hallowed by the great and good,
And trumpeted by Fame,
His mother's prayer rang in his heart,
And filled his soul with joy,
Making a paradise of earth :
" God bless thee, precious boy !"

THE DEATH OF MY FATHER.

The month of song is come,
The murmur of the bee,
The cuckoo voiceful round our home,
The blackbird from the lea :
The skylark in the sky
Strikes his enchanting lyre ;
But gushing tears are in mine eye
For my departed sire !

He fell, and, falling, found
The victory he implored ;
Death's sting had been extracted by
The God whom he adored !
And, with his dying breath,
Sweet words of comfort came :
He whispered, pierced by cruel Death,
His strong Deliverer's name !

Stretched on affliction's rack,
The iron in his bones,
No murmur passed his sainted lips,
No murmur in his groans.
Resigned, submissive, meek,
He waited for the change,
When angel-bands would guide him hence
Through fields of light to range.

I saw him face the foe,
And close his languid eye :—
Sure, fiends at such a scene might weep,
To see a Christian die !
He doffed his weeds of care
For an angelic vest,
And on a Christian Sabbath eve
He gained the promised rest !

My father lives in heaven !
I weep not though he's flown :
I have a sainted parent now
Before the' eternal throne !
O may his weeping wife
And orphan children see
Him feasting in those starry fields !
" Amen ! so let it be !"

He left no wealth behind,
No riches but his name ;
No honour but his honesty :
He was unknown to fame.
His grave is with the poor,
The rude, unlettered clan ;
But from the tomb a voice breaks forth,
" He was an honest man !"

Thank God for such a sire !
He taught my lips to pray,
And bade me bend my infant knee
In childhood's early day.
Thank God for such a sire !
'Tis much to be thus riven ;
But now he strikes a golden lyre,
And swells the songs of heaven !

THE DRESSMAKER'S DAUGHTER.

"Does it rain much, my Andoo?
  Upon the door and see."
"Yes, mother, and the great wind
Roars loudly through the tree;
And it is dark, O very;
  But I don't fear to go
And take the work you've finished
  At once to Mrs. Snow."

Thus answered Ella's daughter,
  Her only one and best:
To-morrow was the Sabbath,
  The day of holy rest.
No food had they or fuel,
  And baby-boy was low:
Through tears the mother whispered,
  "Yes, Andoo, you must go."

Once they had many comforts
  Which earnest toil procured;
Nor dreamt they then of hardship
  Such as they now endured.
Her husband join'd the army,
  Against the foe to stand;
And rumour said he perished
  When fighting for his land.

She took the little parcel
  Bound up secure and plain;
Then wrapped her shawl around her,
  And stepped into the rain:
And soon amid the tempest
  Which everywhere did roar,
She stood, the darling Andoo,
  Before the lady's door.

Within the work was taken:
  It was my lady's ball;
She had no time for Andoo
  To speak to her at all.
Distress and sorrow seized her:
  She wept and trembled too,
And cried in bitter anguish,
  "What will my mother do?"

On through the street she plodded;
  The great big drops came down,
The rain-flood in a river
  Was rushing through the town:
And this her only murmur,
  Which sad and sadder grew,
As she approached the alley,
  "What will my mother do?"

O, need I speak of weeping
  Within that dwelling small?
And this because my lady
  Was busy at the ball!
O, need I speak of hunger?
  O, need I speak of prayer,
And cold, and cry, and darkness
  Within that hovel bare?

The mother kissed the maiden,
  And pointed to the skies:

Even as I think upon it,
  The tears are in mine eyes.
O, she was worn and wasted;
  It was a bitter cup:
"Weep not, my dearest Andoo;
  The Lord will take us up."

Why do the rich thus trifle
  With industry and worth?
Why do they not remember
  The toiling ones of earth?
Why swell the tide of sorrow
  With this neglect, O why?
For which the righteous Giver
  Will judge them by and bye.

Ere midnight there was succour;
  The Lord had answered prayer;
From battle came her father,
  And found his Andoo there;
And found his dearest Ella,
  Who sat so long in night,
And kissed away their sorrow,
  And cheered them with his light.

THE FISHER'S WIFE.

"Look through the lattice, Laura,
  Look out upon the main:
'Tis time your fisher father
  Was at his home again.
The winds are wailing wildly,
  The great waves lash the strand:
O Saviour, save the fisher,
  And bring him safe to land!"

And Laura through the casement
  Gazed o'er the sand-hills brown
Upon the fretted ocean,
  Which rolled in fury down.
No vessel met her vision,
  Or boat, upon the blue,
But hills of foamy water,
  And clouds of pitchy hue.

"Look, look again, my Laura:
  How fast comes on the night!
O how the lightning blazes
  Around the rugged height!
The pent-up rains are falling,
  The thunders meet in strife:
O, when will come the fisher,
  The sunshine of my life?"

And Laura's eyes are gleaming
  Again upon the sea:
No boat is seen approaching,
  Or fisher on the quay.
The sun has sunk in shadow,
  A thick black darkens space:
Her heart beats hard and harder,
  And tears are on her face.

"Now trim the midnight taper,
  And, Laura, let us creep
Together to the doorway,
  And back again to weep.
The storm is raging louder,
  And deeper moans the sea;
The dismal darkness thickens;
  No fisher comes to me."

And when the blush of morning
  Hung on the brightening air,
They early sought the sea-side,
  To weep in sorrow there.
For one a sire and lover,
  And one a husband found,
Washed dead upon the shingles—
  The fishermen were drowned.

You see that cottage yonder;
  The thatch is old and grey:
There Laura and her mother
  Are living to this day.
And one is fresh as summer,
  One wintry, reft, and riven;
And both wear weeds of widowhood,
  And both prepare for heaven.

TO THE OLD HILL.

ONCE more to climb thy rocky brow,
  When early buds are peeping;
Once more to muse where breezes blow,
  And white young lambs are leaping;
To brush thy hair through croft and mead,
  Refreshed with vernal rain;
O, this is luxury indeed,
  And glads my heart again!

Once more, and yet once more, old hill,
  I kneel upon thy crest;
Of all those mountain-peaks around,
  Thou art the brightest, best.
The flowers that gem thy rustling locks,
  And stud thy forehead fair,
Are peering from among the rocks,
  To me beyond compare.

Once more, my native mount, once more
  The welcome Spring is come:
How freshly steal the soft south winds
  Along my mountain home!
And flowers, as when a boy, come forth,
  Clinging to moss and stone;
But ah! they look a different look,
  And speak a different tone.

Once more, within my quiet bower,
  I hear the skylark's song:
How wildly come his warblings down,
  Those bending brakes among!
Blessed be the God of Providence!
  His name will I adore,
Who spares me on my pilgrim way
  To visit thee once more.

THE PARTING SCENE.

THE parting knell was rung;
  A scene of tumult reigned;
Hands clung to hands, and eyes of love
  Were on each other strained.
Those eyes which never wept
  For many, many years,
Were shedding, for departing friends,
  A gush of hallowing tears.

The mighty steamer moves
  Along its watery track,
And oft the weeping emigrant
  Turns round and gazes back.
His friends are on the beach
  Within his misty view:
He waves his hat, and silently
  Breathes forth a last adieu!

A son is in that ship;
  A father on the shore;
And silently he paced along
  Beside the breakers' roar;
And, when the flying bark
  Out of his vision swept,
He turned his furrowed face away,—
  He turned away and wept!

I saw him wipe the tear
  From off his cheek that day;
The secret workings of his soul
  No poet can portray.
He saw his son no more
  Beneath the spreading skies;
And now the tears are wiped away
  For ever from his eyes!

THE ROBIN'S MONODY.

THE silent snow came down,
  Mantling the woods and leas,
And hanging beautiful festoons
  Upon the forest-trees;
Shrouding the hamlet's face,
  Powdering the mountain's locks,
And spreading chaste white drapery
  Over the mossy rocks.

My little ones and I
  Were sitting round our hearth,
Secure from wintry winds without,
  Cheered with the faggot's mirth;
Pitying the poor old man
  Who came that day to beg,
Bringing his scars from Waterloo,
  Where he had left a leg.

'Twas when the storm was high
  Against the window-pane,
Among the feathery, falling snow,
  A little Robin came,

And sang, in melting tone,
His own pathetic lay;
And as his notes came dropping forth,
To us he seemed to say:—

"I'm tired, and hungry too,
In calling here and there,
Imploring food, and getting none,
Because they've none to spare.
I asked my cousin, wren,
Within his mossy shed;
But he looked angry while I spoke,
And shook his feathery head.

"I asked the sparrow, who
Was chattering in his glee,
If he could give me anything
To feed upon—not he.
He ruffled up his plumes,
And scratched himself in ire;
Looking unutterably cold,
He bade me to retire.

"The linnet could not hear;
The blackbird could not stay;
The lark, in music's mellow tone,
Said, 'Come some other day.'
I visited the thrush,—
He might have grain in store:
He had indeed, but not for me
Who was so very poor.

"A finch and I were friends
In summer's flowery prime;
I sang her songs at morning hour,
And holy evening time.
I saw her yesterday,
With meat before her spread;
I nodded, but she knew me not,
Nor word of kindness said.

"O, give poor bird a crumb,
List to the Robin's cry,
And I will sing another song
To you before I die."
We ran and gave him bread
Upon the window sill,
And watched him picking up the crumbs
In his small horny bill.

So then he flew away,
The feathery flakes among,
And 'neath a shining icicle
He thanked us with a song.
I know not when I felt
Half so replete with joy!
O, how much better 'twas to feed
That Robin, than destroy.

TO MY LYRE.

LITTLE music-breathing lyre!
Once again I touch thy wire;
Once again a song I raise,
Pensive warbler, in thy praise.
On my father's broomy height,
In life's morning, clear and bright,
'Neath the craggy rocks, which lie
With white faces to the sky,

Lichened o'er with many a lay
Of the old times passed away,
Stony chroniclers outspread
On my mountain's heathy head,—
In their mystic shadows lone,
First I heard thy plaintive tone;
First my hands essayed to bring
Music from thy trembling string,
And my soul's mysterious fire
Warmed to hear thee, little lyre!

Years have passed away since then:
I among the walks of men
Toil and sweat with wounded heart,
'Neath lean Care's oppressive dart:
But, when digging in the ground,
Oft thy tones are tingling round;
Oft I hear thy simple strain
Floating over hill and plain;
And when Danger's self is near,
And I see the face of Fear
Peering o'er some ragged rock,
Falling with a dreadful shock
In the mine's dark chamber, I
Think upon thee with a sigh.
Little, honest, simple friend,
Be thou with me till the end;
For, unnoticed though thou be,
Thou art more than gold to me!

Oft when evening shades close o'er
Mead and mountain, mine and moor;
When the hedger's task is done,
Through the rushes let us run;
And beside the pool we'll sit,
Where the sportive swallows flit,
And the spotted fishes play,
Watching daylight die away;
And the sparrows on the eaves,
And the robins mid the sheaves,
And the flowers, with garments bright,
All shall minister delight.
Then the night-bird will awake
His low ditty from the brake,
And sweet spirit-notes shall come,
Mingling with the milkmaid's hum.
When we have an hour to spend,
We will haste there, little friend.

In some old cave, dank and dim,
We will chant our vesper-hymn,
When the winds, with angry sweep,
Drive their coursers o'er the deep,
And descends the beating rain,
Falling on the sounding plain.
In the bower where Silence dwells,
We will list the evening bells,
And their merry chimes shall raise
Memories of our April days.
Through the hamlet we will stray,
Where the happy children play,
In the deep romantic glen
Musing on the ways of men.
Over rock, by ruined tower,
In the poet's broken bower,
Under hawthorns white with May,
We will muse at close of day.

THE DEATH OF THE FIRST-BORN.

Night's inky mantle cloaked old Egypt's head,
  Wrapping her towers in gloom : Silence was there,
  And Slumber nodded on the battlements ;
Labour lay down, and pressed his weary brow,
Unclosed his hardened hands, shut his dull eyes,
And fell asleep as sweetly as a child.
The task-galled Hebrew, slumbering on his couch,
Forgot his cruel master's iron yoke,
And ceased to roam the ragged stubble-field.
The babe lay nestled on its mother's breast,
And the young bridegroom clasped his blooming bride,
Deeming the earth a Paradise of bliss !
The music of the lute had died away ;
And he who framed the awe-crowned pyramid
That looks and laughs at the destroyer, Time,
Laid down his chisel and forgot his plan.
The murmur of the ocean came and went ;
And the lone nightingale, on the green palm,
Warbled such music to the crescent moon,
That showers of dew-beads fell upon the grass.
The sporting billows, on the glassy Nile,
Kept up their love-race on its heaving breast,
Kissing the lotos-flowers upon its brink,
And curling round the ancient pottery-float.
Amidst such loveliness, at this calm time,
Forth walked the dark Destroyer, and his feet
Echo alike in corridor and cot !

Armed with dread power, lo ! the death angel comes,
And sweeps away the first-born in his ire,—
The rose-bud opening 'neath its mother's eye,
The school-boy dreaming of his lexicons,
The youth, with all his distant primrose paths,
The bridegroom, and his newly wedded bride,
The middle-aged man, and him who crept
Adown the hill of time, grey-haired and slow ;
The peasant, slumbering on his bed of straw,
And him who trembled on his princely couch ;
The wakeful mourner, sighing with his pain,
And the slow-pacing, silent sentinel ;
The beggar, weeping in his blasted rags,
And him who bended o'er his shining heaps.
All these, in one short hour, death-struck and stiff,
Became the sweeper's prey !

        On, on he goes,
Lopping off branches from the household tree,
Sprinkling the hearth with tears, and pauses not
Till on the door-posts marks of blood are seen ;
For here the Hebrew slumbers ! Pharaoh rose,
And called his servants forth ; and a great cry
Was heard in Egypt, wailing for the dead.
The morning broke, and not a single hair
Was bruised on Israel's head ! The Lord their God
Was leading them into the Promised Land,
And Egypt's spires were dwindling into nought.

FATHER COMES TO-DAY.

"Haste, mother, to the garden gate,
  And look across the moor :
  The train is hurrying by the wood ;
I see it from the door.

Whilst you did rub the pewter cans,
  I heard you softly say
That we must make our cottage neat,
  For father comes to-day.

" And borne upon the wandering breeze
  The engine-puffs are loud ;
And see the steam which evermore
  Doth follow like a cloud.
O Benny, Benny, clap your hands,
  And cease awhile to play ;
And let us watch beside the door,
  For father comes to-day."

Full soon a traveller, staff in hand,
  Came walking o'er the green ;
And oft he paused beside the stile,
  To mark the pleasant scene.
He saw his children by his home,
  And dashed the tear away,
And shouted as they raised their arms,
  "Your father comes to-day."

And then his footsteps quickened so,
  As he drew near the gate,
Like one whom royal duty urged,
  So that he dare not wait.
And soon they felt his warm embrace,
  And on his bosom lay,
While Sarah sobbed amid her tears,
  "Your father's come to-day."

Beside the fire they chatted long,
  How little Pedo's feet
Would take her out no more to sell
  Her cresses in the street ;
And Benny would be clothed and fed
  Beneath affection's ray :
And O what prayers arose to Heaven
  For father come to-day !

'SEED-THOUGHTS.

Adown the lane a traveller hied,
  What time the cuckoo told
  His oft-repeated pleasant tale
Among the green and gold ;
And o'er the white clouds floating slow,
  Their western way along,
The skylark, hidden in the height,
  Poured forth his sweetest song.

A group of children, by a tree,
  Were playing in the sun ;
And much this thoughtful traveller joyed
  To see them dance and run.
In their sweet strain of innocence
  His glad soul took its share ;
As it gushed gladly from their lips,
  And rang upon the air.

And as he joined them in their sports,
  And helped them in their play,
These little seeds from Truth's full store
  He scattered by the way.
"Our Saviour God came down from heaven,
  And died upon the tree ;
He says of children, 'Suffer them
  To come, and follow Me !'"

Then onward down the shady lane,
Near which a streamlet ran,
With holy sweetness in his face,
Passed on that pleasant man.
And in the distant future years,
As slowly on they came,
The seed sprang up, and bore much fruit
To the Redeemer's name.

One gained a Missionary's meed,
A Missionary's grave;
And one a Pastor much beloved,
Who all to Jesus gave.
And one, he was a man of peace,
The pen his battle-blade;
With which he noble victories won,
And mighty conquests made.

And planting thus those seeds of thought,
A large increase was given;
When watered by the Spirit's hand,
And blessed by bounteous Heaven.
Still let the Gospel sower strive
To bless this smitten clime:
For, lo, a mighty harvest waves
Along the vales of time.

HEDGES.

YE living boundary-lines,
Where pensive thought reclines,
And gentle song in moss or ivy bower
Trills strains of music rare
Upon the upland air,
All hail, ye temples where the Muses cower.

I love ye at all hours;
When morn awakes the flowers,
Or when the lark at noontide carols free,
Or Eve her silent song
Sighs the green vales among,
And mystic legends float o'er lake and lea.

In spring, in summer's prime,
In autumn's golden time,
When harvest odes uprise the meads among,
Or when old Winter roars
Adown the hollow moors,
I love to listen 'neath your roof of song.

And when soft rains come down
On corn and common brown,
What joy to hide where honeysuckles crowd,
Or hawthorns snowed with spring,
And ivy tendrils cling,
To drink the poetry of the floating cloud!

The briony is here,
And many a wilding dear,
And gentle whispers heard not in the street,
And fays at eventide
On the long grasses ride,
Or climb the mosses with their velvet feet.

And when the morn of May
Resounds with Nature's lay,
And primroses among your green shoots shine,
Or from your sunned sides drop,
Or smile in troops a-top,
Vision of visions,—O what a joy is mine!

The lively chirping wren,
The cuckoo of the glen,
The blackbird, with his rich, refreshing lays,
The all-melodious thrush,
The sparrow of the bush,
With other songsters, fill your brakes with praise.

And, O, to share the joy
Of village girl and boy,
When blackberries are on the brambles strung;
Pulling your clusters down,
When ye are autumn-brown,
What time the harvester's last song is sung!

And here the bard retires
From tumult's hissing fires,
Nought but the ruin rising on his ken;
And, sheltered in your shade,
He woos the musing maid,
Whose simple sonnets murmur through the glen.

O leave the city's hum,
To the still hedges come,
And learn the lessons taught at dying day;
The voice of the Great Sire
Is heard among the brier,
And silent thoughts come stealing, "Kneel and pray."

THE SAD HARPER.

O'ER the valley's green-robed breast
The evening shadows fall,
The daisy sleeps in its grassy nest,
And the rose-tree 'neath the wall;
While from the tower of the village church
Old Time is heard to call.

In the silence of the falling dews,
By the brooklet through the leas,
A harper wandered, all forlorn,
Whose heart was ill at ease;
And thus he sang his mournful dirge
Under the spreading trees:—

"Why do the loveliest flowerets fade,
And die away so soon?
Why do all gentle things of earth
So perish in their noon?
Ah! why are Beauty's roses dimmed
Even in the morn of June?

"O, one there was whom much I loved,
A darling daughter bright,
Who passed away so suddenly
Into the land of light,
The mystery almost blinded me,—
I grope about in night.

"Don't wonder that the stricken bard
    Pours forth a solemn lay ;
There's nought below, however bright,
    But fadeth with decay."
And the harper's thoughts flow past the stars,
    As he wiped the tears away.

TELLING US OF GOD.

BESIDE a little murmuring stream
    I saw two children play,
    What time still Evening came along,
Clad in her sober grey.
The one a little ruddy boy,
    So beautiful and fair ;
The other was a sweet young girl,
    Fresh as the mountain air.

They ran along the brooklet's side,
    Until they both grew tired :
" What does the stream say, sister dear ? "
    The little lad inquired.
" O, does it of my father tell,
    Who crossed the ocean-wave,
And never, never more came back,
    To weep o'er mother's grave ? "

She gazed into her brother's face,—
    How sisterly ! how dear !
Brushed back the ringlets o'er his brow,
    And kissed away the tear ;
Then raised her flashing eyes to heaven
    From earth's corrupted clod :
" This little streamlet, murmuring by,
    Is telling us of God."

And now, whene'er I stand beside
    A little tinkling stream,
The image of those pretty ones
    Is with me in my dream.
The birds that carol, and the breeze
    That fans the flowery sod,
All Nature's sweetest murmurings
    Are TELLING US OF GOD.

THE DISTRESSED MECHANIC.

THE hawthorn leaves were fading ;
    Its fruit was ripe and red ;
    It dangled down in clusters
From the old tree's prickly head.
Cock-robin only whistled
    Where the autumn berries burned,
As the dinnerless mechanic
    To his hungry ones returned.

He left them in the morning
    With his nightly fast unbroke,
And all day long has laboured
    In the cold oppressor's yoke.

And oft his hungry household
    Would on his vision start,
As he returns at evening
    With a cloud upon his heart.

He was an honest workman,
    And diligent and good,
A sober, loving, pious soul ;
    And yet he wanted food.
O shame upon his country,
    And shame upon his race,
To trample sterling honesty,
    And brand it with disgrace !

O, see him slowly trailing
    His wasted limbs along !
He who was once so brawny,
    So stately and so strong!
A tear glides down the furrows
    Upon his sunken cheek ;
His eyes are lifted heavenward,
    Like suffering martyr meek.

Deem not that unattended
    This faithful man crept on :
No, angel eyes were bended
    Upon this weeping one.
And chimes from Eden's rivers
    Through all his being flow,
Too sweet for ears unholy
    In dells of death below.

Who meets him on the door-step ?
    His own beloved boy :
Drops glitter in his bright eyes,
    Which damp a father's joy :
And in the straw are huddled
    His baby and his wife,
Fading away for fasting
    And feebleness of life.

Once many household comforts
    Were sweetly round them spread ;
But they with these have parted
    To purchase daily bread.
All but a few dear volumes,
    Which stand in sad array,
Like favourites round their chieftain,
    Upon the battle-day.

Now see him clasp his children
    Within his fond embrace :
One up his knee is climbing,
    And one will kiss his face,
In spite of countless tear-drops
    That fall upon the floor,
And echo in the silence :—
    Could monarchs sorrow more ?

And now a prayer is offered
    That God would grant them power
To kiss the hand that smites them
    In this afflictive hour.
His dear ones kneel around him,
    And share in his distress :
The busy world forgets them,
    But He looks down to bless.

THE WIDOW.

WITHIN the house of God,
  I saw her bend the knee,
  And lift her pensive eyes to heaven
In silent agony.
Tears trickled down her face,
  And on the altar fell ;
The varied thoughts that stirred her soul,
  No human tongue can tell !

Perchance she mused on him
  Who from her side had flown,
And left her in this desert land,
  A widow, all alone.
And were it not for One
  Who heard her orphan's cry,
It would indeed be happiness
  To lay her down and die.

Perchance she mused on *home*,
  That land where all is fair,
The peaceful palaces of heaven ;
  Her husband resteth there !
O'er its bright battlements
  She oft had seen him gaze,
Clad in a golden vesture bright,
  And harping hymns of praise.

I know not why she wept,
  But tears ran down apace,
And by her side her little boy
  Gazed in her sad pale face.
And when he heard the sob
  She strove in vain to stay,
I saw him shrink within himself,
  And turn his head away.

Dark mourning weeds they wore,—
  That mother and her love,—
And both knelt down and worshipped there
  The God that reigns above.
The widow's heart was full ;
  No words I heard her speak ;
But evermore the silent tears
  Were stealing down her cheek.

I know not why she wept ;
  She communed there with God ;
Perchance she felt resigned to bear
  The chastenings of His rod.
A peace the world knows not,
  Poor stricken one, is thine,
A calm that smooths life's troubled wave,
  The balm of love divine.

LOST AND FOUND.

THE garden-gate wide open swung ;
  A blooming pair passed by ;
The old man 'neath the beech-tree sat
  With sorrow in his eye.
He heeded not the lark o'erhead ;
  His gaze was on the ground :
For he that morn his daughter lost,
  And she a husband found.

He watched them down the lonely lane,
  And o'er the village stile
Beyond the hollow by the wood
  Where honeysuckles smile ;
And birds were singing by the brook,
  And whistling on the trees ;
And oft the maiden's handkerchief
  Was waving on the breeze.

Full soon beyond the old man's view
  The youthful couple passed :
He dropped his face upon his hands,
  And tears fell free and fast ;
And other days came back to him
  With hopes and fears sublime,
When earth with buds was beautiful,
  And love was in its prime.

And then a mystic stillness fell
  Upon his waiting soul,
And echoes from the higher hills
  Over his spirit stole.
He lifted up his furrowed face,—
  Serene it was and mild,—
And breathed these earnest words of prayer :
  " O Heaven, direct my child ! "

Days passed, and months, and then there came
  A little stranger fair,
With million mysteries in her eyes,
  Soft cheek and shining hair ;
And smallest foot were toddling round
  Upon his cottage floor,
And sunny smiles went up to him,
  And he was glad once more.

And thus the tale of human life
  For evermore is told ;
To-day the sky is overcast,
  To-morrow tinged with gold.
One joy departs, another comes
  To fill the vacant place ;
And so 'twill be till death assails
  The last of Adam's race.

THE HAPPY CHOICE.

A LITTLE boy, one harvest-day,
  Sat under a shady tree ;
And a voice came whispering through the leaves,
  " Child, give thy heart to Me."
" I will, I will," said the little boy ;
  " My Saviour mine shall be."

'Twas a golden choice that boy had made,
  And from the hills of God
A halo seemed to fringe the flowers,
  And glorify the sod,
And hang aloft in the upper air,
  And flame the path he trod.

In a hut among the moorland reeds
A bridegroom and his bride,
What time the moon still evening wooed,
Were kneeling side by side;
And their prayer uprose on the vesper breeze,
As the quivering daylight died.

Beside the fire in an old homestead,
A middle-aged hind,
With a nest brimful of singing birds,
Upon his hand reclined;
And thoughts of harps and streets of gold
Were rushing through his mind.

In a cottage on a craggy cliff,
Like a lone tree stript and bare,
An old man sat with the best of books;
White-silvered was his hair;
And his eyes were turned to the gates of bliss;
For he knew he was almost there.

On a humble bed in a lonely room
A dying saint was laid;
Bright angels came, and bore him where
The rills of Eden played.
'Twas the boy who gave to Christ his all,
And wise was the choice he made.

MY LITTLE MAID WHEN FOUR MONTHS OLD.

My little maid, what joy to see
Thee dancing on thy mother's knee!
Thy fair white brow, how bright it seems,
And from thine eye what pleasure gleams!
O, every random glance that's given,
Seems like a messenger from heaven,
Which here unconsciously hath strayed,
To visit me, my little maid.

My little maid, thou canst not tell
How we are charmed with this bright spell:
Two wanderers o'er the hills of care,
Who love the fields and flowerets fair,
To meet on such a wild as this
A cherub newly dropt from bliss,
It cheers our hearts that here hath strayed
An angel in our little maid.

My little maid, I drop a tear,
To think what thou may'st suffer here;
These earnest beaming eyes of thine
May soon be dimmed with sorrow's brine,
And thy smooth cheek, so soft and fair,
Be furrowed with the plough of care;
The cottage flower may fleetly fade,
And death devour my little maid.

My little maid, this feverish clime
Still changes with the flight of time;
And though thou twinest round my heart,
The moment hastes when we must part.
But, daughter dear, there is a home,
Where change can never, never come,
Where Spring's young roses never fade:
There may we meet our little maid.

My little maid, when all is o'er,
And I am " chained to earth no more,"
When in the dark cold grave I lie,
O come beneath the evening sky,
And bring, O bring the earliest flower,
That blooms within my mountain bower,
An offering to thy father's shade,
And I'll be with my little maid.

THE HEROIC MINER.

The world has real heroes,
Whose minds with truth are stored,
Who never bled in battle,
Who never wielded sword:
True helpers of the people,
In moral warfare strong;
Whose lives have passed unheeded,
Whose names are not in song.

And such I deem the miner
Who, when his work was done,
Ascended in the bucket,
He and his little son.
O, how they fondly chatted,
As up the shaft they sped,
Of those who waited for them
Where their own board was spread!

When, hark! a crack which fills them
With sharp and sudden pain:
The rope, the rope is breaking,—
Two strands are snapped in twain;
One, only one remaineth,—
The strain doth it destroy;
It cannot bear much longer
That father and his boy.

O noble, noble parent!
" Sit still, my child," said he.
" 'Twill bear you up in safety,
And do not grieve for me."
And then that loving father
Sprang out into the gloom,
And found within the darkness
A Christian hero's tomb.

How grand is such an action
In this full world of strife!
Such deeds are deeply graven
Within the Book of Life:
And coming years should honour
The noble miner's name
In metal and in marble
With everlasting fame.

THE AGED CHRISTIAN COUPLE.

" The driving clouds are densely dark,
The moon is looking ill,
The winds are at their wildest freaks
By meadow-stile and mill;

And as I through the lattice-panes
    Gaze out into the night,
I surely see the lightnings gleam
    Along the rocky height.

"You've been complaining all the day
    Of keen rheumatic pains,
And showers at noontide filled the pools
    With water in the lanes.
Our elder son is with us here,
    From voyaging long at sea;
And leaves again to-morrow morn
    For unexplored countrie.

"To kirk we've gone on Sabbath eve
    For forty years or more:
Shall we for once now stay at home,
    And close our cottage door?
Old Time has turned these locks of ours
    As white as driven snow,
And weakness fastens on our frame:—
    Say, Lucy, must we go?"

The old dame placed her Bible down
    Upon the cushioned chair,
And, gazing through her spectacles,
    She said with gentle air:
"Whilst I can travel through the lanes,
    Or walk across the sod,
O let me in the holy place
    With Christians worship God!"

That night, upon an ancient seat
    Within the sacred place,
An aged couple might be seen
    With sunlight on their face:
And while the meek-eyed minister,
    In language sweet and clear,
Told of the rest for those that mourned,
    They felt that heaven was near.

Then hobbling home across the fields
    Beneath the shining moon,
The chatting dame forgot her pain,
    Her heart was so in tune.
Their converse was above the stars;
    For they by faith had striven;
And soon on wings of seraphim
    They gained the highest heaven.

THE BOY BARD.

A THOUGHTFUL lad was missed one day,
    And his mother had felt he was long away;
    So she dropped her work, and closed the door,
And walked a little way down the moor;
And found him musing under a tree,
And cried, "Come home, my son, with me."
And the lad replied, "I will, I will;
I was learning the lore of the gentle rill.
O wist ye not that your boy hath striven
To tune the harp which the Lord hath given?"

And the words which rose on the summer air
Were treasured up by that mother there;
And those gentle tones she ever heard,
Like forest sounds by the breezes stirred,
Whether reading low by the evening fire,
Or spreading the meal for his labouring sire;
Whether she plied her needle bright,
Or milked the cow mid the daisies white,
In dark or light, in calm or storm,
She heard his voice, and she saw his form.

The boy grew up like a floweret wild,
For he was Nature's favourite child.
She taught him with her book of moss,
Her beetling cliff, her crag and cross,
Her sounding seas, her rivers wide,
Her hills and vales where streamlets glide,
The face of man, and blooming boy,
Or maiden, like an April joy,
Till he achieved undying fame,
And won a poet's noble name.

TO MY NATIVE VALLEY.

BEAUTIFUL vale, with thy rippling stream!
    How like a picture of youth dost thou seem!
    Blushing with hope-buds, and sparkling with flowers,
And gushing forth harp-notes from all thy bright bowers!
Beautiful vale, with thy rippling stream,
How like a picture of youth dost thou seem!

On my dear native hill I sit midst the heath,
Gazing down on the tree-covered village beneath,
Where oft I have played, in the spring-tide of youth,
When Nature's sweet voice was the music of truth.
Like birds from their nests thy white cottages gleam,
Beautiful vale, with thy rippling stream!

The swallow floats round, as the grasshopper sings,
And brushes the locks of my mount with her wings!
The sky-lark is mounting to heaven, with his song
Overflowing the dell, as he flutters along;
And with mirth and with music thine avenues teem,
Beautiful vale, with thy rippling stream!

A thousand past scenes, too numerous to speak,
Rush into my eyes, and roll over my cheek.
I think of a brother with whom I have played,—
A sister who sat with me under the shade.
They have crossed the wide sea; but surely they dream
Of my beautiful vale, with its rippling stream!

THE PRODIGAL'S RECEPTION.

"STILL wait we for him, Reuben,
    Although the year is old;
    And down the barren ridges
In wild gusts sweeps the cold:
To-night the stars are hidden,
    The moon has lost her way.
Still look we for him, Reuben,
    And wait, and watch, and pray.

" Five summers have departed,
  Five lingering autumns fled,
Since we one morning missed him,
  And mourned our boy as dead.
Still we for him are waiting,
  Though he in rags may come,
To give him warmest welcome
  To father, mother, home.

" Did not the gate clink, Reuben,
  Beside the rose-tree's stalk ?
And now I hear a footstep
  Upon the garden walk ;
Now at the door a knocking
  As timid as can be :
O ! ope it quickly, Reuben,
  My precious boy, 'tis he ! "

The fire was soon rekindled ;
  The milk was in the can ;
The best cheese on the table ;
  The meat hissed in the pan ;
The china left the cupboard ;
  The lost was in their home ;
The kiss upon his forehead ;
  The prodigal was come.

EVENING PRAYER.

Amid the purple skylight
  Is fading out the day,
  And Vesper through the twilight
Is lighting it away.
Over the pool the swallow
  Is wheeling his last flight,
While in the rushy hollow
  Is heard the bird of night.

A solemn hush is stealing
  Upon the holy air,
As two dear children, kneeling,
  Repeat their evening prayer ;
A sister and a brother,
  With early beauty bright ;
While o'er them bends their mother
  In the religious light.

O, mark this hopeful creature,
  This trustful parent-dove ;
" Our Father," says the teacher ;
  " Our Father," says each love.
And as, like flowerets folded,
  They slept in fond embrace,
Tear-drops by memory moulded
  Were stealing down her face.

Thoughts crowd on one another ;
  Her childhood rises there,
Her Bible-loving mother,
  Her early simple prayer,
All from the past are gleaming,
  Like sunshine through the rain,
As her hot tears are streaming,
  When at her prayers again.

And from that land all shadeless,
  Where there is no more sea,
And freshest flowers are fadeless,
  Bright beings bent to see :
And angel notes are swelling,
  And lyres of glory shine,
Filling that humble dwelling
  With melody divine.

MY GRANNY JOAN.

My Muse has silent been of late,
  Unkindly winds have blown ;
  But once again I court her smile,
To sing my granny Joan.
In boyhood's simple garb attired,
  And hands half filled with broom,
I loved to view her honest face
  Within her cozy room.

And sure a cozy room it was ;
  Let's paint it, if we can ;
The mantel-piece so dazzled me,
  Shining with cup and can.
Small Scripture pictures on the wall,
  King David's sling and stone,
Our Saviour in His manger-crib,
  How loved my granny Joan !

Two items only will I name,
  Which, in my boyish eyes,
In careless grandeur on the shelf,
  I ever deemed a prize.
One served to edge his razor-blade,
  Grandfather Benny's hone ;
The other was the snuff-box bright,
  Which cheered my granny Joan.

How orderly all things appeared,
  Arranged with cottage grace !
She had a place for everything,
  Gave everything its place.
With earnest hands her work was done :
  " It saves us many a moan
To do the thing in proper time,"
  Oft said my granny Joan.

A fire of furze and smouldering peat
  The spacious chimney cheered,
Where she potatoes oft would roast
  When autumn days appeared.
And how I crunched my piece of cake
  Baked on the rude hearth-stone,
With ashes of the moorland turf,
  By my old granny Joan !

O cake was cake in those old days
  Of simpleness and trust ;
Potato-cake, how good it was !
  No stoves to spoil the crust.
At dusk, I mind me creeping in
  With business of my own,
To get my share, and say my prayer,
  And bless my granny Joan.

The whitewashed walls must also be
    Remembered in my lay,
The hour-glass, with its running sands,
    Which told the time of day,
But ceased, as night and rest came on,
    To still the sufferer's moan,
When by her Benny's side she lay,
    And slept my granny Joan.

The dresser held the pewter plates
    Which shone like silver bright,
Used only when the feast came round
    To cheer some famous knight;
And here were teapots great and small;
    And on the peg alone
A paper bag of dried herbs hung,
    Preserved by granny Joan.

One book had she, which, like a lamp,
    Shed brightness on her track:
And here she laid her spectacles
    Upon its green baize back.
The Bible was her constant friend:
    When other helps were flown,
She always found a helper here
    To cheer my granny Joan.

Upon the first fly-leaf appeared
    Her own and Benny's name;
And underneath, their family
    In order as they came;
Their date of birth, their time of death,
    If, 'neath the churchyard stone,
She laid them down in peace to rest,
    All dear to granny Joan.

On the pine cricket, tabby cat
    Would watch the approaching mouse;
When with her broom of heath was swept
    Her cleanly sanded house:
And then she took her knitting down,
    And in her dwelling lone
Who knows what holy visions filled
    The mind of granny Joan?

When day was done, and Benny's hat
    Was hanging on the nail,
She changed her dress, and hastened to
    The meeting in the vale.
There psalms were sung, and prayer arose
    In earnest solemn tone;
And much the burden then would fall
    From off my granny Joan.

Two goats, throughout the livelong year,
    In snowy vests were seen,
Climbing the banks, or cropping bare
    The herbage on the green.
And morn and eve they yielded milk,
    With richness all its own,
Settling upon the dairy shelf
    With cream for granny Joan.

The sparrows, from the thatch, looked o'er
    When summer days were fair,
As she, beside her cottage door,
    Sat knitting on her chair;

And robin on the garden tree,
    When evening shades were thrown
Athwart the halo of the hill,
    Sang loud for granny Joan.

Her strongest beer was water clear
    Brought from the meadow well,
With which made she her cup of tea,
    As tolled the curfew bell.
Poor Benny tippled now and then,
    Till quiet was o'erthrown.
" 'Tis best, I think, without the drink,"
    So preached my granny Joan.

If trial came, or pinching want,
    She uttered no complaint,
She ate her crust with simple trust,
    As thankful as a saint.
With patient hope, her load she bore
    In silence and unknown.
"A better day, though far away,
    Will come," said granny Joan.

In person she was somewhat short,
    With face as clear as day,
Her eyes were black and bright, her hair
    Had fallen into grey;
Her gait was slow, her voice was low
    As any brooklet's tone;
And "everything was for the best,"
    So said my granny Joan.

Whene'er she walked abroad, she wore
    A cloak of burning red,
Whose dimpled hood would nearly hide
    The bonnet on her head:
And how the little ones would run,
    When forth she walked alone,
And cluster lovingly around
    The path of granny Joan!

She never gadded, never housed,
    And never tasted strife;
But patiently would bow and bear
    The trial-blast of life.
And I declare, mid all the glare
    That now-a-day is shown,
I cannot find, among them all,
    A match for granny Joan.

TO THE ROBIN.

LITTLE Robin, tell me now,
    Why thou warblest from that bough.
Nearly all the leaves are fled,
And the branch is sere and dead.
Dropping, dropping, one by one,
Surely all will soon be gone.
Winds are whistling round the latch,
Sparrows trembling on the thatch.
Little Robin, tell me now,
Why thou warblest from that bough.

T

"I'm a winter warbler: when
Silence creeps o'er hill and glen ;
When your summer friends are mute,
Lark and blackbird lose their lute ;
When the linnet and the thrush
Trill not from the holly-bush ;
Then I brave the blasts, and sing
Notes as mellow as the spring."

Little Robin, tell me why
Tears are bursting from mine eye ;
Fire within my bosom burns,
Hope and Memory smile by turns.
Still I strive, but know not why
Tears are bursting from mine eye.

"I'm a little red-breast bird,
And my song is scarcely heard,
When the woods are echoing loud
With the tuneful vernal crowd.
Then the red-breast lives alone,
Then the red-breast sings unknown.
But, when all beside is dumb,
Then I seek thy silent home ;
And, to cheer the winter long,
Pour out all my soul in song.
Then thou hear'st me waxing stronger,
And I'm unknown bird no longer ;
Memory tells thee how a shower,
Sweet as this, in childhood's hour,
Fell upon thy listening ear,
And again thou dropp'st a tear."

Little Robin, thou art mine ;
Little Robin, I am thine.
Art thou hungry ? O, come home !
I will give thee many a crumb.
Then I'll sit, in pleasing mood,
See thee swallow down thy food ;
Screen thee from the frost and snow ;
Little Robin, wilt thou go ?

"No, I cannot ; let me fly
Free beneath the spacious sky ;
Free within my leafy bower,
In the sunshine and the shower.
I will sing when flowers are dead,
I will sing when verdure's fled ;
I will sing when Winter roars,
And King Frost is on the moors ;
When great snow-heaps hide the lea :
Only Robin must be free."

THE POOR WIDOW WORSHIPPER.

CLOUDLESS and blue the summer sky,
  Cloudless and blue the main ;
From east to west, from west to east,
The heavens have not a stain ;
The sun shines on the low church-roof,
And reddens the Gothic pane.

Now peal the bells across the wood,
Across the pleasant lea,
Across the lonely moor of fern

Where rills and rushes be ;
Now up the heights, now down the dales,
On by the village tree.

At such a time the musing man,
When wandering through the mead,
Left to himself and to his God,
Of Nature's self takes heed,
And feels the earth is beautiful,
O, beautiful indeed.

Pass we those graceful linden-trees
Beside the gray church wall :
Now wind among the village graves,
With tombstones quaint and small ;
And now beneath the vaulted roof
We hear the Gospel call.

O, wealth is here in cushioned pews ;
And many a lady fair,
In chains of gold and diamonds bright,
In beauteous braided hair,
And flowing robe of richest silk,
Joins in the solemn prayer.

But who is this, forlorn and sad,
And desolate and poor ?
A weeping widow, clad in weeds,
Inside the sacred door,—
Only just inside ; and behold,
She kneels upon the floor.

The cushioned pews are closed to her,
Not so the gates Divine :
In the dim aisle the Saviour comes,
And whispers, "Thou art Mine ;
And all I have, poor child of want,
Yes, all I have is thine."

None notice her, or mark the tears
That trickle down her face :
The well-dressed rustle by, nor think
To speak to thing so base :
But the great King of Kings draws near,
And stays her with His grace.

And when the earth shall pass away
At the archangel's blast,
And the red sun in darkness reel,
And heaven be overcast,
Her name within the Book of Life
Shall be revealed at last.

THE SABBATH.

HUSH ! 'tis the Sabbath-morn :
  The sun looks o'er the hill :
  The forest-leaves begin to stir
Beneath the blackbird's trill ;
The perfumed breezes play
Around the milk-white thorn,
Fanning the dew-hung locks of Day :
Hush ! 'tis the Sabbath-morn !

Hush! 'tis the Sabbath-noon :'
  The pilgrim kneels to pray ;
Labour has thrown his hammer down,
  And Care has slunk away ;
No peasant plies his spade
  To earn the tempting boon :
Hush! earth is holy now ;
  Hush! 'tis the Sabbath-noon!

Hush! 'tis the Sabbath-eve :
  Hark! 'tis the voice of prayer,
Arising from unnumbered hearts
  Within His temples fair.
Of the blue western hills
  The daylight takes its leave,
Kissing the incensed locks of Peace :
  Hush! 'tis the Sabbath-eve!

GOD'S GREATEST WORK.

ON through the meadow-paths they walked
  Towards the setting sun,
  By hedgerows bright with hyacinths,
That father and his son.
And now the old man raised his eyes,
  And asked with earnest joy,
"Which is the greatest work of God?
  Come, answer me, my boy."

Before them rose a lofty hill,
  With rocks upon its crest ;
A rushing river at its base,
  And woods upon its breast ;
The eagles perched among the crags :
  "O father, it must be
God's greatest work to raise aloft
  The eternal hills," said he.

"O no, my son : the hills are grand,
  And grand they will remain :
But God's great work is grander still !
  Come, answer me again."
Upon their ears came up the sound
  Of sea-waves on the shore :
"Is it yon ocean," said the boy,
  "With everlasting roar?"

"O no, my son : the sea is great ;
  But answer me again :
God's greatest work is greater still
  And grander than the main."
Just then the sun set, and the moon
  Came stealing forth in love :
"O, is it, father," said the boy,
  "The bright blue heavens above?"

"O no, my son : the starry heavens
  Proclaim the Almighty's power ;
And so does every blade of grass,
  And every tiny flower.
But God's great work surpasses these,
  Repeated o'er and o'er,
More lofty than the loftiest skies :
  Come, answer me once more."

The cottar's song came floating then
  Across the dusky dell,
And sweetly solemn music made
  The slow-struck curfew bell.
And holding fast his father's hand,
  As by his side he ran,
He lifted up his voice, and said,
  "God's greatest work is man."

"O no, my son : the greatest, best,
  And noblest work of God
Is giving us His only Son,
  To ransom us with blood.
This far outdoes our highest thought,—
  The great redemption plan,
The fallen world brought back to heaven,
  God's untold love to man."

The teaching on that summer eve
  Was like the gentle shower
That falls refreshing on the grass,
  And cheering on the flower.
And as through life from stage to stage
  With fleeting foot he trod,
It shed a sweetness through his soul,
  And led him up to God.

THE FALL OF SLAVERY.

MUSING by a mossy fountain.
  In the blossom month of May,
  Saw I coming down a mountain
An old man whose locks were grey ;
And the flowery valleys echoed,
  As he sang his earnest lay.

"Prayer is heard, the chain is riven,
  Shout it over land and sea ;
Slavery from earth is driven,
  And the manacled are free ;
Brotherhood in all the nations ;
  What a glorious Jubilee !

"God has answered in the thunder,
  In the strife and carnage dire,
In the mountain rent asunder,
  In the battle roaring higher,
In the massacre of millions,
  In the smoke-cloud and the fire.

"God has answered, fall before Him,
  Laud His majesty and might :
On thy knees, O earth, adore Him :
  Now the black is as the white ;
Hallelujah ! hallelujah !
  Every bondsman free as light.

"God has answered, God the holy
  From His high eternal hill ;
He has stooped to save the lowly,
  As He ever, ever will :
Glory, glory to the Highest,
  Jah Jehovah reigneth still.

"Whip, and scourge, and fetter broken,
  Far away in darkness hurled ; ,
This a grand and glorious token,
  When millennium fills the world.
Hallelujah!   O'er the nations
  Freedom's snowy flag unfurled.

"God has answered! Glory, glory!
  O'er the green earth let it speed ;
Sun and stars, take up the story,
  Nevermore a slave shall bleed ;
Shout deliverance for the freeman,
  Send him succour in his need.

"By and bye he'll sow the clearing,
  In the backwoods lone and dim :
Liberty, so long appearing,
  Is more dear than light to him.
Soon he will be self-supporting,
  Praising God with prayer and hymn.

"Glory be to God the Giver,
  Slavery now shall brand no more ;
From the fountain to the river
  Freedom breathes on every shore.
Hallelujah! Hallelujah!
  Brotherhood the wide world o'er."

I MET YOU ON THE MOOR.

Come, Kitty, near the faggot-brand
  Beneath our chimney-tree :
  I love to hear your needles go,
'Tis music still for me.
They always bring a pleasant thought,—
  You know it well, I'm sure,—
When first, near fifty years a-gone,
  I met you on the moor.

No blushing flower in all the land
  To me was half so fair,
As you were then,—as you are now,
  Though dimmed by age and care.
And O, what trials have we seen !
  What conflicts have we pass'd !
But, Kitty, our great Father's hand
  Will guide us home at last.

I've often thought, and felt it true,
  Whilst travelling to the tomb,
That earth has more of joy than woe,
  Has more of light than gloom.
Like others we've had sorrow-storms,
  But they have soon blown o'er ;
And, Kitty, is it not because
  I met you on the moor ?

Yes, we have had our share of change
  And disappointment here ;
Our sons have come, our sons have gone,
  And all our daughters dear.
In weal or woe, while here below,
  You ever have in store
A portion of that love which first
  Was kindled on the moor.

You know how we beneath the tree
  Stood in the twilight bower,
And that first kiss, so full of bliss,
  Is rapture till this hour.
You did not speak, yet blushed your cheek,
  Your eyes were running o'er,
As lingering still beside the mill
  We parted on the moor.

Now age is come, my eyes are dim,
  Grey locks are on my brow ;
I start to hear the throstle's voice :
  O, how the strong men bow !
But, Kitty, you have been to me
  A comfort evermore :
Ten thousand times I've thanked the Lord
  I met you on the moor.

And when we lay our burdens down,
  As lay them down we must,
One grave shall be for you and me
  To mingle into dust.
And in the land of stars and flowers
  We sha'n't forget, I'm sure,
How in the world we left behind
  I met you on the moor.

TO THE RIVULET.

Little, gentle, murmuring rill,
  Winding round my native hill,
  Pouring forth thy pensive tale
In the silent hawthorn vale,
Kissing many a lovely flower,
Sparkling free in Nature's bower,
Wooing oft the poet's song,
As thou murmurest along !
  How I love thee, little rill,
  Winding round my native hill !

Little, lonely, murmuring brook !
Thou hast lured me from my book,
Lured me from my pleasant home,
And beside thy verge I'm come,
Once again to visit thee,
Sitting 'neath my favourite tree.
Still thou hast a melting song,
As thou murmurest along.
  How I love thee, little rill,
  Winding round my native hill !

Little, limpid, murmuring stream !
Let me by thy margin dream,
Severed from the city's noise,
Severed from discordant joys.
Here the swallow dips his wing,
And the redbreast loves to sing ;
Peace within thy bosom laves,
Zephyrs fan thy silver waves.
Thou hast many a tale to tell,
And I love thee passing well !

THE EMIGRANT'S RETURN.

THE cooling eve stole o'er the earth,
  The red sun sank in flame;
The ploughman eased his weary team,
  And from the furrow came.
The shepherd penned his fleecy flock
  Upon the quiet moor,
And sweet the happy cottager
  Sang by his rustic door.

Down from the copse an aged dame
  Came staggering with her load:
A few stray sticks her apron held,
  To warm her mean abode;
And, sitting on a humble stool,
  The wood securely piled,
Her thoughts were with her absent boy,
  Her only living child.

O, years had passed since one bright morn,
  When flowers were on the lea,
He bade farewell to all behind,
  And sailed across the sea.
Then, kneeling down, she prayed for him,
  All lonely in her shed;
And soon she sorrowed for his sire
  When laid among the dead.

Since then, the blast of time hath blown
  Around her rude and high,
And left her on the strand of change
  With tear-drops in her eye.
So she sits down again to muse
  Upon her wandering boy,
To feed that flame which chance or change
  Or time can ne'er destroy.

O, nought is like a mother's love
  In this rude world of strife,
As pure and holy as the rills
  Around the well of life.
It stronger grows as time departs
  Along his tardy way,
And, as the sun, shines brighter still
  Unto the perfect day.

But hark! a rap is at the door;
  And ere she leaves her seat,
Her wandering boy is in her arms,
  When tears and kisses meet.
And now she sobs, and now she smiles,
  And now she smoothes his hair;
Then kneels, and with uplifted hands
  Pours forth an earnest prayer.

"And can this really be my boy,
  Again returned to me,
With so much kindness in his heart?
  O yes, 'tis he, 'tis he!
Last night I dreamt I saw him here
  Before my gladdened view,
And felt his arms about my neck:
  Now, God be thanked, 'tis true."

And when the glow-worm's silvery light
  Was gleaming by the well,
And on the hills the hush of night
  Was resting like a spell,
The breath of prayer from that rude home
  Uprose in strains of joy,
And Jesus Christ was honoured by
  That mother and her boy.

THE MINER'S WIFE.

HE came not, though she waited still
  Beside her own loved hearth,
  Regardless of external things,—
Her playful baby's mirth;
Regardless of the rushing storm
  That o'er the mountains came,
She sat with eyes intently fixed
  Upon the flickering flame.

He came not, though the young wife wept
  Within her wonted place,
And fast the burning tears fell down
  Upon her baby's face,
Who smiled as though he fain would snap
  The melancholy chain
That manacled his mother's soul,
  And make her glad again.

He came not, though the silent hour—
  The midnight hour—had passed;
And little baby fell asleep
  Upon her lap at last.
She fondled with his golden hair,
  And gazed around her home;
Unseen she breathed a fervent prayer:
  "Ah! will he never come?"

He came not, though the feeble light
  Which hours ago was fired,
And flickered in the socket's cave,
  Had finally expired!
Strange spirit-tones were heard to come
  On every fitful breeze,
And hollow sounds were rushing through
  The autumn-dropping trees.

He came not, though the morning's rays
  Streamed over lea and waste;
But with it came a messenger,
  A messenger in haste!
And his pale visage paler grew:
  She read its import well:
"O God, defend the fatherless!"
  And to the earth she fell.

The church-bell tolled at evening time;
  The mourners left the shed;
And robin sang a requiem,—
  Above the silent dead.
The cold clods fell upon the bier;
  The funeral rite was o'er;
And she who loved him once so dear,
  Will gaze on him no more;

And now he sleeps as peacefully
  Within his humble grave,
And slumbers on as quietly,
  As sleep the blazoned brave.
He fell not on the battle-field,
  By bullet or by blade,
Yet perished as a hero should :—
  Peace to the miner's shade!

In mournful garb of widowhood,
  Across the path she'll hie ;
You know it is the miner's wife
  By tears which dim her eye ;
And, like a bird whose mate is flown,
  She hastens to her nest,
And fondles with her little one,
  And hugs it to her breast !

ON THE DEATH OF MY DAUGHTER LUCRETIA,

(WHO DIED DECEMBER 23RD, 1855, AGED SIX YEARS AND FIVE MONTHS.)

AND art thou gone so soon ?
  And is thy loving, gentle spirit fled ?
  Ah ! is my fair, my passing beautiful,
My loved Lucretia numbered with the dead ?

I miss thee, daughter, now,
In the dear dells of earth we oft have trod ;
And a strange longing fills my yearning soul
To sleep with thee, and be, like thee, with God !

I miss thee at thy books,
Lisping sweet Bible-accents in my ear,
Showing me pictures by the evening lamp,
Beautiful emblems thou didst love so dear.

I miss thee at thy prayers,
When the eve-star is looking through the sky,
And thy lone sister kneels in sorrow down,
To pray to her great Father up on high.

I miss thee by the brook,
Where we have wandered many a summer's day,
And thou wert happy with thy loving sire,
More happy here than at thy simple play.

I miss thee mid the trees,
Where we have hasted in the twilight dim
To wake the echoes of the silent dell,
And mark the glow-worm 'neath the hawthorn's limb.

I miss thee on the Hill,
The dear old hill which we have climbed so oft ;
And O, how very happy have we been
In the still bower of the old heathy croft !

I miss thee at day's close,
When from my labour I regain my cot,
And sit down sadly at the supper board,
Looking for thee, but, ah ! I see thee not.

I miss thee every where,—
In my small garden, watching the first flower,—
By the clear fountain,—in thy Sunday-class,—
Running to meet me at the evening hour.

Farewell, my beautiful !
Thy sinless spirit is with Christ above :
Thou hast escaped the evils of the world :
We have a daughter in the meads of love.

When I and little Jane
Walk hand in hand along the old hill's way,
Shall we not feel thy cherub-presence near,
Singing our sad psalms in the twilight grey ?

Companion of the bard,
Mid rocks and trees, and hedges ivy-crossed !
At morn and eve in Nature's presence-cell
We oft have entered with our musings lost.

How thou didst love the flowers,
The darling daisy and the buds of Spring,
The brooks and birds, the hush of solitude,
The moon and stars, like some diviner thing !

Ah ! thou wert like a rose,
Dropped by an angel on earth's feverish clime,
To bloom full lovely, till December winds
Blasted thy beauty in its morning's prime.

Hush, murmuring spirit, hush !
It is the Lord, He only, who hath given ;
And He hath taken—Thus I kiss His rod !—
The gem, which fell from paradise, to heaven.

THE OLD SLOE-TREE.

THERE is a sloe-tree in the vale,
  A bended, broken bough,
  Half-hid among the holly-brakes,
That overtop it now.
A ragged branch it is, and rude
  As ever branch can be ;
Yet oft a poet's shadow falls
  Upon this old sloe-tree.

He comes when green leaves fill the trees,
  He comes in summer hours,
He comes when wild winds whirl the leaves
  In autumn's withered bowers.
And when the ice is on the pools,
  In winter, there is he,
Wrapped in his mantle, prophet-like,
  Under the old sloe-tree.

Why does he come at closing eve,
  When stars appear above,
And little glow-worms light their lamps
  In nooks he aye will love ?
Why does he come and linger here,
  Away from noise and glee,
And list, as if an angel sang
  Upon this old sloe-tree ?

Just cause has he for musing here
  In solitude, I ween ;
For with him oft his little girl,
  His beautiful, has been.
And when they last walked in this dell,
  Like wandering breezes free,
She plucked the fruit with her small hands
  From off this old sloe-tree.

But ere the white buds came again,
  Ay, ere the leaves were shed,
The gates of heaven let in his child,
  His little maid was dead.
Now all alone, the pensive sire,
  As sad as he may be,
Oft muses on his sainted one,
  Beneath this old sloe-tree.

ONCE MORE AMONG THE BRAKES.

ONCE more among the brakes,
  The golden brakes once more ;
To sit and muse amid the broom,
  As oft in days of yore ;
To drink the pure fresh air,
  That fills those moorlands free ;
And once again to be, O bower,
  A denizen of thee.

Here oft a lonely man
  Comes mid the grasses groen,
Communing with the mystic winds
  That blow their trumps unseen.
But now a pious calm
  Pervades this still retreat ;
And not a zephyr stirs to move
  The flowerets at his feet.

Can he not worship here
  The Great, the Good, the Wise ;
Who clothes the earth with majesty,
  Whose glory fills the skies ?
Can he not worship here,
  As truly as those bands
Who land and magnify His name
  In temples made with hands ?

Yes, God is everywhere,
  On hill and silent glade ;
Know, on the Mount of Olivet
  The world's Redeemer prayed.
And in my mountain bower,
  Beside this mossy stone,
While sportive swallows round me wheel,
  I worship at His throne.

Isaac stole forth to muse
  Beside the river's brim,
When Silence, hid in Canaan's shades,
  Listed the twilight hymn.
And resting on his crook,
  The ruddy shepherd-boy,
The tuneful Psalmist, mid his sheep,
  Did Christian peace enjoy.

My child, my loving one,
  Too quickly passed away :
How often have we loitered here,
  Nor travelled with the gay !
Content to watch the flowers,
  Or emmets in their hill,
Or spider weave his wondrous web,
  Or wren with horny bill.

O let me turn aside
  From care, and toil, and pain ;
To weep where I have often wept,
  And muse on thee again !
This heath is holy now ;
  For, at the twilight hour,
The spirit of my little one
  Is floating through my bower.

THE LONELY MUSER.

THE day had ended, the pale stars
  Were shining through the sky,
As all alone a pensive man
  Mused where the rough rocks lie,
Gazing away in empty space
  With tear-drops in his eye.

The dark-cloaked Reaper had just passed
  Where bursting blossoms smiled ;
Not heeding youth and innocence,
  Or beauty undefiled,
He drew his sickle mid the flowers,
  When fell his darling child.

O, she had grown beneath his eye
  Like some angelic thing :
Their two brief beings mixed in one
  'Neath Love's elysian wing.
She felt a cherished part of him,
  When broke life's feeble string.

And now among the reed he sits,
  That creek and common fills,
Gazing away among the stars
  That gem the heavenly hills,
And deems he sees his angel one
  Beside the Eden rills.

LUCRETIA'S GRAVE.

'TIS where the tree-tops wave,
  And gleam with glory 'neath the summer's sun,
And gentle breathings steal among the boughs,
  When busy day is done.

'Tis where a tiny rill
Glides through the silence with a trickling fall ;
And ivy-leaves, like holy epitaphs,
  Are clinging to the wall.

'Tis where the grass is green,
And daisy flowers in snowy beauty lie,
And songs from fragrant field and forest screen
  Are sweetly gushing by.

'Tis where the village church
Among the dews its solemn shadow throws,
When silvery lyrics o'er the dingles float,
At evening's gentle close.

'Tis where the weary rest,
And Age and Beauty moulder in decay;
And Hope upon the silent green sward sits,
Watching the slumbering clay.

Above it shine the stars,
Around it woods and rocky mountains rise :
O, let it be my silent sepulchre,
When Death has sealed mine eyes !

O FOR A COT IN SOME LONE PLACE !

O FOR a cot in some lone place,
  A calm, unruffled home,
  "A lodge in some vast wilderness,"
Where man might never come !
My soul is sick to hear the tongue
  Of slander day by day ;
O had I but a bird's fleet wing,
  I'd quickly soar away !

And oft I think how sweet 'twould be
  To tend my fleecy flocks,
And sing my pensive pastorals,
  Among the mossy rocks,
With no companions but the birds
  And little hedgerow flowers,
And one, my silver star of hope,
  To gild the darkest hours !

This world is very beautiful
  Beneath the sun's bright ray,
Girt round with belts of freshening green,
  And kissed by flowery May ;
But man drags down his fellow-man,
  Exulting in his woe,
Shrouding the bright and beautiful,
  And sullying all below.

And is there not, in all the earth,
  In ocean, or in air,
A spot where Peace delights to dwell ?
  O lead the wanderer there !
Yes, many such, I'm sure, there are
  In this fair world of ours,
Hung round with crystal innocence,
  And gemmed with tearless flowers.

'Tis in the bosom of the man
  Who walks by faith, not sight,
Who knows and feels from day to day
  That all he does is right.
'Tis in the heart where God is feared ;
  'Tis in the pilgrim's prayer ;
'Tis in the good man's Bible-home :
  O lead the wanderer there !

MY MOUNTAIN HOME.

MY mountain home ! how dear thou art,
  For ever graven on my heart,
  For ever fresh in memory's page,
To be so till my latest age !
How can I, dare I, think to roam
Away from thee, my mountain home ?

My mountain home ! by that sweet word
How many leaves of life are stirred !
My infant gambols mid the flowers,
My childhood sports, my boyhood hours,
My schoolboy days, when I would glide
Elate adown thy shaggy side ;
Nor deemed that I should muse, as now,
In tears upon thy rocky brow.

My mountain home ! thy heathy bowers
Are filled with wild, with warbling flowers ;
Thy pathless brow, with pleasures rife,
Is sweeter than the haunts of strife ;
Thy daisy-pastures all combine
To bind thee to this heart of mine.
Should fate command me o'er the seas,
I'll think upon thy healthy breeze ;
To barbarous climes where blackness lowers,
I'll muse upon thy dear wild flowers ;
To barren isles mid pagan men,
I'll turn and gaze upon thee then.
Where'er my weary footsteps roam,
I can't forget my mountain home.

My mountain home ! the autumn leaves
Are dropping on my cottage eaves,
Are falling in the valley's bound,
With low, hushed, soul-subduing sound ;
Murmuring to Memory's musing ear
The death-dirge of the dying year ;
Recalling scenes of distant date,
And whispering of my future fate.
Sad utterance have those autumn leaves,
Down-dropping on my cottage eaves.

My mountain home ! eve shuts the flower,
And soothes the muser in his bower ;
The mower hastens from the mead,
And I must hush my simple reed ;
The leaves and flowers in days to come
Will bud and wither round my home ;
And twilight's song float through the gloom,
When I am slumbering in the tomb,
Perchance in dark oblivion's deep
To take an everlasting sleep.
But I would, ere I cease to be,
Link something of myself with thee,
That should attract some wanderer here,
To drop upon thy head a tear.

THE RESTORED.

THE gentle south winds softly blew,
  Where Spring's first flowers had birth ;
  And the warm cheering sunlight threw
Its radiance on the earth ;

When from his lowly woodbined home,
  O'ershadowed with tall trees,
A pale man, buttoned to the chin,
  Stole forth upon the leas.

Six weary wintry months had he
  Bowed in his lowly cot,
Nor crossed the threshold of his home,
  Nor murmured at his lot.
Sick, sick, was he, his wasting frame
  Drew near the door of death.
When He who smote him healed his wounds,
  And purified his breath.

Beside the crooked hedge of withs,
  He slowly crept along,
Pausing to look upon the flowers,
  That shone the banks among.
And when the grey lark fleetly rose,
  And carolled o'er his head;
Wiping the hot tears from his face,
  He raised his eyes and said,—

" O what a blessed, blessed boon
  Is the dear gift of health,
More precious far than friends or fame,
  Or what the world calls wealth !
O blessings on this cooling breeze,
  That fans my feverish brow !
Methinks I never felt like this,
  Or prized it so till now.

" How beautiful those marigolds
  Are shining in the grass !
And here the blue-eyed cuckoo-flowers
  Bow to me, as I pass.
Methinks they never looked so fair,
  While robin on the spray
Is singing like a merry bard,
  Under the crown of May.

" O blessed, blessed be His name,
  Who raised me from my bed,
And brought me on those paths once more,
  I have been wont to tread.
I laud and magnify Him here,
  Who fills both earth and sky,
Whose power has raised me up again,
  The Holy and the High."

TREES.

To list the summer breeze
  Sigh through the leafy trees.
As on the grass within their shade I lie,
  In the full noontide free,
  Is such a joy to me,
While through their branches shines the distant sky.

Methinks I always hear
  Wild odes, to poets dear,
Swell through the tree-tops, as I muse below ;
  Whether by day or night,
  Whether in dark or light,
Like organ echoes surging to and fro.

Sway ! sway ! as if they said
  In green robes overhead,
" What music is so rich as that we give,
  When breezes steal along,
  Or when the winds are strong ?
In converse with the elements we live.

" Cold, cold the earth below,
  Cold, cold with wrong and woe :
Pride tramples weakness, glorying in its crime :
  Worth warbles in the shade,
  Neglected, lone, dismayed,
And so we joy the firmament to climb.

" Our boughs the free birds love,
  The thrush, the gentle dove,
The linnet chirping to the murmuring breeze ;
  And every bard true-born
  Lingers at eve and morn,
To treasure up the teaching of the trees.

" We stand near halls of state,
  And by the poor man's gate ;
Our summer branches shade the village well ;
  And lovers breathe their vows
  Under our spreading boughs,
When twilight lingers in the dusky dell.

" Where falling waters play
  On the wide moorland grey,
Beside the thatched cot on the daisy lea,
  By ocean's lonely shore,
  Where rolling billows roar,
And in the city's circle, there are we.

" We give the approach of Spring,
  Of Summer's reign we sing,
Discourse of Autumn brown and Winter drear ;
  True books are we which show
  The seasons as they go,
For evermore the prophets of the year.

" The schoolboy loves us well,
  As, lingering in the dell,
He climbs from limb to limb with shout and lay.
  Young men and maidens fair
  Under our boughs repair,
When labour rests, to talk the eve away.

" Beside her cottage door,
  Upon the rushy moor,
The aged dame sits knitting in our shade ;
  What time the cuckoo's note
  Does o'er the meadows float,
And swallows wheel along the grassy glade.

" The invalid comes here,
  Rejoicing through a tear,
To mark the sky-lark o'er our green heads sing,
  When sounds the pensive bell
  Along the quiet dell,
And the lone shepherd watches by the spring.

"And here in secret prayer
The pilgrim doth repair :
At fading eve, when bright the glow-worms shine,
And we are rustling low,
His vespers from below
Rise o'er our heads and reach the ear Divine.

"We screen the old thatched mill,
Wave high upon the hill,
Roar in the storm, and murmur in the breeze ;
Whether full-leafed or bare,
Our psalm is on the air,
The voice of God is heard among the trees."

Sway ! sway ! And so 'twill be,
Till love o'er land and sea
Shall reign, and discord from the earth be driven ;
When swords and spears are spurned,
And into ploughshares turned,
And earth unblasted shall become a heaven.

DEATH OF THE PRINCE CONSORT.

UPON the damp air wailing,
With startling speed there came
A sound of solemn sadness
It is a pain to name.
The willow by the wicket,
The hawthorn on the brae,
Seem moaning in the darkness,
"A Prince has passed away."

When Sabbath prayers were offered
By many a pious band,
Like a cloud-flash the tidings
Swept o'er the smitten land.
And suddenly we staggered,
As if bereft of light.
O, Death has seized the mighty,
And left us filled with night.

Weep, weep, O prostrate nation,
Pour forth thy burning tears ;
The great, the good, the gracious,
Has filled his list of years ;
And, like a quiet leaflet,
He fell at midnight hour,
Casting a sudden sorrow
Upon each palace-flower ;

Casting a sudden sorrow
Upon a Nation's brow,
Who loved the good Prince Consort,
And never more than now.
O, bards of after ages,
In peaceful, prosperous days,
Shall kindle into singing,
And chant him in their lays.

The striving, honest worker,
The peasant meanly dressed,
The widow and the orphan,
The poor with talent blest,

The poet and the painter,
Ay, all who loved the right,
He patronized, and aided
The struggler in the fight.

In life's meridian glory
The silent Slayer came,
With scarce a sound of warning,
And quenched the vital flame.
He maketh no distinction,
All share one common lot,
And Grief shed tears of sorrow
In castle and in cot.

Not leading on red battle,
Mid flashing steel and strife,
And gore and dreadful groanings,
Did he yield up his life.
But as he lived, so died he,
Where Peace delights to bloom ;
And now fair Art and Science
Embrace above his tomb.

O we will hope the Saviour
Has taken him on high,
Where fever never rages,
And goodness cannot die.
Sad is this dispensation,
Its issues who shall tell ?
God giveth, and He taketh ;
He doeth all things well.

Now lay him down to slumber,
With fame upon his breast,
In all his manhood's glory,
Where Britain's heroes rest.
And coming generations,
As future years return,
Shall love to bless his greatness,
And worship at his urn.

But ONE there is we ever
Upon our hearts will bear,
When morn or evening finds us
Engaged with God in prayer.
The Widow of a Nation,
Whose life and works are seen,
A blessing and a brightness,—
O pray for England's Queen.

AN ODE

ON THE ANNIVERSARY OF THE BIRTHDAY
OF WILLIAM SHAKSPERE,
APRIL 23RD, 1864.

Prize Poem.*

ADJUDICATORS : The Right Hon. Lord Lyttelton, George
Dawson, Esq., M.A., Charles Dray, Esq.

OVER the earth a glow,
Peak-point and plain below,
The red round sun sinks in the purple west ;

* This poem won the first prize at the Tercentenary
of Shakspere, April, 1864, which consisted of a handsome

Lambs press their daisy bed,
The lark drops overhead,
And sings the labourer, hastening home to rest.

Bathed in the ruddy light,
Flooding his native height,
A youthful bard is stretched upon the moss;
He heedeth not the eve
Whose locks the elfins weave,
Entranced with Shakspere near a Cornish cross.

Men pass him and repass;
The hare is in the grass;
The full moon stealeth o'er the hill of pines;
Twilight is lingering dim;
The village vesper-hymn
Murmurs its music through the trembling vines.

Starts up the musing boy,
His soul is hot with joy,
He revels in a region of delight;
The winds are rich with song,
As slow they sweep along,
And earth and sky are full of holy light.

Tongues trill on every rock,
Notes flow from every block;
The hawthorn shines with fairies; the clear rill
With pointed rushes hid,
The pleasant banks amid,
Trickles its treasures tuning down the hill.

A spell is on his soul:
He scans the mystic scroll
Of human passions wakened by the wand
Of England's noblest seer,
Whom England holds so dear,—
Great, glorious Shakspere, loved in every land!

He hears the tramp of steeds,
Sees War in gory weeds,
Roams through the forest, with delighted eyes;
Bends to the tempest's roar,
Weeps for the monarch poor,
And sobs with sorrow when dear Juliet dies.

Thus lay that musing boy,
Whose soul was hot with joy,
Environed in a hemisphere of rays;
And in the mystic light
The genius of the height
Brought him a lyre, which he, enraptured, plays.

He sang of him, the great,
Shakspere, of kingly state,
Who in his boyhood by clear Avon strayed,

gold watch. On the centre of the case is a notable repre-
sentation of the great poet encircled with a wreath of
leaves. It was manufactured by the well-known firm of
Messrs. Rotherham, and was competed for by persons in
all parts of the United Kingdom and also in America.
The MS. is now suitably framed and mounted for preserva-
tion in the Shakspere Museum at Stratford-on-Avon.

Learning the lore of song
From feeble thing and strong,—
The great tree towering and the tiny blade:

The welkin's solemn height,
The lightning's livid light,
The thunder's mutter, the black whirlwind's roar;
The little child at play,
The red-breast on the spray,
The daisy nodding by the ploughman's door:

The hedges, hung in flowers,
The falling, pattering showers,
The dew-drops, glittering in the morning's shine;
The smallest film that be,
Which none but poets see,
All taught him lessons with a voice Divine.

Dame Nature oped her store,
Her secret inner door;
Boldly he revelled through her wondrous cell:
And none the song-lines read
Around and overhead,
Or know the mystic chronicles so well.

He solved the human heart
Like mariner his chart,
And passion's every phase was known to him;
And when the full time came,
Forth burst the mighty flame,
To blaze and brighten till the stars are dim!

This greatly-gifted one
Was Labour's noblest son,—
The people's honour, leader, champion strong;
The glory of the soil,
The towering prince of toil,
The matchless monarch in the realm of song.

Loved now the wide world round,
Where human hives are found;
By prince, and peasant following the plough,
The sailor out at sea,
The yeoman on the lea,
The miner digging in the earth below:

The shepherd in his plaid,
The rosy village maid,
The warrior watching by the red camp fire,
The mother with her child,
The satchelled schoolboy mild,
The college student, daily pressing higher:

The dweller of the street,
In the great city's heat,
The mountaineer, within his lodge of reeds;
The silent solitaire
On the wild desert bare:—
All own his witchery where the daylight speeds.

Three centuries' solemn span
Since his great life began
Have borne their burdens to the hidden sphere;
Each epoch ever found
Him with new glories crowned,
Like the red sun when the wide west is clear.

And so, great bard, to-day
We weave thy natal lay,
And cluster gratefully around thy name :
England will ever be,
Dear Shakspere, proud of thee,
And coming ages but augment thy fame.

OUT OF CORNWALL.

Born among the boulders,
In Cornwallia's clime
An untutored harper
Passed his life in rhyme,
Trilled among the thickets
By the crosses grey,
Until forty summers
Led him on his way.

Sang he of the streamlet
And the clinking mill,
The rich lodes of copper
Running in the hill,
Taught by winds that whisper
Round the peasant's door,
And wild tales that cluster
On the weird moor.

Every feature pleased him
Of his native place,
Bank, and brake, and burrow,
With poetic grace ;
And the more he marked her,
Wandering with his quill,
Ever more he loved her,
As a poet will.

Thus he saw Cornwallia
Like a seraph shine,
Until forty summers
Made her half divine.
Never, never had he
Left her hillocks low ;
Never, never did he
O'er her boundaries go.

Then the steam-horse bore him
One sky-pleasant day
Out of old Cornwallia,
Many miles away ;
Onward, onward ever,
Charmed with sight and sound,
Till his feet at Stratford
Pressed the classic ground.

Then again returned he
To his native place,
Where his wife and children
Joyed to see his face.
Lake and landscape charmed him,
Wood and waterfall ;
Yet he knows Cornwallia
Is the best of all.

SHAKSPERE'S SHRINE.

By his ingle crooning,
Near the Cornish sea,
Sat a simple bardie
Harping in his glee :
When a holy vision
Rose before his ken,
Where great Shakspere rested,
Shakspere, king of men.

Longed he to behold it,
Saw it in his dreams,
Talked of it, when questioned,
Mid the flowers and streams,—
Shakspere's tomb at Stratford,
And the chamber dear,
Where his mother bore him,
By the Avon clear.

Sometimes hoping, fearing,
Darkness spanning light ;
Then the prospect blackened,
Rayless, hopeless quite.
Rose he one clear morning,
Hurried off despair :
Early in November,
Much he wondered there.

Saw he then the cottage,
And the chamber small,
Where his mother bore him,
With its written wall.
Saw he, too, the Avon
Flowing through the grass :
O the crystal Avon,
Clear as clearest glass !

Saw he, too, the chancel
Where the poet sleeps,
By his own dear river
Which for ever weeps.
Saw he hill and valley,
Meadow, tree, and plain,
And "sweet Anne's" dear dwelling
By the twisted lane.

Saw he these and wondered,
Saw he these and wept,
Holy as a vision
Coming when he slept.
Every little daisy,
Like a hermit then,
Spoke of William Shakspere,
Shakspere, king of men.

Turned the Cornish crooner,
Heated as with wine,
Turned he dumb with wonder
From great Shakspere's shrine.
Variously the Giver
Giveth gifts to all :
Use them for His glory,
Whether great or small.

SHAKSPERE'S HOUSE.

I STOOD before it with a joy
  Almost akin to pain,
Nor can I hope, throughout life's race,
  To drink so deep again
As when I pulled the rude bell-wire,
  Which dangled by the door
Of Shakspere's house in Henley Street,
  And stepped the threshold o'er.

The old walls seemed to speak to me
  With a mysterious sound ;
And lyre-chords echoed in mine ears,
  As I stood gazing round.
I bared my head, I know not why,
  And tears ran down my face ;
I felt that I was stealing through
  A sacred solemn place.

Strange that the stones about the hearth
  Should bring to memory's sight
The home where my grandfather dwelt,
  Upon the granite height :
There first my simple song I sang,
  Where ferns and flowerets be ;
Enamoured of my mountain muse,
  Under the hawthorn tree.

O, what a tale the chimney told,
  Where Mary nursed her boy ;
Who grew at last, in strength of song,
  To be a nation's joy !
Methought I saw him sitting there,
  Beside the blazing log,
In knitted hose and petticoat,
  With playful cat and dog.

Then I beheld him gathering flowers,
  The sunny knolls among,
And reading lessons on their leaves,
  Where Avon flowed along ;
Or seeking birds' nests in the lanes ;
  Or, velvet cap in hand,
Chasing the pretty butterflies
  Over the daisy land.

E'en then the music of the woods
  And waters filled his soul,
Whose echoes would, in after years,
  Through all creation roll.
His teachers were the little birds
  That caroled on the tree ;
And the long grass among the ferns,
  Where shining fairies be.

Methought I saw him creep to school,
  With satchel in his hand,
And then rush home, with lay and shout,
  When curfews filled the land ;
And how his mother, wondering, gazed,
  With all a parent's joy ;
A tear appearing in each eye,
  To hear her loving boy.

When the skylark o'er Avon's banks
  Was pouring forth his lay,
He heard it like some angel's voice
  From the bright gates of Day :
And when the thunder crashed, and bolts
  Of ruin tore the sod,
Did not the boy adoring bow,
  And own the power of God ?

With pen and paper next he sat,
  Beside the cheerful fire ;
Attuning with untold delight
  His unexampled lyre.
The notes were simply-sweet at first,
  But preludes to the strong,
Which should arouse the universe,
  To crown him king of song.

Yes, here he piped, and here he played,
  Upon this self-same floor ;
His hands have often touched these walls,
  Now widely written o'er.
And here he slept, when moon and stars
  In Night's dark mantle came ;
Watched by the Genii of the muse,
  And the bright form of Fame.

Oft by this same old door he stood,
  When ice was in the dell ;
Clapping his hands, with thought enriched,
  As fast the snow-flakes fell.
And when the angry storm was up,
  And through the forest roared,
To him 'twas Nature's poet-hand,
  Sweeping her loftiest chord.

O boy, O bard, O house of fame,
  O spot to Britain dear !
From every sea, from every land,
  The pilgrim journeys here.
How did my thankful heart o'erflow,
  When on that blessed morn
I breathed within the written walls
  Where Shakspere's self was born !

SHOTTERY.

O SHOTTERY, dear Shottery !
  Sequestered in the dell,
Far-famed for sweet Anne Hathaway,
  I feel I love thee well.
For thou hast hedges like my own,
  With little glens of green,
Where primroses smile out in spring,
  With violets between.

O Shottery, dear Shottery !
  I oft have thought of thee,
When reading Shakspere in my youth
  Under the hawthorn tree ;
Nor did I dream in those joy-days
  To see thee with mine eye,
And tread thy ever-hallowed ground
  Under the bluest sky.

O Shottery, dear Shottery !
Thy cottage by the lane,
Where Anne watched oft for singing Will
Beside the Gothic pane ;
The garden-gate, the courting-seat,
The chimney, bed, and door,
The walls, three hundred years of age,
Are with me evermore.

O Shottery, dear Shottery !
The breeze that passed along
Was full of sweetest melody,
And every breath was song.
The children playing in the lane,
The sheep upon the lea,
The very stones, the grass, and earth,
Were beautiful to me.

O Shottery, dear Shottery !
From out the well drank I,
Where Shakspere oft has slaked his thirst
When Anne was standing by,—
The well within the garden-ground
Where hide the wicked fays ;
And O what comic tales it told
Of Willie's courting-days !

O Shottery, dear Shottery !
I may forget the mine
Where I have laboured in the dark,
From dawn till day's decline ;
But I can never lose thy face,
'Tis evermore with me;
For thou art like a little child
I've dandled on my knee.

SHAKSPERE'S TOMB.

Drop lightly, footfall mine :
A king lies sleeping in the chancel dim,
And every atom of this sacred shrine
Is telling me of him.

I know not how I feel :
A tide of thought comes rushing, music-driven,
And, but for eyes around, O, I could kneel
In prayer to bounteous Heaven !

He gives, He takes away ;
He thrusts the lofty from the uplifted seat :
He lifts the lowly, like to him whose clay
Is resting 'neath my feet.

Is it some dreamy spell
Which morn will break illusive, though now dear ?
O, no ! this music is the old church bell,
And Shakspere's tomb is here.

On every fresh wind-wave
Encircling Stratford like a gale of song,
From mead and moor, and bush and coppice-cave,
His great name rolls along.

With folded hands I wait,
Resting my feet upon the blue, flat stone ;
And in this span of silence years of weight
Seem mystically thrown.

Flows by the Avon clear,
As murmuring for the sleeper evermore,
Whose name is written on each floweret dear
That shines upon its shore.

In the bright book of Fame,
With leaves graved over now by labouring men,
Foremost of all is our dear Shakspere's name,
Who won it with his pen.

He bore no battle-brand,
But in the realm of Fancy stalked alone,
Swaying the passions with a princely hand,
Who sleeps beneath this stone.

I feel it much to meet
In shades so solemn. Tears are on my face ;
The dust of Shakspere is beneath my feet :
Hush ! 'tis a holy place !

THE WANDERER'S WELCOME.

Around the blazing fire of pine
The son and sire were sitting,
The sisters laid aside their work,
The mother stopped her knitting,
And gazed into the flickering flame
Which up the chimney sputtered,
So silent in her old arm-chair,
And not a word she uttered.

Meanwhile the darkness closer grew,
The misty silence deeper ;
The church-clock sounded on the moor,
O'er many a silent sleeper.
Yet in her chair the mother sat,
In holy calm devotion,
And gazed into the fitful flame,
With neither voice nor motion.

The sisters rose and left their place,
Nor could they converse gladly ;
The brother walked across the room,
And oft he listened sadly :
The father sighed, "My son, my son !"
And then his heart grew chiller ;
While in her chair the mother sat
As silent as a pillar.

When, hark ! the tramp of horse's hoofs,
Which each tick nearer counted ;
The gate is reached, the yard is crossed ;
The rider has dismounted.
The door swings wide ; the wanderer comes ;
O! there is sweet caressing,
As on his mother's neck he weeps,
And feels his mother's blessing.

His brother grasped both hands at once;
His sisters sobbed for gladness;
His father shouted lustily,
"This is no time for sadness:
Serve up the bacon and the eggs,
And bring the elder-jerry;
And sing thy psalm of praise, dear wife,
And let us all be merry."

THE FALL OF THE OLD HOUSE.

THE wintry storm is over; its wrecks are strewn
    around;
Uprooted trees and cottages prostrate upon the
    ground,—
Deserted sheds, that quaked to hear the tempest-spirit's
    call:
But one there is,—my dear old home,—more desolate
    than all.

The blasts of eighty years, or more, have lashed its
    rural roof:
Alone it stood, and seemed to laugh at hurricanes,
    storm-proof.
A thousand snows have whitened it; fierce frosts
    assailed its walls;
But Hope almost a century has carolled in its halls.

The sparrow loved to build her nest beneath its shaven
    eaves,
And darted from the chimney-top among the hawthorn-
    leaves.
Green summers came, and passed, and came; the aged
    sparrows fell,
And young ones built a sparrow's nest, where their
    grey sires did dwell.

Here oft was heard the voice of prayer at holy evening-
    time;
And here the poet swept his lyre at morning's early
    prime.
Here the fond lover told his tale; here friendship
    quaffed its fill:—
O, thou wert all in all to me, old cottage on the hill!

And here, on England's holy-day, old gathering friends
    would come,
And sip the peace-cup joyously within my mountain
    home;
Here strangely talked the eve away with legendary lore,
Until the minstrel's harp-strings twanged:—they'll
    gather there no more!

Mine eyes have seen thy loveliness laid level with the
    dust;
Bright gems, once sparkling in thy crown, are cankered
    with Time's rust.
The roaring March doth howl for thee his highest,
    haughtiest knell;
And, cowering 'neath the wind-god's wing, I strive to
    breathe "Farewell."

There is a rent in Nature now,—a gash where all was
    fair,—
A chasm which old Time himself will never more
    repair,—
A breaking up of that which was so beautiful and
    bright,—
A severing of the soul from earth,—a gathering in of
    night.

The silver moon is gazing down upon thy ruins now,
As here I sit and weep for thee upon my mountain's
    brow.
I loved thee when the sweetest songs were melting
    in thy bowers;
How longed I then to decorate my native home with
    flowers!

The blast has come, the parting blast: how wildly did
    it roar!
I looked,—my dear old home was gone! 'Twill be a
    home no more!
And since all things are perishing beneath the solemn
    sky,
O may I seek a happy home more permanent on high!

CHRISTMAS.

THE good old merry Christmas comes
    With smiling face again,
    And troops of happy young folks sing
    Their carols up the lane.
The yule-log blazes brightly now
    Upon the parlour grate,
And long ere evening friends from far
    Are knocking at the gate.

The old folks round the well-spread board
    Are at their cake and tea;
The jocund young ones dance with joy
    Around the Christmas tree.
And shining laurels deck the screen,
    And from the ceiling fall,
And stand up on the chimney-piece,
    And cluster on the wall.

O, good old merry Christmas comes
    Upon his snowy car!
His horses are the noisy winds,
    His lamps are many a star.
And up the echoing hills he rides,
    And down into the moors;
And every cot and castle-home
    With merry laughter roars.

O, let us learn to pity now
    The man of hoary head
Who trembles through the icy streets
    To beg his daily bread.
And as we sit around the fire,
    We read within the blaze
A thousand golden memories
    Of childhood's early days.

And while the younger members try
  Their ancient game at pins,
We sympathize with those that lose,
  And laugh whoever wins.
O, like a gush of holy light,
  Of melody and rhyme,
Amid the dark of winter's night,
  Is merry Christmas time!

THE OLD MAN ON THE BRIDGE.

AN old man on a bridge
  Stood in the twilight dim,
  When the mountains with grey light
Were mantled over him,
And from the rustling rushes rose
  The lone bard's vesper-hymn.

And the old man watched the waves,
  As they stole upon the strand ;
For the voices of lorn friends
  Came in their music bland ;
And his thoughts flew back to other days,
  His happy boyhood's band.

And they all appeared to view,
  Those days of " auld lang syne,"
When beautiful old Mother Earth
  Shone like a thing divine.
And Innocence and Happiness
  Embraced beneath the pine.

And the songs he oft had heard
  In his ancestral halls,
And the quaint old rhymes the bards rehearsed
  At their merry festivals,
Came fluting in the trickling brook's
  Melodious waterfalls.

And other voices spake
  In the stream's delicious chime ;
Even hers, the loved, the beautiful,
  Who perished in her prime ;
With those who fell like autumn-leaves
  In the dank dells of time.

Thus, resting on his staff,
  With the tear-drops in his eye,
The old man lingered on the bridge,
  Till the stars came in the sky,
When he turned back to his rose-hung cot,
  And laid him down to die.

THE WINDING WYE.

THE Wye, the Wye, the winding Wye!
  Beneath a cold November sky,
  I first beheld its waters clear,
Which stole by meads and orchards dear,
And heard the music of its flow,
As through the vales it wandered slow
With many a song, and many a sigh,
The Wye, the Wye, the winding Wye.

The Wye, the Wye, the winding Wye,
Stealing through glens like maiden shy,
Kissing the green banks by thy brink,
Where little birds stoop down and drink,
And watering many a floweret dear,
Which in the still creeks blossoms here !
How sweet upon thy marge to lie,
The Wye, the Wye, the winding Wye!

The Wye, the Wye, the winding Wye,
With happy Hereford close by !
And whether sleep the eyelids seal,
Or busy hands press round the wheel,
Should pleasures cheer, or sorrows lower,
Thou murmurest of thy Maker's power,
Who never leaves thy channels dry.
The Wye, the Wye, the winding Wye.

The Wye, the Wye, the winding Wye !
Another look and then good-bye.
Beside our sheltered harbour clear,
Wait for me wife and children dear ;
And though to these my journeying tends,
I add thee to my list of friends,
Well pleased to see and be so nigh
The Wye, the Wye, the winding Wye.

THE INVALID OF THE ALLEY.

DAY after day departed,
  The long nights passed away ;
  The pale man still grew paler
And thinner with decay.
His wasted frame still wasted,
  His cough more hollow grew ;
His hands could work no longer,
  Though want uprose to view.

No meal was in the barrel,
  Upon the shelf no bread :
He called his children round him,
  And thus he sadly said:
"To-morrow father leaves you,—
  O do not, do not cry !—
To go into the Union,
  In loneliness to die.

" If I should linger with you,
  The parish will not give
The bread on which my dear ones
  Can only hope to live.
I cannot labour longer :
  So for your sakes I lie
Alone within the Union,
  In solitude to die.

" But oft I'll think upon you,
  When morning comes so slow,
Or when the star of evening
  Is mirrored on the snow :
And as around the altar
  Ye bend the willing knee,
My fancy shall behold you
  Beseeching God for me.

· "And if within its shadow
    My latest hour I spend,
Then God will be your Father
    And Christ will be your Friend.
I lean upon my Saviour
    For grace to live and die,
And hope at last to meet you
    For ever in the sky."

Then Jane, his youngest daughter,
    His fairest, tenderest flower,
Climbed up his knee and kissed him
    In this oppressive hour.
Around his neck entwining,
    Her arms she fondly flung;
And these the simple accents
    That murmured from her tongue:

"O dearest, dearest father!
    I cannot let you go:
Remain with little Janie,
    And Peterkin, and Joe.
We'll kindly wait upon you,
    How ill soe'er you be:
Don't go into the Union,
    But stay with them and me."

The sick man kissed the maiden,
    Then bowed his head to weep:
But when the morrow's sunbeams
    Streamed over dell and deep,
They bore him to the Union,
    The iron gate was barred,
And soon a nameless pauper
    Was buried in the yard.

EDA.

BESIDE the village watering-place
    The beauteous Eda came,
When the setting sun o'er the western hills
    Had flung his robes of flame;
And under the flowery hawthorn tree
    She called on her lover's name.

He long had been in the fabled West,
    That wonder-working land,
Where the precious gold, free, free for all,
    Lay shining in the sand;
And 'twas under this same old tree he last
    Had pressed her fair white hand!

That morn a letter came to her,
    A precious word; and she
Crept here beside the village spring,
    Where they were wont to be.
It said, "To-night we meet again,
    Under our favourite tree!"

A tall form coming down the lane
    Makes the fair Eda start.
"'Tis he, 'tis he!—"I'm come to thee,
    Love, never more to part!
My Eda! my loved Eda, dear!"
    He pressed her to his heart.

"Blest be my heavenly Father's hand,
    That kindly guided me,
That gave me gold, and brought me back
    To fatherland and thee!
O take it all, my Eda dear;
    We'll live and happy be!"

THE PILOT'S WIFE.

THE full moon laboured on through clouds,
    The north blast bent the tree,
Which fell in fearful heavy squalls
    Upon the troubled sea.
Beside the lattice Martha stood
    Beyond the lonely bay,
And sighed, amid her pressing tears,
    "Why does he so delay?"

And then she sought her little room,
    And trimmed her fading fire,
And o'er the cradle bent, where smiled
    The image of his sire,—
Their darling boy, their fair firstborn,
    'Twas luxury to survey.
She kissed his brow, and sadly sighed,
    "Why does he so delay?"

The moon went down, the wind rolled on,
    The trees rocked wilder still,
And like a fire the great sun rose
    Above the eastern hill.
Beside her lattice Martha stands
    In morning's early ray,
With this sad burden on her lips,
    "Why does he so delay?"

The storm blew out, the winds were hushed,
    The sea was rough no more;
The sparrows piped upon the eaves,
    The robin by the door.
The thatcher on the lonely barn
    Shaved the white reed away;
And still she by her lattice sighed,
    "Why does he so delay?"

And then a man came travelling fast;
    His step was on the stone,
His well-known carol in her ear,
    His arms around her thrown.
A kiss was on her upturned face;
    The tear was brushed away;
And Martha sobbed, amid her smiles,
    "Why did you so delay?"

THE MONUMENT OF CHATTERTON.

THE shining ice had bridged the pool,
    And pencilled o'er the pane,
Bringing the last leaf from the tree
    In garden-bower and lane.
The streets were cold through which we passed
    To seek in pilgrim round
The monument of Chatterton
    In Redcliff's solemn ground.

x

Soon wondering near the church we stood,
　Now stained by changing time.
Immortalized by him whose harp
　Grew silent in its prime;
And feelings I cannot describe
　With pencil or with pen,
As mournful as the sighing winds,
　Came rushing o'er me then.

O noble pile! O noble place!
　What deeds to thee belong!
But chief I prize thee for the boy
　Who hung thy walls with song,—
That boy whose soul was like a fire,
　Whose genius like a sun,
Alas! alas! eclipsed in death,
　When life had just begun.

Methinks I see him standing here,
　Beneath thy arches grand,
With boyhood's wonder in his gaze,
　When moonlight filled the land,
And silvered o'er the city roofs,
　Entranced with thought sublime,
Which in the land of lays will live
　Until the end of time.

O boy with noblest gifts endowed,
　How smooth thy path might be,
If Love had reached her kindly hand,
　Just as she ought, to thee!
Who knows but in the way of life
　Thy youthful feet had trod,
And all thine energies been given
　To holiness and God?

When musing mid my mountain meads,
　I oft have thought of thee:
If Bible-light had filled thy soul,
　How bright thy path would be!
Thy mother's heart thou wouldst have cheered
　With long, full years of joy,
And England would be proud of thee,
　Thou poor ill-fated boy.

No friendly tongue to soothe thine ear,
　No light on thee to shine:
How dark this winter of neglect
　To such a soul as thine!
And who more sensitive than he,
　The pensive bard and true?
When thought was budding into song,
　Have I not felt it too?

Even now, where minstrel hath small heed,
　Though crisp my autumn years,
Amid the rustling vest of pride,
　I wipe away my tears.
But He who blessed me with my harp,
　And bade me frame my lay
In honour of His own great name,
　Will guide me on my way.

Poor gifted boy, thy native place
　Had small regard for thee,
Who in a garret's gloom drank up
　The draught of misery.

And now they raise thy monument,
　In boy-weeds looking down,
With mutely mournful sad rebuke,
　On the great smoky town.

O Chatterton! O Chatterton!
　How soon thy race was o'er!
Pale Pity by thy monument
　Weeps tear-drops evermore.
I saw a little beggar-boy,
　With blue half-covered limb,
Under his Gothic pedestal,
　And then I thought of him.

O! learn we not from fate so sad
　That talents great or small
Should be employed with usury
　For Him who giveth all?
O! hear Him from the Book Divine:
　"Whoever honour Me,
And give to Heaven what they receive,
　All those shall honoured be."

THE LITTLE BURN.

LITTLE burnie, burnie clear!
　Murmuring down the dingle dear,
　Let me muse beside thy brim,
Charmed to hear thy gurgling hymn.
What it is we scarcely know
Which thou murmurest in thy flow;
But thy music seems to me
Like the songs of Beulah be,
Where the waters, seraph-fanned,
Steal along the holy land.

Little burnie, burnie clear!
Man has not his dwelling here,
Save the lone house on the lea,
Looking down upon the sea.
Onward, onward dost thou pass,
Speaking to us in the grass,
Talking with the leaves and flowers,
Drinking dewdrops, quaffing showers,
Wooing elves and fairies slim
To the rushes on thy rim.

Little burnie, burnie clear!
Flowing onward year by year,
Through this dreamy, pleasant place,
Chirps the wren to see thy face,
And the sky-lark sweeter sings,
As he o'er thee shakes his wings.
Comes the traveller, and is gone,
Yet dear burnie floweth on,
Ever mingling with the wave
When the grass is on his grave.

Little burnie, burnie clear!
Much of heaven I know is here,
In this temple roofed with fern,
Where the organ is the burn,
And the minister the trees
Shaken by the passing breeze.

O how sweet it is to lie
Here with burnie bubbling by
Down the silent solitude,
When the eve is purple-hued!

Little burnie, burnie clear!
Here might artist, bard, or seer,
Far from man's delusive ways,
Joy to spend their latter days.
O'er thee hangs the shining sloe,
By thee dainty wildings grow;
Glancing wings are heard above,
Filling all the air with love,
Mingling with thy murmurs meek
Down the little sheltered creek.

Little burnie, burnie clear!
Brook-nymphs on thy banks appear,
Chanting odes of tender strain
To the glowworms on the plain:
All the grasses shake with mirth,
Joy in heaven, and joy on earth.
Yet we are alone, my sweet:
Hundreds, hundreds throng the street:
Let them,—I am happy here
With my little burnie clear.

THE GLOW-WORM.

THE mantle of twilight was flung
    Over blossom, and beauty, and bower,
    And clustering dew-beads were strung
Upon rose-bud, and leaflet, and flower.
The moon had begun to look pale,
    The stars had lit up their bright fires,
When I hied to a brook-running vale,
    Where once was a fane of our sires.

Some rocks in the top of the dell,
    Piled wildly, looked o'er it and frowned;
Hard by was a temple, they tell,
    Whose ruins lie bleaching around.
And here, in the rifts of the storm,
    'Neath the ivy so chilly and damp,
In a bower which the woodbine did form,
    A glow-worm had lit up its lamp.

It sparkled alone in the grot,
    Like a star in calm solitude's cell;
I bore it away to my cot,
    Exulting,—I loved it right well.
And long in my window 'twas found
    Emitting at evening its ray;
Shedding mystical brightness around,
    Till somebody stole it away.

Now oft, in the music of eve,
    When the curfew floats over the dale,
My cot by the river I leave,
    To wander alone in this vale.
I love, little glowworm, to muse,
    Where the thyme with thy beauty is starred;
And I ask thee at night to diffuse
    Thy rays on the grave of the bard.

THE IDLE MAN.

THERE'S not on this round globe a thing
    So despicably poor,
    In city home, 'neath cottage roof,
From distant shore to shore,
In all the kingdoms Nature owns
    Throughout her every clan,
Beneath the blue outspreading sky,
    As is the idle man.

Whilst each is labouring on, that each
    May life's best gifts enjoy,
Some on the earth, some on the sea,
    Some in the mine's employ;
He wrings his hands in Misery's chain,
    And gropes about in gloom,
Or be he rich, or be he poor,
    Unhappiness his doom.

Behold, Industry's hand hath reared
    The city by the sea;
On river bank, or mountain side,
    Wherever it may be,
Hath stretched the railway o'er the earth,
    Built up the holy pyre,
And conquered time and space itself
    By the electric wire.

The artisan, with earnest skill,
    Is labouring day by day;
The scholar *thinks* to bless mankind,
    The poet frames his lay;
The woodman clears the forest dim,
    The shipwright builds the bark,
The ploughman whistles as he works,
    Where soars the singing lark.

The farmer cultivates the soil
    Through days of cloud and gloom,
And, by and bye, the seed springs up,
    And deserts bud and bloom.
So is it with the human heart:
    Who cultivates it well
Shal. reap a harvest of delight,
    No tongue of earth can tell.

The thatcher shaves the reed away
    From off the cottage-eaves;
And sweet the reaper's song is heard
    Among the rustling sheaves;
And, on the sea, the sailor's voice
    Rings out upon the gale,
As he steers on his own good ship,
    While flaps the pleasant sail.

Nor does the housewife waste her hours
    To spread each welcome meal;
She counts the moments as they pass,
    And from her quickly steal;
The seamstress stitches on and on;
    And by the road-side lone
The old man brings his hammer down
    Upon the stubborn stone.

x 2

And swift the weaver's shuttle flies
  From dawn till dusk of day;
The printer fills the precious page
  Alike for grave and gay.
The artist paints the hero's deeds,
  Who fame has nobly won;
And grandam, by her cottage door,
  Sits knitting in the sun.

Along the streets, or o'er the fields,
  Or be it sun or shower,
When roses bloom, or leaves decay
  In Nature's yellow bower;
Let hailstones rattle through the dark,
  And thunder shake the town,
The postman, with his shouldered bag,
  Is trudging up and down.

The preacher, from the pulpit, warns
  The wandering sons of men;
The author cheers the path of life,
  And smooths it with his pen.
The lady, by the sick man's bed,
  Reads and diffuses joy;
And Nature, with ten thousand tongues,
  Sings at her rich employ.

And thus Industry's children toil
  Wherever peace is found;
Some with the head, some with the hands,
  To bless the world around.
But, like a blot on Nature's face,
  He groans amid his clan,
Thwarting the purposes of Heaven:
  OUT on the idle man!

ROBIN RIDGE.

"BRING me my Bible, Janie:
  My mind is much cast down;
Misfortunes press upon us,
  And disappointments frown;
These manifold vexations,
  This heavy cross and care,
And wounding of the spirit,
  Seem more than I can bear.

"How fast come rolling onward
  The angry waves of woe!
'Tis darkness, utter darkness,
  Above me and below;
My cup of bitter waters
  Is running o'er the rim:
Bring me my Bible, Janie,
  That I may read of HIM."

And then the holy volume
  Upon the board was spread,
And o'er its words of promise
  Was bent his hoary head.
He reads of many mansions
  Whose walls with glory flame,—
The rest which yet remaineth
  To those who love His name.

He reads of Christ's compassion,
  His pity for the poor,
Who giveth strength in weakness;
  Until his eyes run o'er;
And sweetness soothes his spirit,
  And all his being fills,
The calm of living waters
  From the eternal hills.

O, then life's cares no longer
  Upon their spirit weighed;
Fair forms around them gathered,
  In robes of white arrayed.
Praise rose upon the twilight
  That lingered in the dell;
And Jane and Robin whispered,
  "He doeth all things well."

THE HAYMAKER'S SONG.

"TOSS, toss the hay!
  'Tis beautiful in summer time,
  When sweet July is in its prime,
To carol in the meads my rhyme,
  And toss the hay!

"Toss, toss the hay!
The skylark sings his sweetest song,
The sun is shining bright and strong,
And swallows sport the trees among:
  Toss, toss the hay!

"Toss, toss the hay!
The bard has stretched him in the shade,
And yonder walks the village maid,
In flowers of golden tints arrayed:
  Toss, toss the hay!

"Toss, toss the hay!
Who will, may dig the shining ore;
Who will, may toil on foreign shore;
Who will, may dye their blades in gore:
  We'll toss the hay!

"Toss, toss the hay!
And when our pleasant task is done,
And down has sunk the setting sun,
Among the low stacks we will run:
  Toss, toss the hay!

"Toss, toss the hay!
Long life to all who guide the plough,
Who wield the scythe, and rear the mow,
Or fling the grass, as we do now:
  Toss, toss the hay!"

BATTA BATE.

THE summer sun was on the sea,
  The summer leaf was on the tree;
  The wild grape in the forest hung,
The throstle from the thicket sung;

Sweet murmurs o'er the earth did stray,
Kissing the roses on their way;
But Batta saw not field or fell,
As he lay chained in prison-cell.

A bony man he was and strong,
His hair and beard were stout and long;
His sinewy arms, like cedars sere,
Might hurl Goliath's heavy spear!
His deep broad breast much fame should win;
His fierce eye was an eye of sin,
Which flamed with scorn and pride and hate,
The haughty prisoner, Batta Bate.

And here he lay apart from men,
Like a chained tiger in his den.
I know not what the wrong might be,
Whether 'twas done on land or sea,
Whether it stained the day or night,
Whether in darkness or in light:
But Batta in his cell did start,
For crime lay heavy on his heart.

What sees he here in gloomy nook?
How strange indeed! a well-bound book
Left by a traveller in the cell:
And Batta reads the Bible well.
His sins rise up like spectres grim,
And in the dungeon glare at him,
While conscience cries, "No rest, no rest!"
And fire is burning in his breast.

Then came a monk, and bade him pray
To Mary several times a day;
His beads to count, his eye to fix
Upon the wooden crucifix:
"And very soon," the monk did say,
"Thy load of guilt will roll away."
But aye he felt the leaden weight;
It brought no peace to Batta Bate.

Weary and worn and wan he lay
In darkest doubt from day to day,
Counting his beads till twilight fell,
When, lo, a voice rang through his cell,
"God only can thy sins forgive:
Rise, Batta Bate, believe and live!"
"This is the voice of Christ," said he,
"The Scriptures have revealed to me."

Among his friends he stood once more,
Released from prison damp and hoar.
Before they feared his anger wild,
But now how changed he was and mild!
"The Bible is for all," said he;
"The Bible has done this for me,
Which I have read with tears and prayer,
And found my pardoning Saviour there."

Go, Christian worker, scatter wide
The Holy Book on every side,
By rill and rock, by fount and fen,
On mountain moor or mossy glen,
In city-lane and forest-land,
Or on the desert's shining sand,
Till every nation, every tongue,
The praises of the Lord have sung.

EMMA.

STILL moon by moon she faded,
As in the cold the flower;
And yet her beauty lingered,
Increasing every hour.
We never heard her murmur
At her false lover's deed:
While life's light faded slowly,
Like evening in the reed.

Beside the porch where roses
Hung o'er the garden-rail
She sometimes sat, while sounded
The church-bells through the vale.
O then her mien was saintly,
In meditation deep,
And oft we turned our faces
Among the leaves to weep.

And Emma still grew paler,
As on her bed she lay,
Where the small Gothic lattice
Looked out upon the bay.
In loveliness she lingered,
With prayer in every breath;
Nor ever blamed her lover,
Whose cruelty was death.

And then was given the slumber
Which His beloved know,
Who wake where mystery ceaseth,
And trees of healing grow.
She lieth by the chancel,
And here the robin sings,
The solemn cypress whispers,
The humble daisy springs.

PAUL PARSONS: OR, WHAT NEWS AT HOME?

PAUL Parsons married hastily
The woodman's daughter Nell:
They lived until a babe was born
Beside the village well:
And then the hungry wolf of want
Came prowling round their door;
Paul Parsons bade his wife good bye,
And left Cornwallia's shore.

Long wrought he where the gold lay hid
In many a precious stone,
And heard the songs of summer swell,
The winds of winter moan:
And as the seasons hurried by
Like waters in the dell,
His thoughts throughout his busy life
Were with his babe and Nell.

His bags grew heavier year by year,
Amassed with toil and pain;
And then he left his mates behind,
And home he sailed again.

And now he climbs the craggy hill
    So near his native goal:
"What news at home? what news at home?"
    Slow ringing in his soul.

He gains the old mount's breezy top,
    As sounds the curfew bell;
And sees, through tears that fill his eyes,
    His cottage by the well;
And hastens on with strength renewed,
    Beset with hopes and fears:
"What news at home? what news at home?"
    Still ringing in his ears.

And now he's past the roadside gate,
    Now knocking at the door:
A gentle hand is on the latch,
    A small foot on the floor.
O how he kissed his wife and child,
    O'erjoyed to find them well!
"Good news at home! good news at home!
    God bless my babe and Nell!"

JOHN BUNYAN AND HIS BLIND CHILD.

COME to the bridge of sighs,
    And enter Bedford jail,
    What time John Bunyan lingered there,
    The Dreamer quaint and hale.
The crimson hues of eve
    Curtain the western sky,
And the last vesper of the lark
    Drops through his lattice high.

"The day is waning fast,
    My cell's dank walls grow dim:
Before you hasten home, my love,
    We'll sing our evening hymn."
And, sitting on a stool
    Beside her father's feet,
His little blind child's song arose,
    Pathetic, calm, and sweet.

Down on the cold stone floor
    They kneel together now;
And, clasping her small hands in his,
    And kissing her white brow,
The Christian father prays
    For her beside him there,
And those for whom he toiled that day
    With never-ceasing care.

"Child, take those laces home;—
    Let me kiss off that tear;—
And tell thy mother, little one,
    That I am happy here."
And through the prison-door
    The little maiden sped,
And soon she told this sweetest tale
    Within their humble shed.

Imprison, scourge the saint,
    Chain him in dungeons drear;
Deem not you fetter the free soul;
    It bursts its bonds severe.

That night a light from heaven
    Through his cold prison streamed,
As by the rude lamp all alone
    He of his Pilgrim dreamed.

MAY.

NOW Nature receives a new birth,
    How should we with gratitude sing!
    For tripping along the green earth
Is May with the flower-covered Spring.
How fragrant the lea and the lane,
    While robin, upon the young spray,
Sings louder, and louder again,
    "'Tis May, 'tis the beautiful May!"

The primrose, within the green bower,
    Is wooing us back into dreams,
When we frolicked with many a flower,
    Adown where the rivulet gleams.
The earth-bending violets are come,
    And the snow-crested daisies alway
Sing silently round our dear home,
    "'Tis May, 'tis the beautiful May."

The blue-bells are kissed by the breeze,
    A troop of them dance in the vale,
And buttercups under the trees
    Are all of them telling a tale.
O, millions of other bright gems
    Are leaping wherever we stray,
And warbling their eloquent hymns,
    "'Tis May, 'tis the beautiful May."

'Tis echoed along the blue sky,
    And sung by the wandering fay,
While valley to valley reply,
    "'Tis May, 'tis the beautiful May."
And the wild feathered foresters fair
    Sing on oak-branch, or hill-crag so grey,
With the lark in the fields of fresh air,
    "'Tis May, 'tis the beautiful May."

O, there is a flower-budding clime,
    Which knows not a shadow of blight,
Where blossoms ne'er wither by time
    In the rich glow of heaven's pure light.
Sweet buds on the life-giving tree
    Are fanned with bright pinions for aye:
For ever, and ever, 'twill be
    More fair than the beautiful May.

THE UNSUCCESSFUL MINER.

FAR underground a miner
    Is labouring most severe,
    Blasting the shining marble
In lonely cavern drear.
O how the perspiration
    Is streaming from him there!
And like a wretch expiring
    He panted in his lair.

A month was nearly ended,
 And he severe had wrought
Day after day in darkness,
 And it was all for nought.
The mineral-vein had faded,
 And now all hope was fled ;
To-morrow should be pay-day,
 His children have no bread.

He stood within the office,
 His hat was in his hand;
He spoke, and much he trembled
 Before that busy band :
" I've spent a month in labour,
 A month of toil and pain,
A month of disappointment ;
 No tin was in the vein.

" And now I'm come to borrow
 What surely should be fees,
Till I shall better prosper,
 And pay you if you please.
O, think upon my household
 All friendless and forlorn,
Weeping for bitter hunger
 This golden summer morn."

He hung his head in silence,
 A cloud passed o'er his brow,
As spake the ruddy captain,
 " We've nothing for you now."
Within his soul an arrow
 By those dread words was thrown ;
His body bowed and quivered,
 His soul sent forth a groan.

He slowly turned and left them :
 With feeble feverish pace
I saw him creeping homeward
 With tears upon his face :
And as he neared his dwelling
 Upon the granite hill,
He raised his eyes and uttered,
 " It is my Father's will."

But all that day sad sorrow
 Into my heart did flow,
And oft I seemed to visit
 That poor man's shed of woe.
I heard his children crying,
 I felt the father's pain ;
And still this mournful vision
 Is labouring through my brain.

A NEW YEAR'S IDYL.

Two crones sat by a fire of bog,
 Two crones sat on a pine-tree log :
Without the wind did rustle and roar;
It shook the lattice, and smote the door.
The rafters rang, and rattled the latch,
Out puffed the smoke, off flew the thatch :

Like a cavern dark were the sky and main,
And the earth was wet with a month of rain.
Thus talked the crones by the ruddy braud,
As the OLD YEAR died on the rocky land.

Out spoke the first : " I've searched in vain
For one who knows not care or pain.
Both rich and poor sad sorrows share ;
For trouble is man's enduring heir.
'Tis found where youth and love abide ;
'Tis found where age and want reside.
Its trace is seen on the monarch's brow,
And it walks with him who follows the plough.
'Tis everywhere, 'tis everywhere ;
For all have trouble, and all have care.
But this I feel, and this I know,
That earth has more of joy than woe ;
Has more of good than seeming ill :
There's a sunny side to the darkened hill ;
And 'tis well for us, as on we plod,
To do our duty, and trust in God,
With whom the present is as the past,
And He will make it plain at last.
The stony path leads up the height
Where heaven is shining clear and bright;
And he who works and waits shall mow
The harvest-fields which his toil did sow.
Upon the horizon's rim I see
The blessed year of Jubilee,
When the poor man's wrongs shall be redressed,
And the prayer avail of the oppressed ;
When holy psalms overflow the air,
And men be brethren everywhere.
It comes, it comes, like a flowing sea,
And the wind-harps roll the Jubilee."

The second crone did slowly say,
" Our duty here is to obey ;
To strive, with him who heavenward went,
In every state to be content ;
To sow the seeds of love and peace,
And pray that hate and strife may cease.
The little shining grains of sand
Build up a mountain on the land :
So human efforts structures rear
Which stand for ever high and fair.
Do we not oft this utterance hear,
When skies are dark, when skies are clear ?
The night is hastening fast away,
And soon will dawn a brighter day,
When truth will not be trodden so
By noisy pomp and glittering show,
When worth shall stand where worth should be,
And right shall rule from sea to sea.
It comes, it comes. Day breaks above,
When earth is one great fane of love."

By this the moon rose o'er the mill,
The clouds went down behind the hill :
The rains had ceased, the wind no more
Rattled the casement or the door ;
The stars came out in the blue o'erhead,
And burnt the brands with a glow of red.
Uprose the crones from the ingle place,
And the NEW YEAR came with a smiling face.

THE DYING MINSTREL.

Fold thy leaves, floweret,
   The rain cometh down,
      Shadows are stealing
O'er turret and town.

Fold thy leaves, floweret,
   The eve draweth nigh,
Up from the moorlands
   Ascendeth a sigh,

Over the ruin,
   And by the cool rill,
Down by the rushes,
   And up on the hill.

Fold thy leaves, floweret,
   Strange voices are sighing
From hollow and highland,—
   A minstrel is dying.

Fold thy leaves, floweret,
   God's gifted one lies,
Pluming his wing
   For a flight to the skies.

In the morning of life,
   In the freshness of day,
Like a rose-bud in spring
   Is he fading away.

O sorrow, ye rivers,
   And murmur, ye rills,
And clothe you in sadness,
   Ye song-breathing hills.

Fold thy leaves, floweret,
   From summer's sweet strand
A harper is passing
   To Eden's green land.

SHE NEVER LEFT HER HOME.

She never left her home:
   Life's morning hours were spent
Among those clear pellucid springs
And hillocks, flower-besprent,
Where now, in hoary age,
From Memory's mystic tree
She plucks the clustering fruits of time,
And waits to be set free.

She never left her home:
   Her childhood passed away,
And youth and womanhood; then came
   The joyous marriage-day.
Her own bright children grew
   Where she so long had been,
And chased the golden butterflies
   Over the sloping green.

She never left her home:
   Her kindred o'er the seas
Had sailed, to travel other lands,
   And drink a foreign breeze.

The playmates of her youth
   Were scattered far and wide;
And those who strewed life's path with flowers
   Had vanished from her side.

She never left her home:
   Her sons to manhood grew;
And restless, seeking rest in vain,
   Away, away they flew.
One, in the land of gems,
   A treasure hoard hath found;
And one the crown of fame hath won
   On Alma's gory mound.

She never left her home:
   Her cheerful day's work o'er,
She takes the Bible from the shelf,
   To con its precious lore.
And to the mercy-seat
   She evermore will flee:
" O God, convert my wandering sons,
   And draw them nearer Thee."

She never left her home:
   But O, the power of prayer!
It reached the ear of Deity,
   And found acceptance there.
" O God, convert my sons,"
   Was in her latest sigh;
And they were saved in barbarous climes,
   In answer to her cry.

A SPRING WARBLE.

The setting sun, the purple dell,
   The orchard bud, the tolling bell,
   The violet's eye among the moss;
The linnet chirping by the cross;
The primrose 'neath the old oak-tree:
These sounds I hear, these sights I see.

The winding lane, the bursting may;
The happy children at their play;
The robin's nest beside the stone
With fern and ivy half o'ergrown;
The milkmaid singing from the lea:
These sounds I hear, these sights I see.

The passing peasant's earnest smile;
The lovers loitering by the stile;
The dewy mead with daisies drest;
The ploughboy whistling to his rest;
The twittering wren where blue-bells be:
These sounds I hear, these sights I see.

The stream that tinkles long and late
By crag and creek and meadow-gate;
The sporting lamb, the cuckoo's call;
The halo hanging over all;
The swallows floating up the lea:
These sounds I hear, these sights I see.

But comes the time when I no more
Shall pace these lovely uplands o'er,

When, lying low where worms reside
And sounds of music never glide,
No longer it remains for me
These sounds to hear, those sights to see.

He was an honest man
As ever delved the sod :
Misfortune came, and they turned him here,
To die alone with God.

THE DYING LABOUR-LORD.

HIGH over the whispering pines
The rooks in flocks were flying,
As in the cell of a lone poor-house
A labour-lord lay dying.

His frame was of giant mould,
Which time had partly broke ;
His breast, his shoulders, back, and sides ;
And his limbs like limbs of oak.

Now the mighty man was low,
His life was fleetly flying ;
Old age had bound the village hind,
And the labour-lord lay dying.

Around him strangers moaned,
Not a kindred face was there.
His friends ? The grave had some, and some
Had flown he knew not where.

The daylight streamed through heaven,
The birds sang on the spray,
And the mower was out with his shining scythe,
Cutting the early hay.

And the hedger was abroad,
And the traveller paced along ;
And the bard was stretched in the hill's cool shade,
Piping his pastoral song.

And the white clouds floated high
In the deep blue fields of air,
And the swallows wheeled where the insects hummed
And murmured everywhere.

Men passed along outside ;
The rich, the great swept by ;
But none inquired for the labour-lord
Who was so soon to die.

He oft had tilled their fields ;
He oft had reaped their grain ;
The profits swelled their shining hoards,
But his the crushing pain.

He gave to them his youth,
His manhood's golden prime ;
And now they leave the labour-lord
Wrecked on the strand of time.

None could compete with him
To cut the granite rock,
To guide the plough, or wield the scythe,
Or shear the fleecy flock.

Y

THE TELEGRAM.

"A TELEGRAM! God bless him !
My son has sent to say
That ere the evening's sunset
He'll anchor in the bay.
They said the big sea-water,
When all was tempest-dark
And thunder walked the welkin,
Had swallowed up his bark.

" I never thought to see him
Within his home again,
And mourned him much, as sleeping
Deep in the dreadful main ;
But what a blessed message
Is lying on my board,
Brought by no bird, but thrilled me
On the electric cord !

" Now smooth his snowy pillow,
And air his sleeping-place ;
I cannot stay the waters
From running down my face.
O, bless the Lord who kept him
Amidst all false alarms !"
And soon the son and mother
Were in each other's arms.

THE OLD MAN BY THE STILE.

ONE evening o'er the moorland
I wandered with the Muse,
To revel mid the fairies
Among the early dews.
The red clouds hung above me
In all their crimson dyes,
And holy seemed the common,
And holy seemed the skies.

Then from the distant hamlet
The church bells slowly chime :
Sweet whispers filled the welkin,
And Peace slept on the thyme.
Life's battle for a season
Was echoless and still,
As with my harp I wandered
Along the quiet hill.

So turning down a sheep-path
Stained with the purple light,
I lifted up my eyeballs,
And saw a goodly sight.
A hoary-headed pilgrim
Upon a mossy mound
Beside a stile was sitting
In reverie profound.

Perchance the cup of sorrow
  His God for him did fill ;
And now a lonely mourner
  He travelled down the hill.
So here he crept in silence
  Beneath the golden skies,
And looked into the distance
  With sad and thoughtful eyes.

Perchance amid life's bustle
  He softly stole away
In this sequestered corner
  To meditate and pray.
Perchance he was a poet,
  And here in Nature's fane
He wooed the nymph of numbers,
  And drank her liquid strain.

I watched him till the moonlight
  Fell on the silvered mere,
And beautified the common
  In tissue-robings clear.
Then, like a pleasant vision,
  He passed me with a smile,
And oft appears before me
  That old man by the stile.

WINTER.

OLD Winter is come, spreading ice on the moor,
  And wailing like woe at the cottager's door.
  He has blighted the hare-bell that bloomed on the
    hill,
Stalked down in the valley and glassed o'er the rill,
Sipped up the clear pools with their moss-covered brim,
And placed his cold hand on the daisy's white rim.
Old Winter, old Winter, come, hie thee away,
And let the soft breeze with the daffodils play.

O look on the trees ! they are leafless and bare ;
Not a bud, not a blossom, of beauty is there.
Hoarse wails through the branches eternally go,
And the cot in the valley is covered with snow ;
While down from the eaves hang the icicles cold,
And Cock Robin mourns on the sleety threshold.
Old Winter, old Winter, come, hie thee away,
And let the sunbeams with the gossamer play.

But, ah ! it is vain to invoke him to go ;
For the crest of the hill is a cold wreath of snow.
Wherever I look, 'tis the same to my sight,
Mead, mountain, and moorland are mantled in white ;
In his palace of ice, at the back of a rock,
He moans that the crag-heaps seem rent with the shock.
Old Winter, old Winter, O leave our dear land,
And revel where ice-hills eternally stand.

The grey-headed man, clad in rags as he goes,
And the water-cress girl, with the frost in her toes,
I saw them to-day creeping down the dark lane,
And they trembled with cold, and were weeping with
    pain.

Thou hast but a season, old Winter, to roar,
And then I know surely thy reign will be o'er,
And thou must be off to the frost-bitten zone,
And beautiful Spring have thy sceptre and throne.

WIDOW WARE.

AN honest dame was Widow Ware ;
  She dwelt beside the Fal,
  With fruit-trees by her cottage-door ;
Her only son was Hal ;
A stately youth of twice eight years ;
  His mother's staff and stay ;
With too much spirit for his state,
  And so he ran away.

The Fal, as seasons ever changed,
  Went rushing in its pride :
And Widow Ware oft suffered much,
  Whilst Hal was wandering wide.
Her wardrobe worn and scant became ;
  Her hearth was often cold ;
And yet she waited for her boy
  With hopefulness untold.

The distant hills were growing dim,
  A halo marked the sea,
When at her door a stranger stood,
  "Good evening, dame," said he.
"Methinks," she sighed," I ken that voice :
  O do you know my Hal ?
Who left me, when the woods were green,
  Alone beside the Fal."

He looked upon her saddened face,
  As earnest as could be,
Then rushed into her open arms,
  "O ! mother, I am he ;
My conscience would not let me rest :
  O take your sorrowing Hal !"
And there was princely joy that night
  Beside the flowing Fal.

THE DEPARTURE.

THE OLD MAN shivered in the snow,
  As if he knew not where to go,
  With ice above and ice below.

Far off upon the southern shore
Was heard the raging battle's roar.
O when will rifles ring no more ?

Said I, "OLD MAN, with frozen hair,
'Tis sad to see you standing there :
Come in, come in and take a chair.

" Perhaps you bring good news of peace,
That war and wretchedness shall cease,
And love and purity increase ;

"That wrong and hate shall be no more,
And man to man his right restore,
And worth prevail from shore to shore."

The OLD MAN strangely shook his head,
And not a single word he said,
And, O, he looked as look the dead.

A sadness seized my yielding heart,
Like one who with his friend doth part,
And drops did from their fountains start.

The snow fell faster from the skies,
The northern winds began to rise,
And tears came in the OLD MAN'S eyes.

He turned at last to face his doom,
To meet the midnight in the gloom,
And give the young NEW COMER room.

And then by secret signs I knew
'Twas Nature's order ever true,—
The OLD YEAR yielding to the NEW.

ELLEN DEE.

HE waited in the moonlight
　　Where ash and ivy gleam,
　　Perchance to see her passing
Beside the village stream ;
When down the lane she cometh
　Where folded roses lie,
As graceful as a fairy ;
　　And Nathan's heart beat high.

And then he stepped full lightly
　Forth from the elder tree,
And spoke in words of sweetness,
　" Good evening, Ellen Dee."
She blushed not as she saw him,
　Nor shrank away with fear,
But took his hand, and whispered,
　" O Nathan, are you here ?"

Then on they walked together,—
　Each pleased the other well,—
Where Ellen's reedy cottage
　Rose in the rushy dell :
And by the porch they parted,
　With pressure of the hand,
And other silent symbols
　Which lovers understand.

His rival strove to woo her,
　Too noisy and too bold :
He followed in the sunshine,
　He followed in the cold.

But Ellen's heart was Nathan's ;
　The treasure was his own,
Bestowed without beseeching ;
　They loved for love alone.

O, pure was their affection,
　Like balm which eve distils,
Or honeysuckle fragrance,
　Or silver-blending rills.
For Ellen Dee and Nathan
　The bells were ringing soon,
And long did they remember
　That walk beneath the moon.

SPRING.

COME out into the fields ;
　Come out among the flowers :
　Once more, in Nature's budding time,
　This privilege is ours !
The lark soars up ! up ! up !
　The white-winged clouds among :
Come out into the meadows, come
　And listen to his song.

Ye little smiling flowers,
　Wakening at Nature's call,
Bright buds of promise, hail to you !
　Sweet welcome to you all !
The sun looks forth to-day,
　Gilding your eyelids bright,
Painting your emerald diadems,
　Kissing you into light !

Along the fresh hedge-row
　The sighing zephyr strays,
And in the grassy meadow-bower
　The little lambkin plays.
The spirit of the spring
　Is harping in the air ;
A thousand blended music-notes
　Are floating everywhere.

How softly steals the rill
　Along its pebbly bed !
Murmuring sweet songs of fatherland,
　To which our hearts are wed ;
Reminding us of days,
　In life's awakening spring,
When Hope the sunny future drew,
　Hung round with blossoming !

Come out into the fields;
　Gaze on the violet's eye ;
It blossoms, by the waterfall,
　Blue as the summer sky.
There's nought above, below,
　Shining in heaven or earth,
But tells us of the power of Him
　Who spake it into birth.

FLOWERS.

THE FIRST VIOLET.

HAIL to thee, little flower,
    Within my own dear bower,
Smiling among the wiry broom,
Like Hope's bright star mid clouds
        of gloom !
I bend me o'er thy sweet blue eye,
Dropping salt tears I know not why,
Feeling a warm inspiring fire,
Sweeping my fingers o'er my lyre,
Singing within my heathy bower:
Hail, hail to thee, Spring's early flower !

Yes, thou art come to dwell
    With Memory in her cell,
To call her from her still retreat,
And place Remembrance at her feet.
Though thou art gilt with vernal bloom,
Thou tellest of the dark, deep tomb :
Thou tellest of the wide blue sea,
Where waves and storms are wont to be,
And where upon its boundless tide,
Far, far away, my kindred ride.
Because they hasten from my bower,
Hail, hail to thee, Spring's early flower !

O, could they hear the lark,
    Singing till it is dark,
Fluttering his wings those meads above,
And warbling forth his notes of love ;
And could they, in our meadow's bound,
Gaze on these cowslips scattered round,
See all those daisies on the plain ;
They surely would come back again,
To feast their eyes within my bower
Upon my little violet-flower !

What were the words I said ?
    Thou speakest of the dead ?
Ah, yes ! thou tellest of decay,
How earthly splendours pass away :

An hour or two,—come, smile on me,—
And I shall bid farewell to thee.
Here birds will sing, and flowers will bloom,
When I am hidden in the tomb.
But I would sleep with thee, sweet flower,
Companions in my mountain bower.

And oft my ghost shall roam
    Around my native home ;
And here, beneath the wan moon's light,
Weave garlands for the brow of Night.
Blue herald of a numerous line !
Stamped with the mighty Maker's sign,
The impress of the Hand Divine :
Bending thou seem'st to kiss the sod :
Who sees thee, sees a ray of God.
Because He shines within my bower,
Hail, hail to thee, Spring's early flower !

THE FIRST PRIMROSE.

HAIL to thine opening eye,
    Thou little lonely flower !
    The first that cometh blossoming
Within my English bower !
A thousand griefs are past,
    A thousand tears are shed,
Since on this bank I saw thee last
    Lift up thy yellow head.

Hail to thy timid glance !
    And to thy perfume hail !
And, though the north storm may advance,
    O do not look so pale ;
But bloom and blossom on
    Within thy mossy bower,
Till Winter and his storms are gone,
    Thou little trembling flower !

Thou bringest songs of birds,
    And many a pleasing spell,—
The violet-haunts among the elms,—
    We know them passing well.

A thousand other tales
In thee the poet reads,—
Thy sisters clustering in our vales,
And sparkling in our meads !

Then bloom and blossom on,
And gem our withered isle,
Till Winter and his storms are gone.
And tender sunbeams smile ;
When flowers of every hue
Shall thy companions be,
And millions in my fatherland
Look up and smile like thee !

THE HEATH.

Bell-blossomed spirit of the wild,
Hail to thee ! Nature's moorland child,
Shedding a honeyed fragrance round
The craggy cave and boulder ground.
The gorse-bush woos thy smiling face,
And clasps thee in its sharp embrace ;
A thousand swords peer from their sheath
To pierce thee, unassuming heath ;
Thou fear'st not, looking forth so mild,
Bell-blossomed spirit of the wild !

Thou hast no sister-buds beside
The yellow furze-flowers at thy side,
Or the sweet hare-bell's slender form,
That bends before the rushing storm.
Unnoticed in thy wild attire,
I twine thee round my artless lyre,
Clasping thee in my trembling hand,
Strange offspring of my fatherland ;
For, O ! I love thee like a child,
Bell-blossomed spirit of the wild !

I meet thee on the rough hill's brow,
And in the valley there are thou !
Our Cornish hedges thou dost gem
With gold cups on thy wiry stem ;
From steep to steep, from shore to shore,
Thou listenest to the ocean's roar.
By murmuring stream and hamlet fair,
And lone walk smiling everywhere !
But, heath-flowers on my mountain's side,
I love you more than all beside !

The swallow, sporting round my bower,
Stoops down to kiss thee, little flower ;
And the wild bee thy fragrance sips,
Kissing the nectar from thy lips.
Thou hast been my companion long ;
Hast listened to my earliest song ;
Witnessed my tears for friendship shed,
When loved ones pierced my soul and fled ;
Hast many a weeping hour beguiled,
Bell-blossomed spirit of the wild !

When Twilight wraps the mount in shade,
Flinging its dank robe o'er the glade,
When Silence bathes in silvery light
Beneath the "lady of the night,"

When all is listless and serene,
The fairy leaves the evergreen,
And, with the glow-worm for her bride,
She dances o'er the old hill's side,
Sobbing some faithful maiden's knell,
And tripping o'er thee, heather-bell !

At the sweet evening hour, how oft
I've wandered o'er this lonely croft,
Unknown, unmissed, 'midst noise and glee,
To pass a musing hour with thee !
For, who such stars of living gold,
Thick-clustered round him, can behold,
Bright as the gems in yon pure sky,
And glittering with a rainbow-dye,—
Who can such gleams of glory see,
And not adore the Deity ?

TO A VIOLET IN OCTOBER.

Lonely Floweret, why art thou,
Little violet, blooming now ?
Other flowers have passed away,
And thy sisters died in May.
Scarce a daisy can be seen ;
And the thorn has lost its green.
Robin, on the leafless limb,
Sobs his plaintive requiem ;
Primroses have lost their glory ;
Those that held a place in story ;
And the hill's high head is hoary.
Flowers were there, but they are gone :
Hast thou seen them, loitering one ?
Hast thou with Spring's darlings met,
Lonely, lingering violet ?

Time hath swept, with noiseless wing,
O'er earth's vernal blossoming,
Dashed athwart the blighted leas,
Smote the leaf-decaying trees,
Withered all that's fresh and fair,
Blasted, blighted everywhere :
But thy lovely little form
Looks out in the driving storm,
Though the tempest fume and fret,
Little smiling violet !

Wert thou with thy sisters born
At the vernal-bursting morn ?
Tell me,—for I long to know,—
Can it, little flower, be so ?
Hast thou heard the cuckoo's note
Through my Cornish valleys float ?
Listened to the nightingale
Warbling in the shady vale ?
Has the pilgrim, with his staff,
Left the honeysuckled dale,
Where the new-born flowerets laugh,
And the brooklet tells its tale ?
And, when sadly wandering by,
Has he caught thy speaking eye,
With the dews of evening wet,
Lonely, lingering violet ?

I have mused with thee an hour,
Little, hope-inspiring flower;
And I fain would bear thee hence,
With thy look of innocence,
To my dwelling on the moor,
Planting thee beside my door.
Wilt thou, darling, live with me,
When beneath the cypress tree
Low I lay my weary head
In the chamber of the dead?
Glad am I to meet thee here
At the waning of the year.
Thee I never shall forget,
Little, lonely violet!

WILD FLOWERS.

Fair dwellers of the fields,
White whisperers of the lane,
Sweet poets of gentle Spring!
I come to you again,
Where sighing breezes shake
The brightly-budding beech,
To treasure up for other days
The lessons that ye teach.

I know not why it is,
But sorrow flies, and fear,
And hope lights up my brightened soul,
When musing with you here.
And such a freshness flows
Along the dell and down:
O how unlike the feverish air
That settles on the town!

Give me the quiet mead,
The heath, the sheltered bower,
The lichened cave, the rushy moor,
The forest-tree and flower;
The dear old hawthorn lane,
When Eve with gentle sigh
Reposes on her dewy couch,
With folded hands to die.

So let me linger here
Within the whispering vale,
While purple clouds float down the west,
And kiss your foreheads pale.
Among you throbs a voice,
Your great Creator's speech:
So let me wondering treasure up
The lessons that ye teach.

TO A CLUSTER OF PRIMROSES.

Your graces have been sung
By bards of sweetest strain;
But this shall tune my humble lyre,—
I see you once again!
I see you peeping forth
Beneath the budding trees,
And I adore the Mighty One
Who made such flowers as these!

Stars of the wakening dell,
Ye constellations bright,
How like the eyes of those we love
Ye steal upon the sight!
Blushing in solitude,
Where Peace and Silence reign,
Ye early children of the spring,
I see you once again!

Ye come and pass away,
As gayer roses do!
For many friends, since last spring-tide,
Have passed away with you.
In this untrodden dell,
Ye blossom but to wane:
Thank God for His preserving care,—
I see you once again!

A little while ago,
These banks were very dry;
But now they are the loveliest spots
Beneath the April sky.
And since I see you here,
O let me not complain,
But put my trust in Providence;—
I see you once again!

Chaste, lovely little things!
Dame Nature nurses you;
Ye quaff the breeze that murmurs by,
And drink the falling dew:
And 'tis my faith that He
Who made the woodland flower,
Can raise my body from the dust
To bloom in Eden's bower!

A VIOLET IN MARCH.

And art thou come, pale flower,
Reminding us of spring-time fresh and fair,
When Nature feels its renovating power,
And joy is everywhere?

Hail, nodding stranger, hail!
I joy to see thee on this wakening sod;
And though thou lookest passing pale,
Thou tellest me of God.

The lark above thee sings,
As though he soared into the higher sphere,
And shook the music from his wings,
A shower upon thee here.

I see thee smile alone,
As if thy sisters sent thee on before,
To blush on Winter's tottering throne,
And drive him from our shore.

I've waited for thee long;
And now thou'rt come, I'm loath to turn away;
For I could sing my artless song
And gaze on thee for aye.

The setting sun is bright,
  And all the floating clouds are tinged with red,
Stars peer through heaven's blue height,
  The moon shines over head.

And when the breeze sweeps by,
  Calling thy kindred from the yielding sod,
Shaking the dew-drops from thine eye,
  I hear the voice of God.

How kind it is of thee
  To visit us before thy younger brothers!
Sweet cherub, thou appear'st to me
  Far lovelier than all others;

Hope's kindly-beaming star,
  Beckoning me onward to the cuckoo's song,
When May-flowers sparkle from afar,
  And dance the meads among.

I've crept from man away,
  To kneel, sweet one, beneath thy lowly shrine,
And here to Nature's God to pray,
  And link my fate with thine.

The blast that roots the tree,
  May hurl thee quickly to thy early doom.
'Twere bliss to think that one like thee
  Would blossom on my tomb.

Hail, nodding stranger, hail!
  I joy to see thee on this wakening sod;
And though thou lookest passing pale,
  Thou tellest me of God.

MY PRIMROSE FROM THE HILL.

Look up, look up, my darling;
  I brought thee from afar,
  Where rocks o'ergrown with lichen
And ivied hedges are;
Where gush mysterious idyls
  From breeze and narrow rill,
That steal in Nature's freshness
  Adown my own old hill.

To me 'tis full of beauty,
  Each bending brake and bower,
And like a poet singing
  Is every bank and flower.
Men wonder why I love it,
  A thing so rude and wild,
A cairn so coarse and craggy
  Among the storms up-piled.

The fault must be Dame Nature's;
  For at life's early morn
She wooed me with her numbers,
  Beneath the aged thorn,
And smiled with so much beauty,
  And glanced with so much love,
That my old hill seemed shining
  With glory from above.

And so I dearly loved it.
  And dearly love it still.
Embrace it like a daughter,
  And so I ever will.
The flowers upon its summit
  Look blushing in bright bands,
As if the holy angels
  Had touched them with their hands.

I may forget the volume
  That charmed me when a boy,
Relating tales of castles,
  Of wonder, and of joy;
Of haunted home and hollow,
  Where turned the fairies' mill
But thou art ever with me,
  Old granite-covered hill.

Hence everything is sacred
  Upon its holy steep,
The very mould and mosses,
  And rocks where ivies creep;
And paths where angels wander,
  When evening shadows fall,
Upon the summer forest,
  Upon the city wall.

So I dug up one morning
  A primrose from the lea,
And bore it to my garden
  Beside the sounding sea.
And here it blossoms fairly,
  And seems to feel no loss,
Opening its yellow eyelids,
  As if among the moss.

What bright endearing pictures
  Upon its fresh leaves rest!
Its Maker's name is shining
  Upon its gentle crest.
It tells me of the Muses,
  The rushy moors among,
My home upon the mountain,
  And hours of sacred song.

O thank thee, darling, thank thee,
  Thou scion of the down,
Now blooming 'neath my window
  Within the noisy town.
An angel on thy leaflets
  Bids carking care be still,
And whispers words of healing,
  My primrose from the hill.

THE DAISY.

Bless thee, fair angel of the earth!
  Opening thy silvery eye
On barron hills, whose rocky crests
  Gaze up into the sky;
Or by the little wicket low,
  On sunny slope and plain,
Sweet smiling near the village stile,
  And in the country lane.

O, bless thee in thy snowy fringe
  And crest of shining gold,
Thy polished stem and fibrous roots,
  That grasp the slimy mould!
What troops are dancing in the meads
  And by the farm-house lone,
What time the May-breeze floats along
  With music-breathing tone!

The cowslip comes and quickly goes,
  And blue-bells, once a year;
The violets perish with the spring;
  But thou art always here.
When Summer pants along the moors,
  Or Autumn slacks his pace,
Or Winter roars among the reeds,
  Thou rear'st thy smiling face.

I well remember when a boy
  Within my father's mead
I wandered oft beside the hedge,
  To tune my simple reed.
And my young heart rejoiced to view
  Fair pencilled on thy frame,
Which then inspired my rustic muse,
  Thy great Creator's name.

And how I've watched the floating clouds
  Careering through the sky,
When their dark shadows on thee fell,
  To see thee close thine eye!
Then, if a passing sunbeam kissed
  Thee, dancing o'er the plain,
How didst thou ope thy snowy lids,
  And smile on me again!

So let me woo my constant friend
  At evening's holy chime,
And kiss thy dewy lids once more
  Along the walks of time.
And wandering on my weary way
  In sunshine and in shower,
My heart shall oft rejoice to meet
  My little daisy flower.

THE SNOWDROP.

COME, come again, my darling,
  Come, come again art thou,
Like some good angel shining
  Beneath the beechen bough;
And though the wind of winter
  Is filling up the place,
And snow is drifted round thee,
  A smile is on thy face.

How lovely art thou looking
  Beneath this cloudy sky,
As if the snowy tempest
  Brought beauty to thine eye!
So have I known a poet,
  Beneath his household tree,
Sing sweetest in his sorrow,
  A copyist of thee.

I bend me down and kiss thee,
  Like children at their play,
And take thine image with me,
  Along my weary way:
Thy memory oft will cheer me
  Life's thorny thicket o'er;
The footsteps of thy Maker
  Are heard upon the moor.

We know it; yes, we know it,
  That Spring will soon be here;
Along the gladdened valleys,
  With hyacinths so dear;
She cometh, yes, she cometh,
  The daisy-studded queen,
To chase away the darkness,
  And fill the earth with green.

A VIOLET LYING ON THE VILLAGE LANE.

WHY is it that I meet thee here?
  Come tell me, for I love thee dear.
How carefully I've sought for thee,
  O'er hill and mossy plain,
Among the hedges of the lea,
  And down the sheltered lane!
But here I find thee first to-day,
A-withering on the rough highway.

I've gazed upon the broad blue sky,
And deemed it tinctured with thy dye;
And when the deepening twilight died,
  I've sat within my bower,
With thy fair sisters at my side,
  For many a musing hour;
And when the stars came forth at even,
I called them violets of heaven.

O, I have wooed the fickle Spring,
And quaffed the fragrance from her wing,
And oft have hied me o'er the green,
  And through the lonely land,
To mark the spot where I have seen
  Thy blue-eyed kindred stand;
And what strange joy lit up my face,
To find the firstlings of your race!

But thou art dying, little sweet,
And withering quickly at my feet:
My song is far too rough for thee,
  Thou darling of the year,
Uptorn in dewy infancy,
  And rudely trampled here,
Like worth by want and misery driven,
Unfriended, crippled, crushed, and riven.

Who called thee forth? what hand did fling
Thee on the grassy lap of Spring?
Chance could not penetrate the sod
  With new life-giving power;
None other than the mighty God
  Could make thee, little flower.
Thy form so fair, so full, so free,
Speaks volumes of the Deity.

The white moon now is riding high,
The stars are peering through the sky,
Twilight hath fled. In converse sweet
  We've lingered here so long :

But I have been much cheered to meet
  Thee, harbinger of song ;
For thou dost ever with thee bring
A thousand tales of gentle Spring.

DOMESTIC DITTIES.

LINES FOR MY LITTLE ONES.

OME to me, smiling little ones,
  And prattle in mine ear ;
Don't let it fright you from your
    sire,
  This big, round, falling tear.
It came into your father's eye,
  When coming home to you,
Although the earth was beautiful,
  And the far sky was blue.

You ask me why it gushes forth,
  This sorrow-speaking tear :
In hastening home, sweet cherub ones,
  My thoughts were with you here.
Glad harvest-songs were floating round
  Beneath the summer sky :
In spite of Nature's minstrelsy,
  The tears came in mine eye.

You wonder still why it could be,
  At such a merry time,
When robin's song was blended with
  The happy reapers' chime.
And you were promised such rare things
  When I came home to you,—
Long painted rods of sugar-stick,
  And picture rhyme-books too.

So you've been waiting all this time
  Within my lowly cot,
And gazing through the casement said,
  " He's coming, is he not ? "

Ye run with looks of winning love
  No heart can e'er withstand,
With lips that prattle innocence,
  And open outstretched hand.

I'll tell you why the tear appeared,
  When travelling o'er the mead :
'Tis pay-day, and my hard-earned hire
  Was very small indeed :
Not half enough to purchase food,
  In this dark day of dearth,
For you, my shining olive-leaves,
  That gem my household hearth.

Ah ! when this pittance I received,
  None but our Father knows,
How my first thoughts flew home to you ;
  'Twas then the tear uprose.
So through the market-town I passed,
  Nor anything I had,
No, not a sugar-kiss for you,
  I felt so very sad.

I've plucked those berries from the bush,
  In coming o'er the lea ;
And here they are, my little ones,
  As ripe as ripe can be.
Ye eat them up so heartily,
  And seem so pleased and gay,
I'll smile again, my babes, with you,
  And dash the tear away.

Come, we will sit us down once more,
  And sing the song you love,
Of little Jane, your singing sire,
  And her the mother-dove.
I have no mines of sparkling ore,
  No diamonds of rich dye ;
But ye are gems I value more
  Than all beneath the sky.

And since ye cheer my hours of gloom,
And hours of sunshine too,
I'll clasp ye closer to my heart,
And thank the Lord for you.
Blest be the Hand that placed you here,
Upon my humble floor:
I'll trust His Providence to feed
The flowerets of the moor.

THE TRUANT SCHOOLBOYS.

(A STORY FOR JANE.)

THERE is a little rivulet,
Within a shadowy dell,
Which has been murmuring, on and on,
For years :—I know it well:
For, when a very little boy,
I played beside its brink,
And saw the little singing birds
Hop from the boughs and drink.

I think I love this little stream
Far more than any other,
Because it tells me, even now,
Sweet stories of my brother.
It tells me of your uncle, dear,
Who, in a far-off land,
Will oft look back upon the time
We frolicked on its sand.

I well remember now the day,
A long, long time ago,
When we left school before the hour,
'Twas very naughty though !
To go and catch the little fish,
And make them die with pain,
On purpose to amuse ourselves :
'Twas naughty, little Jane !

We tarried till the sun had set,
And then the stars came out,
But we, beside this little stream,
Were watching for the trout.
Up rose the yellow harvest moon ;
We saw her in the rill,
And turned our faces to our home
Upon Bolennowe Hill.

We stopped, when half-way up its side,
To wipe the mud away :
"Twas then we felt how sad we were,
What we had done that day,—
Deceived our parents, left the school,
And told our master lies,
And killed those pretty little fish :—
The tears came in our eyes!

How very sad we crept along !
Our cottage came in sight ;
We heard our own sweet mother's voice,
We saw the taper's light.

We trembled; for we were afraid
To stand before our sire ;
We knew we had incurred that day
His greatest, heaviest ire!

Our hands we lifted to the latch,
Now trembling more and more,
And soft as ever fairy did,
We stepped across the floor,
And cowered beneath our mother's wing,
With love's sweet odour wet ;
And how she acted to us then,
I never shall forget.

Now, daughter dear, I hope you'll strive
To profit by my lay :
Obey your parents in the Lord,
And speak the truth alway.
Deceive not, though you be deceived ;
Take care of little lies ;
And don't give any needless pain
To birds or butterflies.

And when the waxing harvest moon
Shall rise above the hill,
All bright and beauteous at her full,
I'll take you to the rill,
And show you where, years, years ago,
Your singing father strayed,
Beside this murmuring rivulet,
And with your uncle played.

THE BOY AND THE RING.

WHEEL round your chairs a-near the fire,
And shut the outer door ;
The north winds sweep across the fields,
And through the valleys roar.
I have a truthful tale to tell
About a little boy,
Who lived upon a lonely hill,
His honest parents' joy.

Full early was he taught to kneel
And clasp his hands in prayer
To Him who looks upon the earth,
And knows each traveller there;
That we must never lie nor steal,
Nor break His just command ;
For all offending ones will feel
The anger of His hand.

One morn he left his mother's porch,
Where he had been at play,
And crept into a neighbour's house,
When they were gone away
To worship in the village church
Among the solemn trees ;
The murmur of the tolling bells
Then rose upon the breeze.

He placed his foot upon the stair,
The echo made him start,
And still he climbed, and still he felt
A sinking in his heart:

He scarcely knew the reason why
He thus did onward go,
Until he found a refuse box
In a back chamber low.

Here lay in undisturbed repose
A lot of crazy ware,—
Old covers rusted into holes,
And bolts both round and square,
Nails drawn from doors no longer used,
Which filled him with delight,
And saddle-stirrups, studs of steel,
And buckles seldom bright.

He first snatched up a rivless screw,
Then many a tempting thing,
And threw them back, and strangely grasped
A lantern's simple ring;
Then slowly down the stair he went,
Within his hand the toy;
But every footfall seemed to say,
"O naughty little boy!"

He gained the porch, and sat him down
Beneath the woodbine sweet,
And quickly laid the stolen ring
Upon his playing seat;
And every sparrow chirping loud
On the thatch-eaves for joy
Seemed twittering, twittering evermore,
"O naughty little boy!"

He sought the hearth and climbed again
His gentle mother's knee:
She stroked his hair, and kissed his face,
And bade him happy be;
But like a knell he heard the words,
All comfort to destroy,
Still sounding, sounding everywhere,
"O naughty little boy!"

And so at last he took the ring,
And slowly went away,
And crept the stair, and reached the room
Where the old waste-box lay,
And laid it down, and left the house
As softly as could be;
And when he reached his mother's porch,
How very glad was he!

The sparrows' chirp was music now,
His mother's voice was dear,
And from his face I know he wiped
Away the trickling tear;
And when beside his bed he knelt,
With folded hands to pray,
He asked the Lord to pardon him
For his great sin that day.

God heard his prayer, and blotted out
The little wanderer's stain;
His first offence was all forgiven;
He never stole again.
Resist the first approach of wrong,
O guard your virtue well,
Or it may end in wretchedness,—
How awful, who can tell?

THE LOST CHILD.

(A STORY FOR LUCRETIA, WHEN TWO YEARS OF AGE.)

COME, come, Lucretia, do not cry,
Wipe those warm tears away;
Come sit down on your cricket here,
And list to what I say.
Thought, plumed in Memory's mystic wing, .
Was revelling with the past,
While you were sobbing, sobbing on,
As if it were your last!

Let's kiss that fair round face of thine,
So beautiful and bright,
Thou little tender blossoming,
Gladdening thy father's sight!
For he was once a slender boy,
In cap and waving plume,
Playing life's sunny hours away
Among the golden broom.

There is a little sunny bower
Upon the mountain's side,
Where first I found the coy young Muse,
And wooed her for my bride!
And oft I ran to welcome her
In Nature's flowery dome:
My happiest hours were spent within
Her breezy, heathery home.

A-near this musical retreat
Is a low mossy rock,
Which was the same in grandsire's time,—
A rough, unchiselled block;
Projecting from an ancient hedge,
Where fays and fairies play,
Dancing among the hyacinths
When daylight dies away.

The ruins of our dear old home
Sleep in the daisy mead,
Where your own granny used to go
To see the heifers feed.
That straw-roofed home was standing then,
Our childhood's pride and joy,
The birth-place of your singing sire,
The little mountain boy.

The first thing I remember, dear,
Was, years and years ago,
I wandered from my mother's door
A hundred yards or so,
And lost myself among the flowers
That gem our mountain's head;
Nor knew the way to wander back,
Where I was mourned as dead!

I well remember, soon the sun
Departed out of sight,
And then the gathering dusk came on,
And then the starry night.
I sat me on this same cold rock;
The tears came in mine eye;
I wept:—for I was sorrowful
And sad, I knew not why.

z 2

O how my father searched for me!
O how my mother sighed,
And called and called upon my name,
  And wrung her hands beside!
But I, a hundred yards from home,
  Was lost in this lone place,
Nor could I hear my mother's voice,
  Nor see my father's face.

And when, at last, they found me here
  On this low granite stone,
I sat in perfect solitude,
  And made my plaintive moan,—
A few short words repeated o'er
  And o'er with many a sigh,—
   "There's no one, no one with me here;
    Alone, alone am I!"

If you could understand my song,
  Lucretia, I would say,
"Don't give your mother needless pain
  By wandering far away.
Remain within our garden-bower;
  'Tis wide enough for you;
And then you will not lose yourself,
  As hosts of wanderers do!'"

A STORY FOR ALFRED.

THE naughty Muse won't come, my boy,
  Although for near an hour
I've coaxed the maiden, quill in hand,
  From her sequestered bower.
But she won't come, do what I may,
  And seems to shun the door:
However, let us trim the fire,
  And woo the wench once more.

There is a little mossy dell
  A long way from the town,
Unknown to railway travellers,
  A stranger to renown.
The cuckoo-flowers grow there in Spring,
  And the forget-me-not,
And many other wildings fair
  Adorn this lonely spot.

Once on a time some worthy men
  Within this heathy vine,
Perhaps a hundred years ago,
  Sank pits to seek a mine.
These now are half filled up or more
  By old Time stiff and stern,
And look like beds where fairies sleep,
  O'ergrown with furze and fern.

One summer morn,—the lark was up,
  And singing long and loud,
High o'er the hills and rising mist,
  Which floated like a cloud,—
As to my daily work I went,
  This vale I had to cross;
And in a pit I chanced to see
  A bird's nest mid the moss.

O what a pretty nest it was!
  Built with the greatest care,
With grass and moss and bits of wool,
  And strangely lined with hair.
And four unfeathered birds it held,
  The loving mother's brood,
Which oped their mouths when I looked in,
  As if they asked for food.

A bird's nest in the broken bush,
  Or hedge, or garden wall,
I cannot see but I behold
  The hand of God in all.
O why despise the tuneful bard
  Because he's lowly born,
And like the robin builds his nest
  And sings beneath the thorn?

A week had scarcely passed when I,
  One noontide after rain,
With boyish feeling turned aside,
  To seek that nest again.
Don't blame me for a deed like this:
  By Nature's works beguiled,
With her in truth I know I shall
  For ever be a child.

The birds were gone, the nest destroyed,
  With fragments on the clay,
And footmarks of a cruel boy
  Who bore the brood away.
And underneath the spot where once
  Her callow young she fed,
Without one mark of violence
  The mother-bird lay dead.

My faith is this,—that in the fields
  To gather worms she tried,
And coming back to find no brood
  She *felt* so that she died.
O Alfred, never rob a nest:
  The great God made us all
That we might love each living thing,
  However mean or small.

THE TWO BOYS AND THE LAMB.

(A STORY FOR JANE.)

A LITTLE lamb was feeding upon the mountain side,
  Among the grass and meadow-flowers that
    sparkled far and wide;
A little snow-white lamb, so innocent and free,
Leaped up to kiss the sunshine in my father's daisy-lea.

Two little boys were playing, with wheelbarrow and
    spade,
Where this white lamb was leaping in the bright daisy-
    glade.
Sometimes they carolled lightly, sometimes they
    both would sigh,
And, in a moment, they would weep, perhaps they
    knew not why.

These two delicious urchins, myself and Uncle Will,
Here dreamt away our childhood upon our native hill;
We carolled in the sunshine, we chatted in the shade;
We played beneath the hawthorn, in snow-white
  flowers arrayed.

We had a little iron pick to dig the mountain earth;
Some genius of uncommon strength had surely given
  it birth!
We ran and struck this little lamb with it upon the head,
And, in an instant, down it fell :—we thought it must
  be dead!

The pretty white unconscious thing we in the barrow
  placed,
To wheel it somewhere out of sight, and bury it in
  haste.
We trembled lest the owner's eye our wickedness
  should see;
We looked behind, we looked before : alas! how sad
  were we!

At last we tripped it on the heath, sheer o'er the
  barrow's side;
It felt the shook,—and off it ran in mazy circles wide!
We clapped our hands, we sang for joy, we danced in
  rapturous glee :
If we had got a thousand pounds, we could not happier be!

We promised, creeping hand in hand our father's
  meadows o'er,
That we would strike a little lamb in such a way no more!
We never did. Go where I may in Nature's wildest
  bowers,
I never shall forget the lamb we struck among the
  flowers.

This is a simple circumstance, I grant it, little Jane;
But 'tis a wicked thing to cause unnecessary pain.
The smallest worm you tread upon, the little fly you kill,
Feels equally as keen a pain as I or Uncle Will.

A HOME IDYL.

THE fire is once more burning bright,
  And flickering flames of song,
  And towers shoot up, and castles, too,
The curling smoke among.
With wife and children clustered round
  Within my rhyming hive,
I take my book, and deem myself
  The happiest man alive.

True, I have but small store of gold,
  Nor much of worldly ease,
No lands or titles from my sire;
  But what care I for those?
If health be mine, with those dear birds,
  That in my dwelling sing,
I share my meals, and bless my God,
  As happy as a king.

Indeed, my joy-cup is so full,
  And blessings come so fast,
That oft I think, amid my tears,
  It is too sweet to last.
But my great Father knows the way
  To lead me here below;
And so I give it up to Him,
  Or be it weal or woe.

Ye bloom in beauty round me now,
  Like roses bright and fair,
So that I love to hasten home
  Your healing sweets to share;
But ye will leave me, by and bye,
  To walk the ways of men,
And struggle with the multitude :
  God bless my children then.

My dearest wife is like a brook
  That murmurs through the dell,
Refreshing with her sight and sound
  The home I love so well.
Her presence like a sphere of light,
  Her voice as pleasant now
As when at first I heard her speak
  Under the hawthorn bough.

O what a bliss when evening comes,
  With shadows on the lea,
To cluster round the blazing log,
  The arm of some old tree,
And tell the story o'er again
  My children oft have heard
Of tabby cat, or doggy dear,
  Or busy bee, or bird!

And then to seat them by my side,
  When eve is wearing late,
And supper bread is on the board,
  To eat from off my plate!
No monarch ever felt more joy
  With legions at his nod;
I wipe the pressing tears away,
  And thank the Lord our God.

And oft they lift their hands for joy,
  In innocent amaze
To think our Father made them all,—
  The fields where cattle graze,
The trees, and flowers, and mighty rocks,
  That like huge castles stand,
The hill-top high, the great blue sky,
  The ocean, and the land.

And in their eyes are gleaming thoughts
  No bard can e'er express :
I clasp my hands, and thank the Lord
  For what I then possess.
And when the monster winds are up,
  Tearing from tree to tree,
I sometimes tell my little boys
  What I should like to see.

No drunkard reeling to his shed,
 No dark oppressor's hand,
No sound of war or tyranny
 From farthest land to land,
No beggar shivering in his rags,
 But men be brethren all;
And peace and plenty reign throughout
 This sublunary ball.

And so with health to feed the flock
 Within my cottage fold,
I feel I have a richer store
 Than heaps of shining gold.
O precious Shepherd, praise Thy name
 For Thy great love to me;
O what a paradise is home,
 When governed o'er by Thee!

TO MY CHILDREN.

Joyous, sportive, careless things,
 Floating by, like silver wings,
 Gliding round my humble shed,
Blessings, blessings on your head!
O what golden cords ye twine
Round this bleeding heart of mine!
O! the music of your voice
Bids the mourning one rejoice,

And your sunny glances throw
Glorious summer round my brow.
Blessings on ye! Glide around,
Making home enchanted ground;
Prattle, carol by mine hearth,
Beauteous gems of richest worth!
I will hang upon my lyre,
With my fingers on the wire,
Smiling, through the falling tear,
That ye are so happy here.

What would home, and all its cares,
Be without your simple airs?
Be without your loving kiss,
Sweeteners of domestic bliss?
Ye are all my earthly wealth,—
Stars in darkness, suns in health,—
Flowers whose healing odours rise
Like the gales of Paradise.
If it were my lot to dwell
In some humble cloistered cell,
Poor and needy, friendless too,
I would still rejoice with you.
Blessings on ye! May you be
Friends of want and misery!
May you live, sweet ones, to throw
Nectar on the wounds of woe,
Live the Christian's boon to find,
Live to benefit mankind!

EPISTLES AND LOCAL LYRICS.

BUT ALL THINGS WILL CHANGE.

(AN EPISTLE TO MY BROTHER.)

Most of bad omens, too direful to name,
Have been lashing the bard with their switches of flame.
Last evening, returning from work rather late,
With a scar in my hand, and a rhyme in my pate,

A raven flew heavily over my head,
And gave such a croak that I staggered with dread.
O fell Superstition! how long wilt thou stay?
Spread thy scaly black wing, and fly far, far away!

And, brother, last Friday,—unlucky for me!—
I saw a dread magpie alone on a tree.
I kept on and whistled,—sure, this was no sin,—
But, O, it set up such a terrible din,
And whirled o'er my head:—how awful the sight!
I leaped up on the road, and ran home in my fright.
An omen so fearful implied I might lose
My time-rended jacket or sole-clapping shoes.

The fire has burnt blue several evenings of late,
And puss has been washing her hands in the plate.

The death-watch has clicked on the top of the screen;
An owl has been hooting,—a ghost has been seen.
A primrose has sprung on the head of Old Winter:
A wren has died suddenly on a moss splinter:
And once, on a journey, almost at mid-day,
I found a great pin,—but 'twas turned the wrong way!

What these dark gloomy omens are meant to convey,
'Tis not in my power at this moment to say.
The rhymer's spare laurels, poor fellow! may fail,
And his crown of green heather may utterly quail.
The spirit of music may hasten away,
And rough-rolling prosy may lead me astray,
Through deserts all streamless and songless to range:—
It may be, dear brother; for all things will change.

Already what changes are here, my dear brother,
Since last you shook hands with your father and mother!
The pig has been killed just a fortnight ago,
That pork may be had when 'tis winter and snow.
The sheep and the lamb have been sold to the butcher:
I felt very sad when he came up to clutch her;
For a savage he looked, from his feet to his head:—
In a very few hours they were both of them dead!

Your very old shoe which you wore ere you started,—
You know it,—the tap from the upper has parted;
The irons have fled to some part of our zone;
The nails are all scattered, the string's in mine own;
The hind-part of the upper, behind an old crock,
In a web-hanging hole, lies as still as a stock;
Other fragments and splinters along the broad sphere
Are scattered and whirled:—what a change has been
    here!

Our cart-house—you know when 'twas fresh in its
    prime—
Seems now to be momently crushing by Time.
A pole which the place of a lintel supplied,
Is down on the floor, and it lies on its side;
Some clods from the end's majestical height
Are lofty no more,—they are prostrated quite.
But robin, poor fellow, though rafters break out,
Still flies where you often have seen him no doubt,
And trills his sad ditty so pensively true,
That ofttimes we think he is sighing for you.

If our cart-house is crushed by the finger of Time,
Our cow-house, too, quakes on its basis sublime.
The ropes on the roof, which have been on the wane,
Like Samson's green withs, are all severed in twain;
And now, to keep quiet the storm-beaten pile,
On the top of it slumbers an old-fashioned silo,
Which might have upheld, in this troublous range,
The roof of a grotto:—but all things must change.

Our furze-rick, old Cornish, with bunches of broom,
Is hastening away to the regions of fume.
On our straw-covered cot could you open your eyes,
You'd see it in clouds hurry off to the skies.
I wish you were with us, to mark the bright flame,
Now crackling its mirth-song, lit by our own dame:
But seas roll between, the levinthan's home,
The abode of the mermaid:—farewell till you come!

TO MY OLD SILK HAT.

Poor weather-beaten silker, how slight thou lookest
    now,
From what thou wert seven years ago, when
    perched upon my brow!
Thy shagless top, and silkless rim, how piteous to
    behold!
And sides, that seem crushed cruelly together with the
    cold!

Thou didst not always look like this, poor, ragged,
    wrinkled wight;
When thou wert brought from Paris here, thou wast
    a beauty quite;
Thy glossy silken self might then grace even a noble's
    brow;
But Time hath torn thee in his rage: thou'rt sadly
    altered now.

For seven long years, old holeless friend, we've
    travelled up and down,
And thou hast been content to wane on my rhyme-
    ridden crown.
The angry storms have fought with thee among the
    granite rocks;
And none but silkers such as thou could stand the
    winter-shocks.

Change after change has altered both my old silk hat
    and me,
Since first we met, ay, proudly met, elate in youthful
    glee;
But signs have been for months gone by that thou
    wouldst surely fall,
While hanging in thy wonted place, escutcheoned in
    my hall.

I know not who thy maker was, nor what his name
    might be:
For once he did out-do himself, when he had fashioned
    thee.
A Paris hat to stand the rust and rub of such an age
Adds glory to the Frenchman's name, unknown in
    history's page!

Peace to the memory of the man who smoothed thy
    curly rim;
And may unnumbered silkers more, like thee, be made
    by him!
I lost his honourable name before my song was penned;
But he deserves to blaze in print for blocking thee, old
    friend.

In peaceful bowers we oft have been, far from the
    busy town;
And many a thoughtless canzonet I've scribbled on
    thy crown.
I wore thee on my bridal-day,—that sunny day of days;
But Time hath cudgelled thee in ire, and knocked thee
    several ways.

The showery April morn is come, and thou art doomed
    to be
Thrown with the dirty cast-offs now,—a real friend
    like thee!

So have I seen, on Britain's Isle, in my own Cornish
  glen,
A hundred cast-off things like thee,—NOT PARIS HATS,
  BUT MEN.

THE HOUSEWIFE'S SOLILOQUY OVER HER WANING LOAF.

"Hour after hour, how sad to see
    My loaf so fleetly waning !
    While I so oft am cutting thee,
No wonder I'm complaining.

"There's Joe, whose greedy hands and eyes
  For ever are upon thee ;
And Tom,—he'd eat to win a prize :—
  They've no compassion on thee.

"When evening comes, if all be well,
  Home Herman will be strutting ;
And then there's luncheon for our Nell :
  O me ! they'll keep me cutting.

"My well-baked loaf ! the keen-edged knife
  Goes round a-separating :
It quite unnerves my wretched life
  To see thee so abating !

"'Tis but twelve hours ago, no more,—
  O how the phantom flashes !—
When I, to bolt gaunt Hunger's door,
  Did bake thee in the ashes.

"I never deemed that thou wouldst be
  By such lank wights attended ;
But now, alas ! I plainly see,
  Thy day will soon be ended.

"My beauteous baker-loaf ! I weep
  To see thee ever waning !
The shelf thou canst not, canst not, keep ;
  I cut thee while complaining !

"Dear wheaten loaf ! Now dust to dust,
  Morsel hath morsel followed !
'Tis over : "—and the last dry crust
  Was spread, and quickly swallowed !

TO MY BROTHER WILLIAM,

WHEN LEAVING HIS NATIVE LAND FOR NORTH
AMERICA.

My brother, companion of childhood, adieu !
  Too soon wilt thou haste o'er the waters so blue,
  Too soon wilt thou turn from thy own happy
    hearth,
Too soon wilt thou leave the loved place of thy birth,
To contend with the world and thy sin-smitten kind ;
While thy brothers and sisters are weeping behind.
Too soon must we part. Thou art here but to-day,
And to-morrow art posting away and away.

My brother, I love to look backward, to trace
The sweet smile of childhood that lighted thy face,
When we hied off to school, with our books in our bag,
Nor heeded the sneer of the ignorant wag ;
When we crept to the moor with a rod and a dish,
To dip out the water, and catch the small fish ;
When we trundled the foot-ball, or hoisted the kite,
And played the sun down on our heath-covered height.
O dreams of bright beauty that rise from the past,
Now breaking, now melting, too fleeting to last !
But I weep not for these, nor the touch of decay ;
But to-morrow thou'rt posting away and away.

My brother, when o'er the blue waters you flee,
And gaze with delight on the mystical sea,
Swelling over the grotto, the shell-covered cave,
The haunt of the mermaid, the bed of the brave ;
And see there reflected the stars as they shine,
Like spirit-eyes smiling within the blue brine ;
O think of your mother and father behind ;
O think of your brothers and sisters so kind ;
O think of your home on the crest of the hill,
Where the waters ooze out which are turning the mill ;
And believe we are praying that brother may be
Borne safely and fleetly across the wide sea.
Even now the tears fall while composing my lay ;
For to-morrow thou'rt posting away and away.

My brother, if Providence bless thee with lands,
And richly repay all the work of thy hands ;
Ay, if thou shouldst prosper in basket and store,
Build houses, plant orchards, raise hillocks of ore ;
O do not forget us in friendship's green wreath,
The scions of labour, the sons of the heath ;
But often come forth at the eventide hour,
And muse on our mountain, my moss-mantled bower,
Our reed-covered cottage, thy mother, thy sire,
Thy brothers and sisters, beside the hall fire ;
And surely this dream will sweet feelings inspire.
And if through the forest thy footsteps are borne,
When oak-leaves are dropping, and blossoms are torn,
When flowerets are drooping, and all things decay,
O think of thy brother, and muse on his lay ;
For he then, perchance, may be mouldering in clay.
But if from our crag-covered mountain you roam,
And poverty presses, O, brother, come home :
We'll stretch forth our hands to the prodigal son,
And greet with delight the poor rambling one ;
We'll clothe thee, and feed thee, and solace thy pain ;
Embrace thee, and call thee our brother again.
I weep at our parting, I cannot be gay ;
For to-morrow thou'rt posting away and away.

My brother, how painful thus early to part !
The sadness how heavy that weighs on my heart !
We are anxious for thee. O remember thy God,
And think of the prayers offered up on our sod.
Remember thy Maker : He speaks in the breeze,
And will hear thy soft plaint 'neath the great forest trees.
May vice never lure thee from virtue's sweet track,
To haunts the most gloomy, to scenes the most black !
But walk with the good through this region of strife,
To the land of the angels, the city of life.
'Tis for this that we now would invoke thee to stay ;
But to-morrow thou'rt posting away and away.

My brother, 'tis spring-time, the violets are come ;
The cowslips and primroses shine round our home ;
The grey lark is singing delicious on high,
Like an angel's rich strain gushing forth from the sky ;
The hawthorn is budding, the green blades appear,
And the breezes sing songs to the morn of the year.
But now I am sad at the coming of May ;
For to-morrow thou'rt posting away and away.

My brother, well, go, and at evening's repose
Thy sisters shall gather the dew-dropping rose ;
Thy brothers shall pluck from our favourite lea
A nosegay of wild flowers in memory of thee ;
Thy mother shall call her loved younglings around,
And tell them with tears where their brother is found ;
Thy father shall pace o'er the desolate wild,
Wiping off the salt tears for the thought of his child,
And wonder why thus in the spring-tide of bloom,
When the flowerets of hope shed their richest perfume,
His boy should be bounding away and away,
Like a spirit escaped from its prison of clay.
Go, brother, o'er mountains and woodlands to range :
I knew that this world was a sad scene of change ;
And I knew, though thou ever hast twined round my
        heart,
That sooner or later we surely should part.
But I dreamt not so soon. Brother, why not delay ?
No ; to-morrow thou'rt posting away and away.

My brother, I'm with thee where'er thou may'st roam,
How far it may be from our boulder-built home,
Though bounding away from thy own mountain's breast,
Away to the uttermost wilds of the west.
But I want thee to pluck from the meads of my sire
One dear little violet which I admire,
And take it, and carry it over the sea
Enshrined in thy heart, a memorial of me.
Go, brother ; I'll watch the big clouds rising black,
And pray that their pall may not darken thy track :
And when the wild winds round my lattice shall rave :
I'll ask their great Maker to shield thee and save.
Go, brother. On earth we may mingle no more ;
But, O, may we meet on the sun-lighted shore,
In the glory of Eden for ever to dwell !
My brother, dear brother, farewell, and farewell !
O could I, O could I, invoke thee to stay !
But to-morrow thou'rt posting away and away.

MY COTTAGE HOME.

(AN EPISTLE TO MY BROTHER.)

On our beloved native height,
    Far from the ocean's foam,
Beneath a bank of heath-flowers bright,
    I sing my cottage home.
It rears its straw-thatched roof above
    The rocky mountain's head,
And smiles among the prickly brakes
    With golden furze-buds spread.

O me ! how passing beautiful
    Its reedy roof appears !
Its uncouth chimneys, granite blocks
    Unhewn, I've loved for years.

The time-decaying casements, too,
    Though Gothic they may be,—
The very earth it stands upon,—
    Have charms enough for me.

You ask me why I do not come,
    And share the stranger's feast ;
And why I ever stay at home :
    Think'st thou my joys the least ?—
Through England's flowery meads to trip,
    Forgetting labour's life,
Charmed with the melting voices of
    A mother and a wife.

And when the Sabbath hours are come,
    And Labour's sons are free,
Think not that I am pleasureless,
    That there's no bliss for me.
With joy I hail the rising lark,
    As he his matin sings,
And oft haste forth to see him shake
    The dew-drop from his wings.

There may be woods around you spread,
    With broad and glassy lakes :
Fire-flies may revel o'er your head,
    And parrots in the brakes ;
The mocking-bird's capricious note
    May fall upon your ear,
And butterflies around you float
    That never glitter here.

I care not for your woods of green,
    Your lakes and birds and flies :
You have not England's sunny stream,
    You have not England's skies :
You have not England's holiday,
    When man and beast are free.
It is for these, my boy, I stay :
    They are enough for me.

I tell thee, 'tis the budding time,
    And robin comes again,
Building his nest where first he did,
    High up the stony lane.
Thy sisters on the daisy lea
    Now sit and play for hours,
And little brother plucks for thee
    A nosegay of wild flowers.

The cowslips round our mountain cot
    Like dewy pearls are flung,
And on our ancient garden hedge
    The primrose-buds are strung.
The lambkins crop the tender grass
    Our hilly meads supply ;
And birds and breezes carol sweet
    Beneath the vernal sky.

Two sister-violets I've plucked
    Beneath our hawthorn-tree,
And wrapt them in this music-sheet,
    To send, my boy, to thee.

A A

And, brother, when they meet thine eyes,
　Far, far o'er ocean's foam,
Remember they were gems which clung
　Around thy cottage home.

THE FARMER'S APOSTROPHE TO HIS OLD BLIND HORSE.

"Dost think thy master's so unkind,
　Now thou art spavined, lean, and blind,
To turn thee out in sleet and wind,
　　To die alone, old Golly?

"No, sooner on this wintry night
He'd leave his own dear chimney bright,
And playful bairns that glad his sight,
　　Than drive thee forth, old Golly.

"I think upon thy younger days,
When thou wert all the country's praise
In cart or plough.　On broad highways
　　How thou didst race, old Golly!

"The panting winds thou wouldst outstrip,
Thy way through brake and bramble rip,
O'er bog and hedge, nor spur nor whip
　　Dishonoured thee, old Golly.

"A better brute ne'er drew a load
Along the narrow village road,
The driver's chirp thine only goad,
　　True-footed, firm old Golly.

"And shall I turn thee out to die,
Because no light is in thine eye,
Like yon blind wretch 'neath winter's sky?
　　No; eat thy oats, old Golly.

"Canst thou forget that sunny day
When thou didst draw the wain of hay
High up beyond the castle, eh?
　　Thou brute of brutes, old Golly!

"O'er that seven years' unbroken lea,
When thou wert strong as strong can be,
How thou didst pull the plough to me
　　From morn till eve, old Golly!

"On market nights, astride thy back,
With my week's sirloin in my sack,
When skies were dark and lanes were black,
　　Thou brought'st me home, old Golly.

"There are who, selfish, stalk the earth,
And glut the privilege of Worth;
And when it's old, they drive it forth
　　To pain and want, old Golly.

"But he who owns thy honest hide,
Which once shone bright in youthful pride,
Will never on the common wide
　　Thrust thee to die, old Golly.

"So comfort thee within thy shed,
　Nor fear the wild winds overhead:
I'll see that thou art housed and fed,
　　Till death shall smite old Golly."

PENJERRICK.

(THE COUNTRY RESIDENCE OF R. W. FOX, ESQ., F.R.S., ETC.)

I first beheld it when the wintry clouds
　Were rolling grandly through the murky air;
　And flocks of starlings, wheeling to their home,
Like sound of many waters, murmured there.
Here graceful trees, the green, the rich, the rare,
So chastely grouped, in fairy fringes stand;
And limpid rills, and crystal waterfalls,
Are breathing song like notes from angel-land.
Old Winter here is reft of his command,
Rare roses bloom, and fragance fills the breeze;
Here forest-birds from off a friendly hand
Pick their full meal, and flutter 'neath the trees.
If such, Penjerrick, be thy winter scene,
How Eden-hued in summer's richer sheen!

THE CORNISH CHOUGH.

Where not a sound is heard
　But the white waves, O bird,
And slippery rocks fling back the vanquished sea,
　Thou soarest in thy pride,
　Not heeding storm or tide;
In Freedom's temple nothing is more free.

'Tis pleasant by this stone,
.Sea-washed and weed-o'ergrown,
With Solitude and Silence at my side,
　To list the solemn roar
　Of ocean on the shore,
And up the beetling cliff to see thee glide.

Though harsh thy earnest cry,
　On crag, or shooting high
Above the tumult of this dusty sphere,
　Thou tellest of the steep
　Where Peace and Quiet sleep,
And noisy man but rarely visits here.

For this I love thee, bird,
　And feel my pulses stirred
To see thee grandly on the high air ride,
　Or float along the land,
　Or drop upon the sand,
Or perch within the gully's frowning side.

Thou bringest the sweet thought
　Of some straw-covered cot,
On the lone moor beside the bubbling well,
　Where cluster wife and child,
　And bees hum o'er the wild;
In this seclusion it were joy to dwell.

Will such a quiet bower
Be ever more my dower
In this rough region of perpetual strife?
I like a bird from home
Forward and backward roam;
But there is rest beneath the Tree of Life.

In this dark world of din,
Of selfishness and sin,
Help me, dear Saviour, on Thy love to rest;
That, having crossed life's sea,
My shattered bark may be
Moored safely in the haven of the blest.

The Muse at this sweet hour
Hies with me to my bower
Among the heather of my native hill;
The rude rock-hedges here
And mossy turf, how dear!
What gushing song! how fresh the moors and still!

No spot of earth like thee,
So full of heaven to me,
O hill of rock, piled to the passing cloud!
Good spirits in their flight
Upon thy crags alight,
And leave a glory where they brightly bowed.

I well remember now,
In boy-days on thy brow,
When first my lyre among thy larks I found,
Stealing from mother's side
Out on the common wide,
Strange Druid footfalls seemed to echo round.

Dark Cornish chough, for thee
My shred of minstrelsy
I carol at this meditative hour,
Linking thee with my reed,
Grey moor and grassy mead,
Dear carn and cottage, heathy bank and bower.

AN EPISTLE TO MY BROTHER.

My long-remembered brother! ah, whither dost
thou roam?
Why is it thou hast left so soon thy mother and
thy home,
Kind brothers on the mountain-top that carol blithe
and free,
Sporting among the shelving crags they climbed in
infancy?

I wonder where thou travellest now,—over the rolling
seas,
Gazing upon the swelling wave, stirred by the passing
breeze?
Or art thou rich as Crœsus, boy, on Fortune's golden
hills,
Sheltered from want and pain and care by wood-
o'ershadowed rills?

I wonder where thy thoughts are now,—wandering
along our mount,
And gathering flowers that bathe themselves in
Memory's sacred fount?
And art thou dreaming of thy sire, thy mother's kind
caress?
I know these thoughts will call from thee fresh drops
of tenderness.

Or art thou by the murmuring stream, lone musing on
the past?
And does the tear-drop from thine eye rush o'er thy
cheek at last?
And are thy playmates with thee there, bounding
along the lake?
Thy brothers and thy sisters, too? Ah, no! young
wanderer, wake!

For we are on our mountain's head, watching the
twilight grey,
And wondering why our brother thus so soon could
haste away;
Ay, wondering why he thus could go from home's
long-cherished bowers,
And leave us here alone to cull the Summer's brightest
flowers!

I wonder what thine eyes behold, what now my
brother sees?
O, does he walk at evening-hour beneath the forest-
trees,
Gazing through tears with wild delight on the sweet
vesper-star,
Flashing its beams of silvery light upon him from afar?

I wonder what thy feelings are,—if they are aught like
mine?
It may be so, and I will drop a tear or two with thine.
They fall upon our mountain's head within my heathy
bower,
And hang, as doth the evening mist, upon the sleeping
flower.

How sweet, on this delicious eve, my straw-thatched
home appears!
Methinks 'tis dearer now than erst, because enshrined
in tears.
For every passing zephyr weeps, each flower-bud of
the lea,
And all the little singing-birds sob forth a dirge for
thee.

Thou canst not see my British home, with dusky
twilight crowned;
Thou canst not see old England's hills and valleys lie
around?
Thou canst not see the rising moon peer o'er our
mountain's brow,
How beautiful, how beautiful! But, brother, where
art thou?

O, shall we never meet again? Perhaps on earth no
more:
If not, farewell, until it be on heaven's unclouded shore.

But if below I felt for thee, and loved thee with such
love,
O, how much greater will it be in that bright world
above!

EARLE'S RETREAT, FALMOUTH:

FOUNDED A.D. 1869.

THE dew is on the rose,
Morn in the valleys, sun-streaks on the hills;
And glowing Summer in her robe of leaves
Sings by a thousand rills.

The world o'erflows with praise,
Swelling in wavelets to the doors of light;
And there are echoes which the soft breeze sways,
Steps of the Infinite.

Where the tall foxgloves shine,
And honeysuckles front the southern sea,
Wanders a bright face in the sun's red line,
In boyish ecstasy.

And from the rosy skies
A Voice fell, "It is righteous to obey.
What thou receivest wilt thou yield to Me?"
And George Earle answered, "Yea!"

Then came the shock of years,
The manly muscle, the strong vigorous limb;
And forth he went to wrestle with his fate,
And the Voice followed him.

Yet still he struggled on,
With Hope beside him, with white wings outspread,
And finger pointing to more flowery fields,
With the Voice overhead.

His track lay o'er the seas,
And in the West a settler's home he made,
Where roved the hunter through the forest aisles,
And the Red Indian strayed.

The King who giveth all
Rewarded much the labour of his hands;
And still his goods increased from year to year
In silver, gold, and lands.

And when his cup was full,
That Voice came sounding, "Why so long delay?
What thou receivest wilt thou yield to Me?"
And George Earle answered, "Yea."

He sought his native land,
And laid an offering at his Master's feet,
A HOME to shelter the deserving poor,
A free untaxed RETREAT.

And here the aged dwell;
And here the widow with her thoughts on high;
And here the friendless with their friends above,
Lodged in the quiet sky.

And wisely has he reared
A solemn CHAPEL, where they kneel and pray;
And I have seen them at the name of Christ
Wipe the free tears away.

And prayers go up for him,
When Sabbath glory through the stained glass streams,
And in the west has sunk the god of day,
And the fair Venus gleams.

And prayers go up for him,
When on the hearth the household fire sinks low,
And Age is kneeling in his quiet bower,
And words rise faint and slow.

And prayers go up for him,
Where glides the vessel o'er the boundless main:
The sailor knows his aged mother safe,
And wipes the tears again.

And prayers go up for him,
Where harvests whiten, and where rivers run,
Where smokes the smithy by the old road-side;
And the Voice cries, "Well done!"

And prayers shall rise for him,
And rise for his, from those with bended knee,
When morn awaketh, and when evening wanes,
For many days to be.

Better his honest fame
Than warrior-wreath by blood and battle won,
To smooth the downhill of the Saviour's own,
And hear His glad "Well done."

And from his gift of love,
This faithful index of his honest heart,
An echo rises ever rolling forth,
"Go thou, and do thy part."

Directed by his Guide,
May fruits of love and happiness increase,
Till old age crown him with entire content,
And George Earle's end be peace.

TO MY OLD QUILL.

'TIS long since thou hast been my own,
From what wing gathered is unknown:
I've cut thee to the very bone,
Old Quill!

'Twas on the eve of yesterday
When I to my good wife did say,
"I think I'll stumpie throw away,"
Old Quill!

Methought thou gavest me such a glance
As made my very heart's blood dance;
And so I let thee take thy chance,
Old Quill!

We've long been friends to memory dear,
And proudly I would oft appear
When thou wert thrust behind my ear,
　　　Old Quill.

Letters and lays I've wrote with thee,
And jots that jingle merrily:
So we will never parted be,
　　　Old Quill.

Canst thou forget that loving sheet
We penned at Evening's dewy feet,
When Beauty wept with sighs replete,
　　　Old Quill?

Full many a rhyming deed is thine,
A thought of which now brings the brine
From those tear-saddened eyes of mine,
　　　Old Quill.

For this I love thy honest face:
So, hark ye, never cringe for place,
Nor slime thyself with such disgrace,
　　　Old Quill.

MALVERN IN THE MIST.

Ho! ho! great Malvern, wherefore art thou wroth
　In thy mist-mantle? I have travelled far
　In hope to see thee with a face as bright
As my own mounds with mineral-treasures full,
The pride of old Cornwallia; but alack!
Thou'rt mourning in thy fog-shroud, and we climb
As if the daylight were but half begun,
Though it is noon, the ploughman's dinner hour.

Full suddenly, under the dark trees hid,
We came upon a troop of noisy boys
With patient donkeys saddled skilfully;
And dinning was their native eloquence
That we should hire them: "Take my donkey, Sir!
My donkey has been eating oats to-day:
A fine beast mine; he'll bear you to the top
Without a hoof-slip. Try my donkey, Sir!
That fellow's Neddy is so lean on straw,
He has nought else. Mine has the finest food.
How sleek his sides, and what an eye is his!
How glossy is his coat! Just stroke him down.
Look at his ears. Please take my donkey, Sir!"
And thus they piped away with voices high.
But long had we been journeying on by train
Drawn by the horse of iron, and were glad
To press our feet upon the earth once more.

We leave them in the mist and clamber on,
And when a few feet higher than the Well
Of good St. Anne, with sudden swift delight
We mount above the fog, and the clear sky,
Cloudless and blue, is sun-full overhead.
It was a joy that will not pass away.
How like the Christian toiling sadly on,
In doubt sometimes, until, through faith and prayer,
He soars above the mist and feels the sun,

And treads the darkness underneath his feet!
We saw a little robin on a bough
Open his beak and sing deliciously,
While under him the fog-world sank and rose,
And heaved, and swelled, like a huge billowy sea.

Higher we rose and higher, and the sun
Shone brighter still, and everything was grand.
O, what a throne for bard to rest upon,
The base hill-top, so far away from wrong!
Why, every hollow has a harper in't,
And Health is here reposing on the moss.
City and village, river-face and fen,
Forest and field, on this side and on that,
Gladden the vision, standing nearer heaven.
May never war-cloud blacken such a scene
Now brooded over by the nymph of Peace!
Seek we for music? Here it rolls along
From Nature's organ in a sea of praise.
Seek we for health? The four winds waft it here
In urns of nectar opened on the height.
For solitude and rest? Each grassy rift
Is full of murmurs never heard below.

O Malvern, Malvern! lonely in thy life
Of silent wonder, to the solemn sky
Lifting thy forehead, catching the first ray
Of early morning, and the last of eve:
I thank thee for thy favours. The small mounds
I love so well along my Cornish coast,
With heath, and rush, and rock-heap beautiful,
Were mole-hills by thy side. Another look,
And yet another still. Come to my arms and heart:
We seem so near the dwelling-place of God.

TREGEDNA AND JOSHUA FOX.

Our western isle of broom and brake,
　Of winding stream and glassy lake,
　Of woodland bower and echoing moor,
Where hawthorns hide the woodman's door,
Has nought more fair on fen or fell
Than dear Tregedna in the dell.

Here dwells, amid the laurel green,
The genius of this tranquil scene,
Whose love has won the feathered race
To follow him from place to place,
To flutter through this pleasant land,
And pick the bread-crumbs from his hand.

He knows the tones that fill the breeze,
He knows the language of the trees;
He knows the crystal cascade's sound,
The rose-leaf psalms that tremble round;
The silent sighs from rush and reed
All find an echo in his deed.

And here, when bats float by the eaves,
And glowworms twinkle through the leaves,
When o'er the earth a halo steals
Which oft the waiting spirit feels,
Beneath the boughs of evergreen
His spirit worships the UNSEEN.

And may we not in covert lone,
By silvery stream and silent stone,
In wild-wood shade and forest fair,
Draw near to God in praise and prayer?
O yes, O yes! His presence fills
The whispering valleys and the hills.

I've travelled much the ways of men
O'er shaggy down and rushy glen,
Where cities yawn and hamlets doze,
And listless solitudes repose;
But never music filled mine ear
Like his who feeds the robins here.

O, if it were my lot to dwell
In such a dear poetic dell,
I'd stop my tears, and pass my days
In sweetly singing hymns of praise,
So that the crowd should sometimes heed
The gentle murmur of my reed.

To me this dear retreat how blest,
Who pine so oft in vain for rest,
Chased here and there with careless smart,
With song-tones ringing in my heart!
But I submit to Heaven's decree,
And in the tumult sigh for thee.

Who sees him views a chieftain strong,
A child of nature and of song,
A genuine bard, a man of might,
Whose soul is yearning for the right.
When love shall reign from zone to zone,
And tyranny be overthrown.

Go, hear the wonders of his voice,
And let your bounding heart rejoice.
Go, mark his generous aspect bold,
And think of England's seers of old.
Go, ask yourself, if ask you can,
"Does nature hold a nobler man?"

IT BLOWS A FURIOUS FULL MARCH WIND.

(AN EPISTLE TO MY BROTHER.)

IT blows a furious full March wind,
    With startling gusty cry:
Let's under this old furzy hedge
    To hear it hurry by;
Now tearing off the bud and flower,
    And whirling them in rage,
Now tripping up the ruddy boy,
    Now toppling over age.

Hark how it rends itself along
    Above the ruffled rill,
Twisting the strong branch from the tree,
    The heather from the hill;
Rifling old dikes and reedy sheds
    And slate-roofs with a roar,
And breaking through the bending pines
    Upon the mighty moor.

I know not when the blustering March
    Struck such a tempest-strain:
You scarcely trudge against the wind,
    Or foot it up the lane.
It tumbles, cracks along the vales,
    And writhes around the crags,
Shaking the rich man in his robes,
    The beggar in his rags.

O what a prosy thread I've spun
    To meet my brother's eye!
How full of tangled hurricane,
    That leaves the reader dry!
But, leaping from this windy car,
    I would essay to sing
A bud-besprinkled canzonet,
    A welcome note to Spring.

Among the dead leaves of the moor
    The primrose lifts its head,
And by our humble cottage-door
    The crocus flowers are spread.
The lark arises with a song
    Until the woodland rings;
It trembles o'er the travelling storm,
    As high he soars and sings.

How fresh the breezes flow along
    Athwart the rural glen!
How sweet to him who pines within
    The smoke-god's dangerous den!
I ask not wealth or title-deeds,
    Or self-indulgent ease,
But what the strong yeoman enjoys,—
    The pure air of the leas.

To-day I've thrashed an old tin-rib
    Till I could thrash no more;
While streams of perspiration ran
    Unchecked from every pore.
A fire-cloud drank my spirits up:
    How longed I for the breeze
The hoary-headed woodman quaffs
    Among the forest-trees!

Who would not leave the smoky mine,
    And his unhealthy trade,
To carol on the shepherd's crook,
    And wear the shepherd's plaid?
Ay, brother, I have often thought—
    With lassitude oppressed,
When gasping in its cloudy cells—
    A rag-man's lot the best.

Toil, toil, from morning until night;
    Toil, toil, from night till morn!
Of all the struggling sons of earth,
    I surely feel the thorn.
And though my health is failing me,
    Seared with the sulphur-blast,
The only prospect on before
    Is drudgery to the last.

But, brother, let us not complain,
    Whilst toiling on time's road;
There's many a richer wight, I ween,
    Who feels care's prickly goad.

Let's profit by the ills of life,
Through heat, through winter's cold,
And conquer crooked circumstance,
And turn it all to gold.

TO A MOUSE

WHICH HAD EATEN THE LEAVES OF MY LEXICON.

How darest thou, soft-footed elf,
With tiny open jaw,
To cram such crooked syllables
Into thy greedy maw ?
Would not some common household-words
Such joy to thee afford,
Or crumbs that fall at supper-time
From off our humble board ?

The woodman yonder with his axe
Looks on this book with dread,
Pronounces it an oracle,
And shakes his hoary head.
He would not mar this mystic page,
'Twould cripple his belief;
But thou, fur-covered sinner, com'st
And eat'st it leaf by leaf.

What strange mice-spells thy deeds will wake,
When in your mossy nook,
Surrounded with thy mute compeers,
Thou talkest of my book !
Will not thy grandsire shake his head,
To hear what thou hast done ?
Disturb a poet in his dreams !
O thou degenerate son !

Take care, word-eating pilferer,
What learned meals thou'rt at !
If I can catch thee nibbling books,
I'll give thee to the cat.
Some two-legged mice, like thee, sleek rogue !
Climb where they have no right,
Eat what belongs to other men,
And vanish out of sight.

SAILOR'S CREEK.

INSCRIBED TO N. H. P. LAWRENCE, ESQ.

'Tis with me still, where'er I be,
That little glen beside the sea,
Where woodbines arch the narrow pass,
And rabbits gambol in the grass,
And wild flowers scent the summer air.
And oak trees wave and hawthorns fair,
And fays, with dew upon their cheek,
Swing on the leaves in Sailor's Creek.

As by the stile I pleased did stand,
The waves stole up and kissed the land ;
The swallows wheeled among the trees,
The rushes whispered with the breeze;

A murmur ran along the shore,
As flashed and dipped the boatman's oar;
The white gull rose with shining beak,
And left his note in Sailor's Creek.

From the green uplands stole a rill :
How clear it was ! I see it still,
And hear its murmuring low and sweet,
Where fairies come to lave their feet,
And little elves and glowworms be,
What time the moon is o'er the sea,
Whose light illumines pier and peak,
And robes in silver Sailor's Creek.

How happy he whose home is here
With bush and brake and burnie clear,
And quiet seas, and woody land,
And sea-nymphs dancing on the sand,
Or thronging up the grassy shore !
A bard could wish for nothing more
Than day by day and week by week
To sing his songs in Sailor's Creek.

I love it much, this sheltered scene ;
Here Poetry dwells in bowers of green,
And Fancy free unfettered springs,
And mounts with sun-gems on her wings;
And in the soul deep tones are stirred
Which cannot in the crowd be heard :
The little ferns and grasses speak
And wink their loves in Sailor's Creek.

Said I aloud, "I'll bring them here,
My wife and all my birdlings dear :
They'll joy to pluck—I know it well—
The dainty daisies of this dell,
To list the cuckoo on the thorn,
And tell the tale of Michael Moru,
Who brought his skiff in Passion week,
And bore his love from Sailor's Creek."

GYLLYNGDUNE.

How pleasant here at cool of day
Along the winding walks to stray,
Where ebbs and flows the murmuring main,
Whose music fills the woodbine lane,
High on the beach with shingles strewn,
As rise thy vespers, Gyllyngdune !

It is not meet to pass through life
For ever in the city's strife,
Where noise and clamour bear the sway :
Then, weary worker, come away;
Its gentle calm shall cheer thee soon,
Though thou drop tears at Gyllyngdune !

I care but little for the crowd,
Whose empty caskets rattle loud;
Or towns o'erflowed with selfish men,
Where guilt exists in darksome den ;
Or gilded hall, or gay saloon :
No; rather give me Gyllyngdune.

How fresh the waves break on the shore !
How gently drips the boatman's oar !
How grandly the white sea-gulls ride !
How gracefully the swallows glide !
While floats the sailor's merry tune
Upon the breeze at Gyllyngdune.

And old Pendennis on his height
Looks down well-pleased on such a sight.
There stand he like a warrior bold,
Nor heeds he heat nor heeds he cold,
From burst of morn till night's dark noon,
To guard my lovely Gyllyngdune.

When last I chanced to ramble here,
The winds were still, the skies were clear;
Two lovers sat upon a seat,
With ocean shining at their feet,
Whispering their loves beneath the moon,
Which filled with silver Gyllyngdune.

Dear home of love ! sweet haunt of peace !
Here weary life's dark bickerings cease.
A sacred song is on the air
Which lulls to rest the storm of care,
And lifts the heart to heaven's high noon ;
My beautiful, my Gyllyngdune !

DESTRUCTION OF THE CORNISH TOLMEN.

A DRUID link is broken which long joined
　　The Past and Present, rudely wrenched and
　　　　snapped
By cruel fingers. Shame it is to spoil
This ancient temple for the greed of gain,
To flash and flare it in the eye of heaven
For three whole days with the destroying charge,
Until this throne of wonders toppled o'er,
Leaving a wreck that diamonds can't replace.
Shame ! shame ! the rising echoes of the moors
Cry Shame, and the great hill-blocks Shame ;
And through the air a swift-avenging sprite
With arm uplifted shouts the dark word Shame !
If some fierce Vandal from the shore of wrong
In a wild hour had scathed it where it stood,
We could have better borne it : but to think
The scions of the land of cross and carn,
Our own immediate kinsfolk, who should stand
Resolved to shield it with the sword of Fate,
And guard it like a child at their own hearth,—
That they should drag its glory to the ground,
O this is dreadful.
　　　　Ill canst thou afford
To lose such relics, Cornwall, where at eve
The Roman joyed to ramble, fanned by winds
That travelled music-tracks, and lulled by sounds
From far-off minstrels. Here, when soft airs spake
The fragrant language of the lowly thyme,
Oft stole the Druidess in robe of white,
Like Beauty mid the moonbeams, leaving lays
That linger still among the grand old blocks ;
And here the priest, and here the warrior came,
The Lowman bold whose blood was in his face,

To hear the horrors of the haughty Dane.
These murmur, "Spare the Tolmen." Ah ! their words
Are like the rhyme of poet, overborne
By the fierce flutter of the world for gain.

The coming years will miss it. Anxious eyes,
Stained deep with indignation, oft shall turn
To scan the site it dignified so long ;
And the wild bird, the haunter of the hills,
Shall flounder in his passage, seeing not
His ancient landmark : whirling round and round
In strange bewilderment, with shriek and cry
He'll leave the heights for ever. Much I feel
To lose a boulder from my native moors,
As if a sister perished. Ye who love
The poetry of the mountains, guard, O guard
Our curious cromlechs ! Let no hand of man
Destroy these stony prophets which the Lord
Has placed upon the tarns and sounding downs
With tones for distant ages.

CAPERN'S VISIT TO CORNWALL, 1860.

CORNUBIA TO DEVONIA GREETING.

HURRAH, classic Cornwall !
　　Shout with bardic pride :
　　Devon's thrush has warbled
O'er thy moorlands wide ;
And our hearts were gladdened
　　By his converse strong,
Swelling round our pathway
　　Like an ancient song.

By Cornubia's crosses
　　Devon's gifted son,
With his harp unshouldered,
　　Sang when day was done :
And her gentle daughters,
　　Tuneful as the streams
Running round the rushes,
　　Were his richest themes ;

Musing like a Druid
　　By the cromlechs brown,
Or the Nine Stone Maidens
　　Rising on the down ;
Worshipping with Nature
　　Near the lonely loch,
By a poet's birthplace,
　　On the hill of rock.

Not a flower, my Cornwall,
　　On thy walk or wild,
But he seemed to love it
　　As his maiden child :
And the linnet's carol,
　　And the robin's lay,
Were in sweetest numbers
　　Chanted on his way.

Wildly sang the harpist
　　On the rough Land's End,

And where fairy Kynance
  Wooed him like a friend ;
And by hill and hollow
  In the coming time
Loving lips shall murmur,
  " Here did Capern rhyme."

FALMOUTH.

I saw it first when April shoots
  Were shining on the tree,
And daisies, gladdened by the sun,
  Looked up on lawn and lea.
I left my cot when but a boy,
  And, crossing mead and moor,
Gazed I upon its harbour waves
  Which kissed the pleasant shore.

I never shall forget when first
  It burst upon my view,
And from a neighbouring carn I saw
  Its ships and waters blue,
And tower, and terrace, ocean-girt,
  Which met me from the hill :
'Twas beautiful ! 'twas beautiful !
  And so is Falmouth still.

Like some old poem of the past
  Imbued with Nature's fire,
The more we read, the more we love,
  And wonder and admire :
So is this sea-port of the south
  Yet more and more endeared,
As years fill up the calendar,
  Where now my home is reared.

Here barks from every nation meet,
  With streaming flags unfurled ;
Securely here in peace they ride,
  Each ship a floating world.
Here come the fish in shining shoals,
  The shelly creeks among ;
And sweet it is across the tide
  To hear the rower's song.

How beautiful the country walks
  Along the sea-beach low ;
Where ocean-birds perch on the crags,
  And white waves come and go !
The distant hills are thronged with fays,
  And from each brake and bower
A thousand mystic voices rise
  To laud Jehovah's power.

Oft from the street I turn away,
  As peals the solemn bell,
When Eve, with glow-worms in the moss,
  Sits musing down the dell.
And O, how sweet it is to stand
  Upon the pebbly shore,
And hear across the gathering dusk
  The dripping of the oar !

Can bluer waves, or greener fields,
  Or flowers by zephyrs fanned,
Or fairer face of maid or boy
  Be found in any land ?
O, like a lion in his lair,
  Surrounded with the sea,
Is old Pendennis, castle-crowned,
  A sturdy watcher he.

I've travelled where the waters roar,
  And where the hills are high,
Whose lofty summits seem to soar
  Into the distant sky.
But fairer scene, O Falmouth mine !
  Has never met my view,
Than thy green fields and sloping heights,
  And waves and waters blue.

WHEN YOU ARE BOOKED TO FILLY.

The rains pour down a perfect flood,
  Winds howl, huge oaks are bowed ;
And mid old Cornwall's copper hills
  The thunders mutter loud,
While through the air the god of storms
  Rides on his sulphur cloud.

'Tis pitchy dark : ghosts roam the lanes
  At this rough midnight hour ;
And Cynthia, t'other side the world,
  Is sleeping in her bower.
So I must out in such a night :
  O shield me, mighty power !

The slate is whirled from off my house
  With gusts that utter woe,
And down the chimney rush strange sounds ;
  But to the mine I go ;
For fire-whim buckets must be filled,
  Though houses turn so so.

They say that Peace is come at last,
  With Plenty in her train,
Spreading her olive-branches o'er
  The mountain and the main ;
That Europe's heart is sick of war,
  And sick of myriads slain.

Last night my wife presented me
  With little chubby Joe ;
And through my brain a bran new rhyme
  Is rushing to and fro :
But lays and laddies fall before
  The bucket-work, you know.

A sick friend calls me to his bed,
  The good old poet Willy :
He scarcely can live out the night.
  His fingers are so chilly.
But dying speeches go for nought
  When you are booked to filly.

* This is Cornish mining phraseology.—a corruption of
the words, " to fill," " to fill the bucket."

A RHYME FOR EDWARD BASTIN.

In a land of rock and heather,
    Dark peat and prickly thorn,
Low hedges, hills, and mining pits,
A simple bard was born.
And in his early boyhood
    The gentle Muse came down,
And breathed into his spirit,
    As he crossed the common brown.

He loved the golden sunshine,
    The blue sky and the sea,
The clouds at solemn sunset,
    The flowerets on the lea ;
The birds and trees and rivers,
    His cot upon the height,
The face of man and maiden,
    And all things pure and bright.

You might have seen him wander
    Along his father's leas,
Communing with the ivy,
    And whispering with the breeze ;
The swallows his companions
    In many a sacred nook ;
The hedges were his study,
    And Nature was his book.

Upon the slender grasses,
    The fragile floating seed,
The very smallest insect,
    The most ungainly weed,
The crag, the cliff, the coppice,
    Flowers clinging to the clod,—
Dame Nature's ready pupil,
    He read the name of God.

Then came a day of darkness,
    Of deep poetic woe,
When duty's call was answered,
    And he went down below
Mid slime and burning sulphur,
    The flinty rock to part,
With childhood on his forehead
    And beauty in his heart.

O, how he felt the pressure
    Of this song-chilling gloom,
And longed for breezy hillocks
    Beyond the cavern's gloom !
For in his soul there struggled
    Thoughts burning to have birth,
Which could not all be smothered
    Or buried in the earth.

And so, though crushed with labour,
    He oft lay mid the thyme,
When Eve was weeping dew-drops,
    And wrote his simple rhyme,
Which cheered him as he jolted
    Through life's convulsive jars,
Like hymnings from the highest,
    Or whispers from the stars.

Years passed, and still he struggled
    Where darkness sat enthroned,
And Danger lurked in shadow,
    And weary workers groaned.
And still his hymns he chanted
    In solitude and night,
With none to lift him upward,
    Or cheer him with the light.

Then children clustered round him,
    And wooed his fond embrace ;
Sweet prattlers called him father,
    And kissed his pallid face.
His rhymes began to wander
    Among the walks of men ;
And still he wrought in darkness
    Below the quiet glen.

When, lo ! as God would have it,
    In humble clothing dressed,
Two strangers sought his dwelling,
    And kindly him addressed :
" We've read thy simple poems,
    And thou must understand
That we are come to thank thee,
    And take thee by the hand."

A ray of summer sunshine
    Shot through his gladdened heart :
The great earth teems with beauty,
    And cherubs round him start ;
And from his eyes the waters
    In briny drops did flow,
As forth he went to labour
    With hope upon his brow.

Now singing in the daylight,
    And lighted with the sun,
He feels another era
    Of pilgrimage begun.
And so he blows his whistle,
    On Gratitude's green peak,
A blast for Edward Bastin,
    The helper of the weak.

HELFORD RIVER.

I saw it in its clearness,
    The pleasure of the place,
When May in buds and blossoms
    Was mirrored on its face.
The blue-bells edged its margin
    In many a fragrant rank,
And Trebah, like a temple,
    Was shining on its bank.

O lovely in its brightness,
    When Summer woos the wave,
And Morning, like a seraph,
    Doth in the waters lave,
And cuckoo's voice of welcome
    Is o'er the billows borne,
And wood-dove trills his sonnets
    Of music on the thorn !

I thank thee for the beauty
  Thy crooks did so disclose,
While overhead the skylark
  Was singing as he rose ;
The violets tell their story
  To woo the gentle air,
And sail and soaring sea-bird
  Proclaim thee very fair.

VISIT TO A POET'S FAMILY.

(DR. J. A. LANGFORD, BIRMINGHAM.)

I FOUND them in their city-home,
  With love supremely blest,
A poet and his pleasant brood,
  Like doves within their nest ;
And goodly was the cheer they gave
  From warm affection's hoard,
When I, so many miles from home,
  Was sitting at their board.

The faces of the little folks,
  With eyes of blueness blest,
Were beautiful as April flowers
  By Spring's own fingers dressed.
And what uncaroled bliss to take
  Fair Rosy on my knee,
And stroke her curls, and kiss her cheek,
  And hear her speak to me !

O Rosy ! Rosy ! though between
  Are valley, lake, and hill,
And many an English rood of land,
  Thy form is with me still :
Like a delicious thought it comes,
  In poet-beauty clad,
To nerve me in the struggle-time,
  And cheer me when I'm sad.

Ye dwell within the city's bounds,
  Where commerce loves to be ;
I where the white gull rides the wave,
  Beside the western sea.
But long has friendship made us one,
  Amid the strife of men,
By lays and lines of tenderness
  That issue from the pen.

Methought the pictures on the wall,
  The books arranged along,
The hearth a mother's love made bright,
  Had each a voice of song ;
While Willie, with the face of hope,
  Beside the ingle stood,
And looked more fair than ever did
  The sapling of the wood.

O, blissful is the peaceful home,
  Where joys like these are found,
Where rosebuds open in the light,
  And shed their fragrance round ;
Where children love their mother's voice,
  And climb their father's knee,
And hand in hand they travel on,
  That each may happier be.

Good-bye, good-bye ! when far away,
  Where first my song-flower grew ;
In light, or shade, I know I shall
  Full often think of you.
When buds are green, and birds are gay,
  Or when the leaves are sere,
Your memory is a summer joy :
  God bless thee, Rosy dear !

THE AVON.

THE last retreating autumn-dirge
  Swelled slowly on the air ;
  The leaves were changing on the trees,
The arms of some were bare.
The harvest-sheaves were gathered in,
  And garnered safe and dry,
When first I saw the Avon clear
  Beneath a cloudless sky.

O beautiful ! O beautiful
  Its waters as they glide
Through scenes where Shakspere seems to breathe
  In music by its side !
No solemn vision of the night
  To me was half so dear,
As its bright wavelets glancing by,
  Like glass or crystal clear.

Laving the churchyard wall, it flows
  Along its winding way,
Where he, the prince of poets, sleeps,
  Within the chancel grey.
On, on through meads and greenwood glades
  Serenely doth it run,
Where buttercups and marigolds
  Are blinking in the sun.

Slow pealed the great bells from the tower,
  The organ poured its strain ;
Birds in the waters dipped their wings,
  Rose up, then dipped again.
Our shadows were reflected clear
  Within its glassy deeps :
O, fitting teacher of the bard
  Who near its margin sleeps !

O what a joy it was to muse,
  Its shining surface o'er !
Methought I heard the sound of song
  Along its classic shore ;
Ay, every ripple had a voice,
  Which softly shoreward came,
And the green banks upon its edge
  Were whispering Shakspere's name.

And as I wandered by its marge,
  With wonder in my soul,
Sweet feelings I cannot express
  Unbidden o'er me stole.
I thought how pleasant life would be
  Spent in this music hall,
In song and holy intercourse
  With Him who giveth all.

2 H 2

The verdure of the fields around,
  The robin on the latch,
The daisy by the old field stile,
  The sparrow on the thatch,
The hawthorn on the low lane hedge,
  The lark's delicious lay,
Told of the poet-king who has
  Three centuries passed away.

As then, so now the seasons come
  And go, with sun and shower,
And down the lane the little girl
  Is gathering many a flower.
The merry ploughboy, rein in hand,
  Is whistling on the lea,
As when great Shakspere wandered here:
  Now where, O where is he?

Flow on, dear Avon, ever flow:
  When in my home again,
Thine image, like a crystal thought,
  Shall with me still remain.
And when among my Cornish rills,
  Weaving my simple rhyme,
I'll muse on him who sang with thee
  The loftiest lays of time.

THE DECEIVER DECEIVED.

Roons west of the Cheesewring, a butcher by trade
  Of the pale face of Famine was rather afraid,
  Or envious, ambitious, or something or other:
So he sinfully settled to rob a poor mother;
And, thus to accomplish his purposes evil,
To go if he could in the form of the devil.
He tricked himself off in a bullock's black hide,
And his face was made fearful with charcoal beside;
A tail hung behind, with two horns on his head,
And his large rolling eyeballs looked fiery and red:
And thus he stalked off to her cottage of mud,
As much like Old Nick as he possibly could.
He entered the room through some mystical cranny,
And gazed with a groan on the quaking old granny,
Shook his long bushy tail, while his horns seemed to rise,
And the fire-flaps successively flashed from his eyes,
And the breath of his nostrils with brimstone was knit:
She thought he had come from the bottomless pit.
Approaching her bed, he cried with gruff air,
"I'm the monarch of darkness, the prince of despair;
I don't want your body, though I know you are old,
But I'm come for your money, I'm come for your gold.
I've come a long way from the pit of destruction,
And I must have your gold without any reduction."
"O Virgin, assist me! St. Francis, appear!
O come to my rescue! the devil is here!

The grim-visaged black one, with horns on his head,
O murder! O murder! is close by my bed.
Is he come for my money? I pray, Mr. D.,
What is it? what is it you want here with me?"
"I tell thee, old grandam, I don't want thyself,
But all that I wish is thy long-treasured pelf.
Thy money! thy money! I must have the whole,
Or else I'll devour thee, both body and soul."
"O! what shall I do? Will you leave me to fall?
For I've not a farthing to give you at all:
For in order to save my dear gold from the canker,
I let it all out in the hands of the banker."
"Well, never mind, granny, you can't help it, no,
But get it to-morrow; so now I will go.
And when the next midnight shall be on the wane,
I'll call at your snug little cottage again."
And having so said, o'er the staircase he leapt,
And according to custom up the chimney he crept.
When the butcher had vanished, the old woman arose,
And away to the banker she instantly goes;
Related her story; demanded the gold,
Determined to hand it to hard Mr. Bold;
Resolved the next time the devil should call
To yield him her silver, her copper, and all.
The day passed away, and the night came again,
With its mantle of darkness o'er mountain and main,
And granny lay down on her pillow once more,
And blocked up the window and bolted the door,
Expecting old Satan would come as he told,
And rob without mercy her long gathered gold.
The banker, suspecting some trick was on hand,
Had got two police in her chamber to stand,
To wait the approach of this father of fire,
And try if again they could prove him a liar;
And when the grim goblins were starting from sleep,
And Silence was dipping her locks in the deep,
When owlets were screaming, and sprites filled the lane,
The butcher dropt down through the chimney again,
Equipped as before in his imp-mimicked dress,
A frightful old fellow, and flushed with success.
But no sooner had he settled down on the floor
Than he got a hard rap, and he gave a loud roar;
And granny, suspecting no doubt it was thunder,
And that the black monster had clutched all the plunder,
Wrapped the bedsheet in folds round her grey-hooded head,
And without any motion lay down in the bed,
While the butcher was bleeding and groaning and crying,
And she wished in her heart that old Satan was dying.
Having stripped off his scales, they bound the old wag,
And bore him away on a wind-broken nag
To a part of the town where a structure has risen,
And the joke goes around that Old Nick is in prison!
  1842.

SONNETS.

TO THE SKYLARK.

Hail, sweet musician! At the earliest
    dawn,
Shaking the dew-drops from thy
    fluttering wing;
And O how sweet it is to hear thee
    sing,
And drink thy music, floating o'er
    the lawn!
Hail, harper of the cloud! I bend
    me low
In humble adoration at thy shrine,
Rapt with those spirit-notes that round me flow,
Gushing upon my soul in airs divine!
Hail, harper of the cloud! When new-born Day
Peers o'er the mountain-tops, I'll haste away
To drink thy mellow music. Power is thine,
Beloved minstrel, with thy melting hymn,
Stole from the chimings of the cherubim,
To raise my thoughts above earth's dusty line!

TO THE HAWTHORN.

Flower-covered hawthorn! in thy tuneful shade,
    My day's work done, I lay myself along.
    The shepherd loves thee; hind and village maid
Full often carol here their evening song.
As float the vesper-notes those dells among,
And the red light is streaming through the glades,
I gaze and weep,—weep with excess of joy!
Nature is mine; her features never cloy.
Song-honoured hawthorn, fairy of the mead,
Gem of the mountain, beauty of the vale!
Here the young lover tells his tender tale;
And here the poet pipes his artless lay,
Under thy branches whistling on his reed,
Swelling the music of the dying day.

JANUARY.

The New Year wakens like a peevish child
    In Winter's chamber. Nature, his dear nurse,
    Rocks him upon a rolling cradle-cloud,
While the cold winds lift up their voices loud,
Filling the under world with strainings wild,—
A tempest lullaby! In heaps up-piled
The white snow fills the land, a drapery chaste,
On mead productive, moor, and rocky waste.
Echoes the flail from the old barn of thatch,
The wild duck shelters in the frozen fen,
The redbreast hops upon the wooden latch,
And King Frost lords it o'er the icy glen.
Heap up another log. How sad to be
Abroad in such a gale on land or sea!

FEBRUARY.

Snow-drifts and ice! Hushed is the forest-strain,
    Save the small chirrup of the busy wren.
    And, like a monster moaning as in pain,
The great blast tumbles through the dreary fen,
Sweeps the bare hill, and groans along the glen.
Against the white drift on the frozen plain
The gentle snowdrop rests its drooping head;
Looking so beautiful, as if it came
From that dear land where holy angels tread.
O floweret fair, mid storm and whirlwind bred,
White as the cold snow which around thee lies,
How dost thou tell, when bitter winds are fled,
Of lovely wildings under genial skies,
With dew upon their lids, and sunbeams in their eyes!

MARCH.

With fresh gales rushing through the shivering
    trees,
    Drives crashing March. The white clouds
    southward fly,
And up between them shine blue fields of sky.
The lark's first carol rings among the leas.
Now search the moorlands for the earliest flower,
Timidly blushing 'neath the tempest's wing,
Violet and primrose in the sheltered bower;
While little lambs are sporting by the spring.

Beside their teams the merry plough-boys sing.
Twitter the birds where golden furze-flowers shine;
The crocus blossoms in the garden ring,
And wood and wold are full of lays Divine.
The hopeful sower sows the precious seed,
With trust in Heaven, upon the furrowed mead.

APRIL.

WITH one cheek tear-wet, and the other bright
    With passing sunshine, beauty in her eyes;
    On her green garments buds of richest dyes;
Her fair brow bound with leaflets, in the light
Winking and shining, like a timid maid,
Blushing with freshness, seeming half afraid,
Comes changeful April. Violets fill one hand,
And these she scatters o'er the vernal land,
Studding the hedge-rows by the lone sheepfold,
And hanging gems in Nature's silent bowers.
The other doth an urn of waters hold,
Which, in soft tears, she weeps upon the flowers.
Cowslip and primrose round her neck are strung,
And Spring's first notes gush sweetly from her tongue.

MAY.

BEAUTIFUL vestal clad in freshest green,
    Fragrant with hyacinths and flowerets wild!
    Of the twelve months, come, let me crown thee
        queen.
Lover of murmuring brooks and music mild!
The year has not a fairer, lovelier child.
Now lambs play in the fields with daisies white,
The cuckoo's voice flows full among the leaves,
The lark far up is singing out of sight,
And the glad thatcher whistles on the eaves.
The robin's nest scarce shows among the moss,
From hill and valley rings a gladsome lay,
Which floats, love-laden, over crag and cross,
And moor, and mead, and hawthorn-blossomed way,
While Beauty walks the world. 'Tis melody and May.

JUNE.

GREEN fields and music. Like a cheerful bard
    With song surrounded, gushing where she treads,
    Comes joyous June. The great trees bow their
        heads
Full-leafed. On cliff and common hard
Are marks of Summer's fingers. Beauty-starred
Are all the walks of Nature ; gentle eyes
Peer out from grassy windows, and the skies
Are bridged with feathery clouds where angels glide.
Turn we to earth ? The briony and rose
In the green lane are clustering side by side ;
And clover-scents, in showers, are wafted wide
By village stile, and where the fountain flows.
A thousand lyres ring on the gladdened plain,
Burst from the woods, and murmur from the main.

JULY.

HEAT and hay-making ! Through the scented grass
    The sharp scythe rustles, bringing music dear,
    With pastoral echoes, to the listening ear ;
While, in the sunshine, boy and buxom lass
Raise clover-ridges. As the gate we pass
Leading into the meadow, gales of glee
Come floating breeze-borne over lake and lea.
In the tree's shadow stand the panting kine,
Rambles the angler by the limpid stream :
The earth is full of charity Divine ;
Waves the green corn where glancing swallows gleam.
The lanes are loveliness where fair things dream.
A mystery fills creation. Earth, and sea,
And fen, and forest, whisper, Lord, of Thee.

AUGUST.

RIPE fruits and filberts ! Over all the land
    The hot air travels, bearing music bland
    From shining scythe and sickle. Harvest lays
Rise where the white corn, on a hundred hills,
In the broad valleys, by the sparkling rills,
Bends to the joyous reaper ; whilst a haze
Of insect incense fills the world with praise.
Wheat-waving August, in thy straw-bright hair
And leafy zone, with juicy fruitage bound,
What loveliness can with thyself compare ?
Where dwells a queen so greatly, grandly crowned ?
Where'er thou tread'st, the ripe grapes cluster round.
To Him soars up one universal strain,
Who gives the early and the latter rain.

SEPTEMBER.

BEHOLD the year's fruition ! Hedges high,
    And little mounds, where song-nymphs shelter
        shy,
Are bright with berries. Children shout for glee,
As the hedge-bramble yields them a rich store ;
And ruddy apples on the orchard tree
Hang o'er the stream, or by the peasant's door.
The corn is garnered. Down the pensive moor
The swallows glance and wheel, ere they depart
For warmer regions : skilfully they dart
O'er rock and lichened ruin. Here will I
Sit now and watch them. Songs of praise proceed
From grateful souls, whose hearts are beating high
By the farm-house on many a shaven mead
For harvest mercies sent in time of need.

OCTOBER.

BROWN leaves and berries! The old woods are grand
    With the decay of nature. Traces here,
    Which none but poets can decipher clear ;
And there are lines by the great Artist's hand.
A solemn stillness reigns o'er all the land.
Beside these elms I'll watch the skylark soar,
Which sings as though an angel met his view.

The pilgrim pauses on the pensive moor,
And strains his eyes far up the heavenly blue.
Delightful 'tis, as day is waning now,
And the last wood-bird wheels along the air
To seek his mate upon the sheltered bough,
And spend the night in leafy safety there,
To muse on Eden with its valleys fair.

NOVEMBER.

CLOUDS tempest-strided, heavy-sounding rain,
Wind, darkness, cold, make up thy dismal train,
Gloomy November! How the rivers rise
And echo through the hollows! Sadly flies
The last leaf from the forest, whirling round,
Then hurled in anger on the sodden ground.
Sudden the change! The flowers are drowned with tears;
The pastoral field-paths, muddy, tempt no more;
The plover on the open land appears,
And little redbreast ventures near the door;
The ploughman blows his fingers by his team,
The farmer's cart rolls rumbling down the moor.
Books now, and fire, where happy faces gleam,
And cheerful chat, when day's hard toil is o'er.

DECEMBER.

LIKE the last prophet, dark December comes,
Uttering the doom of all things. Hear, my soul,
And profit by the teacher. List the roll
Of surging waters. Not an insect hums;
Carols no bird; cold gloom fills up the whole.
The trees, leaf-stript, lift up their arms in vain
To catch the struggling sunshine. On their steeds
The winds are mounted, prancing o'er the plain,
Then up the hills, then down the vales again.
Like a tried friend returning through the meads

He loved in childhood, after absence long,
To cheer us with his converse, even so
Comes blessed Christmas with its holy song
To gladden once again this world of woe.

MORNING.

HOW beautiful, beneath yon eastern cloud,
Hung like a porter by the gates of Day,
The breezy Morning opes its eye of grey,
Lifting from the glad earth Night's murky shroud!
How freshly from the mountains comes the breeze,
Fanning the robe of Summer, gemmed with flowers;
Shaking the dew-drops from the forest-trees,
And whispering sweetly in the wakening bowers!
The robin stirs among the trembling leaves,
And up the mountain scuds the timid hare;
The sparrows chatter on the shaven eaves,
O'er which the graceful smoke-wreaths curl so fair;
The rising sky-lark sings to greet the dawn,
And the blithe mower whistles on the lawn.

A THRUSH SINGING IN WINTER.

DARK mist-clouds hang upon the naked hills,
Old Winter moans there in his dripping vest;
Wild through the valleys rush the swollen rills
From creek to creek, nor find a place of rest.
A dull, dank shadow shrouds the earth's cold breast,
And everything without is sad and sere;
But, soothing songster, from yon sloping mound
Thy notes come trembling on my joy-filled ear,
As if a minstrel-spirit, glory-crowned,
Sang from the flower-hills of the higher sphere.
Thus, through this tangled wilderness of care,
Mid clouds of sorrow that around me roll,
Some tuneful echoes murmur in the air
The lays of hope, that cheer my trusting soul.

HYMNS.

I. ONE IN CHRIST.

"For ye are all one in Christ Jesus."
—GALATIANS iii. 28.

AN echo on the mountain,
An echo in the glen,

An echo on the highways,
Thronged with the feet of men:
An echo in the forest,
An echo on the sea,
O Jesus Christ of Nazareth,
That we are one in Thee.

One, one in Thee, O Saviour,
The black man and the red,
And he who has in sorrow
No place to lay his head;
The slave with torture crippled,
The fettered and the free,
The servant and his master,
Are one, O Lord, in Thee.

The worker in the city,
And he on hill-top bare,
The man with swarthy visage,
And he with features fair ;
The prince, the poorest pauper,
The plougher of the lea,
The watchman on the turret,
Are one, O Lord, in Thee.

No matter where we worship,
In twilight's temple grey,
Or in the solemn forest,
At the full noon of day ;
With the great congregation,
Or where the few may be,
Or in the poor man's chamber ;
We all are one in Thee.

O hear our prayer, dear Saviour,
Enthroned in light above,
And draw us with Thy Spirit,
And fill us with Thy love.
Let this evangel travel
From farthest sea to sea,
Till all mankind rejoicing
Feel they are one in Thee.

II. FAR OFF A CITY SHINETH.

"And the gates of it shall not be shut at all by day."—
Revelation xxi. 25.

Far off a city shineth,
Described by bards of old,
Whose walls are many-coloured,
Whose streets are solid gold.
No sin within it dwelleth,
No weakness, woe, or strife,
But those whose names are written
Within the Book of Life.

Race after race departeth,
As centuries steal along ;
The student in his study,
The harper at his song.
Yet there that city shineth
Amid the radiant spheres,
With glory on its turrets
As in the early years.

Up to its shining gateways
In ceaseless throngs they go,
From southward, eastward, westward,
With garments white as snow ;
The rich man from his castle,
The poor man from his hut,
The infant and its mother :
Its gates are never shut.

Here shine the Saviour's mansions,
So exquisite, so fair,
Where the redeemed adore Him :
O, when shall we be there ?

Here sadness never enters,
Or frost or fevers eat,
And beauty ever brightens :
Its gates are never shut.

III. THE HOUR OF REST.

"Cast thy burden upon the Lord, and He shall sustain thee."
—Psalm lv. 22.

The hour of rest is come,
The hour of sweet repose ;
Kneel, weary mourner, kneel,
And pour out all thy woes.
Kneel in thy closet, kneel :
Thy Father hears thee pray ;
And He will give the mourner rest,
And take thy load away !

Kneel in thy closet, kneel,
Now busy day is o'er :
Its sorrows and its cares are gone,
And will return no more.
Thy Father sees thee now ;
His eye is everywhere :
O talk to Him as friend to friend,
At this sweet hour of prayer !

Kneel in thy closet, kneel ;
Though rough has been the day,
Kneel down, and tell thy Father all ;
Kneel, weary one, and pray :
Then on thy pillow dream
Of holier, happier bowers,
Where sinless spirits float among
The never-fading flowers !

Yes, on thy pillow dream
Of that bright world above,
Where all is happiness, and peace,
And pure unsullied love.
Dream of that heavenly rest
Which yet remains for thee,
A holy, sweet, unbroken calm
Through all eternity.

IV. BESIDE THE FLOWING WATERS.

"There is none other name under heaven given among
men, whereby we must be saved."—Acts iv. 12.

Beside the flowing waters
Replete with holy psalm
From Zion's solemn arches,
Within the vale of palm ;
Where Christ's own sheep are feeding,
And earthly tumults cease,
Speaketh the gracious Shepherd,
Amid the vines of peace.

"Art thou of walking weary?
Then come to Me and rest;
But wear no other idol
Within thy faithful breast.
No rite, no priest, no prelate,
No robe or altar-flame,
Must shadow o'er My presence,
Or supersede My name."

The blood of Jesus only
Can wash away our sin :
No other house of refuge
Will take the wanderer in.
"Tis Jesus, nought but Jesus,
The true Foundation Stone :
No church or creed or custom,
But Christ, and Christ alone.

Then hope shall fill the future,
And life all beauteous be,
Sweet roses reach the desert,
Heaven's glory gild the sea ;
And love, surpassing knowledge,
Which death cannot destroy,
Nor dust and darkness vanquish,
O'erflow the soul with joy.

V. IN SORROW, ON MY BENDED KNEE.

I will not let Thee go, except Thou bless me."—
GENESIS xxxii. 26.

IN sorrow, on my bended knee,
I come again, O Lord, to Thee :
The road is rough, the hills are high,
And dangers in my passage lie ;
Dark clouds shut out the cheering sun :
Reveal thy presence, Holy One !

Thou know'st that I have nought to plead,
But utter helplessness and need,
And His great love so full and free,
Who gave His precious life for me.
O, for the sake of Thy dear Son,
Reveal Thy presence, Holy One !

I dare not let my Saviour go
Till some small blessing He bestow,
Although the mountains far away
Are brightening in the beams of day :
Arise, O soul-reviving Sun,
And cheer my spirit, Holy One !

Along life's course be Thou my Guide ;
Till, crossed at last the swelling tide,
I walk the heavenly shores of joy,
And join the angels' glad employ ;
My rest attained, my labour done ;
For ever with the Holy One.

VI. REJOICE, REJOICE! THE LIGHT OF LOVE.

"We have found Him, of whom Moses in the Law, and
the Prophets, did write, Jesus of Nazareth, the son of
Joseph."—JOHN i. 45.

REJOICE, rejoice ! The Light of Love
Has reached us from the realms above,
He whom the bards and seers of old
In strains of wondrous song foretold ;
The great Beginning and the End ;
O ! we have found the sinner's Friend.

The mountain-tops are bright with day,
The clouds before His light give way,
The flowers appear, the streams have birth,
And verdure decks the smiling earth ;
Sweet hymns arise from valleys green ;
O ! we have found the Nazarene.

The prisoner now shall lose his bands,
The chains fall off the captive's hands,
The broken-hearted sigh no more,
The Gospel cheer the bruised and poor,
The blind behold His beams afar ;
O ! we have found the Morning Star.

O ! may we learn to prize His worth
Beyond the dearest things of earth,
And as we travel on our way
Look up to Him from day to day ;
Whose boundless love shall never cease :
O ! we have found the Prince of Peace.

His promise is our only stay ;
He takes the sinner's load away :
He makes the wounded spirit whole,
For none but Christ can save the soul.
O ! may we ever heed His call,
Since we have found our All in All.

VII. LIKE RAIN FROM HEAVEN ON THIRSTY ROOTS.

"For as the rain cometh down, and the snow from
heaven, and returneth not thither, but watereth the earth,
and maketh it bring forth and bud, that it may give seed
to the sower, and bread to the eater : so shall My word be
that goeth forth out of My mouth : it shall not return unto
Me void, but it shall accomplish that which I please, and
it shall prosper in the thing whereto I sent it."—ISAIAH
lv. 10, 11.

LIKE rain from heaven on thirsty roots,
Or snow that melts among the shoots,
Causing the earth prolonged increase,
That bread for man may never cease :
So shall Thy word, Jehovah, be,
Returning with Thine own to Thee.

The hills shall shout in tuneful bands,
The trees lift up their leafy hands,
The fir supplant the prickly thorn,
The myrtle glades of green adorn ;
Which is to Him a solemn sign,
That never, never, shall decline.

The blind shall His compassion see,
The captive's faith shall set him free,
The weary wanderer rest attain,
The broken spirit peace regain,
The high before His footstool fall,
And crown Immanuel Lord of all.

Go forth, and sow the precious seed
On stony ground and fruitful mead,
At morn, at noon, at daylight's fall,
In open space, or crevice small;
With trust in His Divine decree;
And fruit shall wave from sea to sea.

VIII. THIS MAN RECEIVETH SINNERS.

" This man receiveth sinners, and eateth with them."—
LUKE xv. 2.

WERE ever words so tender?
Were ever words so true?
This Man receiveth sinners,
The Gentile and the Jew:
No matter where he dwelleth,
On continent or isle,
This Man receiveth sinners,
The vilest of the vile.

Behold it plainly written
Upon the blue above,
And on the sloping mountain
Where tremble hymns of love;
It floateth o'er the waters,
And through the forest-aisle,
This Man receiveth sinners,
The vilest of the vile.

And when the tall trees murmur
Beneath the rising moon,
And the fresh breeze is blowing
Upon the brow of Noon;
It flows in solemn whispers
Along each deep defile,
This Man receiveth sinners,
The vilest of the vile.

Old age with erring hoary,
And manhood's walk of sin,
The first forsaking footstep
May turn and enter in;
The door of hope is open,
And Mercy pleads the while,
This Man receiveth sinners,
The vilest of the vile.

Thrice welcome, precious teaching!
To Christ's own arms I flee:
This Man receiveth sinners;
Then He receiveth me,
A wanderer in the desert,
An erring child of grace,
Who am the chief of sinners,
The vilest of the vile.

Far down the mighty river
Towards time's setting sun.
In waves of welcome sweetness
This holy theme shall run;
Till every hill and valley
With Sharon's Rose shall smile,
And Jesus claim victorious
The vilest of the vile.

IX. TOILING OVER DESERTS WIDE.

" Thou shalt guide me with Thy counsel, and afterward
receive me to glory."—PSALM lxxiii. 24.

TOILING over deserts wide,
Thou, O Lord, shalt be my Guide,
And Thy counsel my sure stay,
As I travel on my way;
Till the home of rest I gain,
Evermore with Christ to reign.

Like a child, O Prince Divine,
Would I place my hand in Thine;
Not a single footstep take
If Thy presence me forsake:
O how soon my feet will slide
If I leave my heavenly Guide!

Here the way is long and lone,
There with briers overgrown;
Here are precipices high,
With their frontlets to the sky;
Dangers crowd on every side;
Lead me, lead me, heavenly Guide!

Shall I murmur that the land
Is so barren on each hand,—
That no watersprings are near
To refresh the desert drear?
No! I dare not leave Thy side:
It is best to trust my Guide.

Take my hand, and lead Thy child
As Thou pleasest o'er the wild.
What I now receive from Thee
Will at last be best for me,
Till my bark the winds outride,
Anchored safely with my Guide.

X. ALL HIDDEN THINGS, AND THINGS WE SEE.

" Are not two sparrows sold for a farthing? and one of
them shall not fall on the ground without your Father.
But the very hairs of your head are all numbered."—
MATT. x. 29, 30.

ALL hidden things, and things we see,
Are governed by His wise decree.
He feeds the varied living race,
And gives to each its proper place;
Nor does the little sparrow die
Without the notice of His eye.

The very hairs upon our head
Are known to Him who gives us bread;
He watches o'er us day by day,
And guides His people on their way;
Till pain is past and labour done,
The journey closed and heaven is won.

O let this thought our spirits cheer,
While far from home we travel here,
Refreshed sometimes with airs of love
Which greet us from the land above:
He feeds the birds where'er they be,
And He will much more care for me.

O may our faith in Him increase
Whose love and mercy never cease;
And though our path be sometimes dim,
Still let us put our trust in Him
Who feeds the birds where'er they be,
And He will much more care for me.

XI. IT IS MY DAY OF TROUBLE.

"Call upon Me in the day of trouble: I will deliver thee,
and thou shalt glorify Me."—PSALM l. 15.

IT is my day of trouble,
   The sky is overcast,
   The sun withdraws in shadow,
The wild winds hurry past;
Distress o'erwhelms my spirit,
Deep sorrows round me roll;
The melancholy waters
Are come into my soul.

It is my day of trouble,
   The way to walk is dim;
I cannot see my Saviour,
   Yet will I trust in Him.
Lift up Thy lovingkindness,
And chase away my night;
O let me gain Thy favour,
And travel in Thy light.

It is my day of trouble,
   My tears to Thee are known;
My sighs in secret places
   Where bitter waters moan.
Thus come I heavy-laden
With sorrow sore distressed,
Nor seek I aught but Jesus,
Whose love will give me rest.

I plead the mighty promise,
   Thine own Divine decree,—
"Call in the day of trouble:
   I will deliver thee."
Behold me brokenhearted
Before Thy footstool bow:
O answer my petition,
And come and save me now.

The light of life is breaking!
   Deliverance comes to me:
The Saviour whispers pardon:
   My captive soul is free!

My heart shall sing His praises,
   Who to my rescue came;
And ever travelling homeward,
   Shall glorify His name.

XII. IN THE PLACE PREPARED FOR THEE.

"And the Lord, whom ye seek, shall suddenly come to
His temple, even the Messenger of the Covenant, whom
ye delight in."—MALACHI iii. 1.

IN the place prepared for Thee,
   Hear us, mystic Trinity:
   Lowly at Thy feet we fall,
Hiding nothing, owning all;
Seeking pardon for our crimes,
Acted o'er so many times.

O forgive our wanderings wide
For the sake of Him who died;
Show us Thy forgiving face;
Now enrich us with Thy grace.
Wash us in the purple tide,
Flowing from the Saviour's side.

May we at this solemn hour
Feel the Spirit's healing power;
In the silence of the soul
Worship Him who fills the whole,
Looking off from earthly love
To our great High Priest above.

Not that men may hear our prayer
Sounding on the solemn air;
Not to wear a saintly face,
Meet we in this holy place:
Rather would we worship here
In the silence of the tear.

Dear Redeemer, Prince Divine,
On our natural darkness shine;
With Thy erring children stay;
Speak our numerous sins away.
May we feel that Thou art nigh,—
Jesus Christ is passing by.

XIII. FROM HEIGHTS WHERE ANGELS GATHER.

"And what I say unto you I say unto all, Watch."—
MARK xiii. 37.

FROM heights where angels gather,
   From depths where mortals moan,
   Where rills leap down the mountain
From shining stone to stone;
Far up where pines are swaying,
Deep down where waters fall,
"Watch, watch," is ever floating;
The echo is for all.

It murmurs in the laurels
Around the rich man's door,

And by the humble cottage
Upon the lonely moor.
It travels through the city ;
It soundeth on the sea :
"O weary not with watching.
But put your trust in Me."

O may we heed the warning
Of God's eternal Son.
The Lord of life and glory,
Who spake and it was done ;
And evermore be watching
Upon the silent tower
For the bright beams of morning
O'er Eden's holy bower.

What wisdom to be ready
To meet the Man of Might,
Whose summons may o'ertake us
Ere evening's fading light !
Our hearts to Thee are lifted
For guidance on our way :
O precious Intercessor,
Help us to watch and pray.

Though weary oft with waiting,
And the wide landscape dim,
The promise never faileth,
Our hope is still in Him.
The King of glory cometh ;
He will not long delay
Over the earth to scatter
The beams of perfect day.

XIV.   SINK THE DAYS INTO THE SERE.

"And we all do fade as a leaf."—Isaiah lxiv. 6.

SINK the days into the sere,
Pensive, old, decrepit year :
Earth has dampness and decay ;
Sigh the winds along their way :
Like the leaves that round us lie,
So we fade away and die.

In the morn our step is strong ;
Oft we halt ere even-song :
Fail the fields with verdure drest:
This we know is not our rest.
Like the leaves when cold winds sigh,
So we fade away and die.

Teach us wisdom, King of love,
Lift our wandering thoughts above :
O'er our heart's affections reign :
May we all Thy favour gain.
Fit us for our home on high,
Ere we fade away and die.

In the land of light unseen
Hill and vale are over green,
Roses die not by the stream,
Where the living waters gleam.
Jesus, take us to the sky,
When we fade away and die.

XV.   AT OUR HEART'S DOOR THE KNOCKER.

"Behold, I stand at the door, and knock : if any man hear My voice, and open the door, I will come in to him, and will sup with him, and he with Me."—Revelation iii. 20.

AT our heart's door the Knocker
Still strives our thought to win :
He knocketh, knocketh, knocketh ;
O let us let Him in !
His locks are wet with waiting,
He gives one warning more :
Hark ! how He knocketh, knocketh ;
Now let us ope the door.

In spring, in pleasant summer,
When Autumn strips the tree,
When winter snows are falling,
That Knocker knocketh He.
He knocketh, knocketh, knocketh,
Although the wind may roar ;
And still His hand is lifted
To give one warning more.

How oft the solemn Knocker
Is in the firelight heard,
And when the sigh of sickness
Our inmost soul has stirred !
He knocketh, knocketh, knocketh,
When household flowers are fled ;
He knocketh, knocketh, knocketh,
When stars are over head.

He knocketh, knocketh, knocketh,
When verdure fills the trees,
When sounds from summer songsters
Are floating on the breeze :
And when the sleet is driving
In fury up the hill,
And the storm lifts its trumpet,
He knocketh, knocketh still.

He knocks in life's young morning,
In manhood's powerful prime,
And when the locks with watching
Are silvered o'er by time.
He knocketh, knocketh, knocketh,
Still standing at the door,
In wind and rain and tempest
Yet knocking evermore.

Now let us open quickly
And give the Knocker room,
Ere He depart for ever
And leave us to our doom.
He knocketh, knocketh, knocketh ;
Here will we seek His face,
And feast upon His favour,
The supper of His grace.

XVI. STRIPT OF ALL BUT SIN AND SHAME.

" My God shall supply all your need according to His riches
in glory by Christ Jesus."— PHILIPPIANS iv, 19.

STRIPT of all but sin and shame,
Call I on my Saviour's name.
Hear me from Thy home on high ;
May I feel my Helper nigh !
Nought but Jesus do I plead,
He is all the sinner's need.

None who travel to the sky
Can be half as poor as I.
Wandering oft where willows be,
Struggling to look up to Thee ;
I am feebleness indeed,
Yet Thou wilt supply my need.

O the riches of His grace
Now within the holy place !
Though my wants may number more
Than the sands upon the shore,
Christ for me doth intercede ;
Jesus will supply my need.

He is near to quell my fears
When my path is wet with tears ;
He will not desert my side
In the midst of death's dark tide ;
Christ, who for my sin did bleed,
Will supply my every need.

XVII. THE LORD SHALL CHOOSE FOR ME.

" He shall choose our inheritance for us."— PSALM xlvii. 4.

I ASK Thy heavenly guidance
In all things here below :
Do Thou direct my footsteps
The way that I should go.
O teach my heart submission,
Whate'er my lot may be,
Contented that my Father
Should ever choose for me.

With Thee I do not falter
To walk the dim unknown :
The yet untrodden future
Is in Thy hands alone ;
And be it sun or shadow,
Rough waves or smiling sea,
A garden or a desert,
The Lord shall choose for me.

If up the stony mountain
My painful pathway lie,
Or through the darksome valley,
I dare not question why.
The fields may lose their verdure,
And leafless rise the tree ;
All things are ordered wisely :
The Lord shall choose for me.

If in deep shades I wander,
Where clouds obscure the sun,
And flow no streams of comfort,
Thy perfect will be done :
What now appeareth dimly
I soon shall fully see,
Where God's own glory shineth ;
The Lord shall choose for me.

And when the cord of silver
At last shall loose its hold,
And in the strife is broken
The mystic bowl of gold ;
When loving friends are watching,
And earthly shadows flee ;
As heaven's first beams are breaking,
The Lord shall choose for me.

XVIII. BENEATH THE LEAFY BRANCHES.

" But thou, when thou prayest, enter into thy closet, and
when thou hast shut thy door, pray to thy Father which is
in secret ; and thy Father which seeth in secret shall reward thee openly."— MATTHEW vi. 6.

BENEATH the leafy branches
With hues of evening drest,
I seek my silent closet
Where Nature is at rest.
The sighing winds shall strengthen
The ardour of my prayer,
While pensive forest murmurs
Fill up the summer air.

Drip, drip, the falling waters
Upon the pebbly shore ;
Folded in evening's curtain
Now let me shut the door,
And pray to Him who dwelleth
High in the secret place,
Who openly rewardeth
The seeker of His face.

He loved the silent mountain
When stars were on the deep,
And there the precious Saviour
Would oft His vigil keep ;
And now His cheering presence
Is everywhere made known,
Each coppice is a closet,
Each crag an altar-stone.

The mighty murmuring forest,
The fields with flowerets fair,
The green well-watered valleys,
Are all perfumed with prayer.
The universe is hallowed
Wherever man may trace,
And hangs o'er all creation
The mystery of His grace.

Within my quiet chamber,
Out on the lonely hill,
Where honeysuckles clamber
Beside the village mill,

Where busy feet are passing,
In Zion's palmy shade,
On land, or on the ocean,
My closet can be made.

Thus kneel I here where roses
Are bending o'er my brow :
Almighty Resurrection,
Lift up my spirit now ;
Clothe me in holy vestments
From the celestial plains,
And fill this leafy arbour
With high seraphic strains.

XIX. THE DAY DEPARTS, THE SUNBEAMS FLEE.

" Wait on the Lord : be of good courage, and He shall strengthen thine heart : wait, I say, on the Lord."—Psalm xxvii. 14.

The day departs, the sunbeams flee,
Yet wait we here, O Lord, for Thee ;
The dew falls fast on flower and spray,
Yet shall our courage not give way ;
He will all needful grace impart,
And cheer the earnest seeker's heart.

No matter where our prayer may rise,
'Neath temple-roof or spreading skies,
In every place the Lord is near,
To mark the sigh and see the tear,
To make the wounded spirit whole,
And renovate the waiting soul.

We need no words from sin to flee,
We need no words to come to Thee ;
The silent sorrow of the soul,
The sigh that Christ may make us whole,
The waiting heart, the fond desire,
Will bring the peace our minds require.

Thus do we here in silence bow ;
O blessed Spirit, hear us now !
Down at Thy feet we lowly lie,
And wait for Him who passeth by,
Whose love can cheer the weakest heart,
Assured that He will strength impart.

XX. TAKE MY HAND : THE WAY IS STEEP.

" Thou hast holden me by my right hand."—Psalm lxxiii. 23.

Take my hand : the way is steep,
And the mire is dark and deep.
O, I know not where to tread ;
Clouds are gathering over head.
Do not let my footsteps stray :
Dearest Father, lead the way.

Take my hand : my faith is weak :
Let me hear Thee inly speak.

May my spirit drink again
Balm from Gilead's palmy plain :
Now divinest strength impart :
Dearest Saviour, cheer my heart.

Take my hand : the waters roar,
Breaking on the barren shore ;
Shake the branches on the hill :
Jesus, whisper, " Peace, be still."
Light of Life, break forth at length,
Calm the ocean's raging strength.

Take my hand : on Thee I rest ;
Where Thou leadest it is best :
Whether it be foul or fair,
Whether it be bleak or bare,
Over waste or fragrant dell,
Where Thou leadest, all is well.

XXI. THOUGHTS CROWD THE SPIRIT'S PORTAL.

" In the multitude of my thoughts within me Thy comforts delight my soul."—Psalm xciv. 19.

Thoughts crowd the spirit's portal
Of sad or gentler mood,
In daylight and in darkness,
An endless multitude :
When rise the summer vespers,
When falls the chilling snow,
Forth on their mystic mission
In silent ranks they go.

They come with looks of sadness,
They smile with faces bright ;
Some wear the weeds of mourning,
And some are clothed in light ;
Some have the hues of Mammon,
And some display the tear,
With meekness in their features
And gentleness and fear.

Some bear a worldly burden,
Some seek a lowly place,
Some wander mid the shadows,
And some are fraught with grace.
Yet in this mighty army
How very few there be
Which bear upon their banners
Remembrances of Thee !

Amid this busy legion,
Close-marshalled on my way,
This wasting war of silence,
Thy comforts are my stay :
Thy promise is the pillar
Which glitters in the gloom,
The everlasting beacon
To light me through the tomb.

How precious are Thy comforts
Which flow on wings Divine,
In morning's balmy breezes,
Or at the eve's decline !

O come, restoring Spirit!
The wounded heart make whole;
And may the Saviour's presence
Delight my waiting soul!

XXII. LOWLY LET ME EVER LIE.

"Let every man be swift to hear, slow to speak."—
JAMES i. 19.

Lowly let me ever lie
At the feet of the Most High,
In the valley take my place,
Learning lessons of His grace,
His unerring guidance seek,
Swift to hear and slow to speak.

As I calmly onward go
Through this changeful scene below,
May I ever strive to be
Prized when most it pleaseth Thee;
Only strong when I am weak,
Swift to hear and slow to speak.

Seek I here my Saviour's aid
In the lowly valley's shade,
Overhung with Gospel vines,
Where Humility reclines,
Underneath the pointed peak,
Swift to hear and slow to speak.

Thus may I pursue my race,
Thankful for the lowest place;
Though the world may pass me by,
In the valley let me lie;
Ever prayerful, ever meek,
Swift to hear and slow to speak.

XXIII. THOU ART OUR SUN, DEAR SAVIOUR.

"For the Lord God is a sun and shield: the Lord will
give grace and glory: no good thing will He withhold from
them that walk uprightly."—PSALM lxxxiv. 11.

Thou art our sun, dear Saviour,
To light us on our way;
The shield of our protection
In every trial-day.
How sweet to feel Thy favour
For evermore the same!
Thou wilt give grace and glory
To all who love Thy name:

Grace in this lower region,
Where oft Thy people sigh,
Weighed down with tribulation;
And glory in the sky.
O glory which excelleth!
O brightness without stain,
Which man cannot imagine
Nor angel-mind explain!

Grace in the hour of trial;
Grace when the heavens are bowed,
And the far sky of comfort
Is hidden in a cloud;
Grace when the spirit faileth;
Grace when the foe is near;
And glory everlasting
Where never falls the tear.

To those that walk uprightly
The promise is not slack:
No blessing Thou withholdest,
No good thing shall they lack.
Thou wilt give grace and glory
Which cannot be expressed,
The splendour of the city,
The beauty of the blest.

Thus rest we on Thy promise,
Our sure unfailing stay,
Which ever more upholdeth,
And never can give way.
Do with us as Thou pleasest;
Whate'er Thy will may be,
Thou wilt give grace and glory:
We leave it all with Thee.

XXIV. WHEN THUNDERS SHAKE THE CITY.

"I will bless the Lord at all times."—PSALM xxxiv. 1.

When thunders shake the city,
When tempests smite the sea,
When torrents sweep the valleys,
And winds uproot the tree,
When earth is wrapped in shadow,
Through which the lightnings flame,
Amid the great commotion
Still let me bless Thy name.

And when the spirit droopeth
For lack of heavenly rain,
And tribulations thicken
Upon the barren plain;
When sorrow leaves me lonely,
And sickness bows my frame,
Amid forsaken friendships,
Still let me bless Thy name.

And when the harvest faileth,
And there is no supply
To meet the stricken reaper,
And all the wells are dry;
When poverty approacheth
And want assails the frame,
O teach my heart submission;
Still let me bless Thy name.

Sit with me, Great Refiner,
And watch beside the clay:
O purify my spirit,
And take the dross away.
May I be trustful ever,
In life and death the same;
And whether sun or shadow,
Still let me bless Thy name.

XXV. WHERE SHALL WE FLY FOR SUCCOUR?

"Lord, to whom shall we go? Thou hast the words of
eternal life."—JOHN vi. 68.

WHERE shall we fly for succour
But to the Prince Divine,
Whose word is life eternal,
The ever-living Vine?
Thou art the sinner's refuge,
Our only hope and stay:
O none but Christ the Saviour
Can take our sins away!

The name of Jesus only
Is to the guilty given,
To guide us o'er the desert,
And bring us home to heaven.
O precious, precious Saviour,
We at Thy footstool fall,
And worship Thee in spirit,
Our Advocate, our All.

With Thee is present pardon
For all our sinful race;
Thy boundless lovingkindness
Doth all the world embrace.
The voice of Jesus pleadeth,
He waiteth to forgive:
O wonderful compassion!
The worst may turn and live.

How sweet these heavenly tidings
To hearts oppressed with care!
How precious round Thine altar
To kneel in praise and prayer!
The kingdom of the Blessed,
Foretold so long ago,
Through mystic type and shadow,
Abides with man below.

Be with us on our journey,
To guide us in the way:
O do not let us wander!
O do not let us stray!
Till, crossed the rolling river,
We cease our earthly race,
And on the mount of glory
Behold Thee face to face.

XXVI. PRINCE OF PRINCES. GIVE US GRACE.

"And let us run with patience the race that is set before
us, looking unto Jesus, the Author and Finisher of our
faith."—HEBREWS xii. 1, 2.

PRINCE of princes, give us grace
To pursue the heavenly race,
Never in our duties slack,
Never, never looking back,
Life and all things to resign,
Striving for the faith Divine.

Grant us patience day by day,
Step by step along our way:
Guided may we ever be
In the path marked out by Thee:
From our fears and doubtings cease,
Striving after perfect peace.

Lead us on through pastures new,
With the Prince of Life in view.
He the Author, He the End,
Jesus Christ the sinner's Friend;
Who will give us here His love,
And the rest of heaven above.

Lift we now our anxious eyes
To the Ruler of the skies:
O descend our souls to bless,
Clothe us with Thy righteousness.
Let Thy power on us be shown,
Then transport us to Thy throne.

XXVII. SEEK WHEN THE FLOWER IS FRESHEST.

"But seek ye first the kingdom of God, and His righteousness; and all these things shall be added unto you."—
MATTHEW vi. 33.

SEEK when the flower is freshest,
Seek when the morn is young;
Seek when the shining dewdrops
Upon the boughs are strung;
Seek when the heart is tender,
Seek when the world is fair;
Seek in the early dawning:
Bow down to Him in prayer.

He loves the opening blossoms
Which April suns awake;
He loves the smallest effort
Put forth for Zion's sake;
He loves the first fair fruitage
On Reason's sacred tree:
Seek first the Saviour's kingdom,
And all is well with thee.

Seek first this heavenly blessing
Of holiness and peace,
The righteousness of Jesus
Whence pure delights increase;
And favour shall be added,
The bountiful, the free,
From His eternal storehouse,
Whate'er is best for thee.

O leave it to His choosing,
Whatever is thy lot;
It were not well possessing
The idols of thy thought.
In this thou wouldst be erring;
Then let it calm thy breast,
That in thy daily travel
He knoweth what is best.

All needful things are promised
To those who seek His love,—

His presence on their journey,
And purer joys above.
Seek first Messiah's kingdom,
The mighty Prince Divine,
Whose love all love excelleth ;
And everything is thine.

XXVIII. ASK WHEN THE WATER RISETH.

"Ask, and it shall be given you ; seek, and ye shall find;
knock, and it shall be opened unto you :..For every one
that asketh receiveth ; and he that seeketh findeth ; and to
him that knocketh it shall be opened."—MATTHEW vii. 7, 8.

ASK when the water riseth,
Seek when the sunbeams flee,
Knock when the tears are falling,
And Christ shall answer thee :
For every one that seeketh
With all his heart, shall find
The ever-blessed Saviour,
The Friend of human kind.

How positive the promise
The Holy Spirit gives !
The poor awakened sinner
Repents, believes, and lives.
The face of Nature changes;
The darkness flies away ;
And gladdened hill and valley
Bathe in the beams of day.

Ask, and the clouds shall vanish,
Bright sunlight fill the sky;
Seek, and the vine shall flourish,
Although the land is dry ;
Knock, and the door of mercy
Shall open at the sound ;
For every one that striveth
Shall walk on holy ground.

He shall remove the hardness,
The stupor of the soul ;
The precious balm of Gilead
Shall make the wounded whole.
Again we bow in spirit
Before the Great Unseen,
Believing that the fountain
Can wash the foulest clean.

We need no more, dear Saviour,
Here is enough for all :
O may we seek Thy favour,
And listen to Thy call;
Embrace with deep contrition
What Thou dost freely give
To every one that thirsteth ;
Pray earnestly, and live.

XXIX. O COME, MY SAVIOUR, BRING ME LIGHT !

"He giveth power to the faint ; and to them that have
no might He increaseth strength."—ISAIAH xl. 29.

O COME, my Saviour, bring me light :
To-day Thou see'st I have no might ;

My strength is gone, my hands hang down,
And tears shut out the conqueror's crown.
My faith is small, my foes are strong :
O Saviour ! do not tarry long.

I plead Thy sovereign saving grace,
Vouchsafed to me and all my race.
Whoever humbly asks Thine aid
Shall feel Thy healing power displayed ;
The weak shall walk, the low shall rise,
The feeble enter Paradise.

From babes in Christ shall praises rise
Which will confound the great and wise ;
The faint Thy favour shall enjoy,
The widow's heart shall sing for joy,
The drooping pilgrim strength obtain,
Refreshed anew with heavenly rain.

Enough, enough ! The weak shall be
Restored to perfect power by Thee.
I'll take the grace Thou hast bestowed,
And travel on my homeward road,
Although through faintness and through fear :
My Jesus will be ever near.

XXX. THERE IS NO FRIEND LIKE JESUS.

"If God be for us, who can be against us?"—ROMANS viii. 31.

THERE is no friend like Jesus,
Whose own arm sets us free :
If heaven's high King is for us,
Who can against us be ?
Our foes may rise in armies,
Like giants fierce and tall,
In overwhelming numbers :
His breath shall quench them all.

If God, the great Creator,
The everlasting Light,
Uphold us in the conflict,
Support us in the fight,
What foe shall dare withstand us
In travelling to the skies ?
In spite of warring legions
Our faith shall win the prize.

He who in wondrous pity
Restored us from the fall
By His dear Son our Saviour,
Will surely give us all.
The riches of His glory
No human thought can reach,
Nor highest angel utter,
Nor burning seraph teach.

Then let all doubt be scattered
Before His rising ray :
All hail the true Messiah !
Bring in the perfect day,
When lamb and lion fondle,
Where cruelty shall cease,
Within the flowery valleys
Of everlasting peace.

XXXI. THE KING IS COME, FORETOLD SO LONG.

"For unto you is born this day in the city of David a Saviour, which is Christ the Lord....Glory to God in the highest, and on earth peace, good will toward men."—Luke ii. 11, 14.

The King is come, foretold so long :
The earth is now one strain of song :
O'er town and tower the billows swell,
O'er mead and moor, o'er down and dell :
The wilds rejoice, in glory clad,
And every mountain-top is glad.

Behold Him in a manger laid :
The star appears in heaven's high glade :
The shepherds hear the angelic strain,
And leave their flocks upon the plain ;
While overhead bright seraphs sing
In honour of our Saviour King.

O precious, precious guiding Star,
Which cheers the sinner's eye afar,
And lights us through the deeps of time
To regions holy and sublime !
O may we our best offerings bring
In honour of our Saviour King !

Still swells the song through every sky,
"All glory be to God on high !
Good will to men : from shore to shore
Let peace prevail for evermore."
And rivers roll and forests ring
In honour of our Saviour King.

Then let all hearts rejoice to-day
In every cot and castle grey :
The Prince has left His holy place,
To ransom all our fallen race.
Rejoice, rejoice : let nature ring
In honour of our Saviour King.

XXXII. HOW OFTEN ON OUR JOURNEY.

"Weeping may endure for a night, but joy cometh in the morning."—Psalm xxx. 5.

How often on our journey
The silent tear will fall !
A measured sum of sorrow
Is portioned out to all.
The indigent, the wealthy,
The sick man in his room,
The widow, and the orphan,
Have all their share of gloom.

The night of dark contrition,
Of penitence and prayer,
For so much sin committed
With lifted arm and bare
Against the loving Father,
Whose hand upholds the whole,
Will bring a joyous morning
Of beauty to the soul.

A life of inward striving
Till worldly walking cease,
With much of tribulation,
But in the Saviour peace.
A night of solemn weeping,
Of battle and annoy
From foemen in the darkness,
And then the morning joy ;

The melting of the vapours
The glistening peaks above,
The sound of angel-harpers
Upon the shores of love,
The sea of flaming crystal,
The seraph's soaring wing,
The anthems of the holy,
The glory of the King.

Then let us wipe our eyelids,
And lift our hearts on high ;
The golden morning breaketh,
Its tints are on the sky,
When sin and sorrow vanished
Shall cloud the earth no more,
And Christ's abiding kingdom
Extend from shore to shore.

XXXIII. PURSUE THY WAY WITH PATIENCE.

"But go thou thy way till the end be : for thou shalt rest, and stand in thy lot at the end of the days."—Daniel xii. 13.

Pursue thy way with patience,
Whate'er thy lot may be :
Throughout thy earthly journey
Thy God shall choose for thee.
The Lord is thy protector,
He knoweth what is best :
O leave it all with Jesus,
And heaven shall be thy rest.

How rapidly approacheth
The end of all things here !
With Jesus for thy leader
Thou hast no cause to fear :
He strengthens the believer
To walk His blessed ways,
So that with joy he standeth
At the full end of days.

Pursue thy way with meekness,
And nothing shalt thou lack :
Heed not the false deceiver
Who strives to turn thee back.
Thy crown is with thy Captain :
O give Him perfect praise !
He shall reward His servant
At the full end of days.

Then rest upon His promise ;
With God's own truth comply ;
Gird on the Gospel armour ;
Jehovah cannot lie.

The earth, the heavens shall vanish,
In one consuming blaze ;
But in thy lot thou standest
At the full end of days.

Go on thy way believing
Towards the heavenly goal,
And higher revelations
Shall beautify thy soul ;
Till mid the trees of Eden—
Where Israel's prophets sing,
And martyrs chant their story—
Thou walkest with thy King.

XXXIV. WHETHER MY BURDEN PRESSES.

"In all thy ways acknowledge Him, and He shall direct thy paths."—PROVERBS iii. 6.

WHETHER my burden presses,
Whether my load be light,
Whether I sigh in secret,
Or journey on through night ;
Whether my conflicts thicken,
Whether the shadows flee,
In barrenness or verdure,
May I acknowledge Thee !

In things of smallest measure,
In deeds of higher grade,
In all my daily duties,
In travel and in trade,
In lying down, in rising,
Whether engaged or free,
In time, in holy talent,
May I acknowledge Thee !

In winter, spring, in summer,
And when the leaves are dry ;
When painful disappointment
Brings tears into mine eye ;
In health, in solemn sickness,
Thy goodness may I see,
In life, in death, for ever
Acknowledge only Thee !

How like a star the promise
Shines with unfailing ray !
Along the lonely desert
The Lord shall mark my way.
If Him my heart acknowledge,
Direction will be given,
So that my path shall issue
In holiness and heaven.

O help me, Prince eternal,
To follow Thy command,
To seek in each condition
The guidance of Thy hand.
Whate'er Thy mercy orders
For ever be my guest,
Till in the groves of glory
My happy spirit rest.

XXXV. HIDE NOT THY FACE, DEAR SAVIOUR.

"Though He slay me, yet will I trust in Him."—JOB xiii. 15.

HIDE not Thy face, dear Saviour ;
I fall before Thee now :
The tears are on my eyelids,
A cloud is on my brow :
My hands to Thee are lifted,
My heart to Thee I raise :
O come and cheer my spirit,
And let me sound Thy praise.

O help me, holy Jesus,
Out of myself to flee ;
So utterly unworthy
To lift mine eyes to Thee ;
So very, very sinful ;
So apt to turn astray
Amid forbidden pastures,
And leave the narrow way.

O heed a sinner's sorrow,
Whose feet are in the dust :
Come quickly, dear Redeemer :
In Thee is all my trust.
Lift up the feeble-minded :
O draw my thoughts above,
And let me feel Thy favour,
And take me to Thy love.

Although Thine axe descending
Should smite the barren tree,
And slay me in Thine anger,
Yet will I trust in Thee.
Yet will I cling to Jesus
Amid the anxious fight,
Although it waxeth hotter
In darkness and in light.

Thy love no tongue explaineth
Which man and angel drink :
O no, Thou wilt not suffer
My fainting soul to sink.
In Thee the grave is conquered,
And Death has lost his sting :
None other name but Jesus,
My Saviour and my King.

XXXVI. THIS IS THE LAND OF PARTING.

"When my father and my mother forsake me, then the Lord will take me up."—PSALM xxvii. 10.

THIS is the land of parting ;
We go from whence we came ;
Dust unto dust returneth ;
But Jesus is the same.
The hills shall leave their places,
The sea forsake its shore ;
But Jesus Christ the Saviour
Remains for evermore.

How oft our kindred leave us,
And vanish from our track
Over the world's wide surface,
And never more come back !
Near friends, too, may deceive us,
So that we suffer blame,
And sigh among the thickets ;
But Jesus is the same.

And now He loves as truly,
His mercy is as free,
As when He fully pardoned
The poor of Galilee;
His heart is still as tender
As when from heaven He came
To rescue us from darkness :
O ! Jesus is the same.

How are His people strengthened
To take the painful cup !
If father, mother, leave us,
The Lord will take us up ;
Will feed us at His table,
Will give us home and rest
Within His holy mansion,
The palace of the blest.

Then let us labour onward
Till time and toil are done,
And bear the cross with patience
Until the crown is won,
And in the land of prophets
With angels we repose,
Amid the trees of beauty,
The olive and the rose.

XXXVII. THE SLAIN ARE IN THE VALLEY.

" Come from the four winds, O Breath, and breathe upon
these slain, that they may live."—EZEKIEL xxxvii. 9.

THE slain are in the valley,
  Dry bones and nothing more ;
  O they are very many :
Who can this host restore ?
How thickly are they lying
Upon the open plain,
A sadly-silent army,
Whitened with sun and rain !

A melancholy murmur
Arises on the air :
The mother and the maiden,
The old and young are there ;
The ignorant, the scholar,
The wealthy, and the poor,
The monarch and his people,
Are bleaching on the floor.

Who can this mass awaken ?
Who the free unction give ;
Reanimate the carcase,
And bid the dry bones live ?

None but the King Almighty ;
None but the Great, the Wise,
Whose mercy never faileth ;
O speak, and these shall rise.

Ye four winds, leave your chambers,
Waft on the Breath Divine,
And in the gloomy valley
The Light of Life shall shine ;
The song of deep thanksgiving
Arise from hearts forgiven ;
And earth possess a measure
Of purity and heaven.

The distant reeds are shaking,
The joyous pines are stirred ;
The Holy Spirit cometh,
The prostrate bones have heard.
They rise a living army,
The Breath has set them free,
And Christ receives due homage
On every land and sea.

XXXVIII. IN THE SAD RAIN FALLS A SOUND.

" We spend our years as a tale that is told."—PSALM xc. 9.

IN the sad rain falls a sound,
  Echoing o'er the gloomy ground,
  Sobbing on by hearth and home,
Rolling in the river's foam,
Smiting through the dark my brow :
'Tis the OLD YEAR dying now.

Like a tale when fires are bright,
Like a meteor of the night,
Like an arrow swift and strong,
Like the twilight's solemn song,
Like the blossom on the bough—
So the OLD YEAR dieth now.

O renew me with Thy grace ;
Quicken, Lord, my sluggish pace ;
Let me see my Father's hand,
Follow Thy Divine command,
Firmer grasp the Gospel plough—
As the OLD YEAR dieth now.

Looking back as on I go,
I have much to lay me low,
Much to rouse my anxious fears,
Much to humble me in tears ;
Sorrowing at Thy feet I bow,
As the OLD YEAR dieth now.

Shouldst Thou grant me future days,
May I spend them to Thy praise ;
More obedient let me be,
Ever learning more of Thee.
O accept my solemn vow,
As the OLD YEAR dieth now.

XXXIX. IN A CLIME OF FLOWERS I STRAYED.

"Before I was afflicted I went astray: but now have I kept Thy word."—PSALM cxix. 67.

In a clime of flowers I strayed,
Roses hung in every glade,
Health by crystal fountains lay,
Song arose from mead and spray,
Sunshine glimmered through the trees,
Beauty carolled on the breeze.

But amid those pleasant things,
Flower and song and water springs,
Health and friendship's holy ray,
I had wandered far astray,
Heeding not my Father's love,
Lifting not my heart above.

Came a dark mist o'er the scene,
Hiding mount and meadow green,
Rolling up in awful bars,
Shutting out the sun and stars,
Stretching over sea and shore,
And the earth was fair no more.

Felt I then how I had erred ;
Turned towards the living Word ;
Sought a refuge from my woes,
Till the Sun of Love arose,
And my prisoned soul was free :
Thus these ills were good for me.

Saviour, hear a suppliant pray,
Guide me in the narrow way ;
Where Thou leadest it is best ;
Cheer me with the thought of rest ;
Till I gain the upper shore,
And my tent is struck no more.

XL. ALL NIGHT UPON THE MOUNTAIN.

"And it came to pass in those days, that He went out into a mountain to pray, and continued all night in prayer to God."—LUKE vi. 12.

All night upon the mountain
Where dews and damp airs be ;
Within Judea's dwellings
There is no room for Thee.
Although the world's great Maker,
Thy night companions now
Are beasts that leave the thicket,
Or birds upon the bough.

All night upon the mountain,
The great sky overhead,
And burning constellations
Along the wide heavens spread ;
While rivers hurry onward
Through dells of deep renown ;
And o'er the mighty cedars
The cold moon looketh down.

All night upon the mountain,
Alone with God in prayer,
While wings of lofty seraphs
Sweep through the silent air ;
Here clearer visions gladden,
Apart from mortal strife,
And we are nearer heaven
Than in the shock of life.

All night upon the mountain ;
Yes, it is even so :
How often in the darkness
I utter forth my woe !
But soon the morning dawneth,
And daylight comes. Behold,
The glowing eastern portals
Lift up their bars of gold !

Enough that feeble servants
Should as their Master be :
If sorrow smote my Saviour,
It surely comes to me.
Ah ! He who had no dwelling,
No settled place of rest,
Will raise the lowly-hearted,
And succour the distressed.

XLI. TO THY COURTS, O LORD, I FLEE.

"According to your faith be it unto you."—MATTHEW ix. 29.

To Thy courts, O Lord, I flee,
One great good to crave of Thee,
One great favour to request ;
Saviour, now Thy love attest ;
Grant in answer to my call
Faith, the greatest gift of all.

Do not leave me in my woe ;
Thou art all I have below ;
I have none in heaven but Thee ;
Manifest Thy love to me :
Grant in answer to my call
Faith, the greatest gift of all.

As my trust on Thee is stayed,
So Thy power shall be displayed,
So the bitter springs shall cease,
So my life of love increase :
Grant in answer to my call
Faith, the greatest gift of all.

Having this, I need no more ;
Barrenness shall then be o'er ;
Fruit shall flourish, fair to see,
Clustered on the goodly tree :
Grant in answer to my call
Faith, the greatest gift of all.

This the bow which spans the gloom,
Cheers the pathway to the tomb,
Gilds with light the lower shore,
Opens heaven for evermore :
Grant in answer to my call
Faith, the greatest gift of all.

XLII. AGAIN I WALK IN DARKNESS.

"Who is among you that feareth the Lord, that obeyeth the voice of His servant, that walketh in darkness, and hath no light? let him trust in the name of the Lord, and stay upon his God."—ISAIAH l. 10.

AGAIN I walk in darkness,
A mist is on my sight,
High hills shut out the Saviour:
When shall I see the light?
O Thou in heaven that dwellest,
With glory on Thy brow,
Alone in kingly greatness,
Shine on my spirit now!

Shine on this vale of shadows,
Shine on the mist of sin;
O let the beams of beauty
With healing power break in!
So shall the clouds be scattered,
So shall the darkness flee,
And living sunlight gladden
The soul in Jesus free.

Where'er Thy Spirit worketh
He brings eternal day;
The goodly fir shall flourish,
The thorn shall pass away.
Along the moral desert,
O'er all the barren ground,
Shall fruits of love and mercy
And holiness be found.

O what a sign unfailing
Of the Messiah's sway,
Which evermore remaineth
Till sin is past away!
Break in upon my spirit
From purer skies above,
And let me feel Thy presence,
O Sun of perfect love.

I would believe Thy promise,
And rest upon the rod,
Wait patiently before Thee,
And stay me on my God.
I dare not doubt Thy wisdom,
Thou knowest what is best.
O, after sterner conflict,
The luxury of rest!

XLIII. ALL HAIL THE LIVING SAVIOUR!

"Fear not; I am the First and the Last: I am He that liveth, and was dead; and, behold, I am alive for evermore, Amen; and have the keys of hell and of death."—REVELATION i. 17, 18.

ALL hail the living Saviour,
The Christ who intercedes!
He ever for His people
Before His Father pleads.

The tomb has lost its tenant,
The reign of Death is o'er,
And Christ the Saviour liveth
For ever, evermore.

The silent gates which open
Within the unseen land,
His eye for ever watcheth;
The keys are in His hand;
And not a footfall stealeth
Along this mighty shade
Without His full permission
By whom the worlds were made.

How oft, when trouble presses,
How oft, when hope is strong,
When roses kiss the lattice,
And home is rich with song,
When earthly props are broken,
When worldly comforts flee,
The blessed Saviour sayeth,
"Fear not; lo, I am He!

"I am the Resurrection,
The entrance to the sky:
Whoso in Me believeth
Shall never, never die.
I suffered but to conquer
The latest foe for thee,
And purchase heavenly treasure:
Fear not; lo, I am He."

And onward swell the tidings
Along their course sublime,
To cheer the true believer
Until the end of time.
O marvellous Beginning!
O all-absorbing End!
All hail the living Saviour,
Our interceding Friend!

XLIV. A GLORY ON MOUNT TABOR.

"And they feared as they entered into the cloud."—LUKE ix. 34.

A GLORY on Mount Tabor,
A mist of dazzling light!
A splendour which surpasseth,
Too grand for mortal sight;
The halo of the Highest,
The shining rifts between;
A wondrous upper brightness
The world has never seen.

O, Christ the Saviour prayeth,
While breezes round Him blow;
His countenance is altered,
His raiment white as snow.
Mid Moses and Elias
A voice of pleasant cheer:
"Divine and loving Master,
'Tis good to meet Thee here."

And then the glory vanished,
The dreadful darkness bowed,
And feared His loved disciples
To enter in the cloud.
But Christ was in the shadow;
The awful vault is stirred,
And in its solemn chambers
His loving voice is heard.

Even now, when trouble gathers,
And fears start up within,
When gloom hangs o'er the portal,
We fear to enter in.
But Christ is with His people,
To guide them on their way,
Until the light of morning
Shall end in perfect day.

Dear Lord, support our weakness;
If clouds surround the hill,
Still help us onward, upward;
For Thou art with us still.
Above the storm a rainbow,
A voice within the gloom,
The presence of Jehovah
To light us through the tomb.

XLV. HOMEWARD, HOMEWARD EVER.

"And the sheep follow Him: for they know His voice."
—JOHN x. 4.

HOMEWARD, homeward ever,
Slowly day by day,
Guided by our Shepherd
In the narrow way;
Speaks He words of comfort;
On His arm we lean;
In the vale He leadeth
Where the fields are green.

There the living waters
Through the flowerets flow,
Murmuring songs of Beulah,
As we homeward go.
Here are healing fountains;
Here are corn and wine,
And delicious fruitage
From the living Vine.

Long had we been straying
On a toilsome track,
Till the loving Saviour
Gently called us back,
Saying, "I am Jesus:
Endless life I give,
If you keep My precepts:
Follow Me and live."

Now we love to travel
Where the Shepherd leads,
Cheered with pleasant pasture
From the fruitful meads;

And where grapes in clusters
Hang the arches o'er,
Oft He sweetly speaketh,
"Jesus is the Door.

"Do not trust a stranger,
Hang upon My love:
Then eternal glory
Shall be yours above,
In My Father's mansion,
In the land of gold,
Where Divine affection
Never will grow cold."

How our eyes are gladdened
By Thy kingly crook!
Zion music floateth
From the crystal brook,
Rise the sounds of praises
From unnumbered strings:
Holy, holy, holy
Is the King of kings.

XLVI. OFT WHERE SHINES NO SUN OR STAR.

"And Peter followed afar off."—LUKE xxii. 54.

OFT where shines no sun or star,
Follow I my Lord afar,
Where no voice is near to bless,
In a land of barrenness.
More in earnest let me be,
Draw my footsteps nearer Thee.

Why where thorns and thickets are
Do I follow Thee afar?
Where is heard no cheering strain,
Come and break the prisoner's chain;
From lukewarmness set me free,
Draw my spirit nearer Thee.

How I fail like him of old.
Shivering in the outer cold,
Slowly walking day by day
Where the sun emits no ray!
Lowly let me bend the knee,
Draw me, Jesus, nearer Thee.

How amid Thy trees I stand,
Like a shrub upon the sand;
Or the heath upon the rock,
Which the angry seasons mock!
May I Thy perfections see;
Draw my weakness nearer Thee.

Quicken, Lord, my growth in grace,
Show me Thy forgiving face;
Let my footsteps lag no more,
Travelling to the sinless shore,
Where I shall for ever be,
In Thy palace, nearer Thee.

XLVII. UP, AND DO THY DUTY.

" Whatsoever thy hand findeth to do, do it with thy might."—ECCLESIASTES ix. 10.

UP, and do thy duty ;
Time brooks no delay :
Wait not for a morrow
Brighter than to-day.
Whether cloud or sunshine,
To thy Saviour cleave,
Rest upon His promise,
Labour and believe.

Day by day advanceth,
Night succeedeth night ;
What thy Master biddeth,
Do with all thy might :
Stand in Gospel armour ;
Force thy way through care ;
Gain a higher footing,
Breathe a purer air.

Sleep not on thy weapon :
Foes are round thee spread ;
At thy feet is danger,
Danger overhead.
Quick the moments hurry,
Fades the golden light ;
What thy Master biddeth
Do with all thy might.

Sound the solemn warning,
Call thy brethren in,
Bid them heed the Spirit,
Leave the husks of sin :
Feed upon His favour,
In His love delight ;
What thy Master biddeth
Do with all thy might.

Death may come to-morrow ;
O arise and pray !
Call upon thy Maker,
Shake the dust away.
Thou hast but the present,
Gird thee to the fight ;
What thy Master biddeth
Do with all thy might.

XLVIII. OVER THE HILLS A RIVER.

" And there shall be no night there."—REVELATION xxii 5.

OVER the hills a river,
Beyond the river light,
Green palms and stately cedars,
And skies where all is bright ;
A land of golden summer,
A clime beyond compare,
Where verdure never ceases,
And flowers are always fair.

No tongue can tell its beauty,
Or heart its love express ;
Here flow the living waters
Mid banks which angels press ;
Here wave the snowy lilies,
The exquisite, the rare ;
Here dwells the Prince of Glory :
No night is ever there.

No sin is in its valleys,
No blight upon its hills ;
Here sickness cannot enter,
No wasting fever kills :
The balmy breeze is laden
With sweets divinely fair
From richest rose and myrtle :
No night is ever there.

Within it dwells no sorrow,
And tears are shed no more,
No sigh disturbs its quiet,
The former things are o'er :
Here kings lay down their glory
Its loveliness to share,
And walk the golden city :
No night is ever there.

And in this angel-kingdom
Our friends are with the blest ;
Beyond the silent valley
They beacon us to rest ;
In robes of purest whiteness,
Palms in their hands they bear :
O blessed home of Jesus,
No night is ever there !

XLIX. THE EARTH IS HOLY GROUND.

" But the hour cometh, and now is, when the true worshippers shall worship the Father in spirit and in truth : for the Father seeketh such to worship Him."—JOHN iv. 23.

" For the place whereon thou standest is holy ground."—EXODUS iii. 5.

DRAW near in solemn worship
To heaven's eternal King,
Under the leafy arches,
Where nature's minstrels sing ;
By rills where reeds and rushes
And rising rocks abound,
Or where the great sea floweth :
The earth is holy ground.

Whoever gains His favour
Must in the spirit pray,
Beneath the vaulted ceiling,
Or on the moorland grey,
When moonlight fills the cloisters
And gilds the hallowed mound,
Or noon is in its brightness :
The earth is holy ground.

The heart may reach the Highest
From overshadowed lane,
Where ivy holds the ruin
Upon the tangled plain,
And silver water falleth
With a religious sound,
Amid the twilight shadows :
The earth is holy ground.

The plougher in the furrow,
The mower on the mead,
The poor man in his dwelling,
The thatcher on the reed,
The sailor on the ocean
Amid the blue around,
May worship God in spirit :
The earth is holy ground.

And such the Father seeketh,
And such the Father hears,
Whose prayers go up through Jesus
In words, or sighs, or tears :
And sendeth He the answer
Of peacefulness profound,
Which passeth understanding :
The earth is holy ground.

Strong Angel of the Promise,
We at Thy footstool kneel ;
Be present by Thy Spirit,
Our sinfulness to heal ;
Come in a voice of stillness,
Or with a rushing sound,
And let us feel Thy presence :
The earth is holy ground.

L. AND KNEW NOT IT WAS JESUS.

" And knew not that it was Jesus."—JOHN xx. 14.

AND knew not it was Jesus,
Although they felt that day
Their glad hearts burn within them
When talking by the way,
Towards the lonely village,
Among the watching hills,
Where lie the lovely lilies,
Beside the gentle rills.

And knew not it was Jesus,
Though His sweet words of love
Had lifted up their spirits
To higher worlds above :
How Christ their King should suffer
A sacrifice for sin ;
And ope the doors of Zion,
To let His people in.

And knew not it was Jesus :—
Oft when the dawn appears,
And the low willows tremble
Amid the rain of tears,

His presence passeth by us,
Hallowing the holy spot,
Gilding the awful shadows,
And yet we know it not.

And knew not it was Jesus :—
Although in striving long
We walk through secret places
Where floateth holy song,
Faint murmurs from the valleys,
Where heaven reveals its light,
And the strong arm of Mercy
Is guiding us aright.

And knew not it was Jesus :—
Though oft we faintly pray,
And the unfailing Presence
Is with us on our way.
And knew not it was Jesus :—
Until the solemn shade
Is broken by His whisper,—
" 'Tis I, be not afraid."

LI. BY JACOB'S WELL HE SITTETH.

" I that speak unto thee am He."—JOHN iv. 26.

BY Jacob's well He sitteth
When noontide fills the air,
And comes a lonely woman
Bringing her pitcher there ;
A dweller of Samaria
Where Sychar youths rejoice ;
And how her heart is gladdened
To hear the Saviour's voice !

O woman of Samaria,
What sweetness fills thy tale,
When Jesus faint and weary
Toiled onward through the vale !
We see thee by the fountain,
The blue bright heavens above,
Conversing with thy Saviour,
And wondering at His love.

" I know Messiah cometh,
The faithful One and true,
Whose peaceful kingdom maketh
The whole creation new.
How would my song awaken,
This holy Seer to see ! "
And Jesus sweetly answered,
" O woman, I am He ! "

Then thrilled her soul with gladness :
How oft in lonely place
We sigh amid the darkness,
" O could we see His face ! "
Until the living waters
That evermore flow free,
Refresh our thirsty spirits :
" O woman, I am He ! "

E E

Though in a land of dryness
Where roses gem no bower,
And the short herbage withers,
And falls no cheering shower;
Amid the mighty murmur
Of mountain side and sea,
The voice of Love ariseth,
"O woman, I am He!"

When in the dusky chamber
The silent step is heard,
And the pale lips are breathing
The latest loving word;
Along the mystic landscape
Of Heaven's sublime decree,
The voice of Mercy floateth:
"O woman, I am He!"

LII. WHILE THE SUN IS IN THE SKY.

"Buy the truth, and sell it not."—PROVERBS xxiii. 23.

WHILE the sun is in the sky,
While the roses round thee lie,
While thy step is firm and strong,
And the morn awakes with song,
Praise Him for thy lengthened lot:
Buy the truth, and sell it not.

If upon the bed of death
Quickly heaves thy labouring breath,
And the twilight fades away
As thy friends around thee pray,
Praise Him for thy lengthened lot:
Buy the truth, and sell it not.

Have thy days been spent in crime,
Rushing down the march of time;
Herding with the sons of sin,
Though thy conscience spoke within?
Turn and wonder at thy lot:
Buy the truth, and sell it not.

He who traffics here is wise:
This the costliest merchandise:
This the gold that will not rust;
Gems to it are sordid dust.
Christ demands thy highest thought:
Buy the truth, and sell it not.

Better part with all things here,
Friends, and home, and kindred dear,
Health, and strength, and worldly worth,
Life, and all the joys of earth,
Than forego the pilgrim's lot:
Buy the truth, and sell it not.

LIII. NOT BY WORKS WHICH MAN MAY NAME.

"For by grace are ye saved through faith; and that not
of yourselves: it is the gift of God: not of works, lest any
man should boast."—EPHESIANS ii. 8, 9.

NOT by works which man may name,
Not by deeds of might or fame,

Not by hunger, thirst, or pain.
Can we, Lord, Thy favour gain,
Nor by sighs or deep distress.
Toiling through the wilderness.

Though I with my worldly store
Clothe and feed the hungry poor;
Though I in religion's name
Give my body to the flame;
This will gain no meed for me
If I have not faith in Thee.

Not by works, lest man should sin,
Boasting how he enters in;
Not by labour lone and long,
Wrestling with temptations strong;
But by living faith Divine,
In the seed of Jacob's line.

Faith the wing that soars to Thee;
Faith the wondrous golden key;
Faith the Christian's conquering rod;
Faith the greatest gift of God:
Crave I now this precious store;
Having it, I need no more.

This the glorious Gospel plan,
Leaving nought for boasting man.
Thus before Thee, Lord, I bow;
Let my faith be strengthened now;
Every outward arm forego;
Only Jesus would I know.

LIV. LIFT UP YOUR SHINING PORTALS.

"Lift up your heads, O ye gates; even lift them up, ye
everlasting doors; and the King of glory shall come in....
Who is this King of glory? The Lord of hosts, He is the
King of glory."—PSALM xxiv. 9, 10.

LIFT up your shining portals!
The grave has lost its prey:
The mighty King of glory
Has left the tomb to-day;
And heavenward He ascendeth,
That earth may Eden win.
Lift up your bars of beauty,
And let the Conqueror in!

Who is this King of glory?
The Prince beyond compare,
In battle ever mighty,
Whose strong arm layeth bare.
Fall back, ye ranks of seraphs,
The fields of light within:
Lift up your bars of beauty,
And let the Conqueror in!

He cometh up from Edom
With garments strangely red:
The winepress of Thine anger
Did He in sorrow tread.
His own arm brought salvation
From the dark night of sin:
Lift up your bars of beauty,
And let the Conqueror in!

Let your bright heads be lifted,
Ye doors of golden light !
The Lord of Hosts ascendeth,
The awful Man of Might.
His life He freely offered
A sacrifice for sin :
Lift up your bars of beauty,
And let the Conqueror in.

His Spirit through all ages
Shall fall like gentle rain,
And kings bow down before Him,
The poor His favour gain.
He shall endure for ever ;
Subdued are death and sin :
Lift up your bars of beauty,
And let the Conqueror in !

LV. ART THOU TOSSED, MY BROTHER?

"But the ship was now in the midst of the sea, tossed
with waves: for the wind was contrary."—MATTHEW
xiv. 24.

ART thou tossed, my brother,
On the ocean's foam ?
Is thy vessel drifting
Far away from home ?
Roar the billows round thee ?
Rise the waters high ?
Courage, brother, courage :
Holy help is nigh.

There is One who guideth
Every wind that roars ;
O'er the stars He sitteth,
By their silver doors:
His abiding presence
Filleth earth and sky.
Courage, brother, courage :
Holy help is nigh.

Do the billows buffet
With a sound of dread ?
Past those foamy shallows
There is land a-head,
Where the life-tree groweth,
Where the lilies lie.
Courage, brother, courage :
Holy help is nigh.

Leave it with thy Pilot :
Though the tempests swell,
And the foam is flying,
All will yet be well.
Sweetest rest remaineth
In the quiet sky.
Courage, brother, courage :
Holy help is nigh.

Once the harbour entered,
Storm and strife are o'er.
Hark, what cheering music
Floateth from the shore !

Never more to suffer,
Never more to sigh.
Courage, brother, courage :
Holy help is nigh.

Therefore meet with patience
Troubles great and small :
Once within the city
Maketh up for all.
Here no shadow stealeth
O'er the tranquil sky.
Courage, brother, courage :
Holy help is nigh.

LVI. WHY STAND HERE ALL DAY IDLE?

"Why stand ye here all the day idle ?"—MATTHEW xx. 6.

WHY stand here all day idle
Within the market-ground,
Whilst other earnest workers
Are toiling much around ?
There is no time for wasting,
No hours to spend remiss :
All should be earnest purpose
In such a world as this.

Ask what thy Father willeth :
He shall direct thy hand
To train the fruitful branches,
Or plough the stubble land ;
To keep the temple's portal,
To guide the wretched in.
The smallest Gospel service
A rich reward shall win.

Along the world's wide desert
How many pilgrims sigh !
What griefs there are to soften !
What gushing tears to dry !
The aged need thy succour
Far down the shadowy vale,
The widow and the orphan,
Whom winter winds assail.

And in the shed of sickness
Where the light burneth dim,
And sighs the weary watcher,
O speak a word for Him !
Thy ever-loving Master,
The humble sinner's Guest,
He succours those who suffer,
His presence bringeth rest.

Then stand no longer idle
Within the market-ground,
While various kinds of labour
For each and all are found.
The weakest oft are strongest
To spread the Saviour's fame,
And gather holy honours
Which cluster round His name.

LVII. IT IS ENOUGH, MY FATHER.

"Like as a father pitieth his children, so the Lord
pitieth them that fear Him."—Psalm ciii. 13.

IT is enough, my Father,
Thy pity reacheth all,
To every land extendeth
Where light and sunbeams fall ;
And as a loving parent
Doth o'er his first-born bend,
So are Thy tender mercies,
Which never, never end.

Ah ! who can bear the sorrow,
The suffering and the tear,
The ringing cry of anguish,
From infancy so dear ?
Who, if his child in hunger
Ask bread with bitter moan,
Could turn away unheeding,
Or offer him a stone ?

Than love of parent stronger,
Through changing years the same,
Is the Redeemer's pity
For those who love His name.
The firmament shall darken
With Nature's last decay ;
But His Divine compassion
Will never pass away.

Then let this cheer us onward
From rising sun to sun,
Through every tribulation,
Until the heights are won,
And in the blessed kingdom,
Our holy home on high,
We dwell with Christ for ever,
Whose pity cannot die.

LVIII. WITHIN AN UPPER CHAMBER.

"And the same day there were added unto them about
three thousand souls."—Acts ii. 41.

WITHIN an upper chamber
The loved disciples wait,
Until the promised Spirit
Should all things new create ;
When, lo ! like wind He cometh
To run His heavenly race,
The mighty rushing tempest
Filling the holy place.

A radiance brightly golden
Doth with the daylight blend,
The cedar-rafters tremble,
And tongues of fire descend :
The Holy Spirit speaketh,
Nought can His influence stay.
O what a grand awakening,
Three thousand in a day !

Three thousand brought to Jesus :
The swarthy and the fair,
The servant and his master,
Are all converted there.
In other tongues they utter
The wonders of His fame :
Three thousand brought to Jesus :
O glorify His name !

O rich display of mercy
And blessing from above !
How is the truth attested
Of the Redeemer's love !
The Comforter delighteth
With sinful man to stay,
Nor will His power diminish—
Three thousand in a day.

Now pray we for Thy coming,
Thou all-creating Power ;
O bless Thy waiting people
At this devoted hour !
And grant to each believer
A measure of Thy grace,
And let Thy saving presence
Descend and fill the place.

LIX. FORTH FROM THE TANGLED DESERT.

"John had his raiment of camel's hair, and a leathern
girdle about his loins ; and his meat was locusts and wild
honey."—Matthew iii. 4.

FORTH from the tangled desert,
In cloak of camel's hair,
Girt with a leathern girdle,
With strange and stately air ;
His simple food the locusts
And honey of the wild ;
Comes the inspired Forerunner
Of the anointed Child.

His garments smell of cedar,
And the untrodden wood,
Where Nature rears her altars
By forest-arch and flood.
His hair so richly flowing
And lofty gait accord ;
And hues are on his visage
The wilderness afford.

And as he walks he utters
The burden of his lay :
"Repent, repent ! He cometh
Who bringeth endless day.
Prepare His path of honour :
In welcomes warm conspire :
I you baptize with water,
But He with heavenly fire.

"The vale shall be exalted,
Brought down the mountain chain ;
The crooked paths be straightened,
And the rough places plain ;

The thorn shall be uprooted,
New flowers adorn the sod ;
And every ransomed nation
Behold the Lamb of God."

O may we see Thee ever,
Our refuge in distress,
The sum of our salvation,
Our perfect righteousness,
Our gracious strength in weakness!
O hear us when we pray !
In life, in death's dim shadow,
Thou art our only stay.

LX. HOW CAN I DOUBT MY FATHER'S CARE?

"Sufficient unto the day is the evil thereof."—Matthew vi. 34.

How can I doubt my Father's care,
Whose love appeareth everywhere,
In spring's first sigh, in summer's breeze,
In thoughtful autumn's changing trees,
In all I feel, or hear, or see ?
Sufficient is Thy grace for me.

Why should I forward look with fear,
When Christ my King is ever near ?
How dare mistrust His mighty hand,
Who scatters blessings o'er the land,
Whose voice is in the sounding sea ?
Sufficient is Thy grace for me.

Why should I shrink from storms which rise
And gather over distant skies,
Or passes dim where twilight broods
In thickly gathering solitudes,
Or fear the approaching days to be ?
Sufficient is Thy grace for me.

Why should I doubt that powerful Name
When sickness stealeth o'er my frame,
When friends withdraw and foemen reign,
And I alone go forth with pain ?
Amid the swellings of the sea
Sufficient is Thy grace for me.

O let me take my daily share,
And leave to-morrow in Thy care,
Enjoy the sunshine Thou hast sent,
And learn the lesson of content ;
Still trusting, whatsoe'er may be :
Sufficient is Thy grace for me.

Sufficient when the sun is high,
And when it gilds the evening sky ;
Sufficient in the hour of strife,
When death is entering into life,
And heaven appears and shadows flee :
Sufficient is Thy grace for me.

LXI. STRANGE DARKNESS RODE THE WATERS.

" Then they that were in the ship came and worshipped Him, saying, Of a truth Thou art the Son of God."—Matthew xiv. 33.

Strange darkness rode the waters,
A black wind smote the wave,
The ocean tossed and tumbled :
Who can the storm outbrave ?
The little ship is drifting
Upon the angry deep,
While the distressed disciples
Can only wait and weep.

Ere the fourth watch had ended
With anguish on their lee,
The ever-loving Saviour
Came walking on the sea :
And while they laboured greatly,
With doubt and fear dismayed,
" Be of good cheer," He whispered ;
" 'Tis I, be not afraid."

Then Peter trod the tempest ;
But when the winds were high,
He sank into the billows
With a beseeching cry.
And Christ vouchsafed His mercy
In answer to his prayer,
And took him to His favour,
And saved the suppliant there.

And soon the winds were silent,
The waves were rough no more,
The white moon kissed the waters,
Sweet music swept the shore.
Glad voices swelled the murmur
Which o'er the still sea trod
From the rejoiced disciples.
" Thou art the Son of God."

How oft the Saviour cometh
When winds and waves are high,
And stills the mighty tempest,
And bids the darkness fly !
The leaves of hope are freshened,
Bright flowers adorn the sod,
And whispers fill the morning :
" Thou art the Son of God."

LXII. LISTEN, AS THOU JOURNEYEST ON.

" Whatsoever He saith unto you, do it."—John ii. 5.

Listen, as thou journeyest on,
To the voice of God's dear Son,
In the hum of noonday light,
In the stillness of the night.
Whatsoe'er He saith to thee,
Do it with a spirit free.

Does He bid thee climb the hill?
Onward, never standing still.
Heed not what thy fears may meet ;
Tread distrust beneath thy feet. .
Gird thine armour on thy breast:
On the summit there is rest.

Does He lead where in the vale
Sing the thrush and nightingale,
Where the waters sparkle free,
And the land is fair to see ?
On. with thankfulness and prayer:
Jesus wills that thou art there.

Does He call thee to possess
Pain and anguish and distress,
Guiding where prostration pines,
And a blast is on the vines ?
Whatsoe'er He orders thee,
Bear it with a spirit free.

Does He bid thee front the foe ?
Onward to the battle go:
Aim to slay the man of sin:
Call the sons of suffering in
To the Gospel's welcome cheer,
Spread for every sinner here.

There is earnest work for all :
Some are builders on the wall ;
Some are drawers from the well ;
Some are hewers in the dell.
Whatsoe'er He saith to thee,
Do it with a spirit free.

LXIII.   IT IS THE SABBATH STILLNESS.

"And He healed them all."—Matthew xii 15.

IT is the Sabbath stillness,
  A type of heavenly rest :
  A halo crowns the mountain,
And wraps the valley's breast.
The gathering hush is holy
Which thus enfoldeth space,
And every tree a teacher
Of the Redeemer's grace.

Amid the corn He walketh
Along the pleasant land ;
And now His mercy healeth
The man with withered hand.
Behold, the people follow,
And on the Saviour call,
The blind, the brokenhearted,
And Jesus healeth all.

None are by Him rejected ;
To all His love outflows ;
No matter what their sickness,
No matter what their woes.
His great compassions reach them,
And raise them from their fall ;
He bids them go rejoicing :
O, Jesus healeth all.

The hoary-haired transgressor,
Whose deeds are dark with sin ;
The stained in youthful folly,
Whose conscience speaks within ;
Nought is beyond His goodness ;
The worst may on Him call,
And find His full forgiveness :
O, Jesus healeth all.

The heaviest load He lightens,
The saddest heart He cheers :
Ask, and His lovingkindness
In thy behalf appears.
Whoever prayeth gaineth
A blessing great or small,
An influence from the Highest:
O, Jesus healeth all.

LXIV.   ALWAYS WALKING, WATCHING.

" Pass the time of your sojourning here in fear."—1 Peter
i. 17.

ALWAYS walking, watching,
  Serving Thee in fear,
  Knowing that our journey
Quickly endeth here.
Short the longest sojourn,
Fleet the farthest flight :
O for holy wisdom,
Thus to walk aright !

Poor is earthly pleasure,
Like the burning thorn,
Cracking, flashing, dying,
Gone as soon as born.
O for heavenly manna !
O for angels' cheer !
Which the Saviour breaketh
To the soul sincere.

Not with gold and silver,
Not with bread and wine,
Are His people ransomed,
But with blood Divine ;
With the solemn slaughter
Of his precious Son.
Quicken us, dear Jesus,
All the race to run.

May we ever follow
Christ the Lord in fear,
Guided by His presence
On our journey here,
Burning like a pillar
Floating like a cloud ;
Till our sojourn endeth
Where the palms are bowed.

There is earnest labour
For the willing hand ;
Helping on a brother
O'er the silent sand ;
Speaking for the Saviour
On our homeward way,
Ere the night approacheth,
Shutting out the day.

LXV. FROM CARMEL'S SIDE IT COMETH.

"How long halt ye between two opinions? If the Lord be God, follow Him: but if Baal, then follow him."—1 KINGS xviii. 21.

FROM Carmel's side it cometh,
Where Baal's own prophets stand,
And like the strong wind rusheth
Across the thirsty land,
O'er Kishon's silvery waters,
On to the mighty sea:
"Between these two opinions
How long, how long halt ye?

"If Baal be your protector,
Then serve him with your might.
If God be God, then give Him
His undivided right.
Take ye the severed victim,
And lay it on the pyre,
And let the truth be tested
By heaven's descending fire."

How rave these wicked prophets!
They cut themselves, and cry;
And yet no fire descendeth,
No voice is in the sky.
They leap upon the altar;
The stones are scattered round;
Yet unconsumed the victim,
The heavens afford no sound.

The shades of eve are falling
On Carmel's lovely brow:
Elijah wraps his mantle
More closely round him now.
His eyes to heaven are lifted;
His lips have breathed the prayer;
The holy flame descendeth;
Jehovah conquers there.

Why halt ye in your folly?
On this side sorrows rise:
The dreadful hail, the tempest,
The death that never dies.
On that, the trees of Eden,
The waters of His love,
The fulness of the Saviour,
Jerusalem above.

LXVI. WHERE SHALL UTTER WEAKNESS HIDE?

"A bruised reed shall He not break, and smoking flax shall He not quench."—MATTHEW xii. 20.

WHERE shall utter weakness hide,
Save in Christ the Crucified?
What shall utter weakness do,
But rely for succour too,
Feeling ruined and undone,
On the love of His dear Son?

Saviour, see me spirit-bowed,
Toiling underneath a cloud,

Of all heavenly help bereft,
In a land of darkness left.
But, though ruined and undone,
Let me hope in His dear Son.

Still the light of life is dim:
I can scarcely come to Him,
Scarcely see the narrow way,
Scarcely lift my heart to pray.
But, though ruined and undone,
I will hope in His dear Son.

Jesus, come; a suppliant bless;
Pity, Lord, my feebleness.
Never sued for help Divine
One whose weakness equalled mine.
Yet, though ruined and undone,
I will hope in His dear Son.

Breaks He not the bruised reed
On the peaceful Gospel mead,
And the smoking flax shall rise
In a flame to Paradise.
Thus, though ruined and undone,
I am safe in His dear Son.

LXVII. NOT BY BURDENS MAN MAY BEAR.

"What shall we do, that we might work the works of God? Jesus answered and said unto them, This is the work of God, that ye believe on Him whom He hath sent."—JOHN v. 28, 29.

NOT by burdens man may bear,
Heaven is won by faith and prayer.
Build thou not on works of thine,
Rest upon the Word Divine.
Nothing do, and nothing give:
Come to Christ, believe, and live.

Come with all thy sore distress,
All thy woe and wretchedness,
All thy anguish, all thy grief.
All thy sin and unbelief,
To the Son whose side was riven,
And thy wrong shall be forgiven.

Come with all thy load of care:
He the pilgrim's part shall share.
With thy doubt and darkness come:
He shall guide the helpless home.
Wait not for a brighter day:
Clouds shall thicken, shouldst thou stay.

Come to Jesus as thou art;
Now with all thy idols part;
Lay thy burden on His breast;
He shall give thee perfect rest.
He shall make thy weakness strong,
He shall fill thy soul with song.

Come with all thy sin and shame,
Plead the merits of His name.
Nothing mention of thine own,
Cling to Christ by faith alone;
And His love's delicious store
Shall be thine for evermore.

LXVIII. OPEN MINE EYES, DEAR SAVIOUR.

"I see men as trees, walking."—MARK viii. 24.

OPEN mine eyes, dear Saviour,
That I may plainly see
The riches of Thy mercy,
So bountiful, so free.
How weak my aspirations,
Which slowly rise to Him!
How indistinct my vision,
Like trees when woods are dim!

Open mine eyes, dear Saviour;
Me to Thy mercy draw.
O teach my spirit daily
The wonders of Thy law!
May I increase in wisdom,
Still more and more like Him,
Nor longer see His beauty
Like trees when woods are dim.

Open mine eyes, dear Saviour;
Diffuse Thy Spirit's ray.
O may I see Thy glory
In the clear light of day!
May faith's weak hand be strengthened
To touch Thy garment's rim;
Nor longer may I view Thee
Like trees when woods are dim.

Open mine eyes, dear Saviour:
O cheer me with Thy love!
May I behold distinctly
My hidden home above,
The land of living waters,
The clime of harp and hymn,
Where nought on high appeareth
Like trees when woods are dim.

LXIX. WITH THE PROMISED STAFF IN HAND.

"But he that shall endure unto the end, the same shall be saved."—MARK xiii. 13.

WITH the promised staff in hand
Walk we o'er a dangerous land:
And the Saviour's voice we hear
Rising in the desert drear:
"Grace for all is full and free;
Win eternal life through Me."

If we falter halfway o'er,
We shall never reach the shore,
Never gain the home of rest,
Never mingle with the blest,
Never wander where the trees
Whisper over crystal seas.

Ever ready may we be
To endure as seeing Thee,
Guided by Thy perfect love,
Till we reach our home above,

Far from sorrow, pain, and strife,
In the land of endless life.

Only these who persevere
Till has dropped the latest tear,
Till has ceased the aching breast,
Gain the mansions of the blest.
Gracious Saviour, may we be
Saved at last to heaven and Thee.

LXX. WITHOUT THE BUSY CITY.

"What wilt thou that I should do unto thee?"—MARK x. 51.

WITHOUT the busy city,
Beside the broad highway,
Blind Bartimæus sitteth,
And beggeth out the day.
The birds are on the branches,
The cedars bathe in light;
But all to him is darkness,
O, all to him is night.

He hears the children's voices,
He hears the matron's hymn,
And Jordan's murmuring waters
Across the lowlands dim;
When, hark! the tramp of footsteps,
Which quickly draweth nigh;
And how his heart is gladdened,
For Jesus passeth by!

He prays the Lord for pity
In language strong and clear,
Though chided by the people:
"Thou Son of David, hear!"
And casting off his garment
In answer to his call,
He rose and came to Jesus,
And told the Saviour all.

"What wilt thou, Bartimæus,
Poor blind one, at My hand?"
"Let me receive, dear Saviour,
My sight at Thy command."
"Go on thy way rejoicing,
Thy faith hath made thee whole;"
And happiness unuttered
Filled his delighted soul.

O with what joy he witnessed
The lovely earth around,
The hills beyond Judæa,
The fruitful pasture-ground,
The waving woods, the waters,
The human face Divine!
And praises filled the valleys
Above the loftiest pine.

'Twas well the blind man rested
Where olives whispered low,
That, when appeared the Saviour,
He might His footsteps know,

And to the gracious Healer
With earnest zeal apply.
So let my soul be waiting
Where Jesus passeth by.

Christ might have blest the beggar
Without his earnest call:
But this is not like Jesus,
Whose pity reacheth all.
Ask, and His mercy floweth
As freely as the light;
And the kind Son of David
Giveth the blind one sight.

LXXI. EVER LEARNING MAY I BE.

"Learn of Me; for I am meek and lowly in heart: and ye shall find rest unto your souls."—MATTHEW xi. 29.

EVER learning may I be
Living lessons, Lord, of Thee,
From the ever-cheering light,
From the mystery of the night,
From the stars that spread Thy fame,
Whispering through the heavens Thy name.

Let me learn from all things here,
Bird and brook and floweret dear,
Valley low and mountain high,
Ocean vast and spreading sky,
Meadow green and forest tall;
For Jehovah made them all.

Let me in the knowledge grow
How Thou didst abide below;
Wear Thee ever in my heart,
Meek and lowly as Thou art,
Who the scoffer's insult bore,
And the crown of mockery wore.

Let me learn from sin to flee,
More and more to copy Thee,
In Thy pity for distress,
In Thy life of lowliness,
In Thy deeds of love to man,
Perfecting the Gospel plan.

Let me learn from hour to hour
More and more Thy saving power,
More and more Thy counsels sweet,
Sitting lowly at Thy feet;
On Thy steadfast truth rely;
Learn to live, and learn to die.

LXXII. WHERE PALMS O'ERHANG THE SILENT SHORE.

"They that are delivered from the noise of archers in the places of drawing water, there shall they rehearse the righteous acts of the Lord."—JUDGES v. 11.

WHERE palms o'erhang the silent shore,
And noisy archers stir no more;
Where matrons meet with comely grace
Around the ancient watering-place,
Where hangs the richly clustered vine,
Would they rehearse His acts Divine.

Here sound of bow and tramp of steed
Break not among the murmuring reed;
The crystal waters, rippling low,
As o'er the cypress roots they flow,
With whispering winds and waves combine,
Where they rehearse His acts Divine.

O sweet to be delivered here,
Where wavelets sparkle cool and clear,
From wasting noise and rude alarms
Of gathering multitudes in arms;
Where Peace and Piety recline,
And thus rehearse His acts Divine.

So would we gather here to-day,
Beside Life's Fount to watch and pray.
O Saviour, hear us from above,
And feed us with the bread of love.
Now, Holy Spirit, seal us Thine,
As we rehearse His acts Divine.

LXXIII. A FAIR BARK RIDES THE WATERS.

"And so it came to pass, that they escaped all safe to land."—ACTS xxvii. 44.

A FAIR bark rides the waters,
The skies assume a frown,
The fretful winds are sighing,
The angry storm comes down,
A mighty moving tempest,
Which grandly thunders on,
Driving the foam before it,
The great Euroclydon.

The labouring ship was lightened,
The sails were rent away;
The waters rose and rumbled,
And flashed the blinding spray.
All hope of life had vanished,
As they the quicksands neared,
And through long days of darkness
No sun or star appeared.

And then in robes of beauty,
Whose garments wore no speck,
Girt with a golden girdle,
An Angel walked the deck.
O how the cordage glittered
With glory unsurpassed,
Which tinged the surging waters,
And streamed upon the mast!

"Fear not," the Saviour whispered;
"Your lives are in My hand;
The ship alone shall founder,
The crew shall reach the land."
The dreadful tempest conquered,
The vessel ran aground,
And the great sea swept o'er it
With a sublime rebound.

And some were saved by swimming;
Some grasped the floating oar;
Some, portions of the vessel:
And all escaped to shore.

So shall the Church of Jesus,
The days of darkness past,
The toiling and the tempest,
Arrive in heaven at last.

And when we drift in darkness
Upon the roaring wave,
The Angel of the Promise
Is ever near to save.
Across the foamy waters
He guideth with His hand,
And all who trust His mercy
He bringeth safe to land.

LXXIV. THE CRIMSON CROSS WAS LIFTED.

"And sitting down they watched Him there."—MATTHEW xxvii. 36.

THE crimson cross was lifted,
Its foot was on the land;
The thorns upon His temples,
The nails were in His hand.
The scourge had marred His visage,
O sorrowful to see!
And sitting down they watched Him
Extended on the tree.

And then the sun was darkened;
The solemn valleys sighed;
The mighty mountains murmured,
When Christ their Maker died.
The work of love is finished;
The temple's veil is torn,
And type and shadow vanish
Before the perfect morn.

'Tis finished, yes, 'tis finished,
The wondrous Gospel plan:
The King has brought salvation
To erring guilty man.
The flinty rocks are rending,
The startled dead arise,
And angel lyres are ringing
The welcomes through the skies.

Within thy courts, O Zion,
Where palm and cedar stand,
And living waters murmur
Along the holy land,
In humble adoration
We bow the willing knee,
And supplicate Thy favour,
And watch and wait for Thee.

O come with holy comfort
From vales of light above,
And let Thy free forgiveness
Delight our souls with love.
Descend, O promised Spirit;
Our sinful souls restore;
And may we feel Thy presence,
And wonder and adore.

LXXV. FAR BACK, WHEN MORNS WERE GOLDEN.

"Lord, now lettest Thou Thy servant depart in peace, according to Thy word: for mine eyes have seen Thy salvation."—LUKE ii. 29, 30.

FAR back, when morns were golden
With beauty that should be
More bright in the hereafter,
Illuming land and sea,
An old man had a vision,
By God the Spirit given,
That he should see Messiah
Before he entered heaven.

With quenchless hope he waited
As summer sweets disclose,
And the broad olive widened,
And the grand cedar rose.
Yet still with holy patience
His eye was on the star,
Which edged the blue horizon,
And cheered him from afar.

At length the Light of Mercy
Beamed on this world of strife;
Old Simeon saw the Saviour,
The lowly Lord of Life.
Within the temple's halo
He cheered his trusting heart:
"Now lettest Thou Thy servant,"
Said he, "in peace depart.

"Mine eyes have felt Thy glory
Upon my spirit fall,
The Healer of the people,
The Light to lighten all."
And o'er the mountain summits,
Through deserts dark and dead,
On by the whispering waters,
The kindling beauty spread.

So wait we for Thy Spirit,
The Comforter of Love.
O take away our blindness,
And lift our hearts above!
Assist us by Thy mercy
From sin and self to flee,
And in our heart to worship
And wait alone for Thee.

LXXVI. NOUGHT HAST THOU, POOR CHILD OF SIN.

"This is the work of God, that ye believe on Him whom He hath sent."—JOHN vi. 29.

NOUGHT hast thou, poor child of sin,
Pardon, peace, and heaven to win.
Wherefore would'st thou plead delay
When thy Saviour says to-day?
This is what thy work must be:
Trust in Him who died for thee.

What is penance ? What is prayer ?
Daily fasting, midnight care,
Sighs and tears and watchings deep,
Where the waving willows weep ?
If thou hast not in thy plea,
Trust in Him who died for thee.

Leave thy feelings, leave thy fears,
Leave thy labours, sighs, and tears ;
Leave thy burden with thy Lord,
Take the Master at His word :
Let thy work of merit be,
Trust in Him who died for thee.

Then the joy which angels own
Shall be thine by faith alone :
Thou shalt taste the balm of peace,
Feel the prisoner's sweet release,
Enter heaven, where prophets be :
Trust in Him who died for thee.

LXXVII. BELIEVE AND LIVE.

" Believe on the Lord Jesus Christ, and thou shalt be
saved."—ACTS xvi. 31.

HEAR His voice, O child of woe,
Where the Gospel breezes blow,
Where the trees of triumph stand
Mid the lilies of the land,
And the rills of mercy glide
Mingling with salvation's tide.

Sheltered in this sacred place,
Mid the fruitful vines of grace ;
Flows His voice who fills with love
Earth and air and heaven above.
He eternal life will give,
We may now believe and live.

Every star that shines on high,
Every meteor of the sky,
Every flower and changing leaf,
Every bud and blossom brief,
All and each this teaching give :
We may now believe and live.

Higher tidings, holier cheer,
Never gladdened human ear,
Maid and mother, sire and son,
Saint and sinner, every one,
May their hearts to Jesus give,
Hear His voice, believe, and live.

LXXVIII. FREE AS AIR ON LANDSCAPES VAST.

"Ho, every one that thirsteth, come ye to the waters,
and he that hath no money ; come ye, buy, and eat ; yea,
come, buy wine and milk without money and without
price."—ISAIAH lv. 1.

FREE as air on landscapes vast,
Free as waters flowing fast,

Free as ocean's solemn bound,
Free as silence, free as sound,
Free as light, or anything,
Is the mercy of our King.

Offer neither house nor land,
Bring no money in thy hand ;
Corn and oil we need no more ;
For the former state is o'er :
Free as light, or anything,
Is the mercy of our King.

Art thou thirsty ? drink thy fill,
Christ receiveth sinners still ;
He the vilest will embrace,
Give the worst a sheltered place :
Free as light, or anything,
Is the mercy of our King.

Come, the Gospel feast is spread ;
Come, and taste the Living Bread ;
Christ for all His life did give,
Only trust, and thou shalt live :
Free as light, or anything,
Is the mercy of our King.

LXXIX. I LEAVE IT ALL WITH THEE.

" Cast thy burden upon the Lord, and He shall sustain
thee."—PSALM lv. 22.

DEAR Saviour, as from day to day
I travel on my homeward way,
Sometimes in joy, sometimes in fears,
Sometimes in trust, sometimes in tears,
Still let Thy truth my safeguard be,
And may I leave it all with Thee.

Without Thee I am weak indeed,
More brittle than a bruised reed.
Though darkening clouds my pathway hide,
Still may I trust my watchful Guide,
Within His arms for succour flee,
And, Saviour, leave it all with Thee.

All power is Thine, eternal Love,
On earth below, in heaven above.
When worlds on worlds are passed away,
Thy years shall never know decay.
Thou didst endure the cross for me :
How safe to leave it all with Thee !

If pain or want or sharp distress
Assail me in the wilderness,
O, may I trust Thine arm of power
To save me in the trying hour,
And feel, when death shall set me free,
'Tis sweet to leave it all with Thee !

LXXX. MY FATHER! I MAY CALL THEE SO.

" I will be his Father, and he shall be My son."—
2 SAMUEL vii. 14.

MY Father ! I may call Thee so ;
Beset with care, oppressed with woe,

I lift my eyes, my heart, to Thee :
O, hear my prayer : O, come to me !
Forgive my wanderings o'er the wild,
And save Thy sighing, sorrowing child.

O, fill my heart with holy fear ;
Still be Thy presence ever near.
More trustful may my spirit grow,
And weaned from vanities below.
Through Christ my Saviour reconciled,
Most truly may I be Thy child.

More gentle still may I become,
As drawing near my heavenly home :
O, may my thought be oft of Thee.
At morning, noon, and evening free !
Thus may I grow in virtue mild,
And be my Father's patient child.

Thou know'st how rough the road I tread,
How dark the cold sky overhead.
I will not fear : I know Thy hand
Will lead me to the promised land.
So Thou shalt guide me o'er the wild,
And then in heaven receive Thy child.

LXXXI. AMID LIFE'S CONFLICTS DAY BY DAY.

" Come unto Me, all ye that labour and are heavy laden,
and I will give you rest."—MATTHEW xi. 28.

AMID life's conflicts day by day
How sweet to hear my Saviour say,
In tones of gentleness and love,
To lure my wandering thoughts above,
" Come, weary soul : to Jesus flee,
And lay thy heavy load on Me ! "

I come, I come. My Saviour dear,
With healing in my heart appear.
How long the road without Thy light !
How weak my strength without Thy might !
My merciful upholder be :
I lay my load of sin on Thee.

All my distress and grief and care,
My loving Saviour, Thou wilt bear ;
My human weakness, want, and wrong :
And Thou shalt be the sinner's song.
Thy loving voice hath set me free :
I lay my load of guilt on Thee.

Long as I tread this lonely land,
Thou shalt uphold me with Thy hand ;
And in the midst of Jordan's wave
Thy presence shall be near to save ;
And when are vanished earth and sea,
In that great day I'll rest on Thee.

LXXXII. REMEMBER ME.

" And he said unto Jesus, Lord, remember me when Thou
comest into Thy kingdom."—LUKE xxiii. 42.

THERE is a grief I cannot bring
To any but my heavenly King :

And He will listen when I cry,
And hear the mourner's weakest sigh.
From sin and earth I look to Thee :
O Saviour dear, remember me !

Should strong temptation like a blast
Assail me as it hurries past,
And thunders roar, and lightnings fly,
And daylight leave the darkened sky ;
To Christ for refuge may I flee ;
And, Saviour dear, remember me !

O, suffer not my feet to slide ;
Still keep me near my Shepherd's side :
Increase my faith, restore my soul,
And make the wounded wanderer whole.
Thy boundless love is all my plea :
O Saviour dear, remember me !

Then, when the flight of time is o'er,
And sun and moon shall be no more,
When quick and dead, both great and small,
Appear before the Judge of all,
And to Messiah bend the knee,
O Saviour dear, remember me !

LXXXIII. LIFT UP THE HEART, AND PRAY.

" I will therefore that men pray everywhere, lifting up
holy hands, without wrath and doubting."—1 TIMOTHY ii. 8.

WHERE rivers meet and mingle,
Where daisies deck the plain,
Where forest-trees are waving,
Where roses scent the lane,
Where flows the village fountain,
Where gentle lambkins play,
Where silent rocks are rising,
Lift up the heart, and pray.

Within the smoky smithy,
Upon the gliding deck,
Where harvest cheers the reaper,
Amid the battle's wreck,
Down in the mine's dark working,
Out where the fresh winds stray,
Far on the pathless desert,
Lift up the heart, and pray.

Before the full church altar,
Within the cottage small,
Down in the humblest dwelling,
Up in the highest hall,
Forth where the city darkens,
In where the fettered stay,
Low in the deepest dungeon,
Lift up the heart, and pray.

When morning gilds the lattice,
When noontide fills the plain,
When night and stars and silence
Hang over earth and main,
In health, in strength, in sickness,
In nature's last decay,
To Jesus Christ the Saviour
Lift up the heart, and pray.

Throughout the whole creation
We cannot find a spot,
On land or on the ocean,
Where Thou, O Lord, art not.
The prayer of faith is answered,
Wherever prayer may be :
The earth is one great temple
Where we may worship Thee.

The sailor far away from land,
The mourner everywhere,
The fettered captive in his cell,
Through Christ may offer prayer.

O, may our hearts in praises rise,
Whilst journeying on our way,
That He allows the sons of men
The privilege to pray !

LXXXIV.   THERE IS ONLY ONE RETREAT.

" In that day there shall be a fountain opened to the house of David, and to the inhabitants of Jerusalem, for sin and for uncleanness."—ZECHARIAH xiii. 1.

THERE is only one retreat
For the wandering sinner's feet :
Not in creeds, however clear ;
Not in penance most severe :
He can only safely hide
In the Saviour's open side.

Dearest Lord, to Thee we pray,
Take our load of guilt away :
Lift us to a higher place
In the sunshine of Thy face.
May we evermore abide
In the Saviour's open side.

Here when storms and tempests blow,
Here when strives the angry foe,
Here when death is drawing nigh,
Here when trumpets rend the sky,
Safely may the sinner hide,
In the Saviour's open side.

LXXXV.   HOW MERCIFUL OUR LOVING LORD !

" Be careful for nothing : but in every thing by prayer and supplication, with thanksgiving, let your requests be made known unto God."—PHILIPPIANS iv. 6.

HOW merciful our loving Lord,
Who grants us day by day,
Whilst travelling onward to our rest,
The privilege to pray !

In simple words or earnest sighs,
Upon the bended knee,
Or in the silence of the heart,
It is the same to Thee.

Amid the daily toil of earth,
Upon the sick-bed laid,
Or mid the tramp of busy feet,
The prayer of faith is made ;

Within the consecrated fane,
Out on the lonely lea,
Or by the infant's cradle-bed,
Where holy angels be.

LXXXVI.   IS THERE WITH THY PEOPLE HERE ?

"Unto me, who am less than the least of all saints, is this grace given, that I should preach among the Gentiles the unsearchable riches of Christ."—EPHESIANS iii. 8.

IS there with Thy people here
One so weak in faith and fear,
One like me so sorely tried,
Prone to leave my Saviour's side ?
Surely, Lord, this cannot be :
Yet I dare repose on Thee.

O, how slowly I fulfil
My Redeemer's righteous will !
O, how stony is my heart !
Thoughts of Thee so soon depart.
Come and visit me once more
With the balm from Eden's shore.

Holy Spirit, breath of love !
Draw my wandering thoughts above :
Stamp me with the seal Divine :
May I evermore be Thine,
Nearer, nearer Christ my Friend,
Till in heaven my wanderings end !

LXXXVII.   THY WILL BE DONE.

"Father, if Thou be willing, remove this cup from Me : nevertheless, not My will, but Thine, be done."—LUKE xxii. 42.

IN all my conflicts here below,
In all my times of pain and woe,
By His dear hand may I be led
Who had not where to lay His head,
And feel, from rising sun to sun,
Whate'er my state, "Thy will be done !"

Thou knowest, Lord, from day to day
What numerous trials throng my way ;
Thou know'st the tears that silent start,
And every sigh that rends the heart.
Submissive I my race would run,
And bow and say, " Thy will be done ! "

Should tribulation like a sea
Roll its dark waves of woe on me,
And friends depart, and sickness chain
The sufferer to a bed of pain ;
May I draw near through Christ Thy Son,
And meekly pray, "Thy will be done ! "

Nought have I but what God hath given ;
Health, strength, my all I owe to Heaven ;
And if Thou tak'st Thine own away,
O, help Thy humbled child to say,
As props fall prostrate one by one,
"My Father, God, Thy will be done !"

I dare not choose my earthly state ;
Low at Thy feet I calmly wait :
Thy presence only would I crave,
To cheer my journey to the grave.
Till bliss eternal is begun,
In life in death " Thy will be done !"

LXXXVIII. I WOULD BEHOLD MY SAVIOUR.

" The same came therefore to Philip, which was of
Bethsaida of Galilee, and desired him, saying, Sir, we
would see Jesus."—JOHN xii. 21.

I WOULD behold my Saviour
    At morning's early ray,
    And when the evening shadows
Fall on the dying day.
Throughout each changing season,
    In every time and place,
My soul with earnest longing
    Would seek my Saviour's face.

When comes the hour of trial,
    In every time of dread,
When sunshine drives the shadows,
    And joys are round me spread,
In sickness, pain, and anguish,
    By faith, O, may I see
The mighty Man of Sorrows
    Who tasted death for me !

When all around is gloomy,
    When heaven and earth are black,
When hope in clouds is hidden,
    And cares are on my track,
Even then may I remember
    That Jesus is the same,—
He knows the way to lead me,—
    And bow and bless His name.

To Christ the only refuge
    Still may a sinner flee.
In every dispensation
    I would submit to Thee;
Until in faith I finish
    The humble Christian's race,
For ever and for ever
    I would behold Thy face.

LXXXIX. OFTTIMES, WHEN WANDERING LONELY HERE.

" Fear not, little flock; for it is your Father's good
pleasure to give you the kingdom."—LUKE xii. 32.

OFTTIMES, when wandering lonely here,
    How far the heights of heaven appear !
    And when the storm is raging loud,
And cares our souls have earthward bowed,

The golden streets and city new
Seem almost hidden from our view.

'Tis then we sigh so sore distressed,
" O, shall we ever reach our rest ?
Dear Jesus, shall we ever be,
All toiling o'er, at home with Thee ?
So prone to slide, so full of sin,
O shall we ever enter in ?"

And when the winds the waves have stirred,
The voice of Christ is sometimes heard :
"Ye need not fear, My little flock,
But hide you in the riven Rock.
My Father on His changeless throne
Will give the kingdom to His own."

All power belongs to Christ the Son ;
The rich and poor to Him are one ;
And all who seek the Saviour's face
Shall taste the sweetness of His grace.
The word has left the lips Divine,
" Come unto Me, and ye are Mine."

The voice of praise from earth and sea
For evermore ascends to Thee ;
And we would catch the holy flame,
And bless Messiah's sacred name,
Who comes with healing in His wings,
The Lord of lords, the King of kings.

XC. HE DOETH ALL THINGS WELL.

" He hath done all things well: He maketh both the deaf to
hear, and the dumb to speak.'—MARK vii. 37.

FROM earth arises ever
    A solemn strain of joy,
    A beautiful thanksgiving
No discord can destroy ;
In murmurs from the forest,
    In echoes from the fell ;
Such notes no man can number:
    "He doeth all things well."

O, teach us, dear Redeemer,
    Whilst travelling here below,
Should it be through affliction
    In anguish, pain, and woe,
Even when our path is hidden,
    Let not our heart rebel,
But evermore acknowledge,
    "He doeth all things well."

The oil-cruse may be empty,
    No meal the barrel hold,
The tender lambs be taken
    From home's love-guarded fold,
Our worldly store may vanish,
    And sorrow with us dwell ;
But sigh, O chastened spirit,
    " He doeth all things well."

The dumb still sing His praises,
    The deaf His accents hear ;
The blind behold His glory,
    And follow in His fear ;

The dead in sin are quickened,
And now rejoice to tell
How great is His compassion
Who doeth all things well.

O, may our full hearts utter
This holy hymn of joy,
Although the fig-tree wither,
And storms our hopes destroy !
Dear Jesus, still be near us
In Jordan's heavy swell,
And teach our lips to whisper,
"He doeth all things well."

XCI. SWEET SABBATH REST! SWEET SABBATH REST!

" And call the Sabbath a delight, the holy of the Lord."
—Isaiah lviii. 13.

SWEET Sabbath rest ! sweet Sabbath rest !
How welcome to my anxious breast !
Now let me banish worldly care,
And lift my heart in praise and prayer
To Him who leads me on my way,
And gives another Sabbath day.

Sweet Sabbath rest ! sweet Sabbath rest !
Along the meads with daisies dressed,
The solemn bells in music rare
Are calling to the house of prayer,
Whose lingering echoes seem to say,
" Come, worship on the Sabbath day."

Sweet Sabbath rest ! sweet Sabbath rest !
Of days the calmest, brightest, best ;
When angels walk this world of strife
With whispers from the land of life ;
And Christ is near with healing ray
To cheer me on the Sabbath day.

Sweet Sabbath rest ! sweet Sabbath rest !
Dear holy emblem of the blest.
How long I oft, mid toil and sin,
To hear the welcome word, " Come in,"
To spend where love shall ne'er decay
In heaven an endless Sabbath day !

XCII. LONG HAVE WE BEEN WAITING.

" The watchman said, The morning cometh, and also
the night : if ye will inquire, inquire ye : return, come."—
Isaiah xxi. 12.

LONG have we been waiting
For the dawn of day :
Rise, O Sun of Beauty,
Chase the gloom away.

Lead the ransomed nations
With Thy mighty hand :
Let the Rose of Sharon
Perfume all the land.

Still before the altar
We our hands outspread :
Feed us, dearest Saviour,
With the living bread.
Fill us with Thy fulness,
Vine of Judah's stock :
May our feet for ever
Rest upon the Rock.

We are waiting, waiting
For the sunshine clear :
Come, convincing Spirit,
In our hearts appear.
Hark, the song of morning
Breaks among the hills :
Soon Messiah's kingdom
All creation fills.

XCIII. ALL IS TOO MEAN, HOWEVER RARE.

" How sweet are Thy words unto my taste ! yea, sweeter
than honey to my mouth !—Psalm cxix. 103.

ALL is too mean, however rare,
With sacred Scripture to compare.
A well amid the desert sand,
A light within the wanderer's hand,
A lifeboat on the stormy sea,
The holy Bible is to me.

Here turn I when the rains descend,
And angry winds the welkin rend ;
When moon and stars behind the cloud
Are hidden in a wintry shroud ;
When nature groans from pole to pole ;
And light arises on my soul.

And when the ground is parched and dry,
And showers refuse to leave the sky ;
When buds are drooping on the spray,
And dust-clouds hide my weary way ;
In its enclosures fair and still
I drink from Canaan's clearest rill.

Here Sharon's Rose perfumes the gale ;
Here blooms the Lily of the Vale ;
Here fountains flow in brooklets bright
With healing from the hills of light,
My highest, holiest thought to engage ;
And Christ is seen on every page.

Eternal Power, I bless Thy name,
From whom this sacred treasure came.
More precious may my Bible be,
Which shows the sinner's way to Thee ;
And though I health and wealth resign,
Still may I own the Book Divine.

XCIV. PILGRIM, KNEEL: THE DAY IS DONE.

"Let my prayer be set forth before Thee as incense, and the lifting up of my hands as the evening sacrifice."—PSALM cxli. 2.

PILGRIM, kneel: the day is done;
In the west has sunk the sun;
Labour's busy ring is still;
Twilight settles on the hill:
Mid life's endless toiling stay,
Kneel before the Lord, and pray.

O, how oft a Father's care
Has been with His child to spare!
O, how oft in danger's hour
Thou hast saved us by Thy power!
Neath the evening shadows grey
Kneel before the Lord, and pray.

For our duties slowly done,
For our failings every one,
For our sins against Thy love,
Lift we now our hearts above.
Saviour, purge our guilt away!—
Kneel before the Lord, and pray.

Gentle Shepherd, lead us where
Verdant fields are smiling fair:
Mid the pastures of Thy choice
May we heed Thy loving voice,
Guiding us to endless day!—
Kneel before the Lord, and pray.

XCV. THANK THEE FOR THE DAYLIGHT.

"My voice shalt Thou hear in the morning, O Lord; in the morning will I direct my prayer unto Thee, and will look up."—PSALM v. 3.

THANK Thee for the daylight
Breaking on the shore;
Thank Thee that I see it
On the earth once more,
Kindling up the forest,
Lighting up the lea,
Kissing through the casement
Where my dear ones be.

Many are Thy mercies,
Lord of earth and skies:
With delicious slumber
Thou hast blessed mine eyes.
Now again I waken
So refreshed and free,
And my early praises
Would ascend to Thee.

Guide me, dear Redeemer,
With Thy gentle hand:
May each moment find me
Nearer Canaan's land;

And when day is ended
With its toil and care,
May I ever close it
With the Lord in prayer.

Glory to the Father!
Praises to the Son!
Glory to the Spirit!
Ever Three in One!
Help my footsteps onward
In the Christian race,
Till I see my Saviour
In the holy place.

XCVI. WHERE THE HILLS ARE RUDE AND HIGH.

"And they said among themselves, Who shall roll us away the stone from the door of the sepulchre? And when they looked, they saw that the stone was rolled away; for it was very great."—MARK xvi. 3, 4.

WHERE the hills are rude and high,
Where the land is parched and dry,
Where no flowers of comfort grow,
Oft I wander, sad and slow;
Sighing thus from day to day,
"Who will roll the stone away?"

From the mire of sin I cry,
Towards the heavens I lift mine eye:
See, a weeping suppliant see:
God be merciful to me!
Near me in the desert stay,
Roll my unbelief away.

He who died my soul to save,
He who triumphed o'er the grave,
He who lives in heaven above,
Sends the angel of His love,
All my rising fears to allay;
And the stone is rolled away.

Praise I now my heavenly King:
Take the offering that I bring,
Though it be so mean and poor:
May I trust Thee more and more,
Knowing that Thy love alone
Rolls away each hindering stone.

XCVII. LIKE A TRAVELLER WANDERING FAR.

"Eye hath not seen, nor ear heard, neither have entered into the heart of man, the things which God hath prepared for them that love Him."—1 CORINTHIANS ii. 9.

LIKE a traveller wandering far,
Where no kindred faces are,
Absent long from friends and home,
Weary thus alone to roam,
With his face towards the shore
Of his native land once more:

So wo feel whilst journeying here,
Far from Canaan's valleys dear,
Far from heaven and all that's told
Of its towers and streets of gold,
Where the shining seraph sings,
Shaking odour from his wings.

Home of sweet abiding joy,
Nought of change can e'er destroy ;
Songs of earth, however rare,
Cannot show the glory there,
Filling all the heavenly plains
Where Messiah ever reigns.

Lift we now our hearts on high :
Dear Redeemer, hear our cry ;
Wash our robes, and make them white,
Worthy of the land of light;
And when breaks the silver band,
Take us to the golden land.

CVIII. STAINED WITH SIN, AND FULL OF WOE.

" But God forbid that I should glory, save in the cross of our Lord Jesus Christ by whom the world is crucified unto me, and I unto the world."—GALATIANS vi. 14,

STAINED with sin, and full of woe,
Help us, Lord, as on we go,—
Though we oft have cause to sigh,—
Evermore to fix our eye,
With a chastened spirit still,
On the cross on Calvary's hill.

There our precious Saviour bled ;
There He bowed His bleeding head ;
There He heaved His dying groan
For the sins of man to atone.
O, what grief His soul did fill
On the cross on Calvary's hill !

In the hour of woe and wrong,
In the hour when foes are strong,
In the hour of swift decay,
When the heavens shall pass away,
May we view our Saviour still
On the cross on Calvary's hill.

Risen is now our living Head ;
Cruel Death is captive led :
Sits He on His Father's throne,
Interceding for His own ;
And His love all hearts shall thrill
For the cross on Calvary's hill.

XCIX. THE EARTH IS FULL OF JESUS.

" And one cried unto another, and said, Holy, holy, holy, is the Lord of Hosts : the whole earth is full of His glory."—ISAIAH vi. 3.

THE earth is full of Jesus ;
The mountains speak His power,
And glimpses of His glory
Are seen on every flower.

The valleys sing His praises ;
The rivers roll His name,
The everlasting Father,
For evermore the same.

It trembles through the forest
When day is dying fast ;
The winds attest His presence
Upon the desert vast :
The ocean rolls His wonders
Unto the listening land ;
The stars are bright epistles
Engraven by His hand.

His goodness shineth over
In earth and heaven above :
Each season is a teacher
Of the Creator's love.
The monarch of the forest,
The grasses of the sod,
The breeze, the rain, the tempest,
Proclaim the power of God.

O, bow before the Saviour !
To Him due praises give ;
He who upholds creation
Has died that we may live.
This is the greatest glory
That burst the heavens above :
O, crown Him King eternal,
The Lord of life and love !

C. NOT IN THE TOMB FOR EVER.

" And I will raise him up at the last day."—JOHN vi. 40.

NOT in the tomb for ever,
With silence and the shade,
Be it the waters' cavern,
Be it the forest's glade ;
Not bound in frozen fetters,
Never again to rise,
But only there awaiting
The trumpet of the skies.

Not in the tomb for ever :
The sun and moon shall fail,
And ocean's waves grow silent,
As sinks the last great gale ;
The stars of heaven shall stagger,
And swiftly rush through space,
And all earth's wakened sleepers
Leave their still resting-place.

Not in the tomb for ever :
His word has reached our ears,
Whose truth outlives the ages,
Whose glory fills the spheres.
O when the last morn breaketh,
O'er troubled earth and sea,
The dead shall leave their slumbers
At His Divine decree.

Not in the tomb for ever:
The trumpet's sudden roar
Shall cleave the solid mountains
And open ocean's door,
The gathered dust of ages
In one vast throng unite,
And soul and body mingle
Upon the plains of light.

Not in the tomb for ever:
The Son of Man shall come
With His attendant angels,
And take the watchful home.
Below the flames shall rustle,
And roll through heaven above,
The dead in Christ shall triumph,
And scale the hills of love.

CI. WHY IS THY SPIRIT TROUBLED?

"He appeared to put away sin by the sacrifice of Himself."—HEBREWS ix. 26.

WHY is thy spirit troubled?
   Why is thy soul distressed?
    Look up, look up, thy Saviour
Will give the weary rest.
The shadows have departed
Before His healing ray,
And Gospel sunlight gladdens:
O sin is put away!

From hill to hill it streameth,
Deep vales its lustre give,
From isle to isle extending;
Believe and thou shalt live.
None are by Him rejected
Who wait and watch and pray
At Mercy's open portal:
O sin is put away!

Old men with travel weary,
And youths of vigour strong,
The maiden mid the roses,
The poor man in the throng,
The mother and her offspring,
The gentle child at play,
Are all redeemed by Jesus:
O sin is put away!

O precious, precious tidings,
Which lift our lives above,
Where Eden's gateways glitter
And fill the world with love.
The sacrifice is offered
The lifted arm to stay,
And Christ and heaven are purchased:
O sin is put away!

Why is thy spirit troubled?
Come forth into the light,
Behold thy risen Saviour,
And praise Him with thy might:

He giveth joy for mourning,
True beauty for decay,
And life for death's enduring:
O sin is put away!

CII. WE SEE THEE NOW, DEAR SAVIOUR.

"For we shall see Him as He is."—JOHN iii. 2.

WE see Thee now, dear Saviour,
   Where mountain mosses lie,
    In the great forest's fulness,
Throughout the boundless sky;
And not a bud or blossom,
Within the loneliest place,
But it reflects the beauty
And brightness of Thy face.

We see Thee in the rainbow,
Fair herald of the shower;
We see Thee in the dew-drop,
We see Thee in the flower;
We see Thee in the order
That everywhere prevails,
The glory of the sunset,
The grandeur of the dales.

But chiefly in the Gospel
Thy loveliness we trace,
Thy smile of perfect sweetness,
The mystery of Thy grace.
O fairest of ten thousand,
The altogether bright,
Our precious strength in weakness,
The weary wanderer's Light!

But O, when life is over,
And flesh and spirit part,
When in Thy own dear Eden
We see Thee as Thou art;
Where prince and peasant mingle
In Zion's royal realm,
What glory! O what glory!
Our souls shall overwhelm!

Prepare us, gracious Spirit,
For this Divine abode:
O let the Sun of Beauty
Beam ever on our road!
Thy soul-enlivening presence
Delightfully impart,
Until, in heaven's clear vision,
We see Thee as Thou art.

CIII. A DRY WIND FROM THE DESERT.

"O Lord, I am oppressed: undertake for me."—ISAIAH xxxviii. 14.

A DRY wind from the desert,
  A sorrow from the sand,
  A thirsty, voiceless valley,
A darkness on the land,

A rising of the river,
A swelling of the sea ;
And yet my loving Father
Shall undertake for me.

As step by step I travel
Towards my resting place,
My prayer shall be for patience
To run the heavenly race ;
And though the verdure faileth,
And nought but dearth I see,
The Giver of the promise
Shall undertake for me.

Here lie unnumbered perils
My homeward course along,
And there huge hills of trouble
Block up my pathway strong.
The arrows of the archer
From bows of malice flee,
And yet my loving Father
Shall undertake for me.

My path was never darker
Than at the present hour,
When black winds fill the forest
And fall upon the flower.
The promised prop is hidden,
No refuge can I see.
And yet my loving Father
Shall undertake for me.

And in the hour of sickness
And life's extreme decay,
When forth into the future
My spirit wings its way,
In life, in death, in judgment,
I safe in Him shall be ;
For then my loving Saviour
Shall undertake for me.

CIV. THE TWILIGHT DEEPENS AS THE DAY.

"Who forgiveth all thine iniquities."—PSALM ciii. 3.

THE twilight deepens as the day
With all its noise fades fast away.
Now let me close my closet door,
And my imperfect life deplore,
Beseeching pardon for my guilt
Through Him whose blood for all was spilt.

What I have left to-day undone,
Forgive, in honour of Thy Son:
What I have wrongly wrought or said,
By blinded selfishness misled,
Content in barrenness to live,
Forgive, dear Father, O forgive!

Have I forgotten in the race
To speak to him of saddened face,

To cheer the orphan from my store,
To bid the mourner weep no more,
To take the feeble by the hand,
And help him o'er life's burning sand?

Perhaps some lonely child of grief
Has looked to me to bring relief,
And I have not in mildness meet
Gone with him to the Saviour's feet,
To seek in penitence and prayer
What never is denied us there.

Forgive me, Father, O forgive,
And teach me how I ought to live.
Still day by day, and hour by hour,
O may I feel Thy Spirit's power
O'ershadowing me with love benign,
Till heaven and all its joys are mine !

CV. ALL DAY—FROM MORN TILL EVEN.

"All day long I have stretched forth my hands unto a disobedient and gainsaying people."—ROMANS x. 21.

ALL day—from morn till even
Shuts on the western wave,
The arms of Christ the Shepherd,
Are still outstretched to save.
All day—till shadows thicken
Along the distant down,
And silence fills the valleys,
And night comes dimly down.

All day—from youth to manhood,
When noon's bright sun is high,
Till eve's increasing twilight
Falls from the fading sky ;
And age, with garments dusty,
Sits 'neath the shadowy height,
And yearns to reach the city
Where it is endless light.

All day is He beseeching,
In voice of tenderest tone,
The erring sons of sorrow
To walk with Him alone.
The seasons change for ever,
The new year groweth old,
But ceaselessly He wooeth
The wanderer to His fold.

All day—from dusk till darkness,
When fears are round us spread,
And hoary hairs are sprinkled
Upon the pilgrim's head.
O may we yield to Jesus,
And give our wanderings o'er;
He granteth strength in weakness,
And glory evermore.

PEACE POEMS.

TO THE

BARONESS BURDETT COUTTS,

DISTINGUISHED FOR HER LIBERALITY TO THE WORKING CLASSES AND HER CHRISTIAN

CONSIDERATION OF THE TOILERS OF GREAT BRITAIN,

WHOSE GENEROUS NAME WILL GO DOWN TO POSTERITY AS THE BENEFACTRESS OF MANKIND, THESE

PEACE POEMS

ARE BY PERMISSION

Humbly and respectfully inscribed

BY THE AUTHOR.

July, 1872.

THE WAR-FIEND.

MAN! Christian! Briton! up, bestir
        thyself!
Red War is rampant.   From his
        cave of bones,
Of numerous nations slaughtered
        in the fight,
He rushes forth with fury, fire, and
        flame,
With ringing steel, with weapons blood-bedyed,
And fire-winged monsters echoing deeds of death.
Red War is rampant, smearing the high hills
And the low valleys with the gore of men,
Snapping the bond of human brotherhood,
And driving man to kill his follow-man,
Who cuts and stabs him in the awful fray,
To be himself the sport of polished blades,
Handled by those he should embrace and love.
Neighbour has met his neighbour on the field,
And both shoot wildly at each other there.
Foe turns his flashing eyes upon his foe,
Intent to plunge the dagger in his heart.

Forth from his cave he comes, this gory fiend,
Where he so long has fed on human flesh
Mown down for him, mown down in days of yore,
And heaped into his vault by bloody hands:
Forth from his cave he comes with murderous mien,
And the earth trembles 'neath his iron feet.

Dost think the Maker of this lovely world,
The great Designer of the Universe,—
Who built the mighty mountains with His word,
And scooped the flowery valleys with His hand;
Who from the very dust created man,
And in his nostrils breathed the breath of life,
So that he started up a living soul,
And bade him live and greatly multiply,
And people the new world,—dost think that He
Designed at first that man should murder man,
Filling the earth with cruelty and blood,
Making its fairy fields a charnel-house,
And the blue skies to blush at human woe?
Man fell,—and Cain was the first murderer.

Up from thy books, and forth into the fields:
What dost thou hear on the rose-scented breeze?
Beneath those stars that shine so beautiful,
Shedding sweet influence on the man of peace.
That look down in thy face so lovingly,
Like eyes of friends escaped away to heaven,—
Beneath those stars the fearful howl is heard,
And the fierce fighters ply their flashing blades;

Shells burst, and rockets hiss, and cannons roar.
Death on his white horse rushes o'er the land,
Trampling with iron hoofs the forms of men :
Flames from his nostrils rush : proud chiefs are singed,
Smouldering to ashes on his ruin-track.

'Tis night : along the sky huge meteors walk,
Like giants flashing with mysterious blades.
Behind them, on those clouds of gory red
Ride hosts of horsemen, and their flickering swords
Clash and re-clash upon the ear of Night ;
And down the sides of those dark rolling hills
Rush streams of human blood, with fire and smoke.
Unearthly sounds are muttering through the dark :
Men shiver in the streets, and talk of woe :
Dogs howl, the ravens scream, and funeral songs
Wail through the midnight with the voice of death,—
Awful prognostics of the coming storm.

List to the crackling of those tongues of fire,
Leaping from roof to roof, from street to street,
Beneath the cloudy mantle of the night.
A city burns with its inhabitants,
Its holy fanes and sculptured palaces,
Its famed cathedrals, gemmed with daring deeds,
Its noble domes, the boast of royalty,
Its costly magazines of precious wealth,
Its choice museums, rich with scraps of eld,
The pith and marrow of all age and time.
Old men and youths, the father and his flock,
Mother and daughter, widow and her charge,
Lover and maiden, mistress and her lord,
Poet and painter, harper and his lute ;
The rich man grasping hard his bags of gold,
And blasted mendicant in fluttering weeds ;
The wise philosopher, and staring clown ;
The man of prayer, and the blasphemer rude :
The new-born infant, and its grey grandsire ;
The veriest drudge, and prince in shining robes,—
Consume together in a whirl of flame.

Hark how the wind moans through those ancient elms,
Flapping their leafless arms in winter-time,
Like spectres gazing at the flying moon.
Forth from yon dwelling stalks an English knight,
Leaving behind him in that lonely vale
A wife, a mother, and his children dear ;
And on he goes to battle. How his arms
Flash in the moonlight, as he hastes away
To meet the foe, and front him foot to foot
And hand to hand ! O, how his great heart beats
When, standing in the entrance of the wood,
He looks back on the dwelling of his youth,
And the fair sleepers swim before his eyes !
Then, dashing off the tear, his steed's quick tread
Rolls through the solitudes as on he sweeps.

Amid the slaughter of the reeking host,
He grapples with the foe. At the first charge
Which stilled the echoes with its deafening roar,
Shot crossing shot, and blast re-crossing blast,
Sweeping away the foeman and his foe,
He thinks of home and friends, of wife and babes,
Of fire-side joys, of walks at summer-time,
Where rose and woodbine hung, and deeds are done
By which his name will live in martial song,
Till the sun darkens, and the moon is blood.

Genius, and valour, and a noble mind
Led him to laurels Hector might have won.
Learning was on his lip, and in his eye
The fiery flashes of an orator.
His ire was as the lightning of the storm.
Fierce, terrible, astounding earth and heaven.
His soul was like a blazing thunderbolt,
Shivering to atoms all impediments.
He hurled his sword with strong Herculean hand.
And armies trembled at its dreadful glare.
He raised his rifle, and grey heroes fell ;
They and their plumes were trampled in the dust.
By tact, and art, and wondrous stratagem,
He led his troops to certain victory.
But when the shout of the pursuing host
Died on the listening ear, and night came on,
When round the camp-fires hoary veterans met,
And tales of slaughtered regiments were told,
His own great name was reckoned with the dead,
He stiff and cold on the red battle-plain !

Ah ! never more that warrior's noble form
Was seen across the threshold of his home ;
And never more his children climbed his knee,
Or wife gazed on the features of her lord.
He fell in battle, covered o'er with wounds.
Ah ! what avails his foreign monument,
Or all the thunder of the trump of fame,
To him, or those who aye bewail his loss ?
An empty chair is now beside his hearth,
And sorrowing hearts for ever cluster there.
Sweet little younglings look for him in vain.
A shadow rests on all terrestrial things.

On sweeps the War-fiend, on his car of flame,
By hungry coursers drawn, whose iron teeth
Gnash in their fury for a human meal.
On sweeps the War-fiend, shaking his hot brand,
With red hair streaming in the sulphur-blast,
And visage dark with blood. On sweeps the fiend,
Rushing o'er vineyards trampled in the dust,
O'er palaces and peasant homes in tears ;
O'er widows, wailing for their husbands slain ;
O'er children, weeping for their murdered sires ;
O'er friend, left friendless in a world of foes ;
O'er sobbing households, ruined, rent, and riven ;
O'er lover, prostrate on the field of death ;
O'er maiden, weeping for that lover there ;
O'er hamlets drenched in blood, o'er towns destroyed.
O'er cities sacked and burnt to wretchedness ;
O'er plains with corses strewn, or white with bones ;
O'er countries saturate with human gore,
Where shrieked the cormorant his doleful note ;
O'er kingdoms shaken with the thunder-blast,
Ploughed up with ruthless bullets, where the sky
Was hung in clouds of darkest drapery.
On sweeps the War-fiend on his maddening march,
With his stern train of smiting followers.
That stab, and shoot, and chop, and rip, and pierce,
And murder in broad day. Earth groaned and writhed
Beneath the huge calamity it bore.

Among the hills he dwelt, that pensive one,
A loving father, with an only child,
His little daughter, beautiful as Spring.
Among the hills he dwelt, that tuneful bard,
Singing his songs unheard in Nature's ear ;

Unless, perchance, beneath some towering cliff,
Or shadowy rock, or wandering far away
Where flowers were clinging to the rugged ridge,
And silent rills went gliding down the steeps,
Or by the margin of the placid lake,
Whose limpid waters mirrored the tall trees,
Where sang the birds their evening orisons,—
Unless, perchance, when sweetly wandering here,
Leading his little fairy daughter forth,
She caught the burden of his rural lyre.

How pleasant were those days, those walks of song
With music and the Muses! How she loved
Those solitary rambles, by the brook,
In the low valley where the swallows played,
And up the mountain-path, high on the crags
Rent by the wintry blast! through meads of flowers,
Where butterflies were floating in the sun,
And gentle breezes murmured sweetest songs.
O, how she loved those walks, to father dear,
And dear to her, Dame Nature's happy child !
Each spot of secrecy in field or fell,
Where oft her sire would sing his madrigals,
Each little brooklet where he mused at morn,
Each rock and hawthorn visited by him,
Were known to her, companion of the bard :
And oft, when evening came, they wandered forth
To revel in the glow-worm's ghostly light.

Behind the western mountains sinks the sun,
And one by one the kindly stars come forth :
The evening dews descend on hill and dale ;
The rising moon illumes the riven crags,
Pouring her first fair rays into the glen ;
And the last story dies beside the hearth.
Forth in the moonlight shadows walks the maid,
With tears upon her cheek. No sire is there,
No poet with his mystic instrument,
No father with his heart brim-full of love.
He, severed from his only daughter's side,
Is forced into the battle. Far away
Is heard the storm and strife of martial hosts,
With all the roar of horrid musketry,
And groans of dying men in sheets of flame.
Amid the stillness of this summer eve
The echo of the far-off fight is heard,
Borne by the breezes to her listening ear,
Like Thunder muttering in his distant caves.

" Where can my father be ? O, tell me where !
They tore him from me while I lay asleep ;
And when at morning from my couch I rose,
He was not at our hearth. I searched the meads,
Climbed up the mountain, hastened down the vale,
Ran to the arbour by the babbling stream.
And where the hawthorn lures with its cool shade,
Flew to the cliff, and roamed the fragrant heath,—
Where he was wont to be delighted much.—
Calling upon his name. He heard me not.
Among the pretty flowers, whose looks were changed,
I sat me down and wept, and wept again,
Till my heart sank within me. Five long days
And long, long nights have I found me desolate.
No food have I to eat, and my brain whirls :
Yet oft methinks, when hunger pierces me,
I hear the music of my mother's voice,
And wonder why I cannot go to her."

Day after day she drew her wasting form
Into the fields, to look out for her sire ;
And day by day her wasting strength declined,
Till one bright summer evening,—as the sun
Tinged the high summits of the' eternal hills,
Leaving his last smile on the golden clouds
That hung around him like a bannered host,—
Under a hawthorn in her native vale,
Her gentle spirit winged its way to heaven. '

War, raise thy brasen trumpet as thou wilt,
And blow with all thy might a thunder-blast,
So that thy roar o'erturn the solid rocks,
And rend the mountains into chasms huge,
Shaking the cities with thy dreadful shout,
And toppling kingdoms over with thy roar !
Ay, howl with all thy might thy last long howl !
Thy reign of blood must shortly have an end,
Thy day of vengeance surely speed away ;
Thy flaming faggots flicker to expire ;
Thy glaring eye-balls slowly film in death,
Thy car be shattered, and thy last shrill clang
Die on the borders of the universe !

See'st thou this book ? It is the Book of God.
What words are glittering on its sacred leaves ?
" A virgin shall conceive, and bear a Son,
And they shall call His name IMMANUEL :
For He shall save His people from their sins.
His peaceful kingdom ever shall increase,
Stretching from isle to isle, from sea to sea,
Till nation against nation lift no sword,
Beating them into ploughshares, and their spears
Shall all be changed to graceful pruning-hooks,—
Till universal man learn war no more."

Fire-breathing monster, on thy hissing steed,
Pawing the seat of power with lightning-hoofs !
It comes, the stormy tempest and thy last ;
The awful plunge of blades which cleaves thy head ;
The furious fight which lays thee on thy bier ;
The hurricane of blows that breaks thy bones ;
The rush of might that leaves thee marrowless ;
And thou shalt perish with thy weight of woe.
Even now thy red arm, lifted in the fight,
Pulls down the curse of Heaven upon thy head :
The heated cannons roll thy dirge of death,
And the cracked trumpet sounds thy requiem :
The rifles cry upon the field of strife,
" We soon shall be transformed to prongs and spades."
The twanging swords, that gleam, and flash, and blaze,
Startlingly utter, " We shall shortly turn
Into keen scythes to cut the ripened grain."
The spears sharp-pointed, too, have found a tongue ;
And blades of every kind and every name,
Spotted with blood, cry, " War will soon be o'er !"

Even now, when musing in my hedge-row bower,
Hushed by the calm of autumn, when the air
Hangs motionless around the echoing earth,
And the leaves fall away so quietly,
Reminding us of death, and the dark grave,—
Even now, when all alone in this sweet spot,
Communing with the spirits of the past,
Or toiling through the ground, where I am oft
Braised in the cave of darkness, till my bones
Cry in their iron harness, and my soul

Longs to shake off this clay and be at rest,—
Even now an echo breaks upon my ear,
Rolling sublimely o'er those granite crags,
And ringing through the caverns of my mount.
" List, list ! the last great battle-hour is near ;
The final conflict will commence its march ;
The roar of warfare is about to end,
And the last struggle that shall tear the world.
The dove of Peace is stirring in her nest,
To bear the olive-branch to every shore.
The holy Bible wins its widening way,
To teach humanity the lore of love.
The Gospel-morn is breaking in all lands,
To usher in the grand millennium.
Men have begun to throw their spears away,
And grasp the hammer for the soldier's blade.
War shakes with anguish, his rude end is near,
And the grey rocks fling back, " HIS END IS NEAR."
Amen, so let it be ! Thy kingdom come !
And the grey rocks reply, " THY KINGDOM COME."

OLD REUBEN.

" Is the scythe ready, Simon ?
  Just put it on the stone,
  That it may cut with keenness
    The clover fully grown.
I've had no other helper
  Since Charlie went to sea,
A-fighting in the frigate :
    So come, and mow with me.

" If peace were always practised
  Abroad and at the board,
We should not need the soldier,
  We should not need the sword :
More useful is the plougher
  Within the rural glen,
And he who moweth clover
  Than he who moweth men.

" Be this thy maxim, Simon,
  That sword and spear shall cease,
And men of every colour
  Bind the full sheaf of peace.
Then trumps unheard by mortal
  Shall on the heights be blown,
And glow along the valleys
  A glory yet unknown.

" The time is speeding, Simon,
  When strength will yield to worth,
And the delicious olive
  Shall flourish o'er the earth.
Then charity shall conquer,
  As overcome it must,
And every battle weapon
  Be buried in the dust."

The scythe was in the clover,
  Old Reuben's words were there ;
They came with every rustle
  That laid the meadow bare.

In Simon's ears they tingled
  Like some angelic chord,
That charity shall conquer,
  And not the lifted sword.

THE LAST STICK.

" Bring forth the last stick, Marie,
  And lay it on the brands,
  The wintry winds are roaring
Along the barren sands ;
The sleet is cold and cruel
  That driveth down the hill,
And beateth on the casement,
  But man is harder still.

" Bring forth the last stick, Marie,
  And draw your cricket nigh,
While the weak pottage cooketh,
  That we may eat and die.
There's nothing more to cheer us,
  From cupboard, shelf, or chest ;
We'll say our prayers together,
  And look to Heaven for rest.

" Bring forth the last stick, Marie,
  Your sire will come no more,
And Laban with him lieth,
  Where earth is red with gore.
What darkness, and what anguish,
  The war has forced us through !
Bring forth the last stick, Marie,
  'Tis all that we can do."

OLD ABEL.

In his cot, where the Nine Maidens stand on the moor,
  Old Abel sat down by his fire on the floor ;
  Said he, as the wood on the hearthstone did crack,
" I'd give my new buckles if Bobby were back."

Then Abel took down an old book from the shelf,
Where the print was quite large, which he kept for
    himself ;
But his vision grew dim, and he stammered, " Alack !
I'd give my new buckles if Bobby were back."

So he put on his spectacles, turned the leaves o'er,
Threw on a fresh branch, and attempted once more ;
But almost sobbed out, as the letters grew black,
" I'd give my new buckles if Bobby were back."

Then he sat on his chair, with his head on his hand,
And talked to himself with his eyes on the brand :
" Ah, war leaves disaster and wrong in its track :
I'd give my new buckles if Bobby were back."

THE WHITE SHIP.

Came a white ship o'er the sea,
  Very white and fair was she,
  With slender mast, and sails of snow,
Gliding over the waves below.

Not a gun, or pike, or sword,
Or bearded spearman was aboard,
And Bible texts the shrouds did show,
Gliding over the waves below.

There fairest damsels sweetly sang,
And viols thrilled and trumpets rang,
" 'Tis peace, 'tis peace, where'er we go,
Gliding over the waves below."

The echo rose from the peopled strand,
And sweetly spread from land to land ;
" 'Tis peace, 'tis peace, where'er we go,
Gliding over the waves below."

From old and young, from down and dell,
The conquering music rose and fell,
" 'Tis peace, 'tis peace, where'er we go,
Gliding over the waves below."

THE HARPER.

THE moon shone on the boulders
Around the beacon's base,
And Silence mid the ivy
Sat with a thoughtful face ;
When by it sang a harper,
Whose notes were sweet and clear,
" Lift up your heads, ye peoples,
The reign of Peace is near."

The old rocks seemed to answer
As in their lairs they lay,
With moonbeams for their helmets,
Like warriors after fray ;
The pines upon its summit
Awoke the joyous cheer,
" Lift up your heads, ye peoples,
The reign of Peace is near."

The wind that swept the shingle
And shook the holly brake,
The mosses of the moorland,
The wavelets of the lake,
Joined the prophetic music
Which stirred the solemn mere,
" Lift up your heads, ye peoples,
The reign of Peace is near."

The moon went down, and morning
Broke o'er the misty hills,
Fierce sunlight flamed the forest
And flashed the flowing rills ;
Yet there that harper standeth,
And harpeth year by year,
" Lift up your heads, ye peoples,
The reign of Peace is near."

NAT NARDIP.

NAT Nardip disobeyed his sire,
Refused to reap and mow,
And more and more his pride increased,
Till he away did go.

He wandered on from town to town,
Oppressed with want and shame,
Until, through rags and emptiness,
A soldier he became.

They marched him off to Brittany,
Where youth and age were slain,
When Nat, disabled, was dismissed,
And home he came again.
Gray Eve was musing in the withs,
As he drew near the door ;
And the last carol of the lark
Was ringing on the moor.

He waited till the dusk increased ;
And when 'twas growing late,
With trembling step and rising fears
He oped the garden gate ;
And through the window he espied
His father in his nook,
His mother with her knitting-sheath,
His sister at her book.

He raised his hand, and feebly gave
A very low rat-tat,
When Jetty oped the door, and cried,
" O mother, 'tis our Nat ! "
" Come in, come in ! " the old man cried,
" I pardon all thy strife :
The erring wanderer has returned,
Down with the trencher, wife ! "

LIVE IN PEACE.

A LITTLE stream went flowing by,
Where vales were green, where hills were
high ;
And as it murmured on its way,
At eve and morn, it seemed to say,
Still travelling downward to the sea,
" O live in peace, where'er you be ! "

The pretty fishes 'neath the wave
That hide in many a quiet cave,
The bees and flies that sport their hours
Around the lovely ferns and flowers,
Are ever whispering, full and free,
" O live in peace, where'er you be ! "

The rushy vale, the mountain brown,
The swallow wheeling o'er the down,
The solemn tarn, the echoing moor,
The boulders on the great sea-shore,
All whisper, where the echoes flee,
" O live in peace, where'er you be ! "

And there's a mystery on the height,
Which fills with sound the listening Night ;
And in the bosom of the dell,
Who listens oft will hear it well,
The burden of the land and sea,
" O live in peace, where'er you be ! "

A VISION.

WHERE the woodbine and whortle arose,
  And held their sweet cups to the sun,
    I sat in a dingle of rose,
When an evening of June had begun ;
And far o'er the rock-covered wold,
  Where the glory of sunset did lie,
In currents of crimson and gold,
  A vision arose on mine eye :

A country of meadow and stream,
  With valleys of palm-tree and vine,
Where corn in its richness did gleam,
  And fattened the beautiful kine.
The ploughman was on the wide mead,
  The milkmaid was under the tree,
The shepherd was tuning his reed
  Afar on the bountiful lea.

Here Peace, in a halo of light,
  Her sway o'er the populace spread ;
No clamour arose on the night,
  No cry of the orphan for bread.
The sword and the battle-axe then
  Were changed to the glittering share,
And songs from the bosoms of men
  Swelled on the millennium air.

No brother chased brother to death,
  No master did fetter the slave,
No chief-trump received the warm breath:
  O, War had gone down to his grave.
And over the nations a joy
  For ever fresh honours did win,
Which rifles would never destroy,—
  The kingdom of love had set in.

WE WILL EVER BE KIND TO ALL.

WEAKNESS, gentleness, and worth,
  In the ages of the earth,
    Have been left where boasters brawl;
But we'll ever be kind to all.

Should a brother lose his track,
We will strive to lure him back,
Holding up the hands that fall;
For we'll ever be kind to all.

Bird and beast, by steep and strand,
In the ocean, or on the land,
Whether they walk, or whether they crawl,
We will ever be kind to all.

Children playing in the lane,
Driver whistling on the wain,
Travellers great, and travellers small,
We will ever be kind to all.

Old and young, and rich and poor,
In the meadow, or on the moor,
Until rifles rust and fall,
We will ever be kind to all.

THE ORPHANS.

"O WAIT a little, Lucy :
  The moon is o'er the lake :
    Perhaps our dearest mother
May very soon awake.
I never saw her sleeping
  So peacefully as now,
Or witnessed such a paleness
  Upon her cheek and brow.

"Has she not suffered hunger,
  And weariness and pain,
With longings that our father
  Would come to us again ?
Let's wait a little longer :
  Perhaps he may be here,
To comfort us in sorrow,
  And kiss away the tear."

The moon went down in silence,
  And yet no father came ;
And day by day they waited,
  And it was still the same.
Alas ! their soldier-parent
  Will never see them more,
Down trodden in the battle,
  With garments rolled in gore.

THE GUNNER.

THROUGH the fields a gunner came,
  Somewhat scarred and somewhat lame :
    Spoke he under a chestnut tree,—
"This is the home of Molly and me.

"Day by day, as the battle roared,
Fed with famine and fire and sword,
Ever I saw it under the tree,—
This is the home of Molly and me.

" In the fierceness of the fight,
Firing left, and firing right,
Up it rose like a vision free,—
This is the home of Molly and me.

" Up the hill, and down the glade,
Where I've travelled, where I've strayed,
Nought is half so fair to see.
As the home of Molly and me.

" Things will alter by and bye,
Kings themselves should fight. say I :
Rest thee, soldier, under the tree,—
This is the home of Molly and me."

THE SAD LETTER.

"READ out the letter, Susan :
  Where did our Robert fall ?
    Was it by shell or splinter ?
Was it by blade or ball ?

H H

I in my chair will listen,
  Beside the kindling brand,
My feet upon the fender,
  My head upon my hand."

Then Susan read the letter,
  Which from the captain came,
From side to side, all over,
  By the pine-branch's flame.
Upon a stormy rampart,
  One noisy battle-day,
When blood was shed like water,
  His life was blown away.

The old man moaned in spirit,
  Like wind among the waves ;
And Susan's heart in fervour
  Arose to Him who saves.
But no one knows the anguish,
  The bitter cup of life,
Which that sad letter carried
  To Robert and his wife.

HURRAH FOR THE SHARE.

Hurrah for the share, the shining share,
  Where the ploughman breathes the country air,
  Where the daisy blooms by the granite cross,
And the snowdrop muses among the moss,
And the blue-bells hang in their arbours rare :
Hurrah ! hurrah ! for the shining share !

Hurrah for the share ! the shining share !
Which has nought of the soldier's borrowed glare :
No desperate deeds with fire and shout,
No ransacked cities, no homes burnt out,
No states o'erturned, no lands laid bare,
Can ever be placed to the shining share.

Hurrah for the share ! the shining share !
Which doth for the scythe and the flail prepare,
Which bringeth the loaf to the poor man's board,
And addeth its store to the prince's hoard ;
Without it the shelf and the cupboard were bare,
Hurrah for the share ! the shining share !

THE LAME SCHOOLMASTER.

Where four roads met in quaintness,
  Upon the hedgeless moor,
  A lame old man instructed
The children of the poor.
And hanging in his schoolroom
  Was many a curious board :
" Why cannot wrongs be settled
  Without the flashing sword ? "

'Tis said by those who knew him
  That stripes were his disdain ;
He never beat a pupil,
  He never used a cane ;
Yet rich became his scholars
  From wisdom's golden hoard.
Why cannot wrongs be settled
  Without the flashing sword ?

And still the utmost order
  Prevailed throughout the place :
He had some word of comfort
  To cheer the rising race ;
And sang they morn and even
  How peace should be restored,
And human wrongs be settled
  Without the flashing sword.

Forth went that old man's pupils
  Along their several ways,
With peace-stars on their banners,
  Throughout the after days :
Each strove for arbitration,
  Of which we are assured,
When wrongs shall all be settled
  Without the flashing sword.

THE STRONG SMITH BY THE SEA.

In the peaceful days to be
  Worked a strong smith by the sea,
  Chanting thus, with bosom bare,
" The sword I change to the shining share."

Heaps of spears in his smithy lay,
Blades gore-dyed in the fearful fray,
And the sparks rose high on the morning air
As the sword was changed to the shining share.

And loud the monster bellows roared,
Reddening many an ancient sword.
" This is the way," sang the strong smith there,
" To change the spear to the shining share."

The great wind came from the northern moor,
And shook the walls from roof to floor ;
But that steady smith, in the forge's glare,
Still changed the sword to the shining share.

And ever that strong man laboured he,
Summer and winter beside the sea,
With heavy hammer and bosom bare,
Till the swords were changed to the shining share.

OLD JOHN.

" We'll keep the kettle boiling, John ;
  Perhaps our boy will come.
  What gathering darkness has been ours
Since first he left his home !
Heap up another lot of pine :
  Did not the letter say,
That he would leave the hospital,
  And be at home to-day ? "

The old man shook his locks of snow,
  And bowed his reverend head ;
And, sitting in his own arm-chair,
  He very slowly said :—
" Mishaps attend the soldier's life,
  And weariness and pain,
And much that offers fair is false :
  So let us wait, dear Jane.

" I had a vision yestereve
 Of blossoms white and rare :
A little child the lion led,
 The wolf and lamb were there :
No tent of war was on the plain,
 The sounds of strife did cease,
And through the air an angel sang,
 ' It is the reign of Peace.'

" This blessed time will surely come,
 I pray for its advance,
When men shall not each other slay
 With sabre, shot, or lance.
Our boy henceforth shall stay at home,
 And use the sword no more.
I hear a footstep in the lane ;
 Hark ! hark ! he's at the door."

THE FARMER.

No one could stop the farmer :
 He buckled on his sword,
 Brought out his snowy charger,
And crossed the noisy ford.
Then to his little sister,
 Within the lattice light,
He waved his hand at parting,
 And dashed into the fight.

No one could stop the farmer :
 He rode where swords were crossed,
And men of giant stature
 Were wildly hewn and lost.
Blood soaked the ground like water,
 And in red brooklets ran,
And groans arose in anguish
 From dying beast and man.

No one could stop the farmer :
 He passed where sons were slain,
And hoary-headed fathers
 Lay hacked upon the plain.
Blades fell with awful clangour,
 Which heads and helmets broke,
And Carnage sat in terror
 Upon his throne of smoke.

No one could stop the farmer :
 He swept through woods of spears,
With the sharp hiss of bullets
 And steel-points in his ears ;
On, on, with headlong gallop,
 Into the awful night,
Whence he returneth never
 Upon his charger white.

UNCLE JABEZ.

" COME in, Uncle Jabez, the settle
 Awaiteth you in the old hall :
 That very deep scar on your forehead
Was made by a rifleman's ball.

You have been in the wars, Uncle Jabez,
 Where weakness is trodden by might,
And force is the hero in laurel,
 And strength is the author of right.

" Come into the hall, Uncle Jabez,
 And Peggy shall bring you some meat :
Do put your great crutch in the corner,
 And rest on the fender your feet.
Your days with the match-lock are over,
 Your country will need you no more ;
And yet they have left you to wander,
 Forsaken, and homeless, and poor.

" Come into the hall, Uncle Jabez,
 That I may your kindness return :
You saved my life once on the beacon,
 When the thunder-god spoke in the fern ;
And goodness comes back to the giver,
 Although it may seem to delay.
My home is your home, Uncle Jabez,
 And here you are welcome to stay."

The old man advanced at her bidding,
 And sat in the snug proffered place ;
And oft he made use of his kerchief
 To wipe the warm tears from his face.
Then Peggy came in with the platter,
 And placed before Jabez his mess :
He smoothed down his hair, and said softly,
 " Thank God for a friend in distress ! "

THROUGH THE WOODS, AT CLOSE OF DAY.

THROUGH the woods, at close of day,
 Came an old man, worn and gray,
 And he sang with native art,
" Come, sweet Peace, and never depart."

Clear the echo rose and fell,
Over the dingle and over the dell,
Over the moor and over the mart,
" Come, sweet Peace, and never depart."

And the ploughman on the lea,
And the woodman 'neath the tree,
Caught the strain with glowing heart :
" Come, sweet Peace, and never depart."

Children sang where daisies grow,
Men whose hair was white as snow,
Duke, and driver by his cart :
" Come, sweet Peace, and never depart."

Thus the song that old man sang
Through the gladdened nations rang,
Till the demon of war did start :
" Come, sweet Peace, and never depart."

AN ECHO FROM MOUNT LEBANON.

AN echo from Mount Lebanon
 Amid the cedars grand :
 O spears shall change to pruning-hooks
Throughout the peaceful land :

Sharp swords shall into ploughshares turn,
And fighting days be o'er;
All nations learn the arts of peace,
And war shall be no more.

Far down the cycles of the past
This joyful sound has come;
It rings throughout the palace vast,
In every poor man's home:
'Tis heard along the lonely wood,
In ocean's solemn roar,
And spreads from listening vale to vale,
That war shall be no more.

The palms where Israel's prophets trod
Still murmur on the plain,
And prince and peasant lift their heads
To catch the silvery strain,
From Cedron's brook to Carmel's crest,
From Hor to Allion's shore,
From east to west, from north to south,
That war shall be no more.

O this belief shall still be ours,
In spite of spear and shield,
And fighting ships and fighting men;
We cannot, dare not yield.
The beams of Peace will shortly break
Through Morning's golden door,
And stream on all the gladdened earth,
And war shall be no more.

JOE AND HIS MOTHER.

"Is Joe's bed ready, Charlotte?
Smooth down the sheets of snow,
And ope the little lattice
About half-way or so.
Then place some sprigs of myrtle,
Fresh gathered from the stem,
Within a glass of water.
And put a rose with them.

"I'll seek the curious cromlech
Where swallows love to play,
And watch along the willows:
Perhaps he'll come to-day."
And saying this, she hastened
Along the rocky down,
And watched till twilight settled
Upon the beacon brown.

And every day she gathered
Fresh myrtle from the frame,
Then climbed the hill and waited,
And yet he never came.
His bed was always ready,
The pillows placed with care,
Awaiting Joe the soldier,
And yet he came not there.

The widow's hair grew snowy,
As year succeeded year,
In patient expectation,
With faith and hope sincere.

Through wind and rain and sunshine
Still watched the loving dame.
And for her Josey waited,
And yet he never came.

THE CHILD'S PRAYER.

No sound, no sound, from bower or brake,
The crimson light was on the lake,
When a child prayed thus, in her hamlet home,
"O, Father above, let Thy kingdom come!"

The eve star glimmered above the pines,
And the sparrow had nestled among the vines,
As that child prayed soft in her dearest home,
"O, Father above, let Thy kingdom come!"

The moonlight stole through the Gothic panes,
And the bats were out in the woodbine lanes,
And prayed she thus in her quiet home,
"O, Father above, let Thy kingdom come!"

The dew came down in the floweret's cup,
And the leaves of the rose-tree drank it up,
And He heard her prayer in His highest home,
"O, Father above, let Thy kingdom come!"

The sound went forth from rill to rill,
From glade to glade, from hill to hill,
From town to town, from home to home,
"O, Father above, let Thy kingdom come!"

And the warrior's club became a flail,
And the spear was changed to the iron rail,
And peace-strains rose from every home,
"O, Father above, let Thy kingdom come!"

WILLIE AND MEG.

Meg took her pitcher to the dell,
Where ferns like fairies stood,
And then well-pleased she viewed herself
Reflected in the flood;
And thought of one in soldier vest
Who bade her hope and wait,
And when the corn was in the stack
She should be Willie's mate.

But she had waited wearily,
The corn was threshed and sold,
And yet he knocked not at her door
By which the river rolled.
"He may be wounded in the fight;
Or is he dead," thought she,
"And lying where the warriors fell?
For false he cannot be!"

She heard a rustling in the grass
Upon the summer air,
And looking round how struck was she,
For Willie's self was there!

And soon his arms were round her thrown
  In love's untold embrace,
Her name upon his truthful lips,
  His kiss upon her face.

"O Meg, I've seen enough," said he,
  "In camp and tented field,
Where many a warrior slept in death
  Upon his broken shield.
'Tis wrong, 'tis wrong, I'll fight no more,
  My all to thee I bring;
Before another month is past
  Our wedding bells shall ring."

DAME DOLO.

By Mainporth Crag, where the breakers foam,
  Dame Dolo dwelt in her boulder home;
And she was aged, and worn, and weak,
And the furrows were deep on her brow and cheek.

Dame Dolo sat by her fire of peat,
And throbbed her heart in the smouldering heat,
The wind like a war steed paced the Crag,
And smote the water and lashed the flag.

"My bread is done," Dame Dolo said,
"My cans are empty, my silver fled;
But though no way just now I see,
My Father above will care for me."

A voice at the lattice aroused the Dame,
From a soldier man footsore and lame:
With earnest eyes around looked he:
'Twas her own dear Jack, from over the sea.

What his wallet held was mean and small,
Though it served till the generous rector's call;
But his broken health nought could restore,
Till by Mainporth Crag he was seen no more.

A CHILD GREW UP AT NAZARETH.

A Child grew up at Nazareth,
  The Infinite made man,
  Who self-existent long had reigned
Before the stars began.
He spoke by Cedron's flowing brook,
  With lips that cannot lie,
"Whoever takes the sword of war
  Shall fall himself thereby."

Men heard it, but they heeded not,
  And turned their ears away,
Snatched up in ire the battle-axe,
  And perished in the fray.
Yet still the echo rolleth on,
  And filleth earth and sky,
"Whoever takes the sword of war
  Shall fall himself thereby."

And as the centuries come and go
  They oft this fact proclaim,
Where hostile armies armies meet,
  O'ercome with fire and flame.
The sound is travelling through the earth
  As fast as time can fly,
"Whoever takes the sword of war
  Shall fall himself thereby."

O ye who fan the fires of strife,
  And thicken human gloom,
Hear what the awful Judge proclaims,
  Blush at His words of doom.
Away, away with battle-ships,
  Let peaceful pennons fly;
For he who takes the sword of war
  Shall fall himself thereby.

THE BENIGHTED HUSSAR.

'Twas when the gorse was golden
  In fragrance on the moor,
  An old benighted soldier
Knocked at the shepherd's door.
They gave him kindly greeting,
  And offered him a seat,
And he was shortly chatting
  Beside the smoking peat.

The shepherd's little daughter
  Soon hushed her simple lay,
And gazed upon the stranger
  With eyes of tenderest ray.
Then rose, and whispered sweetly,
  As she before him stood,
"This is the man, dear father,
  Who saved me from the flood."

With tears the gladdened mother
  The old hussar addressed:
"Right welcome art thou, soldier,
  We'll feed thee with the best.
Lay down thy simple wallet,
  And take the table's end,
And we will shortly show thee
  How we can feast a friend."

The soldier ate in silence,
  Then spoke, and looked above:
"I've learnt this holy lesson,
  The loftiest power is love.
And he who feeds the hungry,
  At Friendship's generous board,
Is greater than the warrior
  That buckles on his sword."

ROB ROOD.

At Lizard, by the Lion's Den,
  Rob left his youthful wife,
  And donned the soldier's uniform,
And rushed into the strife.

He vainly thought to gain renown,
But lost his limbs and health,
And back at last he feebly came,
A crutch his only wealth.

He gained a gentle eminence
From city home aloof,
And saw the curling smoke ascend
Beyond his cottage roof.
The milkmaid caroled on the mead,
The lark was in the skies,
The ploughman whistled by his team,
And tears came in his eyes.

With his one hand he waved his cap,
As on his crutch he leant,
To Susan standing by the door,
And shouted as he went.
She held her smiling babe aloft,
Who seemed her bliss to share,
So that the honeysuckles kissed
Her soft and shining hair.

He crossed the village bridge at last,
And hobbled o'er the green,
And felt his own dear Susan's kiss
The garden flowers between;
Then sat within his humble home
With baby on his knee :
" O wife ! the sinful sword of war
Is red with guilt," said he.

THE SOLDIER'S WIFE.

" STILL Eve cometh out of her chamber,
With the dew shining bright in her hair ;
And homeward the ploughman returneth,
Half stript of his burden of care.
But, baby, thy father will never
Come back to his dwelling again,
Or kiss the bright face of his darling ;
For now he lies dead on the plain.

" He pressed us so warmly at parting,
And bade us be cheerful and gay,
And when he came back from the battle,
He'd never again go away.
But he fell, so the newspaper sayeth,
When making a gallant attack :
Alas for his widow and orphan,
Alone on a desolate track !

" Hush ! baby, my tears have aroused thee ;
The wind cometh down from the height ;
Strange fingers are moving the lattice,
The mystical murmurs of night.
Thou sleepest ! I'll pray by thy cradle,
Where lieth his last offered toy
Thy father brought home to his darling :
O be not a soldier, my boy."

THE LAST ATTACK.

THE lurid air with shocks was rent :
Arose one heavy, huge lament
From shepherd's shell and warrior's tent.

Great towers lay prostrate in the gloom,
And cities 'neath the foot of Doom,
And Mercy found on earth no room.

The widow wailed her husband dead,
The orphan died for lack of bread,
And love and charity were fled.

Gore dripped from peaks of frozen snow,
And stained the silent flowers below,
Wherever erring man could go.

The battered corpses rose in hills,
And blood rushed down in swollen rills,
And greatest he who greatest kills.

Then came a voice across the dark,
The steady gunner missed his mark,
And desperate swordsmen whispered, " Hark ! "

'Twas Peace, with all her gentle train,
O'er every clan and clime to reign,
And swords were never raised again.

THE SOLDIER'S FATHER.

" LEAD Boxer to the stable, boy,
We'll plough no more to-day ;
And, Abel, see you give the beast
A feed of corn and hay.
I must ride off this afternoon
As fast as we can go,
And get, within the market-town,
A doctor for our Joe.

" He left us when the elm was green,
And corn was in the ear,
For lands where warriors walked the woods,
And watched the passes drear.
Instead of peace he bore a sword,
Instead of meekness, might ;
And in the soldier's lofty plume
He trampled on the right.

" His regiment was overpowered,
And many sadly slain ;
For two long days and longer nights
Joe lay upon the plain.
They brought him to his mother's home,
A feeble, broken thing ;
So I must to the market-town,
And our good doctor bring."

ANNIE AND AMOS.

A DOWN to the well walked Annie,
Humming a pastoral lay,
Thinking of one who had left her
Over the hills and away.
Whom should she see but a soldier,
Looking so weary and worn ?
On the old seat he was sitting,
Under the favourite thorn.

He had deep scars on his forehead,
　He had deep scars on his breast,
And strikingly pale were his features,
　As if he were longing for rest.
He rose when she came to the fountain,
　And asked her to give him a drink;
And while she was holding the pitcher,
　She thought the poor fellow would sink.

At last their eyes met in the hollow:
　The soldier gazed sadly and sighed,
Whilst Annie her white arms uplifted,
　"'Tis Amos! 'tis Amos!" she cried.
And now in the cot of his father
　He trails his crushed foot on the floor,
And knows that for life he's a cripple,
　Whilst Annie peeps in at the door.

WILL WARD.

WILL Ward passed by the farm-yard gate,
　His arm was in a sling;
He had been soldiering in the ranks,
　By order of the king.
They said, 'twas noble thus to wear
　The coat of crimson hue,
And learn to shoot his fellow-men;
　And Will believed it true.

So off he went to fight the French,
　Equipped from head to heel,
With knapsack on his shoulder strapped,
　Bright musket, and sharp steel;
And as he passed the holly-fence,
　The old thatched barn in sight,
He heard his father at the plough
　Say, "Why do Christians fight?"

The cannon roars, the war-steed moans,
　The hissing bullet rends;
And Will came back with broken limbs,
　A burden on his friends.
And hobbling down the garden walk,
　Where roses blossomed bright,
He heard his father at the door
　Say, "Why do Christians fight?"

His sorrowing mother dressed his wounds,
　And Mary came to see,
Who with her thrifty parents dwelt,
　Beside the shepherd's tree.
And oft the old man bent his head
　When Willie was in sight,
As if he spoke to one unseen,
　"No! Christians cannot fight!"

THE WAKENING WIND.

CAME a wind from the farthest hills,
　Giving a voice to the crystal rills:
　"Earth below, and heaven above,
Teach us ever to live in love!"

Through the forest rode the blast,
Shaking the cedars as it passed:
　"Earth below, and heaven above,
Teach us ever to live in love!"

Swept that wind through ocean's caves,
Sounding aloud on the lifted waves:
　"Earth below, and heaven above,
Teach us ever to live in love!"

The nations rose with a gladdened soul,
And threw their swords to the mining mole:
　"Earth below, and heaven above,
Teach us ever to live in love!"

And mother and child, to the farthest vale,
Rejoiced in the sound of that sweeping gale:
　"Earth below, and heaven above,
Teach us ever to live in love!"

ALF ANDREWS.

ALF Andrews sat upon a stool,
　Beside his father's feet;
A pale-faced, gentle-looking boy,
　With scarce enough to eat.
And thus he spoke, with thoughtful eyes,
　And slowly raised his head,
"Why don't you be a soldier, dad,
　And wear a coat of red?"

"No, no, my son. You know the man
　We met the other day
Among the pines upon the peak:
　His arms were shot away.
For years he served on foreign fields,
　With cutlass, pike, and gun,
In cold and heat, in strife and gore,
　And this is all he won.

"I'd rather dwell where peace-flowers grow,
　Apart from human strife,
And feebly aid my fellow-men
　Along the road of life,
Than wear the soldier's crimson badge,
　To gain a hero's name,
In polished brass and printed books:
　Away with such a fame!

"The happiest man is he, my son,
　Who lifts the load of care;
Who takes his brother by the hand
　Along the desert bare;
Who fills the orphan child with bread,
　The widow's heart with joy,
And smooths the evening path of life;
　Be such an one, my boy."

THE REIGN OF PEACE.

THE reign of endless peace is near:
　Away, away, with sword and spear;
　Let needle-guns and cannon lie
In foul neglect beneath the sky;

Or go to aid the wondrous rail
Or iron ships before the gale.

Along the margin of the moor,
Through vines which shade the rustic door:
By temples reared on forest sod,
Where red men meet to worship God;
The morn of peace, in beauty bland,
Is breaking o'er the gladdened land.

The rich and poor secure shall dwell,
Unguarded then by ship or shell;
Sweet rose and olive fill the glade,
The latest warrior sheath his blade;
Sweet peace its living power attest,
And earth repose in perfect rest.

WANA WERTHER.

"SIT down, my loves, to supper,"
  Poor Wana Werther said;
  "And let me give you quickly
  The last dry crust of bread.
I wonder why your father
  Should thus so long remain,
Where Havoc's arm is gory
  Upon the dreadful plain.

"I'll take the road to Mawnan,
  And watch below the tower,
Should any boats be coming
  At this clear moonlight hour.
O, when will Reuben meet me?
  O, when will war be o'er?
Hark! hark! a boat's keel grateth
  Upon the silent shore."

'Tis Reuben, yes, 'tis Reuben;
  But O, how changed is he!
One arm has been shot from him,
  His leg beyond the knee;
A bandage round his forehead
  Half hides a fearful scar.
O, Reuben, soldier Reuben!
  Are these the fruits of war?

'Tis said that in the winter,
  When winds were on the wold,
They perished in their dwelling
  Of hunger, pain, and cold.
And still a woman's wailing
  Is heard along the shore:
"O, when will Reuben meet me?
  O, when will war be o'er?"

PETER PINE.

'TWAS Christmas tide and carol,
  The ice was on the vine,
  When down the lane came lowly
Dear little Peter Pine.

His cap was old and shabby,
  His hair did strangely flow,
His coat had wide rents in it,
  His toes were in the snow.

Nine years was he last birthday;
  And at a roadside door
He told his simple story,
  Which grieved the listener sore.
His father in the warfare
  Was shattered by a ball,
When marching on to conquer,
  As rose the trumpet's call.

His mother pined to hear it,
  Like floweret on the moor,
When sudden frosts come chilling,
  And rising tempests roar.
And day by day she wasted,
  Till all her strength had flown:
Then angels called her to them,
  Where hunger is unknown.

So now he was an orphan,
  Poor little Peter Pine;
For two days had he fasted,
  His pale face showed the brine.
And sang he in his sadness,
  "O lady, give me bread!
O lady, gentle lady,
  I would that I were dead!"

The moon arose at midnight
  Upon the glittering snow,
And flung her robes of silver
  On hill and vale below;
But Death had claimed the orphan
  At that brief day's decline,
As 'neath the squire's low laurel
  Lay little Peter Pine.

MARTIN'S PORRINGER.

"DON'T sell our Martin's porringer,
  Although of low estate;
  But leave it on the dresser shelf,
  Beside the pewter plate.
'Twas his when he long lessons learnt
  Beneath the schoolhouse tile;
And also when a youth he joined
  The army of the isle.

"A thousand memories come to me
  When I behold it there,
How oft I danced him on my knee,
  And half forgot my care;
Or led him forth among the flowers,
  O'er many a rustic stile,
And little thought my boy would join
  The army of the isle.

"How pleased was I at supper time
  To see him in his place!
I felt so happy that the tears
  Would trickle down my face.

I hoped he would have tilled the farm,
And raised the clover pile ;
Nor ever dreamt my boy would swell
The army of the isle.

"Don't sell that simple porringer,
'Tis everything to me,
Since my poor boy, with soldier hands,
Was buried by the tree.
Full oft it lessens loneliness,
Although I weep the while,
For him who joined, misled by fame,
The army of the isle."

AGNES ARROW.

Not far from Helford Passage,
Just up a narrow lane,
Resided Agnes Arrow,
A widow, poor and plain.
Her only son had left her,
The fighting ranks to swell ;
And rumour said he perished,
When England's foemen fell.

So Agnes in her cottage
Lived near the southern shore ;
And thus one eve she murmured,
"'Tis no use waiting more.
I thought perhaps he'd see me,
When the great war was done ;
Yet I am ever lonely
From setting sun to sun.

"'Tis no use waiting longer ;
Yet hark ! there's some one near:
A moving of the wicket
Methinks I faintly hear."
And in another moment
She felt her son's embrace,
And knew it was her Robby,
And praises shook the place.

Yet he was scarcely like him,
Her beautiful, her brave :
She nursed him in her chamber
With what the parish gave.
And when the moon was rising
The crippled soldier died ;
And he and Agnes Arrow
Are sleeping side by side.

EDDY EAST.

"Open the door, mother, quickly,
Our Eddy is down by the gate ;
And O, he is looking so poorly :
He active, and don't let him wait !"
And soon on his neck she was sobbing,
And kissing the face of her son ;
The fire was alight, and the kettle
Its musical song had begun.

His father came down from his threshing,
And vowed he would rather behold
His Eddy once more in the cottage,
Than have any measure of gold.
His sister, the beautiful Polly,
As bright as the forehead of Day,
Was clapping her hands in her gladness,
And dancing around like a fay.

They put him to rest in the settle :
Then said, with a sob, the poor boy,
"I am come home to stay with you, mother,
And have done with the soldier's employ.
The fruit of the battle is baleful,
Whoever the fighter may be :
The glory of war is but glitter :
So the farm and the garden for me."

CRIPPLED WILLIE.

"Who lives in that house yonder,
Where woodbines reach the eaves,
With one small diamond lattice
Where roses rest their leaves ?
Ten years ago, last Easter,
I left my Fanny here,
When for the wars we parted,
And both brushed off the tear.

"We promised to be faithful,
Whatever might betide ;
And when the war was over
She should be Willie's bride.
She hung upon my shoulder
When I was going away,
And kissed my face so fondly,
And wished that I could stay.

"But I had long enlisted,
And thus was forced to go ;
And twenty times I watched her
Along the upland slow.
She waved her snowy kerchief,
Till it was lost to sight ;
A hundred times I saw it
When in the fiercest fight.

"I think I'll ope the wicket,
And hobble to the door,
And stand beneath the woodbine,
A knocking as of yore."
And soon he looked on Fanny,
Alas! another's bride ;
And in a few weeks after
Poor crippled Willie died.

ISAAC ISLE.

'Twas Ember Week, and the lengthening light
Grew more and more on vale and height,
When Isaac Isle and his good wife Joan
Sat near the brands on the wide hearthstone.
Their glasses in their sheath-homes lay,
When Isaac Isle to the dame did say:—

"The ends of the days are stretching, Joan:
I can see from here the Druid Stone.
Pull back the blind some inches more,
We need no candle yet, I'm sure.
And what a blessing again to be
In a few weeks more from lighting free!"

Just then, as the brands a-flame did roar,
A tall thin man came in at the door.
On a crutch he leant, with a trembling gait,
Which seemed to cripple beneath his weight;
And he stood stock-still at his father's moan:
"'Tis Tommy come back from the wars!" cried Joan.

LETTY LORE.

"THE way is lonely, Letty,
    The cold night wind is high;
    No star looks through the blackness,
No moon is in the sky.
The great trees shake with sorrow,
    A sigh is on the snow;
And Letty Lore is weary:
    Ah! whither shall we go?

"Dost hear the thunder, Letty,
    Along the northern height?
The mountain gods are angry
    For deeds of death to-night.
The household head is smitten,
    The child an orphan made,
The peaceful wife a widow,
    To glut the soldier's trade.

"A light in yon small window
    Is shining through the gloom:
Knock, knock, and ask the cottar
    To give the houseless room."
And soon before the faggot
    They whispered in the heat;
While Goody fried the rasher,
    And brought the broken meat.

There are true hearts and tender
    In every Christian clan,
So that sometimes the stronger
    Assists the weaker man.
Nor is affection warmer,
    From farthest east to west,
Or charity more lovely
    Than in the peasant's breast.

AARON ARCH.

"STILL sleeping, dearest mother,
    To the music of the rain,
    Which falls among the roses,
Beside the diamond pane.
Come down, and ope the wicket,
    Undo the iron bar:
'Tis Aaron Arch, your Aaron,
    Returning from the war.

"There is a slender stirring,
    The blind is pushed aside;
O, mother, 'tis your Aaron,
    Now ope the casement wide.
It is her face. I see it.
    O mother! look again:
'Tis Aaron Arch, your Aaron,
    Here standing in the rain.

"I hear a footfall surely
    Beside the stair-head clock;
And now the old key turneth
    Within the birchen lock.
She cometh. Yes, she cometh,
    With many a falling tear.
Her kiss is on my forehead,
    Her voice is in my ear."

And soon the peat was smoking,
    The pewter on the board;
The best the cottage yielded
    Had left the secret hoard.
"Bless God!" the widow shouted,
    And Aaron shouted too:
"I've only one hand, mother,
    But that shall work for you!"

RAGLAN RUBE.

OLD Raglan Rube at even
    Sat silent by the hearth,
    While in his soul's recesses
Mysterious thoughts had birth;
But one above all others
    Rose up, and filled the gloom,—
A son who long had left him
    To face the battle's doom.

Old Raglan's hair grew thinner,
    His feeble step more slow,
His wife was dead and buried
    Beneath the yew-tree low.
Alone he lived, and wondered
    Where human loves could flee;
Why fades the flower of friendship,
    And where his boy could be.

His casement is half-open,
    And some one taps the pane.
Rube raised his head to listen,
    And it was tapped again.
"Come ye with words of sorrow?
    Come ye with words of joy?
Come ye from o'er the mountains
    With tidings of my boy?"

The latch was lifted quickly,
    Ere Rube could leave his place,
And Willie sprang to greet him,
    With scars upon his face.
The clock ticked in the corner,
    The kitten gamboled near;
But Raglan Rube could utter
    No words but, "Willie dear!"

BRETHREN ALL.

ALONG the lawns, when fires are low,
An echo murmureth sweet and slow,
If sunbeams shine, or shadows fail,
That red and white are brethren all.

The stars proclaim it overhead,
The moon within her watery bed,
The clouds that fly the tempest's call,
That red and white are brethren all.

What brooks it if the coat be poor,
And reed-caves hang above the door,
And children on the rush-mats sprawl?
The red and white are brethren all.

O come it will, as sure as day,
When dim distinctions shall give way;
And man with man, the great and small,
The red and white, be brethren all.

THE LAST WARRIOR.

THE ground was red with gore,
Red waves rolled on the shore;
Uncoffined armies stiffened where they fell;
Cities and towns were void,
Deserted, sacked, destroyed,
And creeping things did in their ruins dwell.

Blood trickled down the hills,
Blood oozed into the rills,
Stained the sad valleys, hung upon the reeds,
Dripped from the shattered plough,
Stared on the battery's brow,
And crimsoned was the verdure of the meads.

Ships home or outward bound
Foundered, or ran a-ground;
The harbour waves moaned sadly on the strand;
Corn-fields were burnt with fire,
Orchard and vine, and dire,
Dark desolation frowned on sea and land.

Wild War had dared his worst,
The red earth lay accurst,
Death had hewn clans to silence,—life had fled.
Now the hot waste was o'er,
And Havoc raved no more,
But sat with Misery gloating o'er the dead.

The sky waxed wild and frowned
Upon the gory ground,
And sad the requiem the great rain-drops made,
As the last warrior strode
Along the lonely road,
His right hand holding loose his broken blade.

A voice is in his ear,
It echoes loud and clear:
He pauses as the heights it thunders o'er:
"The day of Strife is done,
The crown of Peace is won,
And love has conquered,—war shall be no more."

He flung his blade away,
And, travelling day by day,
O'er vale and mountain, reached a peaceful clime.
No sword or spear was there,
No war-shriek rent the air,
No brand of battle till the end of time.

Here grew the shining pine,
The box, the clustering vine;
The lion took the leaves from the child's hand;
And, "Praise to God's dear Son!
Heaven is on earth begun,"
Arose for ever from the joyful land.

Hasten that happy day,
Let not Thy chariot stay,
O blessed Prince of Peace, when love shall reign
In every human soul
From joyous pole to pole,
And earth pour forth one loud thanksgiving strain.

THE CANNON IN THE LANE.

A DOWN a lane, with trees embowered,
A musing hour to pass,
Where bloomed the dainty violets
Like blue eyes in the grass,
I turned one evening, when the light
Was fading into grey,
And to his nest the forest bird
Was wheeling on his way.

Close by some stone steps and a gate,
Not far from Falmouth town,
A clear stream, from a cannon's mouth,
Was sweetly purling down.
I stood to view this watercourse
In old Trevethan lane,
Which murmured from the iron gun,
And flowed along the plain.

Perchance, by some old bark 'twas borne
Across the 'whelming tide;
Or hewn from some strong battery's breast,
The haughty conqueror's pride;
Perchance, it has a history strange,
As most of its compeers,
Whose actions might be graved in blood,
And steeped in human tears.

And as I gazed, methought, a voice
Rose from the gentle rill,
"The time will come when cannons all,
Like this, shall cease to kill;
When hissing shot, and shrieking shell,
Shall never more be hurled;
And sweetly shall the tide of peace
Flow over all the world.

"O what a clime of happiness
Our jarring globe will be
When every gun in every place
Is laid as low as thee;

When not a missile more is driven
  Against the brow of love,
And dwells the human brotherhood
  As angels do above!"

THE RED CHIEF.

THE angry storm had rent the royal ridge,
  And smote the stately pines upon the moor :
  Gone from the river was the rustic bridge,
Nor pilgrim feet would press its worn planks more.
Shaken and shattered was the peasant's door,
The farm lay trodden overgrown with brier ;
And in the distance boomed the cannon's roar,
Down-dashing solemn fane and princely pyre ;
And Ravage roared unreined, full-fed with flame and
  fire.

Through the thin mist that round the ridges hung
Peered the still arms of a retreating band ;
And rended banners on the wind were flung,
Stained and deviceless, by some mystic hand.
A nameless silence filled the rocking land,
Like that which oft precedes the earthquake's roar,
And sated Havoc sat upon the sand,
With corses heaped along the lonely shore ;
And Death paused on the crags, with huge hands red
  with gore.

The sun went down in his full wealth of gold,
Until the crimson skies were all a-glow,
Shedding a richness o'er the lonely wold,
And deserts deep where men but seldom go.
Then came the Twilight, with soft feet and slow,
Linked arm in arm with ruminating Eve ;
When from the welkin floats an utterance low,
Which with the fern-brakes did itself inweave,
As glow-worms with their lamps their cells of mosses
  leave.

The hare was out a-feeding with his mate,
Nor started they that solemn sound to hear ;
The bat wheeled by the lonely forest gate,
And glided up and down the rushy mere ;
The owl was muttering on an alder near ;
A lone thrush whistled his retiring lay ;
The gentle brooklet glided seaward clear,
With murmuring music, on its winding way ;
And gentle voices hummed the dirge of dying day.

The voice increased in strength from hour to hour,
Until from every point of heaven it came :
It filled with holy sound the poet's bower,
And shot across the hollows like a flame.
From star to star, from zone to zone, the same ;
A universe of melodies sublime,
Which thrilled the soul like Zion's loud acclaim,
When conquering faith has entered on its prime,
To cheer for evermore the sorrowing sons of time.

No human language can avail to paint
That swell of echoes over hill and dale,
Which only could be pictured by a saint
Of highest order in green Eden's vale ;

And from the gloaming peered forth faces pale,
With twisted scars upon their battered skin ;
And ever and anon arose a wail,
That shook the pine-tops with its powerful din :
Then ceased, then rose again, a surging sea of sin.

And then behold above the rippling lake
The white moon rose with sweetness in her face,
Weaving her tissues with the lonely brake,
The fern and flower, and hallowing all the place.
The sounds of sorrow left the scene apace,
While more melodious grew the floating psalm,
That filled with jets of joy the listening space,
For woe and wrong a universal balm ;
And Silence left her bower to breathe the heavenly calm.

"The sorrowing earth hath seen enough of strife,
Enough of horror on the field of spears,
Enough of battle and the waste of life,
Enough of orphans' cries and widows' tears,
Enough, enough, of fighing privateers,
Of ransacked towns and cities flaming higher,
Of swordsmen, pikemen, lusty cannoneers,
Girding the globe with desolation dire,
Yoked to the car of Death with Hunger, Thirst, and Fire.

" Enough, enough, of hosts in dread array,
Of soldiers tramping down the household bower,
Of bearded warriors strangely taught to slay,
And pluck before its time the lovely flower ;
Causing the tears to issue in a shower
From eyes which watched the nursling on her knee,
Lulling her child asleep at evening hour,
When lonely shadows lengthened on the lea.
And angel wings were heard slow-sweeping through
  the tree.

" Enough, enough, of camp-fires in the gloom,
Of keen eyes watching for the wary foe,
Of metal bullets dashing down to doom,
Where towers lie shattered and red rivers flow.
Enough, enough, of war, and want, and woe,
The rifle-ranger and the whetted blade,
The hail of anger hissing overthrow.
The braying war-trump, the gay-clad brigade,
The sinful soldier-craft, the cruel soldier-trade.

" Enough, enough, of enmity and strife,
Nursed into rage which only blood can quell,
When hosts rush madly to the sharpened knife,
And cut, and hack, and lop, and pierce pell-mell,
Which only lowest demons could excel.
Enough, enough. The curse has reached the sky,
And through the air the awful moanings swell,
As far as light can reach, or sound can fly.
Enough, enough, enough, the blushing heavens reply.

" There is a power more potent than the sword,
A chain far stronger than great links of steel,
Which binds more firmly than the stoutest cord,
And holds for man his share of human weal.
In homely guise she oft will onward steal
Through quiet lanes, and groves, and hamlets fair,
With eyes upturned, which she cannot conceal ;
And from her lips ascends an earnest prayer,
That war may never more the lovely earth lay bare.

" Among the Graces on the holy Book
Her name is greatest in the heavenly train ;
From Him hath she her gentle nature took,
Whose loss for us becomes eternal gain.
O blinded earth ! let Charity now reign,
And feuds shall cease, and fighting be no more ;
Then corn and cattle shall bedeck the plain,
And nations live in peace the great globe o'er :
And Love her tendrils twine from fruitful shore to shore.

" Put down the spear, and lay the sword aside ;
Change the war-weapon to the shining share.
He is thy BROTHER, though he may abide
'Neath torrid skies or frigid boulders bare ;
Then honour him, embrace him, and forbear.
Kindle no strife within his beating breast :
Thou savest thyself if thou thine anger spare ;
In blessing thou assuredly art blest ;
And giving love for hate thou shalt thyself find rest.

" If charity o'ercome the world with good,
How would the earth rejoice in summer flowers,
The thorn and thistle quite desert the wood,
And kids and tigers play in rose-hung bowers !
Delicious life and love would then be ours ;
The heavens look down on cultivated plains,
Watered with rills and soft refreshing showers,
Where milkmaids caroled to rejoicing swains,
And Peace walked forth well-pleased to hear the gentle
        strains."

Among the blue lakes of the wilderness
Ratagoe dwelt within his dear wigwam.
Not much of worldly wealth did he possess :
An only daughter, a sweet forest lamb,
White-fleeced and mild, which never knew its dam :
A cat and dog, a rifle and a knife,
A birch canoe, which on the Huron swam,
Rowed by the Indian like a thing of life,
Mid cliffs, and creeks, and coves with Nature's wonders
        rife.

Of his red tribe Ratagoe was the chief,
Though now alone amid their silent graves ;
And he would tell, with voice subdued with grief,
How oft he led a host of fearless braves,
Who roamed the woods and crossed the river-
        waves.
Gay ostrich plumes adorned his lofty crest,
And shining shells from fabled forest caves ;
The belt he wore with gilded beads was dressed,
And a rude leopard's skin flowed loosely from his breast.

His wants were few. He drank from gentle rills
That trickled music by his cabin door ;
He trapped the coney on the wooded hills,
The hare and squirrel in the forest hoar ;
And now a deer would wander to the shore,
Which oft became Ratagoe's welcome prey ;
Or wood-dove found his nest, to escape no more ;
Or fish was caught in the secluded bay ;
Or larger game would then his watchful walk repay.

Thus dwelt he here among the whispering pines
Free as the birds that caroled in the brake,
Or breeze that warbled through the bending vines,
Or kissed the wavelets of the crystal lake.

To the deep glen his way he oft would take,
And where the grove was thickest strangely rest ;
But not a single word the red chief spake,
Nursing the thought in his untutored breast,
While crimson clouds hung round the doorway of the
        West.

In every rustle of the musing Eve,
In every whisper from the tangled bower,
Where briony and woodbine sweet inweave,
And odours rise from many a forest flower,
He the Great Spirit heard with solemn power.
Laying his hand upon his beating heart,
Soul-saddened with the mystery of the hour,
That gently drew him from his child apart,
And quicker forced his blood with tedious tingling
        smart.

Much wrong and suffering was Ratagoe's lot,
In days gone by, among the dingles deep.
His wife and babe one sultry morn were shot
By hostile Indians as they lay asleep ;
For he was hunting on the farther steep,
And just returned to see the smouldering fire
Of his own wigwam lying in a heap,
And the two bodies underneath the brier,
With death upon their brows, down-trodden in the
        mire.

His other daughter hid herself the while,
Yayfoe by name, as beautiful as light,
Whose gentle bosom was as free from guile
As forest-nymph, or fairest river-sprite.
She came at last to glad Ratagoe's sight,
And kissed his cheek, and pointed to the west,
That she his better feelings might incite,
Where now the mother and her babe did rest,
In goodliest hunting-grounds and gardens of the blest.

They buried them within the cypress shade,
With faces fronting the retiring star,
And their strange dirge filled up the listening
        glade,
And floated through the murmuring pines afar.
' The gates of light, ye snowy hands, unbar,
And let the Prairie Rose and Petal in,
Where richest glens and clearest fountains are,
And garments grander than the tiger's skin,
Than whitest snow more pure, than lily-leaf more
        thin.

' Plucked is the Petal from the household tree,
And gone the ripe Rose from Ratagoe's bower ;
The sun and moon may often come to me,
But never more these treasures of an hour.
A great cloud now does on the valleys lower,
The light of home is quenched in kindred gore.
Come, Yayfoe, come, let us the green woo l scour,
And seek for peace on some far river's shore,
Where Nature dwells alone, and tread this waste no
        more.

"Yes, seek for peace. The blind, ungoverned foe
Has turned our day into the darkest night ;
Yet lift I not a hand to strike a blow,
Or shoot an arrow in the fearful fight.

We'll send to them a flag of purest white,
To show that blood is not what we desire.
May be their heart will soften at the sight,
And the war-brand grow feeble and expire,
And Love be ours for aye, clad in her pure attire.

" O never more shall they their vigil keep,
And watch for us when southern stars are bright,
When a great silence settles on the steep,
And wandering voices fill the shades of night.
No more will they sing in the wood-fire's light,
When rich with spoils I seek it from the chase.
To view its roof-top was extreme delight,
Which would inspire me with a quickened pace,
And drew the sunshine forth upon my gladdened face.

" Come, Yayfoe, come. The forest paths are free,
The prairies boundless, and the horizon clear.
The rivers run by many an ancient tree,
That woodman yet has never ventured near.
Each changing moon shall watch them sleeping
    here,
The Prairie Rose with Petal in her arms,
While we in glades will hunt the timid deer,
Where darling Nature spreads her choicest charms,
Returning love for hate, and peace for war's alarms."

Two silent shadows through the dusky brake
At falling twilight-time were seen to glide,
On, on, and on, by level land and lake,
Through regions rare and pensive prairies wide ;
Nor ever turned they from their track aside,
Or lingered long upon their western way,
The storm-struck maple their unerring guide,
And moss-trunks rising mid the shining spray.
On, on, still farther on, where giant branches sway.

And so these children of the solitude
Passed into realms as air or ocean free.
The savage warriors, once so fiercely rude,
Were now delighted their true friends to be,
And presents came—wolf-skins and hominy ;
And never more awoke the battle-throe
Against the dwellers of that household tree,
Or fell in wrangling war another blow ;
But like the moorland stream so did their summers
    flow.

Around them hostile tribes at variance rose,
And man met man with the uplifted knife ;
But not a missile in the butt of blows
Glided across the pathway of their life.

Hereafter they were sweetly free from strife,
Because not striving in their little sphere,—
A maxim with philosophy more rife
Than warlike kings will often pause to hear :
As true for empires wide as lonely mountaineer.

The wild woods taught them, more than mouldy
    books,
How love is stronger than the fiercest hates,
Than pikes, or swords, or bayonets, or hooks,
For small communities or mighty states ;
That time it was to shut the iron gates
Of brutal force, and rend its massive bars ;
Which Charity in white robes advocates
For rising feuds and miscellaneous jars ;
And Peace assert her reign beneath the smiling stars.

And Yayfoe loved, and was beloved in turn ;
The forest birds came fluttering at her call
To pick the scattered fragments by the burn,
On its lone way towards the waterfall ;
And squirrels scrambled from the fir-tree tall,
And wood-doves dropped upon the cabin eaves,
To list her love-song by the ivy wall ;
While robins followed mid the harvest sheaves,
Or winked with knowing nod 'neath the mangolia
    leaves.

Thus lived Ratagoe till his hair was grey,
And his slow step grew feeble as a child,
Supported by Yayfoe from day to day,
And loved by all, the Peace Man of the wild ;
And when he died a thousand warriors filed,
And threw their arms into the mighty stream,
To fight no more, but practise virtues mild,
Directed ever by fair Mercy's beam
Through fields of corn and kine, where richest land-
    scapes gleam.

Then from a simple wigwam of the west
An Indian chief came o'er the woodlands wide ;
Nor did he give his gay moccasins rest
Until he stood erect by Yayfoe's side,
And claimed the maiden for his own dear bride :
When back she went with him the lakes among,
Where roses bloomed, and slender saplings sighed,
And birds awoke her with their morning song,
And Peace sat in their bower, and sang the whole year
    long.